Times and Seasons

Seasons of Blessings

BEVERLY LAHAYE
TERRI BLACKSTOCK

TWO   BOOKS   IN   ONE

Times and Seasons

Seasons of Blessings

ZONDERVAN®

ZONDERVAN.com/
AUTHORTRACKER
follow your favorite authors

ZONDERVAN

Times and Seasons / Season of Blessing
Copyright © 2010 by Beverly LaHaye and Terri Blackstock

Times and Seasons
Copyright © 2001 by Beverly LaHaye and Terri Blackstock

Season of Blessing
Copyright © 2002 by Beverly LaHaye and Terri Blackstock

Requests for information should be addressed to:
Zondervan, *Grand Rapids, Michigan* 49530

ISBN 978-0310-32977-0

Published in association with the literary agency of Alive Communications, Inc., 7680 Goddard Street, Suite 200, Colorado Springs, CO 80920. www.alivecommunications.com

Interior design: Melissa Elenbaas

Printed in the United States of America

10 11 12 13 14 15 16 • 20 19 18 17 16 15 14 13 12 11 10 9 8 7 6 5 4 3 2 1

Times and Seasons

Dedication

This book is dedicated to parents of prodigal children, searching the horizon for their loved ones to come home.

Acknowledgments

Special thanks to Jim Woodall, who helped us get our facts straight regarding Nicaragua. Thanks, also, to Terry Bartlett, who offered valuable insights about the juvenile prison system.

He urged them to plead for mercy from the God of heaven. . . .
Then Daniel praised the God of heaven and said:
"Praise be to the name of God for ever and ever; wisdom
and power are his. He changes times and seasons;
he sets up kings and deposes them. He gives wisdom
to the wise and knowledge to the discerning. He reveals
deep and hidden things; he knows what lies in darkness,
and light dwells with him."

DANIEL 2:18–22

CHAPTER One

I'm telling you, Mark, it's a sorry idea."

Mark Flaherty turned from his bedroom window and glanced back at Daniel. His best friend still wore his church clothes from this morning—a button-down blue shirt neatly tucked into khakis. The clothes made Daniel look older than fifteen as he stood with his arms at his sides, preparing to fight him if he tried to push past. "You always think my ideas are sorry."

"You've already been arrested once," Daniel said.

Mark turned back toward the window with a clear view of Cedar Circle, in full summer bloom. His mother was next door, revving up for the wedding shower the neighbors were giving her. Brenda Dodd and Tory Sullivan had been talking about it for weeks, and Sylvia Bryan had come all the way back from her mission work in Nicaragua to host it in her home. It griped him that his mom had insisted on the men in her life being there. Showers were for women, and he had better things to do. It was only early June, and the wedding wasn't until July 4th. The shower was just a lot of trouble for nothing, in his opinion.

"I'll be back before anybody knows I'm gone," Mark said. "I'd have to be crazy not to do this. It's easy money." He turned back to his friend and reached for the small bag of marijuana he'd bought from a friend at the baseball park last night. "Chill out. I won't get caught, okay?"

The words sent a little jolt of memory through him, for he had said them before. Just over a year ago—months after his mother had freaked and got Miss Brenda to home-school him. He had sneaked out of his dad's house in Knoxville and gone joyriding with a kid—in a car he didn't know was stolen. They'd been caught spray-painting graffiti on the side of a school building. Mark had been charged with car theft and vandalism, both in one night. The judge, who'd had a fourteen-year-old kid of his own, had let him off with probation.

But this time was different. He had turned fifteen last week, and he wasn't following the crowd anymore. He was in control here. He had this figured out.

"You're just mad because you won't be able to buy a concert ticket," Mark said. "But I'll be there in the front row. I'll buy you a T-shirt."

"Your mom will go ballistic," Daniel said. "She won't even let you go to that stupid concert, and you know it."

"She won't know," Mark said, stuffing the bag into his pocket. He heard a horn honk and looked out the window. Ham Carter and some other guy waited in his jeep at the end of the driveway. "Gotta go. He's here."

Daniel's cheeks were blotched pink as he tried to block the way. "Man, I'm telling you, you're making a mistake."

"I have to go," Mark said. Though Daniel was a little taller, Mark knew he could take him if he had to. "Move!"

Daniel stood there for a moment, then finally moved aside. Mark pushed past him to the stairs and bolted down, Daniel right behind him.

Eighteen-year-old Annie stood in front of the wall mirror at the bottom of the stairs, dressed like Barbie's evil brunette twin. Rick, his twenty-year-old brother, waited by the front door, tugging at his collar.

"Mom said to wear a tie," Annie told Mark. "Hurry up and get ready, or we'll be late."

"I have to go somewhere," he said. "I'll just be gone a few minutes."

"Gone *where?* We're supposed to *be* there!"

"I have to run an errand," Mark said.

"What kind of errand?" Rick asked with that tone he got when he tried to be the man of the house.

Daniel didn't wait for Mark's answer. He shot out of the house, leaving the screen door to bounce shut behind him. Mark watched him cross the street, ignoring the two guys in the jeep. That was just as well.

"If I'm not back in fifteen minutes," Mark said, "go on without me. Just tell Mom I'm coming."

"No way!" Annie cried. "Mark, you're going to get her mad at all of us. I was counting on her being in a good mood later when I hit her up for concert money—"

Mark grinned. He didn't have to hit her up. "She will be," he said, pushing open the screen door. He took off down the driveway, smiling at Ham and his friend. As he jumped into the backseat, he patted his pocket.

"Hey, guys. I'm kinda in a hurry, okay?"

"Sure, man."

Mark grinned as they pulled out of Cedar Circle. This would be the easiest money he'd ever made.

CHAPTER *Two*

Cathy Flaherty kicked her pumps into the corner of the kitchen and wondered why she'd gone to the trouble of getting her hair done this morning. Her blonde strands were already wisping out of the French twist, and the guests hadn't even arrived yet. She should have come in her jeans and lab coat, the veterinarian's garb she wore every day. She would have been more comfortable with her hair in a ponytail and sneakers on her feet.

But that would have disappointed the friends who were throwing this shower. Brenda Dodd and Tory Sullivan, her neighbors on Cedar Circle, had been working on this for weeks. And if that weren't enough, Sylvia Dodd had left her mission work in Nicaragua to come back and host it. It was as if Sylvia had to see it to believe it, Cathy mused.

"Hold still and I'll fix your hair," Brenda said, coming at her with a comb.

"I'm not used to having my hair up," Cathy said. "Shoulda known not to go fu-fu."

Brenda moved a bobby pin, catching some of the escaped wisps. "Tory, does that look okay?"

Tory turned back to them with her fifteen-month-old daughter, Hannah, asleep in her arms. Her body rocked from side to side, as if she swayed to some imaginary beat that only a mother could hear. "Looks good," Tory said in a voice just above a whisper. "I think I'll run home and put her down. Barry can watch her if she's napping."

"When your hands are free, you can help me put out these flowers," Sylvia said. She had several vases of fresh flowers, probably cut from her garden. Cathy had trouble growing weeds, yet Sylvia still had beautiful blooming jasmine, impatiens, petunias, periwinkles, and a dozen other floral varieties around her house, when she didn't even live here to care for them. But Cathy knew Brenda and Tory weeded and watered Sylvia's yard. In March, Brenda had taken her home-schooled children over to plant new annuals in the front garden. She'd considered it a science project. Cathy's son Mark, who was home-schooled with Brenda's four children, had taken great pride in his green thumb. Now, in June, the yard overflowed with blooms, showing evidence of their care.

The Gonzales family had done a good job of caring for the home while the Bryans were on the mission field. In early May, they had finished Carlos's seminary training and returned to Nicaragua, so the house was empty again. It was clear Sylvia had enjoyed being back in the home in which she'd raised her children and that she loved launching Cathy's new life with this shower.

Tory was on her way out the front door when Annie and Rick burst in. "Steve's in the driveway," Annie said. "He and Tracy are on their way in."

"But Mark is AWOL at the moment," Rick said.

"AWOL?" she asked, going to the door and waiting for Steve and Tracy. Tracy was all dressed up, and her hair had been braided with little white flowers. Steve had taken her to get her hair done this morning.

She switched her thoughts back to Mark. "So where is he?"

"Went to run an errand."

"An errand? In what?"

"In Ham Carter's jeep," Annie said. "He said he'd be back in a few minutes. Right."

Steve came up to the porch, dressed like a financier, and grinning like an Oscar winner. Cathy matched that grin and reached up for a kiss. "So we're gonna go through with it, huh?" he teased.

"I wouldn't get too excited," she said with a wink. "It's just a shower." They had postponed the wedding two other times. One was after Mark's arrest, the other after they'd realized how hard it was to blend parenting styles. This time, they had sealed their plans with work—building an addition onto her house. She let Steve go as Rick grabbed a monstrous handful of peanuts, dropping some onto the floor as he shoved them into his mouth. "Rick, please. They'll think you haven't eaten in a week!"

Sylvia came over and gave him a hug, and Brenda bent down to pick up the fallen peanuts. "It's good to see a healthy appetite," she said. "Besides, who cares what we think?"

"That's what I was thinking, Mom," Rick said with his mouth full. "You've just got to get over this constant worrying what other people think. Are you going to wear shoes?"

Cathy tried to remember where she had left them, then hurried to slip them on. Annie was right behind her. "Your hair looks funny, Mom. It's falling on one side. Looks kind of like somebody jabbed some pins in trying to hold it up."

"Okay, so I'll never be able to work as a hairdresser," Brenda said, throwing up her hands in mock defeat. "Annie, help her."

"I'll help!" Tracy shouted, bouncing up and down. "I can fix your hair, Cathy!" The eleven-year-old was already reaching for the bobby pins.

"Tell you what." Cathy started pulling pins out and letting the hair fall around her shoulders. "Forget the fu-fu do. I'm coming as me."

Steve grinned and stroked the silky hair. "Suits me fine."

"Me, too," Brenda said. "Just run a brush through it, and you'll look like a catalogue model."

The front door came open, and Cathy turned hoping to see Mark. Instead, Tory stood just inside the door, looking tired and slightly out of breath. "Okay, let me at those flowers," she called to Sylvia.

Sylvia handed her two vases, and the women began placing them. The smell of white roses and lilies wafted on the air. Cathy looked around at the house full of memories—gold gilded photos of Sylvia's children on the walls, an eight-by-ten of her new grandbaby, and multiple pictures of Sylvia and Harry with the children they loved in Nicaragua. A dried vine wound over and between the pictures, creating that thread of life that had never been broken. Not in this family.

Cathy wished her vine wasn't broken. There was something strange, unnatural, about having a wedding shower when you were forty-two years old. But the events of her life had not always been her decision.

"So where's Mark?" Steve's question turned her around, and she thought of lying and saying that she'd sent him to get something. She didn't want to see that look of *he's-at-it-again* pass across Steve's face, and she didn't want to start him down the *are-we-doing-the-right-thing* road again, either. She'd been down that road enough herself.

Besides, she wanted to be free to hear Mark's reasons for being late, *before* she lambasted him. Her reaction to the children was different when Steve was around. She found herself responding the way she knew he would want her to, with consistency and discipline—all the right things, but for all the wrong reasons.

But the truth would come out soon enough, anyway. "Mark seems to have disappeared with Ham Carter. We're expecting him to be back soon." She turned to Annie. "This Ham Carter. How old is he?"

"At least sixteen, I guess," Annie said. "Can you believe his parents are letting that loser drive? They ought to announce it on the evening news or something just to give everybody a chance to get out of his way. Cool! Cake."

"Annie, don't touch that. We're not ready to cut it."

Annie looked insulted. "So what do you think I'm gonna do? Just grab a handful?"

Cathy glanced at her son, who had just about finished off the bowl of peanuts. She thought of pointing out to Annie that the only thing she could expect from her children was the unexpected. She stepped into the kitchen, where Brenda and Tory were busy decorating plates of pastries. Steve followed her in and leaned against the counter. He reached for a pastry.

Sylvia slapped his hand. "The guests will be here soon," she said. "Just a few more minutes. Then, after you and Rick and Mark make your introductions, you can go watch football until we need you to help carry everything home."

"Might be a long wait, then," he said. "When did you say Mark would get here?"

"Few minutes," Cathy said.

Steve looked at his watch. "Mark knew what time the shower started, didn't he?"

"Oh, yeah, he knew. In fact, I even picked his clothes out for him and told him to get dressed before I left. Annie, he was dressed in those clothes when he disappeared, wasn't he?"

Annie shrugged. "Not his tie. Not yet."

Steve stiffened, and that pleasant look on his face was replaced with concern. "Why would he do this today of all days? Do you think this is some kind of psychological plea for us not to get married? Because every time we've set a date, something has happened."

"No, he's not lashing out. He's just being thoughtless."

"Cathy, any psychologist would have a field day with your youngest child running off *today*."

"Well, thank goodness no one's analyzing it." She took a brownie and bit into it. "Come on, this is not a crisis. Mark's been disobedient, and I'll take care of it when I see him. But I don't want it to ruin the party. So let's not mention it again, okay?"

Steve locked looks with her, threatening to say more, when Tory walked up between them. "Why'd you take your hair down?" she asked. "Cathy, it was beautiful up!"

Grateful for the change of subject, Cathy handed her the brush.

When Tory had finished lacquering Cathy's hair, they emerged from the bathroom in time to see Tracy barreling for the door.

"Grandma's here!" she shouted, and Cathy looked out the window to see Steve's mother and sister getting out of the car in the driveway. "Let me get it!" she shouted. "Please, can't I?"

"All right," Cathy said. "Have at it." She turned to Steve and struck a pose. "So give it to me straight. How's it look?"

A gentle smile softened Steve's features.

"Like cool water in hundred-degree heat. As usual." He leaned down to kiss her. "How'd I get so blessed?"

Tracy threw the door open, and her grandmother and aunt came in with a flourish of gifts and hugs. Sylvia turned on some piano music on the old stereo system Harry had left behind. As more guests arrived, Cathy greeted each one as if they were her old best friend. It bowled her over that anyone had actually taken the time to come. When there was a lull in the number of women arriving, Cathy went to look for her children, who had retreated into the kitchen. "You guys come out here and be polite now," she whispered. "Speak to every guest, and when I open gifts, ooh and ah over everything. And no cryptic comments about what I get."

"Do you believe this?" Annie asked Rick. "She's asking us to lie."

"I'm not asking you to lie," Cathy said. "I'm just asking you to be polite."

"So what are you going to do to Mark?" Annie wanted to know.

"I'll deal with him when the shower is over. One thing at a time, okay?"

The doorbell rang again, and she heard more guests coming in. "Come on, now. We have to get out there."

The smell of fruit punch and sugar icing hung on the air, along with that of melon balls and a dozen different pastries that Brenda had concocted. Cathy owed them big-time, she thought. She just hoped she wouldn't have to move out a couple of rooms of furniture to get all the gifts into her house.

She and Steve had thought of moving to his place, but she hadn't been able to stand the thought of leaving her little neighborhood. Sensing her reluctance, he had offered to move into hers and build a couple of extra rooms, so they would have a little more square footage in which to spread out. The foundation had been poured last week, and the contractor said it would take a couple of months to get the rooms up—not in time for a July 4th wedding. But that hadn't bothered them. They would go ahead with the wedding and move Steve and Tracy into her house, as it was. That way they could put Steve's house on the market while they waited for the new master bedroom and the extra family room to be finished, and they could take their time decorating Cathy's room for Tracy.

The doorbell rang again, and Tracy flung it open. Her excited face changed to surprise, and she stepped back and called over the crowd, "It's a policeman!"

Everyone got quiet and turned to the door, and Sylvia rushed to the foyer. "May I help you?"

"Could you tell me if there's a Cathy Flaherty here?" the officer asked.

Cathy started to the door, not certain whether this was some kind of prank her friends had played on her, or something more serious. She glanced at Tory and Brenda and saw that there was no amusement in their eyes.

"I'm Cathy Flaherty," she said. "Is something wrong?"

"Mrs. Flaherty, I need for you to come to the police station as soon as possible."

If she hadn't still been standing, she would have been certain her heart had stopped beating. "Why?" she asked. Something told her she didn't want everyone to hear this, so she stepped outside. Steve followed her out, then Annie and Rick bolted to the door.

"It's your son, Mark," the police officer said. "I'm afraid he's been arrested."

A wave of uncertainty and denial washed over Cathy, and she took a step back and bumped into Steve. His arms came around her, steadying her.

"For what, officer?" he asked.

"The charge was drug distribution."

Cathy couldn't get her voice to function, and she felt Steve's hand squeezing her arm. Tears blurred her vision, and she thought she might tip right over and collapse on Sylvia's front porch.

"No way," Rick said, finally.

"My brother was selling drugs?" Annie asked, as if to make sure everyone in the house had heard.

"He was picked up on Highland Avenue," the officer said, "after he tried to sell marijuana to a plainclothes officer."

The world seemed to grow dim. Cathy was going to throw up. Her head was going to explode. Her heart was going to give out. Her knees were going to buckle.

But she just stood, letting the words sink in like some kind of toxin, seeking out every vulnerable cell in her body.

She heard Steve taking charge, finding out where they were holding Mark, asking Rick to get the car, telling Sylvia to call off the shower. For a few moments, her thoughts remained scattered. Only one seemed to motivate her to action.

Her son needed her.

CHAPTER *Three*

What was he *thinking?*" The shock etched itself on Cathy's face, making her look older and less like a bride-to-be. She had given up on her hair and pulled the pins out again, and now it was in her way. She swept it behind her ears.

Steve clutched the steering wheel with both hands. He had been quick to get his mother to take Tracy home, as if hearing about Mark's rebellion would influence the child somehow. Cathy wondered what he would do when they all lived together. How would he shelter Tracy from Cathy's kids then?

In the backseat, Rick and Annie sat with their arms crossed, staring out opposite windows. She didn't remember their ever being this quiet before. But she wanted answers.

"Where did he get drugs to sell, for heaven's sake? I tried to separate him from all the kids who were leading him in the wrong direction. He's home-schooled! He must have gotten it in Knoxville when he was with his dad last weekend."

"Mom, he could get it anywhere," Annie argued. "You don't know if he got it in Knoxville."

"But that's where he got in trouble before! Hanging around with car thieves. He could have gone to prison!"

"Mom, he didn't steal a car," Rick said. "His friend took his stepfather's car, and the guy pressed charges. Mark didn't even know he didn't have permission."

"My son was *charged* with car theft—and vandalism of that kid's school. It should have been a wake-up call, but your father didn't wake up. I told him not to let him hang around with them . . . and now he's selling drugs!" Her face tightened, and she felt the arteries at her temples throb. She slammed her hand on the dashboard. "I thought once you got your life right that things were supposed to fall into place! But they're not falling into place! How can my son be selling drugs? He just turned fifteen last week. He's just a child!"

"Mom, he's not a child," Rick said. "He's mobile now. His friends have cars."

"And he's not the little angel you think he is," Annie added.

"I never *thought* he was an angel," Cathy said, turning around in her seat. "Believe me. I've known for years that he was far from an angel. When I was taking him to his probation officer once a week, I knew he wasn't an angel! When Steve and I canceled our wedding twice last year because of Mark's behavior, I knew he wasn't an angel! But I didn't think he was a criminal, either!" She shifted in her seat and turned her accusing eyes to her children. "Why didn't you tell me what he was doing? This doesn't even seem like a surprise to either of you."

"Mom, we didn't know," Rick said. "Don't you think we would have told you if we knew our brother was selling drugs?"

"Then why did Annie say that about him, that he wasn't an angel?"

"Because he's not, Mom," Annie said. "I mean, I've known for a while that Mark was headed in the wrong direction. Even with the home-schooling and everything, he's just a bad kid."

"He is *not* a bad kid!" Cathy said through her teeth. "I will not let his own siblings label him like that!" She turned back around and glared out the windshield.

Steve reached across and gave her shoulder a reassuring squeeze. She wondered when he would jump in and agree with the kids.

"I'm just saying that he doesn't pick the greatest guys in the world to be his friends," Annie said.

"They're trouble if you ask me," Rick said. "All except for Daniel."

"*I* could have stopped him from seeing them!" Cathy shouted. "I could have made him quit going to visit his dad if his father wouldn't control him. Why would you keep something like that from me?"

"Mom, it wasn't Knoxville. It was here, too. At the baseball park . . ."

"So I was wrong to let him keep playing on a baseball league? I thought he could be home-schooled and still be athletic. I thought he could be trusted at least that far."

"Guys like Mark can get into trouble no matter where they are," Rick said.

Cathy breathed out a bitter laugh that only resulted in tears. "I will not accept that. I . . . will . . . not . . ." Her voice broke off, and she pressed a fist to her mouth. "Maybe he's innocent. Maybe it's all just a stupid mistake."

Steve didn't respond, and she knew he wasn't buying it. Everyone in the car knew Mark had probably done exactly what he was accused of. Everyone except Cathy. She still held out hope that this would all be cleared up by the time they reached the station.

Mark had been such a pure, happy little boy. He had been the one who skipped everywhere he went. He hummed a lot, little kid songs from nursery school. He brought stray animals home and nursed them back to health. She remembered the turtle he'd found dead in its bowl. He had cried for hours, then arranged a burial and a solemn ceremony, in which they'd all crowded around to pay their last respects.

Was this some sort of burial ceremony for his future? Were they all supposed to gather at the station with solemn faces and mourn the loss of the child who could feel things so deeply?

What had happened to that little boy?

She would not believe that he had turned bad, that there was no hope, that he was destined to go down the wrong path for the rest of his life. She would not believe that he had hardened into a criminal who would break a law just to make a buck.

It had to be a mistake.

CHAPTER *Four*

She found Mark sitting in an interrogation room with swollen red eyes, as if he'd been trying to cry his way out of this. It had worked when he was four, when one forbidden match had resulted in flames swallowing up the yard. She remembered that Jerry had lambasted him at the top of his lungs, and Mark had cried and cried until Cathy's focus had shifted from punishment to comfort.

But he wasn't four anymore.

She came into the room alone, because they wouldn't allow Steve, Rick, or Annie to accompany her. Instead, they sat in the waiting area for her to come back.

When she saw Mark, she followed her first instinct to pull him out of his chair into a crushing hug. He clung to her as he hadn't in years, and her mother's heart melted at the fear she felt in his embrace. "Mark, what's going on?"

"Mom, I didn't mean to," he said. "I swear I didn't mean to."

"You didn't mean to *what?*"

"Sell drugs," he said. "It's not like I'm some kind of dealer standing on the corner looking for little kids to mess up. I just trusted Ham Carter. You know, the catcher on my team. He called me and told me to meet him. And all he wanted was a bag, Mom. It's not like I keep an inventory or something. I thought I could make a few bucks so I could go to the concert next week. I knew where to get one for him—"

"Mark!" The word yelped out of her mouth, shutting him up. Had he just admitted that he'd done exactly what they said? Had he really bought drugs so he could sell them to someone else? She grabbed a chair and shoved it under the table, as if it was in her way. Trembling, she made herself turn back to him. "Where . . . did you get it?"

"Never mind," he said. "I just got it, okay? And the reason I was going to sell it to him was because he was going to pay me real good. You know, if you gave me a decent allowance, I wouldn't have to do stuff like this."

Her finger came up level with his gaze, and her eyes snapped caution. "Don't you dare blame me for this." Her voice broke, but that finger kept pointing. Through her teeth, she whispered, "Allowance?"

The sad humor in that word made her feel suddenly weak, and she dropped her finger and turned away. Her hair seemed too hot against her forehead, so she pushed it back and held her hand there. "How could this happen?" The words came in a whoosh of emotion. "How *could* you? *Selling drugs?* They put people in jail for that."

"But I didn't think I'd get caught. I thought I could trust him. I didn't know he had some cop with him when he came to get me. The guy looked young. They set me up, Mom. They tricked me."

She dropped her hand and turned back around. He was still wearing the khaki pants and dress shirt she had ironed for him this morning. The tie was probably still hanging on his door-knob. The coat was probably on his bedroom floor. Today was supposed to have been a good day.

She leaned back against the wall and looked up at the ceiling. "That's what they do, Mark. That's how they catch criminals."

"But it's not fair. I'm *not* a criminal."

"Depends on your definition." The words didn't come easy.

"Come on, Mom. I'll make this up to you. I promise I will. I'll work every day this summer at the clinic, and you don't have to pay me or anything."

Suddenly she realized that Mark just didn't get it. He was standing there looking at her, pleading, as if she had a decision to make. "Mark, don't you understand? You've broken the law. You're sitting in a police station. *I'm* not the judge! It's out of my hands."

"It's *not* out of your hands," he said. "You can get me a lawyer."

"Of course I'll get you a lawyer, but that doesn't mean you're going home."

"But you're my mother. They can't hold me here. I'm only fifteen. It's not like I shot somebody and have to be tried as an adult."

"Mark, don't you understand what you've done? This isn't like when you broke a rule at school and got suspended. This is the law. You broke it, and you've been arrested. They have evidence."

"But it's practically my first offense."

"It is *not* your first offense. It's your *third* offense. There were those little matters of car theft and vandalism."

"But I didn't do those things, Mom. I didn't steal Craig's old man's car, and I didn't so much as pick up a can of spray paint at their school. I just got run in with them. I was practically an innocent bystander."

She wanted to break the closest thing she could reach, but since that was Mark, she pulled the chair back out and sat down. Mark slowly took the chair across from her. She sat there, face in hands, staring at her son. Was he really oblivious to what lay ahead of him?

"Mark, I don't even know any lawyers in Breezewood. I haven't needed a lawyer since my divorce, and that was in

Knoxville. Steve is working on trying to get one. He knows somebody at our church. But I can't believe I'll have to hire a lawyer to defend you for selling drugs."

"Mom, I've learned my lesson, okay?"

She dropped her face back in her hands and squelched the urge to scream. How could he treat this like it was a traffic violation? She leaned forward and locked onto his blue eyes. They looked so soft, so innocent. He was too young to be facing a charge like this. Too young to commit this kind of crime. Too young to grasp the reality involved.

Her mouth trembled. "Mark, I was so proud of you last week," she said. "You hit a home run the night of your birthday. And then just a week before that you finished the school year with Brenda and made all A's and B's. I thought maybe we were finally seeing light at the end of the tunnel, that there was hope that you'd gotten through that rebellious phase, and that now you were trying to buckle down and do the right things. I didn't know you were out buying drugs and selling them."

"So I guess now you're not going to let me go out of the house for the rest of my life."

Her eyes shot up like a backdraft blaze, and she almost dove across the table. "Mark, don't you understand? The State of Tennessee may not let you out of the house! You may be locked up in the juvenile detention center. Do you understand what you've done?"

"No!" he said. "Mom, they don't lock you up for doing a favor for one friend who turns out to be a Benedict Arnold."

She wanted to slap him, but she knew better. Holding her hands in the air, she cried, "*Yes, they do!* They caught you red-handed. You sold drugs to a police officer, Mark. It's your third offense. Don't you get it?"

"I didn't know he was a police officer. He had long hair and a goatee, and looked like a kid. Isn't there something called entrapment?"

"Mark, you did it. You did it, and that's all there is to it. They caught you."

"Okay, so you've made your point," Mark said. He looked down at his finger as he rubbed at a spot on the table. "Mom, I'm really sorry, okay? I'm sorry I messed up your shower. I'm sorry I trusted Ham Carter."

"Mark, they said the judge won't see you until the morning, so you're stuck here at least one night, and I hope that's all. For the life of me, I hope it's not going to be longer than that."

Mark sprang out of his chair, his mouth wide open. "Mom, you've got to be kidding! No way can I stay here all night!" He got to his feet, and she saw that he still didn't get it. His ready-to-leave posture indicated that he thought she was bluffing.

He was still small for his age. He hadn't been given the height that Rick had. Even though he had just turned fifteen, Mark looked thirteen. She wondered why in the world he would think he could play among criminal types with his stature. Maybe his height was part of the problem. Maybe he was playing the part of big shot to make up for his lack of height.

"Mom, I'm telling you—you can't leave me here," he said. "Do you know what happens in these places? You took me to the juvenile center—that River Ranch place—yourself last year. *You* told me how horrible it was."

"I thought it would be a deterrent. Never, in a million years, did I think—" She closed her eyes, unable to stop the thoughts of what she had seen there. Kids with rap sheets as long as their arms had filled up those cells. Some had committed violent crimes; others had been in isolation over and over for fighting with other inmates. She shook her head as tears rolled down her face. Maybe they wouldn't put him there tonight. Maybe he'd be safe . . . in a cell alone.

The door opened and a burly police officer came in. "We're ready to take him over to River Ranch," he said. "That's our juvenile facility."

"I know what it is," Mark spouted.

Mark's reaction to the officer set off a small explosion within Cathy. "Mark, if you know what's good for you, you'll talk to him with respect," she said. "You're not in a position to go spouting off."

"Mom, please. You can't let him take me."

"I'll be back as soon as I can get a lawyer, Mark. But I can't promise anything."

"But I didn't *do* anything. They trapped me." He turned to the police officer. "It was a *trick!*" Mark insisted, as if that would make him change his mind about taking him away. The officer wasn't impressed.

"Mom, please!"

But there was nothing Cathy could do.

CHAPTER *Five*

Tory Sullivan wasn't good at keeping secrets, but she felt that Mark's arrest should be kept quiet. As new guests arrived for the shower, she tried, with Brenda and Sylvia, to make excuses for the couple.

"They had an emergency with one of the children," she told a group of women who had shown up together.

"Oh. Is someone sick?"

"No, no one's sick. We're not really sure what the problem is, but we're going to have to cancel the shower."

"It's not Annie, is it? The way that child runs the roads in that car of hers, she's bound to wreck one of these days."

"I really can't say." Or actually, she *wouldn't* say. If her child had been arrested, she would have wanted as little passed on to her acquaintances as possible. She tried to show Cathy the same consideration, even though she knew word would be all over town before sundown. Cathy was the most popular veterinarian in Breezewood, and everyone knew her.

When the last of them had left, Brenda started covering the food. "Maybe we could reschedule the shower," she said. "Freeze the food and try it again in a few days."

Sylvia shook her head. "I have to get back to León in just a couple of days. Besides, everyone left their gifts. Another shower would be kind of anticlimactic."

Tory looked around at the gifts that had filled up the table and lined the wall. Cathy would have had so much fun opening them. "So what are we going to do with them?" Tory asked.

"I have a key to Cathy's house," Brenda said. "We could just take them over and set them in her dining room."

"I'll get Spencer's wagon," Tory said. "It'll take several trips, but we can carry the gifts over in that."

"Better yet," Brenda said. "How about if I get David's truck and back it up in the driveway? We could fill it up with the gifts, then take it to Cathy's in one trip."

"You're a genius," Tory said.

Tory and Sylvia waited outside as Brenda crossed the cul de sac to get the truck. The trellis at the front of Sylvia's yard was covered with a rose vine and jasmine, and the scent seemed to hover in the air as the warm, gentle breeze stirred it. A beautiful day for a shower.

"Poor Cathy," Sylvia said. "This was supposed to be such a happy day. I was so looking forward to it."

"So was she," Tory said as Brenda backed the truck into the driveway. "Leave it to Mark."

Brenda got out and opened the tailgate. "Why would he do this, today of all days?"

"Because he's a brat, that's why," Tory said.

"Tory!" Brenda said.

Tory realized that Brenda had a stake in Mark's life, since she had home-schooled him for the last year and a half. He had turned Brenda's peaceful, ordered life into something unpredictable. Mark's disruptive influence had forced Brenda to come up with skills she'd never thought she'd need. But Tory had to hand it to her. She had done a good job with him.

And now this.

They unloaded the truck at Cathy's, counting thirty-two gifts, which they laid on the dining room floor. Maybe the gifts would cheer Cathy up when she got home, Tory thought. Maybe it would be a good distraction from the boy's trouble.

When they were finished, Tory hurried home and burst in, expecting to hear Hannah's weary cries. But there was no wailing. Instead, she heard Hannah's giggle.

She hurried into the living room and saw Barry lying flat on the floor, with the baby draped on his calves. He was doing leg lifts with her, holding her hands and raising her up, then lowering her quickly.

The baby was gurgling with laughter.

But Tory didn't find it funny. "Barry! What are you doing?"

Her words startled the baby, and Hannah started to cry. He sat up and lifted the baby. "You scared her. Why did you yell like that?"

Tory crossed the room and took the baby from him. Hannah was still small; she looked ten months old, rather than fifteen. Her development was slow. She couldn't sit up alone or crawl yet, her muscle tone was weak, and her joints were loose.

It took a moment for the baby to realize she had changed hands, and her crying ceased as Tory kissed her and bounced her. "Barry, you can't roughhouse like that. She's too fragile. Her neck isn't strong enough."

He got to his feet. "It's not going to get strong unless she uses it. I was doing it just like the physical therapist told me. She was fine."

"But you were being too rough."

"She liked it, Tory. She's not a doll. She likes to have fun just like Brittany and Spencer did." He pressed a kiss on the baby's plump cheek. "We had fun, didn't we, Hannah? Daddy was making you fly."

Tory saw her smile, and she tried to calm down. "I'm sorry I yelled," she said. She shifted Hannah in her arms, so that she held the baby's legs together instead of allowing them to straddle her hip. They had to make accommodations for Hannah's loose hips, in hopes of avoiding a brace.

"Tory, you have to trust me. She's my daughter, too."

"I know," she said. "I'm overprotective. Tell me how to stop and I will." The hurt look on Barry's face registered, and she quickly changed the subject. "Well, the shower was canceled. Mark got arrested."

Barry's jaw dropped. "What did he do?"

"He was charged with drug distribution."

"Is this a joke?"

"No. Who knows what the real story is?" She sat down in the rocker with Hannah. The baby's mouth opened, and her tongue slipped out. Tory touched it to make her pull it back in. "Anyway, Cathy and Steve ran off to the police station, so we had to cancel." She leaned her head back. "I don't know why I'm so tired when I didn't do anything."

"You're tired because you don't sleep. You worry too much about Hannah." He took the baby out of her lap, carefully holding her legs the way the physical therapist had taught them. "Why don't you go lie down? Hannah and I were all geared up for a dad and daughter afternoon. You have a couple of hours to kill."

She didn't want him to know how uneasy it made her to let anyone else care for the child. "I'm not that tired," she said. "Besides, I need to do her exercises with her."

"She doesn't want to exercise," he said. "She wants to play."

"Well, I'll exercise her and try to make her *think* she's playing."

"That's what I was doing." He was getting angry, and Tory wondered why he had to take this so personally. They were both trying to do what was best for their child.

"Did you feed her?"

"Does she look hungry?"

"Barry, can't you just answer me?"

"Of course I fed her. And I changed her diaper twice and gave her her medicine *and* a breathing treatment, which is why she's breathing so well. If you weren't obsessing so, you might notice."

The baby yawned, and Tory took her back from him. "I'll just rock her for a minute. Maybe she's sleepy again."

He surrendered her unhappily, then headed for the door. "I'm going out to check on the kids."

Tory didn't answer. She made no apology for being a good mother. Barry was just going to have to get over it.

CHAPTER *Six*

Brenda lingered on her porch before going into the house. She wondered if Daniel knew about Mark's problems today. He had been at Mark's house when she left for the shower.

She glanced at the front door and saw the shoes lined up there. Leah's and Rachel's were missing, since they were at Sandra Hogan's birthday party. Joseph's small ones were next to his father's big ones, and off to the side were Daniel's, parked toes pointed in. At least she knew he was home.

How had this happened to Mark? He was rebellious, but deep down he was a good kid. There had to be some mistake.

A year ago, when he had first gotten into trouble with the law, Brenda had sat Mark down, looked him in the eye, and asked him what would cause him to follow those kids into trouble.

"We were bored," he said. "I was in Knoxville at Dad's house and he was playing golf. And the guys came by and we went out. There just wasn't anything to do."

"So you decided to paint curse words on the walls of the local high school?"

"I didn't know what they were painting. I was just standing guard."

"You knew they were painting," she said. "You know that was against the law. I've taught you enough about civics that you had to know what you were doing."

She was sure she saw genuine shame on Mark's face. "You gotta understand, Miss Brenda. When I'm in Knoxville there's this different me."

"No, Mark. There's only one you. You make choices wherever you are."

"But it's *like* I'm two people. I'm different in Knoxville than I am in Breezewood."

Brenda screwed up her face, trying to follow his reasoning. "So you want me to believe that the Knoxville you is not as intelligent as the Breezewood you?"

"It doesn't have anything to do with intelligence," Mark said.

"Doesn't it? How intelligent was it to go with a kid who stole his stepfather's car? How smart was it to ruin public property?"

"Well, maybe I'm just as dumb there as I am here, okay?"

"Sorry," Brenda said. "I'm not buying that, Mark. I know better than that." She had been teaching him for six months at that point and knew he was as smart as any of her own kids. "But I will believe there's an element of dumbness in the Knoxville you." She couldn't believe she had said that. She usually tried to make everything into a positive. But it was hard to make anything positive out of what Mark had done that day.

She had patted herself on the back often and told herself she was doing well with him. That the evil had been purged, and that he was maturing into a decent young man who liked to learn.

But what had gotten into him this morning? Boredom, on the day of his mother's shower? Was it another case of his friends having an idea that he thought would be fun? A case of not thinking he'd get caught? And how had Daniel been involved?

She looked for Joseph, and through the kitchen window saw that he and David were in the workshop. She hoped Joseph hadn't forgotten to wear his mask, to keep him from breathing sawdust. Ever since his heart transplant two years ago, he was prone to respiratory infections and pneumonia.

She went into the computer room and found Daniel pounding on the keyboard.

"Daniel?"

The word turned Daniel around, as if he'd been caught at something. She saw the guilt on his face. "Hey, Mama."

"Daniel, what do you know about Mark's arrest?"

He gasped so hard that he had to cough, and he got up and gaped at her. "Arrest? Oh, no. He didn't, did he? You're just kidding, right?"

He did know. She stepped toward him, her eyes searching his for a clue that might break her heart. "Daniel, tell me everything you know."

"I *told* him not to do it, okay? I begged him. Bullied him, even. But he's so stubborn." He looked like he might cry. "Mama, what happened?"

"The police came and got Cathy. Told her he was arrested for drug distribution."

He slapped his hand against his forehead and looked up at the ceiling. "I can't believe this! He wanted money for that stupid concert ticket next week. How could he be so stupid? I *told* him!"

Brenda watched the genuine reactions passing across his face, and she realized that he had not been involved. At least, not in the actual act of selling the drugs. "Daniel, you should have gone to someone if you couldn't stop him yourself."

"I thought about it. I really did. But he was so sure he had it all figured out . . ."

"Then you were at his house when he had drugs?"

Daniel looked at her with those blotchy cheeks, as if he knew he was in trouble now. He opened his mouth to speak, then stopped and looked down at his bare feet. "Okay, yeah, I saw the drugs," he said. "It was a bag of marijuana. I should have left right then. But Mark's my friend, Mama, and I thought I could talk him out of selling it. Maybe get him to flush it or something. What good would it have done him if I'd told on him?"

"He wouldn't be in jail right now."

Daniel sank back into the computer chair and slumped over, staring at the floor. "Oh, no. What is he gonna do?"

Brenda sat across from him. "I don't know." She saw the shame in his shoulders and in the way he hung his head, and felt sorry for him. "Honey, I don't mean to accuse you of causing this. But you're not ever supposed to be in a house where someone has drugs. If something illegal or dangerous is going on, you should tell an adult immediately. You know that, don't you?"

He nodded. "Yes, ma'am. I should have called Miss Cathy or something. Instead I just let him get in that jeep and take off with those guys."

She sighed and slumped, too, pressing her forehead against his. "I've been there. I've dealt with Mark for over a year. I know how frustrating it can be."

"But I'm his best friend. I should have stopped him. Even if I had to knock him down, I shouldn't have let him go."

"I'm not sure knocking him down would have helped." She pulled Daniel's face up and looked him in the eye. "Why would he think of doing this?"

"Like I said, to buy the stupid concert tickets. He said it was easy money." He caught his breath and straightened. "Mama, it's the first time he's ever done this. Mark is not a drug dealer. They'll go easy on him, won't they? They'll see that he's just a stupid kid . . ."

"I don't know, Daniel. They went easy on him the last time."

The back door opened, and she heard the heavy sound of David's footsteps through the kitchen. He came to the computer room door and looked surprised to see her.

"Shower over already?"

"Dad, Mark got arrested," Daniel cut in.

David's eyebrows shot up, and he looked at his wife. "What happened?"

"He was charged with selling marijuana to a police officer."

David took an astonished step back. "I can't believe it," he whispered. "You would think his father would have made him sever his ties with those kids by now."

"It wasn't the Knoxville kids," Daniel said. "It was a kid from the baseball team. From around here."

David got quiet as he realized Daniel knew the story. He met Brenda's eyes, and she gave him that silent communication that husbands and wives sometimes have. It said that there was more to tell, that she was taking care of it, that she would fill him in later.

"All we can really do now is pray," Daniel said. "Maybe the judge will let him off."

David looked down at his hands. Brenda knew that he didn't believe in prayer. To him that was the same as doing nothing.

"He'll probably get off," David said, changing the subject. "The juvenile facilities are overcrowded as it is."

"But what he's done is pretty substantial," Brenda said. "I mean, they don't take it lightly when you're selling drugs."

"Could it be a mistake?" David asked. "Wrong place at the wrong time kind of thing?"

Daniel shook his head and looked back down at his feet.

"Oh." David's word brought his eyes back to Brenda, silently beseeching her to hurry up and fill him in.

"Mama, please don't start thinking that he's influenced me. You know I don't let him do that. Besides, he's not that bad when he's here."

"You're right," Brenda said. "He's come a long way. But do you remember what he said when I was talking to him about being a different person in Knoxville than he was in Breezewood?"

"Yeah, I remember," Daniel said.

"We don't know what the other Mark is like. The one that lives here can sometimes be a real handful."

"But he's gotten better, Mama. You know he has."

"I know," Brenda said, "but the judge doesn't care about any of that."

"We can be character witnesses," Daniel said. "You and I, we can vouch for Mark. Dad, too. Can't you, Dad?"

David had never cared that much for the boy who had brought so much disruption into their lives. But he shrugged. "I guess so," he said.

Brenda nodded weakly, hoping it wouldn't come to that. She wasn't sure any of them honestly *could* vouch for the boy who was so intent on messing up his life.

CHAPTER *Seven*

Cathy was silent as she rode home in Steve's car, her two teens brooding in the backseat. "He'll be okay there for one night," Steve said.

She recognized his effort to comfort her, but it was futile. "He will not be okay," she said. "He's in jail. He's fifteen and small and clueless, and he's with gang members and drug addicts and thieves."

"I meant that I think they'll keep him isolated from the others. He won't be in any danger. If I'm wrong, then they'd have lawsuits up to their ears, parents suing them for putting their children in harm's way."

"The parents are mostly powerless," she said in a dull voice. "Children get beaten up at River Ranch all the time."

"I'll bet you're wrong about that. I'll bet they have more control over things than you realize."

She didn't want him to be wrong—but she couldn't entertain a conversation that accepted that Mark was in jail. She couldn't stand the thought of his sleeping in a cell full of gang members and criminals. She couldn't stand the thought of the guards yelling at him, or of a cell mate who might be stronger or bigger or angrier. She couldn't stand the thought of him lying there, afraid, all night.

It sounded so homey and safe—River Ranch. But it was still a jail. She had toured it with Mark herself, hoping the threat of it would be a deterrent. Apparently it hadn't frightened him into good behavior. But it had frightened her.

As Steve turned his car into Cedar Circle, Cathy's three neighbors were huddled on Brenda's front porch, as if waiting for her. She wished she could have just gone into the house unnoticed, without saying a word to anyone. She wished she could just crawl under the covers and bury her face in her pillow.

But while the kids headed into the house, Steve lingered beside her as the three women headed over. Sylvia was in the lead, her face drawn and sympathetic. She just pulled Cathy into a hug. Brenda was next, searching her face for an answer about Mark. Then Tory came up, holding Hannah in her arms. "Where's Mark?" she asked.

"Had to spend the night in jail," Cathy said, leaning back wearily against the car. She was still wearing the pink suit she had worn to the shower, and the pumps were killing her feet. She wondered if they would let Mark keep his clothes, or if they had some kind of uniform for him. She wondered if she should take some clothes to him. "Steve called a lawyer," she said. "Slater Hanson from church. You know him, don't you, Sylvia?"

Sylvia nodded. "He'll do a good job. What did Mark say?"

"That he did it," Cathy said matter-of-factly, though there was nothing matter-of-fact about it. The corners of her lips trembled as she added, "He didn't *mean* to. Just wanted to make a few bucks. You know, for the concert." The sarcasm in her words left a sour taste in her mouth.

The look on Sylvia's face was as sick as Cathy's, but it seemed to Cathy that Brenda wasn't all that surprised. Maybe Daniel had said things.

Tory just shook her head. "Someone influenced him, Cathy," she offered.

Cathy shrugged. "Well, it sure wasn't me. Or Brenda, either, for that matter. The only people who have any influence over Mark are his friends."

"Some of his friends," Brenda whispered.

"Yeah, I had hoped his friendship with Daniel would make a difference." Cathy sighed. "Does he know?"

Brenda nodded.

Cathy rubbed her face, trying hard not to cry. She didn't want to look weak, beaten. Steve put his hand on her shoulder. She was thankful that he hadn't said much.

"We brought your gifts home," Tory said in a quiet voice. "They're all in the dining room. Thirty-two of them."

Cathy looked down at the concrete beneath her feet. A sprig of grass was growing up through a crack. "Thank you for taking care of that. I hope everyone understood."

"We just told them you'd had a family emergency," Sylvia said.

Cathy met her eyes. "It'll be all over town by morning, anyway," she said. She blinked back the tears. "Even if the judge lets him out, his reputation is shot. Not that it was that good to begin with." She reached for Steve's hand on her shoulder, laced her fingers through it, and squeezed hard.

His grip was strong, reassuring. It promised help and peace in the face of chaos.

She wished she could believe that promise.

She reached out to hug Sylvia, then pulled Brenda and Tory into her outstretched arms and held them for a moment. Then she let them go and took a step back. "I need to go in now. I need to talk to the kids, and . . . I have to call Jerry."

They said their quiet good-byes and promised to pray. Slowly, she headed into the house. Steve was right behind her.

When she turned back and met his eyes, he reached out. "Come here."

She went willingly into his arms and soaked in the feeling of love as he held her so tightly that she couldn't breathe. His face was rough and warm against hers, and his brown hair was soft beneath her fingers. He smelled of early summer and wind and the slightest trace of cigarette smoke from the police station. She tried to blink back her tears but became vaguely aware of how they wet his shirt.

"When Mark was a baby," she managed to get out, pulling back from him and looking up into his eyes, "and I was still married to Jerry, he had all these dinner parties and conferences we had to go to together. He insisted I go with him, but I didn't want to leave my kids so much. I spent three weeks interviewing baby-sitters before I would leave Mark with one of them."

She got a glass out of the cabinet, half-filled it with tap water, and swallowed it down. Staring at the glass, she said, "When he was old enough for nursery school, I literally toured fifteen places before I chose one. I was so careful who I left him with. Even in the last year, I've only left him with Brenda. And now he's there with a bunch of kids who stab and shoot each other."

"Maybe not," Steve said. "Maybe they're just like him."

She leaned on the counter, trying not to let herself fall apart. "He's little, Steve. He can't defend himself against some of those guys."

"Honey, this might be the longest night of your life. I don't have any Band-Aids to put on this. All I can say is that tomorrow maybe things will turn out better than you think. Maybe he'll come home and this will be the wake-up call he needs, the scare of his life that will turn him around."

"I thought that would happen when he got arrested last year," she said. "It didn't work." She stepped toward the door and looked out the screen, as if she would see Mark heading up the driveway. "If I could just go to that place and sleep outside his cell, I would. Just to know he was all right . . ."

She drew in a deep breath and stood straighter, wiped her eyes. "Well, I can't, and that's that. Meanwhile, Tracy is probably worried sick, and you need to go update her and relieve your mother." She covered her eyes. "Oh, I hate for your mother to know this about my son."

"My mother's realistic. She understands what some teenagers go through."

"And she knows Mark," Cathy said.

He didn't seem to know what to say to that, so he said nothing.

"Go," she said. "You need to take care of Tracy, and I need to talk to the kids and call Jerry. Really, I'm going to be all right."

"I know you are." He crossed the room and took both of her hands in his, brought them to his lips. "I love you," he whispered. "Call me when you can. If you don't, I'll call you. And if you need me, I can be back over in ten minutes."

As he headed out to his car, she leaned against the door and stared into the garage.

She imagined all manner of doubts rushing through his mind as he drove home. He hadn't bargained for a criminal stepson, or the roller coaster that was Cathy's life. And he hadn't bargained for a mother's confusing mix of rage and grief, self-recrimination and crushing disappointment.

What would Mark's situation do to their plans?

She couldn't think about that now. Wedding plans didn't seem so important when her son was sitting in a jail cell.

CHAPTER *Eight*

Annie and Rick came into the den when they heard Steve leaving. Rick looked slightly shell-shocked. Annie had been crying. They both sank onto the couch, sudden allies.

"Mom," Annie said. "He's just a kid. He's not ready for this."

"We really didn't know," Rick said. "Really. If we had, we would have told you. We wouldn't have let Mark get himself into this much trouble."

She sat down across from them. "I'm sorry I yelled at you in the car on the way there. It was uncalled for. I was just upset."

"We know, Mom," Annie said. "You always yell when you're upset."

She stared down at her knees for a moment, trying to get a grasp on her emotions. "Well, I need to stop it," she said. "Maybe that's part of the problem."

Rick let out a loud sigh and jammed his elbows into his knees. "I knew you were going to do this."

"Do what?" she asked.

"Blame yourself. You blame yourself for everything. It's not your fault, Mom."

She pressed her fingers against her tear ducts, but her hands trembled. "I just feel like so many things should have been different in this family."

Quiet settled around them again, and she knew they were each counting the ways things could have been different.

"Mom, somebody needs to call Dad. He needs to know."

Cathy had planned to do that, but she couldn't stand revealing her emotions to her ex-husband. "I need for you to call him and tell him, okay? Rick? Annie?"

"Why can't you?" Annie asked.

"Because I'm . . . a little volatile right now. If you think I yell with you . . ."

Rick frowned. "Mom, you're not blaming him, are you?"

She threw up her hands and felt anger quaking through her as tears spilled down her face. "Sometimes I can't help but wonder what you guys might be like if you had a father in the home. You and Annie, you had him longer than Mark did. He was pretty small when your dad left. I can't help thinking that if Jerry had just been here, just his presence in the home might have made a difference."

Annie's voice was weak. "I know families with both parents in the home and they still have kids that turn out wrong and do stupid things. Even kids who were raised with big doses of the Bible every day can still turn out bad."

"I know that's true," Cathy said, her voice wobbling. She wiped the tears with the pads of her thumbs. "I know you're right. But I'm not the most rational person in the world right now. Just please . . . do this for me. Tell him what happened, and what time Mark appears in court tomorrow," she said. "I'm going to be in my room."

She hugged each child in turn before she left the living room. As she got to her room, she sat down on her bed and kicked off her shoes. This day had started out so differently. She had gone to church, floating on an air of anticipation, then her hairdresser had done her the favor of fixing her hair on Sunday. She had been excited about the shower, had looked forward to seeing so many friends and hearing their good wishes for her future. Tonight she was supposed to be taking inventory of the wonderful gifts she'd gotten and working on the wedding that was just around the corner. Now what would she do about that?

She heard the kids on the phone in the living room, and her thoughts went back to her ex-husband. He had played such a part in this, by playing so *little* a part in their family. She knew the kids didn't want her to blame him, and she had no right to do so in front of them. But hadn't he robbed her and the kids of something critical in their lives? Something they may not even know they were missing until an event like today's occurred?

Mark was paying dearly for their father's failings, and Rick and Annie had paid, too. They had all paid.

But they were paying for their mother's failings, too.

She lay back on her pillow, staring up at the ceiling through misty eyes, and thought back to that pivotal week in the life of her family when Jerry had announced he wanted the divorce, that he was leaving her for another woman. There had been no reasoning with him. No logic could have turned his head. It was not something she had counted on in life, nothing she had expected. He didn't want to be married, so *she* had been left alone.

Ironic, that need of his to end the marriage was only to begin another one just weeks after the divorce.

She had tried to forgive him, especially in the past couple of years since she'd given her life to Christ. But forgiveness was a hard concept. It didn't come through lip service or intention. It took her heart—and whenever her heart got involved with her ex-husband, it always came out on the wrong side of Christianity.

Sylvia had said that God would be a husband to Cathy, that he was a husband to widows and orphans, and she supposed, by some stretch of the imagination, that was what she was. A widow with three orphans. She had no doubt God had sent her Steve, a man who would no more betray her than Christ himself would. But if God was ordering things in her life, why had things become such a mess?

No, it wasn't God. It had to be her own failure again. She had done so many things wrong. Prayers of repentance couldn't undo any of them.

And neither could Mark's own remorse.

Now it was all in the hands of God and the circuit court judge.

CHAPTER *Nine*

Cathy recognized the knock the moment it started. It wasn't the polite, neighborly kind of knock, which said comfort was coming, and it wasn't Steve's knock, which had a gentle eagerness about it. It was Jerry's knock, loud and hard and announcing that he was here and they'd better hurry and answer the door.

Cathy heard Annie get to it first. "Dad! What are you doing here?"

She heard muffled voices as Rick jogged down the stairs, and quickly she got dressed. She had been lying on the bed in her pajamas, trying to work the whole thing out with God. But she knew Jerry hadn't made the two-hour drive from Knoxville just to say hello to the kids.

She went into the living area of the house and saw the drawn, angry look on his face as he spoke to their children. Annie swung around as Cathy came in.

"Cool," she said. "I haven't seen you two together in the same house in years."

Cathy didn't find that particularly refreshing *or* amusing. "Hi, Jerry. Guess you heard."

Her ex-husband was sunburned, as if he'd gotten the news on the golf course. He was dressed in a white polo shirt and a pair of khaki shorts. She hadn't seen him in a long time and was surprised that his dark hair was receding. A couple more years, and he'd be as bald as his father.

"Kids, I need to talk to your mother."

Rick looked insulted. "Dad, I'm almost twenty years old."

Annie stood firm, too. "We kind of wanted to hear what you're going to do about Mark."

She recognized and understood the look of helplessness on his face. "What I'm going to do." He breathed out a laugh. "Right."

He stepped into the living area and looked instantly out of place among the pieces of furniture they had bought together. Cathy remembered how they had agonized over the couch, because they wanted something that would last for years. He looked down at it now and ran his fingers across it thoughtfully, as if to see if it was holding up better than their marriage had.

"How could he have done this?" he asked, bringing his eyes up to Cathy.

She didn't want to share this pain with him, didn't want to commiserate or mourn together. She had cut off her feelings for him long ago, had prayed for God to anesthetize her to him in spite of her vows to love him for life. Years ago, God had been merciful and answered that prayer.

"What did he say about it?" he asked when she didn't answer the first question.

"He said that he was trying to make enough money for a concert ticket," she said in a dull voice.

"A concert ticket?"

"It was Third Eye Blind," Annie said, as though that would explain everything. "They're coming next week. The tickets are sold out, but if you can get them from a scalper—"

"So he sold drugs to pay for them?" The words came on an incredulous note of accusation, as if Annie had just condoned what he'd done.

"That's his story. Dad, don't look at me like I did it, because I didn't. I'm just telling you what he told Mom."

Cathy sank down into a chair, and Jerry took the couch. "I want to know what he said to you."

Cathy sighed. "He said that he had been set up. That his friend asked him to get him a bag of marijuana, and when he came to buy it, he had somebody in the car with him. Mark didn't know it was a cop."

"Set up." Jerry had always been a repeater, as if he had to say the words to process them. "And Mark *had* a bag?"

"He got it somewhere," Cathy said. "Bottom line, they're keeping him tonight, and his arraignment is tomorrow."

"What is he pleading?"

"I've been on the phone with the attorney trying to figure that out." It had been difficult trying to work this out herself. She had to admit that she was glad Jerry could help make the decision. "If he pleads innocent, he's lying. It's his third offense. Plus, they caught him red-handed. If he pleads guilty, maybe they'll go a little easier on him. Maybe community service. It's also possible that he could plea bargain. In exchange for a guilty plea, maybe they would reduce the charge. And if we could get him to name the person who gave it to him—"

Jerry was on his feet and laughing bitterly, hands on his hips. "How does he even know people like this?" He turned back to Cathy. "Don't you watch him?"

She sat rigid, stunned that he could accuse her of neglect when he played golf on his visitation weekends. "Yes, I'm watching him," she said. "He's home-schooled, for heaven's sake. I took him out of school to get him away from the kids who were influencing him. But I thought I could still let him play baseball. I didn't know he was at the park making drug deals!"

"If you'd been there, maybe he couldn't have. Do you even go to the games?"

Now she felt like a volcano near eruption. "Yes, I go to the games," she said, her voice rising. "Every one of them. Unlike you!"

"Hey, I live in Knoxville. What do you want from me?"

"How about a little fathering?" she said angrily. "Forget the full-time stuff! How about every other weekend? Or is it too much to ask that you miss a day at the golf course just because your children want to be with you?"

"Mom—" Annie said, trying to stop her. She had confided those things to her mother, and Cathy knew it was a betrayal to use them against him. "Dad does spend time with us."

"Don't defend him!" Cathy cried. "You told me that there wasn't any point in your going every two weeks anymore because you only see him for a couple of hours. Mark and Rick even tried taking up golf so they could spend time with him, but he didn't want to be bothered!"

Annie gave her father a stricken look. "Dad, that's not exactly what I said . . ."

"If I wanted to play golf I'd play golf," Rick cut in. "Dad didn't have anything to do with my quitting." He headed for the stairs, his face flushed, and Cathy knew she had hurt him. "I'm going upstairs." Neither child liked to admit that their father had chosen anything over them, and they didn't like for him to know they cared. Cathy had known better than to say that in front of them.

She was instantly sorry she had.

Annie just stood there, her eyes locked on her father's face. "Dad . . ."

"Go upstairs, Annie," he said. "I told you I need to talk to your mother."

She swallowed hard, looked back at him, then started up the stairs. "You'll say good-bye before you leave?"

He nodded and turned back to Cathy.

Cathy waited for her to disappear at the top of the stairs. "Don't you try to make it sound like *she* did something wrong," she said. "All she did was confide to her mother the fact that her father didn't seem interested."

"She exaggerates everything," he said. "You know it. And I don't appreciate the implication that my son has become a drug dealer because I'm a bad father."

"Of course not," she shot back. "He did it because *I'm* a bad *mother*. Isn't that where you were going with the baseball accusations? When have you ever seen your son play, Jerry? You could have made that drive once or twice."

"And that would have changed everything. If I'd just come to a stinking game."

"No, Jerry. If you'd just showed up *in their lives*. If I hadn't done it all myself!"

"Hey, you wanted custody. You got it. Now it's too much for you?"

"We had those children together, Jerry. I never expected to parent them alone."

"You haven't parented them alone. That's why I'm here tonight."

"And some comfort you are."

"I didn't come to bring comfort," he said.

"No kidding. Just a spotlight to shine in my face."

He started to the door. "Do you want my input on this or not? Because I can walk out of here and let you make the decision, and hope that, for once, you have clear judgment, since Mark's life is at stake—"

"Clear judgment?" she shouted. "What are you talking about? I'm the one who stayed, Jerry! I'm the one who raised these kids and nursed them through sickness and helped with their homework and drove them everywhere and went to every game—" Her voice broke off, and she kicked a chair. "*You* were the one who wanted your space! And *I* have poor judgment?"

She had seen it before. That look he got when she'd stopped getting through to him, when he'd shut down and tuned her out, like some hysterical woman. He might as well have his hands over her ears. He gave her that smug are-you-finished look, and changed the subject. "Do you want to talk about Mark's arraignment or not?"

Her chin was so tight, she thought it might pop out of place. "I think he should plead guilty and hope the judge gives him community service."

"I have to talk to the lawyer. Do you have his number? Maybe I'll even meet with him tonight."

"Of course." She tore down the hall and to her bedroom, where she got the number off the pad on which she'd been taking notes. She returned to the living room and thrust it at him.

He looked down at it, drew in a long, deep breath. "I can't believe my son needs a criminal lawyer."

"Neither can I."

"Well, he can't go to jail. That's all there is to it. No son of mine is going to jail."

She didn't answer. She wanted to believe the same thing, but somehow she knew that it could be exactly where he went.

He looked at the card again, then went to the stairs. "Annie, Rick, I'm leaving."

Rick didn't come, but Annie came quickly, as if he would disappear if she didn't hurry to the bottom of the stairs. "Bye, Dad. Will you be in court tomorrow?"

He kissed her easily, then hugged her. The gesture surprised Cathy. She hadn't pictured any affection between him and the kids. Not since they were little.

But then, she hadn't seen them together since Rick started driving because she no longer had to meet Jerry halfway.

Annie hugged her father, kissed him again, then walked him to the door. "I'll be at the Best Western," he said. "I'll call if there's anything we need to discuss after I talk to the lawyer."

Cathy sat back down, wrapping herself in her numbness, as he headed out to his car.

CHAPTER *Ten*

Late that night, when Annie and Rick were sound asleep in bed, Cathy gave up trying to sleep. She went into Mark's room, saw the clothes thrown on chairs and across the bed. CDs lay scattered around the table, and his stereo had been left on. She turned the power off and sat down in the middle of the mess. What was Mark doing tonight? Was he in a cell alone, or in a room with others, scared to death that harm might come to him? He didn't even like spending the night away from home much. He said there was something about sleeping in his own bed.

Was he repenting of his crime? Or was he merely looking at this with the logic of a child, wishing his mother would come and rescue him, or hoping his father would ride in on a white horse?

She wondered if a mother had any chance of getting inside River Ranch tonight.

"Oh, Lord, please don't let any harm come to him," she whispered. "Please take care of him."

She wasn't one to get down on her knees when she prayed. She'd always believed that God wanted her to be comfortable, like a child in the lap of her father, when she talked to him. But somehow the gravity of these prayers knocked her to the floor.

Her knees were cushioned on a pile of T-shirts and underwear, and she leaned up on the bed, her elbows on a pair of wadded blue jeans. She prayed morning would bring Mark's release. If she could just get him home, she told the Lord, she knew she could straighten him out. All he needed was one more chance. All he needed was an opportunity to start over.

But as night wore on and turned into morning, Cathy knew that his crime had a penalty. And she couldn't pay it herself.

CHAPTER *Eleven*

The next morning, Jerry waited for Cathy in the hallway outside the courtroom. He looked like an older version of Rick, only more comfortable in a suit and tie than Rick had ever been. He paced and perspired, cracking his knuckles as if preparing for a boxing match.

Cathy always felt awkward and uncomfortable when she came face-to-face with her ex-husband. If she smiled and acted civil, it seemed too familiar. Their relationship felt better at arm's length. Soft or fond feelings were strictly forbidden, for she had long ago counted them futile. Besides, too many bitter, hostile memories had buried themselves deeply in her heart.

Last night he had called her after a lengthy telephone conversation with the lawyer, and he'd agreed that a guilty plea was probably the best course of action. She'd spent the rest of the night second-guessing the decision and wondering if they were doing the right thing for Mark.

They both looked tired, strained, and had little to say to each other as they waited there for the attorney to show up.

"He's late," Jerry said.

Cathy looked at her watch. "He's not late. We're just early."

Annie went to stand beside her father. Rick lingered in the middle of the hall. "That him?"

They all looked up and saw the man starting toward them with a briefcase in his hand. "Yes," Cathy said. "That's him." She met him halfway up the hall.

"Cathy?" he asked.

"Yes." She shook his hand. "I recognize you from church now. Thanks for coming."

"Steve filled me in on Mark's case, and I did a little checking last night after I talked to your ex-husband."

Jerry pushed off from the wall. "I'm Jerry Flaherty."

"Slater Hanson," the attorney said, shaking his hand. "They'll be bringing Mark. We can go in this room right here."

He opened a door and ushered them in, but Cathy asked Annie and Rick to wait in the hall.

The attorney sat down and opened his briefcase, shuffled some papers around. He seemed so rushed and distracted that Cathy got the feeling he had twenty other clients down the hall waiting for him. She silently prayed that he wouldn't take this case lightly.

The room seemed so cold that she expected icicles to be hanging from the folding chairs. They should have something more comfortable, she thought, when people were awaiting the fate of their children.

By the time Slater Hanson had fished Mark's paperwork from his briefcase, the door opened and Mark was escorted in. He was dressed in a bright orange jumpsuit and wore handcuffs. His hair was greasy and hung in his eyes.

"Mark!" Cathy burst into tears at the sight of him and pushed his hair back from his eyes. When they removed his hand-cuffs, she hugged him, and he clung back. Jerry stood off to the side, looking down at the floor, fingers jingling the change in his pockets.

The attorney interrupted the hug and reached out to shake Mark's hand. Cathy stepped back.

"Mark, I'm Slater Hanson, your attorney. How was your night?"

"Horrible," he said. "Mom, you can't believe where they put me. I had a mattress that was like two inches thick. It was noisy. There were people yelling all night, cussing up a storm. You just wouldn't believe it. They had me in a little cell that wasn't any bigger than our bathroom."

"You were alone?" she asked through her tears.

"Yeah, I was alone."

"Well, maybe that was a blessing."

"*None* of this is a blessing! Mom, get me out of here." He looked up at his father. "Dad, can't you do something?"

Jerry pulled out a chair roughly and sat down. "Mark, that's what we're here for. We're trying to undo the damage you've already done."

"Dad, I didn't know. I didn't mean to do this. I just—"

"Shut up, Mark," Jerry said. "Sit down."

Cathy didn't know whether to come to Mark's defense or join in on the tough love that Jerry seemed intent on practicing. They all took their seats, and she pulled out a Kleenex and dabbed at her eyes.

"So how does it look?" Jerry asked the attorney wearily.

"You have to know that we're going up against Judge Massey today, and he's one of the toughest judges in the city."

"Oh, great," Mark said. His face looked as if his blood wasn't circulating well.

"Look at him," Cathy said. "He's fifteen years old. It's not like he was standing on a street corner selling crack through car windows."

"In the district attorney's eyes he did," Slater said. "He did it of his own free will, and no one coerced him."

"Come on," Mark said. "I just wanted to make a few dollars."

"Mark, enough with the few dollars," Jerry said. "You've dug yourself in deep enough. Just shut your mouth and don't say another word."

"But he's my lawyer! I'm supposed to talk to him."

Jerry ignored him. "He's just a kid. So he experiments with drugs occasionally, and yesterday he was going to do a favor for a friend. You're going to let them throw him in prison for that?"

"Of course not," Slater said. "I'm going to do the best I can to get him out. I'm just telling you what the possibilities are."

"So what do we need to do?" Cathy asked. "Just tell us."

"Well, neither of you has given me a clear answer on what you want Mark to plead."

"Innocent," Mark said quickly. When his parents were quiet, he looked from Cathy to Jerry. "Come on. I'm nothing like the guys they're trying to get off the streets. It was my first time to do anything like that, and I was set up."

"If you plead not guilty, there will be a trial if the judge thinks there's enough evidence. From the looks of things, I'd say there is. And you have to know that if there's a trial, there's a possibility they'll keep him incarcerated until the trial date. Frankly, that could be longer than the sentence if he pleads guilty."

Were they really talking about her child, this little boy who had had curly hair and skipped everywhere when he was two? Were they really discussing trials and guilty pleas and convictions?

"So let me get this straight," she said. "If he pleads guilty, he's got an automatic conviction, but they may just give him probation again, right? Or community service or something like that?"

"That's a possibility," the attorney said, but seemed tentative.

"But if he pleads innocent, he'll have to go to trial, and the trial may not be for months and months, and he may have to stay incarcerated until then. Is that what you're saying?"

"But, Mom, they *might* let me out," Mark said. "I might get to go home today and then we can figure out what to do next."

Cathy leaned across the table, locking into her child's eyes. "Mark, even if they let you come home and you have to stand trial, we'd have to hire lawyers, and somehow we'd have to prove that you didn't do it. There's a big problem with that, because you *did* do it."

"What do you recommend we do?" Jerry asked the lawyer.

He looked down at the file, flipped through a few pages, then glanced up at Mark, meeting his eyes. "Son, I want you to be straight with me. Did it happen like they said?"

"Well, yeah," Mark said, "I mean, I sold the drugs and everything, but I didn't know it was a cop."

"Did the cop who was with your friend talk you into selling the drugs?"

"No, he didn't say much at all. Just sat there, waiting to bust me."

"He didn't coerce you at all? Convince you to make the sale?"

Mark shrugged. "No . . . When Ham called, I told him I had gotten one bag and I'd sell it to him. There wasn't much conversation about it once I got there."

"Did the cop talk to you on the phone?"

"No. Just Ham."

The lawyer jotted a few notes, and Cathy wondered where he was going with this. "So you're guilty of doing exactly what they said?"

"Yeah, but it's not the way they made it out. I'm not some kind of junkie."

The man took a deep breath and looked from Jerry to Cathy, then back to Mark. "A trial would be expensive, and the chances are you'd lose, anyway. And, like I said, you still might not get to take Mark home today."

Mark slammed his hands on the table and threw himself back in the chair. "I am *not* pleading guilty," he said. "I am *not* going to go in there and say I sold drugs."

Cathy dropped her face into her hands. "But you *did* sell drugs."

"But, Mom, I've got to deny it as long as I can. People get off all the time. We can say he didn't read me my rights, that there was an illegal search and seizure. Something." He looked at Slater. "That's your job, man!"

"Mark, they have evidence. I have the police report right here," Slater said. "There weren't any of those things."

Cathy closed her eyes and, for the first time, wondered if it had been wise to get a Christian attorney. Maybe she needed someone shrewd and cutthroat who would go in there and lie through his teeth to get her son cleared. She had only wanted someone who would do the best job he could, who would care about the young boy whose life hung in the balance.

As quickly as those thoughts skittered across her mind, she banished them and whispered a prayer of repentance. God would honor their honesty. If her short time as a Christian had taught her anything, it was that.

Jerry seemed to be struggling with his own emotions as he stared down at the table. She didn't think she had ever seen him quite so distraught.

"The upside of this," Slater said, "is that he's not old enough to be tried as an adult. The juvenile detention center isn't a place where you'd want to raise your kids, but it's not the worst place in the world either. It's certainly better than prison."

"Prison!" Mark said. "You've got to be kidding! All I did was—"

Jerry's hand came down hard on the table, making them all jump. "All you did was sell drugs," Jerry bellowed. "Don't you get it, Mark? You don't have a leg to stand on. You have humiliated me and your mother and your sister and brother. You've broken the law, and they have evidence against you that we can't refute. You've acted like a juvenile delinquent, because that's exactly what you are. And that's why they're going to put you in the juvenile detention center if we don't get you off. That's where you belong!"

"*Jerry!*" Cathy's shock radiated through the room, reprimanding the man she had once called her husband. "My son is *not* a juvenile delinquent. He broke a law and he got into trouble, but it seems to me I remember you breaking a few laws in your day, too. Some people just never get caught."

Jerry met her eyes. She knew that he knew exactly what she referred to. Back in their teenage days he'd been known to smoke a joint or two, and she knew there'd been a couple of times when he'd even sold some of his own stash to a friend. It was no different than what Mark had done.

"I was never arrested and charged with drug distribution," Jerry said. "My father never had to come to the police station and discuss my defense!"

Slater looked at his watch, then began loading his papers back into his briefcase. "Why don't I leave you alone with this decision? I have another client to see. I'll come back before we go into court and see what you've decided."

Cathy looked up at him, stunned that he would leave them at this juncture. "Well . . . okay. If you're sure you'll be back."

"Before you know it," he promised, then hurried out of the room.

When the door had closed, Mark got up. "Great!" he said. "My lawyer cares more about some other client." He dropped back down, leaned his elbows on the table, and raked his hair back. "I can't believe they're doing this to me."

"I can't believe you're doing this to us," Jerry said.

"That's enough, Jerry!" Cathy bit out. He shot a look at her, as if daring her to speak that way to him again. The look only made her wearier. "It looks like we have a few choices, Mark. They're all equally bad. Most of them require taking huge chances with your life in the next few months, and there are no guarantees."

"So, what do we do?" Mark asked.

She let out a rough breath and looked at her ex-husband. "Jerry, do you have any constructive ideas, or just more snide comments?"

"He deserves whatever he gets," Jerry said.

Cathy wanted to throw something. "That may be true, but don't we all? Some of us never have to pay for what we've done."

Jerry cursed under his breath and got back up, striding to the window at the back of the room.

"Mark," Cathy went on, "the only thing I can suggest is that you go in there and face up to what you did. You plead guilty and we pray that the judge will have mercy on you."

"But, Mom—"

Jerry turned around. "Much as I hate to admit it, I think she's right," he said. "I have a feeling that if you do that, the judge will probably let you go home with us today. That doesn't mean you won't be on probation, that you won't have a conviction on your record, that it won't affect all of our lives. But it might be our only hope."

Mark's face burned as he stared at his dad. "You're not doing this just to save money, are you, Dad?"

The words seemed to ricochet across the room. Cathy flinched.

"Because if you're gambling with my life just so you won't have to pay an attorney, then that's pretty sleazy, Dad."

That artery in Jerry's neck looked as if it might burst, and he took a few steps toward his child, wearing that expression that suggested he could break him in two. "You really think I'd gamble with your future to save a buck?"

She held her breath, hoping Mark had the good sense to say that he didn't, so they could get on with business. Mark just stared him down, too prideful to reveal any intimidation or vulnerability.

Finally, she watched Jerry turn to a barred window and peer out. His shoulders rose and fell with seething breaths.

Cathy tried to clear her brain of accusations and inflammatory memories. "This isn't getting us anywhere, Mark."

"Then what should I do?" he asked. "Just go in there and surrender to them? Let them take me off?"

"Lots of people are in there praying for you, Mark. If you plead guilty, maybe God will show you mercy."

"The whole neighborhood probably showed up, didn't they?" Mark said, further accusation in his voice. "Best entertainment around, Mark getting convicted of drug dealing."

"You didn't hear me, Mark," she said. "I told you they're praying for you. You should be glad."

"Yeah, big hurrah."

The comment turned Jerry around. "That's it," he said. "You've gone far enough, Mark. If you don't want to help with this decision, then we'll make it for you. You're pleading guilty, you're facing up to your crime, and you're taking whatever it is the judge hands down to you. And if you go to jail, maybe you'll learn something your mother wasn't able to teach you at home. Respect."

"Dad, I do have respect," Mark said as tears came to his eyes. "I'm just scared."

"So am I." Jerry strode to the door, opened it, and looked around for the attorney. He turned his dull eyes back to Cathy. "I'll go tell him he's pleading guilty," he said. He closed the door behind him, leaving mother and son alone.

Mark looked small as he stared in the direction his dad had gone. But Cathy couldn't think of a thing to add to what Mark's father had said.

CHAPTER
Twelve

The courtroom smelled moldy, and paint peeled off the walls. A big crack cut through the ceiling plaster, and the industrial tile on the floor looked as if it needed a good washing with Lysol.

It was a depressing place, where lives changed with the strike of a gavel.

She saw Steve sitting with Rick and Annie, and on the other side of them, Jerry had slipped in. Behind them, Brenda, Sylvia, and Tory sat together. Little Hannah lay asleep in her stroller next to Tory. The court was already in session, and those with traffic violations were quickly being processed. Quietly, Cathy slipped into the row between Steve and her children. Brenda leaned up. "How do things look?" she whispered.

Cathy drew in a deep breath and indicated that she really didn't know. Before Cathy could respond, a side door opened, and those charged with criminal offenses were paraded in, all dressed alike in their orange jumpsuits.

Annie made a noise and covered her mouth. Her shocked eyes fixed on her mother, as if asking if she was going to allow this.

Cathy couldn't take her eyes from her son.

He sat next to a boy with a goatee and colored tattoos of serpents down each arm. The boy smiled as he saw some of his friends in the back of the courtroom, and she saw that two of his teeth were missing. He looked as if he'd recently lost a fight but hadn't learned from it.

Steve held one hand as she waited for their turn, and Annie latched on to her other one. The toothless kid next to Mark was called, and she watched as his teenaged wife got up and limped to the front of the courtroom.

After the case was read out, the judge regarded the girl. "Want to tell me what happened to your face?"

She looked at her boyfriend. He gave her a threatening leer that no one in the courtroom could have missed. But little hinged on the obvious, Cathy thought. It was all about paperwork and lawyers making the right motions.

She turned back to the judge. "I fell," she said. "That's all. I just want him out of here."

The judge gave a long hard look at the boy, who obviously had little respect for the girl next to him. "You're charged with Assault and Battery. How do you plead?"

The kid's proud chin came up. "Not guilty."

The judge gave the lawyer a look of disgust. "If she won't talk, my hands are tied. Case dismissed." He pointed a finger at the kid. "But I'd better not see you back in here. Do you hear me?"

"Yes, sir," the boy said, his chin held high. A grin cut across his face as they let him go.

And then came a case with a drunk driver who'd killed someone, and then a car theft followed by several other drug charges.

Finally, it came to Mark.

He looked like a little boy as he stood up and shuffled to the front. She thought he was about to cry. Wouldn't the judge see that this wasn't an everyday occurrence for Mark? Wouldn't Mark's young features soften his heart?

"What do you plead?" the judge asked.

"Guilty," Mark choked out, then glanced back over his shoulder at his mom. Cathy nodded her head, hoping to give him some strength. When Mark looked at his father, Jerry looked down at his hands.

The judge flipped through the pages again, studying the file. She wanted to tell him to forget the papers and look at the boy. She wanted to get up and tell the attorney not to just stand there, to do something and do it quick.

"Your Honor," Slater told the judge, as if her very thoughts had prompted him. "My client is only fifteen years old. His record will show some prior offenses, but it's worth noting that both of them occurred on the same night a year ago. There haven't been any since."

"Until now," the judge said, peering at the attorney over his glasses. "And if I let him off the hook this time, then he'll do it again. Trust me. I see these kids over and over."

"No, Your Honor!" Mark blurted out. His attorney tried to silence him, but the judge looked up as if he couldn't believe someone had dared speak out of turn in his courtroom.

"I won't do it again," Mark said. "I swear. You can ask my mom. She'll probably ground me from now till Christmas."

Cathy closed her eyes. She knew he was making himself look more naive and clueless, as if he still didn't understand that months of his life behind bars was not the same as being grounded in his bedroom. Annie squeezed her hand, and she clung to it, trembling. The judge took a deep breath, as if the very thought of what was about to happen pained even him. He leaned forward, pressing his elbows into his leather inlaid desk.

"Young man, what you did was a very serious offense. And you may have heard that in my courtroom people don't get off the hook. Not guilty people."

Mark looked over his shoulder at Cathy again, and she let go of Steve's and Annie's hands and slowly brought hers to her mouth. A feeling of terror rose up inside her.

"I'm going to sentence you to a year at River Ranch Juvenile Correctional Facility."

Mark swung around, his mouth open, and looked at his mother. She got to her feet and looked across to Jerry. He looked as stricken as they did.

"*No!*" Mark shouted. "*You can't.*"

The judge banged his gavel and ordered Mark to be quiet.

"Your Honor," Cathy shouted. "*Please!*"

"I will have order in my courtroom!" the judge insisted, banging the gavel again. The bailiff came to take Mark out of the room. He turned back with tears on his face, waiting for someone to run to his rescue.

When no one could, he cried, "Mom!" as if she had let him down. "Dad!"

Cathy had never felt more inadequate in her life. Jerry was standing now and looked as helpless as she.

Steve got to his feet and pulled Cathy against him, and she felt as if the world were going black. It all became shaky as he helped her out of the row of spectators and led her out of the courtroom.

CHAPTER
Thirteen

Cathy fought her way down the hall and to the door where they had led Mark out. Annie, Rick, and Steve ran to keep up with her. She tried to catch Mark, but they had already gotten him into the processing room.

"I want to see my son!" she yelled to the bailiff who was coming back to the courtroom.

"You can't see him right now, ma'am. I'm sorry, but he's being processed."

"He is my son!" she shouted. "You can't keep him from me!"

"He's not yours right now, Mrs. Flaherty. He's a ward of the state."

"How dare you!" she shouted. "You can't keep me from talking to him!"

"You can talk to him later, but right now there are things that have to be taken care of."

She started to lash out at the bailiff, who could have picked her up and snapped her in two, but Steve stopped her.

"Calm down, Cathy," he whispered. "This man's just doing his job."

"Well, his job stinks!" she said. "They can't take a child away from his own mother."

"Of course they can," he said. "They do it all the time."

She turned on Steve, as if he had declared the verdict himself. "Not to *me*, they don't!"

She saw Jerry coming up the hall and jerked out of Steve's hands. All the rage that had built over the last twenty-four hours tornadoed toward the man who had fathered these children, then left her to raise them on her own.

"*You!*" she shouted as he came toward her. "This is your fault! *You* did this to us!"

"Did what?" Jerry asked. "Mark did this to himself."

"He needed a father!" she screamed. "He needed somebody he could count on. He needed a man to show him how to be a man. Do you even know how, Jerry? Do you even know what that means?"

"Quiet, Cathy. You're making a scene," Jerry spat out. "I don't have to listen to you talk to me that way."

"No, you never have to listen, do you?" she shouted. "All you have to do is walk out, just disappear, and nobody will hold you accountable. Nobody will expect anything. And then when they come visit you on weekends and you let them run wild just because you don't want to have to deal with them, then you can blame *me!*"

Jerry pointed at Annie and Rick, who leaned against the wall with tears on both their faces. "Hey, these two turned out fine," he said. "Apparently they weren't too badly warped by my leaving you, so you can't blame Mark on me."

"Well, I do!" she said. "I blame you, and I blame the divorce, and I blame that little wife of yours that broke up our marriage! And I blame every morning that Mark woke up without a father in the home. I blame every night that he went to bed without knowing what it was like to have a male role model!"

Steve touched her shoulders, trying to calm her down, but she couldn't be comforted.

"I've tried to forgive you, Jerry Flaherty," she cried. "I've tried my hardest. I thought I had."

Jerry's eyes narrowed. "I don't want your forgiveness, and I don't need it."

She opened her mouth to lash back, but Steve put his arms around her and stopped her. "Come on," he whispered in her ear. "Come on, Cathy. Just walk away. Come on."

Summoning all the strength she had, she shook out of Steve's arms and took another step toward Jerry. She was trembling and felt as if something inside her would explode, that they would have to pick up the pieces and declare the end of her. "You're going to be accountable one day, Jerry," she said. "You're going to have to face God with what you've done for your kids. He's going to ask you where you were all those years, and if your little mistress was really worth it."

Jerry shook his head and walked away. She thought of going after him, grabbing him and making him listen to what he didn't want to hear. But she couldn't make him take the blame, or the pain, or the guilt that wasn't supposed to be shouldered alone.

She leaned against the wall and wept. Steve stood just off to her side, not touching her, but quiet as he waited. "I hope I'm there when God holds him accountable," she said. "I hope I get to hear the answer, because I really want to know . . ." She brought both hands to her head. "I can't take 365 nights like last night! I can't live like that!"

"I know, honey."

She covered her mouth with both hands and turned to her children. Rick and Annie hugged her as she wept out her anguish. Steve was behind her again, touching her back, stroking her hair. She knew that she was distressing him as much as the judge had distressed her, but there was nothing she could do. It was not a time for comforting. It was a time to mourn.

Finally, Steve tapped her shoulder and said, "I'm going to go check on Mark."

He was gone for a few minutes, and she just stood there with Rick and Annie, desperately trying to hold herself together. She was at the end of her rope, about to let go and fall and fall and fall . . .

When he came back, she stepped toward him. "Where is he?"

"They've already taken him."

She slammed her fist against the wall. "Taken him *where?*"

"To River Ranch. Cathy, they said you can't see him until Wednesday night. That's the next visitation."

"No!" the word came out in horrified grief. "No, no, no!" Steve pulled her against him and held her.

"Cathy, I'm so sorry," he whispered.

Her body racked with despair. She had to stop them, she thought. She had to *do* something. She pushed out of Steve's arms and bolted up the hall. He followed on her heels. She turned a corner and ran into Tory, Brenda, and Sylvia. "Cathy, are you all right?" Sylvia asked.

"No!" she said, pushing through them. She grabbed Rick and Annie. "Come on, let's go home," she said. The two fell into step behind her as she hurried out to her car. She got into it and sat behind the wheel and looked back up at the courthouse. Steve stood on the sidewalk, hands on his hips, watching her with that helpless look on his face. She knew she was hurting him, but she couldn't help it. She just had to get away, close herself in her room, and weep and cry and pray.

Rick got in the front seat and Annie in the back, and she started the car and pulled out into the traffic.

"Mom, are they really going to keep him for a year?" Rick asked.

"Yes," she said through her teeth, "and there's not a thing in the world I can do about it."

Silence passed for the next five minutes, and finally, Annie spoke from the backseat.

"Mom, what you said to Dad..."

She almost couldn't see through the blur of her tears. "I shouldn't have said it in front of you."

"Why not?" Rick asked. "Everybody else heard it."

Again, silence ticked between them, and she had to force herself to drive more slowly than she felt like driving. She tried to replay the tape of what she'd said to Jerry in the courthouse. How condemning had it been? How upsetting for the children?

"I'm sorry I said those things. I've tried all these years not to talk bad about your father in front of you, and I know I haven't always been successful at that. Sometimes I've just seen red and I just rant and rave and say whatever comes to my mind. Today was one of those days."

"It's okay, Mom," Annie said. "Maybe those things needed to be said."

Cathy looked in the rearview mirror and saw that Annie had tears on her face. She was wiping them away.

"And maybe they didn't," Rick said.

She glanced over at him and saw the bitterness in his gray eyes. He hadn't let the tears fall, and she could see that the grief was eating him from the inside out.

"You know, Mom, Mark made that choice on his own," Rick said. "It's like you always say. We can make choices in our teen years that affect the rest of our lives. This one's going to affect Mark."

Her face twisted as she turned the corner to get them home. She shouldn't even be driving. It wasn't safe.

"I know you're right," she said. "Your dad didn't do this. I never should have accused him." But as the silence followed, those accusations rose in her mind again. Maybe if Jerry had been around to tell Mark to stay away from drugs, he would have listened. Cathy had told him a million times, but sometimes a mom's word wasn't as powerful as a dad's. Maybe he wouldn't have been so willing to follow his friends, to seek their approval, if his dad had been there for him.

As she turned onto Cedar Circle and pulled into her driveway, she knew that bitterness was eating her up. And no words were going to cure the sin in her heart. It had been deeply planted and cultivated, and Jerry fertilized it every time she saw him.

Before the kids had even gotten out of the car, she got out herself, ran into the house, and hurried for her bedroom where she could lock herself in.

CHAPTER
Fourteen

Mark braced himself against the profanity spewing from the kid behind him in line. Surely the words would erupt into action, he thought, and someone would get hurt. He stood stiff with trembling, clammy hands at his sides.

The pale, greasy kid behind him looked like he'd lost a recent fight. His orange jumpsuit, identical to the one they'd issued Mark, was dotted with blood from his busted lip and broken front tooth.

This was all a mistake, he thought, desperately fighting tears that would mark him as a loser. He wasn't like the ones in this line, with their foul mouths and fighting wounds. They'd kill him as soon as they knew he was weak. He would be an open target—the home-school kid from suburbia. His conviction was a death sentence.

A yellow school bus with bars on the windows came to the curb. A guard with the build of a bouncer began ushering them on. It had been a long time since he'd ridden a school bus, a year and a half at least since his mother had taken him out of the public school and trusted him with Brenda to educate. He wondered what Miss Brenda thought of him now. Had Daniel told her how innocent the whole stupid thing had been? That he'd never in a million years thought he'd wind up here?

It was a joke, he thought. It had to be.

He got onto the bus and took a seat on the courthouse side. He watched the door of the old building, certain that his mother would come along, point to him, and say, "Gotcha!" Then he could get off and lose these handcuffs. It had to be one of his mother's object lessons. A year and a half ago she'd been so mad at him after he got suspended from school that she had taken him to River Ranch for a tour. Maybe this was just a step up from that. Maybe she just wanted him to know what it was like to get arraigned and convicted. Maybe it was all a conspiracy and the whole neighborhood was part of it. It was a pretty cruel way to teach a lesson, but he wouldn't hold it against them.

But his mother didn't come out, and no one lingered at the curb waiting to get him off the bus. Then the doors closed and the guards got on, and the bus started moving. It was not a trick, and it wasn't one of his mother's lessons. He was on his way to the state's teenaged version of prison.

The bus smelled of body odor, unwashed hair, and stale vomit. Mark stole a look around. Some of the prisoners had been here before, and their faces held dread but no mystery or fear. They sat like powder kegs ready to ignite. Others looked as thought they'd just been shoved off a cliff. One kid up at the front was so pale that Mark thought he needed medical care.

Mark thought he was going to be sick, too.

Where was his mother? Why hadn't his father done something? The bus turned down a dark, tree-covered street, moving farther and farther and farther from anyone who cared.

After a while, they came upon the facility that he had seen only as a spectator a year and a half earlier. Even when he'd been arrested last year, they hadn't locked him up. He'd had friends who'd spent a little time here. His friend Jayce from Knoxville had a droopy eye because he'd gotten in a fight in the center and it had damaged a nerve in his eyelid. They were mean here, he'd warned him, but Mark had had no intentions of ever confirming that fact.

They were taking this punishment thing too far, he thought as his lungs tightened. He wouldn't do it again if they'd just let him out. He would study and clean his room and respect his mom.

The bus stopped, and an angry guard stepped on and walked up and down the aisle. "Stand up!" he shouted, as if he'd told them a dozen times and was tired of it. "On your feet!"

Mark got to his feet.

"Hustle, now. Single file! Mouths shut!"

Mark shuffled off the bus and looked up at the Conan-sized guard waiting to take them inside. "Excuse me," he whispered. "This is all a mistake."

The man gave him a look of mock amazement, then shot another guard a look and started to laugh.

"No, really," Mark said. "I'm not supposed to be here."

"Course not," the guard said. "But till they discover their mistake, how about you just line up with all the other mistakes?"

Mark closed his eyes. "But you don't understand. My mother's going to get my lawyer to do something. She'll never let this happen. I'll be out of here before dark. There's no point in going through any more of this."

"What's your name?" the man boomed, making Mark jump.

Mark straightened and looked around. The other guys were getting a laugh out of this. "Mark Flaherty."

"Let's see," the guard made a ceremony of checking his clipboard. "Mark Flaherty, Mark Flaherty. Oh, *yeah*, here it is." His eyes widened and he looked up at Mark. "You know, you're right. It is a mistake. Good clean kid from Breezewood don't belong in no juvenile facility. Says it right here. Whadda you know?"

Mark's heart soared and he looked over at the clipboard for the place where the man pointed. Then laughter spat out, and the guard doubled over. The inmates around them snickered

with bitter superiority. Mark felt like an idiot. They were playing him, he thought. They didn't understand, but they would as
soon as his mother came and did something about this mess he
was in. And if she didn't, his father would. He knew they
wouldn't let him stay here another night.

His mother had jerked him out of public schools because
he'd been hanging with people like this. If she'd known what
he'd been doing in Knoxville, she would have had every lawyer
in town working to keep him from going there again. No, she
would never sit still for this.

But he could do nothing except go along now as they
marched them into the facility.

CHAPTER
Fifteen

Tory had neither the time nor the energy to attend Sylvia's luncheon presentation at Cathy's church—but she'd had so little opportunity to hear about Sylvia's work that she and Brenda felt obligated to go.

Tory hadn't wanted to leave Hannah at home, so she had brought her with her. She was exhausted from battling Hannah's ear infections and bronchitis the night before, but this afternoon they had sessions with the physical therapist, the respiratory therapist, and the occupational therapist.

She had brought Hannah's stroller and hoped the baby would sleep through the meeting. But before she had taken her seat, she heard her name shouted over the ladies filling the room.

"Tory Sullivan!"

She looked up and saw Amy Martin, an old friend who lived next door to her in the duplex where she and Barry lived before they'd had children. "Amy!" she said, and threw her arms around the woman. "I didn't know you went to church here."

"Six years," the woman said. "Look at you. You're so thin and perfect, just like you always were." She bent down to the stroller and smiled at Hannah. "A baby? What is this? Your third?"

Tory grew tense. "Yes, my third."

"Oh, what a sweetie!" She reached into the stroller and tickled Hannah's stomach. The child's mouth was open, and her tongue was hanging again. Tory wished she would pull it back in. "How old is she?"

Tory thought of lying, then was instantly ashamed. "Fifteen months."

"Fifteen?" The word came out a little weaker, and Amy eyed the baby again.

"She has Down's Syndrome," Tory said quietly.

Amy raised back up, her face stricken. "Oh, Tory! That's awful. I'm so sorry, honey."

Tory didn't know what she'd expected. Maybe the usual change of subject, or some benign words about how Down's Syndrome kids were such sweet children. Those things always made her angry, because she didn't like stereotypes any more than dismissal. But the sorrow was a new one. No one had expressed sadness over Hannah's birth in a long time.

Brenda stepped up to the stroller and found Hannah's pacifier. She gently put it in her mouth. "She's a precious child," she said. "Tory is a world-class mother. No child with Down's Syndrome was ever more blessed." She smiled that smile that instantly put people at ease. "I'm Tory's neighbor, Brenda Dodd."

"Amy Martin," the woman said. She turned her sorrow-filled eyes back to Tory. "We need to get together sometime and catch up, Tory. Over lunch, maybe."

There it was. The dismissal. Tory realized that Amy couldn't win. Anything she said would have made Tory angry. This wasn't her friend's problem. It was hers.

"Let's do that," she said, then looked up and saw that the chairman of the ladies' group was heading to the stage. Sylvia was about to be introduced.

Brenda took a seat near the back, but Tory felt tears choking her. She lifted Hannah out of her stroller. "I have to change a diaper," she whispered to Brenda. "I'll be back."

Brenda watched her retreat. Tory knew her neighbor read every crushing thought on her face and would have done anything to fix it. But this couldn't be fixed.

When Tory was in the hall, she held Hannah close, as if to make up for any slight the baby had faced. The pacifier fell out and rolled across the carpet. Tory bent to get it and slid it into her pocket until she could wash it. Hannah looked up at her with her mouth open. "She didn't mean it," Tory whispered to the child. "She doesn't know what a treasure you are."

As hard as she had fought to encourage Hannah's development, part of her hoped the child never grew aware enough to feel shame over something she couldn't control.

Then again, she wanted her to be normal, and be aware of everything.

She couldn't have it both ways.

She heard the group applauding as Sylvia got to the stage. Tory listened from the hallway as Sylvia told about her work in León, first with the orphans, then with the food program for the poor. Then she introduced the slides she had to show them.

Wearily, Tory went back in. She returned to the back row next to Brenda, Hannah in her lap, hugged back against her.

The woman operating the slide projector took her cue, and the first picture flashed on the screen. "I want to show you a few slides of the children that come to us for food," Sylvia said. The face of a starving, malnourished boy flashed onto the screen. He was dirty and had crusty mucus under his nose and greasy tangled hair. Rags hung off his body, as if his clothes had been made for someone much larger. He had a look of hopelessness on his face, and his eyes held a glint of despair. His little belly swelled above bony legs.

"This is Miguel," Sylvia said, her voice catching. "He's my little friend. His father was killed in the hurricane along with two of his sisters. His mother and he come each night hoping that we'll have food. We've been feeding him for about a month now, mostly beans and rice, since that has a lot of nutritional value and it doesn't cost very much. We figured out that we can feed a hundred to a hundred-fifty children like Miguel on $400 a month. Think about it, people," she said. "That's a little over two and a half bucks to as high as four dollars a day to feed a child like Miguel for a month. What better use can you think of for your money?"

Tory sat straighter, her arms tightly wrapped around Hannah. Another face flashed on the screen. This boy had bright, alert eyes.

"This is also Miguel," Sylvia said. "I took this picture the day I left. Notice the difference. His little belly isn't as swollen. He has a twinkle in his eye. He's actually smiling now. He connects. Not only has the food filled his hungry belly, but it's helped him physically in so many other ways. But that's not all," she said. "We had a Bible school last week in León, and little Miguel gave his life to Jesus. His mother brought him to church last Sunday. I have every faith that soon she'll come to Christ, too."

Applause erupted over the crowd. Tory could see that she wasn't the only one moved by the pictures. She glanced at Brenda and saw the tears on her face.

Sylvia showed several other slides, equally dramatic photos of other children she knew by name, their mothers and fathers, their baby sisters and brothers. When the slides were finished, Sylvia leaned on the podium, her eyes sweeping over everyone in the room.

"I know that Nicaragua seems a long way away," she said. "It did to me when my husband first came home and told me he wanted to go to the mission field there. And these faces, you don't know them. You've never seen them. Chances are, you'll never meet any of them. But I can tell you, they're real. They're my family now. They live where I live, and they're victims of the hurricane that has just destroyed the economy, taken away their homes and their businesses, ruined their crops. I know that the Lord sent me there to help in the aftermath of Hurricane Norris, and my husband and I are willing to make as many sacrifices as we can to help those people. But I came here today to ask you to help, too.

"Think about it. Four dollars or less will feed one child for a month. What do you spend four dollars on?" she asked. "When I lived here, I spent four dollars a day on the sodas I drank. It was nothing to run through McDonald's and pick up a burger and fries for under four dollars. But if you think about it the next time you go through that fast food window and realize that there's a child in another part of the world, with a distended belly and skinny little arms and a look of hopelessness in his eyes, then maybe you'll choose to spend that money on him, instead."

Tory smeared a tear across her face. Sylvia was right, she thought. Here Tory sat in her perfect little world, worrying constantly about her imperfect little child. But Hannah was happy and she was healthy and she was a joy, even if others couldn't see it. What if they'd had a hurricane sweep through the land and destroy their homes and businesses? What if they didn't have enough food to eat and had to rely on the kindness of people like Sylvia to feed them? What if that was all her children could hope for?

When Sylvia asked for pledges from the people there to help support the food program in León, Tory wanted to fill out a card. But this wasn't her church, she thought.

"We have to get our church involved," she whispered to Brenda.

Brenda's eyes glistened, too. "I was just thinking the same thing."

They were quiet as they got back into the car and drove home. "That was really good, Sylvia," Tory said. "Really, really good."

"Thank you," Sylvia said. "I get a little nervous when I get up in front of all those people like that. But then I remember it's not for me."

"What can we do, Sylvia?" Brenda asked. "How can we help?"

Sylvia smiled. "Well, to tell you the truth, I *had* planned to hit you up for something."

Tory grinned. "What?"

"Well, when I made it known I was coming home for a few days, I started getting a lot of invitations to speak to other churches about the work I was doing. I had to turn some of them down. But I was thinking that maybe you and Brenda and Cathy could go around and do it for me. I could leave these slides for you and some of my notes. If you could just go and make a presentation, tell them about the work we're doing, maybe you could get them to raise some money, too. We need all we can get. If we don't get it, we'll have to turn children like Miguel away. We'll have to tell their mothers and fathers that we can't help them. Then they won't want to hear the gospel, and they'll never get what they need most."

"I'll help," Brenda said. "But I'm not too good at public speaking. I kind of go weak in the knees. I break out in hives."

Tory grinned. "No, you don't."

"I do," Brenda said. "I have this fear of throwing up right on the stage."

"Brenda Dodd?" Tory asked. "The woman who has it together better than anyone I know, except Sylvia?"

"Well, sorry to pop your bubble," Brenda said. She was growing pale just talking about it. "I'll do what I can. I mean, I can try . . ."

"Me, too," Tory said. "I don't know what I'll do with Hannah. But I'll figure something out. Maybe we could do it together. Brenda could hold Hannah and work the slides, and I could speak."

"I could do that," Brenda said.

"Don't forget Cathy. I want her to get involved, too. It might help her get her mind off of Mark."

"I don't think anything is going to help get her mind off Mark," Brenda whispered.

"I've never heard her yelling like she did at the courthouse today," Tory said in a quiet voice.

"She seems so well-adjusted. You'd never know she had all that anger . . ."

"She's probably been wanting to say those things for years."

"I just wish she hadn't said it where the kids could hear," Brenda said. "They need to think their father's their hero—even if he's not."

"Brenda's right," Sylvia said. "No matter what a father does—or doesn't do—the children need to see him on a white horse. If they don't, how can they believe that God the Father is their rescuer and redeemer?" She looked out the window at the hazy mountains overlooking Signal Mountain. "Some of the children in León are so wounded by their fathers being absent during the hurricane. Little children and their mothers had to fight to survive on their own, when the father's strength might have made a difference. I can't fathom why men don't know how important they are." She dabbed at her eyes and glanced from one friend to the other.

"I'm glad I came home for the shower, even if it wasn't what we planned. But to tell you the truth, I can't wait to get back. I miss the children, and the eagerness in their faces, the sweet expectation when they look at me."

"Then it *was* a calling," Brenda said. "A couple of years ago you fought it tooth and nail."

"Yeah, but the Lord changed my heart. And now I don't think I could ever come back."

"Don't say that, Sylvia," Tory said. "Let us go on thinking that someday we'll have you back to sit with us on Brenda's porch and mentor us into women of God."

"You're already women of God," Sylvia said. "But who knows what the Lord had in mind?"

CHAPTER Sixteen

After a lunch of plain ham sandwiches, the guards herded Mark and the others into a room they facetiously called the beauty shop. The sound of buzzers startled him, and he saw three of the inmates sitting in the chairs. Burly guards, who looked as if they had no barber experience, shaved the hair off the inmates' heads. Mounds of blonde, brown, black, and red hair lay on the floor around the chairs.

Mark thought his heart was going to burst through his chest.

"No way, man," he bit out to the boy in front of him.

The kid turned around. "Shut up," he whispered. "Don't get us all in trouble."

"I'm not getting anybody in trouble," he whispered harshly, "but they are *not* shaving my head!"

"Watch them," the kid said.

This was too much. Mark had done everything else they had required. He had filled out all the paperwork they had requested and taken the obligatory shower complete with lice shampoo.

He had listened quietly through the rules as they were read out to him and had kept his mouth shut while they'd gone over the schedule. He couldn't believe any of this was constitutional. He made a note to look it up in his civics book when he got out of here. He was an American citizen. He had rights. They couldn't treat him like he was some subhuman, just because he'd made a mistake.

His frightened, angry gaze fixed on the foulmouthed boy who had been causing so much trouble since they'd loaded him onto the bus. But there wasn't anything even that kid could do about the hair being mowed off his head. He looked like an Army recruit.

To Mark, this seemed a more binding act than riding the bus here, putting on the clothes, using the lice shampoo. If they shaved his head and his mother still came and got him out, he'd have to return home like that. He didn't want to look like a doofus—and he didn't want to have the mark of a convicted criminal.

The guard called his name, and Mark backed away. "No, man, they're not shaving my head."

"Oh, yes, they are, pal." The guard grabbed his arm and jerked him toward the barber, but Mark resisted. Two more guards came to help, and Mark finally realized that he didn't have a chance against these people. He had to do what they said or suffer the consequences. He gave up and let them put him in the chair. He closed his eyes and, as the buzzer moved across his head, swore to get even.

It was his mother's fault. She should have been here sooner. It served her right to have a son who looked like this. It would show her. Every time she looked at him she'd remember what he'd been through.

Yes, maybe it was all right after all. He could get a lot of mileage out of this. But as he got down from the chair and rubbed his hand over his head, he realized what had been taken from him. Then he looked ahead into the hall—and saw that more was yet to come. It dawned on him with vivid clarity that he had lost all control of his life.

The guards moved the newcomers into what was called Building A. They had been issued special outfits: orange striped pants, like something the Cat in the Hat would wear, and white pullover shirts. They all looked alike with the stupid clothes and their heads shaved. None of them looked cool, and they were anything but tough. As they lined up on a yellow line drawn on the cement floor, he realized he was a clone of all of these other kids who had come in here with him. His life was not his own anymore.

Building A was a huge room with fifty beds lining the walls. At one end, high above the floor, was a wall of windows, behind which was an elevated room like those you see in drugstores. From this room, the guards kept close watch and took care of business. Mark realized that his days of privacy were gone. He had forty-nine roommates now. Even showers were not private.

They handed him a schedule of daily activities, and as his eyes ran from the five o'clock wake-up to bedtime at nine-thirty, he realized that he'd also lost control of his time. If he had thought Brenda was bad, giving them so little free time during her school day, he realized this was much worse. Not more than thirty minutes at a time was given for one to think. Even the school schedule was more grueling than what he'd had in either public school or at Brenda's house. He supposed it was all designed to make him miss what he'd left back home.

But instead of wishing for what he'd had, he fed the anger festering inside of him, making him angrier at his mother for failing to fix the situation. It was her job to get him out of this mess. It was the height of neglect for her to leave him in here, and he would never forgive her for it.

He only hoped he would see her soon so he could tell her.

CHAPTER
Seventeen

Cathy drove slowly down Pinewood Boulevard, searching the numbers on the houses for 352. She was so tired that her muscles ached, for she had lain awake all night, trying to picture where Mark was being kept, how frightened he must be, how full of remorse... and worrying about the arraignment and Mark's future.

Though he had confessed to selling the bag of marijuana to his friend Ham Carter, he hadn't told her much else. She had questions, like why the kid had picked Mark to set up. Why he'd seen fit to get a police officer involved. Whether it was really the first time Mark had done such a thing.

She found 352 and pulled into the driveway. A Jeep and the blue Lumina she had seen his parents drive to ball games sat in the driveway, so she knew she had the right house.

Her face hardened as she got out of the car and looked up at the yellow house with navy shutters. She hoped Ham was home, so she could look him in the eye and find out what he knew.

She stepped up on the porch and rang the bell, then knocked hard. The house shook with footsteps as someone crossed the floor, and the door came open.

"Yeah?" His face changed as he recognized her, and he started to close the door.

She stuck her hand out, willing to have it crushed to keep him from shutting the door. "No, you don't," she said. "I have to talk to you. Stand there like a man and look me in the eye."

Reluctantly, he stepped outside and pulled the door shut behind him. She wondered if his parents were inside. Why didn't he want them to know of his heroics in getting such a reprobate arrested?

Her mouth quivered as she looked up at Ham, who was taller than she. "I understand you had something to do with getting Mark arrested," she bit out. "I want to know what happened."

He shrugged. "Look, I'm sorry about Mark going to jail. I didn't know . . ."

"You didn't know *what?*"

"That he'd get a year. I didn't know he had two other offenses. He's a good guy. I don't have anything against him."

She realized she wasn't following him very well. Maybe her mind was too tired. Maybe her senses were dull. "Explain this to me," she said. "Did Mark or did he not sell you marijuana?"

"Yes, he did."

"And was it the first time?"

"Yeah."

"Then why did you call him and ask him to sell you some? What made you think he'd do it?"

"It was just a guess."

"A guess? What? You were bored that afternoon? You thought you'd spice up your life a little by putting Mark together with an undercover cop?"

"It was a deal we made, okay? I had to deliver *somebody.*"

She still couldn't understand. "A deal who made? You and Mark?"

"No." He got quiet then and looked through the windows into the house. Satisfied that no one could hear, he whispered,

"Me and the cop. He nailed *me* first, okay? It was my first offense, but I knew my dad would kill me if he knew. I mean, he'd *kill* me. He can't find out about this."

Cathy's eyes narrowed as the words sank in. "So why aren't *you* in jail?"

"Because the guy ... the cop ... he said that he wouldn't book me if I could give him somebody bigger. A dealer."

"A dealer." Cathy repeated the words in a monotone as her eyes grew wider. "Are you telling me that you gave him Mark?"

"I didn't *have* a dealer, okay? At least, not one I could name. I got mine from this guy who was at the ballpark one night. I didn't know if I could find him again. I had to come up with somebody. I knew Mark would have some ..."

She thought she might throw up. The air seemed stagnant, useless, and perspiration dotted the back of her neck.

"I figured Mark would sell us a joint, he'd get arrested, and they'd let him off since it was a first offense. Nobody told me Mark stole a car last year!"

"He didn't steal a car," she said in a metallic voice. "His delinquent friend took his stepfather's car without asking." She didn't bring up the other charge. It didn't matter now. All that mattered was that this kid had been trying to get himself out of trouble, and Mark had taken the fall.

She knew she should be rabid with rage. She should slap the kid and parade him in the house before his parents, let them hear what he had done. "My son is going to spend the next year of his life in a juvenile prison," she managed to get out. "A year. Do you know how long that is?"

"Yes, ma'am."

"Well, I hope you're sleeping well. I hope you're able to look yourself in the mirror."

He looked down at the boards beneath his feet, and she turned her back to him and started down the porch steps. Her knees wobbled and her hands shook. Finally, she turned back to him. "This can't be legal," she said. "I'm going to the police. I'm going to tell them what this cop did. Trading you for my son."

The kid got a pleading look. "Getting me thrown in jail isn't going to make up for what happened to Mark," he said.

"Maybe not," she whispered. "But it would sure make me feel better." Slowly, she made her way to her car.

By the time she reached the attorney's office, her anger was at a red-alert level. She stormed in, demanding to see him.

Slater heard the commotion and came to the door of his office.

"My son was set up," she said. "I just found out that he was a trade. A minor possession charge against his friend was dropped if he could lead the police to a dealer. Since the kid didn't know any, he figured he could turn Mark into one. Doesn't that constitute entrapment? Isn't this deal-making illegal?"

Slater took her into his office and sat down behind his desk. "Cathy, I know this must be upsetting. But the bottom line is that the police do make deals to catch bigger fish."

"If this isn't entrapment, then what is? I thought that entrapment was when a police officer tricked someone into committing a crime."

"Not exactly. I thought it might be entrapment, too, when I first heard about it. I even spoke to the arresting officer and got the lowdown, then talked to that Ham Carter kid to get the other part of the story."

"When did you do this?"

"The night Mark got arrested. Right after I got Steve's phone call, I started working on it. I didn't want to mention it to you when I interviewed Mark before the arraignment, because I had already figured out that it didn't fit the definition of entrapment. There's no entrapment unless the officer persuaded Mark to commit a crime he ordinarily wouldn't have committed."

"But he did!"

"No, he didn't. The Carter kid called Mark and asked him to sell him the bag. Mark never spoke to the police officer. Even when he got in the car with them, the cop never asked him to sell him the drugs. The Carter kid did all the talking."

"But it was planned! It was part of a deal. It wasn't Mark's idea. He never would have done it if it hadn't been for the deal."

"But the police never coerced Mark, so we don't have a leg to stand on there. All they did was give him the opportunity to commit the crime."

"The cop lied to him about who he was!"

"Yes, but that's legal. Police officers are allowed, by law, to operate undercover."

She got to her feet and rubbed her forehead, blinking back the tears in her eyes. "My son would not have done this on his own." Her voice cracked. "It was *their* idea, not his. You could, at least, have tried."

"I would have if I'd had the proper evidence," he said. "Instead, I had lots of evidence to the contrary. Mark was more than willing to make this transaction, he worked it out with one of his peers instead of a cop, and he anxiously took the money. It was his third offense, which didn't help matters any. Believe me, Cathy. If I could have used the entrapment defense, I would have. But they had Ham Carter's statement, and Mark confirmed it in his own statement to the police. They asked him point-blank if the cop persuaded him to sell the bag, and he said no, that the guy was pretty quiet."

"There *must* be a way. There has to be something we can do."

"If he hadn't already had three offenses . . . if it hadn't been a violation of his probation . . . maybe . . ."

"If he were *your* son . . ."

"If he were my son, and he had the same record, and made the same transaction, he'd be right where yours is tonight. As badly as I'd want to, there wouldn't be anything I could do. I'm sorry."

She drove home, feeling the pain of fatigue and frustration, and the ache of those tears that had swollen her eyes. Her son had been betrayed by a friend. Despite his own behavior, she knew the fury he must feel right now.

He was counting on her to get him out.

But there wasn't a thing she could do.

She went home and headed for her bed, fell to her knees beside it. She began to pray, the deepest, most earnest prayers she had ever prayed.

But there was a wall between her and God, keeping her from connecting. Sickness rippled through her stomach, and fatigue pulled at her body like metal weights.

Why wasn't God answering?

Had she constructed these walls, or had he? She remembered what Steve had said about her not being able to trust her emotions. She tried to run through what she knew for sure about God.

He would never leave nor forsake her.

So why wasn't he helping?

He was just.

So why had he allowed Mark to be tricked?

He was merciful.

So why couldn't she get another chance for her son?

Maybe she wasn't righteous enough. Maybe she had been too hate-filled, too angry, too unforgiving. Maybe he was punishing her for the way she had talked to Jerry today.

The bitterness and anger and hatred that she had harbored for Jerry had spilled out when she was tipped over, and now she realized that if she was to be forgiven, she was going to have to forgive him. If she wanted her prayers heard, prayers for protection of Mark in this dark time of his life, then she was going to have to agree with God that her words and her behavior with Jerry had been sinful, that the blame she tried to cast on him was not helpful either to him or to the children, or to herself for that matter. Christ had forgiven her so many times, and now she was being called to forgive Jerry. Again.

She took the bitterness and bundled it up like a package. Mentally, she laid it on the altar for God to consume. Along with it, she bundled up the anger she felt toward Ham Carter. She hoped she'd gotten it all. She could only surrender it through the power of Christ. She wondered if he knew how hard this was for her.

When she finished praying, she sat back on her bed. Her eyes ached from the weeping she had done that day, and her lips felt dry and raw. She hadn't learned about the pathology of tears in veterinary school, but she knew there was something cleansing about them, something comforting in their aftermath.

She took a deep breath, feeling as if she were a little child being prodded along by God to do the right thing. She picked up the phone and dialed Jerry's number. His wife answered, and Cathy breathed another prayer of deliverance from the bitterness directed at her.

"May I speak to Jerry, please?" she said.

The woman recognized her voice and didn't answer, just gave him the phone.

"What do you want?" he asked.

She closed her eyes. Her hand was shaking as she clutched the phone.

"Jerry, I just wanted to apologize to you for the way I spoke to you today. It was uncalled for."

"What happened? Did the kids hear it and get angry? Is this apology because you want to show them you're really a big person?"

"No," she said, "they're not here. I'm apologizing because I'm a Christian now and I'm supposed to be more aware of what God has done for me. I'm not supposed to go off half-cocked and rant and rave against people who have hurt me. I'm supposed to understand that there are plenty of people I have hurt, too."

"Your point?" Jerry asked.

"My point is that I'm sorry for the things I said. It didn't help anybody. It only upset the kids."

"So you're admitting that it wasn't true, that it wasn't my fault that Mark turned out the way he did?"

"Mark hasn't turned out any way," she bit out, her voice rising. She closed her eyes and prayed that God would help her through this. She just couldn't do it on her own. "He's only fifteen. We don't know how he's going to turn out yet. I haven't given up on him, and I'm not going to. I will not surrender my child to the world."

She heard a deep sigh on Jerry's end. "I'll ask you again, Cathy. What is it you want?"

"I told you," she said. "I wanted to apologize. It's up to you. You can accept it or not. Your call. I just wanted to offer it."

She heard the click on the other end and knew he had hung up. She knew she shouldn't feel this way, but the severed line of communication gave her relief. She lay back on the bed and looked up at the ceiling, wishing she could see God's face there. Was he nodding that she had been obedient and done the right thing, or was he shaking his head because she still didn't get it?

"I'm trying, Lord," she whispered. "I'm trying, but I need your help."

Wednesday she could go and visit Mark. She wondered if he'd had anything to eat today or if he was too upset to choke anything down. Sometimes when he pouted, he went for days without eating. She remembered when he was much younger, when she and Jerry had told the kids they were getting a divorce, she had heard Mark a little while later throwing up in the bathroom. She wondered if he was throwing up now.

She heard a knock on the door and called, "Come in." Annie opened the door.

"Mom, I was just wondering. Can I go with you to see Mark Wednesday?"

Cathy saw that she had been crying, too. Her eyes were as red and swollen as Cathy's. The thought surprised her. Besides apathy, Annie's main emotion concerning Mark was disgust. She never missed an opportunity to insult him, and one of her favorite pastimes was making him feel like an idiot. Why would she cry for him now? She supposed that was the paradox of siblings. They loved each other, even when they didn't act like it.

"Annie, I think I need to go by myself the first time. There are going to be plenty of times when Mark's going to need to see you, but I think right now he's probably too upset."

Annie swallowed hard and looked at her mother with misty eyes. "Mom, what am I going to tell people?"

"I guess the best thing would be the truth. It's going to come out anyway, if they don't know already."

"But when I think about having a brother who's been convicted of a crime, I just think of scumbags and sleazeballs. Not Mark. He's just some little mixed-up kid. He doesn't know any better."

"He knows better," Cathy said. "He absolutely knows better. Don't ever fool yourself into thinking he doesn't."

"But, Mom, he's just dumb, that's all. He does stupid things. He always has. He shouldn't have to pay with a year of his life."

"Well, maybe if I'd made him pay a little more when he broke those little rules, the government wouldn't have to make him pay now."

Annie wiped her eyes. "Well, I guess that means you're going to really crack down on Rick and me now. Turn into some kind of Hitler."

The thought had crossed Cathy's mind. "No, honey, I'm not going to do that. You don't have to worry. You haven't done anything wrong, and neither you nor Rick is headed for prison."

"Well, thank you for that, at least," Annie said, falling onto the bed next to her mother. "I'm glad you agree. As a matter of fact, I've spent most of the day patting myself on the back 'cause I'm not in jail."

Cathy almost laughed, but the humor quickly melted into despair. Annie hugged her. It was something the girl rarely initiated, and it moved her. "I can't believe he did this on the day of your shower," Annie said. "That was really low."

Cathy laughed without humor. "There's really no good time to break the law and wind up in jail."

When Annie went back to her room, Cathy went to bed and stared at the ceiling, wishing for sleep. But it wouldn't come. Peace was a gift that God had withdrawn from her. She didn't know if she'd get it back in the next year.

CHAPTER Eighteen

Wednesday finally came, and as Cathy prepared for her first visit with her son in prison, she took great pains with her appearance. She knew that her grief would be apparent on her face, but at least she could look like someone who knew how to get along in society. She didn't want anyone mistaking her for the mother of a houseful of criminals.

How would they process the visitors? Would they take her purse and search her clothes? Would she have to pass through a metal detector? Would she be able to sit side by side with Mark, hug him, kiss his cheek, cry with him? Or would they have them separated by glass and make them talk on telephones? How was a mother to behave when she visited her son in juvenile detention?

All of those questions would be answered soon enough. And she knew Amy Vanderbilt hadn't covered them in her etiquette book. Steve had asked to go with her, but Cathy had felt it was best if she went alone this first time. Mark would want to vent, and she didn't want anyone there to interfere with his freedom in doing so. But she had to admit, the thought of going alone terrified her.

She would just have to feel her way through this, and pray that God would accompany her every step of the way.

Because it wasn't a maximum security prison, the guards only made the visitors walk through metal detectors and asked them to leave their bags in a holding room. Anything they wanted to bring to the inmates had to be approved, and to get it approved, they were forced to stand in a long line in a poorly ventilated room.

But Cathy hadn't brought Mark anything, so she went into the visitation room and took a table. She was the first one there, and she looked around, thankful that she would be allowed to sit at a table with her child and hug him, even though the guard had given them each a stern warning about public displays of affection. That *couldn't* apply to mothers—if so, the guard would just have to call her down.

She sat fidgeting at the table as other visitors came into the room to wait for the inmates to come in. A teenaged mother of three took a chair at the back of the room. The baby cried a hungry cry, but the girl ignored it as she tried to keep her two- and three-year-olds corralled.

Next to her table, a grandmother came in with a stack of books she had gotten permission to bring. At another table, two boys who looked like they might belong here themselves slouched in chairs tipped back on two legs.

The door opened, and a guard began escorting inmates in. She watched their faces, watched them head for their families. When Mark stepped into the doorway, she almost didn't recognize him. She hadn't been prepared for the shaved head. It startled her, and she knew her surprise showed on her face.

She got up and waited for him to approach her, and all the emotions of the day he'd been arraigned came rushing up again. She reached out for him, but he shook her off.

"Don't touch me."

Without waiting for her reaction, he stormed to the table, scraped a chair back, and dropped into it. Wearily, Cathy accepted his rebuff and sat down.

"Mark, how are you?"

His eyes bored into hers. "Look what you got me into."

Cathy sat back. "*I* got you into? What are you talking about?"

"I'm talking about the guilty plea. You're the one who made me do that, and if I hadn't, maybe I would have gotten off. A year, Mom! I'm in here for a year! Do you have any idea what this place is like?" He lowered his voice as he looked around. "These other guys, they'd just as soon slit my throat as look at me. The same kind of people you wouldn't let me hang around with before, now I've got to live with them. They put me in this big room with like a hundred other guys. I'll never have any privacy. I can't keep any stuff because they'll take it. I have this tiny little locker where I can keep my shoes at night when I sleep. And a change of these stupid orange pants. I can't believe you did this to me!"

"Mark, I didn't do this to you," Cathy said. "You did this to yourself. You broke the law. The guilty plea was a gamble. You're right. We didn't know what we should have done. Nobody had any answers or guarantees. We did the thing that we thought was best."

"So are you going to appeal this or what?" Mark asked.

Cathy's head was beginning to throb. "Honey, there's nothing to appeal. You got caught red-handed. You pled guilty. The prosecutor has lots of evidence. The judge has made a ruling."

"But I can't stay here, Mom!" He burst into tears and grabbed her hand. "Mom, please. If you'll just get me out of here, I swear I'll never do it again. I'll never see those guys again. I'll just hang around with Daniel 'cause he never gets into any trouble. And I'll study hard and I'll make straight A's with Miss Brenda. You'll see. I'll start helping you in the clinic every day for free. And I'll keep my room clean and I'll even start supper sometimes. Please, Mom!"

As hard as she tried, Cathy couldn't hold back her tears. "Mark, there's nothing I can do. Don't you understand?"

"Of course there's something you can do," Mark said. "You're my mother. They can't decide where I live. I have the right to live with my family."

"You don't have any rights when you break the law," she said. "You gave up those rights when you decided to sell those drugs."

He pressed both fists against his temples. "If this is one of those lessons where you're trying to teach me something, trying to scare me to death so I'll straighten up, it's working, okay? You can stop it now. You can just go tell the guy that I'm finished, I'm changing. I'll do anything I have to do, but please get me out of here."

"Mark, this is not something I've chosen for you. You're stuck here for a year, because of what *you* did, not because of anything else. And, honey, I know it's horrible. I know you never even dreamed that this could happen. But it did. And I'm not able to do anything about it."

"I wish they had the death penalty for something like this," he said. "Maybe I'll just kill myself and get it all over with. Then I won't be a bother to you or Dad or anybody, anymore."

"Mark, don't talk like that."

"Why not?" he said. "Why should I care? If I've got to spend the next year of my life in this place, I might as well be dead. A year is practically an eternity."

"No, it's not an eternity," Cathy said. "Do you want to know what eternity is? Eternity is a billion times longer than the sentence you're serving in here, and then some. And, Mark, when you do die you're going to stand face-to-face with God. Whether it's sooner or later, I'm not going to be able to stand there with you any more than I was able to stand with you in front of that judge."

"Don't talk to me about God," Mark said. "If God cared about me, I wouldn't be here in this stupid place."

"God does care about you, Mark," Cathy said, "and he's a better parent than I am. If I had any power at all, I'd jerk you out of here so fast these people wouldn't know what hit them. But I don't have that power. I don't have any power at all."

She rubbed her face and tried to calm herself down. "Come on, Mark, can't you just tell me about the place? What's it like? Who are the people in that room with you? What are they here for?"

"Want to know what it's like, Mom?" he asked. "They treat me like dirt, that's what. And then they put me in the room with more dirt. And what are those guys in for? For acting like dirt. And for the next year that's all I'll be. Dirt. And when I come out, I'll still be dirt."

"You're not dirt, Mark," Cathy said. "You are my son."

"Well, enjoy it, Mom, because your house will be empty as soon as Annie goes to college. Then you won't have me to kick around anymore. It'll be just you and the empty house. Oh, and yeah, your new husband and his perfect kid. This is pretty convenient, isn't it? Get rid of the kid who's probably going to make the most problems in your marriage. Then you don't have to be bothered."

Cathy felt as if he had struck her. She sat back hard in her chair and gaped at him through her tears. "Mark, I know you're upset," she managed to choke out, "but you can't possibly think for a minute that either of us wished this on you. I did everything I could to keep you away from kids like that, to keep you from walking down the wrong path, but you went anyway, Mark. It wasn't my fault, and it wasn't Steve's fault."

She felt that tugging on her heart and obeyed it. "And it wasn't your father's fault either," she added. "It was *your* fault, Mark. And if you don't own up to it, you're never going to get over this. Never. It will be the longest year you've ever lived."

Mark drew in a deep breath as if filling himself with strength, then pushed himself up out of his chair. "I guess I'll just have to do what I can to get along here," he said.

"What does that mean?" Cathy asked.

"That means I'll act like dirt. I'll be what everybody expects." Then he turned around and headed back to the guard.

Cathy tried to stop him. "Mark, don't go. Come on back. We can talk." Some of the others turned and looked, and she sank back down, trying to be less conspicuous.

"I don't have anything left to say to you, *Mom*." His emphasis on the word was filled with sarcasm.

As the guard took him back through the metal door, she looked around at the other families visiting at the tables. They looked very much like her. Some were having pleasant conversations. She supposed they were the ones who accepted their plight. Others were crying, just as she was. How had she wound up here? This wasn't how her life was supposed to turn out. This wasn't where her son was supposed to be at age fifteen.

Feeling nauseous, she headed to the door, anxious to get out of this place, but devastated that she had to leave her son behind.

CHAPTER
Nineteen

When she got home that night, Steve was sitting in his car, waiting in her driveway for her. As soon as she pulled into her garage, he got out and came to meet her, a look of caution on his face.

"How was your visit?"

She was too tired to cry any more tears, and as she reached out to hug him, she let herself lean on him for the first time since the arraignment. "It was about as bad as you could expect," she said. "Mark's blaming everybody, even you."

"*Me?*" Steve asked.

"Oh, yeah." She took his hand and led him inside. She dropped her keys and purse on the table with a clash. "He even had this scenario in his mind that you and I were secretly delighted that this had happened, because when Annie goes off to college it will leave my house empty, then you and I will be free to get married with no problems. The only child in the house will be Tracy. Where is she, by the way?"

Steve seemed momentarily confused, as if he couldn't concentrate. "Oh—I got a baby-sitter to come stay with her after she went to bed. I wanted to come over and see if you needed me. He actually said that?"

"Yeah, but I think it just came to his head as he was talking," Cathy said. "He also blamed his friends . . . and God. And, of course, he blamed me from several different angles. Just one wouldn't do." She tried to stop her tears. "I don't know how I'll get through this, Steve. I really don't."

"I'll help you," he whispered. "I'll be here for you."

She breathed a laugh and pulled herself away from him. "Steve, you can't be thinking that we can still get married, can you?"

She saw that look of dread coming across his face. "Of course I am, Cathy. What do you think? That *I'm* going to call it off just because of what's happened?"

"No," she said. "Maybe you should be thinking that *I'm* going to call it off. I mean, I can't think about getting married when my son is sitting in a prison."

"It's not a prison, Cathy," he said. "He'll be all right."

She knew he didn't mean to downplay her grief, but the comment made her angry, anyway. "That's easy for you to say," she told him. "It's not your child that's in there."

His face instantly softened, and he stepped toward her. "Cathy, I didn't mean that you shouldn't grieve. And I hurt when you hurt. I love Mark, too."

That made her even angrier. "You can't love him," Cathy said. "You don't love somebody just by saying it. His own father doesn't even know how to love him."

He dropped his hands to his sides, frustrated. "What do you want me to say, Cathy?"

"I don't know," she said. "I guess maybe we ought to just call off the wedding for now."

"Until when?" Steve asked. "Cathy, it's time. Please don't do this again."

"It can't be time," she said. "Not when my son is in trouble. I can't *think* right now, Steve. I can't plan. Everything feels like it's just hanging in limbo somewhere, like it's all going to come crashing down on me."

He breathed out a laborious sigh, then dropped into a chair and stared at the wall for a moment. Finally, he slapped his hands on the armrests. "All right. We can postpone it, but I won't call it off. I'm going to marry you, Cathy."

"Fine," she said. "We can postpone it. That's all I want."

"And you'll keep wearing the ring?" Steve asked.

She looked down at the diamond he had given her for Christmas over a year ago. It was beautiful and had been such a sweet surprise. Neither of them had known just what they were getting into at the time. The ring sealed the promise they had made to marry each other when the time was right. But she wondered if it ever would be.

"Yes, I'll keep wearing the ring," she said. "I just need some time right now. I need for you to understand."

"I do understand," he said, and she saw the emotion battling for control of his face. "I'm disappointed. Tracy will be disappointed. *Everybody* will be. And I don't really see how waiting will make things easier for you. If we could just combine our households and become man and wife, I could be here with you night and day to support you and be with you when you're upset. I could help you through this."

"Won't you, anyway?" she asked.

"Of course I'll help you." He got up and crossed the room and looked into her eyes. "I'll do whatever I can, but it's not the same. I won't be in your bed at night to hold you when you cry." He tipped his head to the side and gazed down at her. "Cathy, I love you. It's hard to wait."

"I know it is," she whispered. "But I just need more time."

"How much?" he asked.

She shrugged. "How long will you wait?"

He sat down on the couch and leaned his head back, thinking. She wondered what was going through his mind. Was he wondering if it was even worth hanging on?

"I guess I'll wait as long as it takes," he said.

"Well, if he's going to be in there a year . . ."

He looked up at her with that look of dread again.

"I don't want him coming home to a whole different family, to a household that's not what he left. I don't want to jolt him like that, make him feel like he lost a whole year out of his life. Or give him the feeling that he's not a part of things here."

"If he feels *that* way, Cathy, it has nothing to do with you. He's losing a whole year out of his life no matter what you do. There's no way around that."

"But if we could just wait until he got out, set the date for some time after that. We could do it, Steve. I know it'll be hard. It's been a hard wait already, but we can wait. Can't we?"

He looked like a child who had just been told Christmas wouldn't come until July.

"Steve, look at it this way. If you marry me now, you marry all my problems. You marry my kids. You marry the smart-aleck remarks and the screaming fights. And you marry this prison sentence that I can't even deal with yet. You and Tracy are so much better off without us right now. This is not what you bargained for when you gave me this ring."

"I bargained for you, Cathy," he said. "I wanted you, and I knew everything that came with it."

"You didn't know about jail."

"No, but neither did you," Steve said. He grabbed her hand and pulled her down next to him. Framing her face with both hands, he looked into her eyes. "We're going to get through this together whether we're married or not, Cathy. Okay?"

"Okay," she whispered.

"Will you count on me?" he asked. "Will you lean on me? Will you let me help and stop being such a tough guy?"

"I'll try," she said.

He held her with his eyes a moment longer. "I'm not promising to wait a whole year." He smiled then, and she saw the mist swelling in his eyes again. "That doesn't mean I'm walking out on you. What I mean is that I'm going to try my best to talk you out of waiting until Mark gets out. I don't think waiting that long will do him *or* us any good. Maybe the time will come before then when you'll feel more peace about it. Maybe when you see light at the end of this tunnel. Besides, if we break up, we have to return all those gifts."

She smiled. "I can't open them, you know. I don't know whether I should return them now or not."

"You don't have time," he said with a grin. "Just leave them right where the neighbors put them. They're not in the way. And since the wedding was going to be so small, we don't have a lot of planning to undo. My mother was going to make the cake, so that will be easy to cancel. I'll call our guests and cancel the florist. Meanwhile, I'm going to go on acting like a man about to get married."

He stayed a while longer. By the time he left, she felt a little better. But depression quickly fell back over her.

She walked aimlessly around the house, trying to straighten things up. Rick and Annie were out, and her every movement seemed loud and hollow. She avoided Mark's room, knowing that there wasn't comfort there—only more recriminations.

The blinking light on her answering machine told of stored messages. She dreaded hearing them. Most of them were probably shocked reactions from friends as they heard about Mark's mess. But what if his lawyer had called with a new idea for getting him out?

She pushed the button and cringed at the first pity-filled platitude from the women's minister at her church. She pressed fast-forward, and made her way through several more. When Sylvia's voice came on, she sat back and listened.

"Honey, it's me, Sylvia. I came by before going to the airport, but you weren't home. I hope you're all right."

She could hear Sylvia pause to control her voice.

"Tory and Brenda are taking me. I have a 9:00 red-eye flight, so I can get there in the morning. I don't know when I'll see you again. But I love you, and I'll be praying. Hang in there, honey."

Cathy pulled her knees up on the couch and closed her eyes. Tears squeezed out. She felt lost, as if she'd let her life raft slip out of her reach.

Sylvia was leaving, and she didn't know when she'd see her again. It could literally be years.

She looked at the clock, saw that it was only eight-thirty. If she hurried, she might make it to the airport before Sylvia left.

She grabbed her purse, stumbled into her shoes, and bolted out to her car.

It had begun to rain, and the scent of wet summer was heavy on the air. Darkness fell over Breezewood like a good-night blanket tucking them in.

Mark slept hard when rain pattered against his window. She wondered if he could hear it tonight.

She reached the airport and parked at baggage claim, then checked the monitor for Sylvia's gate. Then dashing up the escalator without waiting for it to carry her to the top, she checked her watch.

Nine o'clock.

She ran down the wide hall, checking gates, until she came to one overflowing with people. Her eyes fell on Sylvia, Brenda, and Tory, huddled in the corner.

She was breathing hard when she got to them. "I thought I'd missed you!"

Sylvia sprang up. "Cathy! Oh, honey, you didn't have to come!"

"Yes, I did. I couldn't let you leave without saying good-bye." She pulled Sylvia into a crushing embrace.

Brenda laughed. "Well, this just couldn't be more perfect. Sylvia's plane is late because of the weather."

"Looks like a God-thing to me," Tory said.

Sylvia pulled Cathy down into the chair next to her. "We can sit here and visit and pretend it's one of our porches. Did you see Mark?"

Cathy sank into the seat and leaned her head back against the wall. "I saw him. He's angry. Blaming me. I don't know what to do."

"It could be a long year," Sylvia said. She looked down at her knees. She was wearing a pair of shorts, and Cathy noticed that her legs were thinner than they'd ever been. Sylvia was working too hard in Nicaragua, she thought. She wasn't getting enough to eat.

"I was thinking about how awful this was today," Sylvia said, "and then I started thinking back on Joseph's illness, and Tory's pregnancy. We thought both of those were horrible crises, too."

"They *were* crises," Cathy said. "No way around it. Don't try to sugar-coat it. They were awful."

"Yeah, they were," Tory said.

"But remember when they were all over?" Brenda cut in. "That night in the hospital, when we all sat around and talked about the best moment of the crisis, the pivotal ones where we learned something and grew?"

"I'm tired of learning things and growing," Cathy said.

"Well, aren't we all?" Sylvia agreed with a smile. "I was tired of learning and growing in the fourth grade when we started doing multiplication tables, but I still had to learn them." She gave Cathy a thoughtful look. "We did it again with Tory, you know. After Hannah was born and all was well, we were able to look back and think of the best moments. There were lots of them."

Cathy knew what she was getting at, but she rejected it. "Sylvia, there aren't going to be any best moments when my son is in jail. I'm not going to grow from this. I'm not going to learn from it. I'm just going to grieve for a very long time."

"That's what I thought," Tory said, "but Barry came back . . . and we have Hannah. As hard as things have been with her, I wouldn't undo any of it."

"If we learned anything from those days," Brenda said, "it's that sometimes God uses crises to bless us."

"Thanks, guys, but this isn't just your run-of-the-mill crisis."

"No crisis is run-of-the-mill," Sylvia said. "And we know you're in pain. I'm not trying to make it sound easy. I'm just saying that I think some day, maybe not so far away, we'll all be able to sit around and think back on this year and what happened with Mark, and we'll see some things that we can't see now. Who knows, Cathy? Maybe this will be a wake-up call for Mark."

"I wish I'd taught him better," Cathy said. "I should have taught him responsibility. I should have taught him consequences. I shouldn't have waited for the state to do it."

"You tried," Sylvia said. "Don't kid yourself. You haven't been sitting around letting him off the hook."

"You haven't, Cathy," Tory said. "Every time I'm at your house, Mark's been grounded for something. And for the last couple of years he's been home-schooling with Brenda because of what he did in the public school. You did the best you could to keep him away from the friends who were a bad influence."

Brenda nodded. "He's building a testimony, Cathy, and you have to let God finish the work that he started on him."

Cathy wanted to believe that God had a plan in all of this, that things were going to turn out well, but she knew Mark's heart was not where it needed to be. She wasn't sure he was going to allow God to work in him.

The ground clerk's rapid-fire voice amplified across the terminal. "Ladies and gentlemen, Flight 531 from Memphis has arrived at Gate 15. We will begin boarding momentarily."

The reality of Sylvia's departure hit Cathy in the heart, and she grabbed Sylvia's hand. "Don't go," she whispered.

Sylvia smiled. "I have to. I have work to do."

Tory pulled a tissue from her purse and dabbed her eyes, and Brenda struggled valiantly to hold back the tears welling in her own eyes.

"But there's a mission field right here in your own neighborhood," Cathy said. "You don't have to go to Nicaragua to find people who need help. All this time you had a criminal living right next door and you didn't even know it."

"Don't say that," Sylvia scolded. "Honey, don't ever say that about your son again. You need to learn to bless Mark, not curse him. The words that come out of your mouth, even if he doesn't hear them, are more powerful than you think."

Cathy wondered if there was a cave nearby she could crawl into for the next year. "Maybe my words are exactly what got him to this point," she said. "Maybe without even knowing it, I've cursed his entire life."

"There you go again," Sylvia said, "blaming yourself. You've got to stop that. All you can do is say that from this moment on things will be different."

"But how?" Cathy asked. "How do I make them different? Sylvia, you don't know how many times I've gotten on my knees and prayed and asked God to make me a better mother, to make me stop finding reasons not to teach them the Bible, to stop letting the television dictate our evenings. I've prayed that God will empower me to do that and make me want to when I'm lazy. But I'm still me. I still say things I wish I hadn't said. And I still do things wrong. How do I change? How do I make myself the kind of parent that would raise godly children? None of this is working for me."

"Do you remember the story Jesus told about the vine and the branches?"

Cathy was thankful that was one part of the Bible she was familiar with.

"Jesus said that we should abide in him and that through him we could bear fruit. Do you understand what that means, Cathy?"

"I think I do," she said. "It means that we get our power from God."

"Don't you know that a branch that's not attached to the vine is going to die? The leaves wither, and it doesn't bear anything. There's no fruit."

"So you think I've fallen off the vine?" Cathy asked.

"No," Sylvia said, patting her knee. "I think you're still on the vine. I just don't think you're using the vine for your power. You see, in a vine all the branches get all their energy and all their life from that vine. Every piece of fruit, every leaf on the branch, comes from that vine. The branch can't do it alone. There's no way. If it falls on the ground it just withers up and dies. That's what Jesus was trying to tell us. All you have to do is abide in him. You have to soak up the life that he gives you. You have to soak up the power. You have to use it."

"And how do you do that?" Cathy asked. "By reading your Bible every day?"

"Not just reading it," Brenda said. "By soaking it up. Studying it. Meditating on it, thinking about it, turning it over in your mind, living with it, breathing it."

"That takes a lot of effort and a lot of time," Tory said. "It's not so easy when there are kids running through the house demanding your time and attention."

Cathy allied herself with Tory. "Or when you've got a clinic to run and people who need things done, when you're trying to keep a fiancé happy. Life just wears me out. I'd love to spend all day every day reading the Bible, but that's just not realistic. I really do want to feel that power and authority that comes from Jesus. But I'm new at this, and I'm slow growing. I guess I should be a lot further along by now, but I'm not." She shoved her hand through her hair. "I guess God's pretty disgusted with me."

"He's not disgusted," Sylvia said. "He'll feed you milk as long as you need it. But eventually you've got to take solid food."

"If I'd taken it sooner," Cathy said, "then maybe Mark wouldn't be in this position."

"And maybe he would," Brenda said. "Do you believe that God is a good and loving parent?"

"Yeah," Cathy said. "And a wise one, too. He always knows what's best. When I just parent in fits and starts, trying and failing and trying again, God gets it right."

"You have to trust him with Mark," Sylvia said. "He's coming of age, Cathy. He's at the point where there's very little that his mother can tell him. God's got to get his attention. And he's in a place right now where he can."

"How can you say that?" Cathy asked. "He's in there with criminals and thieves and drug addicts!"

"Maybe he needs to look around and see what he could turn out to be. Or maybe God has just strategically positioned him there for a very important reason. Maybe he's going to use him."

"Yeah, right."

"Just wait," Sylvia said. "Just wait and see what God can do. I can't promise that everything will turn out exactly the way you want, but I can promise that you'll be amazed at the way God works through this."

Cathy stared off into space for a moment, trying to picture it, but she failed. Finally, she reached out to hug her friend. "I'm going to miss you," Cathy whispered.

"And I miss you already," Sylvia said. She turned back to Brenda and Tory, and they all got up and hugged.

When they separated, Sylvia smeared her tears across her face. "I wish I could come back for the wedding."

"Well, maybe you can," Cathy said. "We postponed it again. Indefinitely."

"No!" Tory cried. "Cathy, you can't."

"It's just not a good time," Cathy said. "But it's okay. We're still in love. I'm still wearing the ring. And according to him, he's still going to act like a man about to get married."

The boarding call piped across the terminal, and Sylvia framed Cathy's face. "Don't you throw everything away because one bad thing happened," she said. "Steve's a good man. An answer to prayer."

"I know," she said. "I won't forget that."

Sylvia picked up her bag. "And if you need me . . . any of you . . . I'm just down the continent."

They laughed through their tears and hugged again, none of them in a hurry to let go.

🐟

That night, unable to sleep, Cathy got out of her bed and knelt down beside it. She put her elbows on the mattress and folded her hands in front of her face.

"Lord," she whispered, "I know I don't even have a clue what it means to abide in you. I can say I'm doing it—but when I try to read the Bible . . . the words just rattle around in my brain, and ten minutes later I forget what I read." She hated admitting that. "Change me, Lord. I'm talking a major makeover. I want to be able to pray for Mark the right way, in a way where you can hear me and honor the prayers and answer them. I don't think I've been taking prayer seriously enough, especially not the prayers about my children." Her voice wobbled.

"I need you to put me back on the vine, Lord, and give me that life that I know you have. Pump it through me and help me." She wiped her tears. "And, Father, be a parent to Mark, so he has at least one good parent who knows what he needs. Because I sure don't."

The words tightened her throat, and she sat back on her heels and leaned her face into the mattress.

There were no more words, no more petitions. She had nothing left to say, but she hadn't finished praying. She felt as if God's hand touched the back of her head, stroked her hair, like a daddy comforting a hurting child. He was here with her, her father and her husband. He was her provider and her sustainer, her teacher and her comforter. He had revived her branch on the vine.

Neither her church nor Steve, nor Sylvia, nor any of her godly friends could do that for her. Only Christ could. And he could do it for Mark as well.

Time passed without any marking. She never looked at the clock nor yearned to get back in bed. She was still praying, even if the words weren't coming. This time, she was listening, receiving. And God was not locked away somewhere in some inaccessible throne room, silently registering her prayers. Instead, he was sitting here with her, holding her in his lap, loving her like the child who had finally come home.

CHAPTER *Twenty*

After changing planes in Atlanta and San Salvador, Sylvia arrived in Managua at ten the next morning. Weary and stiff, Sylvia got off the plane and ran into Harry's arms. He looked tired, as always, but his eyes danced with the joy that he'd found since coming to Nicaragua. His work here was effective, she thought. People were impacted and lives were changed.

Her life most of all. An hour hadn't gone by back in Breezewood that she hadn't wondered what the children in the orphanage were doing, and if they missed her. Their lives were already so uncertain, and sometimes so tragic, that she dreaded causing them any more sadness.

"Did you bring the pictures?" Harry asked.

She knew he wasn't asking about the shower, but rather about the grandbaby Sylvia had stopped off to see before she'd gone to Breezewood. "I took six rolls of film," she said. "She's the most beautiful baby you've ever seen."

"And the shower?" he asked.

She sighed. "Well, there's bad news. Mark got arrested. He's going to serve a year in the juvenile facility."

"*Cathy's* Mark? What did he do?"

"Drugs," she said. "He was selling them."

Harry touched his heart. "I don't believe it."

"Believe it. Cathy's a wreck. She postponed the wedding again."

"After the shower and everything?"

"There was no shower. We had to call it off. Everybody still left gifts, but Cathy hasn't even opened them."

Harry quietly took the news in as he escorted her to the secondhand car they had bought when they'd first gotten to León. It was a 1975 Fiat Berlin. Half the time it wouldn't run, but somehow it had gotten Harry to Managua today. A piece of plastic was duct taped to where the back window should be, since it had fallen out shortly after they'd gotten it. They hadn't been able to replace the glass. He'd had an order in for a year now, but they despaired of ever getting it replaced.

She got into the old car and sat on the torn vinyl seat. As they drove the distance from Managua to León, she told Harry everything that had happened with Mark. When they reached León, instead of getting him to drive her home, she asked him to let her off at the orphanage. She needed to see the children.

She hurried in, and some of the kids spotted her and screamed, "Mama Sylvia!" She fell to her knees and hugged them all at one time, kissing them and exclaiming how she had missed them.

Julie, the other missionary wife who ran the orphanage, hurried into the room, as glad to see her as the kids were. Sylvia could see from Julie's tired eyes that she was in need of a reprieve. Sylvia got to her feet and hugged her.

"Thank goodness you're back," Julie said. "Little Juan is sick. He's been crying for you."

"What's wrong with him?" she asked. Juan was a four-year-old who had been abandoned by his mother, and he was continually struggling through an illness of one kind or another.

"Dr. Harry said strep throat. He gave him a shot this morning, but he's still sick. I've had to try to keep him isolated from the other kids, but it isn't easy."

"Where is he?" Sylvia asked. "I want to see him."

"He's in the sick room," Julie said.

She went into the room and found the little boy lying limp on his side. There were dark circles under his eyes, but his eyelids were swollen from crying, and a pink flush mottled his cheeks. She pulled up a chair, sat beside him, and stroked his hair until his little eyes came open.

"Mama Sylvia," he whispered weakly. She reached down and gave him a hug so tight it lifted him into her lap.

"I missed you," she told him in his language. "Tell me what feels bad."

He didn't have much energy to talk, but he gave her a rough sketch of his ailments, probably embellishing just a little. She could feel that he was burning up with fever. Harry had already given him Tylenol and had tried to cool him down, but now all they could do was wait until the fever broke.

She felt him relax in her arms, and she started to sing a hymn. "Jesus, name above all names, beautiful Savior, glorious Lord . . ." His eyes came open and he focused on hers for a long moment, then finally they closed, and she felt him drifting off to sleep. Poor child. Julie had undoubtedly been so busy with the other thirty kids in the home that she hadn't been able to give him much attention. But now Sylvia was here, her heart almost bursting for this child who had been feeling so poorly, with no one to attend to him personally.

When she got to the end of the song, she pressed a kiss on the little boy's forehead. "Get well now, Juan," she whispered. "Mama Sylvia is here."

CHAPTER
Twenty-One

Incarceration was nothing like Mark had envisioned. He had pictured himself lying in a cell alone, flat on his back on a bunk bed, listening to the radio with nothing to do all day but read and watch TV. Instead, he had to rise at five A.M., clean up his sleep area, and wait for a ruthless inspection. Then, like enlisted men in the military, they walked single file into the shower, bathed, dressed, then headed for breakfast—at which there was no talking allowed.

At seven A.M., they headed for their first meeting of the day, an affirmation meeting that Mark dubbed "spill-your-guts time." Mark usually sat there with his mouth shut, listening to his cell mates talk about their drug addictions and their withdrawal, the babies they had fathered by several different girls, the foster homes they'd grown up in or the grandparents who had raised them, and Mark began to feel more and more different . . . even while he felt the same.

All their pasts were different, all their addictions and their demons. Mark found himself fighting the realization that everyone here had made choices that had landed them right where they were ... including him. He didn't want to admit that yet. He still wanted to blame his mother. She wasn't going to get off the hook that easy.

He glanced at the kid named Lazzo, who slept in the bunk next to him. He was trembling more than usual today. He kept rubbing his hands on his pants legs and jerking his head as if to sling his greasy hair back ... except that he didn't have any hair anymore.

Mark looked over at him and whispered, "What's the matter with you, man?" Lazzo didn't answer. He just kept fidgeting.

The counselor leading them noticed that Mark had spoken. "Mark, do you have something to say?"

Mark shrugged. "No, not really. I was just watching Lazzo. He's kind of freaking out over here."

"What do you mean, freaking out?" the leader asked. He looked at Lazzo and saw the sweat dripping down his face, the trembling in his hands. "You having withdrawal, man?" he asked.

Lazzo just stared at him for a moment, then said, "Man, you gotta help me. I ain't gone this long before."

So Lazzo was an addict, then. Mark had no idea what kind of drugs the boy was addicted to, although he knew Lazzo would tell him if he asked. "It's going to get worse before it gets better, man," one of the guys said.

Mark didn't know why everyone just accepted this. "Isn't there something you can do? I mean, don't they have some kind of medication or something?"

"He'll be all right," the leader said with a dismissive shrug. "Time to line up for movement to the school, everybody."

Mark got up and watched Lazzo push himself to his feet. His face had a look of desperation on it, and Mark wondered how he was going to get through this dark tunnel if it really did get worse before it got better.

"I need to go to the infirmary," Lazzo said.

The leader shook his head. "Sorry, kid."

"But I ain't feeling good," Lazzo said. "My heart's pounding. I need some help."

Mark looked up at the guard blocking the door, wondering what he would do if Lazzo had a sudden heart attack and dropped right there. "Man, let him go to the infirmary," Mark said.

"We'll keep an eye on you, Lazzo," the guard said. "If you get really sick we'll take you, but you don't get to go just for the jitters."

"But I can't study like this, man," Lazzo said, wiping his hands on his pants legs again. "Come on, you gotta help me."

"In line, Lazzo!"

"Man, I'm telling you. I can't go!" he shouted. "I have the right to go to the infirmary."

"Buddy, you ain't got no rights," the guard said. "You in jail now. Did you forget? You give up your rights when you come through those doors. Now get back in line or you really *will* need the infirmary."

Lazzo spat at him and uttered a profanity, and suddenly there were three guards on him, throwing him down on the floor as he fought and kicked and screamed for help.

Mark backed away, watching with horror as the closest thing to a friend he'd found in this place was subdued by three huge guards with weapons and handcuffs. But Lazzo didn't stop. He just kept yelling and cursing and spitting and kicking with all his might as they wrestled him out of the room. It got quiet, as the remaining inmates lined up.

"Where are they taking him?" Mark asked the kid in front of him.

"To disciplinary, probably," the kid said. "He ought to know better than to act like that even if he is withdrawing. Ain't nothin' worse than disciplinary."

Mark frowned, wondering if Lazzo would be locked in a room that Mark had seen a year ago when he'd come here with his mother. Everything was steel and bolted down, and there wasn't even a mattress on the bed. Maybe the guards feared that the inmates would tear off the cloth in strips and use it to hang themselves.

"I'm not going to make it here," he whispered under his breath. But he didn't dare say it out loud, for he feared that the guards would descend on him as well and teach him a lesson about the trouble his mouth could get him into.

But the altercation had given him an idea. Maybe if he was sick, they would let him go to the infirmary, and then he could sleep all day and just hang around and get out of school and work and all these stupid meetings. Maybe then life would be a little more tolerable.

As he sat in class that morning, studying the work that the prison teacher had given him, he tried to figure out some kind of illness he wouldn't have to prove. Then he'd have easy street, at least for a day or two, before he had to get back to work.

Mark could vomit if he needed to. When he was little, he'd used that talent against his mother when he wanted her to feel sorry for him. She had thought he was just a sensitive child, when all along he'd just been pulling her strings.

He choked back a whole cup of water when they had their break, and when nobody was looking, he spat it out on the floor with a retching noise that drew the guards.

"I'm sick," he said, on his knees and clutching his stomach.

"No, you ain't. Get up and clean up this mess."

"But I'm sick, man!" he said. "You don't throw up unless you're sick."

"He ain't sick," a kid named Miller shouted. "I saw him gulping down his water and looking around to see if anybody was looking."

Mark didn't know what it was inside him that exploded, but he looked at the little snitch and decided he could take him. Without warning, he launched across the floor and head-butted him, knocking him down. The kid yelled and got back up, and his fist flew into Mark's face.

Before he knew what hit him, Mark was beneath the rabid boy, fighting for his life. The guards broke it up before the kid could kill him.

"All right, that's enough! Both of you, to disciplinary."

Mark felt as if he was really going to be sick now, as he dabbed at his bloody mouth and let the guards drag him out.

CHAPTER
Twenty-Two

As soon as Sylvia was able to leave Juan, she hurried to the food kitchen where one of the ladies from town was already engaged in making the beans and rice they would serve for that evening's meal. Maria was thrilled to see her, for she had been trying to do the work alone for the length of Sylvia's vacation.

When the children and their parents began to arrive for the evening meal and Sylvia saw how many more now there were than when she'd left, she wondered why she had ever decided to stay away that long.

She dripped with perspiration and her heart was pounded with panic as they spooned out the last of the food—long before the line had ended. How was she going to tell these people that they couldn't be fed tonight?

She looked into the eyes of the little boy who was next in line and realized she couldn't do it. She would not turn him away. She tried to formulate a sentence in her mind, but her Spanish was too confusing, so she looked at Maria. "Tell them they're going to have to wait a little while," she said, "until we can make another pot."

Maria looked up at her. "But there's no more," she said in Spanish. "That was all we had."

"I have some at home," Sylvia said. "I'll go home and get it." Even as she spoke, she wondered if she had enough. There were at least twenty more people in line. She knew this was the only meal some of them would eat all day.

Harry was in the kitchen when she got home. "I just came home to get something to eat," he said. "Do you want me to make you something, too?"

"No!" she said. "There're too many people at the kitchen. I've got to feed them—but we've run out of food. I didn't realize we were out. I should have gotten some in Managua while I was there. I should have spent every penny I had ..."

Harry rubbed his eyes. She wondered how long it had been since he'd slept. When she wasn't there to nag him into taking care of himself, he never gave himself much thought. "I'll send somebody back tomorrow to see if they can get some more supplies."

She went to their pantry and started unloading the bags of rice and dried beans that she had stored there in case of another emergency. "I'll feed them this," she said. "They have to eat. You should see these children. They're skin and bones."

"I know," he said. "I've treated most of them." He went to the doorway that led to the little garden in the backyard. Sylvia hadn't had much time to work in it, so she knew Harry was looking at more weeds than blooms. She doubted, though, that that was causing the sadness she sensed in his slumping posture. "What's wrong, Harry?"

He turned back, leaning against the casing. "Sylvia, we've got to find a way to get the cash to buy more food."

"I brought back a little," she said, "but most of what I got from those churches was pledges. The money should be coming in soon, but we've got to find a way to get by until it does."

"I was thinking ..." He paused. "Maybe it's time to sell our house."

Sylvia almost dropped the groceries she'd been gathering in her arms.

"The Gonzaleses are out, and it's empty," he went on. "I know you probably left it spotless. We could call a realtor and have it listed."

"Oh, Harry. I just don't think I can do that! You should see it. It's exactly the way we left it. You wouldn't even know the Gonzaleses had lived there. Brenda and Tory took care of the flowers. And all the memories . . ."

"Our life is here now."

"But I wanted to keep it in case we ever went back," Sylvia said. "I just don't feel right cutting off that connection."

"Sylvia, think how many children that house could feed. And we don't intend to ever go back, do we?"

Sylvia looked down at the food in her hands that represented the needs that had brought her to this country. She knew the Lord was using her here and would use her as long as she was willing. "No, I don't intend to go back, either," she said. "Being back just made me miss this place, and all the children . . ." She closed her eyes. "I can't think about it right now. I have to get back to the kitchen and cook for those families."

"Yeah, I'm going to go back to the clinic as soon as I eat," he said. He reached up and touched her face. "Think about it, honey. The kids are all grown and settled. We're here. There's no point in keeping that beautiful home when we could sell it and raise enough cash to keep the pantry stocked for several years. And with the money coming in from the churches, we'd never have to turn anybody away again. Maybe we could even hire people to work in the kitchen. These people need jobs."

"We'll see," she said. Then she scurried out of the house and back to the kitchen to feed the starving children.

CHAPTER
Twenty-Three

Cathy still felt God's presence Sunday afternoon as she went to visit Mark again. Though the visit had ended badly the Wednesday night before, somehow her prayer time had convinced her that she could handle it today. Maybe the interval had mellowed Mark and made him realize that he needed his mother.

But the moment he came into the visiting room and she saw his busted, swollen lip, she knew that her hopes were in vain. She tried not to look shocked as she stood up and met him halfway across the room.

"Mark, what happened to you?"

"I got in a fight with some jerk who thinks he owns the place," he said. "They're animals here, you know. I'm the only human being in the whole place." He threw himself down in a chair at the table.

She found she was having trouble breathing, and it was suddenly very hot. "Mark, I want you to tell me what happened."

"I told you. The guy had an attitude problem and he thought I was in his way just because I breathe and exist."

She wanted to scream out that an injustice had been committed against her son, that someone had to *do* something. "Did you tell the guard?"

"He was standing right there. He saw the whole thing."

"He didn't stop it?"

"Of course he stopped it, but by the time he did, I was already like this. I'm telling you, Mom. Animals. That's who I'm living with now."

He leaned forward, his eyes entreating her as he went on. "Mom, can't you go to the lawyer today and explain to him that I got beat up last night, that I'm not going to make it in here? Because I'm really not. I'm going to die in here. If I have to stay here for a whole year, somebody will kill me or I'll starve to death."

She tried not to let him know how affected she was. "I know they feed you, Mark."

"Yeah, but do you know *what* they feed me? I mean, we're not talking pizza and hamburgers here. Who needs Weight Watchers? They ought to just send fat people here and they'd lose weight in a few days. My stomach's been nauseous since the first thing I ate."

"That's because you're nervous."

"No, it's because the food makes me gag."

She closed her eyes. She had to keep this in perspective. They were playing by a new set of rules. "Mark, there's nothing an attorney can do. I've tried."

Mark slammed his hand on the table. "Then try something else! Wake up! Look at me. You're walking around like you're in some kind of daze, like you have to accept everything that comes down. You don't accept other things. You didn't accept it when Joseph was dying, and when Tory and Barry split up, you didn't accept that. You didn't accept it when the school system was passing out condoms. You fought like crazy that time. Why can't you fight for me?"

She wanted to tell him that she *would* fight for him, that she would fight anyone she could, that she would gladly trade places with him to get him out of here. But the fight was over, and Mark had lost. "There comes a time, Mark, when fighting is not appropriate and accepting your guilt is."

He opened his mouth in astonishment and banged his hands on the table. "Great, Mom. What about *your* guilt? How come you never have to pay?"

She knew this line of accusation. It came as no surprise. "Mark, I'm not gonna sit here and take this. I want to see you, talk to you, but I'm not gonna take your abuse. So you can stop throwing your accusations at me. I haven't done anything wrong."

The words angered him more, and his face turned crimson. "Why don't you just get out of here?" he asked.

She drew in a deep breath. "What?"

"I said get out of here. If you're no good to me, then don't come. I don't want to see you."

Her eyes flashed. "Mark, you don't mean that. Later today, you're going to regret saying it."

"I'm not going to regret it," Mark said. "I hate you. You don't love me, and I don't love you. If you can't help me, then get out of here." He got up and headed back to the guard who stood at the door.

"*Mark!*" she called.

"I mean it," he told her, swinging around and pointing a threatening finger at her. "Unless you have something good to say to me, don't even come in here. I don't want to hear anything else."

The guard took him out of her sight and the door swung shut behind them with a clash. Cathy just sat in her chair, staring at that metal door and wondering where she had lost her little boy.

After a moment, she realized he was not coming back, so she headed back to her car, feeling as if every ounce of energy had bled right out of her. She drove home in a fog of numbness.

When she pulled into the cul de sac, she saw that Brenda was in the car across the street, with Daniel behind the wheel. Tory sat on her porch with Hannah, watching. Cathy wondered whether either of them had anything better to do than sit outside while their children romped and played around them.

And here she was, grieving the loss of her child, while a child across the street—exactly the same age—did the things that fifteen-year-old boys were supposed to do.

It was as if Mark had died a week ago, and something or someone else was occupying his body. She didn't know how to relate to him or how to reach him, and his anger reached much deeper than the love she could show him.

She got out of the car and started inside, unable to talk to the friends she knew cared about her. She had no energy left to vent right now. She just needed to lie down and cry about her lost son.

CHAPTER
Twenty-Four

As frightening as the prospect of speaking in public was to Brenda, she would have taken on a coliseum full of hostile hecklers rather than ride in the passenger seat when Daniel was driving.

It wasn't that her fifteen-year-old was a terrible driver. She couldn't have said that for sure, since he hadn't yet made it more than a few feet without slamming on the brakes.

Her hand gripped the door of her minivan, and she silently thanked the Lord for their anti-whiplash headrests. Her knuckles were turning white, and she was beginning to get a rare headache.

But she didn't want to discourage him.

"Daniel, your spatial skills just amaze me," she said.

Daniel grinned over at her. "Sure you won't let me off the cul de sac?"

"Not yet, honey," she said too quickly. "You need a little more practice."

He let his foot off the brake and stomped on the accelerator, thrusting the car forward again.

"Not so hard, Daniel!" she shouted. "Let off the gas a little!"

He took his right foot off the gas and slammed his left one on the brake, making the car jerk again. She checked the street for children in harm's way.

"Honey, you can't drive with both feet. You have to drive with your right one."

"But I'm left-handed," he said. "I drive with both feet."

Brenda closed her eyes and leaned her head back, wondering where she could buy a neck brace. "You can't drive with both feet, Daniel," she said, "not with an automatic transmission. Only people who drive standard transmissions can drive with both feet. And then they only do it because there's a clutch."

"What's a clutch?" Daniel asked.

"Something we don't have." She glanced back at the house. "You know, maybe your father ought to be the one teaching you to drive. He doesn't get to spend enough time with you and—"

"But I'm doing a good job," Daniel cut in. "I haven't hit anything yet."

She thought about how much money her van had cost and wondered if the insurance would cover her son. He had just passed the written test and gotten his learner's permit, and it wouldn't look good if he totaled the car on his first day out. She looked out the window and saw Tory sitting on her porch with baby Hannah in her lap. Spencer and Brittany were standing in the yard, jumping up and down, cheering for Daniel. She was glad the van was pointed away from them.

"If I agree to drive with my right foot will you teach me?"

She cleared her throat and wondered if these palpitations could do serious damage to her health. "Daniel, don't do it for me. Do it because that's the way it's done."

There she went, getting negative. She should have learned more patience after dealing so long with Mark. "But go ahead and drive to the corner. Nice and smooth."

He shifted the car into overdrive and gave it gas again. They thrust forward.

"Why did you put it in overdrive?" she asked. "You can't do that."

"Dad does that sometimes."

"Only when he's going up a steep mountain. We don't need to do that right now. Stop, Daniel! Stop!" They were coming up on the stop sign, and his foot was nowhere near the brake. "Daniel, I said *stop!*"

He slammed on the brake, and the car jerked again. Her head was beginning to throb.

"Daniel." She wished she had a paper sack to breathe in. "I think maybe we need a bigger space to work in, some place where there aren't houses and other cars and mailboxes and little children."

Daniel was injured. "Mom, you think I'm going to hurt somebody," he said. "I made 100 on the learner's test."

"But driving is different on paper than it is in real life," she said. So much for being positive. "Honey, I want you to keep your foot on the brake and put the car in reverse. Then slowly let off the brake and back up until you get to our driveway. *Very* slowly."

Daniel breathed out a defeated sigh and did as he was told. The car inched back until it was right in front of their yard.

"Now," she said, "just put it in park and get out. I'll pull it in the driveway."

"No, Mom," he said. "I can't let everybody see me handing it over to you for something as simple as parking. I can do it. Just let me try."

"Spencer and Brittany are little children. They don't know the difference."

"Well, Joseph and Leah and Rachel do. They'll make fun of me, too."

"They're your brother and sisters. They always make fun of you. You've never let it bother you before. Come on, honey. You're not ready."

"But how am I ever going to learn if you don't let me try?"

She looked at his hands clutching the steering wheel, his foot on the brake, and glanced back at the driveway. It couldn't be that hard, she thought. Maybe he could do it, after all. She didn't want to destroy his confidence or give him the idea that she didn't expect the best of him. So her head would hurt, and she'd wear a neck brace for a few weeks. Mothers had to make sacrifices. "All right," she said, fearing that she would regret this. "I want you to put it in drive and slowly turn the car in a circle, and then pull into the driveway very carefully with your foot on the brake the whole time."

"Score!" he shouted, as if he'd just made a touchdown. "I wish Mark was here to see this." He put the car in park and carefully gave it some gas. She was pleased as he gently turned the car around and pointed it toward the driveway. Maybe he could do this after all. Maybe he wasn't as bad a driver as she thought.

The front bumper scraped the concrete as he took the pitch of the driveway too quickly. "Slow down," she said. "On the brake, Daniel! On the brake!"

But instead of the brake, his foot pressed the gas. The car bolted up the driveway, dragging the back bumper as it went over the gutter.

"Daniel, that's the gas! The gas!"

Panicked, he stomped the accelerator.

"Look out for the truck!"

Brenda threw her arms over her face as the van crashed into the truck—an awful sound of metal smashing metal and thousands of dollars' worth of vehicle being crunched like empty Coke cans. The impact flung them forward. Seat belts jerked them back.

When she had uncovered her eyes, Brenda surveyed the damage, her heart still in panic mode. Daniel froze, clutching the steering wheel and staring at the smoke rising from the van. "Oops," he said.

"Daniel, are you all right?"

"Yes, ma'am," he said. "At least, until Dad sees."

Brenda tried to open her door, but it was jammed. She thrust her shoulder against it, forcing it open.

Leah and Rachel came running across the lot next door, bouncing up and down as Brenda got out.

"Daniel wrecked the van!" Leah shouted. "Go get Daddy!" Rachel dashed around the house.

Having heard the crash, David was already out of his workshop and halfway to the driveway. He stopped at the sight and stood with his hands hanging at his side as his face betrayed his shock.

"What in the name of all that is good happened here?" David asked through his teeth.

"Dad, I'm sorry," Daniel cried, getting out of the van. "Mom said to hit the brake and I accidentally hit the gas."

"I can see that," David said. "Son, this is our *family* van. I've had that pickup truck for twelve years. How could you do that the *first* time you got behind the wheel? Don't you know the difference between the brake and the gas?"

Brenda touched his arm to calm him down. "He didn't mean to, David."

"Didn't mean to?" David asked. "Daniel, didn't you learn anything when you were studying that handbook?"

"Dad, I was trying, okay? I did really well when I was turning the car around. Didn't I, Mom?"

Her head hurt so badly that she didn't know if she had enough Tylenol to get rid of it. Joseph had come around the house now and was laughing his head off at Daniel's plight. Daniel looked like a little boy as he walked around the van, assessing the crumpled metal, as if he could fix it somehow.

"I'm really, really sorry."

"Just go in the house, Daniel," David said. "Just . . . go."

Daniel walked up the front porch steps. That old protective maternal instinct kicked in, and Brenda's heart surged with compassion for the boy.

When the front door closed, she turned back to her husband. He was still gaping down at the van, as if wondering if he could fix it.

"It's my fault," she whispered. "He wasn't ready."

"It was not your fault," he flung back. "How could he ram the truck in the *driveway?*"

"At least no one was hurt." She knew the statement was weak, that it didn't really help matters at all.

"I don't believe this," David said again. He started into the house. "I'm going to call the insurance company."

"It's Sunday," she said. "They won't be open."

"Right," he said. "Well, let me go in and look up our deductible. We may not even be able to afford to get it fixed."

She followed him in. Daniel was waiting just inside the door. "Dad, I'll pay for it myself," he said. "I'll get a job and I'll pay every penny back."

David wasn't in the mood to hear. "Daniel, go to your room."

"But I didn't mean to—"

"Just go upstairs. Your mother and I are going to need a little time here."

Leah and Rachel had their hands over their mouths and were muffling their laughter, and Joseph was running along beside Daniel like a paparazzo trying to get the dirt.

"Joseph, Leah, and Rachel—go to your rooms, too!" David yelled.

"But we didn't do anything, Daddy," Leah piped in.

"Just do as I said."

Slowly, they all climbed the stairs and retreated to their bedrooms.

"Go easy on him," Brenda whispered. "He really didn't mean to do it. This is not a punishable offense. It's just really bad driving. Really, *really* bad. Why do they even let teenagers drive?"

"Do you think we could get the state to take back his learner's permit?" David asked. "You know, just because the law allows it doesn't mean *we* have to."

She drew him into the kitchen and got them both a glass. As she poured David some ice water, her hand came up to touch her aching head.

David took her wrist and brushed her hair back from her forehead. "Did you hit your head?"

"No. Just a headache. I had it before the wreck."

He kissed her forehead, then let her go, and she poured her glass and sat down. David followed.

"So what do we do now?"

David shook his head. "I guess we call the insurance adjuster to come look at it tomorrow, and we see if it can be fixed. Let's hope it can, because we can't afford another car right now. Maybe I *should* let him get a job and help pay for it."

"No," Brenda said, "he's too young to work. He's just barely turned fifteen."

"Hey, I was working at fifteen."

"Yeah, but that was different. He has a lot to do, and I don't want him having that kind of commitment right now."

"You just don't want him having to go to work and be surrounded by people who aren't Christians."

Brenda wished they could talk about this later. "David, you know that's not true."

"Of course it's true," he said. "You're used to sheltering him."

"What is wrong with that?" Brenda asked. "Would you rather he hung around with drug dealers and wound up in jail like Mark?"

"No," he said, "I'm not saying that you've done wrong. You've done a good job with him. But I'm telling you that it's not going to hurt him to be exposed to other types of people. Especially when he just totaled our car and we need help paying to get it fixed."

She ran her fingers through her hair and looked out the window at the two damaged vehicles. "Well, the truck's not in bad shape. Maybe it still runs."

"We can't transport six people in a pickup truck," he said.

"Well, maybe we won't all need to go somewhere at the same time. I'll just have to hold my driving down a little."

"Brenda, it won't hurt him to pay for what he's done."

"But it's not like he broke the rules or was disobedient," she said. "He just doesn't know how to drive."

"We'll talk about it later," he said, heading to the computer room where they kept the file cabinet. "I've got to find the insurance policy and see what our deductible is."

Brenda lowered her face into her hands as she awaited the verdict.

CHAPTER
Twenty-Five

Spencer played fast and hard with a friend who had come home from church with him, and Tory wondered if she should coax them from the front yard into the back. It seemed somehow disrespectful to have her son playing out in the open, where Cathy would see and be reminded of her own child, locked in a jail.

The thought of forbidding her children to play in public seemed a little overreactive, but she had no clue how to make things easier for her grieving neighbor.

And just across the street, both of Brenda's vehicles sat crumpled and possibly disabled. Tory wondered if the strain this put on the family finances might send Brenda back into the workforce. Again, she wished there was something she could do.

Sylvia would have known exactly what to do. She would have shown up at Cathy's doorstep at the perfect time, would have known when to hug and when to speak and when to be quiet. She would have known whether to cook a meal or call on the phone or send a note.

And she wouldn't have spent a moment wondering if she was doing all the wrong things. She would have known that it wasn't about her.

Tory was still learning, but she would have given almost anything to have Sylvia still here to teach her.

And the first thing Sylvia would tell her was that she didn't need to borrow trouble from the neighbors up the street, because she had enough of her own.

The physical therapist was on her way over for a rare Sunday visit, since she was going to be out of town the next day and couldn't come to work with Hannah. Every visit carried potential for progress, and Tory took it seriously, each time praying and hoping that Hannah would have a victory on that day.

Tory moved from her rocking chair to the floor of her porch, and bent down until she was face-to-face with her daughter. "Today's the day you're gonna sit up for her, isn't it, Hannah? We're going to surprise Melissa and show her what a big girl you are. That you're very high functioning."

Hannah smiled and shoved her fist into her mouth. Tory ran her thumb along the baby's chin.

"What if Mommy let you go, and you had to sit up by yourself? What if I did that?" She asked the questions in a soft, teasing voice, and Hannah's eyes locked onto hers.

Tory opened her fingers and started to let her go, but Hannah fell back and let out a wail. Tory caught her and scooped her up. "It's okay," she whispered, angry at her own disappointment.

"What'samatter with her?" Spencer yelled from the street. He abandoned his little bike with a clatter and stepped through the impatiens to get to the porch.

"Spencer, use the steps, not the garden," Tory said. "She was trying to sit up but she fell over. It scared her. No big deal."

But it was a big deal to Tory. She told herself that it didn't matter, that she'd had no reason to think Hannah would be able to hold herself up this time.

Spencer's friend, Andy Holloway, dropped his bike with a crash on the sidewalk and clomped up the steps.

"How come she's so scared?" he asked. "My brother's walking and climbing now."

She looked down at the boy whose mother had been pregnant at the same time as Tory. His brother had been born two months after Hannah.

"Babies develop at different rates," she said, as if that would mean anything to a six-year-old.

"Ain't Hannah crawling yet?"

"Crawling?" Spencer shouted. "Duh. She's not even sitting up yet. Her back's not strong."

Andy just stared at Hannah as if he didn't understand, and Tory wanted to take her inside so she wouldn't have to answer any more questions. But the child meant no harm.

"Miss Tory, how come Hannah doesn't do nothing?"

She tried to smile. "Andy, Hannah does plenty. She's just having a little trouble sitting up."

"But my brother did that a long time ago, and he's younger than her."

"Not that much younger." She was getting defensive now, and she reminded herself that he was a child.

"I know how to make her crawl," he offered. "You put her down on her hands and knees and rock her back and forth. Want me to show you?"

She swallowed back the retorts that came to her mind, retorts that she might have given to an older person who wouldn't leave her alone. "No, Andy, I don't. Hannah's got some problems with muscle tone, and her backbone isn't as strong as your brother's. She'll sit up and crawl and walk when she's ready. We just have to be patient."

Andy considered her pensively again. "What if she doesn't?"

Tory wanted to scream that she would, that she *had* to, that they still had every hope that Hannah would be one of the Down's Syndrome children who was high functioning. The physical therapist had predicted that, as soon as she sat, other things would quickly follow.

She realized that her idea about sending the kids to the backyard was a good idea, and not for Cathy's emotional state, but her own. "Spencer, why don't you take Andy and play in the sprinkler?"

Spencer let out a whoop and took off running around the house, wiping out the marigolds and periwinkles on his way. Andy forgot his concerns about Hannah and followed.

Tory went back to the rocking chair and leaned back with Hannah on her lap. Her heart ached for the baby . . . and for herself. "Please help her sit up today," she whispered to God. "Please give us that."

She saw the little yellow Volkswagen Beetle pulling into the cul de sac. The physical therapist, Melissa, putted up to the front of their house and, dodging Spencer's bike, parked and cut the engine off.

Melissa, in her early twenties, had perky eyes and an expressive face that Hannah responded well to. Tory tried to point Hannah's gaze to the car to see how long it took the child to recognize her visitor.

The young woman got out of the car and bounced up the yard. "Hi, Hannah!" she said in a voice dripping with baby delight.

Tory answered for the baby and made her wave. It didn't yet appear that Hannah had recognized her.

"Thanks for letting me come on Sunday," Melissa said.

"That's okay," Tory told her. "Hannah's ready to work. I think she just might sit up today." She turned her pleading eyes up to Melissa. "She just has to, doesn't she? Soon?"

Melissa took Hannah from Tory's arms and headed into the house. "We'll see what we can do, won't we, Hannah? But we don't want to get our expectations too high."

Tory followed them in and closed the front door behind them. Brittany was sitting at the kitchen table, drawing a cartoon picture of a puppy she had copied from a magazine. "See my puppy, Mommy?"

Tory muttered that it was nice, then went into the den where Melissa was setting up. "If you don't expect anything, you won't get anything," Tory said. "I've always found that to be true."

Melissa handed Hannah back and opened the mat they kept in the den for her work. She spread it out on the floor. "Well, with Down's Syndrome, all the rules change." She said it as though it was a little thing that wouldn't affect Hannah's entire future. Tory laid Hannah on the mat. The baby kicked her legs up at her. "Look how aware she is today," Melissa said. "She knows me. Look at those smiling eyes."

Hope fluttered back to life in Tory's heart. "Really? I'm around her all the time, so sometimes I think it's my imagination. Some of the babies at the school aren't aware of anything yet. They just stare at their mothers without any real response. But Hannah seems pretty aware to me. Wouldn't that indicate that she was high functioning?"

"High functioning is a relative term," Melissa said. "Let's just take one step at a time. How have her exercises been going this week?"

Tory's heart sank again, on the downhill spiral of that roller coaster she rode. No one would tell her that Hannah was high functioning, primarily because they didn't know. But Tory *needed* to know.

"They were fine," she said.

She glanced out the back window and saw Spencer and Andy dancing in the water of the sprinkler, while Barry read the paper on the swing. She thought of Andy's hurtful words about his own normal baby brother, who was developing the way babies were supposed to. She longed to see Hannah do some of those things . . . to pull up and climb and walk and run from her mother.

She longed to hear her talk. She longed to know that everything was going to be all right with the child.

But there were simply no guarantees in life.

Not about anything, it seemed.

CHAPTER
Twenty-Six

Rain set in with as much force as the depression in Cathy's heart. She curled up on her bed, listening to it pound against the roof and the bare foundation behind her house, where they were supposed to build the addition—blending houses as they blended families.

But the house addition wasn't a source of joy or excitement anymore.

The doorbell rang. It was probably Steve. She had promised to call him after her visit with her son. But Mark's attitude had knocked the wind out of her.

She got up as the bell rang again, and went in sock feet to the door. She felt small, weak, as she opened it to let Steve in.

"Cathy, are you okay?" he asked.

"I couldn't call you," she said. "I was upset." She looked around the house and realized how cluttered it was. Dishes filled the sink, and shoes littered the den. She didn't know they had that many shoes.

"Did your visit with Mark upset you?"

She nodded, grabbed a wadded paper towel off the counter, and tossed it into the trash can. "It was awful. He told me he hated me. Doesn't want to see me again."

Steve's face changed. "He said that? That he hated you?"

"He meant it, too," Cathy said. She curled up on one end of the couch, her arms around her knees. "He does hate me. In his mind, I've let him down. I've betrayed him by making him plead guilty, and now he's stuck there and I'm not doing a thing to get him out. But I've tried, Steve, and there's nothing I can do."

Steve sat down next to her and closed his hand over one sock foot. "He shouldn't have talked to you that way."

"Well, he did." She looked curiously at him, noting the crinkles next to his eyes where laugh lines had carved character into his face. But those eyes looked angry now.

"I've felt sorry for him, and I've prayed for him," he said. "I've lost sleep worrying about him. But I've got to tell you, I don't like it when anybody treats you like that. He had no right."

"He had every right," she said, hugging her knees tighter. "I'm his mother. I'm supposed to be abused."

"Actually, you're not. And Mark needs to learn that his own frustration and discomfort aren't grounds for disrespect. I can't even imagine saying those things to my mother."

"But you were raised by Mrs. Cleaver," she said. "Why would you say it?"

"So you're saying that you deserved it because you're not Barbara Billingsley?"

"Well, let's face it—"

"Cathy, you are a devoted mother, and if you don't think so, it's because you've been buying into Mark's attitude. How dare he treat you that way after what he did!"

"He's more concerned with what I did . . . or didn't do."

"Well, don't let him throw stones at you."

Sighing hard, she got up and went back to the kitchen. "This isn't about me, Steve. It's about him. I'm not real concerned with my feelings."

Steve followed her. "That's *because* you're a good mother. But look at you. You're a wreck. He has no right to put you through this."

"I'd like to see what kind of shape you'd be in if Tracy was taken away from you and locked up for a year. You wouldn't be trying to make a point about disrespect. You'd be wringing your heart out."

"I'd be in terrible shape," he agreed. "I'd be just like you. But I guarantee you she wouldn't talk to me like that."

It was the same old argument they'd had many times over the past year. He always thought her children were disrespectful. He tried to defend her, only to make her feel more torn apart. Nothing new.

"You know, I really can't deal with this right now," she said, "and since you and I have called off the wedding, there's no use in you trying to change my kids now. This is not the time. I'm trying to deal with a crisis in my family, and I don't need your criticism about my parenting skills. I've had enough of it. I've given *myself* enough of it all night."

"I'm not criticizing you," he said. "I'm criticizing Mark. I think you need to nip this in the bud early, let him know that your visits are a privilege, and if he can't treat them like that, you won't come."

"No, I will *not* do that," she said. "I'm going to be there for him if it kills me. The state is teaching him about disrespect and rebellion. He's locked up in jail for a year. What do you want from me?"

He stood quietly for a moment, then got up and came around the counter and took her hands in his. "What do I want from you?" he repeated. "How about a smile? I want to see joy back in your face again. I want to hear that laughter that lights up my heart."

She didn't want him to be soft and sweet. She wanted to lash out. She needed to be angry. But his fingers came up to caress her face. "I love you, Cathy, and for the rest of my life I'm going to defend you from any unnecessary pain."

"I don't need defending from my son. He's upset, okay? Give him a break."

"I'm not trying to bully you, Cathy. I'm not trying to force you to do anything you don't want to do with your children. But I take it real personally when you're mistreated."

"And I love them and take it real personally when you try to stifle my maternal instincts. I have to be free to love them the way I need to. The balance is off here. You're not Mark's father. You didn't change his diaper when he was little, or hear him say his first word. You don't have that image that I have in my mind ... of him chewing on a biscuit when he took his first step. One hand clutching that piece of biscuit like it was holding him up, crumbs all over his face, curly hair flopping all over his head ..." She choked off the words and swallowed. "You can't love him as if you were there. You never will. So how can you tell me how to treat him? How can you know what he needs?"

He backed away, slid his hands into his pockets. "You make it sound so impossible."

"It is impossible. I mean, isn't it?"

"No. I think with God's help we can be a family. Nothing is impossible with God."

"You say that so confidently, until the first time I criticize Tracy and tell you to do something that contradicts your parenting instincts. And then you'll be torn between keeping peace with me and loving her the way you need to."

"I'm not trying to get in your way, Cathy. I just want to be your protector."

"I don't want protection," she said. "I just want to have the freedom to bless my children. Like you want the freedom to bless yours."

"Okay," he said. "I'm sorry I said anything."

"I'm sorry you did, too."

That guarded look returned to his eyes, and he went to the door, opened it, and gazed through the screen door into the rain.

"I've got to get on back to Tracy," he said quietly. "I left her playing at Shelly's house. I just wanted to see if you were okay.

I'll call when I get her to bed. And I was thinking about going to visit Mark myself Wednesday."

"Steve, please don't give him more to be upset about. If there's ever any hope for us, I want you to build a relationship with him, not make a bigger rift."

He looked helpless as he stood at the door. "I want to help you, Cathy. I just don't know how. I want to be there for you and comfort you, and I also want to be there for your kids, all three of them. And that means going to visit Mark and doing what I can while he's in there. He's not a lost cause, Cathy. You can't give up on him."

"*Me* give up on him?" she asked. "What makes you think *I've* given up on him?"

"I think if you start letting him get away with everything, you're giving up on him. Acting as if it's too late to change anything about him. You've got a captive audience there, Cathy. Use it."

As she heard his car pulling out, she plopped on the couch and stared at the door. She hoped that, when he went to see Mark, nothing erupted. She didn't know how much more Mark could take. And frankly, she didn't know how much more she could take, either.

The old axiom that this, too, would pass seemed unlikely. She was locked here in this nightmare that was destined to go on, and there wasn't a thing she could do to stop or change it.

CHAPTER
Twenty-Seven

It was still raining on Monday when Tory took Hannah to the Breezewood Development Center for the class she took with other mothers of Down's Syndrome babies. The class, originally supposed to have been such a comfort for her, had become something she dreaded. Some of the babies in the class had surpassed Hannah, and that fact depressed her more each time they came.

One child, a little younger than Hannah, had started walking just last week. Another one, only ten months old, was starting to crawl.

Most of the mothers were struggling to get their children to do simple things like sit up and reach for or hold a spoon, and Hannah seemed more functional than a few, who lay limply on the mat, never making any progress at all.

She had considered quitting and just taking all her therapy at home, but the benefit of belonging to a group like this outweighed any downside—at least as far as Barry was concerned.

Barry had warned her that she needed to stop comparing Hannah to babies outside the class who were normal, *or* babies within the class who might be doing things differently or better. Hannah was Hannah, and she had her own pace and would not be pushed.

But Tory felt it was her own personal challenge to make her baby everything she could be. And if Hannah didn't sit up, Tory considered it her own fault. She hadn't exercised Hannah enough to strengthen the muscles in her back or hadn't held her right, enabling the joints to do their job.

Tory hadn't bonded much with the other mothers because of that sense of competition. She looked jealously at the mothers whose children were walking and crawling and had bitter thoughts about how superior they thought they were. The truth, of course, as Tory dimly realized in her best moments, was that those mothers, like her, were simply grateful for any progress at all. Their children still had Down's Syndrome, no matter what they were able to do in class.

Tory tried to concentrate on the day's classroom activity— guiding their children through a series of exercises to music as the physical therapist who worked with them wandered through the room, encouraging and offering advice.

Tory heard a tap on the hall window and looked up. Barry stood there, smiling in. Hannah caught his eye, and he waved at her. Her mouth came open in delight. Tory looked around, hoping one of the other mothers had caught that. It meant that Hannah was aware of her daddy, that she responded appropriately to the sight of him. She allowed the thrill to alter her mood and picked up Hannah's hand to make her wave at her daddy.

"Don't you want to do a trick for Daddy?" Tory whispered to Hannah. "Come on, baby. You can do it."

She sat Hannah up in front of her and tried to make her balance. The child raised her hands in excitement at her daddy's face, apparently forgetting that she was making the effort. Tory balanced her on her little rump, sat her up, then tried to let her go. Always before, Hannah had gone limp and fallen back against her. But this time Tory could feel that there was a little muscle tone there, a little balance. Her heart rate quickened, and slowly she let Hannah go. Barry's smile faded and his eyes widened as he saw what she was doing.

Slowly Tory pulled her hands away. Hannah was sitting up on her own, waving her arms and laughing up at her daddy in the window!

Tory held her breath as the child sat there for ten, fifteen, twenty seconds. Tory wanted to scream out that Hannah had done it, but she knew it would startle her. So she sat there, frozen, counting off the seconds.

Finally, Hannah seemed to realize what she was doing, and wilted back against her mother. Tory snatched her up and let out a loud whoop. Everyone in the room turned around and Barry burst through the door.

"She did it!" she said. "She sat up! Did anybody see her? She sat up! Barry, did you see it?"

He came into the room and took Hannah from her, swung her around, and the baby laughed.

"She did it!" he said. "That's my girl!" They were both crying and laughing at the same time.

Other mothers in the room cheered for Hannah and made their babies clap along with them. Joy danced in Tory's eyes, until she saw the looks in the eyes of the mothers whose children were older, yet had not passed that milestone. She knew how it felt.

But this was Hannah's time. Her baby had sat up! That meant she was progressing, developing. Next, she would crawl—and then walk. Maybe there was hope. And as Barry clung to his youngest child, Tory threw her arms around his neck and hugged them both.

CHAPTER
Twenty-Eight

Tory couldn't wait to tell Brenda. She didn't even go inside when she got home, just let Spencer and Brittany out and hurried over to the Dodd's house. The wrecked minivan still sat in the driveway, along with the dented truck. She went to the door and gave a light knock, then stepped inside, carefully carrying Hannah.

She found Brenda in the kitchen. "Brenda, you'll never guess what she did. Hannah sat up by herself!"

Eyes wide, Brenda clapped her hands. "Hannah, you're such a big girl! You sat up for your mommy?"

"It was so great," Tory said. "Barry was there, and she was laughing and reaching up at him, and it was like she just forgot I was trying to make her do something. You know, sometimes I think she just doesn't want to do it for me. Like she's tired of the constant exercises and just doesn't want to work. But today she forgot she was working."

"See? I told you she'd do it in her time. Relax, Tory. Hannah's gonna be all right."

Tory let out a breath and looked down at the food covering the stove. "You're cooking supper already?" she asked. "I don't even know what I'm going to fix tonight. I was thinking pizza sounded good. I want to celebrate."

"I'm actually making this for Cathy," Brenda said. "You know how it is. When you don't know what else to do, make food."

Tory picked a cut cucumber out of a bowl and crunched on it. "I didn't know what to do either. I thought of food, but didn't know if she'd even feel like eating." She shifted Hannah in her arms. "How do you do it, Brenda? How do you always know what to do?"

Brenda dropped a fork in the pan and turned around to Tory. "I hate it when you make me out to be some kind of angel," Brenda said. "I'm not like that at all, and you know it. We're supposed to love our neighbors and that's what I'm doing. Just trying to love my neighbor."

"I love her, but I don't know whether to show up at her door or take her food or write her a card or visit Mark or what."

Brenda put aluminum foil over the fried chicken piled up on a platter and covered a Tupperware dish full of mashed potatoes and a little Cool Whip container of gravy. "You know what Sylvia would say. If you err, err on the side of too much food. It's sustenance, energy. It's also sometimes comfort." She stacked another Cool Whip container of green beans and a bowl of corn on the cob. "Could you help me carry this over?"

"Sure," Tory said, shifting Hannah again. "Is she home?"

"I don't think so. I saw Annie and Rick drive up a little while ago. We'll just leave the food."

"I'd love to tell her about Hannah," Tory said. "I know she'd be excited. She knows what a step this is."

"You'll have a chance soon. Cathy's not the type to wallow in depression. If I know her, she'll be over here laughing and praying with us again soon."

"I don't know," Tory said. "We haven't watched Cathy deal with anything this serious. All the rules might change. The pain from our children's hurts can really do us in. They can be downright debilitating."

"But God doesn't leave us," Brenda said, "and he won't leave her. He'll tell us what to do."

CHAPTER
Twenty-Nine

Steve had struggled between anger and compassion all week long, and Wednesday as he sat in the visitation room at River Ranch, waiting for them to bring Mark to him, he told himself that he needed to go easy on the kid. By now, Mark was probably pretty shaken up at what his own actions had cost him.

The door opened. Steve looked up and saw the guard standing a foot taller than the kid he ushered in. For a moment Steve didn't recognize Mark. His lip was cut and swollen, and his head was shaved.

Mark searched the room, then caught Steve's eye. Steve saw the look of profound disappointment pass across his face. He got to his feet and reached out to shake Mark's hand as the kid came closer.

Mark ignored the outstretched hand and sat down. "They told me my dad was here."

Steve gave the guard a frustrated look. "I didn't tell them I was your dad. I don't know why they'd think that." Steve put his elbows on the table. "So, how you doing, buddy?"

Mark shrugged. "How do you think?"

"Well, you don't look so good. How's the other guy look?"

Mark didn't find that amusing. "He looks just fine, okay? He's had more experience than I have."

"I talked to one of the guards while I was waiting," Steve said. "They said you threw the first punch."

"There's only so much a person can take before he snaps."

"I'm sure that's true," Steve said.

Mark looked surprised that Steve would agree with him. Suspicion narrowed his eyes.

"What do you want from me?" Mark asked. "Why are you even here?"

The sudden question surprised Steve. "I'm here because I care about you," he said. "I don't like to see what's happening to you. You're too good for this."

"You don't think I'm good. You're probably glad to get me out of the way."

"You're wrong about that," Steve said. "I'd take your sentence myself to keep your mom from going through this."

"My mom? I'm the one going through it."

"Actually, she's trapped in prison, too. She's impacted by this more than you'll ever know. I worry about her."

"You're not even married to her yet. What are you trying to do? Score points with her or something?"

Steve swallowed back the retort that flashed into his mind. "I love her, Mark. I can't stand to see her heart breaking."

"My mom can stop this. She doesn't have to leave me here. If her heart is broken, it's her own fault."

"Wrong again, Mark. Your mom feels completely helpless. And you should have seen her when she came home last week, after you told her you hated her," Steve said. "She doesn't deserve that, Mark."

Their eyes locked and held each other off for several moments, and finally Mark looked away. "Well, thanks for this visit," he said, getting to his feet. "Feel free to come any time, but next time don't make them think you're my dad."

Mark headed out of the room. Steve sat still for a moment until his heart rate settled. It was going to be a long year. And it was going to take every resource he had to get through it without doing any serious damage.

CHAPTER *Thirty*

The food that Brenda had brought over was a godsend. Cathy hadn't thought as far ahead as supper, and now, as Rick and Annie sat down with her to eat, she wondered if any part of the day could be salvaged.

It was getting warm in the house, but just before they sat to eat, Rick had opened all the windows and left the door to the garage open, as if they needed fresh air to blow out the cobwebs and the sadness from their home. They all ate in relative quiet. Finally, Annie spoke up.

"This is the worst day I've ever had in my life."

Cathy tried to look interested, but Annie was prone to exaggerations and melodrama. "Any special reason?"

"Yeah, a special reason," Annie said. "The fact that my brother's in prison."

"It's not prison," Cathy said. "Don't call it that."

"Jail then," Rick said.

"It's not that, either. It's a correctional center. A school, really."

"Oh, yeah, that's a lot better," Annie said. "It was all over town. Everybody's heard about it by now. Even at the church, that was all they could talk about."

When Annie had taken a job at the church helping with the summer day camps, Cathy had seen it as an act of God. The jobs were coveted, and the fact that they'd chosen Annie had given Cathy hope that the girl would enter a deeper level of commitment to God. Would Mark's situation change all that?

"Well, you'd better just get used to it," Cathy said. "There's no use hiding."

"They act like *we're* convicts," Rick said. "I had a date with Rebecca Farmer for Saturday night, and would you believe, her mother made her break it!"

Cathy looked up. "Why?"

"Because she found out about my brother and figured I was the same way. She told Rebecca she doesn't want her going out with a druggie."

"A druggie?" Cathy said, throwing her fork down on her plate. "I have a good mind to call her myself and tell her that no one in this family is a druggie."

"It's ruining our social lives, Mom."

Cathy sat back in her chair. "Well, I'm sure Mark is devastated to have a part in that, Annie. And if the judge had only known, I'm sure he would have given Mark a lighter sentence."

There it was again. The sarcasm. She didn't know where it came from or why it seeped into her tone so quickly. She thought about being on her knees the other night and repenting and asking God to put her back on the vine. Why was it that she kept falling off?

She rubbed her face. "I'm sorry. I'm just under a lot of stress right now, Annie, and I have a few more things to worry about than your social life."

"Hey, Mom, people kill themselves over their social lives, okay?"

"Well, I'm just going to have to trust that you're not planning to do that."

"Well, you wouldn't care if I was."

Cathy got up from the table, trying to keep herself calm.

"Annie, I don't have the patience for your games right now." She took her plate to the counter and left it in the sink. "Since you have so much energy to keep pounding me, why don't you just clear the table when you're finished and come do the dishes?"

"Mom, that's not fair," Annie said. "Rick never has to do anything."

"Yes, I do," Rick said. "I do more around here than anybody else does. Why do you have to be such a jerk?"

"Don't call me a jerk," Annie said. "I'm sick of you calling me names. Mom, make him stop calling me names!"

"Rick, why don't you go out and mow the yard when you're finished eating?"

"Mow the yard? I just mowed it a few days ago."

"It grows," Cathy said, and she threw her dish towel down and started out of the room.

"What is it with you, anyway?" Rick demanded. "You're acting like Annie and I are in jail ourselves. We haven't done anything wrong."

"She's not acting any different than she always does," Annie pouted.

"Annie, go to your room," Cathy said.

"How can I if I'm supposed to be doing the dishes?"

Cathy was getting confused now. She brought her hand to her head. "Get up and do the dishes and *then* go to your room."

"Well, I'm still eating and so is Rick. I can't very well take his plate from him when he's still eating, can I?"

"Annie, why don't you shut up?" Rick asked. "You're making it worse for both of us. She's going to jump all over us no matter what we do."

"I don't jump all over any of you. I respond to the things you say to me!" Cathy shouted.

"Well, why don't you just respond to somebody else!" Rick returned. "I'm sick of taking the heat for what everybody else does around here."

It was at that moment that the screen door flew open and Steve stepped inside.

Cathy was startled. She hadn't heard his car pull up, hadn't known he was standing there listening to the exchange. "Steve, I didn't know you were here."

"Obviously," he told her, "and neither did they."

"Oh, great! Here it comes," Annie said. She got up and took her plate to the sink and turned on the water, as if to drown out whatever Steve might have to say.

He just stood there, hands in his pockets, looking down at the floor as if he had lots to say but was restraining himself.

"I'm sorry you heard that," Cathy said. "I lost my temper."

"No problem," he said in a strained, quiet voice.

She just stood there, looking at him, wondering if he was judging her, condemning her. She stepped outside with him and closed the screen door behind her. In the garage, she turned back to him with her hands on her hips. "So just say it. I'm a terrible mother because I talked to my kids that way."

"No, that's not what I was thinking."

"What then?"

"I was thinking that they shouldn't talk to *you* that way. You're their mother, not a paid servant. Not an equal. They're supposed to respect you. All of them—Annie, Rick . . . and even Mark. But if you don't require it of them, if you don't *expect* it of them, then they're not going to do it."

He started back out to his car.

"Wait!" she said. "Where are you going?"

"Home," he said. "If I go back in there, I'll say something that won't be constructive." He got into his car and drove off.

Feeling as if the wind had been knocked out of her, Cathy went back in.

"You know, Mom, I heard what he said out there," Rick spoke up. "If you ask me, he's gotten way too power-hungry. He's not our father, and he has no right to tell you how to treat us."

"Go to your room," Cathy said. "Now."

Annie just threw her hands up. "The dishes? Excuse me?"

"I'll do the dishes myself," she said. "Go to your room, both of you. I don't want to see you again until I tell you you can come out."

The kids scurried off as if they were getting away with something, instead of taking punishment. As Cathy began to clean the kitchen, she felt as if she had failed again.

CHAPTER
Thirty-One

Steve was pensive and still nursing his anger when he picked up Tracy from her friend's house that afternoon. He fixed them a light supper and tried to pay close attention as the little girl rambled about her day, and all the friends who had done silly things, and the way Matthew Rutledge had made fun of Susan Murphy until everyone on the playground had been cracking up. It all seemed so simple, he thought, when he listened to Tracy talk about her grade school problems and her friends who were too young to break their parents' hearts.

He realized that he and Tracy had it pretty easy. Yes, they had had trauma in their lives when his wife died of cancer. It was the worst two years of his life, but they had come through it together.

That night, he sat on her bed, brushing out her braids and thinking how precious she was to him. What would it be like when they were all living together as a family? Cathy's three kids and Tracy. Some part of him felt as if he was sacrificing his own child on the altar of that family life. That instead of her children becoming more respectful and better behaved, Tracy would be the one to decline.

"Daddy, why did Mark have to go to jail?"

He brushed her hair and stroked the silkiness of it, wondering how much longer she'd let him do this. "He's not really in jail, honey. He's kind of in a home. It's a place where they're going to teach him not to do the things he did."

"I already know what he did, Daddy," Tracy said. "He took drugs and he sold them to somebody."

"How do you know that?" he asked.

"I heard everybody talking at the shower after the policeman came. And then Annie told me. Why do people take drugs if they're going to go to jail for it?"

He didn't know how to explain to his child that not everyone went to jail, that only the ones who got caught did, that many, many others got away with the act to the detriment of their own bodies. He hated for his daughter to be exposed to such things. Would there be any preventing it, once he and Cathy got married?

"I don't know, honey. Sometimes people do pretty stupid things."

"Are you still going to marry Miss Cathy?"

"I hope so," he said.

"I want you to," Tracy whispered. She crawled under her covers and lay flat on her back, looking up at her dad. "She's really sad right now, isn't she?"

"Yeah, she's worried about her son."

"I don't like for her to feel like that," Tracy said.

Steve's heart melted. "I don't either."

"Then we'll just have to cheer her up, won't we, Daddy?"

He swallowed the emotion in his throat and leaned down to kiss his little girl. They prayed for Cathy together, then for Mark and the others, and finally he left her alone and went into his own bedroom. He lay on top of the bedspread, staring at the ceiling.

Was he doing the right thing even wanting a marriage to Cathy? Wasn't he just taking on a whole barrelful of problems? He would forever be at odds with her children, biting his tongue and cringing every time they spoke to her in the tone that suggested that she was a subordinate. And then she would be mad at him for his anger at them. It would be an endless cycle, like so many other stepfamilies he'd encountered.

He didn't know if he had the constitution for it. But then he thought of life without her, and he realized the alternative was no better.

Sleep came hard that night, but finally he dozed, still wearing his clothes. Sometime in the middle of the night, he heard Tracy crying. He got up and ran to her bed.

"I had a dream, Daddy," she cried. "He was in there trying to get me! I saw him in the kitchen!"

"Saw who?" Steve asked her.

"Somebody," she said. "He was coming to get me!" She was crying and trembling, so he lifted her up out of bed and held her. She wrapped her arms around him, clinging with all her might.

"It's okay," he whispered, "Daddy's here."

He sat down in the rocker across the room from her bed, and slowly rocked her back to relaxation. He could feel the tension seeping out of her, the fear dripping away. All was well, he thought, because he was here.

He realized that Mark hadn't had his father to comfort him when he was afraid. Annie and Rick hadn't had their dad to guide them with a firm hand. But he knew it was too late for him to fill Jerry's shoes. They wouldn't have it, didn't want it . . . and he wasn't certain he had enough love in his heart to bridge those gaps their father had left.

As he rocked his daughter to sleep, he closed his eyes and tried to imagine whether he had the strength to enter into this marriage when Cathy said it was all right.

But wouldn't it take even *more* strength to walk away from the woman he loved?

He put Tracy back to bed, tucked her in, kissed her good night, then went back to his own bedroom. His picture of his wife sat on the table beside the bed, and he picked it up and gazed down at it. Why had she died and left him to make such decisions? Why was he in the position now of having to take a family that was broken and lost and blend it with his? Could two families ever really blend?

He wasn't sure. But he was committed. Living with Cathy and being her husband might outweigh the hassles and dread of living with her children, and maybe God would teach him something in the process. Maybe he would actually make a difference in their lives. Maybe they would make a difference in his.

He took it to God before he went back to sleep, laying all his concerns and feelings on the altar, asking for God to show him what he was to do, how he was to help. Before he said "amen," Steve was hit with the overwhelming sense that there *was* one thing he could do. He couldn't be Mark's father, but he could help Mark's father give him what he needed. It was a start.

Tomorrow he would go and see Jerry in Knoxville and try to get him to visit his son in jail. Maybe then Mark could start his road to recovery. Maybe then Steve could help him fill the empty places that no stepfather would ever be able to fill.

CHAPTER
Thirty-Two

Steve didn't tell Cathy he was going to Knoxville. He didn't want to give her another source of worry today. He had business of his own to handle in Knoxville; then, when he'd finished what he needed to do wearing his account manager's hat for the telecommunications company he worked for, he navigated his way to Jerry Flaherty's office, hoping he was there.

He stepped up to the secretary's desk, hands in his pockets.

"May I help you?" she asked.

"I'm here to see Jerry Flaherty. Is he in?"

"Do you have an appointment?"

He shrugged. "No, I was just in town and thought I'd stop by and talk to him. I won't take long."

She picked up the phone and dialed a number, then told Jerry that he was here. "Could I get your name, please?" she asked.

"Steve Bennett."

She said the name into the phone, then glanced at him again. He wondered if Jerry had asked her if it was the Steve Bennett who was his ex-wife's future husband.

Hanging up, she said, "You can go on back. It's that door right there."

He went to the door she was pointing toward, knocked, then opened it. Jerry was on his feet coming toward him.

"Steve," Jerry said, shaking his hand. "Didn't expect a visit from you. I saw you at the courthouse the other day, but it didn't seem like a good time to introduce myself."

Steve gave him a weak smile. "Cathy doesn't know I'm here."

"I see," Jerry said, dropping down into his own executive chair. He leaned back, tapping his fingertips together in front of his chest. "So, did you come here to get advice on how to handle her?"

Steve shifted in his seat. "Actually, no. Cathy and I get along just fine. It's about the kids."

Jerry's eyebrows came up as if he finally understood. "I see." He laughed and set his arms on their rests. "Well, I might have expected this."

Steve frowned. "Expected what?"

"I should have known you didn't want to marry Cathy and all her kids, so you thought you'd come here and make a little deal with me, maybe to have them in Knoxville a little more often."

The remnant of Steve's smile vanished. He got to his feet and looked down at the man who had broken Cathy's heart. He had never liked him, but he disliked him more intensely now.

"No, actually, that's not what I want. Cathy would be brokenhearted ... devastated ... if she didn't have her kids with her. I would never do that to her."

"Well, it hardly matters now, since Annie and Rick will be going off to college in a few weeks, and Mark's otherwise detained."

"You don't have to worry about my relationship with the family," he said. "We're doing just fine."

Jerry grinned, as if he knew better. "Then what brings you here?"

Steve sat slowly back down. "I came here to talk to you about Mark. Have you seen him since he's been at River Ranch?"

Jerry's face hardened. "No, I haven't."

"Well, Mark's really angry right now. He's very upset. He's at a turning point in his life, and he doesn't know which way to turn. I think he needs your support."

Jerry stiffened. "You have a lot of nerve, coming here and telling me how to be a father to my son."

"I'm not telling you how to be anything," Steve said. "I'm just telling you what Mark needs. I saw him yesterday, and he's right at the end of his rope. He's rabidly angry about what's happened. He desperately needs to know that he's still loved, in spite of what he did." He stopped and leaned forward, setting his elbows on his knees. "Look, I'm not divorced. I'm new at all the dynamics that go on in a divorced family. All I know is that when I went to see him, they told him his father was there, because they thought that was who I was. You should have seen the look on his face when he saw me, instead of you. He was crushed."

Jerry glared at him for a long moment. "You know, your fiancé—my beloved ex-wife—made it out to be all my fault," he said. "She claimed that if I had been there in her home as Mark was growing up none of this would have happened. Like Mark did all of this to get my attention or something. But I'm not buying it. Mark did what he did because he's a selfish, bratty kid, and he's been getting away with murder. His mother has no backbone and no discipline and no consistency."

Steve felt his hackles rising. "And you do?"

"I have more than she has."

"Well, what exactly are you consistent *about?*" Steve asked. "Your golf game? Because the kids claim you don't spend time with them even on your weekends. So where do you get off criticizing how Cathy has brought them up?"

Jerry got to his feet, dismissing him. "Glad you could come by," he said.

Steve was happy to leave. He started for the door, then stopped before walking through it. "You know, it doesn't really matter if Cathy was wrong or right about your part in this," Steve said. "The bottom line is that your son is in trouble. He needs you, and I came here to ask you to go to him and be what he needs for you to be. One time in your life."

Jerry pointed to the door, as if Steve had lost his way.

But Steve didn't leave. "Just tell me one thing. Are you going to go visit your son or not?"

Beads of perspiration dotted Jerry's upper lip. "As long as my son wants to humiliate and disgrace my family, he can't count on my support. Respect and approval have to be earned, and he hasn't done a thing to earn it."

"A child needs respect and approval whether he's earned it or not," Steve said. "Maybe your attitude is just what's wrong with this picture."

With that, Steve left the room and went back to the elevator. He seethed all the way down.

CHAPTER
Thirty-Three

Steve was troubled all the way back to Breezewood, and it took the whole two-hour drive to cool his anger. No wonder Cathy had such trouble dealing with her ex-husband. Some part of Steve had expected him to be a good guy deep down. After all, Cathy had chosen him once. She had been in love with him. She'd had children with him. Steve had expected him to have some redeeming qualities, and maybe he did. If so, they were pretty well hidden on first impression.

He thought of Mark and the disappointment on his face yesterday when he realized that Jerry hadn't come after all. The kid might go through the whole year of his sentence without one visit from his father. It wouldn't surprise Steve a bit. He wondered how a father could turn that cold against his son. The thought made his heart swell with compassion for the boy.

If he was going to marry Cathy, then he had a responsibility to Mark. He had an obligation to help him as much as he could. Cathy deserved it. She couldn't do this alone.

He racked his brain, trying to find a way that he could have more of an impact on Mark, build a relationship with him, mentor him while he was in jail. But Steve was limited by the visitation hours—and by Mark's attitude.

Maybe he could mentor Mark through the mail. Mail call was probably an important time for the inmates. Maybe Steve could use the mail to do a Bible study with him or something. Maybe Mark would read it.

Then again, maybe he wouldn't. It was no substitute for a father. And as hard as Steve tried, it wasn't in his power to give Mark that.

CHAPTER
Thirty-Four

The kids were gone, Rick to work and Annie to a movie, and Cathy found that the house was quiet. She paced from one room to another, straightening here and cleaning there, wondering why she hadn't heard from Steve today.

Part of her wanted to reach out and lean on him, but another part of her, the pride-filled part, wanted to handle things herself. She had done it for years.

She walked around the house aimlessly, cleaning up little bits of clutter, wiping counters, folding laundry. Suddenly, she had a sense of how purposeless her life had become. She went to work every day to take care of people's pets, animals who couldn't say thank you or pass her kindness on to others. And then she came home early to be there for her children. But being there wasn't all they needed, and now she wondered if she might as well have worked longer hours and made more money, for all the good coming home early in the afternoons had done her.

When the doorbell rang, she ran to answer it. It was Steve. "I tried to call you," she said. "Where have you been?"

"Long story," he said, coming in. "I went to Knoxville."

"Knoxville? Was it last minute? You didn't say you were going." She closed the door. "You want something to drink?"

He went to the couch and sat down. "No. I'm fine. And I didn't tell you I was going, because I didn't want you to stop me."

She stood looking at him for a moment, then slowly lowered into a chair.

"I went to see Jerry."

"You *what?*"

"I went to see Jerry. I wanted to tell him how hurt Mark was that he hasn't visited. I thought I could appeal to him father to father."

She only gaped at him, her mouth open. "I can't believe you did that." She got up. "Why didn't you tell me? Why didn't you *ask* me? What did you think? That you'd pop in and have a nice talk over lunch? Find out that my ex really isn't such a bad guy? Solve all of his problems with his children?"

He looked down at his clasped hands. "Well . . . yeah. I hoped. But it turned out not to be true." He looked up at her, registering the anger on her face. "Cathy, I was trying to help. I wanted him to know how disappointed Mark was when I came instead of his dad yesterday. I thought if he heard that—"

She turned away and crossed her arms. "This is incredible. You and Jerry . . ."

"It's not like we talked about you behind your back," Steve said. "Come on, Cathy. I'm going to be your husband. I'm going to be your children's stepfather. I wanted to do the most effective thing for all of you. I thought visiting Jerry would do it."

She turned back around. "And what did he say? Was he receptive, or did he have security escort you out?"

Steve got up, fighting the slight grin on his face. "Well, he did get a little hot."

She didn't say anything, but her eyes changed, as if she tried to picture the scene.

"He's not going to visit Mark," he said softly. "At least, not soon. He said that Mark hadn't earned his respect."

"Perfect," she said. "Well, at least we know where we stand."

"Yeah. Guess we can prepare Mark. Let him know not to look for his dad."

She shook her head and dabbed at the corner of one eye. "I can't do that. I'm not going to tell Mark to give up on his father. He's just going to have to figure it out."

Steve reached for her hand and pulled her next to him. Then he pulled her into a hug. She closed her own arms around him, laying her head against his chest.

"Mark was hateful to me again last night," she said. "You think he was disappointed to see *you*? He ranted the whole time I was there."

He moaned. "Why didn't you call me when you got home?"

"I was too upset, and I didn't want to hear what you would say about it."

He touched her chin and made her look at him. "Cathy, you know I'd be right."

"You're confusing me, Steve. One minute you're his knight in shining armor, defending him to his dad. The next minute you're telling me I need to come down harder on him."

"To me, it's all about you," he said. "I want you to be okay. I want you to be treated with respect. And believe it or not, I want him to grow up to be a good, productive citizen. Not a smart-mouth who treats his mother like pond scum."

"What do you want me to do? Abandon my child just like his father has?"

"No. I think you should withhold your visits until he apologizes."

"He won't know why I didn't show up!" Cathy said. "I can't just not come."

"I can go and tell him. Make him understand that your visits are a privilege. They have phone time. He could call and tell you he's sorry. Or he could write you a letter."

"A letter will take three days to get here. And what if he doesn't write it right away? What if he waits a week? He's a stubborn kid. He doesn't do anything anybody expects. Not until he absolutely has no choice."

"Just try it," Steve said. "Let him miss you; let him realize that he's blessed to have a mother who comes faithfully. You've got to show him, Cathy. You've got to teach him that he can't talk to you that way, that he has to treat you with respect along with every other adult who makes an effort to come see him."

"He's just angry, Steve. He's been through a trauma."

"You don't think he's put *us* through a trauma?"

"Yes, but we're adults. We can handle it. He's just a kid."

"He's a kid who needs to learn some things. He's a kid who needs to suffer some consequences."

The word made something snap inside her. "Consequences?" she said. "He's going to be in jail for a year. You don't think that's enough of a consequence?"

"Not yet," he said. "Not when he's still throwing things in your face like he has."

She paced the room, looked down at the floor, shaking her head frantically. "Steve, what you're asking me to do is to punish him for being punished. Make him pay another penalty when he's already paying the dearest one of his life."

"No, I'm asking you to teach him to treat you with respect."

"But this isn't about what I need, okay? This is a critical time for Mark. He needs someone. Jerry has abandoned him. I won't do it."

"Cathy, you can't sacrifice yourself on the altar of Mark. You can't let him treat you like you're some subordinate that he can kick around."

She ran her hands through her hair, unable to believe what he was asking her. Part of her knew that he was right, that she had to teach Mark these lessons sometime. She didn't like being treated the way she'd been treated the last couple of times she'd visited him, but in her mind, it was a sacrifice she had to make for her son.

"Steve, when I was first divorced, I made myself a promise," she said. "I promised myself that I would never choose a man over my children. I promised myself that I would never let a man's influence cause the destruction of my relationship with them. And I'm not going to start now."

He looked as if she had struck him. "So what about when we're married, Cathy? Is my opinion never going to count? Are you never going to take my advice about parenting?"

"Steve, we're not married, and the reason we're not married is because of this. I'm not willing to give the reins of my children over to you. I'm still their mother. And no matter how long we're ever married or what we ever mean to each other, you are not their father."

"Their father has abdicated his seat."

"Then I'll be *both* parents like I've been for the last few years," she said. "I can do that."

"You don't have to," Steve said.

"Oh, yes, I do. I do have to when you issue ultimatums like this. I'm not going to turn my back on my son, Steve. Not because you tell me to. Not for any reason. Mark is not going to get the impression from me that he can blow it with his mother. Because he can't. Never. Not ever. Just like Tracy could never blow it with you."

"Tracy wouldn't treat me that way. She wouldn't rebel this way and then blame others for it."

The comparison slashed across Cathy's already-open wounds. "That was low, Steve. The lowest yet. Tracy's a great kid. I'll give you that. But I don't need for you to hold her up like some standard by which I measure mine. I love my children as much as you love yours. And I'm committed to them above my work, my friends, and my love life. If you can't see that—if you can't allow me that—then I don't see much hope for marriage with you." She took off her engagement ring and handed it to him.

He took it, cleared his throat, and rubbed his face hard. "Do you mean that?"

"Yes, I mean it. I'm not finished being a mother yet. And that's enough of a fight."

Staring at the ring in his hand, Steve let out a deep, broken sigh. "I love you, Cathy. I'm not finished with you, unless you're finished with me."

She couldn't answer him or even look at him.

Then, without another word, he walked out the door and headed to his truck.

Cathy waited until he was out of the driveway and had turned from the cul de sac before she let herself burst into tears.

CHAPTER
Thirty-Five

Cathy had hoped Mark's disposition had improved, but the moment he was ushered through the door into the visitor's room, Cathy knew that he was in a worse mood than he had been the time before. She got up and reached out to hug him, but he shrugged her away.

"What do you want?"

Too weary to fight, she plopped down in the chair. "Mark, don't treat me like that. I've worried about you all week, and—"

"You know what the guy in the bed next to me did?" he butted in.

She tried to follow his change of subject. "What, Mark?"

"He's a thirteen-year-old kid who stabbed his brother."

She felt the blood draining from her face.

"And he's out to get me."

She tried not to respond the way he was hoping. "He's just bluffing."

"Well, you know, he's used to people calling his bluff."

She wondered where the closest bathroom was. She felt an urgent need to throw up.

"I used to think I was different from the kids in places like this," he bit out, "but now I know we have something in common."

She shouldn't egg this on, she thought. It wasn't healthy. But she wanted to have a conversation with him. If she didn't engage, she didn't know how she would maintain a relationship with him.

"What do you have in common, Mark?"

"We all have scummy mothers."

The urge to swing her hand as hard as she could and slap him across the face overcame her, but she stopped herself. Suddenly, the blood was pumping back through her face again.

She got up. Clutching the back of the chair, she bent down. "Mark, do you want me to keep visiting you or not?"

"I don't care," he said. "Why don't you just stay home from now on?"

He was bluffing, she knew, but if that was the game he wanted to play, she suddenly felt she had the strength to play it. She got to her feet. "Mark, I'm leaving, and I'm not coming back until I'm strong enough to handle these visits. I don't know when that will be."

He didn't say anything, just looked down as if he didn't care. Her throat constricted, and she found herself unable to speak again. Tears sprang to her eyes.

"Annie and Rick are coming later. Try not to abuse them, okay?" Without saying another word, she left him sitting there and headed out of the visitation room.

Cathy wept as she drove to Steve's house, hoping she would find him at home. He had every right to go out and find something else to do. What made her think he would be sitting around pining over her? But when she got there and saw his car in the driveway, she was grateful.

She knocked hard at the door. After a moment, he answered. "Cathy!"

All the emotion she'd been trying to contain in the visitor's room at the prison just came pouring out. "I don't want to hear

I-told-you-so. I just miss you and realize that you're the one I want to run to when I have to run somewhere."

He pulled her hard into his arms and crushed her against him.

"He called me scummy. He said I was just like all the other mothers. He hates me. I left him there, just sitting at that table. He didn't care."

He slid his fingers through her hair. "I'm sorry, Cathy. So sorry."

"And I told him I'm not going back until I shore up strength for those conversations. I don't know how long I can stay away, and I'm not playing games, trying to make him think I could turn my back. I just . . . don't know what to do."

"I know. I understand." He kissed her forehead and wiped her tears. "Whatever you do . . . I'm behind you. Not criticizing, Cathy. Not comparing. I'm sorry for what I said about Tracy not acting like that. I don't know how she'll act when she's fifteen."

"It's okay," she said. "This can't be easy for you, either. None of it."

He took her hand and pulled her into his kitchen. "Have you eaten?"

She tried to think back and realized she hadn't eaten since the half bagel she'd had for breakfast. "No."

"Then our first order of business is for me to feed you," he said. "Sit down."

Then he began preparing a meal that she had no appetite for. But something about eating it and having him care for her gave her a warm sense of comfort. She found the tension leaving her body, though the grief kept its foothold. She wondered if she would ever get over it.

When she'd finished eating, she found that she felt better. "I didn't realize how much food could help. I've had a headache for days. I think it's finally going away."

He touched the lines on her face as if his fingertip could erase them. "But those lines are still there," he whispered.

"They're going to be for a while, Steve," she said. "I hope you can get used to them. I can't feel good when Mark is there."

And she was thankful he didn't demand that she did.

CHAPTER
Thirty-Six

Mark brooded as he sat in the schoolroom off the main room of Building A, waiting for mail call. Mail call was one of those privileges that you had to earn. Some of the kids only got mail once or twice a week because they hadn't worked hard enough to earn the privilege on the other days.

Since they claimed he hadn't been "cooperative" at his job in the cafeteria, they'd taken his mail privilege away for the past couple of nights. It qualified for cruel and unusual punishment, he thought. Since his mother hadn't visited Wednesday night, he really felt the need for some mail, some contact with the outside world. He must have several letters saved up from her, Rick, and Annie. Maybe even Brenda and her kids. He wouldn't be surprised if Sylvia had written from Nicaragua.

He waited as they called out the names one by one, and people cheered as they got their letters from home. He watched as Lazzo, who had the bunk next to his, scrambled up to get the letter from his girlfriend. Even Beef, who seemed like a guy who would mock anyone who foolishly wrote him, got two or three envelopes. But they never called Mark's name.

As the other inmates shuffled out of the room, Mark sat stunned. He had been *cheated* out of his mail! They were holding out on him. How else could this have happened? How could no one in his family have written, none of his friends, none of the neighbors?

"Nothin' for you, man?" Lazzo asked him, slapping his own envelope against his palm.

Mark got up and started out of the room. "I hate mail. I didn't want it, anyway."

Lazzo followed him in and pulled his bed covers back. With a groan, he dropped onto the bed, propped his feet up, and began reading his mail.

Mark lay down and stared at the ceiling. "My mom's boyfriend probably talked her out of writing. He can be a jerk."

He heard Lazzo folding his letter back up, cramming it into the envelope. "So what has that dude done to you? Beat you up?"

Mark gave him a sour look. "No, he doesn't beat me up."

"Beats your mom up, then?"

"No!" he said, getting angry. "He doesn't do anything like that."

"So why is he a jerk?"

"I don't want to talk about it, okay?" He kicked his covers away and turned on his side, wishing they'd turn the lights out.

He shouldn't have been so hateful to his mother. That had been a mistake. He had to admit that he missed her. He hadn't gone a day in his life without her, except for the weekends when he was at his dad's. And now here he was, locked away from everyone he was used to.

They were forgetting all about him, and he didn't blame them. Some people could only take so much before amnesia set in. It was how they stopped hurting, like painkillers or alcohol.

He wished he could forget. But he was stuck here, with no one but himself . . . and the other forty-nine convicts in his room.

CHAPTER
Thirty-Seven

Brenda sat—weak and dejected—on the steps of the front porch, watching the insurance adjuster's car pull away. Behind her, she heard the front door open, and Daniel stepped out. "What did he say, Mom?"

"Deductible is what we thought," she said. "A thousand dollars for each vehicle. Thank goodness the truck still runs. I can drive it beaten up."

He looked sincerely distraught. "I'll get a job," he said. "I'll pay for fixing both of them."

"I don't want you to get a job," Brenda said, reaching for his hand. She pulled him down next to her. "You're too young."

"Why am I too young? It's summer and I don't have anything else to do, anyway."

"Daniel, do you know how many hours you'd have to work to make two thousand dollars?"

"I'm willing, Mama," he said. "Please. Dad's never going to let me learn to drive if I don't take responsibility for what I've done. I don't want you to give up on me."

"I haven't given up on you," she said.

"Then why did you ask Dad to teach me to drive?" Daniel said. "I don't want him to. He's still mad about the wreck. Besides, you're a lot more patient than he is."

It was one time when Brenda wished she didn't have that gift. She didn't have the patience to get back in a car with Daniel, and putting him behind the wheel of their only running vehicle seemed crazy.

"Look, Daniel, I think we all need a little more time before we get you behind the wheel. Why don't you just stop worrying about it for a while? Your dad and I will take care of the thousand dollars to fix the van. We can wait on fixing the pickup." She kissed his cheek and stroked his hair back. "At least neither car is totaled. But we can't get the van fixed until we have the deductible." She patted his knee and got up. "We'll figure something out, honey."

Feeling very tired, she went into the house.

CHAPTER
Thirty-Eight

Daniel opened the driver's side door of the wrecked minivan and sat behind the wheel. He felt like a failure. He couldn't believe he'd done such a terrible job of driving his first time out. He had always pictured himself driving flawlessly with one elbow out the window and his wrist on top of the steering wheel. He had pictured the radio playing and himself turning corners as smoothly as a Nascar driver. He had even pictured himself getting his own car and driving Joseph, Rachel, and Leah around when his mother didn't have time. Maybe even going on a date or two.

His dreams were shattered now.

"What's up?"

He turned and saw Rick, Mark's older brother, crossing the grass.

"Hey," Daniel said.

"Looks pretty bad." Rick stepped to the front of the van and evaluated the damage. "I saw some man over here. Was that the insurance guy?"

Daniel moaned. "He said we have to come up with a thousand dollars for each."

"Tough luck," Rick said. He came around the van, dragged the passenger door open, and slid into the passenger's seat. "You know ... I was watching out my bedroom window when you were driving, and I could see right off what you were doing wrong. First off, you were nervous, and it was showing."

"It was my first time." He should have known Rick would see him. He should have waited until the older boy had gone to work.

"You have to have a light touch," Rick said, demonstrating with his hands, "just barely touch the accelerator until you get used to it. Just ease into the accelerator and the brake, real slow like." He nodded to Daniel. "Go ahead. Put your foot on the accelerator. Just push it down real slow."

Daniel did as he was told. "Man, if I just hadn't punched the accelerator when I meant to punch the brake."

"Yeah, big mistake," Rick said, "but I bet you won't do it again."

"I won't have the chance," Daniel said. "My parents will probably never let me drive again. I'll be forty-two years old and still riding my bike. I'll have to get my mother to come drive my kids to school."

Rick chuckled. "Come on, it's not that bad. We've all had our wrecks."

Daniel glanced over at him. "You?"

"Sure," Rick said. "My mom tried to teach me how to drive, and you've never heard such yelling in your life. The first day I got my driver's license, I scraped a pole on my way out of the parking lot."

"No way," Daniel said, a grin illuminating his eyes.

"I did," Rick said. "I did great through the driving test and he gave me my license. Man, I was all proud, struttin' around.

And then we got back in the car, and I took off driving a little too fast and took a corner too close. Next thing I knew, there was this terrible sound—concrete scraping metal. My mom almost had a heart attack. And then there was that time I ran into the garage and busted my headlight. That was back when I just had my permit."

Daniel was captivated. "You hit your own garage?"

"Yeah, there's still a black mark there to this day," he said. "I thought Mom would never let me drive again. And then she turned me over to my dad, and he never had time to teach me. When he did, he had this idea that he could do it in three easy lessons. When I didn't learn just like he wanted me to, he went ballistic."

"How'd you finally learn?" Daniel asked.

"Dr. Harry," Rick said. "Miss Sylvia told him all the problems I was having, and he took me to the parking lot at the city auditorium for several Saturdays in a row, and we drove around there until I got the feel of things." Rick's eyebrows shot up. "Since Dr. Harry's not here, you and I ought to do that."

Daniel gaped at him. "Really? You would teach me?"

"Only if your parents said it was okay. But in the parking lot, you couldn't do too much damage. And you could drive my car."

"You would trust me with your car?"

"Sure," Rick said. "I'm supposed to be teaching Mark how to drive anyway, and since he's not here, I might as well teach you."

Silence settled like bereavement between them. "How's he doing?"

"Not so good," he said. "He got beat up the other day. They busted his lip. You know Mark. He's going to fight this kicking and screaming. If he settles in there before a year is up, it'll be a miracle." He looked out the cracked windshield. "Man, I can't believe he would be so stupid."

"Yeah, me either," Daniel said.

"I can't stand the thought of people knowing that my kid brother's in jail. Makes our family look like a bunch of losers."

"You're not losers. You didn't do anything."

As if he didn't want to talk about it anymore, Rick opened the door and got back out. Daniel followed and met him in the yard. "So when are you going to take me driving?"

"I don't know," Rick said. "Talk to your folks about it. Then I'll talk to them, and we'll see."

Daniel slid his hands into his pockets. "I was thinking that maybe I could get a job, and then the state would give me my hardship license so I could drive there and back. That way I could make the money to fix the minivan and maybe buy my own car."

"A job, huh?" Rick asked, a thoughtful grin creeping across his lips. "You ever thought of bagging groceries where I work?"

"Are they hiring?"

"Sure, they're always hiring. And I have a little clout. I've been there three years. I can get you hooked up."

Daniel looked up at the house. "I don't know if my parents would let me."

"Talk to them," Rick said. "You can convince them. You're a smart kid. You know, you're gonna want to date sometime soon, and a car would help things out."

Daniel's face blushed pink. "Where am I ever going to meet a girl?"

Rick shot him a grin. "We have some cute ones checking groceries," he said.

Daniel's eyes widened. "Yeah, I've seen some of them."

"Talk to the folks about the driving and the job, then get back to me. I can work you in," he said. "And if you want an application, I'll bring one home from work."

"Yeah," Daniel said. "Bring one. That way I can fill it out and have it ready to turn back in as soon as they say it's okay."

"All right." Rick held out his hand, and Daniel slapped it. "It's pretty fun most of the time. And sometimes you get tips."

"Tips?" It sounded too good to be true. "Thanks, Rick. I really appreciate it."

"No problem, man," Rick said as he went back across the street.

CHAPTER
Thirty-Nine

Everyone had forgotten Hannah's triumph by Thursday, when Tory returned to class. Cynthia Harrison's year-old baby had said the word *Da-da*, and everyone was lauding him as if he'd just recited Lincoln's Gettysburg Address. Elisa Marshall's baby was walking as securely as any of the adults in the room, and Peg Jenkins's baby had started crawling. Hannah still lagged behind.

When the occupational therapist met with them for their twice-a-week appointment after the class, Tory proudly demonstrated Hannah's progress. "This is a great sign, don't you think? I mean, don't you think she'll be crawling soon, now that she's got the muscle strength to sit up?"

The OT was a woman in her fifties, built like a linebacker. Her name was Tilda, and she was compassionate and sweet to the babies, but stern and demanding with the mothers. She was trained in neurodevelopmental treatment and was never as concerned with what Hannah was doing, as much as she was with *how* she was doing it.

"I don't really like the way she's sitting," she said, studying the positioning of the baby's back, hips, and legs. "This could cause problems when she starts to crawl and walk. You need to check these joints when she sits up. Make sure her posture is right, that her legs aren't too far apart . . ."

Tory's heart rate went into overdrive. "She's sitting, okay? That's major progress! I've been working with her to do this. Can't you say anything positive?"

Tilda's smile seemed condescending. "I know this looks like a big step . . . and of course, it is. But if you don't watch her positioning, the rest of her development could be slowed."

Tory tried to bite back the rest of her reactions to Tilda's instructions, and her weariness and frustration nearly brought her to tears.

But on the way home, she stewed and told herself enough was enough. She wasn't going back to that class, and if the doctor insisted that she keep seeing Tilda, she would have to come to the house like the rest of the therapists did. Tory couldn't stand comparing Hannah to other Down's Syndrome babies. She couldn't stand knowing that she was always a little behind, even in a class of children like herself. She couldn't stand seeing the joy on the faces of the moms who saw more progress than she.

No, she and Hannah could do this alone. She would just work harder with the baby, exercise her more, spend every waking moment trying to stimulate her into talking and reaching and crawling.

If she just worked hard enough, she could make Hannah as close to normal as it was possible for her to be.

Then they would all see what a high-functioning baby she was.

CHAPTER
Forty

The next few days crept by for Cathy like the long, empty days following a funeral, when grief gets its foothold. Because both Rick and Annie worked afternoons, she stayed at the clinic instead of rushing home at three o'clock, as she had done when Mark was home. She tried to concentrate on the animals in her charge, but found herself calling her answering machine every fifteen minutes, just to see if Mark had used his telephone privilege to repent of his treatment of her. At lunchtime, she rushed home to check her mail, hoping he had written her a remorseful letter.

But nothing ever came.

Sunday, she decided to go back and suffer whatever abuse he had for her, but a storm of tears assaulted her in the parking lot, and she couldn't go in. The words "scummy mother" played through her mind like a broken record, and disappointment and anger turned her back.

As she drove home, she couldn't honestly say whether she was following Steve's advice to teach her son respect or simply nursing her wounds. Whatever her motives, she prayed that Mark would miss her and regret the things he'd said.

But as soon as visiting hours were over, she was sorry she hadn't gone. She hurt for him. He must feel abandoned, forsaken. But there was nothing she could do except wait for Wednesday.

She ran purely on nervous energy, trying to get through the days without breaking down. She spent a lot of time on her knees asking God to do a mighty work in Mark, asking him to enable Mark to take the blame for his own actions, asking him to show her what she should do.

Wednesday dawned like the bright morning after a long, miserable night, and she prayed once more about whether to see him that night.

The call came at the clinic just before noon, and her receptionist answered and called her to the phone. "I think it's Mark," the girl whispered.

Cathy attacked the phone. *"Mark?"*

"Uh ... Mom?" His voice cracked on the word.

"Honey, are you all right?"

There was a moment of silence, as if he struggled with every syllable. "Mom, I'm sorry."

Relief flooded over her. "Mark, it's okay."

"I didn't mean to be disrespectful," he went on, as though he'd practiced the words and had to say all of them. "I was just so mad. I felt like everybody was against me, and I hated the world. I still do. But not you, Mom. I don't hate you."

"I know, honey," she whispered. "I know."

"Will you come back and see me tonight?"

"Yes, honey, I'll be there tonight, as soon as visiting hours start."

She could hear the relief in his voice, and she would have given anything to reach through the phone and hug him. "Thanks, Mom. I gotta go now. There's a line waiting behind me."

"See you later, baby," she said. "Can I bring you anything?"

"Maybe my Bible," he said. "The one I used at Miss Brenda's. It's got notes in it and stuff."

She closed her eyes and tears pushed out. "Sure, I'll bring you your Bible. Anything else?"

"If you can find any books you think I might like. It gets pretty boring in here during free time. And maybe some paper to write on."

"I'll do it, honey. I'll bring them tonight."

He said good-bye, and she heard the click. Then, collapsing against the wall, she held the phone against her chest for a moment. "Oh, Lord, thank you," she whispered. She covered her face and wept.

Her spirits soared as if they were lifted by angels, and she went through the rest of the day watching her clock. She couldn't wait to put her arms around her son again.

CHAPTER
Forty-One

Annie begged to go with Cathy that night, so Cathy acquiesced and took her along. It took her a while to get through the checkpoint with the books, Bible, and paper, but finally, she and Annie made their way to the visitation room. She would never have believed she'd be happy to see it again.

When Mark came in, she saw that his countenance had changed. The defiance was gone, and in its place was a wide-eyed vulnerability that told her he was on the edge of tears. Cathy hugged him first, and he clung to her in a way that reaffirmed his remorse.

Annie got up and patted him roughly. "How's it going, kid?" she asked.

Mark patted her back and sat down. "Okay, I guess."

"Have you made any friends?" Cathy asked.

"Mom, he's in jail," Annie cut in. "It's not like he's the new kid in school."

"I've made some friends," Mark argued. "There are fifty of us in the same building. You'd have to be a real dork not to make any friends."

Annie leaned up with great interest. "So what are they in for? Did anybody kill anybody?"

Mark grinned. "Yeah, there's this kid who killed his teenaged sister."

"Mark!" Cathy said.

But Annie laughed. "Don't lie." She pointed to a guy talking to his family in the corner. "Like, what's he in for?"

"I don't know, Annie. Probably drugs, too."

"Anybody you know in here?" she asked.

Again, he rolled his eyes. "Yeah, Annie, three kids from my kindergarten class, and a guy from my English class last year."

"Really?" Annie asked on a shocked whisper.

"No, not really," he said, mocking her tone. "They're all new faces."

"Are any of them—"

"Nice?" Cathy butted in.

Again Mark grinned, and she could see that he was getting more comfortable in the place, that it wasn't as much of a horror as it had been the first few days.

"Some of them haven't tried to beat me up, if that's what you mean."

"Oh," she said, trying to sound enthusiastic. "Well, good."

His grin crept broader. "Mom, you don't have to worry," he said. "The guards sit up above us in this little room with glass all around it, and they watch us 24–7. If anything ever happens, they're on us like flies at a picnic."

"Then how come you got beat up the first week?" Annie demanded.

"Long story," he said. "I know what not to do now."

He sat back in his chair and looked around the room. "So, have you heard from Dad?"

Cathy exchanged looks with Annie. "No, not since court."

"Me, neither," he said quietly. He looked down at his clasped hands on the table. "Guess he's pretty hot about what happened. I tried to call him yesterday, but he wouldn't take my call."

Cathy felt that flame rise up in her chest again. "Wouldn't take it? Are you sure?"

"Well, they said he wasn't there. I told them to leave him a message I had called. It probably embarrassed him."

"Do you blame him?" Annie said, and Cathy kicked her under the table. She didn't want any confrontations today. Nothing negative.

"So . . . I brought you some books," Cathy said, changing the subject. "And your Bible, and some paper. Boy, they really check things out in here. It takes an act of congress to get them through."

He glanced down at them, and Cathy got the impression that he didn't care much about them. She wondered if he'd just asked for the Bible to make her feel better about things.

Annie looked at her watch and got up. "Well, I've got to go. I have a date picking me up."

"What else is new?" Mark asked.

"The guy," she said, lifting her eyebrows. "It's Jimmy Donovan."

He feigned shock, and she laughed. Cathy knew he was glad Annie had come. His sister leaned down and kissed his cheek. Cathy hadn't seen that in years, and her heart jolted. "Hang in there, kiddo," Annie said. Then she straightened. "See you later, Mom. Don't get mugged in the parking lot."

"Annie!"

She watched her daughter prancing out and shook her head. Then she turned back to Mark. She saw the pleasure in his eyes. Annie's visit had done him good. "Mark, do they have chapel in here?"

"Yeah," he said. "I went Sunday."

Her eyes brightened. "You did?"

"Yeah. There's no TV or anything. When we do have free time there's nothing to do."

"What do you do with your time?"

"Well, during the day they work us to death," he said. "If we're not doing schoolwork—which, by the way, is a lot worse than what Miss Brenda used to teach, and a whole lot less interesting—then they've got me in the hot kitchen helping with the cafeteria food."

"That's the job they gave you?"

"Yeah. It's not so bad. You get to munch on snacks once in a while."

She sat back. She should be grateful that he wasn't out on a highway median picking up trash like she'd seen adult prisoners do.

He looked down at his hands. "Mom, I want you to know that I'm not one of those guys that's going to keep coming back here. I'm never going to do this again. I mean it. I'm not just saying that."

"Well, good, Mark. I hope that's true."

"And when I get home, I'll appreciate my room and my privacy, and I'll keep my clothes picked up. Really. These guards in here, they watch us constantly. You can't burp without getting into trouble."

"Well, be glad for the guards, Mark. They just might save your life."

"Tell me something I don't know," Mark said.

Cathy leaned forward and took his hand, kissed it and squeezed it, and Mark squeezed back. Then she started telling him about some of the animals she'd recently treated at the clinic, what the score of the ball game had been the other night, and the letter they'd gotten from Sylvia and Dr. Harry.

Before she knew it, visiting time was up. Choking back tears, Mark initiated the hug this time. Cathy tried not to cry as she watched her son being taken away from her again.

CHAPTER
Forty-Two

When Annie came in that night, she climbed onto the bed next to Cathy. "Feeling better, Mom?"

Cathy smiled. "I feel more relaxed than I have since this first happened."

"Yeah, it was a good visit."

"I've been thinking a lot about all this." Cathy fluffed her pillow and sat up in bed. "About my part in Mark's being in jail."

"Mom, you didn't *have* a part in Mark being in jail. You did everything you could to keep him from getting involved with those kids. It's not your fault."

"I know, but I still keep thinking that maybe . . ."

"Mom, you can't do that to yourself. Rick and I didn't wind up in jail, did we?"

"It's not over yet," Cathy said with a grin.

Annie slapped at her playfully, and Cathy laughed.

"You have to have faith in us, Mom," Annie said. "Rick and I, we make good decisions all the time."

"You do?" Cathy asked. "Like what?"

"Like, don't you realize we've had ample opportunity to go out and get drunk on Saturday nights?"

Cathy's stomach knotted again. She realized this conversation wasn't going to help her stay relaxed. "I had a hunch that you might have the opportunity."

"Well, we don't do it. Even Rick doesn't. I mean, most of the time he's hanging around with some of the straightest kids in Breezewood."

"He is?" she asked. "Really?"

"Yeah. The ones he works with at the grocery store. I mean, there are some partyers in the group, but they're not the ones Rick hangs with."

Cathy decided this was good news. "Well, what about you, Annie? Who do you hang with? I don't know enough about the guys you date. And some of your girlfriends, well, I can only judge them by what I see. I don't quite like the way they dress. But then I haven't always been real crazy about the way *you* dress, either."

"Big surprise," Annie said. "But really, Mom, some of the kids I hang with are partyers, but that doesn't mean I do it."

"Are you ever in the car with them when they're drinking?"

"Not if they're driving," Annie said.

Cathy closed her eyes, wishing her daughter had simply said no. "Honey, why do you want to be in their presence if they're drinking? Why can't you just hang around with people from church?"

"Well, I do a lot," Annie said. "A lot more than I ever thought I would. I mean, you know me. A couple of years ago, I wouldn't have gone near that place, and now some of my best friends are from there. I just don't feel like dropping my other friends like hot potatoes. I mean, aren't we supposed to make a difference in our world?"

"Yeah, but first I think we need to be grounded in our faith. I'm not so sure you are."

"Well, I'm working on it, Mom. I mean, I'm better off than I used to be. All that Scripture memorizing you used to make us do."

Cathy moaned. She was embarrasssed and ashamed that, a couple of years before, she had routinely made her children memorize Scripture when she was mad at them. Brenda had pointed out that that was no way to make them fall in love with the Bible. She hadn't done it since.

"You know, they do make us memorize some Scripture in youth group. And it comes in handy every now and then."

"Really, Annie?" Cathy asked. "Are you serious?"

"Sure," she said. "When I took the SAT test I was really nervous. I thought I was going to blow it. And I started quoting to myself, 'Peace I leave with you, my peace I give to you. I do not give to you as the world gives. Let not your heart be troubled and do not be afraid.' It's from John 14:27. Mike taught it to us in a song. I remember the tune and everything." She sang a line of the song, and Cathy smiled.

"And then last week when all this happened with Mark and we were all so upset, I kept quoting to myself over and over, 'Consider it pure joy, my brothers, whenever you face trials of many kinds, because you know that the testing of your faith develops perseverance.' That's from James 1."

Cathy's eyes filled with tears, and she rolled over and hugged her daughter. "Annie, I can't tell you how much this means to me."

"Well, Mom, why do you always assume that I'm out on the street somewhere emptying beer bottles and making drug deals?"

"I don't assume that," Cathy said. "I have never assumed that."

"Well, I'm just saying you should quit making yourself out to be this horrible neglectful mother who's done everything wrong. Because apparently you've done a few things right. And if you had to weigh which one of the three of us you've done the most right with, I'd have to say it was Mark."

Cathy sat up and looked down at her. "Why?"

"Because look what you did. The minute you saw signs of trouble, you took him out of school, got him in with Miss Brenda, and had her teaching him Scripture. And, Mom, let's face it. Ever since you became a Christian, you've had us in church every time the doors open. A person doesn't have a chance to reject the gospel when you put it in front of us every time we turn around."

"Oh, people have plenty of chances to reject the gospel," she said. "Just because people are sitting in church doesn't mean they're Christians."

She had been worried about Annie, because none of her children had made a profession of faith or walked down the aisle and joined the church. Yet she had seen subtle changes in both Annie and Rick.

"I know that. I'm just telling you that you've done a good job."

Cathy lay back down, considering that. "Annie, have you got a personal relationship with Jesus? I mean, more than just knowing about him and quoting Scripture?"

The lamplight cast dark shadows on Annie's face. "Well, yeah. I use it in my life, okay? I put it into practice."

"But have you accepted Christ? Do you understand about what he did for you?"

Annie sat up and hugged her knees. "Mom, you don't have to preach to me. I'm not Mark, okay?"

"The gospel isn't just for Mark. It's for you, too."

"And I have," she said. "One night at a youth rally. I talked to Jesus that night for the first time, and he and I have had a thing ever since."

Cathy couldn't have scripted a better answer. "Annie, I thought I was going to worry about you when you started college this fall, but now I know you're going to be all right."

Annie flopped back down and looked at the ceiling. "Oh, yeah. College."

She had noticed a coolness in Annie's voice whenever the subject of college came up. She had enrolled at the local community college for the fall, but Cathy knew she was looking for a way out. "Annie, why aren't you excited about college?"

"Well, I just don't know what I want to do yet. It seems like such a waste of time."

"An education is never a waste of time."

Annie slid off the bed. "Can we talk about it later? You need to sleep."

Cathy wasn't fooled. The college conversation could wait, but she sensed that it would be a difficult one when it came. She sat up and kissed Annie good night, then watched as her daughter left the room. She slid to her knees and whispered a prayer of tearful thanks for the night of affirmations.

CHAPTER
Forty-Three

Tory couldn't wait to open the package that came from León, Nicaragua. She wondered what Sylvia had sent her. She tore into the package and pulled out the little rolls of film in plastic cylinders. Frowning, she pulled out the letter that came along with it. One short note was addressed to Tory individually, and the other was to all three neighbors. At the top of the letter were explicit instructions not to read it until they were all together.

She folded the long letter back up and stuck it in her pocket, then skimmed through the short one that was addressed to her.

Dear Tory,

It cost too much to get film developed here so I was hoping you wouldn't mind if I sent you the film. These are pictures of other children who have come here to get fed. I thought you and the girls could use them in your presentations if you wouldn't mind getting them made into slides. Give your precious little

Hannah a kiss for me, and Brittany and Spencer, too.
I love you,
Sylvia

Tory looked down at the cylinders. Here, she knew, were priceless pictures that would move people into helping. But how would she work this around her schedule with Hannah? She supposed she could give up a little more sleep.

"Spencer, Brittany," she cried. The two kids came running from the back of the house. "Get in the car. We've got to go get some film developed."

"Can we get candy?" Spencer asked.

Tory checked Hannah's diaper. "No, no candy."

"Potato chips?" Brittany asked.

"It's too close to suppertime." Cradling Hannah, she headed out the door. "Come on, kids."

"Where are we going?" Brittany asked.

"To the mall, to that one-hour photo place. Miss Sylvia sent us some pictures, and I want to see them as soon as we can."

Tory paid extra to have the pictures developed quickly, and as soon as they walked out of the photo shop, Brittany begged to see them. Tory put little Hannah in her stroller, then sat on a bench with Brittany and Spencer on either side of her, and started flipping through the pictures. One by one, she saw the faces of hungry children with glazed looks in their eyes, swollen little bellies, toothpick legs.

"What's wrong with them? Are they sick?" Brittany asked.

Tory shook her head. "They're hungry. They don't have enough food to eat."

"Why not?" she asked.

"Because they're poor."

"Why don't they just go to the grocery store?" Spencer asked.

"Because they don't have them there. At least, not like we have. Miss Sylvia said that the stores there have a whole bunch of one thing but not enough of everything."

"One thing like what?" Brittany asked.

"Like hats or something," Tory said. "But not food."

"Hats?" Spencer asked. "Why aren't they wearing them?"

"Well, I didn't mean hats, for sure," Tory said. "I was just using that as an example."

Spencer grabbed the next picture and studied the little boy. "He's not wearing a hat."

"I know. I was just telling you . . ."

"None of them are wearing hats."

She couldn't help laughing. "I was trying to explain that, instead of having a lot of different things on the shelves of the grocery stores, they only have a few things. Those things are usually things they don't need."

"Well, why don't they just get food?"

"It's a long story," she said, "but we're trying to help Dr. Harry and Miss Sylvia get money so they can buy it and feed these children. It's real important."

She looked into the envelope; yes, the box of slides was there too. They would need them for their presentations.

"Why are there children who don't have food?" Spencer asked. "Why can't we give them some of ours?"

"That's a good question," Tory said, "and that's exactly what we're going to try to do. We're very blessed, you know. We never have to go hungry, and we have those wonderful grocery stores with everything in the world."

"You don't think they're wonderful," Brittany said. "You always hate to go."

"I always say I hate a lot of things, but then I find out that somebody is worse off than I am, and I feel really bad about it."

As she loaded her children back into the car, she resolved that she was going to stop whining. There were people with genuine problems, much worse than hers. Even Cathy's problem was monumental compared to Tory's. She had been a terrible neighbor. She needed to do what Brenda had done and take Cathy a meal.

She changed her mind about heading home and pulled into the parking lot of the grocery store she frequented.

"What are we doing here?" Spencer asked. "Getting candy?"

"No," Tory said. "I need to pick up a few things. I'm going to make a casserole for Miss Cathy tonight."

"Is she hungry, too?" Spencer asked.

"Probably," she said. "But that's not why I'm doing it. Food is a good way to tell her I love her."

Brittany and Spencer pondered that as she unloaded them again and headed into the grocery store.

CHAPTER
Forty-Four

Sylvia was exhausted by the time she had fed all the orphans in the school and all the families that had come to eat that day. It was way past dark when she finally made it home. She found Harry sitting quietly in his recliner, reading his Bible through bifocals in the light of a lamp.

She went to stand in front of him. "Okay," she said. "I'm ready."

"Ready for what?" he asked, looking up at her.

"I'm ready to sell the house," she said. "There's no other way. We've got to do it to raise the money. More and more families are hearing that we've got provisions, and they're coming to get food. Harry, we're going to run out, and there's no way on this earth that I can tell those people I can't feed them."

He closed his Bible and dropped his feet. "Sit down," he said. "You look really tired."

She sat down and realized how little energy she had left. She'd been on her feet most of the day. "So what do we do? What's the next step?" she asked.

"I guess we call the States and get a realtor to put a sign up."

She thought about that. "I have to tell the girls first."

"Okay. When?"

"Soon," she said. "We can't wait. We have to do something quick."

Harry took her hand and pulled her onto his lap. Holding her, he said, "I'm really surprised that you would come to this decision on your own. I didn't think you were going to agree to it."

She put her arms around his neck and laid her head on his shoulder. "I don't know," she said. "I should have been willing to turn it over in the first place. There are so many things we need here. It was my last hold on home, almost like a lifeline to Cedar Circle. But I don't need the house. I still have the girls."

"Yes, you do," he whispered. "They're not going to cut you off just because you're not a property owner in the neighborhood anymore." He kissed the top of her head. "I'm proud of you, you know. This means you're totally committed to your work here. Completely, unequivocally, without looking back."

"What was it that Jesus said?" Sylvia asked. "'He who puts his hand to the plow and looks back is not fit for the kingdom of God.'"

"He did say that," Harry agreed.

"Well, I've got both hands on the plow," she said, "and all I can see is a field of children who are starving to death. I might as well send that treasure to heaven. There's no sense in holding onto it."

"All right," he said. "I'll get the ball rolling with the realtor as soon as you've told Brenda, Tory, and Cathy. Now you go on to bed."

With that decision made, Sylvia dragged herself to their room and fell into the bed.

CHAPTER
Forty-Five

Cathy could count on her kids for overlapping crises—after all, she had three of them, and they had each vowed not to let their mother's life get dull. So when Annie walked into Cathy's clinic just before it closed and announced that she wasn't going to college that fall, Cathy wasn't all that surprised.

Her daughter made the announcement as calmly as if she were telling Cathy that she was going to a friend's house or getting her hair cut. She stood there happily, her hair pulled up in a flip ponytail, and big dangly earrings slapping against her face. She was chomping on a piece of gum.

"Annie, you're already enrolled. What do you mean you're not going?"

"I'm going to get a real job and skip college."

She blew out her impatience. "Annie, a full-time job is no picnic. And I'm not going to let you loaf. A few months of having to support yourself and you'll be begging to go to school. You'll hate the routine of a job."

"Well, *you* don't hate your job," Annie challenged.

"No, I don't," Cathy said, "but I happen to have college degrees, so I'm able to do something I love. What are you able to do, Annie?"

"I don't know," she said. "I could get a job at the mall."

"And do you ever intend to move out and get an apartment of your own, maybe get married, have a family?"

"Well, yeah, sure. Someday."

"And how do you plan to support yourself?"

She twisted her face and leaned back against the wall. "I don't know. I haven't thought that far out. All I know is I hate school and I don't think I can stand it for four more years. This thing with Mark has just reminded me how precious my freedom is. I don't want to be institutionalized."

Cathy rolled her eyes at the melodrama. "Institutionalized? Annie, school can hardly be compared with juvenile detention."

"But I bet it *feels* the same. Mom, I just don't want to go to college."

Cathy was getting flustered. She hadn't prepared for this. She raked her fingers through her hair, feeling her spirits sinking again to their level before the breakthrough with Mark. "Look, could we talk about this later? I'm really kind of busy right now."

"Sure," Annie said and popped her gum. "How 'bout we talk about it in September after I've already missed registration?"

"No," Cathy said, "I meant that we'll assume you're going to college this fall until I'm miraculously convinced otherwise. You see, it's like this. You live in my house and you do as I say. I'm not sacrificing another child to the world. You either go to college or you find a way to support yourself, period."

Annie looked at her as if she'd disowned her. "You would think I came in here and told you I was pregnant."

"No, Annie, if you came in here and told me you were pregnant, there would be a marked difference in how I responded. Trust me."

Annie smiled, as if she wished she could pull that particular string. "So when are you coming home?"

"In a few minutes," Cathy said. "I just need to finish up some paperwork."

"Well, Miss Brenda left a message at home for you to call her. She said that Miss Sylvia is going to call tonight, and she wants to talk to all three of you."

"About what?"

"She didn't know," Annie said.

Cathy shuffled the papers on her desk and got up. "Well, okay. I guess I'd better get home. I don't want to miss that." She took off her lab coat and hung it up. "Annie, I'll meet you at home."

"After the big phone call, can we talk some more about college?"

"We'll see. But I'm not changing my mind, Annie. You're going to college."

"What if I get a job? I could get one tonight, you know. Between now and suppertime, I could join the military or get into a management program at the mall. I could be earning more than you before the day's out."

Cathy retrieved her purse from its hook on the wall and dug for her keys. "Tell you what, Annie. If you get a job making more than I make, you can skip college. But it has to be legal and moral."

"Oh, right," Annie teased. "There you go laying down a bunch of conditions."

Cathy escorted Annie out of the clinic and locked the door behind them.

CHAPTER
Forty-Six

Cathy and Brenda gathered at Tory's house at seven that night, when Sylvia had promised to call. Tory laid out the pictures of the Nicaraguan children on the table, and they tried to organize them into the right order for a slide show. Cathy would take the first speaking engagement for the following Sunday afternoon, since Brenda went weak in the knees at the prospect, and Tory had committed to speak at another church that evening.

They were certain that was what Sylvia was calling about. It was probably a pep talk, Cathy thought, or she was making sure that they got all the details right. They'd kept in touch by e-mail about the requests coming in for them to speak, and she supposed Sylvia was afraid they would blow it.

When the phone rang, they each picked up on a different extension in Tory's house. "Hello?" Tory said.

"Are you all together?" Sylvia asked. Her voice sounded so clear she might have been next door.

"Yes, we're here." They each gave their greetings, and she spent a few valuable minutes asking about Mark and Hannah and the wrecked cars in Brenda's driveway. Then she got to the point.

"I wanted to talk to you girls and let you know something before you heard it from someone else."

Cathy didn't like the sound of that. Her chest tightened. "What is it, Sylvia?"

"It's the house."

Cathy glanced at Tory, who stood across the room holding another phone to her ear.

"The house? What house?"

"My house. The empty one?"

All three women got quiet.

"Girls, we've decided to sell it."

"No!" Tory's cry carried through the house. "Sylvia, you can't."

Cathy sat down, and Tory leaned back against the wall.

"Sylvia, this is a big step," Cathy said. "Are you sure you've given it enough thought? This is your *life*. It's your history."

"No, *this* is my life now," Sylvia said. "And I'll have my history no matter what I do with the house. It's the future I have to think of now—of these children, and the fact that we don't have enough money to keep feeding them. I have to think of the starving parents and the medicine Harry needs for these people."

"But we're raising money, Sylvia," Tory said. "Both Cathy and I have speaking engagements Sunday. We were just organizing the slide show. We're on it, Sylvia."

"I know you are," she said. "And I need for you to go ahead with that, because it might be a while before the house sells. But Harry's calling our realtor tomorrow, and she's going to list the house and put up a sign. I just wanted you to be prepared. I wanted you to understand."

Cathy looked at Tory and saw the way the light caught the tears in her eyes. Brenda came out of the back room with a cordless phone to her ear. "Sylvia, please don't," Cathy said.

"We were hoping you could come back when you retire," Brenda said in a cracked voice. "It's your house. Nobody else can fill it."

"That's sweet." She could hear the tears in Sylvia's voice. "But I have to do what I've been called to do. And we need this money. It would do so much for the children. And I can come back there and visit and stay with one of you."

"But you won't," Tory said. "Your own kids don't live here anymore. You'll go to see them when you're in the States. You won't have time to come here, if you don't have your house to bring you back."

"It's not the house that makes Cedar Circle my home," she said. "It's you. Your families. I love you and I *will* come back to see you. And I'm going to keep in touch as if you were all still my next-door neighbors."

Silence weighed heavily over the line. Finally, Brenda spoke again. "We understand, Sylvia. You do have to follow God's leading. We're just a little sad for us. But how wonderful that you've come from not even wanting to go to Nicaragua, to being willing to sell your house for those people."

"That's how you can know it's God," Sylvia said. "It's not like me at all."

Later, when they'd gotten off the phone, Cathy, Tory, and Brenda sat around the pictures on Tory's kitchen table, staring at each other with smudged eyes. "It was one thing to have the Gonzales family living there," Tory said. "They were temporary. Just house-sitting, sort of. I always thought Sylvia and Harry would come back."

"What kind of people do you think will buy it?" Cathy asked. "Retired people? People with children?"

"Maybe they'll have kids the ages of ours," Brenda said. "Maybe they'll fit right in."

"And maybe they'll be antisocial and let their grass grow to their hips," Tory brooded.

"Maybe it'll be an axe murderer," Cathy said, and as her eyes met Brenda's and Tory's, a slow smile broke out on her face. The others smiled, too.

Brenda took both of their hands. "We've got to support her in this," she said. "Sylvia's being obedient to God. He never said it wouldn't hurt."

"Maybe the house won't sell," Tory said.

"Yeah." Cathy grinned again. "Maybe we could put up road-blocks. Make the neighborhood look less attractive. Hey, I'm willing to let *my* grass grow."

"I'm doing my part," Brenda said. "I have two beat-up cars out in the driveway."

"And I'm the mother of a convict," Cathy said. She tried to smile at the flippant remark, but it didn't feel funny.

"And I could always sic Spencer on them," Tory said. "Let any lookers know that Dennis the Menace comes with the neighborhood."

They all laughed, then wiped at their tears again. "At least we still have Sylvia, no matter how far away she is."

"But I don't look forward to seeing someone else's furniture being carried into that house," Tory said.

"Or hers out," Cathy added. "Boy, will that be painful." She set her chin on her hand. "Feels like a new era. Like things will never be the same again."

"They won't," Brenda said. "But maybe they'll be better. Maybe God wants us to turn this corner. Maybe he has something special waiting. And if he doesn't, the house won't sell."

"We can hope," Cathy said. "And raise money like crazy while we're waiting. Then maybe she won't need to sell it anymore."

That was the best idea any of them had come up with yet, so they set about organizing their photographs and planning speaking engagements.

CHAPTER
Forty-Seven

As Cathy crossed the cul de sac to return home, an old pickup truck pulled up to her curb, with an elderly weather-beaten man behind the wheel. Annie was just pulling into the driveway, and she got out of her car and met Cathy in the yard before the man got out.

"Mom, I know you and Steve are kind of on hold, but really, you can do better than that."

Cathy elbowed her daughter in the ribs. "Who is he?"

"Like I know?"

Cathy crossed the yard to meet him as he got out of the truck. He smiled at her, flashing a decaying front tooth. "May I help you?" she asked.

"Yes, ma'am," he said. "Sorry to come by so late, but I just need to scope out the backyard and make sure everything's ready for tomorrow."

"Ready for tomorrow?" Cathy asked. "What's happening tomorrow?"

"We're starting work on the new addition on the house, that's what," the man said. "Ain't nobody told you?"

She frowned. "Well, no. I mean, I thought we postponed it."

"Can't postpone it," he said. "You got a contract."

Cathy thought back to the document she and Steve had signed with the contractor weeks ago. The man had so much business that he'd put them on a long list and promised to get started at least a month before the wedding. He had the slabs poured weeks ago, but he was late beginning the construction. Neither Cathy nor Steve had thought to tell him the wedding had been called off.

"Well, your boss has so much business it won't matter to him. He can tear up the contract, can't he?"

"No, ma'am," the truck driver said. "Never heard of him tearing up one yet. He's got him a lawyer, though, that presses pretty hard when it comes to breach of contract."

Cathy gaped at him. "Are you telling me that you're going to start work on my house tomorrow whether I want you to or not?"

"All I'm doing is following orders, ma'am. He told me to come and make sure everything was ready to start."

"How do you mean, 'ready'?" Cathy asked. "Apparently it's not 'ready,' since I don't want it done—at least not yet."

"Take it up with him. Mind if I walk around to the back and look at the foundation?" He started around the back before she could answer.

"Excuse me!" She trotted behind the man. "Do you have your boss's phone number on you? I need to talk to him immediately."

"Yes, ma'am," he said. He pulled a leaky ballpoint pen out of his ink-stained pocket. "Got something to write on?"

She didn't, so she stuck out her hand. "Here, just write it on my hand. I'll go in and call him right now."

He seemed amused that he was writing on flesh, but he jotted the number down. Then scanning the work that had already been done, he said, "Tell him it looks okay. Won't be no problem starting in the morning."

"There definitely *will* be a problem starting in the morning," Cathy said, "but I'll take care of that right now."

She went into the house and dialed the number. A man yelled hello into the phone, and she could hear something like a jackhammer buzzing behind him.

"Mr. Barksdale?" she asked.

"Yes, ma'am."

At least he was polite. "This is Cathy Flaherty over on Cedar Circle."

"Yes, ma'am," he said. "Sorry it took us so long to get to your house, but I sent my man out there tonight to check to make sure we could start in the morning."

"Well, that's just it. He's here," Cathy said. "Look, about that contract. I was wondering if there was any way we could just cancel it. We'll do another one later when we're ready to build."

"Cancel it?" he asked. "What happened? Your boyfriend dump you?"

She caught her breath. "No, he didn't dump me!"

"You dumped him, then?"

"No! Nobody dumped anybody. We've just postponed the wedding for a while."

"Well, I'm sorry, ma'am. After the foundation was poured and everything."

"Yes, well . . . We'll build eventually, but I just can't handle it right now."

"I understand completely," he said, though that jackhammer buzzing in the background made her wonder if he could even hear her. "No problem, ma'am."

"Then you can refund our money?" she asked.

He hesitated. "I'm sorry. Come again?"

"I asked if you could refund our check," she yelled.

"Well, now, nobody said anything about that."

"I just did. I said it. If we're not having the work done yet, then we shouldn't have to pay."

"But there's a contract, ma'am."

"But you just said we could get out of that. You just said—"

The jackhammer on his end stopped. "Oh, I'll postpone the building," he said. "Even cancel it entirely, if you want. But I can't return the money." He chuckled, as if the whole concept was absurd. "If I did that, I'd have folks pulling out on me left and right. Contracts are binding, ma'am."

"But you have business coming out your ears! You're already weeks later than we agreed. It won't hurt you to let this go. I've been having some personal problems. If you have any compassion at all . . ."

"Ma'am, if my business hung on people's love lives, I'd be bankrupt in a month."

"My personal problems have nothing to do with my love life!" She wadded the roots of her hair in frustration. "Look, would you call my fiancé and let *him* explain this to you?"

"Fiancé? Thought you said you weren't getting married."

"I don't know what we're going to do. Just call him, will you?" She spouted out his number at work, then hung up the phone.

"Mom, that man's out there spray-painting the yard," Annie said.

"Spray-painting it?" Cathy asked. She ran to the back door and flung it open. The man was painting lines on their grass with bright orange neon paint.

"Why won't they listen to me?" She swung around to Annie. "Am I invisible? Can people not hear me?"

"I hear you, Mom, loud and clear," Annie said. "I've never had any trouble hearing you."

Cathy looked back in the yard again. "Okay, if he wants to paint up our yard, that's fine. I'll just go rinse it off as soon as he leaves. I don't have the energy to fight with him again."

She sat down at the kitchen table, her fingers threaded through her hair.

"He's leaving," Annie said, still peering out the window.

Cathy listened until his old truck started up, vibrating the neighborhood.

"Crisis passed," Cathy said with a sigh. "Steve will take care of it. That was all I needed. A construction project in the middle of everything."

"Maybe I could get a job doing construction," Annie said thoughtfully as she stared at the backyard. "Instead of college, you know? I can paint lines in neon."

"Yeah, and you're sometimes just as deaf as those guys are." She got back up and went to the box she'd brought home with the pictures of the Nicaraguan children. "I'm just going to forget about it. Steve will take care of it. I have to organize these pictures. Annie, will you help me?"

Annie looked at her watch. "Right now?"

"You weren't doing anything," Cathy said. "You've been hanging around talking about construction work." She went to the closet and got out the slide projector, set it on the coffee table, and focused it on the wall.

Annie shrugged. "Well, I guess I could help for a little while," she said. She sat down on the couch next to Cathy and started flipping through the papers that were stacked under the slides. "So what are these?"

"They're Sylvia's narratives," Cathy said. "I've got to figure out which thing goes with which slide and make sure everything's in order. It's for the presentation I'm doing Sunday."

"Cool," Annie said. "Yeah, I'll help." She put the first slide in, and they saw the group of orphans who lived at the school where Sylvia helped. It looked like any other class of children, only the kids' clothes were less elaborate, more faded.

Cathy ran through the narrative that Tory had given her about the picture. Annie changed slides—a close-up of three children who didn't look quite as healthy as the ones in the previous picture. Their hair was dirty and messed up, stringing in their eyes. They were barefoot and dressed in clothes with holes and dirt.

"Who are these?" Annie asked.

Cathy searched through her notes. "These are kids from the community who come to get food," she said. "Look how skinny they are."

Annie's eyes grew serious. "They are skinny," she said. She turned to the next slide: a little boy with toothpick legs and a distended belly. His eyes were dull.

"Says here his name is Miguel," Cathy said.

"Miguel?" Annie asked. "What about him? Is he an orphan?"

"No, he's got a mother, according to this. But they don't have food. His father was killed in the hurricane, and his mother hasn't been able to make a living. It says she brought him to the orphanage for Sylvia to keep until she could get on her feet." Annie stared at the little boy who looked no more than four. "Mom, that's awful. Don't they have, like, welfare or something?"

"No, Annie, they don't. That's an American thing. Besides, the Bible tells us that we're supposed to help people in need, not wait for the government to do it. So that's what Sylvia is trying to do, and that's why we're trying to raise money. So little boys like Miguel won't have to suffer."

She changed slides and saw Sylvia holding the little boy on her hip. He had his arms around her neck and was kissing her on the cheek.

Annie smiled. "He looks better here, doesn't he?"

"Yeah," Cathy said. "Go to the next slide."

Annie switched slides, and a picture of the same little boy came up on the screen. His eyes had a twinkle in them now, and his stomach wasn't swollen. His little legs had fattened up to normal proportions.

"Oh, look," Cathy said. "This is after they've been feeding him for a month. He looks so much better. Look at his eyes."

"He's in there now," Annie said. "He just looked like a little shell, before."

"He's just one example," Cathy said. "Go to the next one."

They went to the next one and saw another "before" picture of a little girl with stringy hair, dirt on her face, and a chipped front tooth. She was wearing a smock dress that was too little for her. In the next picture, she saw her with Sylvia, playing with some other children. Then there was a picture of her eating beans and rice out of a bowl . . . then an "after" picture a couple of months after they had been feeding her. She looked normal and healthier and had that same sparkle in her eye that Miguel had had.

"Mom, that's amazing," Annie said. "I always thought of Sylvia being over there just preaching to people, standing on street corners and passing out tracts or something. I didn't realize she was really helping people."

Cathy gave a dry laugh. "Annie, how can you say that? Sharing Christ with people *is* helping them!"

"Oh, I know it is," Annie said. "I mean, in theory. But the truth is she's doing more than that. She's filling their little stomachs."

"Well, not for long," Cathy said. "If we don't get people to send her money, she's not going to be able to fill anybody's stomach. She and Dr. Harry have decided to sell their house to raise it."

"No way! Mom!"

"I know. It makes me sick. But maybe if we raise enough money through the churches, they'll reconsider."

Annie switched slides, and Cathy came back to sit down beside her. They saw Sylvia and some of the other missionaries working in the orphanage, teaching school to the children who were grouped according to their ages. They were all clean and well cared for.

"They didn't come to her like this," Cathy said. "Look at the next one."

Annie put the next slide in and flashed it on the wall. It was a shot of some of the same children she had just seen, only they were in rags and covered with dirt and mud, sores and scrapes. Some of them were crying, and their noses were crusted with mucus. They were all hopelessly skinny and looked desperately afraid.

Cathy swallowed. "That was when they came to her after the hurricane," she said. "Her friends, the other two missionaries, thought they were going down there to build a school. They couldn't get any students to come to it, but then the hurricane hit and orphaned children started showing up, brought by people who had no way to care for them. And they finally realized that God hadn't sent them there to build a school at all. He sent them there to build an orphanage."

Annie's eyes rounded as she looked at her mother. "Mom, that's awesome," she whispered.

"Yeah, only they need lots more workers. They don't have enough. And they need money."

Annie looked back at the slide. "And we're sitting here so fat and happy."

Cathy grinned. "Annie, what do you weigh?"

"A hundred ten pounds." She giggled. "Well, I didn't mean literally fat. I just meant that we have everything we need. And even most of the stuff we want."

"Sylvia said they can feed 100 children—maybe even 150—on $400 a month," Cathy said. "One child, for four dollars at the most. For a *month*. Isn't that amazing?"

"Yeah," Annie whispered. "Awesome."

Cathy saw the tears in her daughter's eyes as she flipped through the slides, watching the images on the wall as if these people were coming to life before her. It moved Cathy to see that Annie could be touched this way.

"So do you want to come help me at the luncheon Sunday?" she asked. "I'm going to need help with the slide projector, and since you've already been through the slides, you'd know what to do."

Annie dabbed at the tears dotting her eyes. "Sure, I can do that," she said. "It's the least I can do, I guess. I have a date with Jimmy, but I can get out of it." She considered the next slide. "You know how I've been saving for that new CD player?"

"Yeah," Cathy said.

"I don't need it," Annie said. "What if I just send the money to Miss Sylvia? Would it help much?"

"How much is it?" Cathy asked.

"I've got about $100 so far."

Cathy smiled. "Annie, do you think feeding twenty-five kids for a month is 'doing something'? Because that's how many kids a hundred dollars would feed. Maybe even more."

"Well, yeah, but I mean, is that really true, or is that just a figure Miss Sylvia made up to make it sound dramatic?"

"It's true, honey," she said. "Send her the money, if you want to. It'll give you a lot more satisfaction than the CD player."

"I will," Annie whispered. Her face softened even more as she watched the images Sylvia had sent of the rest of the children.

CHAPTER
Forty-Eight

Saturday night, Annie got dressed for her dinner date with Jimmy Donovan, one of the most sought-after guys at the community college. She had pined after the "older man" her entire senior year of high school, but it wasn't until she'd graduated that he'd finally asked her out.

When he showed up in a pair of shorts and tennis shoes and announced that they were going to the soccer field to meet his friends rather than to the restaurant, she was a little miffed. Still, he was the most eligible college guy she knew, so she figured he was worth changing clothes for.

It also made her feel a little better about canceling her Sunday afternoon date with him.

"Jimmy," she said, trying to get his attention as he tossed the Frisbee toward his friends. "Could you give it a rest for a minute? I need to talk to you."

"Yeah? What about?" He caught the Frisbee and spun it back.

"Would you be terribly mad at me if I don't go to the swimming party tomorrow afternoon?" Annie asked.

Jimmy turned to her as if she had slapped him.

"What do you mean, you can't go? You have to go. You *said* you would." He missed the Frisbee as it flew back to him and gave it an annoyed look.

"Well, I know, but something's come up. My mom needs me to help her with a luncheon. We're trying to raise money . . ."

He set his hands on his waist, looking disgusted. "If you couldn't go, you could have told me earlier so I could have gotten another date."

Annie grunted. "Well, excuse me. I didn't think it was that big of a deal."

"Well, it is, okay?"

"Come *on*, Donovan!" his friend J.J. shouted from across the field.

Jimmy retrieved the Frisbee and threw it back. "So does this have something to do with your jailbird brother?"

Fire ignited in Annie's eyes, and she intercepted the Frisbee before he could grab it and held it at her side as she turned her furious face to his. "No, it is not about my brother," she said, "and if you ever call him a jailbird again, you're going to regret it. It just so happens that I'm going to help my mother speak at a luncheon about our friend Sylvia's missionary work in Nicaragua."

He rolled his eyes as if he couldn't believe she would come up with such a lame excuse. "You have got to be kidding. You'd choose that over a swimming party at Sara Beth Simpson's house?"

She wondered if he could really be that shallow. "Jimmy, Sylvia's working with these little kids over there and they're starving to death. They're malnourished; they have bloated bellies and toothpick legs. And she's got to raise money so she can feed them. Sylvia's already gone back to Nicaragua, but my mother's going to stand in for her at a church that invited Sylvia to speak. I'm going to help with the slides. I'm going to show pictures of sad little children who have nothing. And, yeah, I'm glad to say that I consider that a little more important than splashing around in Sara Beth Simpson's pool."

"Hey, your mother can do this without you. She's just trying to keep you away from me."

"She doesn't even know you," Annie said. "Why would she do that? My mother didn't force me to cancel this date. I'm doing the slides, and I sure would like to think that you had enough depth to understand."

"Fine!" He grabbed the Frisbee out of her hand and ripped it back with all the anger he felt. "You just go ahead. And I'll see if I can find another date to go with me to Sara Beth's."

Annie set her hands on her hips. "Well, you just do that, Jimmy. Have fun."

He looked at his watch. "Wonder if Karen Singer's home? Maybe she still doesn't have a date."

"Karen Singer?" she asked. "You're going to take Karen Singer to the swimming party?"

"Hey, I've got to take somebody. I'm not going to show up by myself."

"Heaven forbid," Annie said. "That might ruin your reputation as a player. You know, I don't think I wanted to go with you, anyway. You'd probably just be watching all the girls in their bikinis and ignoring me, anyway."

"Hey, you're lucky I even give you the time of day, little high school twerp."

"Little high school twerp?" Annie repeated. "I can't believe you said that. Take me home."

"No," he said, "I'm playing Frisbee with my friends."

"Fine," she said. "Then I'll walk."

She heard him laugh as she started off over the hill and back down the road that would lead down Signal Mountain. Maybe there would be a pay phone somewhere along the way, so she could call her mother and have her come get her. If not, she could get home on pure fury. She was sorry she had invested so much time in Jimmy over the past year, pining away for him and dreaming of the day he would ask her out. When he had, she had felt so privileged. But not privileged enough to forsake hungry kids to show up like a trophy on his arm. *How dare he?* She wiped her tears away, determined not to cry another one for him. There were other guys. She was better off.

But as she stormed down the street, the tears pushed into her eyes again. She smeared them away and told herself this was a small price to pay.

The thought of the little boy Miguel propelled her faster, each step giving her new purpose. There were other little boys like Miguel, other little girls with sick stomachs and dull eyes who didn't even know that they needed help. It was the least she could do. The very least.

CHAPTER Forty-Nine

Cathy was nervous during church the next morning, wondering why she had agreed to speak at the luncheon that afternoon. She had enough stress in her life. She was a veterinarian, not a speaker. If those poor Nicaraguan kids were depending on her, then they were in deeper trouble than they knew.

But true to her commitment, she left her church after the service and hurried over to the church where the luncheon was being held.

"You can do it, Mom," Annie said as they pulled into the small parking lot.

"I'll be glad when it's over," Cathy told her. "I just hope I'm not wasting my time and all of theirs."

"You're not," Annie assured her.

They pulled into a parking place. Cathy's hands shook as she gathered up the stack of things on the seat next to her. Annie got the box on the floor at her feet.

A wave of dizziness washed over Cathy, and she leaned back in her seat. "I've got to stop a minute," she said. "I need to calm down."

"Okay," Annie said. "Just take a deep breath. You'll be all right."

Cathy looked up at the front doors of the church. "I don't know anybody in there. Do you think they know about Mark?"

"I don't know. Did you tell them?"

"No, but most of the people in this area know me. I treat their animals. Mark's arrest was in the paper, and everybody in town is talking about it."

"Well, they probably do know then, Mom," Annie said. "But that doesn't mean they won't listen to you."

Cathy forced herself to get out, but she leaned against the fender of the car and closed her eyes. She heard Annie's door close and sensed her daughter coming to stand beside her. "I don't know why I ever agreed to do this," Cathy said. "They don't care about any of this. They just have this luncheon once a month, and they needed a speaker. That's all."

"You agreed to it for little Miguel," Annie said. "That's all the reason you need. And if they don't care now, they will. Now come on. Let's go. I didn't miss that swimming party for nothing."

Cathy opened her eyes. "What swimming party?"

Annie shook off the question and shifted the box with the slide projector. "Just some stupid swimming party at Sara Beth Simpson's house. I was supposed to go as Jimmy's date."

Cathy's eyes widened. "That was the date you cancelled? For me?"

"Not for you, Mom. For Miguel, and for Sylvia, and all those other little kids."

Cathy's heart rate settled, and she stood straighter. "Annie, I'm so proud of you."

"Don't be," she said. "It's really a pathetic trade-off. They're starving, so I miss a swimming party. It's not a big sacrifice, Mom; I wouldn't get excited about it."

"But just the fact that you would do something like that. It's unselfish and mature. I'm just so surprised."

Annie grinned and looked up at the sky. "Come on, Mom. You're making me sound like a heathen. You raised me to be a decent person, okay?"

"Well, decent people sometimes choose swimming parties over slide shows."

"I know," Annie said. "But I made my choice. Now come on. Let's go in. I'm sweltering."

"Wait." Cathy grabbed her hand and stopped her. "Let's pray. I don't think I can go in there without it."

"Okay, Mom," Annie said. "Whatever you say."

Cathy closed her eyes, and Annie followed suit. Cathy asked God to help her through this, to give her the words, and to work on the hearts of those who heard and watched. When she said "amen," she felt peace wash over her where dizziness threatened just a moment ago. It was going to be all right.

"I'm ready now," she said. Annie was quiet as she followed her inside.

An hour later, Cathy stood at the front of the room, amazed as the hundred people in attendance began passing their checks forward, along with pledge cards and notes of encouragement for Sylvia. She stood at the front as, one by one, they came up and told her how much the slide show had moved them, and how much her scripted words had convicted them.

She looked through the audience to find Annie. There she was—over to one side, talking animatedly to a group of people as if she, too, were selling them on the idea of helping Sylvia. It amazed Cathy that her daughter could have an intelligent conversation with adults concerning something other than herself or her social life. Maybe Annie was growing up.

It was over an hour more before the fellowship hall emptied of the guests. As Cathy gathered up the slides she had so carefully laid out for Annie, she saw Annie flipping through the stack of checks.

"Mom, you're not going to believe this," she whispered.

"What?"

"Well, if I'm counting right—it looks like we have almost three thousand dollars here."

"Really?" Cathy eyed the stack. "Are you sure, Annie?"

"Yeah, I'm sure. Mom, you did great. In fact, one of these checks is mine. I had planned to give it to you so you'd feel like you raised something, even if no one else gave." She laughed. "Guess you did okay without me."

Cathy grinned. "You decided to give them your CD player money?"

"Decided?" she asked. "How can anybody decide not to? I was thinking of selling my clothes and all my shoes just to raise more. That's how good you were."

"That's how good the Holy Spirit is," she said. "Annie, you don't know how much this is going to mean to those kids."

"I think I do," Annie said.

Cathy hugged her, then gathered up the rest of her things and loaded them into a box. "So, is there still time for you to make that swimming party?"

Annie looked away. "No, I don't think so."

"Come on, they're probably still there. It's early."

"Yeah, but I don't want to go. Jimmy's a jerk, and I don't want to be around him. Besides that, he's got another date."

"Are you kidding? He got another date just because you backed out?"

"Yep. That's the way he is," she said. "But it's good I found out now. I don't want to invest any more time in him. He's definitely high maintenance."

Cathy smiled. Prayers were being answered about her children. She hoped God was answering the ones for Mark as powerfully as he was the ones for Annie.

CHAPTER Fifty

Tory was already busy when Barry got up for work, giving Hannah a breathing treatment to break up the phlegm in her lungs. As the child lay in her seat with the breathing mask strapped on her face, Tory held her feet and made pedaling motions.

"Do you ever stop?" Barry asked, standing rumpled and groggy at the living room door.

Tory glanced back at him. "She was up and rattling. She has to breathe."

"I'm not talking about the breathing. I'm talking about the exercising. Aren't you afraid she's overdoing it? Won't you get her worn out before her class?"

Tory hadn't told him of her decision to quit the class. She knew he wouldn't understand, and she couldn't risk having him insist. "She'll be okay," she said.

He bent over her and moved his face close to hers. "It's you I'm worried about."

"Me? I'm fine."

"I never see you when you're not working with her. You need a break. Just wait and do it in class today."

She thought of telling him, but the words lodged in her throat.

"Tell you what." He straightened up. "I'll take my lunch hour during her class, and I'll take her so you can have some time off."

She looked up at him, knowing she'd been caught. "Well, uh ... ordinarily ... that would be fine ... but to be perfectly honest..." Her voice veered off, and she searched for the right way to say it so that he would agree with her.

She laughed. "It's the funniest thing. See, that class—" The medicine attached to Hannah's mask began slurping, and she cut the machine off. "I was planning to keep her home today because of her cold."

"She always has a cold." He took off Hannah's mask and lifted her out of her seat.

"But today it's worse than usual. I just thought it wouldn't hurt to miss."

He kissed Hannah's fat cheek. "Well, I guess that's reasonable. Isn't it, Hannah?" He cradled her and kissed her belly, and the child smiled. "Here, go to Mommy," he said. "Daddy has to shower for work."

Tory took her, and as Barry left the room, she felt that familiar surge of guilt that she hadn't been honest about quitting the school. But by the time he found out, Hannah would have progressed so far that it would be clear she'd done the right thing.

Then, instead of protesting, he'd praise her.

As she took Hannah to the kitchen to feed her before she got Spencer and Brittany up, she told herself she was doing the right thing.

CHAPTER
Fifty-One

Thursday morning Cathy woke to the sound of voices in her backyard, loud hammering, and a drill that sounded as if it were boring right through her bedroom wall. She leaped out of bed and ran for her robe, pulled it on, and dashed to the window. She bent the blinds down and peered out. The yard was full of workers.

"What is *this!*" she shouted. "I *told* them!" She rushed out of her room to the back door and stepped barefoot out into the yard.

"What are you doing?" she shouted. No one seemed to pay much attention to her. "Excuse me!" she yelled, clutching her robe tight. "Where is Mr. Barksdale?"

"He ain't here," one of the workers said. "He's over at another site."

"No! This is not acceptable!" she cried. "I want everybody to stop what they're doing. Just freeze, okay?"

Most of them stopped their work and looked up at her, but a drill continued to clatter. She looked around, following the sound. The worker who ignored her wore headphones. He was drilling into the bricks on the back of her house.

She ran barefoot across the yard and pulled his headphones off. The grinding stopped, and he looked startled. "I told him we weren't going to build yet! I told him we wanted to postpone it! My fiancé spoke to him and told him!" She turned back to the crowd of men gaping at her. "Hold it right here. Don't hammer one more nail. Don't chip off one more brick. I'm going into the house to make some phone calls."

She bolted back inside and dialed Steve's number. He sounded too perky for six-thirty.

"Hello?"

"Steve, *they're here!*"

"Who's here?"

"The workers," she said. "They're banging holes in my house, breaking down the bricks, digging up the yard."

"Oh, no," he said.

"You said you would take care of it!"

"I did take care of it," he said. "Barksdale told me he'd check his schedule to see if he could shift us around. He never got back to me, so I assumed that he had."

"But I didn't want to be shifted around. I wanted to cancel it until we were ready."

"But if we cancel, we'll lose the money. Cathy, I borrowed money for this. I was trying to find a way to keep from forfeiting it."

"Do you mean to tell me that I have no choice in this? They're going to start tearing up my house whether I want them to or not? We're broken up! I gave the ring back."

"But I don't plan to keep it," Steve said. "I was waiting for the right time to put it back on your finger."

"What were you going to do? Drug me and make me set a date?"

"Maybe." She could hear the smile in his voice. "Something like that. So I was thinking it wouldn't be the worst thing in the world if they went ahead and got started."

"*Steve!*" she shouted. "You tricked me."

"No. It's not a trick, Cathy," he said. "And if, for some reason, things don't happen, and you meet Mr. Casanova and decide to dump me—"

"Does Mr. Casanova have a contractor?"

He laughed, then quickly cleared his throat. "Cathy, I'm paying for the renovation, and if for some reason you refuse to marry me, you'll have a nice house that's worth a lot more than it was when we started. If you think about it, I'm the one who might get taken here."

"Right," she said. "This is all my clever ploy to get a bigger house."

He laughed again.

"Steve, it's not funny. I don't want contractors here. I have too much going on."

"Just ignore them. Act like they're not there."

"But I can't. They're digging up my backyard and banging down my walls."

"They're not banging down the walls," he said. "They're just taking off the bricks. They're not going to make doors into the house until they've almost finished everything else. We talked about that."

She let out a frustrated scream.

"Mom, what's going on?"

Rick was standing, groggy-eyed, in the doorway to the den.

She put her hand over the receiver. "My life is out of control," she said. "That's what's going on!"

"What time do you go to work?" Steve asked.

She looked at the clock. "Well, I have to be there at eight."

"Fine. Just put on some headphones or something, turn the hair dryer on, do anything you can to get your mind off the men in the backyard. They'll be gone before you get home from work today. They get started early so they can knock off early and miss the hottest part of the day. You can pretend they were never there."

She opened her mouth to give him a retort, but nothing came out.

"I love you," he dared say.

She wanted to break something.

"Cathy, I know you're under a lot of stress right now, and I promise to make this as easy as we can. Most of the mess will be in the backyard, and except for early mornings, I really think they'll stay out of your way."

"Do I have a choice?" Cathy asked, falling back onto the couch.

"Of course you do. You could call it all off and let me eat that fifty-thousand-dollar loan. Hey, it's only money."

She threw a cushion off of the couch, then kicked it. A horrible noise erupted in the yard, making it impossible for her to hear. "I can't hear you!" she shouted. "I'll call you back later."

She hung up the phone and let out a frustrated yell again. The noise stopped before her voice did.

"Mom?" Now it was Annie, standing in her gown.

"Go back to bed," she said. "They're just destroying our house. Don't worry about it."

"You're letting them?"

"Unless you have fifty thousand dollars on you." She flung the cushion again, then started back to her room. "I have to get ready for work."

CHAPTER
Fifty-Two

Cathy heard from her children a dozen times that day, complaining about how the workers sounded as if they were tearing the house down, how they were digging up the yard and blocking the driveway with their trucks. Each time, Cathy told them to call Steve at work and let him handle it.

A sense of dread crept over her as she doctored the animals that came to her for attention. She had postponed the wedding because of Mark—or had she? Was it really Mark's situation, or was it a much broader fear? If Mark could bring this much stress on them, she couldn't imagine what it would be like to be married and still dealing with the frustrations of smart-mouthed kids and attorney bills.

The thought that she would have so much responsibility for Tracy, a child at the very age where she had probably started making the most mistakes with her own children, frightened her to death. The constant comparisons that she knew were inevitable for Steve frightened her even more. How would the love she and Steve had for each other endure such hard times?

Then again . . .

It would be nice to have a partner in life, someone who had a stake in what happened, someone who could grieve with her and for her, someone on whose shoulder she could cry. And Steve was more than that. He was someone who made her laugh and brought joy back into her life.

The thought of losing Steve frightened her even more than the thought of marrying him. If he gave up and went his own way, she doubted that she would ever get over it. Yes, she was strong. Yes, she had been through grief before and come out on the other end. But she didn't want to do it again—not alone.

She went into her office and pulled out the file that held the blueprint they'd made of the addition on to her home. It would be a beautiful home when they were finished. Steve had thought of everything.

This would be the first time she'd have a master bedroom with bookshelves. She'd always wanted that. And their bathroom would border on luxurious. They needed that family room, especially with four kids and all their friends coming and going in the house. Even when all the kids had left home, the family room would come in handy for grandchildren and visits back home.

The thought that she had a future like that and someone to share it with filled her with warmth. Maybe it was a good thing the builders had gone ahead. Maybe God was intervening with her postponement, telling her that it wasn't necessary.

Yet how could she get married when Mark was behind bars?

She decided not to deal with any of it today. She would wait until she got home and see what happened. Maybe this was a good thing. She would try to hang on to that thought.

Pulling into her driveway that afternoon, Cathy saw that the trucks were all gone, just as Steve had promised. Some supplies had been left behind, but at least they were all stacked in a pile on the side of the house. That was probably as good as she could expect.

She went into the house and put her things down. Annie was sitting in front of the television. "They finally left, Mom. But you should see what they did to the backyard."

She closed her eyes. "Should I even look, or should I just pretend I don't know anything about it?"

"I think you should look," she said.

Cathy headed to the backyard. At first sight, she was torn between feeling a thrill that her house was going to turn into something wonderful, and a little kernel of dread that this was going to get worse before it got better. In the early stages of drawing up the plans, she had asked the architect for things she had never thought she could have. With two incomes, there would be room in her life for a few luxuries ... and more contributions to Sylvia.

She looked at the lumber stacked at the side of the yard and the other supplies that would soon be made into part of her home.

She was surprised to see Rick at the edge of the yard, squatting in the dirt where she had spent last spring planting a garden on her weekends. Her heart sank again as she saw what had been done to it.

"They dug up my flowers," she said.

"Sure did, Mom." Annie was behind her, egging her on.

Rick looked up at her. "I was thinking of maybe putting them in some pots before you got home. I didn't want you to go crazy."

"Good idea," she said. "Maybe it's not too late. Are they dead?"

"No, they still look alive and kicking," he said.

"Come on, Annie," she said. "There's some potting soil in the storage room. Drag it around here and get some pots."

As they worked together to get the flowers into pots, she realized that no real harm had been done. The workers had been more respectful of her property than they had been of her schedule.

"So, Mom, I was thinking," Annie said. "About this college thing ..."

Cathy gave her a warning look. "Annie, you're going to college."

"But Mom," Annie said. "I told you, I can't stand the thought."

"Then get a full-time job that will support you," she said again. "Annie, education matters. You can't do anything in life unless you're educated for it. It's worth the hard work."

"I know," Annie said, "but my problem is that I don't know what I want to do, okay? I don't have a clue. And I don't want to just float through college like Rick's doing, taking all those classes that don't mean a thing to me."

"Hey, I'm not doing that," Rick said. "I'm about to declare a major."

"Yeah? Well, what is it?" Annie challenged.

Rick shrugged. "I'm going to come up with it by the end of summer, okay? Get off my back."

"That's just my point," Annie said. "Why should I go spend all this money at college and take all these classes and keep studying for four more years when I don't even know what I want to do?"

"Annie, I'm not going to let you skip college," Cathy said. "I told you how it's going to be."

"Well, I had another thought," she said. She abandoned the pot she was working on and sat back on her bottom, not even heeding the dirt stains that she was going to have to deal with later. "Mom, listen to me," she said. "I have a plan. A really great idea."

Cathy looked up at her and braced herself. "Okay, shoot."

"Well, you know those pictures of those kids that Sylvia's working with? You know, they really moved me. The truth is that Sylvia needs help from *people*, I mean, another pair of hands, more than she does money."

"She needs both," Cathy said.

"Well, I was just thinking about what I'd be giving if I went to college. I mean, what I'd really be accomplishing, especially since I don't know what I want to do yet. And I was thinking that maybe if I went to Nicaragua . . ."

"Wait a minute," Cathy said. She got to her feet and dusted off her hands and rump. "Annie, if you're going to start asking me to send you to Nicaragua on some glorified vacation, I'm just as sorry as I can be. I don't have the money for it, and I don't have the patience to talk about it."

"No, wait," Annie said. "I don't want to go on a vacation. I'm not interested in seeing the landscape. Oh, I mean it'll be cool and all, but that's not it."

"Then what do you want, Annie?"

"I want to help those children."

Rick started to laugh. "Here it comes."

"Shut up!" Annie said. "I'm serious."

Rick snorted.

"Mom, that little boy, Miguel. The way his eyes came to life after they'd been feeding him . . . it really surprised me and made me think. It takes so little to meet somebody's needs."

"But it's not just about meeting their physical needs, Annie. It's about meeting their spiritual ones."

"I know, Mom. But I want to help with both."

She had never heard Annie talking this way before, and something inside her stirred in gratitude. She gazed in surprise at her daughter. "Annie, are you serious?"

"Mom, I was thinking that if I could just lay out of school for one year and go over there and help Sylvia with the orphans and the children who need to be fed, the hundred dollars I was going to give to help her buy food could help pay for sending me. And don't worry, Mom. I know I'd have to raise my own support, buy my own airline tickets, get over there myself."

"Annie, have you really given this any serious thought?"

"Yes," she said, "ever since I started looking at those pictures. I thought how bad I want to go over there and pick those children up and hold them and work with them."

Cathy looked at Rick. He was leaning against the fence, his mouth stretched into a huge grin as if he couldn't believe his ears. "Annie, a missionary? You've got to be kidding me."

"Hush, Rick," Cathy said. "She sounds serious about this."

"I am serious, Mom," Annie said. "Why would I make this up? Most kids are anxious to go off to college. You know me. I love the social part of school, and I love camp and I love being with the youth group and I love hanging out with my friends. That's part of what college is all about. But I don't want it."

"I know, Annie, and I really don't understand it."

"Well, maybe this is why. Maybe God wanted me to do something else this year. And then when I come back, I can go to college, and by then maybe I'll know what I want to do. It'll give me time to think, and time to get out of Cedar Circle where everything's nice and pat. I can get over there and actually help people. I don't think I've ever helped anybody before, Mom."

"But, Annie, for you to really be able to help people the way they need to be helped, you have to have a certain spiritual maturity. I'm not sure you've really grown into that yet."

"Mom, how am I going to if I never stretch? Let me go."

Cathy sat back down in the dirt and realized that tears were stinging her eyes. "Annie, I'm not ready to send you halfway across the world on a whim."

"It's not a whim, Mom."

"She's gone insane," Rick said. "It won't last a week."

"It will, too," Annie said. "Shut up, Rick. If I get over there, I can't afford to come back until it's time."

Rick chuckled and went back to his potting. "Let her go, Mom. It's about time she got out of my hair. And then you could just give Tracy her room and not worry about fixing up yours."

"No!" Annie said. "I'd be back. It's still my room."

"Of course, we'd keep it, Annie," Cathy said.

"Then you're going to let me go?"

She felt broadsided, unprepared. "Annie, I have to think about this. It needs a lot of prayer."

"Well, we have time before school starts, Mom. I don't have to go right now. I can go whenever Sylvia thinks it's best."

"That's another thing," Cathy said. "I've got to talk to Sylvia. She may not want you to come."

"Why wouldn't she? She needs help."

"Well, I know, but she remembers you as this teenaged kid floating around from social event to social event. She might not actually believe that your heart is right in this."

"Mom, let me talk to her," she said. "I can convince her. When I raise the support, she'll know I'm serious."

"And how are you going to do that, Annie?"

"I've got lots of plans," she said. "I've learned a lot from you. When you fought with the school board, and last year when you collected clothes for the clothing drive. I know how it works, Mom. I'm willing to go door-to-door if I have to and ask people to sponsor me. Trust me. If I can't raise the money, then it's not meant to be."

"You'll understand that?" Cathy asked. "You'll believe it?"

"Yes, Mom."

"Because I'm not willing to spend your college money on this. I'm not giving up on that."

"That's fine, Mom. I promise, I'll come up with the money. And if I don't, I won't go." She laced her hands together. "Just say you'll talk to Miss Sylvia."

"I will. And I have to talk to Steve."

"Why Steve?"

"Because," Cathy said, "my future's tied up with his, even if we've postponed things."

"It doesn't look like you've postponed it much," Rick said, looking around.

"No, it doesn't." She sighed and dug into the dirt. "All I do know is that I want to spend the rest of my life with Steve. You and Annie, you'll be out of here before I know it, wherever you decide to go. And Mark, well, he's where he is. Steve is for me. He's mine. He's someone that I believe God sent me to make my life more complete. And I want to consult him about things going on in my life."

"Fine," Annie said. "Consult him. I think he'll probably be glad to get rid of me. Two down, one to go, if you can ever get Rick to move out."

"*Hey!*" Rick said, no longer amused. "I'm leaving in August."

"I know the time is coming," Cathy said, "and I know God has a plan in both of your lives. I don't want to cling. But I've got to know it's right, Annie. I've got to consult God and make sure it's his plan and not yours."

"Okay, Mom," she said. "Just know that I'm praying, too, and my prayers might cancel out yours."

"Thank goodness it doesn't work that way." She touched Annie's face with her dirty hand. "I'm very proud of you, Annie, for even considering this. Even if I don't let you go."

Rick stepped toward them but didn't commit by touching either of them. "It is pretty cool, Annie. If you really do it."

It was the most tender moment they'd had as a family in a very long time. Cathy only wished that Mark was here to share it.

CHAPTER
Fifty-Three

Brenda was starting across the street to see Cathy when Rick began carrying the potted plants to the front yard. "Hey, Miss Brenda," he said.

"Hey, Rick. What's going on with the construction? Did your mother change her mind?"

"They kind of changed it for her."

The front door of the Dodds's house slammed, and Daniel bolted out. "Hey, Rick," he called. "Did you get that application?"

Brenda turned back to her son and watched him loping across the street. "What application? Daniel, did you—?"

"I got you one," Rick said. "And guess what? There's an opening right now for a bag boy at the store. I talked to them about you, and I think if you go by there tonight they'll hire you."

Daniel looked as if he'd just won a lottery. "Thanks, man."

"What?" Brenda asked. "Daniel, we didn't say—"

"Come on, Mom," Daniel said. "I need a job so I can pay the deductible on your car. I can do it, Mom. I promise I can. Then you can get the van fixed."

"Daniel, it'll take months for you to save up a thousand dollars."

"Still, it's something I can do, Mom. And I need some spending money. After I pay the deductible, I could save for a car, and then you and Dad wouldn't have to come up with extra cash. I can even help buy groceries and maybe make part of the house payment."

Brenda looked a little embarrassed that he would say such things in front of Rick. Daniel had no idea just how little minimum wage really was. But his heart was right. He was trying to take responsibility, and she didn't want to stomp it out. "Honey, they don't pay *that* much."

"But it's not bad for a first job," Rick said.

"Oh, Mom, please!" Daniel said. "*Please* let me do it."

"I'll talk to your dad again," Brenda said. "That's the best I can do right now."

"But I have to go up there tonight. If I don't, they'll hire somebody else."

She looked at Rick, wishing she had never walked over today. "I'll think about it, Daniel. If your dad says it's okay, we'll drive you there ourselves."

"That's okay," Rick said. "I can take him."

"Yeah, Mom," Daniel said. "I don't want my parents hanging around when I'm applying for my first job. It wouldn't look good."

"Well, don't you think they know that a fifteen-year-old boy has parents?"

"Mom, please."

Brenda closed her eyes and decided she was entering a new phase of life that she hadn't counted on quite so soon. "I'll go talk to him right now," she said.

But as she walked back across the street, she tried to formulate her argument so that David would agree with her that Daniel wasn't ready to enter the workforce just yet.

CHAPTER
Fifty-Four

It took a couple of days for Cathy to get Sylvia on the phone, but when she finally did, she told her what Annie wanted to do. "So, what do you think?" she asked Sylvia. "Do you think you can use her?"

"It's an answered prayer, that's all there is to it," Sylvia said. "We need her, Cathy. She'll be a big help to us."

"Are you sure?" Cathy asked. "Let's face it, she's not the most spiritually mature person in the world. She's a little self-centered, as we both know. She's never done anything for anyone on this scale."

"Neither had I, when I came here," Sylvia said. "She'll be fine. She can stay right here in our house with us. Harry will be thrilled to have her around."

"She doesn't have to stay the whole year if you don't want her to."

"Well, we'll leave that open. If she can get herself here and home, then we'll take care of her while she's here. Don't worry about a thing. I think it's the best way she can spend this year before she goes to college, anyway. You'll see. It'll change her life."

"For the better, I hope," Cathy said. She heard the pounding outside. The workers seemed to be in a demolition phase, but she couldn't think what they were destroying. She propped her chin on her hand, wondering why her life seemed to be moving so fast these days. "I seem to be going through a lot of transitions right now, but I'm not sure it's all going to be for the best."

"This one will," Sylvia said. "Trust me. And trust God. If he's put this on Annie's heart, you know it can't be from any selfish motive. Let her come, Cathy. You'll be glad you did."

Later that evening when Steve came over, Cathy sat with him on a stack of lumber. "I feel like my life is out of control," she told him.

"How so?"

"Well, I have no control at all over what's done with Mark. He's a ward of the state now, and they're calling the shots. I only get to see him twice a week. I don't know what's happening to him in between. Rick's moving to campus this fall. And now this with Annie."

"This with Annie is a good thing," Steve said. "It's the best thing that could happen to her. You wait and see."

"Yeah, well, that's out of my control, too, pretty much. I may be sending her off to Sylvia for a year, and she'll be the one taking care of her."

"Don't you trust Sylvia?"

"Well, of course, I do. I trust her parenting a lot more than I do my own."

"Annie's not a little girl anymore," he said. "She's eighteen. Technically, her childhood is behind her."

"Technically, maybe," Cathy said, "but we both know there's still a lot of immaturity there. I don't know if she can take this. I'm almost worried that Rick is right, that she'll want to turn around and come home after she's gotten a good look at the sights."

"Maybe not," Steve said. "Maybe she'll surprise you. Maybe this is God's way of showing you that the same parent who could raise a child who would wind up serving time could also raise a missionary."

She looked up at him, her eyes glistening with the tears that seemed to come too often these days. "You know, I've thought of that myself. Isn't that amazing?"

"Sure it is, and we don't even know what will happen to Rick yet. It could be anything."

"He's really been sweet with Daniel," she said. "Almost like he's doing penance for all the mean things he did to Mark. He's going to teach him how to drive, and he's trying to get him a job."

"There's a lot of good in your kids, Cathy. You just need to have a little more faith in them."

"I know," she said.

He drew in a deep breath and looked at the work being done on the house. They'd gone too far—there was no turning back.

"This is costing a lot of money," he said, "and I know it's one of the other areas where you feel out of control."

Cathy sighed. "Even the good things seem out of control. The house, and Annie's plans. But I don't know why I'm so worried about her. She may not even raise the money."

"I was thinking maybe I could help her."

Cathy looked up at him. "Steve, I can't ask you to do that."

Steve shrugged. "It's no problem. I hocked your engagement ring today. I'll just use that money—"

"*Steve!*" Cathy sprang to her feet. "How could you?"

He doubled into laughter then and stood up. He dug into his pocket and pulled out the ring. "See? I knew you still wanted it."

She swung at him, and he ducked and leaped over some piping. "Oh, no! I dropped it," he said.

She stopped chasing him and looked down at her feet. "Where?"

"Just kidding," he said, and held the ring up as he came back toward her. Amazed that she had fallen for it, she grinned and took the ring, gazing down at it. "That was low, Steve."

He took her shoulders and touched his forehead to hers. "Maybe so. But if you don't put that back on your finger right now, I'm going to the pawn shop. Annie needs that money."

She grinned and slapped playfully at him. He caught her hands, took the ring back, and held it up, as if he needed a finger to put it on.

She provided hers. Steve's smile faded, and his eyes grew serious as he slid it on. "Thank you," he whispered, then his hand came up to cup her face. He kissed her, making her melt like a candle.

"Nicaragua is a good cause," he whispered, "but marriage to you is a better one."

"Annie'll get over it," Cathy said.

"Maybe she won't have to." He pulled her back to sit next to him on the lumber. "I'm still going to help her. I won't give her all of it. I think it would be good for her to try to raise it on her own. That way we'll be able to gauge her level of commitment. But I was thinking maybe I could pitch in a few hundred dollars. Maybe that would go toward half of the airline ticket or something."

"She'll be grateful."

"I know she will," he said, "but I don't think I'm going to mention it to her until after she's raised the rest. Let's just keep watching to see how she does."

"I've been thinking, too," Cathy said. "At first, I told her I wouldn't use any of her college money to help her pay for the trip. I thought this was just a ploy to get out of going to school. But now, I'm thinking that if I did dip into it and help her, I could work a little extra to help her out with this. Maybe stay open all day on Saturdays and stop knocking off at three. What do you think? Would that be spoiling her?"

"Like I said, see how much she raises before you do that. And I'm sure there'll be times when we'll be sending money while she's over there."

"We?" Cathy smiled. She touched the diamond. It felt good on her finger. "I like the thought of 'we.'"

He slid his arm around her and pulled her close. "I love you, lady," he said. "I'm going to marry you. I'm going to move into your house. And you're going to have a beautiful bedroom and a huge family room, and we're going to live happily ever after. And your daughter is going to be a missionary, and your son is going to be a successful executive somewhere."

"And Mark?" she asked.

"And Mark's going to come out of jail a stronger person. Who knows? Maybe he'll even find Christ in there."

"Do you think so?"

"I do," he said. "And we have to make sure during this down time in Mark's life that Christ is exactly who he's thinking of. I'll help with that."

Her eyes filled with tears again as she touched his face. She loved the way his stubble felt against her palm. It was amazing how much she loved him and even more amazing that he could love her through all this.

"Marry me, Cathy," he whispered.

"I will," she said. "I'm just not sure when."

"Marry me on July 4th, just like we planned," he said. "Let's go in there right now and open all those presents."

She smiled. "Oh, so that's what this is all about? You just want to open your presents."

He grinned back. "Well, some of them did look pretty interesting."

Her smile faded, and she gave a great sigh. "Steve, July 4th is just a few days away. You know that's too soon. It's just a bad time. And I don't want to open the presents until we've set a date. I may have to wind up returning them all."

"I'm not going to let you return them," he said, "and I'm not going to let you stop work on the house. And I'm not going to let you cancel our wedding. Not until you convince me that you don't love me and you don't want to spend your life with me."

"I could never convince you of that," Cathy said, "because it wouldn't be true."

It was clear he already knew that. "I'll wait for you. I know you're going through a tough time with Mark. I'll even be here to help you. But make no mistake. This is *we*, not *you*. It's our problem, not your problem. I'm here for you, okay?"

"Okay," she whispered.

"And, like I said, if you get sick of me and want out, then you'll have this great big nice house and you won't have to pay for any of it."

"I didn't mean for you to have to pay for everything," Cathy said. "I was really going to help."

"As far as I'm concerned, it's all about to go into the same pot, so it really doesn't make any difference," Steve said.

The feeling of warm relief washed over her like an ocean tide, and she realized that God had sent her one of the most precious gifts in her life the day she'd looked up at a parents' meeting and seen Steve standing at the door.

"Be patient," she said. "I'll marry you as soon as I know the time is right."

That'll have to be good enough, then," Steve said. He pressed a kiss on her lips, then on her forehead, then pressed his forehead against hers and combed his fingers through her hair. Cathy knew that, no matter how bad things got, she wasn't alone this time. God had sent Steve, and he was standing beside her.

CHAPTER
Fifty-Five

Brenda and David sat in their car at the end of the coliseum parking lot and watched as Rick taught Daniel to drive.

"I should be doing that myself," David said. "I shouldn't have overreacted to his wrecking the car."

"Don't be so hard on yourself," Brenda said. "There are some things that other people can teach your children better than you can."

He looked over at her and grinned. "I can't believe this is you talking, the definitive mother hen."

She grinned back at him. "I'm not a mother hen, just because I home-school. At least I admitted that I can't home-school him in driving. Look at him! He just made a U-turn."

David squinted. "Are you sure that's him driving?"

They both broke out laughing, but Brenda's mirth quickly faded. "There's a lamppost coming up." They both braced themselves, breath held.

He easily swerved around it. They both breathed.

"Rick's a miracle worker," Brenda said.

David leaned back in the pickup truck and started to relax. "I say we let him take the job."

Brenda closed her eyes. She didn't want to hear this. She had decided on her own that it was too soon, and there were too many reasons not to let Daniel work. "Why, David? He's too young to go to work. When we start school again he needs to study."

"Come on. He's doing great," he said. "You've already got him at an eleventh-grade learning level. He needs a little time to socialize."

"He does socialize. He socializes at church. He plays baseball."

"I know, but he needs to learn responsibility. He needs to learn what it's like to earn money. And it sure won't hurt him to have to pay off this deductible. I guarantee you, once he learns to drive, he'll always be careful if he knows how much the insurance is going to cost. And, hey, if he's able to save up for a car ..."

"Come on, David. At minimum wage? How much do you think he'll be able to save?"

"Don't underestimate him," David said. "He can do it. I did it when I was young."

"But what if he starts going overboard with it? How do we draw the line? What if he starts working nights and weekends and overtime?"

"We can put our foot down anytime we want to. Besides, it's not going to be such a novelty for that long. After a while, he's going to get tired of it and want to work less, not more. Mark my word."

Her gaze drifted back to the car creeping along the edge of the parking lot. "I'm just not ready for this," she whispered.

"Well, be glad you're not Cathy sending him off to prison."

"Oh, don't even say that," she said. "David, I've been sick about Mark. It's made me want to cling even harder to Daniel."

"I know it has," David said, "but we've got to let him go."

The car screeched, and Daniel jerked to a halt. Brenda threw her hands over her face. "I can't look," she said.

"Oh-oh, he's coming toward us," David said.

She opened her eyes again and sat straighter, grabbing David's hand. "He's coming too fast!" But almost as soon as the words were out of her mouth, Daniel slowed, then inched forward toward them.

"I'm too old for this, David," she said.

He nodded his head slowly in agreement. "That's why we have Rick."

CHAPTER
Fifty-Six

Cathy took Rick and Annie with her when she went to visit Mark Sunday afternoon.

When Mark came into the visiting room and greeted everyone, Annie made her announcement with a flourish. "I've decided to be a missionary in Nicaragua. I'm going to spend a year with Sylvia in León."

"No way," Mark said. "Mom, is she?"

"Maybe," Cathy said. "If she raises the money to get there."

"I'm going," Annie said. "It's practically a done deal." She reached into her purse and pulled out snapshots of the children in Nicaragua. She flipped through until she found the picture of little Miguel.

"You think *you* have problems," she said. "Look at this little boy. See how swollen his stomach is, how vacant he looks?"

"Vacant?" Mark asked. "When did you start using words like *vacant?*"

"Since your room became vacant, okay?" Annie said irritably. "Look at him, how sick and miserable he looks. And in this one, after he's been eating at Sylvia's kitchen for a while, he's gotten healthier. Do you see that?"

Mark leaned up and looked at the picture again. "Yeah, I see it."

"Sylvia's making a difference in people's lives, and I'm going to go help her."

"Don't they have, like, rules? Standards? That sort of thing? They let just anybody go to the mission field?"

"They're letting her," Rick said. "Go figure."

Annie smiled. "Hey, I'm called by God."

"You sound like Dan Aykroyd in the *Blues Brothers*," Mark said. "What is it with her, Mom? Does she know some guy that lives there or something?"

"Hey, I'm going for the children," Annie spouted.

"No way," Mark said again. "There's something in this for her, Mom. Better figure out what it is before she costs you a fortune."

"It's not costing me anything, Mark," Cathy said. "Annie's raising her own support."

"I've already raised three hundred dollars," Annie said.

Cathy shot her a look. "Are you serious?"

"Yeah, Mom. I went to the families of each of my friends from my youth group and I told them what I was doing, and they wrote me checks on the spot."

"Why didn't you tell me?"

"Because I've been so busy doing it I haven't had a chance." She turned back to her brother. "So, see? I'm not going for any mercenary reason. I'm seriously doing this because I want to help the children."

Mark just stared at his sister for a moment, as if waiting for her to get to the punch line.

Annie rolled her eyes. "Just forget it. You'll see, when I'm writing from Nicaragua."

His eyes finally changed, and he regarded his sister with a serious look. "Well, if it's true, I think it's pretty cool. But, Mom, what are you going to do with both me and Annie gone?"

Cathy looked down at her hands. "Rick and I will get along somehow, until he leaves in August."

"The house will keep her busy," Rick said. "They've started building."

Mark looked at his mother. "Really? You're going ahead with it?"

Cathy's heart sank. She didn't want Mark to know of all the changes being done without him, anticipating how depressed he would feel after they left, when he went back to his cell and sat staring into space, aware that the world was revolving at full speed without him.

"We had sort of a run-in with the contractor. I wanted to postpone it, but we would have lost the money."

Mark didn't say anything. He just looked down at the table. "So you two are going to go ahead with the wedding?"

"No," Cathy said, "we're not. We're postponing it until you get out, Mark." She watched his reaction, hoping he would say that waiting was ridiculous, that they should go ahead. Instead, he just kept looking down at his hands clasped in front of him. She wondered what was going through his mind.

"So, tell us how it's going in here," she said finally. "Are you getting along with the other guys?"

"Yeah, they're okay, some of them," he said. "You just figure out who to avoid."

"Have you been going to chapel?"

"Yeah. The Christians love us. We're a captive audience. They can't pass up the opportunity to preach to us every time we turn around. Of course, the Muslims and Hindus and Buddhists have chapels, too, but I don't go to those."

Annie brought her gaze back to Mark. "You talk about Christians like they were another group. I thought you were one."

"Yeah, I am," Mark said with a shrug. "I mean, I'm not a fanatic or anything like Mom, but, hey, I believe there's a God."

To Cathy, those did not sound like the words of someone who knew Christ. But lectures from her weren't going to change what was in his heart. That would take prayer—and a work by the Holy Spirit.

Later that night, as Cathy and Steve sat out on the pile of sheetrock in the backyard, looking at the new work done by the construction crew, Steve came up with an idea. "I think I'm going to do a Bible study with Mark on my own," he said.

"How?"

"Well, I can do it through the mail," he said. "Mark likes to get mail. I can just write him letters, give him things to look up, kind of disciple him like a correspondence school or something."

"I think that would be great. But prepare yourself. It may all be a waste. He may not even read it."

"Maybe not now," he said, "but at some point he might pull them out and study them. And with the Christian groups coming to him a couple of times a week, it could turn out to be really good, you know? Maybe I could supplement what they're doing somehow through the mail and then work with him one-on-one on visitation days. I don't want to take away from your time with him, but I think it could work out."

Emotion assaulted her, and tears sprang to her eyes.

"Did I upset you?" he asked.

She smiled and shook her head. "No. I was just sitting here wondering why God's blessing me so with you."

"July 4th will be here before you know it," he said. "The church is still free. The pastor's still available."

She smiled. "Not yet. It's just not time."

He didn't say any more about marriage for the rest of the evening, but she knew her delay was costing him. Even so, she couldn't think of marrying him until things had fallen more into place. Things were just too rough, too rocky right now. She was on the downward slope of a steep roller-coaster ride, and she didn't want to bring two more people into that. No, there had to be a better time to get married, a time when the problems were fewer and the path seemed straighter. Second marriages brought enough problems. She just hoped Steve wouldn't give up.

CHAPTER
Fifty-Seven

Brenda didn't sleep at all the night before Daniel started his new job, and then she got him up early and fixed him a healthy breakfast before dropping him off at the grocery store. She found it hard to do anything that day, because she kept thinking about her baby entering the work world, earning his own money, getting to know people she didn't know, taking orders from bosses whose motives she couldn't predict.

Around noon, she decided she needed a carton of milk.

"Where you going, Mama?" Joseph asked her.

"To the grocery store," she said, distracted as she gathered her checkbook and truck keys. "I need some milk."

"But Daniel's there," he said. "Don't show up at the store on Daniel's first day! He'll be embarrassed."

"He will not be embarrassed. I go to the grocery store all the time, anyway. I'm not going to quit just because Daniel's working there."

"Okay," he said, "but I want to go with you. I gotta see this."

They both got into the pickup truck and headed off to the store. As Brenda went in, she searched the checkout counter for Daniel, hoping he would be up front where she could find him. When he wasn't there, she went down the meat aisle, then the produce, then the canned soup.

" Mama, this isn't where the milk is," Joseph said.

"I know."

"You're looking for Daniel, aren't you?"

"Why would you say that? I was just trying to remember a couple of other things I need to pick up." She peeked around a stack of cereal and still didn't see Daniel.

"Mama, what are you going to do? Go search the back for him?"

"Well, where is he?" she asked. "He's supposed to be in here bagging groceries. Why isn't he up front? He's not supposed to just disappear like this."

"Mama, he's working."

"I know he's working, Joseph," she said. "And it's wonderful that he's got a job here, but when he gets a job bagging groceries, he should be up front bagging groceries."

"Mama, you know I'm okay."

Daniel's voice came from behind her, and she swung around as if she'd been caught stealing a ham. "Daniel!"

His cheeks had that mottled, burning look. "Mama, I can't believe you're here on my first day on the job. You'll embarrass me to death. Please don't let anybody know you're my mom."

Brenda's heart crashed. Her children had never uttered those words before, and she hadn't been prepared for them. It sounded like something Mark would say to Cathy—something insensitive and ungrateful. Maybe she'd made a dire mistake in letting Daniel spend so much time with Mark.

"Daniel, I just wanted to make sure everything was going—"

"Mama, it's going fine," he whispered. "I was stocking canned goods on aisle four. You can't check on me. It's just not right."

"Daniel, I shop here. I'm not checking on you. I needed a carton of milk."

"Well, the milk is in aisle thirteen," he said.

She started toward it, as if she didn't have time for chit-chat. A man who looked like he had a little authority was standing at the end of the aisle, looking to see what Daniel was doing.

She suddenly wanted to cry. "Joseph, let's just get the milk someplace else."

"Good," Daniel whispered. "You can shop at the Jitney on Monroe Street."

Brenda tried to blink back the tears pushing into her eyes. "I'll pick you up at three," she told Daniel, then hurried out of the store with Joseph running to keep up.

"Mama, I know he didn't mean that," Joseph said.

She touched the back of his neck and tried to smile. He was her most sensitive child, the one who seemed to read her thoughts most clearly. He would never speak to her the way Daniel had. "I know he didn't mean it," she said.

They got into the dented truck, and she sat for a moment, staring at the steering wheel.

"You're not going to cry, are you?" Joseph asked in a soft voice.

"No, of course not," she said. "I'm so proud of Daniel I just don't know what to do. Working, having so much responsibility . . ." Despite herself, she felt her mouth quivering. "It just chokes me up."

"You're not crying because you're choked up, Mama. You're crying because he said that to you."

"No, no, it's fine," she said. "He's right. I embarrassed him." She started the engine and pulled out of the parking space. "I think this is going to work out just fine. This is a good job for Daniel." But as she drove to the other grocery store, she wondered what this job would do to her son. Would he start treating her more like an embarrassment than a protector? Would he dread seeing her, instead of calling for her?

She had always known her children would grow up, but she hadn't expected for it to come in such a painful way.

CHAPTER
Fifty-Eight

July 4th came without a wedding, and as Cathy made an effort to celebrate with barbecued chicken and sparklers in the cluttered backyard, it was clear that she was melancholy about what the day could have been. Steve tried to be festive for Tracy's sake. But that night, after he'd put her to bed, he sat at his desk in his spare bedroom and asked God to help him with the feelings of loss. There would still be a wedding day, he vowed. And in the meantime, there were things that had to be done.

He felt a clear calling to do something for Mark, so he searched through his Bible for just the right study to begin sending to him. He racked his brain for something that would get through to the boy and make him really think about the messages God had given him. Steve thought of starting with the parables. Did Mark have the ears to hear or eyes to see?

Or he could start with the gospel of Matthew. But would that just seem like a history lesson that didn't apply to him?

No ... no, he needed to start with a baby step, something simple yet profound, something Mark could relate to.

He sat back, thinking of Jerry Flaherty, and Mark's disappointment that his father still hadn't come to visit. That was it—the perfect story: the prodigal son, a father searching the horizon each day for his child, waiting for him to return home.

Yes. That was it. Mark would be able to understand and relate to it, and maybe it would make a difference in his life.

He turned to the passage in Luke 15, then closed his eyes in prayer. He pleaded with the Lord to let the Holy Spirit work in Mark's heart through these words. Then he got out a piece of paper and started to write. "Dear Mark ..."

Two hours later, he signed the letter and sat back and looked at it, wondering if he had just wasted his time. No, God had promised that his Word would never return void, and Steve believed it.

He addressed the envelope and applied postage. He would mail it on his way to work tomorrow. Maybe Mark would have it by Tuesday. But that wouldn't be the end of it. Steve had a lot more to teach Mark, a lot more than he could put into letters. And when Mark went to mail call, he'd be glad to get something. He would probably take the time to read it, no matter what it was.

Before he went to bed that night, Steve prayed again for the boy who was spending time in jail without a hint of real repentance in his heart.

CHAPTER
Fifty-Nine

By Tuesday, Tory's fatigue was like an alien invading her body, turning her into a cranky shrew so irritable that she couldn't even stand herself. Her schedule for Hannah had every fifteen-minute segment of the day filled in, but the work she was doing to make her child progress kept her from time with Brittany and Spencer.

As a result, both of her older children spent most of the day whining and misbehaving.

Hannah screamed every time they began a new exercise. But there were too many things that needed to be done if Tory was to make up for the classes they weren't attending anymore, and she was determined not to wilt under the pressure.

She could do this.

Over Hannah's cries, she heard the garage door open. The kids weren't supposed to come in that way, so she prepared to call them down as soon as they stepped over the threshold into the kitchen.

But it wasn't Brittany or Spencer who came in. It was Barry.

She looked at him like a child caught running in the street. "Barry," she said in a weak voice. "You're home early."

He crossed the kitchen, came into the living room, and leaned in the doorway as he looked helplessly at his screaming child lying on her exercise mat. "Tory, what are you doing?"

"Her exercises," Tory said.

He came into the room and scooped Hannah up. She stopped crying instantly.

The sudden quiet washed over Tory like a hot bath.

"I skipped eating lunch so I could go to the school and watch Hannah's class," he said.

Tory dropped her face in her hands. She had known he'd find out. She had planned to tell him before he did.

"Tory, why didn't you tell me you'd quit?"

"Because I knew what you'd say. You would tell me to take her back, that it's good for her. But it's not, Barry. The competition is ridiculous, and the babies that are doing better . . ."

"You think *she* cares who's doing better? Tory, Hannah's not having a problem with the school. You're the one who's in competition. She's just a little baby, doing the best she can."

"She can do better," Tory said, "if I just work harder with her and don't have all those other babies distracting her. I can do it. I have a schedule, and the way I've figured it, she's going to progress much faster this way."

"Tory, Hannah needs that class. *You* need that class."

"No, we don't." She took Hannah out of his arms, and the little girl laid her sleepy head on her shoulder. "We're going to do fine, Barry. It's just been a bad day, but this is no big deal. I've already seen progress."

"She's miserable," Barry said. "Brittany and Spencer are miserable. *You're* miserable."

He saw her schedule on the end table and picked it up. "I should have known you'd schedule it out like this. You've broken her life down into fifteen-minute segments. There's not one break for you, Tory, and there's not a break for her. She'll start hating her therapy."

"You're exaggerating," Tory said.

"Yeah? Then lay her back down on that mat and see how she reacts."

Tory had to accept the challenge. She slowly approached the mat, got down on her knees, and laid the baby down.

Hannah began to wail.

Barry picked Hannah up. "Honey, you're turning our house into a developmental laboratory, and it's not right."

Tears filled Tory's eyes. "What do you want me to do? Go to that class and wallow in the frustration? Some of the babies her age are walking now. Some are talking. All she can do is sit up."

"Well, a month ago, she couldn't do that. I'll take sitting up," he said. "Let's enjoy that for a while before we start to panic."

"It's not panic, Barry. I just want her to be high-functioning."

"Well, what if she's not?" He sat down on the recliner and cradled Hannah in his lap. Her eyelids were heavy, and Tory knew she was about to drift off to sleep. It wasn't time for her nap. A nap now would throw the whole schedule off. She fought the urge to take her from Barry.

"What if she's low-functioning?" Barry asked. "Just like Nathan?"

They had been all through this during the pregnancy. Nathan was Barry's autistic brother, who sat in a wheelchair all day, staring into space and whistling. He had never been able to walk or talk, hold a job, or connect with another human being. At least, not on a level most people would recognize.

"If she is, that's fine," Tory said. "If I know I did every single thing I could to push her to her full potential, then I'll accept whatever level she reaches."

"And how will you know if you've really done everything?" he asked. "When will enough be enough?"

She looked at the mat, trying to think of a stopping point.

"I'll tell you when," he said softly. "Never. Whether she can walk or talk, she'll be the most miserable child ever born with Down's Syndrome, because you'll never accept anything less than normal."

She got up, went to the couch, and dropped wearily down.

"I'm not criticizing, Tory. I know you're doing what you think is best. But I'm one of Hannah's parents, too. I need a say in this. If you plan to drop out of the school, you need to talk to me. If you just need a break from the competition, maybe I could arrange my schedule so that I take Hannah for a while. But she needs to stay in the school. She's really going to need it later, when she gets older. And the work they do there is good, Tory. You know it is."

"Then how come I feel so crummy every time I leave there?"

"It's pride, Tory. You want your baby to be the best. The smartest. But God didn't give us Hannah to pump up our pride. Maybe he gave her to us to *teach* us about pride."

Tory wiped her tears. She couldn't remember ever being this tired. "Barry, I don't want her to *be* the best. I want her to *have* the best."

"So do I! And I happen to think that class and those therapists up there *are* best for her. Look what they've done so far. They've shown us what to expect, how to handle things, how to cope. They've helped her get over milestones that might have taken a lot longer."

"But I can't stand it, Barry. Tilda didn't even celebrate Hannah's sitting up. She just criticized her positioning. Said her legs were too far apart, that her hips weren't right ..."

"Tory, she's trying to keep Hannah from having to wear a brace some day. Even if it rains on your parade, it's best for Hannah. That's what we pay her for."

"I know. I was just so mad ... I thought I could do it." She got up and crossed the room and kissed Hannah's forehead. Hannah looked trustingly up at her, and Tory took her again and hugged her tight. "I didn't hurt her," she said. "I would never hurt her."

"Of course you wouldn't." Barry got up and stroked Tory's hair, then kissed her temple. "It's not Hannah I'm worried about," he said. "It's you. You're missing everything, Tory. Hannah's miserable, you're exhausted ... Brittany and Spencer are bouncing off the walls ... You haven't even been to one of Spencer's ball games this summer."

"I have Hannah," she said. "She's had ear infections and bronchitis. Besides, I don't want her to get sunburned."

"The heat won't hurt her ears, and she's over the bronchitis. And we can put up an umbrella over her stroller. She'll be all right. She'll love it."

"But ... people stare at her. I hate that."

"People stare at all babies," he said. "They're cute and soft. Hannah's no exception to that."

"They look at her like that at first," she said, "but then they see that there's something wrong ... and they get this sad look on their faces and start getting nervous. I always get so defensive ..."

"You've got to get over that," Barry said. "We have a long way to go with Hannah. She's going to have people stare sometimes. You can't shelter her from that."

"But I don't want her hurt. I don't want her to know she's being talked about, made fun of ..." She hiccuped a sob and wiped her face.

"We'll teach her to forgive. But you have to learn to relax and enjoy her. No baby wants to grow up in a laboratory. I say throw the mat out, and get rid of that schedule, and just try to get our family back to normal. The therapists are still coming, the classes still go on, but you don't have to be Hannah's constant teacher/therapist/speech pathologist/doctor. All you have to do is be her mother. And that, I know you can do."

His words brought a healing balm that Tory desperately needed. She leaned into him, and he pulled her into his arms and held her.

Maybe it wasn't all up to her, she thought as she wept against him. Maybe she could relax a little, after all.

CHAPTER *Sixty*

Tuesday afternoon, Mark scored big at mail call. He got letters from Rick, Annie, Tracy, Steve, and his mother. When he got to Steve's letter, he saw that it was a Bible study from a passage in Luke. He rolled his eyes and folded the envelope back up, crammed it into his pocket, and turned, instead, to the letters from his sister and brother.

When he got back to his bunk, he shoved Steve's letter into the Bible in his locker without reading it. He was bored, but he wasn't that bored. Grabbing his textbooks, he headed to the classroom for another hour of cruel and unusual punishment, in the form of a math class.

❧

Steve joined Cathy, Rick, and Annie Wednesday night on their visit to Mark. On the way to River Ranch he told them of the Bible study he planned to provide for Mark.

"He probably got the first one yesterday," he said. "Don't expect any overnight changes, but you can be praying that something I wrote will reach him."

Cathy gave him a skeptical look. "It wasn't anything theological, was it? Nothing real complicated?"

"No. I knew better than that. I just started with the Prodigal Son. I thought he could sink his teeth into that."

"He won't read it," Annie said, leaning to see into the rearview mirror. She twisted her hair and clipped it. "He probably threw it away. You're wasting your time, Steve."

He glanced at Annie in the mirror. "Well, maybe he'll surprise you. Don't forget how bored and lonely he is."

"Pretty cool that you'd do that," Rick threw in.

Cathy smiled and took Steve's hand. "Yeah, pretty cool," she said. "With work and Tracy and church and everything, I don't know how you found time."

"I'm taking time," Steve said. "Mark's too important to let fall through the cracks."

The kids got quiet in the backseat as he drove, and Steve figured they didn't buy a word of it. Once before, he'd been accused of using the kids to score points with Cathy. Rick and Annie were so young to be so cynical.

Then he told himself that Annie had come a long way in the past few months. She had chosen to go to the mission field, and had done a valiant job of raising money. Maybe she had stopped jumping to the wrong conclusions. And Rick was growing up, too.

Maybe they saw that he was honestly concerned about Mark.

Since he couldn't stand the heavy silence, he changed the subject.

"I was thinking about a swimming pool."

Cathy shot him a look. "What?"

"A swimming pool, in the backyard. I mean while they're building and everything. What do you guys think about putting in a pool?"

"All right, Steve!" Annie shouted. "We *need* a pool, Mom. We've always needed a pool!"

Cathy looked like he'd just suggested getting a pet elephant. "Steve, we can't put a pool in. It's too expensive."

"Sure it is, but it's worth it. I mean, wouldn't it be nice to come home from a hard day's work at the clinic and take a nice cool swim?"

"Sure, it would be nice," Cathy said, "but I have enough things to take care of without having to complicate my life with keeping a pool clean."

"I'll take care of the pool," Steve said. "Don't worry about it."

"Yeah, Mom," Annie cried. "We'll take care of it!"

"What are you talking about?" Rick said, laughing. "You're not even going to be here. You're about to hit some third-world country for a year."

"But when I come back I'll want to swim."

Rick shook his head. "She's insane, Mom, but no kidding. We could use a pool. I could invite my friends over."

"Yeah, maybe he'd finally get a girl," Annie said.

"And how do you guys think Mark would feel about that?" Cathy asked. "It's bad enough that he knows the house is changing and he's not there to see it, and that the family may change before he gets out, that his sister's going off to another country and his brother is moving into the dorms. How do you think he'd feel if he knew we were building a pool?"

"He'd probably be anxious to get out so he could swim," Annie said.

"No," Cathy said. "We're not building a pool. I don't want to hear any more about it."

Steve shrugged. "Oh, well, it was worth a try."

"Don't give up that easy," Annie said. "You're the man. You've got to stand up for yourself."

"Well, since I don't own your mother's house, I'm thinking I'd better defer to her on this."

"Hey, you are going to own it," Rick said. "When you get married, what's hers is yours and what's yours is hers, right?"

Cathy couldn't believe they were switching sides just for the sake of a pool. "You guys are priceless, you know that? Not *once* have you encouraged us to go ahead and get married. In fact, you both seem pretty content with the status quo. But the minute there's something in it for you . . ."

"Well, sure, Mom," Rick said. "That's human nature. There's something in it for you, too. Think about it. A cool swim after a hard day's work . . ."

"It's only you we're thinking of, you know," Annie added.

"Yeah, right." Cathy smiled at her kids in the backseat. "Sorry, no enchilada. We're not getting a pool."

"*Man!*" Annie slapped her hand on the seat. "I should have known it was too good to be true."

"Sorry I brought it up," Steve said.

They reached River Ranch and pulled into the usual parking lot. The visitation room was crowded tonight, full of mothers and sisters and brothers, and several children fathered by the teenaged boys.

When Mark stepped into the room, he looked around and quickly found them at the table. His face lit up.

He looked pale and had dark circles under his eyes. Steve wondered if he'd been sleeping.

Mark greeted them all with hugs for the women and handshakes for Steve and Rick, then sat down and bantered with his sister and brother for a while.

Finally, Steve saw an opening. "So did you get my Bible study?"

Mark frowned. "Your what?"

"You know, the letter I sent you with the Scripture verses to look up?"

Mark looked down at his hands. "Oh, that. Yeah, I got it."

"Well, did you read it or did you make paper airplanes out of it?" Rick asked.

Steve wished Rick hadn't said that. It might have given Mark a new idea.

"I skimmed it," he said. "It's in my locker."

Cathy looked embarrassed. "Mark, Steve went to a lot of—"

"I'm doing it, too, you know," Rick cut in, propping his chin.

"Doing what?" Mark asked.

"The Bible study."

Steve gave him a confused look. What was he talking about?

"Steve's about to start working with me on it, too," Rick said. "I'd hate to get so far ahead of you that we had to stop and wait for you to catch up."

Steve saw the interest pique in Mark's face. "No way," Mark said. "You're doing a Bible study with Steve?"

"Yeah. It might be over your head, though."

Mark was insulted. "It's not over my head."

Steve decided to seize the moment and hold Rick to his word. "Yeah, we're going to start with the Prodigal Son, which is what I sent you. Then we'll go back to some of the more exciting events in the Old Testament."

"Yeah, that Jericho's pretty cool," Rick said.

Cathy looked shocked, but she rallied well. "Yeah, it's one of my favorites."

"Those walls falling down and all," Rick said. "And God telling them to march around the city and blow the trumpet. And they never had to fire a shot."

"Mark, you remember," Cathy said. "Didn't Brenda talk about the walls of Jericho with you?"

"Yeah, I remember," Mark said. "I know all about Jericho. But the trumpets are a little fuzzy."

"Look it up," Rick said. "I'm not doing your work for you."

"It'll be in the next installment of letters," Steve promised. "I'll mail it tonight."

"Then I'll get it tomorrow?" Mark asked.

"Or the next day," Steve said.

Mark considered his brother, and Steve could almost see the spirit of competition coloring his face.

"So what kind of schedule are you and Rick on?" Mark asked him.

"We'll work together twice a week," Steve said, and Rick turned and gave him a surprised look. Steve only grinned.

"But if that's too fast for you . . . ," Rick said.

"No, it's fine," Mark said. "I can do that."

Steve sat back in his chair and decided he owed Rick a big one. Who would have thought a challenge from his brother would have piqued Mark's interest this way?

As the bantering went on, Steve's mind reeled with possibilities. He would have to make it something that Mark could discover on his own. He'd give him Scripture to look up, ask him hard questions, get him thinking. This could work even better than he'd expected. And even if it didn't, the time he'd get to spend with Rick, bonding and mentoring him, would be well worth it.

It gave him hope for the first time in a long time that this group of separate individuals might some day actually blend into a family.

On the way home from the jail everyone was quiet until Annie erupted with her latest idea. "Mom, I've got an idea to raise a lot of money for my mission work."

"Does it have anything to do with a pool?" Cathy asked with a grin.

"No, for real. I was thinking of having a party, maybe renting the church's family life center or something, have music and food and let it go all night like one of those junior high lock-ins."

"Well, how's that going to raise money?"

"I could charge everybody twenty bucks. If I invited twenty people, that would be $400 right there. Forty people would be $800. Fifty people would be $1000. I'd have the money I needed before the party was over."

Cathy twisted to look at her daughter in the backseat. "Back in my day we used to work for our money."

"Well, I'm in a hurry, okay?" Annie said. "I want to get there before August so I don't have to go to school."

Cathy shook her head. "And here we were, thinking you were anxious to get there and help the children."

"Well, that, too," Annie said. "But, come on, Mom. If I don't go by August, you know you're going to make me enroll. I really want to do this. Will you help me with it?"

"I'll help," Cathy said, "but I'm not planning it, Annie. I'm not doing this *for* you. If you want to do it, you can call the church and ask them if the room is available. You find out what the rental is. You invite everybody and you buy the food and line up the music and all that. I'll be there as a chaperone. I don't mind that, even though going without sleep is definitely not on my list of fun things to do."

"It's for a good cause, Mom."

"I know," Cathy said, "but I'm telling you, I'm not planning this for you. This is part of your money-raising efforts, and if the Lord wants you to go, he'll help you with it."

"That's fine," Annie said. "I can do it."

"All right, but don't be surprised if people don't want to come. Twenty dollars is a lot of money for a kid to pay."

"Watch," Annie said with a satisfied grin. "You'll see. They'll come."

CHAPTER
Sixty-One

Days later, Mark heard about the party his sister had planned in record time, and a letter from Daniel suggested that everybody in the world was going to be there. It was turning out to be the party of the year. Annie had all sorts of things planned, and she was calling it the "Help Me Help the Children" party. Mark figured his household was abuzz with activity right now as they made the final arrangements. He was missing it all. He wondered how many more events like this he would miss before he got out of jail.

He had trouble sleeping that night and lay on his back on the thin, lumpy mattress. Around him, the other guys slept, and through their glass booth, he could see the guards watching TV as they kept their eyes on the room.

He wondered what was on.

He stared up at the ceiling, wishing he could fall asleep so he wouldn't be dog tired the next day, but dreary thoughts of his life passing him by kept him awake.

A tear rolled down his face. He wiped it away quickly, hoping no one would see. Others cried, sometimes, at night. He could hear sniffles from across the room, but never could identify exactly whose they were. If anyone ever did, they made fun of the guy mercilessly. A lot of the guys in here were too hardcore to shed a tear.

Another tear came, and he wiped it away.

He wished he could sit up, turn on the light, and get those letters from Steve out of the locker. He'd already read them each once, but they were the kind of things you had to think about a while. Steve had asked him questions and challenged him to find answers through his own search of the Bible. He just hadn't done it, even though he knew Rick was getting ahead of him.

But he couldn't sit up now and work on it, because the guards wouldn't allow it. Everyone had to go to bed at the same time. They had to get up together and work together and study together, and there was never a moment's privacy, none at all. He didn't look forward to the thought of paging through a Bible in front of those guys.

No, the only time he could do that was in Bible study or chapel where others were doing it at the same time. Then, it was understood that they all did it to get out of the building.

He turned to his side and tried to get comfortable, closed his eyes and tried to fall asleep, but the thoughts just kept circulating through his mind like a repeating tape on a reel.

He was a coward, he admitted. If not, he wouldn't have cared what the others thought. He would have searched the Bible as much as he wanted to. Maybe it could really offer him help. Maybe God did care.

Loneliness wrapped him in its cold cocoon, making him more miserable than he'd been before. In the bunk next to him, Lazzo snored. Beef, across the room, mumbled curse words in his sleep. J.B. wheezed and coughed. So many around him, yet he was so alone.

Finally, he reached out to the only person who could hear him at the moment.

"Help me get out of here," he whispered to the Lord. He didn't know if God heard, if he cared, or if he listened, but Mark said it nonetheless. It was the first time he'd prayed in a long time. He wasn't sure he'd ever prayed from his heart. It had always been mechanical before, the "Now I lay me down to sleep" kind of prayer, or "God is great, God is good." None of it ever really sank in, but now his plea came from his heart. He hoped God was listening. He hoped he had the power to answer.

CHAPTER
Sixty-Two

Somehow, Annie had conned Tory and Brenda into helping with the food for the "Help Me Help the Children" party. Annie had set up a screen as part of the decoration so she could flash pictures of the children on it all night, so that everyone could see the ones she would be helping.

At first, she told Cathy that fifty kids were coming, mostly from their youth group and school, but when Friday night arrived and they opened the doors, dozens more came. Friends had brought friends, and *they* had brought cousins and acquaintances and people they'd met at the mall. Word had gotten out all over Breezewood that this was the party of the year.

The church had agreed to let Annie pay for the family life center from the proceeds. They had also given her the condition that there would be no alcohol and no secular music on the premises, so she'd spent the whole week trying to find good Christian contemporary songs that could be played. One of Rick's friends from college played disc jockey and kept the music going.

Cathy thought the music selection was a God thing in itself, for Annie had discovered some Christian groups that she might never have noticed otherwise. Cathy couldn't have been prouder of Annie as the night wore on.

By two A.M., she and Steve were exhausted, and they left the gym and went into the game room where it was cooler and quieter. They plopped onto the couch there and dropped their heads back on the cushions.

"It's going well," Steve said.

"Yeah, I'm really proud of her," Cathy said. "But you know what this means, don't you?"

"It means she's going to be leaving soon."

"Yes. Soon. Like in the next week or two, maybe. A month, tops."

"That's right," Steve said. "How are you going to handle it?"

She looked at the ceiling. "I don't know. I guess I never really thought it would happen. I mean, Annie raising her own support? No way. But then she came up with this ingenious plan, and look at her. She's made money hand over fist tonight."

"She's let a few people in free."

"Yeah, but most of them have brought the money. And some of the parents even wrote bigger checks. It's kind of unbelievable."

"Maybe she'll be an entrepreneur."

"And all this time, I thought she'd be a con artist."

Steve laughed. "You did not."

She grinned. "No, but I never thought God would use her like this. I mean, I was just hoping she would walk straight and do right. I never expected her to bear fruit."

"Well, you should have expected it," Steve said. "She's God's child, too. That's what he wants from her."

"But I never dreamed it would happen this young. Look at her," she said. "She's in there, more concerned about the kids seeing those slides of the children than she is about how she looks. That's always been her first concern, before."

"You raised her right, Cathy. It finally kicked in."

Cathy gave a harsh laugh. "Hey, I don't think I had anything to do with this."

"Yes, you did," he said. "I want you to open your eyes and look, Cathy. God's giving you rewards."

Cathy touched his face, and her eyes glistened with tears. "I think you're one of those rewards."

"You bet I am." Steve slid his arms around her. "I've been waiting for you to notice."

"Oh, I noticed," she said.

"Then when are you going to marry me, Cathy?" he asked close to her lips.

"I don't know, Steve." She kissed him, but he pulled back.

"I don't want you to marry me until you're thrilled and excited about it, until planning it is fun. I don't want you to do it until you're ready to open those gifts and giggle over every single one."

She thought about those gifts still stacked on her dining room floor. She had gone back and forth between sending them all back and tearing them open. "I don't want to get married until I feel that way either, Steve," she said. "I did feel that way until Mark got arrested. Everything's changed."

"I know it has," he said, "and there's not a lot I can do. But I want you to think about it, Cathy. We don't have to wait a year. God's not requiring that of us. And I don't think Mark is, either."

"I'm going to have to hear that from him," she said.

"So you need permission from your child before you make a life-changing decision?"

"Not in every case," Cathy said. "In fact, not in most cases. But in this case I'd have a lot more peace about it if I did."

He let her go and sat back on the couch, closing his eyes. "Okay," he said. "Then I'll just have to be patient."

"You'll wait, won't you?"

He smiled and threw her a frustrated look. "I can't break up with you now," he said. "I've got way too much invested."

She grinned and poked him in the ribs, and he grabbed her hand and pulled her close. As his lips descended to hers again, he whispered, "And might I add, it would break my heart in two?"

Cathy pulled him back into a kiss and knew that hers would break, too, if Steve wasn't in her life.

CHAPTER
Sixty-Three

Mark spent the little free time he had for the next few days digging through the Scripture that Steve had sent him. The first day, he'd hidden the Bible under a stack of papers, and no one had noticed. The second day, Lazzo had seen it.

"Man, what you doin' with that Bible?" he'd whispered. "You let ole Beef see you with that, you'll be an open target."

"I'm not scared of Beef," Mark lied.

Lazzo gave him a long look, and Mark could have sworn there was admiration in his eyes. It gave him the courage to uncover the Bible. Even when Beef, the gang leader who could have been a bouncer or linebacker, headed his way, Mark kept reading.

"Man, you trying to impress the guards?" he asked. "They don't believe it when nobody gets religion. Been done."

Mark looked up at him. "I'll take my chances."

"Well, let me know if it works. I might get me one."

Mark didn't say anything, just went back to reading. When Beef ambled away, Mark looked up and saw Lazzo grinning at him as if he'd just performed some heroic feat.

Mark went to bed feeling better about himself that night. And when he tried to pray this time, he felt more of a familiarity with the Creator of the universe.

Wednesday night, Annie's appearance alone at visitation surprised him. His mother would be coming later, Annie said, but Annie had been anxious to share her pictures of the party with him. She told him of everyone who had asked about him, and he felt that familiar sense of shame.

"But I wanted you to see these pictures from Nicaragua, too," Annie said. "Miss Sylvia sent them to me the other day. She just wanted me to have more of a taste of what I was in for. Look at these." She showed him some of the children who lived in the orphanage, whose parents had been killed in mud slides and tornadoes, or structural collapses when the hurricane had come. Others had parents, but they were starving and hung around the orphanage hoping to get a meal.

Mark looked at the snapshots one by one, trying to picture his sister among them, working with the children, showing responsibility, thinking of someone other than herself.

"This is pretty cool, what you're doing, Annie," he said.

Annie smiled. "Yeah, I think it's pretty cool, too. Who would have ever dreamed?"

"I guess Mom's pretty proud of you."

"Says she is."

"One kid in jail and another who's a missionary. Thank goodness she has Rick to keep things balanced."

Annie's serious gaze locked with his. "You're going to get out of here some day, Mark," she said. "You're not going to be a convict all your life."

"No, after this I'll be an *ex*-con."

She gave him an apologetic look. "Well, you know what they say."

Mark frowned. "No, what do they say?"

He could almost see the wheels in her mind turning as she tried to think of something compassionate to say. "Well, I don't know," she said finally. "But they must say something."

He couldn't help laughing, and she grinned.

"I'm sorry, okay?" she said. "It's just a bummer all around. I'm fresh out of Band-Aids."

For some reason, he didn't feel so bad about it. Annie had cheered him up, in her flaky kind of way. "So tell me about your love life." The question surprised even him.

"You never cared about my love life."

"Hey, it's entertainment. Who's the guy of the week?"

"Well, if you have to know, nobody. I'm scared to go out with anybody. Knowing me, I'll fall in love and it'll mess up all my plans. Besides, the guys all seem like such jerks right now. Nobody understands what I'm doing. It's kind of hard to explain."

"Yeah, I guess." Mark tipped his chair back and looked down at the stupid striped pants they made him wear. "You think I'll ever have a shot at doing something like that?"

"Sure you will," she said. "It's your choice, Mark."

"Yeah. I made stupid choices before. Trust me," he said. "When I get out of here, I'm never touching a joint again."

"I believe you," Annie said. "And I think by the time you get out, you'll really mean it."

"I really mean it now," Mark said.

"Well, if you do, then maybe you'll do that Bible study Steve gave you."

He brought his chair back to all fours. "I have been," he said. "So do you know how far Rick is on it yet?"

"I don't know. I think they're still talking about Jericho," Annie said.

"No," Mark said. "We're finished with Joshua. We're studying David now."

Annie looked shocked. "Cool."

He was glad she didn't make a big deal over it. He stacked the pictures and handed them back to her. "So, when are you leaving, anyway?"

Annie's face lit up again. "Two weeks from tomorrow."

"No way," Mark said.

She smiled. "Yep. There's no use waiting. I've got all the money I need to get there and back, and even a little bit to keep me going in between. Mom's a little freaked out that it's so quick, but she'll get over it."

"It's going to be a hard year for her."

"Yeah," Annie said. "I really kind of wish she was going ahead and marrying Steve. That way I could wait and leave right after the wedding, and she'd have him to keep her busy. You know, we'll all three be gone come August," she said. "I'll be in Nicaragua, you'll be here, and Rick will be moving to campus. You know why she's not marrying Steve yet, don't you? It's because of you."

"Hey, I didn't stop anything," Mark said. "That's her choice. If she doesn't want to marry him . . ."

"She thinks you'll be worried the family is changing too much, that everything will be different when you get home."

"Well, everything will be different. They're already working on the house."

"But your room will be the same, Mark, and everything is still in place. It's just going to be bigger, better."

"Well, maybe I don't want our family to be bigger and better."

"I wish you'd think of Mom instead of yourself," she said. "Steve's really good for her."

"Well, I'm not so sure about that," he said. "She thought Dad was good for her. She was wrong about that."

Annie looked down at her hands. "So, has Dad been to see you yet?"

"No."

She shook her head. "I don't get that."

He glanced around the room, trying to look like it didn't interest him. "So have you seen him?"

"Yeah, I've seen him some. He's real touchy when the subject of you comes up."

"He's really mad at me," Mark whispered. He leaned his elbows on the table. "I totally blew it."

"You blew it?" Annie asked. "Mark, he's our dad. You're not supposed to be able to blow it with your dad."

"Well, it's not like he's an ordinary dad. I mean not like Mr. David or Barry, always home. I wouldn't even know what that was like," he said. "If I don't do everything right, he just pretends he doesn't know me."

"That's not true," Annie said. "He's our father."

"Well, he's not acting much like it. I mean, where is he when I need him?"

"He'll come around," Annie said. "He's just having a hard time."

"Well, so am I!"

"I know," she told him. "And Rick and I have tried to talk to him, but you know how stubborn he is."

"Yeah," Mark said. "I guess that's where I get it."

"You get your fair share from Mom, too," Annie said. She glanced at her watch and slid her chair back. "Well, I've got to go. I'm supposed to meet some people. Mom will be here in a little while."

He stood up as she did and crossed his arms awkwardly. "So . . . are you coming back before you skip the country?"

"Sure I am." But something about the way she hugged him and waved good-bye told him that this was the last time he would see her for a while. Annie wasn't into long good-byes, and she didn't like crying in front of others. He hoped he was wrong about that, because he wasn't ready to say good-bye to his sister for a whole year.

He watched her leave the room, then turned back to the table. She had left the pictures. He picked them up and took them back to his building with him.

Lying down on his bunk, he looked at them more carefully, studying the faces of the hungry children, seeing the difference the food had made in their lives.

He felt sick that he would never be able to do anything as good as what Annie was doing. He had messed up his life and ruined any chance he'd ever have of making a difference.

He didn't know why a real God would spend any time with him. He supposed that God, like his father, was turning his back on him, unwilling to pay attention until Mark had somehow made up for what he'd done. For the life of him, he didn't know how to do it from in here.

He pulled out his Bible and read back over the parable of the Prodigal Son again. He couldn't imagine the father searching the horizon for the kid who had messed up so bad. He looked up some of the verses Steve had given him again, and tried to understand what kind of father God was.

When he'd exhausted all the Scripture verses in the Prodigal Son letters, he turned to the next letters about the walls of Jericho and tried to imagine the walls of this place falling down. Rick was right. This Jericho thing was pretty cool. This God was pretty cool. Mark still wasn't sure he believed, but there were smart people who did. He supposed they must know something.

That night, when it was time for lights-out, and he lay on his bunk staring at the ceiling again, he went to God. It was starting to become a habit.

"If you're really the God from the Bible," he whispered, "then show me how to get my dad's love back. He's not like the father in the story. He's not looking for me at all, 'cause he knows right where to find me."

He felt as if the words fell on deaf ears, and he turned onto his side and wiped a tear away again. He wished his father could be more like Steve, writing him letters every day and worrying about his soul. Steve was even coming to visit him at almost every visitation, but his father hadn't contacted him once. Mark knew he might not hear from him for the rest of his sentence.

It wasn't like his dad was used to having him around and missed his sudden absence. In his dad's eyes, Mark was always absent. For most of Mark's life, he'd only seen him every other weekend. There was nothing to miss. Not from where his father sat.

Mark didn't know why all of this suddenly mattered so much to him, but it did.

He fell into a restless sleep, dreaming of his father standing at the edge of the horizon, watching it and looking for him as he came, muddy and clothed in rags, tromping up a hill toward home. But just as his eyes connected with his dad's, he saw Jerry turn and walk away.

The Prodigal Son was not welcome home. And Mark couldn't say he blamed his father.

CHAPTER
Sixty-Four

Tory threw away her carefully calculated schedule and immersed herself in prayer about her pride and her expectations for Hannah. Forcing herself to relax, she went back to the school on their next assigned day. This time she made a conscious effort to see the class as a support system she sorely needed, and laughed and played with Hannah as if they were in no hurry to reach that next milestone.

They both came home happier.

That evening, Barry brought home a bouquet of roses. She gave him a suspicious grin as she took them. "What are these for?"

"I just thought you deserved flowers," he said, kissing her. "And a date for the first time in a very long time. We haven't been out without the kids since Hannah was born."

Tory's face changed. "Barry, you know how I feel about leaving her with baby-sitters. Her chest is rattling again, and there isn't a baby-sitter who knows how to hold her right. Her neck still isn't strong ..."

Barry brought his finger to his mouth, shushing her. "It just so happens that there are a few people who do know how to hold Hannah. And I've paid one of them big bucks to baby-sit."

"Who?" she asked.

"Melissa."

Tory caught her breath. "Her physical therapist? Barry, she's a professional. You can't ask her to baby-sit!"

"I can, and I did. For a hundred bucks, she decided to come. I'm taking you to dinner and dancing, so go get ready. You have two hours before she'll be here."

The shocked look on Tory's face slowly gave way to a smile as the information sank in. She could leave Hannah with Melissa. After all, she was the one who'd taught Tory how to hold Hannah. She was the one responsible for much of the baby's progress. She had been a twice-a-week fixture in their lives since Hannah was born, and the baby knew and enjoyed her.

"Come on," he said. "You can't back out. I've paid her in advance." He took Hannah from her and guided her toward the bedroom. "Take a long hot soak in a bath, and then put on that black dress I like. Our reservations are at seven."

She laughed aloud with relief that everything had been done for her. The baby-sitter, the reservations, even the decision about what to wear. Reveling in the orders to relax, she took advantage of the quiet to soak in the tub.

CHAPTER
Sixty-Five

The day Annie was to depart for Nicaragua, most of her youth group from church gathered at the airline gate with her, as well as all of the neighbors from Cedar Circle. Cathy had moped for the last week as she anticipated this day, and she had deliberately put off saying good-bye. She had been on the verge of tears the whole day as they'd packed, pulling together all the things Annie would need for a year's stay in León.

But now she wished she'd had a talk with Annie before they'd headed to the airport, that she had sat down and told her how proud she was of her, how hard she would be praying for her, what high hopes she had for Annie's future now that she was following the Lord's path. But all of that went unsaid as Annie went from friend to friend and from neighbor to neighbor, hugging each one and saying good-bye.

When the boarding call finally came, Annie grabbed up her carry-on bag, and Cathy saw her big, misty eyes rapidly seeking her out in the crowd. When she found her mother, their eyes locked in dread. Cathy burst into tears and pushed through the people, got to her daughter, and threw her arms around her.

Annie clung a little longer than she'd expected. "I'll miss you, Mom." Her voice cracked.

"I'll miss you more," she said. "Honey, I'll be praying for you." She took a step back and looked into Annie's wet eyes. She felt self-conscious with everyone's eyes on them, but she couldn't let anyone deprive her of this moment. She wiped the tears on Annie's face, then her own, and pulled her daughter close again.

"I'm so proud of you," she whispered in her ear.

"Don't be, yet," Annie told her. "I might turn into a wimp and come running back home."

"And you might not," Cathy said. "You might make a difference in a thousand children's lives."

It was all she could do to let Annie go, and she stood on the other side of the rope as her daughter stepped across the threshold to the jet bridge all alone. Annie paused and turned back, looked at Cathy again, then swallowed hard and disappeared down the hallway.

Brenda and Tory came to Cathy's side, putting their arms around her while she waved good-bye. She felt Steve's hands on her shoulders from behind.

Annie was gone, but she was in good hands. God would get her there, and Sylvia's arms would be waiting on the other side of the trip.

She had to learn to let her children go and trust God to take things up where she had left off. He, after all, was a better parent than she.

CHAPTER
Sixty-Six

Cathy couldn't sleep that night. She put off going to bed, and instead, walked from room to room in her house, looking for evidence of her children. Rick was out late with friends, and the house felt empty. She went to the back window and peered out onto the construction work, on the foundation that had been laid weeks ago and the boards that were going up to form the framework of her new life.

She tried to picture her new bedroom with Steve, him sitting in the rocker pulling on his shoes, combing his hair, shaving over the sink. It had been a long time since she'd had a husband. She wished she could just marry him and bring him into the family, with his strong hands of support, his broad shoulder to cry on when she thought of her empty nest. She wished she had Tracy's little-girl laughter filling up the silence.

But she couldn't marry him yet. Not until Mark felt better about things.

She went to the cabinet and found the old home videos that she and Jerry had made when Mark was just a little boy, and she chose one of Christmas when he was only three. She popped it into the VCR and sat down across from the television, intent on finding the little boy her son had once been, the little girl to whom she had just waved good-bye, and the firstborn who was preparing to move away in just days.

She watched Mark skipping along, holding his father's hand . . . and Jerry waving at the camera. That skipping had always made Jerry smile.

She watched as the father picked up the child and put him on his shoulder, then acted as if he was going to buck him off. Mark screamed and squealed with laughter. Annie bounced up and down next to her dad.

"Do me next, Daddy!" she cried. "Do me."

Rick, only seven, tried to act cool while awaiting his own turn.

Then the picture changed, and Cathy saw herself at a younger age. She tried to imagine what she had felt like when she'd had a man in the home, a father for her children, an intact family unit. It had been a very long time.

She put in another video, shot when Mark was a little older. Cathy studied it for his facial expressions, the bounce in his step, the smile in his eyes. He had stopped skipping when his father left. The twinkle in his eye had dimmed then, too. Was that where his life had turned? Had he been headed, ever since then, toward the prison that now held him? She couldn't say for sure, didn't even want to try. But he had lost his innocence a long time ago.

At just after midnight, she heard the car door slam in the garage. She looked up as Rick came into the house and closed and locked the door behind him.

"Mom, what are you doing up? You have to work tomorrow."

"I know," she said. "I just couldn't sleep."

He studied her as if he had caught her at something, then glanced at the TV screen. "What are you watching?"

"Just an old video," she said, "of when you and Mark and Annie were little. I was just watching Mark's face. It's hard to remember him that young and carefree."

Rick smiled at the picture on the screen. "He used to skip," Rick said. "Do you remember?"

"Yeah," she whispered. "I was just thinking about that."

He sat down opposite her and regarded her for a moment. She recognized the concern on his face. "Why didn't Steve come over tonight?"

"He had to get Tracy to bed," she said. "We talked on the phone, but he has to get up early, so he went on to bed."

Rick looked from her to the video, then back again. "You okay about Annie?"

She smiled. "Yeah, Annie'll be fine."

He sat there a moment, letting silence fall like wet dew between them. In a weaker, more doubtful voice, he asked, "You okay about Mark?"

Her smile faded. She frowned slightly and looked at the video again. "I'm getting there."

He tipped his head and gave her another gentle look. "You okay about me?"

She thought about that for a moment, then took in a deep breath. "I don't think I've told you how proud I am of you, Rick. I mean, with Annie going to the mission field and Mark getting a lot of the attention, I've just mostly been grateful for you. But I haven't said it enough."

"Why? What did I do?"

"You're just a good kid," she said. "I'm proud of the way you're helping Daniel learn to drive, and how you got him that job, and how you're mentoring him."

"Mentoring?"

"Yeah, you know, the big brother kind of thing. He needed that, I think."

"Well, I just kind of felt like it was a way to help, since I couldn't help Mark."

"I know," she said. "It was a good thing. You're a sweet boy. You're going to make somebody a wonderful husband. And some day you're going to be a great father."

He looked at her as if she were crazy. "Me?"

"Yes, you," she said. "I raised you. I know what you're like. Why would that surprise you?"

He shrugged and looked back at the screen. "Well, it's not like I've had a great role model. For being a father, I mean."

Rick rarely said anything negative about his father, so the observation surprised her. "You don't think so?"

"No. I'm disappointed in him," Rick said. "The way he's acting toward Mark. I just don't get it. I think he might just not want to be bothered. And he's acting funny to Annie and me, too. He doesn't want us to bring up Mark's name because he knows we're going to hound him about visiting. And then he didn't even show up today to see Annie off."

"She told me they said their good-byes last weekend," Cathy said. "It is kind of awkward, you know, having the ex-husband and ex-wife there alongside each other."

"Get over it, Mom," Rick said. "That's the way things are. You'll both be at our weddings. When my first kid celebrates his third birthday I'm going to invite both you and Dad. You're going to have to learn to get along with each other."

"I know," she said, "and I will."

He stared down at his feet for a long moment, and she wondered if he was trying to picture it. His own home with a wife and children. His mother and father standing across a birthday cake from each other. "Why don't you go to bed, Mom?" he asked finally. "You're going to be wiped out in the morning."

She nodded, clicked off the television, and wearily got up. "Guess I will."

She kissed him good night. As she stepped into her bedroom, she heard him turning on David Letterman. The bedroom felt big and lonely and cold, and she longed to have Steve there beside her, helping her to relax in the safety and security of his arms, knowing she wasn't alone, that someone who loved her dearly was there beside her and would be there when she woke up.

She got into her bed and lay on her side for a moment, knowing sleep wasn't going to come easily. She looked at the phone and thought about calling Steve, just talking to him into the night, as if they were teenagers in love. She knew it would wake him up, and that wasn't fair. But the longer she lay there, the lonelier the room became.

Finally, she picked up the phone and dialed his number.

He answered with a hoarse, groggy voice on the third ring. "Hello?"

"I woke you up," she whispered. "I'm so sorry."

She heard sheets rustling, as if he was sitting up. "Cathy. You okay?"

"Yeah, I'm fine," she said. "Just lonely for you."

"You sure, for me?" he asked, and she could hear the smile in his voice. "Not for Annie, or Mark?"

"Them, too," she whispered. "But mostly you right now."

"Then I'm glad you called."

"You sure?" she asked. "Because it was really selfish of me, waking you up. I should have just laid here and toughed it out."

"No, you shouldn't," he said. "You never have to tough it out again, Cathy. Your lonely nights could come to an end real soon. All you have to do is marry me. Then you can just turn over and nudge me in the side, and I'll wake up."

"I know," she whispered. She turned on her back and pulled the phone with her. "I was just watching videos of Mark, thinking back to when he was a little boy. Trying to figure out where the road turned."

"Don't do that to yourself, Cathy."

"I had to remember," she whispered. "I had to see it, so I'd know I hadn't just made it up in my mind."

"I love you, Cathy. I wish I could give you back all the years Jerry took away from you."

She smiled. She knew he would do that if he could, no matter the cost. Just the knowing made her feel better. "You're a good man, Steve Bennett. I'm going to let you go back to sleep now."

He sat there a moment like a teenaged boy who didn't want to cut the connection, and finally he whispered, "Good night. Call me back if you need me, okay?"

"Okay," she said.

"Promise?"

"Promise."

"'Cause I'm just seven digits away. You know that, don't you?"

"Yeah," she whispered, and quietly hung up the phone.

The calming balm of Steve's voice helped her fall asleep, and she rested despite the images of her kids as young children, skipping and begging for their turn . . .

What was Mark thinking right now?

Had Annie landed yet?

She thanked the Lord that one of her chicks was still in the nest, even if he wouldn't be there much longer. The knowledge that someone was in the house gave her great peace, and finally she drifted into a restless sleep.

CHAPTER
Sixty-Seven

Annie's stomach tied itself in knots as her plane touched down in Managua. For the last few weeks, her life had revolved around her preparation for *getting* here. She hadn't given much thought to *being* here. She tried to swallow the knot in her throat as she clutched her duffel bag and stood in the aisle, waiting for the passengers to move off the plane.

Spanish conversations were exchanged all around her. She'd heard them all the way here, and it had seemed like a novelty at first. Now she realized that *she* was the foreigner, in a country where she didn't speak the language. She should have paid more attention in Spanish class. Or at least bought tapes and brushed up before she came.

A tear dropped to her cheek, but she brushed it away. She thought of little Miguel and the other children she would get to know. She didn't feel much older than they. What on earth did she have to offer them?

She followed the passengers up the aisle and off the plane. As she walked through the jet bridge, she wondered what she would do if Sylvia wasn't waiting for her? How would she call her? How would she get to León?

But as soon as she entered the terminal, she saw her favorite neighbor across the crowd, laughing and waving as if she bubbled over with delight at the sight of her. "Annie!"

Annie's fears melted away, and she ran to Sylvia and threw her arms around her.

"You're here!" Sylvia cried. "Bless your heart, you're here!"

Annie's tears vanished as her purpose returned.

When Sylvia pulled her car up to load her bags, Annie thought she was putting her on. "Sylvia, this is not your car!"

Sylvia gave an amused look at the beat-up Fiat they had bought when they'd first come here. "Sorry, but it is. I told you there were no frills here."

Annie tried not to look shocked as she pulled on the passenger door handle. It stuck.

"I'll get it," Sylvia said. She got in on the driver's side and gave the passenger door a good kick. It jolted open. "You just have to know how."

Annie stood there a moment, looking into the car as her dignified older neighbor ducked slightly in the front seat to avoid the dented roof. She struggled to get her feet back in front of her.

Annie didn't mean to, but she started to laugh. She tried to stop it, tried to get serious, but the harder she tried, the funnier things seemed. Sylvia began to laugh, too, and Annie leaned against the car to support herself.

"You used to drive a Cadillac!" Annie screamed with laughter. She took a deep breath and tried to stop. "I'm sorry, Sylvia. I just can't picture you driving this."

"You're about to, honey." Sylvia wiped the tears her laughter had produced and came around the car. She picked up Annie's suitcase and crammed it into the backseat. "You should have seen me when Harry came home with it. I laughed, too.

Thought it was one of the best jokes he'd ever played on me. Then I cried, until I realized it really was all we could get. And it runs okay. We haven't had many problems with its engine."

Still laughing, Annie tried to help her wedge the suitcase behind the seats, but Sylvia had some bags piled up, and they were in the way. They fell against each other laughing.

Sylvia let go of the suitcase and put her arms around the girl. "Oh, it's going to be good to have you here. Harry and I need more laughter." She let her go and shoved at the suitcase again.

Annie sighed and let her laughter die. "What's all this stuff?" she asked.

"Bags of beans and rice," Sylvia said. "I picked some supplies up before I came to the airport. It should get us through a few days. I wish I'd had more room. I thought of tying some on top but I was afraid we'd have to do that with your luggage." She pulled the seat back. "There. It's in."

Annie eyed the car again. The thought of riding in it didn't seem quite as amusing as it had at first. "Will this get us all the way to León?"

"It'll have to," Sylvia said. "Don't worry. It has every time before."

Annie got into the car and stuffed her carry-on bag in front of her. She sat with it at her feet, trying to get comfortable.

"That door may not close well once you get it open," Sylvia said. "Here, let me do it."

She came around and slammed it several times, trying to make it click. When it finally did, she warned her not to lean on it. She got in and started the car, then looked over at Annie. "I told you it's not like Breezewood."

Annie just grinned. "I was about to say that the bags and the suitcase are keeping you from seeing out the back window ... but you can't, anyway, with the plastic taped on like that."

Sylvia chuckled and started to pull out into traffic. Annie felt as if she needed to swing her body forward to help give the car some pickup. "That window was one of our biggest frustrations the first few months we were here. Someone smashed our window to steal something out of the car. We ordered a replacement window, but it never came. Still hasn't come, to this day." She patted Annie's leg. "It's no Cadillac, but it gets us where we need to go."

"So the place where you live, is it kind of like the car?" Annie asked, bracing herself.

"Oh, no, honey. Don't worry about that. We have a nice place to live. We make our sacrifices where we have to, but sometimes they're not required."

"Thank heaven," Annie said, leaning her head back on the torn seat. "I was picturing an adobe hut with plastic windows duct-taped on."

Sylvia burst out laughing again and patted Annie's hand. "No, our windows are real glass," she said, "and they're all in one piece so far. It's not Cedar Circle, but it's home."

They chattered all the way to León, about Mark and Rick and Daniel's accident and Cathy and Steve.

But as they reached the city of León, Annie got quiet and looked around at the red-roofed houses up on the mountains on one side of the town, and the lush green vegetation coloring the landscape.

"We're not going straight to the house," Sylvia said. "We have to go by the clinic to let Dr. Harry see that you made it okay, then we've got to go over to the food distribution center and start cooking for the evening meal."

Annie shot her a look. "People are coming tonight?"

"You bet they are. They heard I was getting fresh supplies in Managua, so there'll be more tonight than usual. We've been real low on supplies lately, and we've had to turn people away."

"That's awful."

"I know," Sylvia told her, "but we're working on selling the house, and as soon as we do, we shouldn't have that problem anymore."

Annie got quiet.

"What is it, honey?"

"Well, it's just my mom. She's lost an awful lot lately. I hate to see her lose you, too."

"She's not going to lose me. Heavens. She'll never lose me."

"Well, I know, but your house sitting there was kind of a symbol of you. Once you sell it, it's not going to be *you* anymore. I don't know how she can handle that on top of everything else."

"Well, as soon as you write home and tell her about all the great work you're doing with the money we make on the house, she'll know it was the right choice," Sylvia said.

They ran by the clinic, and Dr. Harry made a big fuss over Annie, taking her around to meet all the people who worked there with him. Then they got back into the car and headed over to the food center. Since it was in a building adjacent to the orphanage, several of the orphans helped to cook the evening meal.

Annie's heart broke when she saw the real faces of the children she had only seen in pictures. Again, she wished she'd spent more time trying to learn their language.

They had barely started preparing the meal when the children from the community began showing up. She saw the hungry faces, the skinny little children with their ribs showing and their bellies distended. She felt as if she was in over her head as Sylvia and the Nicaraguan women who helped her hurried to make enough food to meet everyone's needs.

As the crowd of hungry people grew, Annie was overwhelmed. She counted two hundred children and at least a hundred adults. She watched their faces as they devoured the only meal some of them had had that day.

The children didn't change before her eyes, and she didn't receive accolades or applause for her work. But that night, when Sylvia finally took her to the home that would be hers for the next year, she realized it had been the most rewarding evening of her life. She had fed the hungry, and it felt pretty good.

She only hoped she'd have a little beach time before she had to go at it again.

CHAPTER
Sixty-Eight

Steve went with Cathy to visit Mark at the next visitation, and Mark floored them both with his question.

"So what's this stuff about the loot in Jericho?"

Steve tried not to look shocked. "The loot in Jericho? I thought we were studying David."

"I finished that and started over," Mark said. "How come they couldn't take the loot there after the walls fell down and they took possession of the city? But in the next city they could?"

Steve glanced at Cathy. Was this a sign that Mark wasn't just doing it out of competition with his brother? Had the Scripture itself drawn him back?

"I think it had to do with giving God the first of what they had," Steve said. "God calls that 'firstfruits.' Like the farmers when they have a harvest, he wants them to give the first bit of it to him. It's kind of a sovereignty thing—God's way of reminding them that they wouldn't have any of it without him."

"Well, they sure wouldn't have any of Jericho," Mark said. "But then how come they got to take loot in the other cities?"

"Because those weren't the firstfruits," Steve said. "God wanted Jericho, and he gave them the rest. But sometimes we're so anxious to take all we think we deserve, that we lose out on the better things he has in store for us."

"Well, that guy who got killed sure did. I mean, all he did was steal a few things, and the next thing you know his whole family is paying for his crime."

"God means business," Steve said. "What can I say? He wanted to show them that when he gives them an order, they'd better follow it. He wanted to show them who was in charge. Somebody's always in charge, you know."

"Tell me about it," Mark said. He looked around at the guards.

Then Mark changed the subject to Daniel's job and the letters he'd gotten from him about his work and his driving. Steve sat back in his chair, listening to Cathy's exchange with her son and trying not to look as excited as he felt. Mark's interest was a giant leap forward. He'd actually been studying his Bible, thinking about it, and now he was asking questions.

He wanted to jump out of his chair and leap for joy, wanted to pull the kid up and swing him around. But he knew that if he made a big deal out of it, Mark wasn't likely to do it again soon. So he played it cool and didn't make a scene. But in his heart he was dancing; God was already answering his prayers.

Later that night, when Cathy and Steve had gone home, Rick came by to see Mark for the last thirty minutes of visitation. They made small talk about baseball season and who had made All-Stars. Then Rick got serious.

"Hey, Mark, I was thinking about Mom the other day," he said. "About how lonely she is, what with Annie gone and you gone and me getting ready to move out. She's there all by herself.

I came in the other night after midnight and she was up watching videos of us when we were little kids."

Mark tried to picture it. The thought of his mother sitting up alone in the middle of the night, strolling down memory lane, disturbed him.

"Mark, I think you need to tell her to get married."

"*Me* tell her?" Mark asked. "Why do I have to tell her? She's not waiting for me."

"She is too," Rick said. "She feels like it would hurt you if the family changed that much while you're in here. She doesn't want to do it without your approval. But, Mark, you need to start thinking of her. She never deserved to be alone in the first place. It wasn't her idea to get a divorce all those years ago. You were little, but it's no secret that Dad left her for Sandra."

Mark shrugged. "I'm not stupid."

"So how come Mom's the one that had to be alone all these years? It's not fair, Mark. And now there's a man who loves her and wants to take care of her, and she won't marry him."

"She will marry him," Mark said. "Or else they wouldn't be adding onto the house."

"But she won't marry him as long as you're in here, not unless you tell her to."

"Yeah, like she'd really listen to me."

"She'll listen to you if you say *that*," Rick said. He looked around at the visiting families at other tables, then lowered his voice and leaned in closer. "Mark, I'm asking you to do something for somebody else for a change. Think about what Annie's doing, going down there to feed all those kids. Come on, I know there are times when you sit there and think, 'I ought to be doing something like that.' Because I sure do."

Mark looked astonished that Rick had those same feelings.

"Well, you *can* do something like that," Rick said. "You can give Mom her freedom to marry Steve. You can tell her that you want her to. It's not even that big of a sacrifice for you. Not like going off across the world or something. Just say the words."

"But they would be a lie," Mark said.

"Then make it be the truth," Rick told him. "Just work on yourself until you really feel it. Mom's been through a lot. She deserves happiness."

Mark's face grew hot, and he glanced at the door where the guard stood, wondering if he should just get up right now and walk out of there. He didn't have to listen to this.

But he didn't. "You think I don't know what Mom deserves?"

"I think maybe you don't care," Rick said. "Sometimes things are all about us, you know? This time let's make it about her."

Mark leaned on the table and looked around the room with angry eyes. "So you really want Steve walking around in our house in his underwear with his little twerp girl running around like she owns the place?"

Rick shrugged. "I'm hardly ever there, anyway. What difference does it make? And it's kind of nice to have Tracy in the house. She's real upbeat, you know? Everything's an adventure to her. Mom's always in a better mood when she's around. And Steve's a good guy. He'll take good care of her."

"I never said he wasn't a good guy."

"Then think about it," Rick told him. "Maybe you'll have to work on yourself a while, sort of psyche yourself up. But do it, okay? For Mom's sake."

Mark rubbed his eyes. "I'm not promising anything."

Rick snorted. "I didn't expect you to."

Later that night, as Mark lay in bed, he turned the words over and over in his mind and wondered what it would really cost him if his mother got married. Would it really hurt that much? Was it his feeling of being left out of the family that bothered him most? Or was that just an excuse, one more way of manipulating things to his advantage?

He didn't want to be like that anymore. He wanted to be thought of as one of the good kids, not the criminal that everyone had to work around.

But he just wasn't ready to tell her to do it. Not yet. He needed more time.

CHAPTER
Sixty-Nine

Annie didn't get near the beach for the next several days. Instead, she spent time working with the children at the orphanage, playing games with them, holding them when they wanted to be loved. In the evenings, they would assemble at the food distribution center, where she would sweat over a hot stove of beans and rice, then feed it to the children, the same thing day after day. Sylvia said it was nutritious and had everything they needed, and she could see as the days progressed that some of them really were improving.

But newer, scrawnier children showed up each day.

The fact that Sylvia took every chance she got to share the gospel of Christ surprised Annie, especially when they were working hard to get things done. Sylvia was never too busy to stop and have a one-on-one, heart-to-heart talk with anyone who would listen.

Just that day, one of Sylvia's converts had come by to tell her that he had decided to give his life to ministry. Sylvia had almost danced for joy.

"See this, Annie?" she asked. "This is how it works. You lead someone to Christ, and before you know it, they're leading others, and the next thing you know there are hundreds and thousands of people who know Jesus. That's more important than the food we're giving them. Do you understand that, Annie?"

Annie stopped stirring and wiped the sweat from her forehead. "Actually, no. It seems to me like the food is more important right now. I mean, the spiritual stuff is good and everything, and yeah, they need Jesus. But I guess I don't see it as first in importance."

"Jesus said he was the Bread of Life," Sylvia said. "He's the Living Water. We can feed their bellies all we want to, but we've got to feed their souls, or it doesn't do them any good."

Annie thought about it that evening when she dropped exhausted into bed. Just before she fell asleep, she realized that Sylvia was right. There were millions of people in America who had full bellies ... but they still seemed hungry. It wasn't until they knew Christ that their focus shifted and they were finally filled.

Just before she drifted to sleep, she asked the Lord to help her to make a deeper commitment to him, so that she would have the nerve and the courage and the enthusiasm to distribute her faith among the needy, just as she was helping distribute the food.

She wanted to be as excited about that part as Sylvia was. She knew the children of Nicaragua needed the Bread of Life. And maybe she was the one to give it to them.

CHAPTER
Seventy

David Dodd hadn't been to the grocery store in years. Although he considered himself an equal partner with his wife and didn't necessarily hold to traditional roles for men and women, he always let Brenda take care of the food in their house. There always seemed to be everything he needed, so he never had reason to shop for groceries.

But today he found reason.

He needed bread, he told himself, and if Daniel happened to be working at the time, so be it. He wasn't a father checking up on his son. He was just a customer who had a purchase to make.

He came, glanced at the cash registers, and saw Daniel at the end, bagging groceries as fast as he could. Pride swelled in David's heart. His son was a hard worker, just like he had taught him to be.

He slipped on past the cash registers and went down the produce aisle, searching for the bakery. Thirteen aisles later, he found the bread aisle. He stood there for a moment, looking at the wide array of breads. Whole wheat? White? Rye? He grabbed the wheat, because he recognized the wrapper. Then he headed to the cash register.

He tried to pick an aisle where his son wasn't working, hoping that maybe Daniel wouldn't notice him. But their eyes met as he reached the line. Daniel's face fell, just as Brenda had described the other day. David just lifted his hand in a wave, trying not to embarrass his son.

Daniel looked relieved and turned back to his work. David made his purchase, then gave his son a wink. Daniel smiled.

David grinned all the way out to the car.

For the rest of the day, David couldn't stop thinking about his son working hard at his first job. Despite Brenda's protests, he had allowed Daniel to work almost every day. At this rate, he would have the insurance deductible paid soon. Within a couple of years, he might even be able to save for a car.

He hated to make Daniel wait. Maybe there was some way he could help out. They didn't have much money, but maybe a little could be allotted for a car for the boy, now that he was learning responsibility.

David didn't mention it to Brenda; he just turned the idea over and over in his mind, wondering how it could be worked out. He worked with his budget for several days, trying to see if a hundred dollars could be spared here, another hundred there, a couple of hundred somewhere else. The car didn't have to be that good—just reliable enough to get him to work, church, baseball practice, and back.

He was out cutting the front yard one night when Steve drove up at Cathy's. They waved at each other and, as he often did, Steve stepped across the street and shook his hand. "How's it going, David?"

"Pretty good," David said. He cut off the lawn mower and leaned on it, taking a breather. "So how's this wedding thing going with you and Cathy?"

"Well, right now it's not," Steve said.

"Oh, yeah? Well, then why all the construction?"

"Going out on faith," Steve said. "But I'm hoping we're getting closer."

David chuckled. "You know, Rick's been a real good kid, helping Daniel the way he has with driving and all."

Steve smiled. "That's good to hear. I'll tell Cathy you said it."

David glanced across the street and saw that Steve was driving a newer model pickup than the one he'd last noticed him in. "Get a new truck?"

"Sure did," Steve said. "I have a friend who owns a used car lot on the other side of Breezewood. He gave me a good deal, so I decided to upgrade."

David studied the truck. "Gave you a good deal, huh? Did he have any older model cars that might be good for a teenaged boy?"

Steve lifted his eyebrows. "Sure. Had a bunch of them."

"I wonder if I could get a deal. I can't afford much, but I sure would like to get something for Daniel. He deserves some wheels, as hard as he's been working. Maybe we could take out a little loan, let him pay the notes."

Steve grinned. "Tell you what. I'll take you down and introduce you to my friend. Maybe he can work you up a deal, too."

"Sounds good," David said. "When do you want to go?"

Steve looked at his watch. "Couple of hours?"

"He's open at night?"

"Sure is," he said. "That's the only time I have to look."

David couldn't believe his luck. "Sounds good to me, Steve. That'll give me a chance to finish what I'm doing and get showered. Then we can go take a look."

"All right," Steve said. "I'll see you then."

David grinned as he finished mowing the yard.

CHAPTER
Seventy-One

There were at least two cars on the lot that would work well for Daniel, and that night as Steve drove them home from the car lot, David seemed excited. "He'd be thrilled to have either one," he said.

"Can you convince Brenda?" Steve asked. He knew how worried Brenda always was about money, not to mention her worry about Daniel driving on his own.

David sighed. "Well, I'm not sure. The money will set us back a little each month, but as hard as Daniel is working, he could pay the notes. I could work a few more hours a week to finish up the kitchen cabinets I'm building. If I get them installed for the customer before my deadline, that could pay for it right there." He looked out the window. "I don't blame Brenda if she doesn't go for it, though. I'm always telling her how we're having trouble making ends meet. But sometimes a father just needs to reward his son, you know?"

Steve nodded. "Yeah, I guess I do." He glanced over at David. "Wish Jerry Flaherty felt that way."

"Cathy's ex?" David asked.

"Yeah. He hasn't come to see Mark yet. He's completely written him off. So I've been trying to fill the void, best I can. I've started doing a Bible study with Mark and Rick, and it's given us something to talk to each other about." He glanced at David, wondering how he'd react. He knew David didn't put much stock in Christianity, much less Bible study.

But David's response surprised him. "I guess it's something."

"I figured it was a good way to bond with them, you know?" Steve said. "I mean, it's not so easy to blend as a family. When we get married, there are going to be enough problems. And this was a great way to bridge the gap. We're bonding. They need a dad, and I'm trying to be there for them."

David shot him a look. "So how does their dad feel about that?"

The question surprised Steve. "He couldn't be less interested."

David frowned. "Are you sure?"

"Well, there's plenty of evidence," Steve said. "In the beginning, I went there one night to visit Mark by myself, and he comes out all expectant, thinking it's his dad. When he saw me, you should have seen the look on his face."

"Does his dad know Mark is looking for him?"

"Oh, yeah," Steve said. "I told him myself. Went all the way to Knoxville to confront him. He didn't appreciate it one bit. He can be a real tough case sometimes. Meanwhile, Mark still looks for his dad every visitation and every mail call, but he hasn't so much as written him a note. The last conversation they had was angry, and Jerry made it clear that he was ashamed of Mark. That he had disgraced him."

David's gaze drifted back out the window.

"I'm just trying to take up the slack," Steve said. "I really feel like I'm supposed to do the best I can to fill Jerry's shoes when I marry Cathy and be what he's supposed to be in this family."

"I don't think you can."

The quiet declaration hit Steve like cold water. He tried to rally. "Well, technically, it's probably impossible, but I can at least shoot for it, you know? I believe that, with God's help, I can do anything."

David looked skeptical. "Maybe you're jumping the gun, Steve. I don't mean to downplay your faith or anything, but you know I don't share it. And even if you're right, and God could help, I don't know if he'd really want you taking their dad's place."

They came to a red light, and Steve looked over at him. "Why do you say that?"

"Sometimes fathers get mad at their kids. They say things they don't mean. Sometimes they *mean* things they don't mean. Later, anyway."

Steve tried to think that over, but he found it hard to fathom. He'd never gotten that mad at Tracy, not mad enough to tell her that she had disgraced him and made him ashamed. But then again, Tracy had never sold drugs or stolen a car or vandalized a school.

"Like when Daniel crashed the car," David said. "I was so mad at him I could have bitten his head off. I yelled at him, said some things that I meant at the time, but now I wish I hadn't said them."

"Well, don't you think after the number of weeks Mark's been in jail, that Jerry would have had a chance to feel some remorse and come around to make up with his son?"

"Yeah, you would think," David said, "but don't jump to conclusions. That won't help."

"And what conclusion would I be jumping to?" Steve asked.

"The conclusion that his dad doesn't love him."

"That's not *my* conclusion," Steve said. "I think it's Mark's. And what else is he supposed to think?"

A horn behind them honked, and Steve realized the light was green. He stepped on the accelerator.

"I know it's a natural conclusion," David said, "but the truth is that Mark needs his dad, and you'd be making a mistake to try to push him away."

"Hey, I haven't pushed him away," Steve said, trying not to sound as aggravated as he felt. "I've tried to pull him in. *He's* the one pushing away."

"That may be," David said. "And maybe I'm way out of line. But I'm speaking as a kid who grew up without a dad."

The anger in Steve's heart faded. David had never shared that with him before. It made all the difference in what he was trying to say. Steve tried to hear it without letting his pride get in the way. "How old were you when you lost him?"

"He left when I was eight," David said. He swallowed and looked out the window, letting the silence play between them.

Finally, David spoke again. "Mark needs him. Even if he's not what he hopes he is, and even if he doesn't respond the way Mark wants him to. Even if he's a bona fide jerk, Mark needs him. That's all there is to it. You can try to replace him, you can be there all you want, but when it comes right down to it, that relationship with his real dad is vital. If there's any way to salvage it, do it."

Steve clutched the steering wheel harder as he navigated his way up the mountain toward Cathy's home. "Well, then, I'm not sure what my role is supposed to be as a stepfather. I want to be everything that I'm supposed to be, but how do I know when I'm overstepping my bounds?"

"If you start coming between Mark and his dad, or enabling Jerry to stay out of the picture," David said, "then you've overstepped your bounds. Your role as Cathy's husband will be to help *her* love her kids the best way she can. Just don't get in her way when you think she's doing it wrong. Don't try to control the way she loves them. I've seen too many blended families that have messed up that way. The step-parent gets in the way of the birth parent, interrupts the love relationship between the parent and the child—maybe disapproves of it somehow—and the next thing you know, the parent is full of resentment and confusion, and the kid is a mess. On the other hand, you can let the kids set the tone. When they need you, be there."

Steve let the silence fall between them as David's words sank into his mind. "That's good advice, David," he said finally. "I'll try to follow it."

"It won't be easy."

"Don't I know it." Steve had a lot to think about as he pulled into Cedar Circle.

CHAPTER
Seventy-Two

Dear Mark,

    I know it's not like me to spend my time writing my kid brother when I could be out living it up with the Nicaraguan hunks, but the truth is I haven't met any. And even if I did, there wouldn't be time. Sylvia works me day and night, and I fall into bed exhausted. But like Mom said that day when we worked so hard at the fair to raise money for Joseph's heart, it's a good kind of tired.

    I've been thinking a lot about what you're going through, and in some ways we're both in the same boat. I'm kind of stuck here, even if I decide I want to come home, and most of my time is structured for me. The thing is, I know that some day I'm going to look back, and it's going to be one of the best years of my life. Maybe you can't say the same thing, but who knows? I've been seeing God do some pretty amazing things.

    There's this kid named Chico who came to Dr. Harry first because he had pneumonia and some kind of horrible rash on his legs. He was one of nine kids in his family, and none of them got much to eat. You could tell by their ribs—you could count every one just by looking. And he had crusty stuff under his nose, all raw and dirty. It made me just want to gather him up and take him inside and give him a bath. But his mother was with him, and I didn't want to insult her.

Dr. Harry got him going on antibiotics—a miracle of God, believe me—and then Sylvia started feeding him. His mother brought him back every day to Dr. Harry for two weeks, and every time he'd get his dose of medication, Dr. Harry would send him over to us and we would feed him. He's well now, and he comes around every day asking if there's anything he can do to help us. He couldn't be more than seven years old. But Sylvia told him about Jesus, and he understood. She thinks telling him about Jesus is more important than filling his belly or making him well. When I first got here, I didn't think so. I thought we needed to do everything we could to get these people well and keep them from being hungry. But they're hungrier for God than anything I've ever seen. One of the men came back the other day after Dr. Harry had treated him and told us he wanted to be a pastor because there weren't enough churches around here. Dr. Harry was so happy he cried. Sylvia set to work right away finding someone to train him to pastor a church.

I felt kind of bad because I should know a lot more about the Bible than I do. But I guess I'm taking it one day at a time and learning just like these people are. Sylvia surprises me every day by leaning on God when we're almost out of supplies, and all of a sudden somebody will show up with some cash or some supplies. Then we have enough for one more day.

She says if she ever sells the house, she'll be set, but it doesn't look like the house is selling. I know Mom will be happy about that. But she wouldn't if she understood where the money was going to go.

Well, I hope all's well with you, and that you're not getting into any fights or getting yourself into any more trouble. Give Mom a hug for me when you see her. I'll send you pictures of little Chico as soon as I have time to take some.

Love, Annie

Mark folded the letter back neatly and put it in its envelope. He leaned against the table at the center of the room in Building A and thought about his sister down in Nicaragua, working with orphans and hungry children and not getting very much back. He'd never seen Annie that way before, and he had trouble imagining it now. It could only be considered a God thing, he thought. Annie on the mission field.

He looked around him at the inmates going about their own business in their free time. Steve had said that this, too, was a mission field, that God could use him here. But he doubted that. God couldn't use him anywhere, not with his heart the way it was.

He reached into his locker and pulled out his Bible, got the letters out that Steve had sent him, and went over them again. The story about King David being a man after God's own heart, after he'd killed a man so he could steal his wife, really puzzled him. He turned back to it and studied it again, trying to figure out exactly how God's forgiveness had come. Was that whole story some great myth, or was it reality that applied to his life today? Could a repentant man really get the approval of God? Could someone weak and spoiled and tainted like him really ever become a man after God's own heart?

He envied Annie for knowing who she was. She had said that some day she'd look back on this year as one of the best of her life. What would *he* look back and remember?

The pensive thoughts stirred up his soul, disturbing him, but there was no comfort to be found. Not when he rejected the comfort that his mother and stepfather-to-be offered him. He wondered what advice his own father would give. He supposed he would never know.

He stuffed the letter back into his Bible and returned it to his locker. Then, mentally, he tried to compose a list of questions he wanted to ask Steve the next time he saw him. A few things he wanted to clear up in his mind.

He just wanted things to make sense.

CHAPTER
Seventy-Three

Tory was late for Spencer's T-ball game because it had taken her so long to prepare Hannah before she took her out in the hot sun. She had put a bonnet on her to keep the sun out of her eyes and a cool little sunsuit with brand-new sandals that matched. She brought Hannah in her stroller with the sun shield up and pulled a lawn chair up next to the bleachers.

Spencer saw her coming and yelled, "Hey, Mommy!" from the dugout. She laughed and waved, wondering how she could have stayed away for so long.

Hannah grew fussy, so Tory pulled her out and set her up on her lap. Barry, who was standing at the fence next to the dugout, tore himself away from the field and came over to give Tory and Hannah a kiss.

"How's my girl?" he said, and lifted Hannah from Tory's lap.

Tory glanced around at the others on the bleachers. Everyone's eyes were on their children on the field. Two young children, around the ages of three and four, sat spooning up dirt. It reminded her of Spencer not so long ago.

Barry gave the baby back. "Has Spencer batted yet?" Tory asked.

"No, he's up next," Barry said. "You made it just in time."

She looked past him to her son, coming out to practice his swing next to the dugout.

"Mommy, look at me!" he shouted and demonstrated his prowess with the bat.

She clapped for him. She looked around and saw Brittany at the snow-cone stand. It was probably her second one of the night, and she had only been here half an hour.

"Look at the baby!" She heard the little four-year-old in the dirt and told herself not to get defensive. Little children loved babies. They weren't staring at Hannah because she had Down's Syndrome.

The children got up and came running over to see Hannah. Hannah kicked her feet and shook her arms, delighted to have people around her. The little boy reached out to touch her with his dirty hands, and Tory resisted the urge to push him away.

Spencer walked over to the fence, forgetting the game. "That's my sister," he said proudly.

The boy turned around. "How come her tongue's hangin' out?"

Tory recognized the fulfillment of her worst fears, as some of the parents turned to look. The mother of the child looked more horrified than Tory. "Jonathan!"

The child ignored her and kept standing there. Tory tagged Hannah's tongue, and the baby pulled it in. But it only stayed for a second, and her mouth fell open again.

"It came back out," the kid said. "Does she have a stopped-up nose?"

Tory started to answer, but Spencer did it for her. "No, her nose ain't stopped up," Spencer said. "Her chin just doesn't work so good."

Tory wanted to tell Spencer to leave it alone, that he didn't have to defend his sister.

But Spencer didn't mind. "See, she's special," he said, leaning on the fence. "Not just anybody could get a baby like that."

"Why not?" the little boy asked, his eyes wide with fascination.

"'Cause," Spencer said. "God gave her to us because he knew she would need a lot of help. Doesn't she, Mom?"

Tory managed to smile. "That's right, Spence."

"But we take good care of her," he said, swinging his bat as he spoke. "And one day she'll keep that tongue in." He made a face at his sister. She recognized her brother and started kicking harder.

"I can't take you now, Hannah," he said. "I've got to bat." He turned back to the field and saw that it was almost his turn. Without another word, he headed back to his place. Tory looked up and met Barry's eyes. He gave her a wink.

She relaxed back in her lawn chair as Hannah kicked her arms and legs and watched her brother hit a double.

She couldn't express the pride that she felt in her little boy, but not because he'd been a good hitter. He was the best PR person Hannah could have had. Tory knew that, as long as he was around, Hannah was going to be just fine.

CHAPTER
Seventy-Four

Mark woke up at two A.M. and stared at the ceiling. He knew better than to get up. The guards didn't look favorably on people wandering the floor in the middle of the night. They usually assumed you were trying to steal something.

He'd seen it happen a couple of times before. They'd put them in disciplinary for a week, and it only took one time in isolation for Mark to know he didn't want to go there again. These kids that he lived with now weren't his top choice in companions, but they were better than nothing. And in isolation, that was exactly what you got. Nothing.

A faint glow from the guard's station lit up the room. No wonder he couldn't sleep, he thought. Back home, he used to close his door and turn out the light and sleep in the pitch black. But there wasn't such a thing here, any more than there was privacy or choice. He just lay there on his back, staring up at the ceiling. He knew it by heart. He could have reproduced it himself if he'd been given the proper tools. He knew where every little hole was placed, every crack in the plaster, every place where the paint was thinning.

He thought about his father, who still hadn't been to see him. Mark had written him a couple of letters but hadn't mailed them. He figured his dad wouldn't open them anyway. He'd really blown it with him. He couldn't believe what a fool he'd been.

He wondered if anything would change when he got out of here. Would his dad act like nothing had ever happened and pick up where they'd left off? Or would he hold it against him for the rest of his life, passing the grudge down to his grandchildren? Would Mark forever be the black sheep of the family?

He started to cry, something he hadn't done in a while, and he covered his face, trying to muffle the sounds that would give him away in case anyone else lay awake tonight.

He thought back over the way things had worked out since he'd been in here. If God was trying to get his attention, he had certainly succeeded. Mark had been to every chapel since the first week he'd been here and had worked at every Bible study that Steve had sent him.

He could tell from the way that God kept getting in his face that he hadn't given up on Mark. He had been there, knocking and knocking on the door. Steve had shown him a verse that said that Jesus stood at the door and knocked, and if anyone opened it, he would come in with them and dine with them. Mark figured that was pretty cool. Thinking about somebody as powerful as God wanting to sit down with him over a burger. That was pretty friendly. Not just anybody would do it, not with a kid who'd messed up so badly and wound up in jail.

His heart melted at the thought of God standing on the horizon, scanning it as he waited for his child to come home. His problem before had always been that he'd assigned his dad's face to that father on the horizon, and he couldn't picture it, not since his father had forgotten about him and left him in here to rot. But the Bible said that God would never leave or forsake him. If that was the case, then God was nothing like his dad. He wouldn't disappoint Mark, and he wouldn't just decide not to show up when Mark needed him. He wouldn't turn his back on Mark or hold onto his anger, refusing to forgive.

For the first time in his life, Mark got it. He understood about that father running to meet his son, kissing his face, bringing out a robe to put on him so that others could see him as royalty, putting a ring on his finger, restoring him in good standing to the family. He felt like that boy standing among the pigs, wishing he had what they were eating to fill his empty belly.

And then he remembered what Annie had said about their bellies not being the hungriest part. It was true with him. He had all he needed to eat, but his soul was so empty.

He began to weep harder, and as he did, he looked up at that ceiling again as if somewhere behind the tile he could see God's eyes on him, weeping and waiting with his arms spread wide. He pictured God running toward him, and his own feet falling into a trot, hurrying toward his home.

"I'm sorry, God," he whispered. "I shouldn't have been so stupid. If I had just done what you wanted . . ." He wept and felt his Father throwing his arms around him, lifting him off the ground, swinging him around, kissing his face and weeping with joy. He felt the love in that royal cloak being thrown around his shoulders, felt the authority and the inheritance of that ring as it slipped upon his finger. For the first time in his life he understood the love of Christ, that profound fill-up-your-heart kind of love that didn't go away or turn its back. It was the kind of love that would enable someone to lay his life down for someone else. The kind of love that could turn Mark into something useful, even in prison. The kind of love that could make this the best year of his life, just like Annie's, if he gave his life over to God.

"I'm yours, Jesus," he whispered into the night. "I'm yours a hundred percent. Do whatever you want with me. I just want to do what you say. I want to keep wearing the robe and the ring on my finger. I want to change. Please help me to change."

And as he wept into the night, he knew that it was an answered prayer already. God was already at work changing him. It was a done deal.

CHAPTER
Seventy-Five

Mark was the first one in line for the telephone the next day. He dialed Steve's phone number at work, the number that had been printed on office letterhead Steve had used to write him. He called collect, hoping no one would refuse the charges before the call was routed to Steve.

"Steve Bennett."

Mark sighed with relief. "Steve," Mark said, "it's me, Mark."

"Mark, is everything okay?"

"Yeah," he said. "I just had a few minutes and a chance to use the telephone. I thought I'd call and tell you something."

"Okay," Steve said. "What is it?"

Mark hesitated for a moment. He looked around at the people standing near him, waiting to use the phone. Nobody was really paying attention.

"I just wanted to thank you. I mean for all the letters you've been writing and the Bible studies and all that."

"Well, you're welcome."

"'Cause I've been reading them and everything, you know," Mark said, "and I've been thinking about a lot of it. And I sort of woke up in the middle of the night last night. I kept thinking about the Prodigal Son, and I felt like that kid who wound up wallowing with the pigs and then came home. You know how his father was waiting for him with that robe and that ring? That was all pretty cool."

He could hear the emotion in Steve's voice. "Yeah, it was, Mark."

"I just sort of decided I was that kid coming home," he said, his voice wobbling. "And I sort of ran to God, told him I was sorry."

He heard Steve suck in a breath. "You did that?"

"Yeah. And, well, I realized what Jesus did for me and everything. And what a dope I've been, kind of throwing it back in his face the way I have. Running from it like there was something else I could get. I'm not gonna be like that anymore."

Steve's voice moved into a higher, emotional pitch. "Thank you for telling me, Mark. You don't know what this means to me."

"Well, I just thought you should know first," he said, "since you had so much to do with it."

"Are you going to tell your mom?"

"Yeah, the Bible says we're supposed to say it out loud, aren't we? Guess I need to do that. But I don't get another phone call, and besides, I want to tell her face-to-face."

"I'm going to let you tell her," Steve said. "It's the best thing you could give her, Mark. It's even better than Annie going to the mission field."

"No way," Mark said on a laugh. "You think?"

"Hey, I know. You tell your mom this and the jail, the drugs, all the rest of the stuff, she'll completely forget about it. She'll be so thrilled to know that you've got Jesus."

Mark swallowed the lump in his throat and blinked back the tears. "Well, I gotta go. There are people waiting to use the phone."

"Tell her, okay, Mark?"

"I will, next time I see her." He hung up the phone and stood there a moment, thinking of calling his mom right now, but those in line were growing impatient.

"Hey, man, move on. You've had your turn."

He turned around and saw Beef, and he handed him the phone. "Go ahead, man. I'm finished."

Beef grabbed the phone and pushed him out of the way, but Mark didn't react. He just hurried to the cafeteria to get started on his day's work.

CHAPTER
Seventy-Six

Cathy noticed a change in Mark as soon as he walked into the room for visitation Wednesday night. His eyes were brighter than she had seen them in months, and he smiled as if he had a secret that he couldn't wait to share.

Pleasantly surprised by his new demeanor, she said, "You must have had a good day."

"It's been a good week," he said. He leaned up with his chin on his palm, fixing his eyes on her. "So what's going on with you? Have you heard from Annie?"

"I got a letter from her this week," she said. "She's doing really well, Mark. I'm so proud of her."

"Me, too," Mark said.

The words surprised Cathy, and she lifted her eyebrows.

"What about the house?" he asked. "How far have they gotten?"

"Well, they've got the frame up, and the wiring's been done. They put the insulation in yesterday. They're starting on the drywall tomorrow. Once that's up, it shouldn't be that much longer."

"Three weeks? A month?"

"Maybe," she said. "They're working at it pretty hard. Steve got a good contractor, despite everything."

Mark leaned back in his chair and kept his smiling eyes on his mother. *He has a secret*, she thought. "What is it, Mark?" she asked, finally. "There's something going on."

He nodded, and his face got serious. "Mom, the other night I woke up in the middle of the night and I started thinking about the things Steve has sent me."

Her eyes widened, and she took his hand. "Really?"

He went on. "Mom, I called Steve the other morning, and I told him what had happened."

"What?" Cathy asked. "What happened? He didn't say anything."

His smile faded, and his eyes grew serious. "I gave my life to Christ," he said. "I finally got it about the Prodigal Son and that guy's dad standing there watching for his son. I finally realized about the robe and the ring, and I decided I didn't want to be going in the wrong direction anymore. I wanted to come home."

It was the first time he had said the word *home* without a plea behind it, and she knew that this wasn't another desperate attempt to make her get him out of here. Tears rushed into her eyes, and she covered her mouth.

"Mark, you're not just telling me what I want to hear, are you?"

"No, Mom. It's the truth." Tears glistened in his eyes, and he wiped them away and reached into his pocket for a folded piece of paper. Slowly, he opened it and ironed it out with his hand. "I drew this yesterday, when I was thinking about the son being like the father. I kept getting hung up on Dad, you know, and the way he's turned against me."

"Mark, he hasn't turned against you."

"Mom, the best you can say is that he just doesn't care one way or another. But that's okay. It's not so much about him. It's about God. I'm *his* son, too. And I want to be like my Father."

She looked down at the picture and saw the silhouette of a man, with a smaller silhouette of a boy just inside it.

"At first, this was Dad and me. We were both angry and disappointed. And then I realized it didn't have to be Dad and me. It could be God and me. And God had gotten over the disappointment. He could see some hope for me."

She reached out for her son and wept as he held her.

"I want you to have the picture, Mom," he said as he pulled back. "It's not great art or anything. But maybe it'll remind you that I'm not a lost cause."

She choked back her tears. "Thank you, Mark." She pondered the picture again. "So you gave your life to Christ, and you called *Steve?*"

"Well, I wanted to tell you in person. He sent me all those letters, and I saved them up, you know, and kept reading them and studying them, and even talking to God about them. When I finally did it, it seemed like he should know."

"And he didn't tell me?"

"He wanted you to hear it from me. He's a pretty good guy, Mom."

Cathy wiped the tears on her face with the fingertips of both hands. "I know he is, Mark."

"Then why won't you marry him?"

Her mouth fell open. "Mark, I was waiting for you."

"You don't have to wait for me, Mom," he said. "I think you need to go ahead and do it. I'm fine in here. And when I get out I'm going to need some stability in my life."

She started to laugh through her tears. "Stability? You?"

"Yes," he said. "You know, it's not always so great to have everything stay the same. I think he's going to be an improvement to our family. I can handle it. I'm a big boy."

She couldn't find words to answer him. Finally, she grabbed his hands and brought them both to her mouth. "Oh, Mark," she whispered.

"So you'll do it?" he asked. "You'll marry him?"

"Of course I will," she said. "I've been *wanting* to. But I thought it would be kind of a betrayal to you until you got out of here."

"Hey, you can videotape it, okay?" he said.

She shook her head. "I don't know what to say, Mark."

"Just say you'll do it," he said. "I don't have much to give you as a wedding gift, but you can take this."

She smiled and wept some more as she let the gift from her son sink in.

CHAPTER
Seventy-Seven

Cathy almost ran two red lights trying to get to Steve's house when she left the prison that night. She left her car door open, bolted up the porch, and banged on the door. Tracy flung it open.

"Hi, Cathy," she said in that voice so full of enthusiasm.

"Tracy!" Cathy grabbed the girl and swung her around.

Steve came running into the foyer. "Cathy! What is it?"

Cathy set Tracy down and threw her arms around him. "You didn't tell me about Mark!"

He pulled back and looked down at her. "What did he tell you?"

"That heaven was having a celebration and I didn't even know about it!"

Steve's smile cut from ear to ear. "I wanted him to tell you himself. I figured if he did, that it must be true—not just something he felt for a few minutes."

"No, he meant it!" she cried. "He was excited, and he told me. And you'll never guess what else he said!"

"What?" Steve asked.

"He said we should go ahead and get married, that there was no point in waiting for him. He *wants* us to go ahead."

Steve caught his breath, and Tracy began jumping up and down, whooping with delight. "You can do it, Daddy! You can marry her now. We can move into the house as soon as it's finished, and ..."

But Steve wasn't listening to Tracy. His eyes were focused on Cathy, and he touched her face with both hands. "Will you, Cathy?" he asked. "Will you marry me?"

"Yes!" she said. "Yes, I will. Let's set a date. How about ... four weeks from now?"

He ran for a calendar and turned to September. "That would be the 26th."

"September 26," Cathy said. "Our anniversary will be September 26." She threw her arms around him, then embraced the bouncing girl. "Let's go home right now and open all those presents."

"Yeah!" Tracy said, and jumped even higher. "Come on, Daddy. Please, can we go?"

"Get in the car," he said. "I'll get my keys."

And together they all headed to Cathy's house to open the presents that had been sitting in her dining room for too long.

CHAPTER
Seventy-Eight

The telephone connection between Breezewood and León, Nicaragua, seemed as close as if Annie was just in another house around the corner. "Mom, I checked into it, but I really don't think I can come home for the wedding and still afford to come back here. Would it upset you if I missed it?"

There wasn't much that could shake Cathy's joy now. "Well, no, honey. I know it's short notice."

"I want to come and everything, but right now we're so busy and I really don't think Sylvia can do without me. I know she did before, but now she's depending on me, you know?"

"I was hoping she could come, too."

"Well, she can't. We're just swamped. Besides, it costs a lot of money and she doesn't want to spend it on airfare when she could be spending that money on food. You know, they haven't sold their house yet. And until they do, we're just making it hand to mouth, giving the kids as much as we can each day. It's really hard to spread the food out among all of them. So neither one of us can come, Mom. So much wouldn't get done if I left."

"Honey, that's the best wedding gift you could give me. You just stay there and do your work. We'll be okay. Rick is going to be the best man and Tracy will be my little maid of honor."

"What about Mark?" Annie asked.

"Mark is great. In fact, I'm thinking about having the wedding in the chapel at River Ranch if I can work it out. That way Mark can be there."

"That's a great idea, Mom. And you have to videotape it, 'cause I really want to see it. Do Tracy's hair up real nice, with flowers in it and everything." Her voice cracked. "I wish I could be there."

"Don't worry. I'll send you pictures and tell you all about it. And I'll even videotape the house before we move Steve and Tracy in just so you can see all the changes as they take place."

"That's what life's about, Mom," she said. "I'm finding out it's all about change. You don't have to worry about me coming back and having everything different. It might sting for a minute, but it'll all be for the best. Won't it?"

Cathy couldn't swallow the tears down. "How'd you grow up into such a wonderful young lady, with a mother like me?"

"Mom, with a mother like you, how could I lose? You should see some of the kids here who don't have moms. It really makes a difference. It just breaks my heart. I wish they could all have a Cathy Flaherty in their lives."

Cathy wiped the tears from her face as she let those words seep into her heart.

CHAPTER
Seventy-Nine

September flew by as Cathy took care of the wedding details, and when the 26th finally came, the wedding was everything they had hoped. It was small and brief, but beautiful. The singles' minister that Steve and Cathy had gotten to know at their church performed the wedding in the prison chapel, and Mark was allowed to attend.

When it was over, Cathy kissed her new husband, then his little girl, then turned to Rick and pulled him into a hug. Finally, she turned to Mark.

"Thank you, Mark," she whispered, touching his face. "You're turning into a very nice young man."

He smiled, teary eyed. He hugged his mom, then turned to his new stepfather and gave him an awkward hug. "I'm sorry I've disgraced everybody the way I have, but some day I'll make it up to you," he said. "I'll be even more useful than Annie. You'll see. Some day I'll make everybody proud of me. Even my dad."

Steve made the silent vow to be everything he could to fill in the blanks for this boy. But he would need God to help him discern where his boundaries were.

🦎

Rick stayed in Knoxville with his dad while Cathy and Steve honeymooned in Gatlinburg. Steve's parents kept Tracy, and the contractors had been given strict orders to finish the construction while they were gone.

Rick's visit with his dad was awkward, for Rick hadn't gotten over the fact that his dad had refused to communicate with Mark. But it was time to mend fences, he told himself, and if he could help mend fences between Mark and their dad, then it was worth the time.

Rick waited until Jerry was feeling good about a golf game with one of his partners. Jerry stood at the grill in his backyard while the steaks sizzled, describing the shot he'd made at the fourteenth hole that morning. Rick listened and pretended to be interested.

"It was beautiful," Jerry was saying. "You shoulda been there. I'm telling you, ESPN would have loved this."

"Too bad we don't have it on video," Rick said. "Mark would love it, too."

His dad got quiet and opened the grill and seemed to concentrate on moving the steaks off of the flames.

"You know, Dad, he's changed a lot since he's been in jail." Jerry didn't look up.

"No kidding. He's a different person. You wouldn't believe it. He's made all these promises about when he gets out. He doesn't want to ever go near drugs again."

"You like T-bones, don't you?" Jerry asked. "Sandra's been marinating them. Smell."

Rick slid his hands into his pockets and went to stand beside his dad. "Dad, he's become a Christian. He's been doing a Bible study and praying a lot, and I think he's able to look at his future now and see some hope."

He got a reaction then. Jerry closed the grill and stared at the top of it for a long moment. "Well, that's *something*."

"Yeah, I thought so," Rick said. "I know you're not big on religion and stuff but, you know, it's really changed him. Oh, and I have some pictures of him at Mom's wedding."

Jerry rolled his eyes, as if the last thing he wanted to see was pictures of his ex-wife's wedding, but Rick pulled them out and showed him the ones of just Mark. "See how tall he's getting? And his hair's growing out a little. Did you know they shaved his head when he first got in there? But I think he looks pretty good right now. You wouldn't know him. He looks clean-cut, like he could actually get a job or something."

Jerry took the pictures and looked down at them, as if he didn't recognize his son. "They let him go to the wedding?"

"Well, Mom and Steve got married at the prison chapel. You know, it was actually Mark's idea that they go ahead and get married. They were holding off, waiting for him to get out, but that meant a whole year, and Mark didn't think they should do that. I thought it was pretty mature of him."

Jerry looked up at him, pensive, and Rick wondered what was going through his mind. The fact that his dad even acknowledged what Rick was saying was a good sign.

"Dad, he'd really love to have a visit from you. I think every visitation on Wednesdays and Sundays he secretly hopes you're going to come."

Jerry opened the grill again, letting a puff of smoke escape. "I don't have any experience with this, Rick," he said. "Visiting my child in prison, knowing how to act toward somebody who's disgraced the family this way ..."

"Well, it seems to me that it's Mom he's disgraced more than anybody," Rick said quietly. "I mean, the policeman came to tell *her* about it when she was at her own wedding shower. All the people who know him mostly are from Breezewood instead of Knoxville. A lot of people don't even know he has anything to do with you. But Mom hasn't turned her back on him."

Jerry turned around and gazed at Rick. "So what's it like in there? What are the other prisoners like? Are they a bunch of hoods from the ghetto or something?"

"Actually they're all pretty straight right now," Rick said. "When they're not on drugs they're pretty decent people. They all look clean-cut right now, except for those silly suits they make them wear. I think the whole experience has made Mark stronger. He's found out there are consequences to his actions and that those consequences can change his life. And he's learned about people of all different kinds and how to get along with them. Plus he's working in the cafeteria and studying, because they have classes during the day."

Jerry flipped the steaks over and stared down at them for a moment. Rick thought he was going to ask more about the prison, or maybe even about Mark. Instead, he said, "Go in and ask Sandra for the pepper, would you?"

Let down, Rick took that as a dismissal of the conversation, and he knew his father wasn't going to engage any more. Well, Rick had said his piece, given his dad all the information he needed, even made a plea for Jerry to go visit Mark. But there was nothing more that he could do without straining his own relationship with his dad, and he wasn't sure that would accomplish anything.

"Yeah," he said, finally. "I'll get it." And as he did, he said a silent prayer that God would take care of the rest.

CHAPTER *Eighty*

Cathy and Steve spent the first day of their honeymoon lounging around the condo in Gatlinburg, and the next day they went rock climbing in Pigeon Forge. The day after that they traveled to North Carolina to a place called Horse Pasture Creek and spent the day playing in waterfalls that took their breath away.

Each night they ate in charming little restaurants and had romantic evenings in their condo. Cathy couldn't believe how blessed she was, how covered with God's grace, as she got used to Steve being her husband.

Steve and Tracy moved into the house the day they arrived back in Breezewood. Tracy seemed a little moody and emotional about all the changes in their life. Steve's parents helped them move in, and Cathy allowed his mother to help Tracy organize her room.

That night, when everything was in the house but not yet put away, and the grandparents had gone home, and everyone was exhausted, Cathy went to put Tracy to bed. She found her curled up on her new bedspread, leaned back against the wall, with tears rolling down her face.

"Oh, honey," Cathy said, and sat next to her on the bed. "What's the matter?"

"Nothing."

"Have we been ignoring you?"

"No, ma'am," she said.

"Then what's wrong?"

"I don't know."

She looked at the little girl and realized that, for the past few days, she'd been without her father. That, in itself, could have been slightly traumatic, especially since she anticipated so many changes coming upon their lives. Even though Tracy had wanted it, had looked forward to moving into her new room and having Cathy as her new mother, the whole thing was probably a little overwhelming.

"Do you want me to put you to bed?" she asked.

Tracy shrugged. "Where's Daddy?"

Cathy started to tell her that Daddy was busy hanging pictures in their room. But then she realized that Tracy wasn't ready to switch gears on her parent just yet.

"I'll go get him," she said. "Maybe you and Daddy need to spend a little time together, just the two of you. What do you think?"

Tracy's eyes lit up. Cathy reached down and hugged the little girl, then went back out and found Steve in the new master bedroom.

"How do you like this picture here?" he asked with a nail between his teeth.

She smiled. "It's perfect. But why don't you do it later?"

He turned back to her and grinned. "What have you got in mind?"

"Tracy," she said. "She needs a little time alone with her daddy. I think all the moving and all the changes are getting to her, and she's sitting in there in a new room feeling a little overwhelmed."

Concern instantly filled his eyes, and he took the nail out of his mouth. "Well, thanks," he said. "I needed to know that. I've been so busy I haven't paid attention."

"Just go in there and read her a story or something, lie down with her until she goes to sleep. I can take it from here."

He gave Cathy a sweet kiss, then headed back to the bedroom to be with his daughter. Cathy had plenty to keep her busy.

After a while, Cathy drifted back to Tracy's bedroom and saw the father and child lying together on the bed. He was reading to her from *The Lion, the Witch, and the Wardrobe*, making funny voices and talking in a British accent.

Tracy's tears had dried and all was well. Her eyes followed the words as he read. Cathy wished she had a camera ready to take a picture of that, but she wouldn't have interrupted it for the world. Her heart swelled to the point of bursting at the love that had been brought into this home.

If they were careful, if they nurtured it, if they did things right and didn't push too hard, some day the family would be one instead of two fractured pieces. Some day, with God's help, maybe they would all be comfortable and used to each other and think of each other as siblings and parents instead of steps. But she didn't want to hope for too much too soon. There were limitations, and she had to be aware of them and work around them. But those limitations weren't as great as the potential benefits. She couldn't be more thrilled with the new arrangement.

She only wished her children could have grown up with a father like Steve instead of a father like Jerry, but she supposed there was nothing she could do about it now. All they could do was pick up from this point and move on the best way they could.

CHAPTER
Eighty-One

By the grace of God, Mark's incarceration went by more quickly than they could have expected. Though Jerry still kept his distance from Mark, Steve continued to disciple Mark through the mail and in his visits to River Ranch. As Cathy and Steve settled into their marriage, they saw a genuine maturity developing in Mark. Winter passed, then spring. As summer approached, Cathy began to look forward to Mark's homecoming with joy and almost painful anticipation. By the time June came and his sentence had ended, she had come to see the year of his incarceration as a blessing instead of a crisis. Never before had Mark been such a willing subject, listening to the things she wanted to teach him, puzzling over them, studying them, digging for them, and understanding.

Just last week, he had sent her a letter with a Scripture passage in it, and she had wept at the depth of his understanding. It was Proverbs 2:1–5. Mark had written, "Mom, look what the Lord showed me today." Then he'd quoted the verses: "My son, if you accept my words and store up my commands within you, turning your ear to wisdom and applying your heart to understanding, and if you call out for insight and cry aloud for understanding, and if you look for it as for silver and search for it as for hidden treasure, then you will understand the fear of the LORD and find the knowledge of God."

"It works, Mom," he wrote. "I tried to tell Lazzo. I think he's listening lately."

Just weeks before his release date, Steve had come up with an idea. "You remember the first letter I sent Mark with the Bible study in it, the one about the Prodigal Son?"

"How could I forget?" Cathy asked. "It wound up making such a difference in his life."

"Well, when he called me that night to tell me that he'd accepted Christ, he talked about the robe and ring. And I've just been thinking. What if we threw him a celebration when he gets out? We could do it here, in the house, and invite everybody we know, show him that we're not disgraced, that we're as proud of him as we can be."

Cathy threw her hands over her heart. "Oh, Steve, that's a fabulous idea. We could have a sport coat made for him, sort of like the robe the father gave to his son. And we could make him a ring."

"And that picture he drew for you. The one with the father's head and the son's head inside it? Maybe we could have it duplicated for some kind of insignia to put on the pocket and on the ring. He'd always remember what it meant."

"Yes! It could be even bigger than Annie's party. We could call it his Prodigal Son Celebration."

She threw her arms around her husband and almost danced a jig. "I'll get started on it right away. Boy, is Mark going to have something to come home to."

CHAPTER
Eighty-Two

Not everyone was as excited about the Prodigal Son Celebration as Cathy was. A phone call from Jerry the night before Mark's release told her that *he* was anything but thrilled.

"What's this Rick tells me about some big party you're having?" he asked.

Cathy's hackles came up as she got ready to defend herself. "I'm throwing my son a party to welcome him home. We're calling it our Prodigal Son Celebration. Do you have a problem with that, Jerry?"

"Well, I have a problem with Steve doing it. He's not his father."

"And neither are you, last I heard," she threw back. "You haven't visited Mark one time in a year. He's given up looking for you. Steve has been there at least once a week, sometimes twice. He's discipled him with Bible studies and patience. He's taught him things that will benefit him in life. What have you done, Jerry?" The passion in her words surprised her, and she realized that she hadn't dealt very well with the anger she had toward him.

"I don't care what you say," he told her. "I am still Mark's father, and I'm not going to have a party thrown where Steve steps into my shoes and pretends he's the conquering dad."

"Well, would you like to do it, instead?" she asked.

"No, I don't think we should throw a party for a kid who's spent the last year in prison. Welcome him home, Cathy, but for Pete's sake, he doesn't deserve a party."

"Well, he's changed, Jerry. You'd know that if you had visited him. And I'm throwing the party whether you like it or not. You're welcome to come if you want, but I'm not going to tell Steve to stay away from him. He's been too big a part of Mark's life in the last year. He's made a difference, and I'm grateful to him. Mark needed a positive male role model."

"Oh, thanks a lot," Jerry said. "Like I'm not one?"

"Figure it out for yourself, Jerry," she said. "Positive role models are there where people can look at them and imitate them. There's nothing that Mark's been able to imitate in you."

"I'm just saying that I don't think we should call more attention to the fact that he's been in prison. It just disgraces the family more."

"Not *my* family," Cathy said. "I'm proud of Mark. I'm proud of how far he's come. And you're missing it all, Jerry, every bit of it. Your occasional weekends with Rick aren't making up for what you're missing in their lives. They're all changing and growing and becoming adults. If you want to be part of their lives, if you want a say in what goes on around them, then you have to be there."

She hung up the phone and sat there beside it, realizing that forgiveness was much harder than she thought. How did one forgive someone who was so unrepentant? Still, she got down on her knees and turned it over to God, asking him to work in Jerry's heart for the good of her children. And she begged him to work in her own heart to help her forgive.

CHAPTER
Eighty-Three

The long year was nearing its end, and Annie knew that it was time for her to go home. She had known it as soon as her mother told her about the Prodigal Son Celebration. But it would not be easy to leave the children she had come to think of as her own family.

Sylvia hadn't been feeling well and had been growing tired a lot more quickly than before. Dr. Harry was worried about her, Annie could tell, and arranged for Sylvia to accompany Annie home so that she could see a doctor in the States. Annie worried too, but Sylvia didn't have time to worry. She just tried to work around the fatigue and her limitations.

The day they were to head to the airport in Managua, Annie wept her heart out and said good-bye to each child individually, both the ones in the orphanage and the ones from the community who hung around waiting for handouts. She would come back and visit them someday, she promised, and when she did, she would bring them goodies from America. She would also see to it that others from Breezewood kept sending money so that the work could continue.

She wept throughout the flight home, but just as the plane landed in Houston, her heart began to lift. It was time to move ahead with her life, to make plans for her own future. Her time with Sylvia and Harry had given her a hunger for the Word, and now she realized that she wanted to major in Bible at a Christian college, then head to seminary. Someday, she hoped to return to the mission field. Whatever God's plan for her was, she wanted to make a difference. She didn't think she could ever return to a mundane, fruitless lifestyle again.

As they boarded the plane from Houston to Breezewood, Sylvia grew faint and had to sit down in the jet bridge. She lowered her head, and a flight attendant got her some water. Annie tried to fan her off.

After a moment, Sylvia had gotten slowly back to her feet and boarded the plane. Annie prayed all the way home that the doctors would be able to quickly find whatever was wrong with Sylvia and cure it. There was so much work to be done. Maybe Sylvia just needed a rest. In a way, Annie was thankful that their house hadn't sold yet. Sylvia would be able to sleep in her own bedroom on her own mattress with her own linens, surrounded by her own things, with her neighbors fussing over her. Maybe within a week she'd be back to normal.

It had been good of Sylvia to come home to celebrate with Mark. Annie hoped that, when she got married and had a family of her own, she'd live in a neighborhood with friends who loved her and cared for her and celebrated her triumphs with her.

Yes, life held so much. Annie couldn't wait for whatever came next.

CHAPTER
Eighty-Four

Mark woke up on the day of his release and realized that everything was different. Even before he climbed out of his bunk, he already felt free—and with a sudden grin he remembered how much he had to look forward to. When he'd first been told of the Prodigal Son party that his family had planned for him, he'd had to go into the bathroom to hide his weeping. He had immediately begun working on the speech his mother had asked him to give. He must have written it a hundred times in the days since then, adding things, deleting those things that sounded lame. He'd tried to organize it the way Brenda had taught him to write papers. He wanted everyone at the party to see that he had changed, that the experience of being in jail had not hardened him. Instead, he was a stronger person for it, a man of integrity and purpose.

But as he dressed that morning, Mark felt a sharp regret for leaving his prison friends behind. He went around to each of them, shaking hands and saying good-bye. He saved Lazzo till last. The boy couldn't meet his eyes as Mark shook his hand, and Mark knew that Lazzo was sorry to see him go.

"You'll come back and visit once in a while, won't you, man?" Lazzo asked, picking at a piece of lint on his blanket.

"Sure I will," Mark said.

Lazzo shook his head. "People say that all the time. They say they'll do it and then they don't."

"No, man. I'll really do it. And I was thinking I might write to you."

"Write to me?" Lazzo asked. "Yeah, right, like you're going to have time to sit around writing letters to your old pals in jail."

"No kidding. I will." He went to his locker, opened it, and pulled out all the papers Steve had sent him, with all the Bible studies and all of Mark's notes. He handed them to Lazzo. "You can have these, if you want them. They're pretty cool, if you do them."

"That Bible study?" Lazzo asked.

"Yeah. If you don't want to do them, I'll take them, but if you want them—"

Lazzo took them out of his hands. "I'll take 'em," he said. "Might fill up some time."

"Worked for me." He cleared his throat and took in a deep breath. "You know, if you ever wanted to do more, well, uh . . . I could send you stuff . . . or bring it by."

"Yeah, man. Thanks."

He packed the few things that he had been allowed to keep and dressed in a new pair of khakis and a button-down shirt that his mother had brought him. Then he met her in the visitation room where they'd talked across the table so many times before. She wept as soon as she saw him come through the door.

Though he had seen her twice a week for the past year, he held her in a crushing embrace, a hello hug. But he couldn't help looking over her shoulder to see if his father had come. There was no one there, but Mark wasn't surprised. He had grown numb to that kind of disappointment months ago. At least, he told himself he had.

"So what time does the party start?" he asked his mother.

She wiped her face. "We're going straight there," she said. "I hope you're ready."

He nodded. "So who's going to be there?"

"Everybody."

She smiled and began to roll his suitcase toward the front door. He took it out of her hands and carried it as he walked out the door, an inmate no longer.

"Just brace yourself," she said as they drove home. "You're not going to believe this party."

When they pulled into the driveway, the house looked exactly the same from the outside as it had when he left, except for the cars parked along the cul de sac and pulled up into the empty lot between the Dodds and the Sullivans. He got out and dusted off his pants and realized he was pretty nervous. He wondered if he would remember his speech and if he would embarrass anybody.

But as his mother walked him into the room, his breath caught in his throat. The room was full of friends, old and new, kids he'd gone to junior high school with, kids from the youth group, relatives from his mother's side of the family, some of Steve's relatives he'd met briefly, and the chaplains he'd worked with at River Ranch.

His mouth shook with the emotion rising up inside him, and he told himself that he had to be a man, had to keep his eyes dry and his hands steady, at least until he was alone in his own room tonight.

"Mark?"

He heard his mother's voice at the front of the room. She was holding a navy blue sport coat with an insignia on the lapel. He studied it—the insignia was the picture he had drawn months ago of the father and his son. He had almost forgotten it, though it was packed with meaning for him—about his new heavenly father, and the fact that Mark was growing in his image, and was always on his mind.

"Come on," she said. "Put it on."

It was the robe, he realized. The robe from the Prodigal Son. He wove through the crowd to the front of the room and slipped his arms into the sleeves of the new coat. It fit him perfectly.

Everyone got quiet. His mother turned to the crowd, her eyes full of tears. "This coat represents something really special," she said. "It represents Mark putting on Christ and the life that comes with that choice. And it represents his right standing in our family. In the parable of the Prodigal Son, the father brought out a robe and put it on his son so that everyone would know that he was an heir."

She smiled. "I don't have much of an inheritance to leave." Everyone chuckled. "But I have a family to give Mark, and he's one of us. And I just wanted him to know that he's welcome back."

And then she pulled out the ring that she had had carefully made for him with the same emblem carved in gold. "And I had this made for Mark, too," she said. "Whenever he wears it, he can look down at it and remember how much his Father in heaven loves him, how much he searched the horizon waiting for him to come home, and how clean his slate is."

Mark burst into tears, in spite of himself.

"Mark, you have so much ahead of you," she said, as she slipped the ring onto his shaking finger.

The crowd parted, and Annie pushed through. She looked thinner, taller, healthier than she had before. Her face was more mature, more full of purpose. He'd never seen her more beautiful.

He met her halfway, and she threw her arms around him and began to cry. He buried his face in Annie's neck. Then Rick came up behind her, and he hugged his brother with the same crushing strength.

Then Sylvia came up, and Brenda and Tory, and their husbands, Barry and David. One by one, he hugged Daniel and Joseph and Leah and Rachel, Spencer and Brittany. Even the baby Hannah, who was walking with the help of her parents, who each held a hand. He hugged Tracy, who was jumping up and down with excitement.

And then he came to Steve. He looked at him awkwardly. He had thanked him before, but he wanted to do it again. He just didn't know how. Steve shook his hand, then pulled him into a rough hug.

The moment was broken when someone began tinkling a bell to get their attention. It was Rick, standing on the hearth.

"We have a few people who want to say some things," Rick said. "The first one is from Dr. Harry. He sent it with Sylvia from Nicaragua. If everybody would listen, Mark, you especially ... You need to hear what Dr. Harry has to say."

They turned on the video, and Mark listened as Dr. Harry gave him a blessing such as he'd never received before. And then Rick got up to speak and said things about Mark's childhood, how he used to skip and make everyone laugh. No one who spoke seemed to recall that Mark had once been arrested for stealing a car, for vandalism, for drugs, for distribution. No one seemed to remember his spending the past year in jail. Instead, you would have thought he was getting an award for feeding the homeless or saving souls.

He couldn't believe the grace of it all.

Steve hadn't yet spoken, but Cathy felt moved to say a few more words before he addressed the crowd.

"One more person has a few things to say," she called out, quieting the crowd. "But before he comes up, I just want to say how proud I am of my son." She met Mark's eyes. "I know that what you've been through in the last year has been really hard, Mark. And at the beginning, I was ashamed and upset, but today I couldn't be prouder of you if you had cured cancer or invented some kind of modern gadget that changes the whole world. I love you." She kissed her fingertips and blew it to Mark.

The door from the kitchen to the garage opened, and she glanced over to see who was coming in. She saw Jerry sticking his head slightly in, looking around with purpose ... and anger.

Her heart crashed. How could he come here and make a scene, on Mark's day? How could he ignore the joy and dig up only the things that affected him? Was he going to heckle Steve's speech? Challenge his right to stand in the place of father?

Their friends and neighbors kept their eyes on her, as Mark did, so no one else saw Jerry. He backed out and closed the door. Great, Cathy thought—now he was out there like a ticking bomb, volatile and waiting to explode. Something was about to happen, and she couldn't predict what it was. Her eyes met Sylvia's in a moment of panic.

"But before we hear from Steve," she said, "I want Sylvia to come up and say a few words. Ladies and gentlemen, our resident missionary who's been mentoring my daughter for the last year—Sylvia Bryan."

Sylvia looked surprised, but she rose to the occasion and came forward, weak and pale. As the crowd applauded, Cathy whispered to Sylvia, "Jerry's in the garage. Stall while I calm him down." Sylvia nodded and started to speak. Cathy hurried through the crowd, grabbed Steve's hand, and pulled him toward the door.

"Jerry's here," she whispered. "He's going to ruin your speech. Come with me to talk to him."

They hurried out the side door.

Jerry was waiting in the garage, leaning against the wall, hands in his pockets. "What are you doing here?" Cathy asked.

Jerry stiffened. "I'm his father."

"So what are you going to do? Just come in here and tell everybody not to welcome Mark home, that he's an ex-con and he doesn't deserve any of this?"

The anger was clear on Jerry's face, and he took a step toward Cathy.

Steve stepped between them. "Cathy, let me handle it, okay? You go on back in. Mark's going to come looking for you, and we don't want to upset him."

Cathy drew in a deep breath, then lifted her chin. "All right," she said, "but so help me, Jerry, if you mess any of this up, you're going to pay. None of your children will ever forgive you." With that, she went back into the house.

She tried to act as if nothing was wrong, but her hands trembled. Sylvia's speech was heartfelt and spontaneous, and she realized that it was a God thing that she had let her friend get up. Sylvia kept talking until Steve stepped back in alone. Then she shot Cathy a questioning look. Cathy nodded grimly and started back to the front.

As Sylvia turned it back over to her, Cathy tried to swallow the tension in her throat. She drew in a deep breath, afraid of what was about to happen.

"There's one other person who'd like to speak," she said in a shaky voice. Everyone looked at Steve expectantly. He only looked down at the floor.

"He's someone who's had a huge impact in Mark's life, someone who's loved him and grieved over every step of this process. Someone who's celebrating now, just like God is in heaven."

She looked across the room at Steve and saw him shaking his head. She frowned and started to urge him to come on, when the door opened and Jerry stepped inside. He took a look around at the crowd, his face reddening.

She started to launch toward him, but Steve held up a hand to stop her. He nodded that it was okay.

Slowly, Jerry pushed through the crowd.

CHAPTER
Eighty-Five

Mark slowly turned and saw Jerry moving to the front. His mouth came open, and his eyes looked so vulnerable Cathy thought they might shatter.

"Uh . . ." Jerry cleared his throat. "I feel kind of out of place in here." He coughed nervously and looked down at his son. "Mark . . . just look at you."

Mark slid his hands into his pants pockets and looked down at his new shoes.

"I'm not very proud . . ." He stopped and cleared his throat again. Mark brought his eyes back up, and Cathy moved next to Mark and touched his shoulder. "I'm not very proud of the way I've treated you over the last year," he said. "Even though I'm your dad, I was mad, and I didn't want you to think I would reward you for what you'd done. But I was wrong, Son."

Cathy covered her mouth against the muffled sob.

"I've missed a lot," Jerry went on. "I haven't been there for you. But tonight I've been standing outside the door listening to what the people said about you. To tell you the truth, I came here to confront your mother and Steve, who I thought was trying to fill my shoes. And standing out there, I heard all those great things that everybody's been saying, and I realized that I've missed an awful lot. Not just for the last year, but for your whole childhood."

Mark's mouth twitched at the corners, and Cathy could see the Herculean effort he was giving to not falling apart. But *Jerry* was falling apart.

"Mark, I hope you can forgive your old man," he said, "because when I look at you right now, I'm prouder of you than I've ever been in my life. I love you, Mark."

Before he had a chance to say another word, Mark bolted forward and embraced his father. Cathy saw Jerry dip his head down and kiss Mark's neck, just like the father had done to the Prodigal Son.

She watched father and son descend back into the crowd, watched the others patting his back and shaking his hand, watched Annie and Rick as they embraced their dad, celebrating the fact that he had come to do this thing for their brother.

Stunned, Cathy pulled back out of the crowd and stepped outside to calm herself. She leaned back against the garage wall, exactly where Jerry had been moments earlier. The door opened, and Steve slipped out.

He looked at her with worried eyes. "I hope you're not mad," he said.

"Mad? About what?"

"That I let him in, let him go talk in my place. Let him speak publicly like that to Mark."

"How could I be mad?" she asked, wiping her tears. "It was exactly what Mark needed. It's what he longed for all this time. Here I was thinking you were going to step up and make him feel so proud and bless him in a way that he needed so badly. But you did more than that. You gave him back his dad."

He held her as she wept with joy for what her son had gained, when so many times before, she had wept over what he had lost.

And then the doors opened again, and David Dodd stepped out. They broke the embrace, and Steve whispered, "Why don't you go on back in? I need to talk to David."

Cathy went back inside to find her son.

❧

David reached out to shake Steve's hand. "That was very moving," he said in a cracked voice. "I know it wasn't easy."

"It was your idea," Steve said. "I appreciate it."

"You know," David said, struggling to control his voice, "what happened in there . . . all the symbolism, the coat you had made for Mark, the ring on his finger, that little insignia, and then watching Mark and his father embrace the way they did. It was a real good picture to me, Steve."

"A picture of what?" Steve asked.

"A picture of God." He rubbed his jaw hard, trying to cover the trembling of his mouth. "I just need to think about all this for a while."

"I'll pray for you, man," Steve said.

David nodded. "You know, that didn't mean a whole lot to me a while back, but I think I'm starting to see that maybe there's some good to praying. It always seems to work."

"Every time. Not always the way we want. But I have no regrets."

David swallowed hard. "If Brenda comes looking for me, tell her I went home, okay? I have some thinking to do."

"Sure, I will."

And as David walked down the driveway and crossed the street, Steve prayed that David would see his own Father scanning the horizon, waiting for him to come home.

CHAPTER
Eighty-Six

When the party was over and all the guests had gone home—and Cathy's kids had gone out for a bite with their father—Sylvia, Brenda, and Tory stayed behind to help Cathy clean up.

The kitchen was almost clean when Sylvia had to sit down. It was jetlag, Cathy thought, on the tail end of a couple of years of the hardest work of her life. Sylvia would rest, and they would take care of her, and by the time they put her back on the plane, she would be fine.

"You haven't been taking advantage of one of God's greatest gifts," she said, bringing Sylvia a mug of coffee and sitting down beside her.

Sylvia sipped, looking puzzled. "And which gift is that?"

"Rest," Cathy said, kicking off her shoes and pulling her feet up to the couch.

"You're right," Tory agreed. "Rest is a gift."

"One of many," Brenda said. She set her mug down on the coffee table. "Think where we were a year ago, when Cathy thought everything had come crashing down."

"But it hadn't," Cathy said. "Look what came of it."

"It's been a full year," Sylvia said. "A year with a lot of good moments. One of mine was when Annie got off the plane in Managua and saw the car I drive." She threw her head back and laughed. "You should have seen her face, Cathy. It was priceless. She was trying not to laugh, but then she fell against the car and laughed until she cried. Wish I'd gotten a picture of that." She sighed. "We loved having her there. It was a good time."

"But I'm glad you brought her back," Cathy said. "I missed her. But I have noticed that she's appreciated driving my little car. Not one complaint."

"That's just because it has real windows instead of duct tape."

"She said you were so tired from pedaling your car," Cathy said, and they all laughed again.

"So what was your best moment in the last year, Brenda?" Sylvia asked.

She thought a moment. "Mine was getting Daniel *his* car," Brenda said. "It's probably not a whole lot better than yours, Sylvia, but it suited him fine."

"Mine was the date with Barry," Tory said, "when he arranged the sitter and took me dancing."

"The wedding was nice," Cathy said, feeling that sense of well-being that comes in the wake of joy. "The marriage is even nicer. Best moment? When Mark told me he'd found Christ."

Sylvia nodded. "When Annie understood that Christ was better than food."

"When David was so moved today by the picture of the Prodigal Son," Brenda whispered.

Tory swallowed and drew in a cleansing breath. "When I understood that life's family joys are more important than my pride."

"Oh, yeah," Cathy said, relating too well. "Or when Jerry understood that." She dropped her feet and leaned up, as if amazed all over again. "The look on Mark's face when his dad told him he loved him." Her heart ached with that sensitive joy that always comes with tears. "*That* was the best moment," Cathy whispered.

"You're right," Brenda whispered. "It was."

"Yeah," Tory said as tears rimmed her eyes. "I'll never forget it."

"Neither will he," Sylvia said. "What a precious gift."

CHAPTER
Eighty-Seven

That night, Mark enjoyed settling back into his messiness, as he had not been allowed to do at River Ranch. He took his shirt off and threw it over the basketball hoop on his door, then pulled on a pair of jeans, relishing the feel of them in place of his Cat-in-the-Hat pants.

He plopped down onto his bed and stretched out on the thick mattress.

And then he thanked God that he was out of jail, that he wasn't the stupid, stubborn kid who went in, that his family had welcomed him back . . .

He had never expected to feel this sense of well-being again, but tonight all seemed right with his life.

❧

Cathy woke up in the middle of the night and reached over to touch Steve's chest. He slept soundly, with that rhythmic breathing she had come to depend on. Carefully, she slipped out of bed and walked barefoot across the plush carpet in their new bedroom. She went into the living room and down the hall to Tracy's room. The child slept with four stuffed animals and a nightlight on. Her hair lay like a blanket across her face, and Cathy pushed it back from her eyes.

Quietly, she slipped out of the room and went up the stairs. Rick's door was open, and she stopped in the doorway and saw him buried under his covers. He was almost too big for his bed, she thought. She hadn't noticed it before. But she supposed there was no point in getting him a bigger bed when he had such a small bed in his dorm. She stepped close to him and saw the perspiration on his face. He was too hot. She'd have to adjust the thermostat.

She went back out and stopped at Annie's room. Her daughter had already fallen into her habit of cluttering her room with clothes and shoes and makeup, as if she'd waited a solid year to spread out again. Photographs of the children in León were already framed and placed around her room. Cathy stepped close to the bed, where Annie lay like the little girl she had once been, all innocent and sweet and full of life. She was still that girl, Cathy thought with gratitude. Annie was tangled in her covers, with something clutched in her hands. Cathy looked to see what it was.

It was the picture of a tiny little girl Annie had come to love. Cathy swallowed back the emotion tightening her throat.

Then she went on to Mark's room and stepped inside. He was sound asleep on his bed, still wearing his jeans. He looked like the little skipping boy that Cathy had lost, with his bare chest and bare feet, and his arm carelessly flung over the side of the bed.

She went in and pulled his covers up over him. Love and unspeakable gratitude filled her heart so full that it almost hurt. She knew just whom to thank.

She looked up at the ceiling, as if she could see her Lord smiling down at her. "I owe you a big one," she whispered.

They had all turned out right. In spite of her flawed mothering, in spite of their broken home, in spite of everything that had gone wrong in their lives . . . God had filled in the blanks.

He had raised her children right and had seen them all the way home.

Season
of Blessing

*This book is dedicated to cancer patients everywhere,
and to those whose lives have been altered because
someone they love has fought this disease . . .
and to the Great Physician,
who sometimes cures here on earth . . .
and sometimes heals by taking us home.*

Acknowledgments

Special thanks to Dr. Bobby Graham and Dr. Sharon Martin for being our consultants on this book. Your help was invaluable, and we couldn't have done it without you.

We'd also like to thank our agent, Greg Johnson, for the vision he had for a "Best Years" series, which ultimately evolved into these four books. He also had the vision to introduce us to each other in hopes of forming a partnership. That partnership has worked beautifully, and we've both been blessed by it.

And we must thank our editors at Zondervan—Dave Lambert, Lori Vanden Bosch, and Bob Hudson—for their tireless work to make sure these stories are the best they can be. And thanks to Sue Brower, who is responsible for letting our readers know that the books are out. This whole team does a wonderful job.

And finally, thanks to you, our reader, for giving us your time and attention as we spun these tales. Thanks for all your letters of encouragement, and for sharing tears and laughter with us as we've grown with Brenda, Tory, Cathy, and Sylvia.

May all your crises be blessings, and may you have many, many, many "best moments."

I will sing to the Lord all my life;
I will sing praise to my God as long as I live.

PSALM 104:33

CHAPTER *One*

Sylvia Bryan had always considered the words *early detection* to have more to do with others than herself. She'd never had anything that needed early detecting, and if she had any say in the matter—which apparently she did not—she would just as soon jump to the best possible conclusion, and proclaim the lump in her breast to be a swollen gland or a benign cyst. Then she could get back to her work in Nicaragua and stop being so body-conscious.

But Harry had insisted on a complete physical because of her fatigue and weakness, and had sent her home from the mission field to undergo a battery of tests that befitted a woman of her age. She had been insulted by that.

"I hope I don't have to remind you that you're a *man* of my age," she told him, "so you don't have to go treating me like I'm over-the-hill at fifty-four."

Harry had bristled. "I'm just saying that there are things you're at greater risk for, and I want to rule all of them out. You're not well, Sylvia. Something's wrong."

She'd had to defer to him, because deep down she'd been concerned about her condition, as well. It wasn't like her to be so tired. She had chalked it up to the brutal August heat in Nicaragua, but she'd weathered last summer there without a hitch. For most of her life she'd had an endless supply of energy. Now she had trouble making it to noon without having to lie down.

So he'd sent her home to Breezewood, Tennessee, to see an internist at the hospital where he'd practiced as a cardiologist for most of his life. After just a few tests, he'd diagnosed her with a bad case of anemia, which explained her condition.

But then he'd gone too far and found a lump in her breast.

She'd gone for a mammogram then, certain that the lump was nothing more than a swollen gland.

The radiologist had asked to see her in his office.

Jim Montgomery was one of Harry's roommates in medical school, and he came into the room holding her film. He'd always had an annoying way of pleating his brows and looking deeply concerned, whether he really was or not. He wore that expression now as he quietly took his seat behind his desk and clipped the mammogram film onto the light box behind him.

Sylvia wasn't in the mood for theatrics. "Okay, Jim. I know you want to be thorough and everything for Harry's sake, but my problem has already been diagnosed. I'm badly anemic, which explains all my fatigue. So you can relax and quit looking for some terminal disease."

Jim turned on the light box and studied the breast on the film. With his pencil, he pointed to a white area. "Sylvia, you have a suspicious mass in your left breast."

Sylvia stiffened. "What does that mean ... 'a suspicious mass'?"

"It means that there's a tumor there. It's about three centimeters. Right here in the upper outer aspect of your left breast." He made an imaginary circle over the film with his pencil.

Sylvia got up and moved closer to the film, staring at the offensive blob. She studied it objectively, as if looking at some other woman's X ray. It couldn't be hers. Wouldn't she have known if something that ominous lay hidden in her breast tissue? "Are you sure you didn't get my film mixed up with someone else's?"

"Of course I'm sure." He tipped his head back and studied the mass through the bottom of his glasses. "Sylvia, do you do self breast exams?"

She felt as if she'd been caught neglecting her homework. "Well, I used to try. But mine are pretty dense, and I always felt lumps that turned out to be nothing. I finally gave it up."

"Not a good idea. Especially with your history."

She knew he was right. Her mother had died of breast cancer when Sylvia was twenty-four. She should have known better than to neglect those self-exams. But she had been so busy for the last couple of years, and hadn't had that much time to think about herself.

"Well, I have tried to have mammograms every year since I turned forty ..." Her voice trailed off. "Except for the last couple of years when I've been out of the country."

"Well, it seems that the last couple of years were what really mattered."

She looked at him, trying to read the frown on his face. "But it's okay, isn't it? You can tell if it looks malignant ..."

He looked down at her chart and made a notation. "You need to get a biopsy tomorrow, if possible."

The fact that he'd averted his eyes alarmed her. "You just evaded my question, Jim. And you know Harry is going to want to know. Does it look malignant to you or not?"

He leaned back in his chair, crossing his hands over his stomach. The frown wrinkling his brow didn't look quite so melodramatic now.

She set her mouth. "Be straight with me, Jim. You see these things all the time. I want the truth."

"All right, Sylvia." He sighed and took off his glasses, rubbed his eyes. "It does have the characteristics of a malignancy."

For a moment she just stood there, wishing she hadn't pressed the issue. Malignancy meant cancer, and cancer meant surgery, and then chemotherapy and radiation and her hair falling out and pain and depression and hospice care and death.

Her mouth went dry, and she wished she'd brought her bottled water in from the car. She wondered what time it was. She had to get to the cleaners before it closed.

Her hands felt like ice, so she slid them into the pockets of her blazer to warm them. "Come on, Jim. I don't have cancer. I've been tired, that's all, and they already figured out it's from anemia. There is no possibility that I have breast cancer. None. Zilch."

"Sylvia, you have to get this biopsied as soon as possible."

"Okay." She looked down at her blazer and dusted a piece of lint off. "Fine. I'll get the biopsy, but I'm not worried about it at all."

"Good." But he still wore the frown that said it wasn't good. He turned and jerked the film out of the light box. "And you're probably right. But if it is cancer, you may have detected it early enough that you'll have an excellent prognosis."

As Sylvia drove home, she realized that, along with *early detection*, she hated the word *prognosis*. It was not a word she'd ever expected to have uttered about her own body. This was just a minor inconvenience, she thought. She did not have time to be sick. The Lord knew how hard she worked for him in Nicaragua, and how much the children in the orphanage there needed her. They were probably already grieving her absence.

The Lord surely wouldn't cut her work off when she'd been bearing so much fruit. He cut off barren branches and pruned those who needed to bear more. But when she spent her life giving and serving, wouldn't he want her work to continue?

So she determined to push the news out of her mind until she'd actually had the biopsy. She knew in her heart that the mass was benign.

And if the biopsy proved her wrong, she would deal with it then.

CHAPTER *Two*

Brenda Dodd wiped the white paint off of her hands and threw the rag across the plywood limousine. She hit Daniel—her sixteen-year-old—in the face.

"No fair! I wasn't looking."

He flung it across the prop and hit Leah across the forehead. She slung it at Rachel, her twin sister, leaving a smudge of paint across her cheek. Rachel tossed it at Joseph.

Preoccupied, twelve-year-old Joseph hardly noticed. He stood in front of his father, watching him sand the steering wheel that would go inside the car. "It seems like an awful lot of work to go to, Dad, if you're not even going to come to church and watch the play Wednesday night."

Brenda's smile faded, and she looked at her husband. David had that tight, shut-down look that he got whenever the subject of church came up.

"I don't mind."

"But, Dad, I'm the star. I play the Good Samaritan who drives into town in his limousine and helps the guy who got mugged. How can you not want to see that?"

David cleared his throat. A cool breeze blew through their yard, ruffling his wavy red hair, but he still had a thin sheen of sweat above his lip. "Son, you know how I feel about church."

"I know, Dad, but it's not like something terrible will happen to you if you come."

"I'm not a hypocrite."

"But I want you to see me. I've practiced so hard. And I'm good, aren't I, Mom?"

Brenda knew better than to get involved, but she couldn't let her child down. "He is good, David."

"It's not that he's good." Fourteen-year-old Leah slopped more paint on her shorts and bare legs than she did on the car. "It's just that he's such a ham. He's a terrible show-off."

"I am not."

"Are too." Rachel came to sit beside Leah. "I thought they were going to have to pry that microphone out of your hand the other night at rehearsal. They wanted you to sing one verse, but you sang three."

Joseph snickered. "Hey, I felt moved by the Holy Spirit, okay?"

Rachel laughed. "Yeah, moved to stand in the limelight just a little longer."

"Okay, guys." Brenda got up and went to the other paint can sitting on the picnic table. "Leave Joseph alone. He's a talented performer, which is why he was chosen to play the Good Samaritan."

Joseph struck a pose. "And Dad isn't even going to see."

"Enough, Joseph." David sanded the steering wheel, blew the sawdust off.

Joseph shrugged and grabbed a paintbrush and stuck it in the black paint.

Brenda winced as he dripped it across the lawn. "This paint's for the windows, Joseph, and we might not have enough. Be careful not to let it drip."

"I won't." With great care, he began to outline the windows. "But really, Dad. I know you don't want to come to church because you don't believe in Jesus, but I don't see why you couldn't just fake it every now and then."

David sanded harder. "I don't fake things, Joseph. You don't fake your feelings just to please other people."

"But *why* don't you believe? I mean, it's just so obvious to me."

David shot Brenda a look. "Joseph, could we drop it?"

"But why, Dad? You always say that we should ask questions when we don't understand."

Daniel turned to see his father's reaction. Rachel and Leah stopped painting. Brenda said a silent prayer that their son's probing would make David think. If anyone in the family could get away with questions like these, Joseph could.

David set the steering wheel down. He looked at Joseph, then at Leah, Rachel, and Daniel.

"Okay, here's the thing." He sat down on the bench and leaned his elbows on his knees. "Your mother is a believer, and I'm not. I'm a facts kind of guy. She's more . . . spiritual. Ever since she became a Christian a few years into our marriage, I've agreed that she can raise you guys in church. I figure if she's wrong, it doesn't hurt anything. And you guys seem to like it. But ever since I was a kid, I've hated church. It's just a personal thing."

That didn't satisfy Joseph. "But you wouldn't hate our church. It's a good church."

"I'm sure it is."

Brenda knew that David would never tell them that he'd been the son of a preacher who had run off with the church organist, or how the church had thrown his mother and him out of the parsonage—leaving them homeless—in order to take a moral stand against the divorce that resulted. He would never tell the children how the church members had insisted that he was demon-possessed when his anger about his broken family surfaced. His father had died with a shipwrecked faith, and just five years ago, his mother died without ever forgiving his father—or the church.

Brenda didn't blame David for being bitter about the church.

"But, Dad, if you're a facts man, then how come you can't see the true facts? It wasn't so long ago that I was dying, and Jesus healed me. Now I'm perfect," Joseph said.

"Perfect?" Leah grunted. "Get real."

"I mean my body is perfect. I'm healthy and normal, except for all the medicine I have to take. But I was dying, Dad. God didn't have to give me a heart transplant, but he did."

David met Brenda's eyes again. She knew Joseph had put him in a tight spot. They had agreed that he would never denigrate the children's belief in God. But how could he defend his own beliefs without doing that?

"Isn't that proof, Dad?" Joseph demanded.

David swallowed. "To some people it is."

"But not to you?" He went back to the paint can and got more paint on his brush. "Dad, it's like this. You know how I was dying, and I couldn't be healed without a heart transplant? Somebody had to die so I could live?"

"Yeah."

"Well, that's a lot like what happened with God. We were all dying, and we had no hope. So Jesus came and died in our place, so that we could have a new heart and a new spirit. So that we could live."

"I know how it works, Joseph." David's aggravation shone clearly on his face.

"But how could you not want to live?"

David gazed down at his son. "I think I am living, son. Don't we have a good life?"

"Well, yeah, but it's not just this life that you have to consider."

Brenda suppressed her smile and caught a black drip cutting down through the white paint. She doubted David had ever had the gospel presented to him in such a clear way. She knew that seeds had been sown, whether they took root or not.

Joseph was getting sloppier with his painting, but Brenda didn't dare interrupt. His words to his father hit dead center.

David reached out and tousled Joseph's hair. "I appreciate your concern, son. I really do. And I'm proud of you for being able to make your case that way. Someday you'll probably be a lawyer. If I ever have to face a judge, it's you I'd want speaking for me."

Joseph's face betrayed his sorrow as he looked up at his father. "When you face the Judge, Dad, I won't be with you. You'll have to answer him for yourself."

CHAPTER *Three*

Up. . . . down . . . up.... down...."

Tory Sullivan mouthed the words with Melissa, the physical therapist, as she moved Hannah's legs in an effort to tone her weak muscles. The small woman sitting on the classroom floor had become like a member of their family, ever since Hannah had been born with Down's Syndrome. Now, at twenty-two months, the child was just beginning to make the effort to stand on her own. Watching the other Down's babies at the Breeze-wood Development Center had been an encouragement to Tory, reminding her that these children did develop, even if they did it slowly.

But the struggle didn't get easier for Tory. A former Miss Tennessee, she had always expected near perfection from herself and her family. Her home was immaculate and decorated like something out of *House and Garden*. Brittany, her ten-year-old, was into frills and curls, ribbons and lace, just as Tory had been at her age. Eight-year-old Spencer was a textbook boy—

athletic, outgoing, and definite leadership material, even if he was sometimes a handful.

And then there was Hannah. It was almost like the Lord had declared Hannah the one to be imperfect in the Sullivan household, just to remind her that not everything could line up under her checklist of expectations. Everything didn't have order and logic. God's order often came without explanation.

Hannah had taught Tory to lean on God more than she ever had before . . . to lower her expectations . . . to exult in the unexpected.

Still she longed to know that Hannah would walk, talk, learn . . . That she would live a happy life without daily battles to function . . . That she would develop and grow and progress to her full potential.

The truth was, she wanted everything for Hannah that she wanted for her other two children. But Hannah had challenges that Spencer and Brittany would never have. She always would. But Tory considered it a miracle that the baby had come this far when just a few months ago she hadn't believed she would ever even sit up alone. She knew the walking wouldn't come for a while yet, maybe even a year or two, but the fact that Hannah tried to pull up now gave her great hope.

A knock sounded on the classroom door, and Mary Ann Shelton, the director of the school, stuck her head in. "What are you guys doing here so late? It's after five."

"My fault," Melissa said. "I had a dentist appointment this afternoon and had to reschedule Hannah."

Mary Ann came into the room. "I'm just glad I ran into you, Tory. I was going to call you. Can I talk to you in my office for a minute?"

Tory smirked at Melissa as she got up from the floor and dusted off her pants. "Oh, boy. Hannah hasn't been cutting class again, has she? Is that why I'm being called to the principal's office?"

Mary Ann laughed. "No, I just wanted to talk to you about a job we've had that just came open."

Tory couldn't imagine what a job opening had to do with her. Mary Ann knew that raising Hannah took up every moment of her time.

But the director led her into her office and sat down behind her desk. Tory sank onto the plush easy chair, feeling as if she had forgotten something important. She realized she had never been in here without Hannah on her lap.

"So what's this about a job?" Tory asked.

Mary Ann's eyes inspired excitement, whether she talked about school tuition or the janitorial staff. "We've had an opening for a part-time teacher's assistant in the older children's class, ages six to nine, and I was thinking that maybe you would be interested."

Tory frowned. "Oh, I don't know, Mary Ann. I haven't really thought about getting a job. I'm so busy at home with Hannah."

"Well, that's just it." Mary Ann set her hands palms-down on the desk. "You could bring Hannah with you and she could play in the nursery while you work with the older kids. I thought it would be an encouragement for you to see how these older children are learning. And I can tell from watching you with Hannah that you'd be a godsend for these children as well."

Tory had never considered working with the older kids, but the truth was, she spent a lot of time standing outside the door of that classroom, peering through the window at those older kids who could walk and dance and talk and sing.

"You wouldn't have to do any planning or preparation. Linda, our teacher in that room, would do all that. You'd just help two mornings a week, Tuesdays and Thursdays. I've gotten another parent to commit to three mornings, and we have a couple of teenagers who help in the afternoons."

"Two mornings a week," Tory repeated. "That wouldn't be so bad. Might even be fun."

"And of course, it wouldn't interfere with Hannah's class." Mary Ann caught her breath. "Oh, I forgot. It pays too. I don't want you to think it's a volunteer position. And it might be good for Hannah to play with some of the other babies without you around. I don't mean that in a bad way. It's wonderful to have you there. I wish we had more mothers as involved as you. I'm just saying that maybe she needs to start socializing a little and learning to separate from you."

Tory knew that was true. Even now she had a hard time leaving Hannah with a baby-sitter, even at church.

"I'll need to think about it." She got up, anxious to get back to the child. "I need to talk to Barry and pray about it some. Can I get back to you?"

"Sure," Mary Ann said. "Take your time. I will need to hire someone by the end of August. But you were my first choice."

Tory ran the possibilities through her mind as she drove home that evening, and wondered if taking the job would indeed be good for everyone involved.

CHAPTER *Four*

Cathy Bennet sat at her kitchen table, her patchwork family feasting on tacos, as if they had never been touched by divorce or remarriage or jail. Having her new family all together was a dream come true.

She didn't know why Mark had chosen to ruin it.

"What do you mean, you don't want to go back to school?" Her taco crumbled in her hand, and she threw it onto her plate. "Mark, I know you had school in jail, but you didn't finish. You still need a diploma. I want you to go to college. I thought you were finally getting your head on straight."

"I am getting my head on straight, Mom!" Mark chomped into his taco, and shredded cheese and ground beef avalanched out.

"Then what are you talking about?"

Mark swallowed the bite in his mouth without enough chewing. "I didn't say I planned to drop out altogether. I just want to get my GED, that's all. Then I can go to college *or* get a job."

"A job?" Steve leaned up on the table, studying the boy who sat across from him. "Mark, what kind of job do you think you can get without an education?"

"I *have* an education."

"A complete education." Steve wiped his hands on a napkin. "Mark, you have to think of what kind of money you could make without finishing school."

Tracy tapped her spoon to the side of her glass, drawing all eyes to herself. "If he quits school, I get to quit, too."

Steve shot his twelve-year-old daughter a disgusted look. "You can think again, buckaroo."

"Why? In some countries kids are finished with school before they ever get to my age."

Nineteen-year-old Annie pushed her food around on her plate. Since she'd come back from Nicaragua with Sylvia, she had gone on a health food kick and refused to eat anything that even looked like it had calories. "You should see the kids in Nicaragua, wandering the streets digging through trash for food. They'd kill to be in a school like yours."

Cathy turned her gaze back to Mark, her blonde ponytail waving with the movement. "Why don't you want to go to school, Mark? I thought after being in jail for a year you'd want to go back to normal."

Mark dropped his taco and wiped his hands on his jeans. "Don't you see, Mom? I can't go back to normal. I've changed. I can't go back to public school because the guys I got in trouble with still go there."

Cathy met Steve's eyes. "Well, at least he sees that."

Steve leaned up on the table. "So why couldn't you go back to home schooling with Brenda's kids? She's already said she'd take you back. And she needs the money we'd pay her."

"Man . . ." Mark propped his face on his hand. "I feel like I've grown up past that. Going to school with little kids and having her hovering over me. I don't have anything against her. I really like Miss Brenda. I do. But I just need to get on with things, you know?"

Cathy started to tell him that he wasn't as grown up as he thought he was, when Rick's cell phone rang, injecting life into the otherwise silent twenty-one-year-old who sat staring at his food. He pulled the phone from his belt clip.

"Hello? Yeah. What's up, man? Nothing much."

Steve met her eyes in silent encouragement to rebuke him.

Cathy touched Rick's arm. "Rick, could you please take that somewhere else? We're trying to have dinner conversation here."

He didn't answer, just got up from the table and strode to another room. She watched him leave, wishing she'd made him turn off the phone before they sat down to eat. Since he lived on campus for summer school, he seldom came home to eat with them, and she hated calling him down when he did.

She turned back to Mark. "Mark, let's say you did get your GED. You're only sixteen. You're probably not ready to jump right into college."

"I told you, I'm not sure I even want to go to college. I'm tired. I need some freedom after being locked up for a year."

Tracy started drumming her fingers on the table.

Steve reached out and stopped her hand. "But, Mark, there's no freedom in having to work without a college degree. It's hard. Why would you want to put yourself through that?"

"Steve's right," Cathy said. "Honey, school is the best place for you now."

"Okay, but where?" he asked. "Do you want me to go to public school or do you want me to go to Brenda's and study with Leah and Rachel and Joseph?"

"And Daniel," Cathy said. "Don't forget Daniel. He's exactly your age."

"But he's different, Mom. He's a good friend and all, and I'm glad to have him as my buddy, but he's basically clueless. I've been in jail for a year. I've been around people who are hard to get along with."

"Then this should be easy for you."

"I don't want to be baby-sat all day and hovered over. I can take a GED course and get out of school and have some freedom."

Steve got up and took his plate to the sink. "Mark, you don't even have a driver's license yet. You're kidding yourself if you think this is going to give you extra freedom. And I think you need to define what freedom is."

"I know what freedom is," Annie piped in, flipping her dark hair back. "Freedom is just another word for nothing left to lose."

Cathy smirked. "Thank you, Annie, for bringing the wisdom of Janis Joplin into this conversation."

Rick came back into the room just then and took his place at the table. "Freedom? Oh, freedom. That's just some people talking." He broke into singing "Desperado," and Annie joined in. Mark threw his napkin across the table. Annie deftly caught it in the air and threw it back.

Cathy ducked. "Hey, not at the table. Come on, guys."

Tracy wadded one of her own and threw it smack into Cathy's face. Cathy caught it in her fist. The girl cracked up at the hit.

"Nice going, Tracy." Annie high-fived her. "Only I wouldn't recommend you repeat that."

Cathy waited for Steve to call Tracy down, but his eyes were still fixed on Mark.

"Mark, you must have given this job thing some thought. What kind of jobs are you thinking of?"

"I don't know. Maybe something like an electrician."

Steve came back to the table. "Electricians are trained. Some of them go to college. If they don't, at the very least they go to vocational school."

Mark shifted in his seat. "They need assistants, don't they?"

"Well, yeah, but that's a minimum wage job. And you've got a background, Mark. You've got a few strikes against you since you've been to jail. If you offset that with a college degree, people will forget about it and think that maybe you were irresponsible as a kid, but you grew up. But if you don't even finish high school and you get your GED and then try to get a job just a few months after getting out of jail, the chances are that you'll have to take some crummy job that you hate just to make a living."

"Well, it's not like you guys are going to throw me out in the street, is it? I can stay here for a while, can't I?"

Cathy took Mark's hand. "Of course you can, honey."

Steve crossed his arms. "You can stay here, Mark, as long as you're working toward something. If you're going to school . . . if you have a plan . . ."

Cathy turned to her husband, her eyes lashing him. "Steve, he's only been out a week."

"Yeah," Mark said. "It's not like I've been sitting around doing nothing."

"Honey, I think he's entitled to a few days of rest," Cathy said.

Steve looked as aggravated as she. "Of course he is, but now he's telling us he doesn't want to go to school, and if he doesn't, then we need to know what the plan is. There has to be a plan, Cathy."

Cathy turned back to her son. "Honey, he's right. You do need a plan."

Mark scowled. "I will have a plan, Mom. It doesn't have to be *his* plan."

Cathy winced and stole a look at Steve. His face had that hard, tight look it got when he was angry. "He didn't mean that the way it sounded," she said weakly.

"Yes, I did." Mark got up from the table and shoved his chair back. "I've already talked to my dad about this. He's all for it. He thinks the GED is a good idea."

Cathy bit her tongue. It wouldn't do to remind him that his father's ideas were usually bad. His involvement in Mark's life had left way too much to be desired. It didn't surprise her that the one time he advised his son on anything, he'd encourage him to drop out of school. Not certain how to proceed from here, she moved her gaze back to her simmering husband. He stared down at the table, the little muscle of his jaw popping rhythmically in and out.

Rick bottomed his can of coke. "Hey, Mark can come stay with me on campus."

Mark's face lit up. "Can I, Mom?"

"Of course not." Cathy pinned Rick with a look. "You're not helping matters."

Rick looked as if she'd slapped him. "Excuse me for trying to help. Excuse me for coming home for a nice family meal. Excuse me for daring to open my mouth."

Steve's teeth came together. "Don't talk to your mother that way, Rick."

Rick threw up his hands. "What way?"

Steve heaved a loud sigh.

Rick got up. "I'm finished eating. Can I go?"

Cathy wondered how long it would be before she could get him back again. "I guess so."

Rick got up and left the house, and Mark took off up the stairs. She heard his door close hard.

Annie and Tracy sat watching their faces, as if anxious for the next round.

"We need to talk about that door slamming," Steve bit out.

"He wasn't slamming it." Cathy rubbed her face. "He just closed it too hard. Boys do that. They walk harder, open cabinets harder, close doors harder."

"I used to be a boy." Steve grabbed Tracy's plate and dropped it hard in the sink. "I don't do that."

"Well, he's still learning." She gathered the rest of the plates and followed him to the sink. "You're used to raising Tracy, and she doesn't slam and make a lot of noise."

"One time I slammed my door," Tracy said, "and Daddy took it off the hinges for two weeks."

"You didn't slam it again, did you?" Steve pointed out.

Tracy grinned and shook her head.

Cathy followed him to the sink. "Please, Steve. Don't do that to Mark. He's had a rough year, and he came home to a changed family. I only want him to be comfortable here."

"And I'm making him uncomfortable?"

"No, that's not what I said. I just don't want you coming down hard with the rules. Give him some adjustment time. He's only sixteen. He's not supposed to have his whole life mapped out already."

Steve turned the water on full blast. "I'm not asking him to map it out. School is basic. You must agree with me on that."

"It is basic," she said, "but I can see where he's coming from. I can understand why he doesn't want to go study with Brenda's brood."

Annie rounded up the glasses and took them to the counter. "If you ask me, he's matured a lot since he got arrested. He's had life experiences ... not good ones. It's got to be hard for him, coming back to his old life and everybody expecting him to be the same guy that went away. Only he's a year older and a year wiser. And he's a Christian now. And he just doesn't quite know how to fit his new self back into the old skin. You know what Jesus said, about putting new wine into old wineskins?"

Cathy just stared at her daughter. "I'm not sure exactly what you just said, but I understand the concept." She looked at Steve. "She may be right."

"Well, if that's true," Steve said, "it only means he needs a little more guidance. That's what we're here for. Not just to throw him out in the world to make more mistakes."

Annie folded her arms. "I'm just saying to cut him some slack. It's got to be frustrating coming back with everything changed. I know it is for me."

Cathy gaped at her. "Frustrating? Why?"

"Well, the house is different. The renovation changed everything. And you and Steve all chummy and romantic, like two peas in a pod, and before you were just dating ... Rick gone and me getting ready for college in the fall ... Tracy in your old bedroom. Mark was the youngest in the family when he left, and now Tracy is. The birth order has changed. I read all about that in an article."

Steve wasn't buying. "Amateur psychology notwithstanding, Mark Flaherty is still only sixteen. And if my parents had let me make my own decisions at sixteen, I'd be a fry cook alcoholic with children in every state."

Cathy couldn't picture it, but she didn't tell him so. She was getting a headache and didn't want to talk about it anymore.

CHAPTER *Five*

When Cathy crossed the yard to Sylvia's for the prayer time they had scheduled earlier, Tory and Brenda were already there, leaning against the kitchen counter as Sylvia bustled around making her favorite dip.

Tory, who seemed not to know what to do with her hands since Hannah wasn't on her hip, munched on a carrot. "So she asks me if I want to work there part-time two mornings a week, helping with the six- to nine-year-olds."

"You going to do it?" Brenda asked.

Cathy came and stood in the doorway, and Tory picked up the vegetable plate and thrust it at her. "Here. Eat."

Cathy shook her head. "Can't. We just had a family dinner. There were few survivors."

Sylvia looked up from the dip. "Oh, no. You didn't have a family squabble, did you?"

"Well, yeah ... sort of. Long story."

Brenda slid up onto the counter. "We've got time."

Cathy grabbed a celery stick and bit into it. "But I want to hear what Tory decided."

"Haven't decided yet," she said. "Part of me wants to do it, but the other part feels like I'd be neglecting Hannah. But Mary Ann thought it would be good for me to work with the older kids. She thought it would encourage me about the things that Hannah will eventually be able to do."

Sylvia opened a jar of salsa and poured it into a bowl. "I think it's a wonderful idea. And you know Hannah will be cared for. She'll be right down the hall."

"I'm thinking about it." Tory took the vegetable plate and a bowl of chips to the living room, set them on the coffee table. Cathy followed with the dip, and Brenda brought the glasses.

Cathy plopped wearily down into an easy chair, and Tory and Brenda sat on the floor near the food. Sylvia came in, dusting her hands. "Okay, what am I forgetting?"

"Nothing," Brenda said. "Come sit down."

"Drinks!" Sylvia hurried back to the kitchen. "I forgot your drinks. Iced tea okay for everybody?"

The three agreed that it was, and she hurried back with a tray. "Now, that should do it."

Cathy watched Sylvia as she sat down. Her face looked tight and preoccupied, and dark shadows beneath her eyes spoke of her fatigue. "Sylvia, are you sure you didn't overdo it today?"

"I'm sure." But as she said it, she averted her eyes.

"So what did you find out at the doctor?"

Sylvia's smile faded. Pink blotches colored her neck. "Just a bad case of anemia. That's what's causing me to be so tired and weak."

"What do they do for that?" Tory asked.

"Iron and vitamins. I'll be all right in no time."

Cathy laughed. "Well, what a relief! I was worried it was something more serious."

Brenda looked as if she didn't quite buy that diagnosis. "Are they sure that's all?"

Sylvia grew quiet and looked down at her fingernails. "Well ... not completely."

Cathy sat up straighter. "What is it, Sylvia?"

Sylvia snapped her face back up, forcing a smile. "Well, you know how doctors are. If they'd stopped at the anemia, it would have been just fine with me. But no, they have to keep looking until they find something else."

"What did they find?" Dread flattened Cathy's voice.

Sylvia picked up her glass and a napkin, wiped the dampness off of it. "It's probably nothing. I shouldn't have even told you. I'm not worried about it in the least."

Tory got off of the floor then and looked down at Sylvia. "And?"

"It's just that they found a lump in my breast."

"Oh, no." Tory's whispered words voiced what Cathy was thinking. But she told herself that it could be nothing. She'd had lumps in her own breasts, and they'd turned out to be nothing.

"Did you go for a mammogram?" Brenda asked.

"Sure did." Sylvia sipped her drink. "It's there, all right. I saw it myself."

"What are they going to do?" Brenda's voice held steady.

"Well, tomorrow I'm going for a biopsy. I'm really optimistic, girls. I mean, just think about it. I've got so much work to do in Nicaragua. The children need me so badly, and Harry ..." Her voice broke off, and she swallowed back her emotion. "I don't believe the Lord would afflict me with breast cancer right now, so it's not even something I'm worried about. I'm going to go for the biopsy, find out it's benign, then go on back to my work. I refuse to worry about it until I get the results."

"I had a lump in my breast once." Brenda's voice was too quiet to inspire confidence. "It turned out to be just a cyst. No big deal."

Sylvia nodded. "See? That's exactly what this is. I guarantee you."

But Cathy wasn't satisfied. "What did the radiologist say?"

Sylvia looked at her as if she'd been caught.

Cathy leaned her elbows on her knees and locked onto Sylvia's face. "I know you talked to the radiologist. Harry knows every doctor in town, and if anyone would get personal attention it would be the wife of a cardiologist who worked in this town for twenty-five years. So what did the radiologist tell you?"

She shrugged. "He just showed me the lump, that's all. There it was, smiling at us, right from the X ray. It was really very creepy."

Cathy knew from her own experience with breast lumps that the doctor could tell a great deal from the mammogram. Cancer had specific shapes and characteristics . . . She knew he would have an opinion.

But Sylvia stuck to her story.

"He just set me up for a biopsy and that was it. Now who wants a piece of pie? I'd like to say I made it myself, but I just went by Kroger and picked it up. My sweet tooth was really acting up, and I figured I'd lost enough weight that I could stand to stuff a few calories into me. I also bought some red meat so I could start getting the iron back into my blood. I cooked myself filet mignon for dinner."

Cathy looked from Tory to Brenda. They each had volumes written on their faces.

"Nothing for me, thanks," Tory said.

"Me, either." Cathy swallowed.

"Have you told Harry?" Brenda's question mirrored Cathy's thoughts.

Sylvia groaned. "I wish I could hold him off until I've gotten the biopsy back. But I guess there's no chance of that, because he knows I went to the doctor today. I really, really hate to make him worry."

"He's a doctor," Cathy said. "He can take it."

"Trust me. He's not that objective when it's his own family. I'll never forget when Sarah's appendix ruptured. You would have thought it was his fault somehow, that he should have seen it and prevented it. He hovered over her in the hospital for days, worried sick."

Sylvia got up and hurried to get the pie. "It looks good, girls. Sure you don't want some?" she called from the kitchen.

Cathy looked at Brenda, saw the worry in her eyes.

Tory's hand came up to her heart, and she sent a stricken look to both of them.

Sylvia fluttered back into the room with four slices. "You don't have to eat it. But one bite and you'll be a goner."

She took a bite and closed her eyes. "Mmm. This is the best thing I've ever put in my mouth," she said. "You girls don't know what you're missing. Cathy, come on and get a piece. Oh, I've missed American food."

Cathy took a piece, just to make Sylvia feel better, but as she ate, she couldn't help watching Sylvia and wondering what burden she hid behind her smile, refusing to share with them.

CHAPTER *Six*

*It was eight*when they finished praying together. Brenda walked out with Tory and Cathy, and all three seemed lost in thought as they crossed Sylvia's yard.

"She's keeping something from us," Cathy said. "I'm afraid the radiologist gave her some bad news."

Brenda locked her eyes on Cathy's face. "Would he really have been able to tell anything?"

"He could tell by the shape of the mass whether it looks like cancer. It's not one hundred percent accurate, of course, and in some cases it's nothing more than a guess, but it's an educated guess, and I know he told her something."

Brenda looked toward Sylvia's house, wondering if her friend sat in there, struggling with the fear and anxiety that she refused to share with them. "Why wouldn't she tell us?"

"Because she's Sylvia," Tory said. "She would think more of us than herself, and she wouldn't want to worry us."

Brenda felt helpless. "Wouldn't you think she'd need to talk?"

"Sure she does," Cathy said. "But she's not going to. Not if it gets us upset."

"Well, I hope she tells Harry."

Cathy shook her head. "She'll probably tell him as much as she told us. We really need to pray for her. And tomorrow, I'm going to close the clinic and go with her."

Tory nodded. "Good idea. She doesn't need to go through this alone."

As Cathy headed back to her house and Tory back to hers, Brenda stepped across her yard. David's light shone in the workshop, and she knew he was working late to make up for the time he'd lost working on the limousine. She opened the door and stepped in, smelling the scent of sawdust and lacquer. Her husband, with his red curly hair and freckled skin, stood over the cabinets he worked on, examining them with a critical eye.

"What do you think?" he said. "Is this my best work, or what?"

She ran her hand along the sandy wood. "I think your customer will be delirious."

"I think so, too. Maybe one of these days I'll make a set for us."

She laughed. "I'm not holding my breath. You've got too much paying work."

"Well, I can dream, can't I?"

She sat on one of the counters, watching him crouch down to screw the hardware onto the doors. "I was just over at Sylvia's."

"Nice having her home, isn't it? Too bad she can't stay. When's she planning to go back?"

"I don't know. She had a little disturbing news."

He looked up at her. "What was that?"

"They found a lump in her breast."

David unfolded from his crouch and stood up. "Oh, no."

"Yes. She's acting all upbeat about it, like she's not worried at all."

"But you know better."

"Yeah, I know better." Brenda slid off her perch. "The doctor says her fatigue and weakness are caused by anemia. But it worries me a little, David."

"Why?"

"Because if they're wrong, and anemia is not the thing causing her fatigue and weakness, then maybe she does have cancer, and if it's already affecting her that way, it could be really advanced."

"You're borrowing trouble," he said. "Who was it that said today has enough trouble of its own?"

She smiled. "Jesus."

"Oh." He turned around and fiddled with the tools behind him, got what he needed, and squatted back down. "Never thought you'd hear me quoting the Bible, did you?"

She didn't answer him. There was no point. "Well, I guess I'd better get inside and see if the kids did the dishes."

He got up and pressed a kiss on her lips. "You okay?"

"Yeah." She laid her face against his chest, and he closed his arms around her. "I'm a little concerned, that's all. But I'll pray for her tonight, heavy-duty prayers. God will listen."

He didn't respond, just turned back to his work as Brenda left the building and walked across the grass to her house. She whispered a quiet prayer that she knew was familiar to God's ears. "Take the veil from his eyes, Lord. Please help him to see."

The fact that God did not answer immediately didn't daunt her at all. He hadn't for the many years that she'd been praying for David. She knew one day the prayer would be answered. It had to be, in God's timing. God had promised that anything she asked according to his will would be done. Saving David would glorify the Lord, so how could it not be in his will? There were no ifs, ands, or buts about it. She only wished the Lord's timing was more like her own.

CHAPTER *Seven*

Later that night, Cathy found Mark sitting at his computer. She leaned in his doorway. "What are you doing?"

He looked at her over his shoulder. "He influences you too much."

"What? Who does?"

"Steve."

She sighed and pushed off from the doorway. "Of course he influences me. He's my husband."

Mark kept typing. "But he's not always right. Sometimes he could be wrong, you know."

She knocked some wadded clothes off the edge of his bed and sat down. "Mark, we're a team now. We're married. He's my husband. He's your stepfather."

"But he's not my real father." Mark kept his eyes on the monitor. "I have one of those, and he happens to like my ideas."

Again she restrained herself from making a deprecating comment about her ex-husband's wisdom. "That's fine, Mark, and we'll look into it, okay? I just need some more information. We need to think this through and pray about it."

"I have been praying about it," he said. "I really have."

"For how long?"

He finally turned away from the computer and faced her. "Since I've been home, okay? Since it's gotten so close to school starting." He got up and kicked his way through the clothes on his floor. He had only been home a week. She couldn't imagine how he'd already accumulated so much laundry.

"I really do want to have a plan, Mom. But there he is, telling you what to think, what to do . . . and what *I* need to be doing. It's just not right."

"It *is* right," she said. "Mark, he's the head of this household now."

Mark grunted. "The head of the household? Mom, it was just you before. You were the head of the household, and we did just fine."

"That's because I didn't have a husband. But now that I do, he's the leader."

"But that doesn't even make sense, Mom, because he's not our real father. He's not supposed to be *my* leader."

Cathy wasn't sure how to respond to that. The Bible was clear on the marriage roles—it just didn't address stepfatherhood. "Mark, you know from all the time he invested in you while you were in jail that he cares about you. Don't you know that?"

"Well, yeah. But that's different. He can care without being so hard-nosed."

"He just wants things to go well for you."

"Things will go well for me, if he lets me get my GED and do what I want."

"Doing what you want is what got you in jail in the first place."

"But I'm not like that anymore, Mom! You know I'm not. I've changed. I'm a Christian now. I have a purpose. And I'll never get within ten feet of any kind of drugs again. I'm not ever going back to jail, and I can promise you that."

"I believe you, honey." She sighed and set her hands on her knees. "I don't want you to worry. It's going to be all right. We'll work all this out. We just don't want you to waste your life."

"You can be a worthwhile person without going to college, Mom."

"I just don't know why you're in such a hurry to grow up."

"I already *have* grown up."

He had a lot to learn, but Cathy didn't want to tell him so. Instead, she reached over and gave him a hug. "I'm really, really glad you're home."

"I am, too." He kissed her cheek. "And don't get me wrong. I do like Steve. I'm glad you married him. He's good for you. I just wish he'd stay out of it when we're talking about me."

"He's not going to stay out of it, Mark. He's a wise man and I admire him and trust him. I welcome his input. I wish you would, too."

"I do to some extent," Mark said, "but he's wrong this time. I'm trying to get my life back on track, but that doesn't mean I have to do it Steve's way."

Cathy got up and started back to the door. "I'll talk to him. We'll figure something out."

Mark followed her. "I think I might go and talk to Daniel."

She walked down the stairs with him, then stepped outside as he started through the garage. "Mark, are you sure you don't want to go back to home schooling with Brenda? Wouldn't it be fun to be learning with Daniel all day?"

Mark stuck his hands in his pockets and looked down at his feet. "Mom, the truth is that I'm too far behind. Daniel's way ahead of me academically, but he's way behind me in maturity."

"Why do you say that?"

"Because it's true. He was always smarter than me."

"Only because he's been home schooling all these years. You're smart too, Mark. You can catch up."

"Mom, I've been exposed to things that Daniel can't imagine. He's still just a kid, you know? But I'm not."

Cathy felt as if her heart had swollen too big for her rib cage, as the grief she'd struggled with for the past year ached inside her again. "I wish that wasn't so, Mark."

"I know you do. But it is. I've been in juvenile detention with kids who have been on drugs since they were four years old. Guys who've practically raised themselves. They've seen their dads and moms beat each other up. Most of them have been abused since they were toddlers. A lot of them are hard and they don't care about right or wrong. Some of them have killed people. You learn to tolerate different kinds of people ... to get along with people you might have been afraid of before. It makes *you* different. And Daniel can't understand that. I mean, who could?"

She didn't want to cry in front of him. "But don't you think your experience could help Daniel? And his academics could sure help you."

"Mom, twelve-year-old Joseph is probably ahead of me academically. I never applied myself in school. I never listened. I was just a washout. I can't start it all over and do it right. I might as well just make the best of it and move on."

"Mark, you're settling. I don't like for you to settle. You have too much potential."

"Mom, I'm not settling. I'm just trying to find my place. Work with me on this, okay? Trust me."

She crossed her arms and leaned against the garage wall. "I trust you, Mark, but I don't trust your judgment, not yet. You're too young."

"Well, at some point, you're going to have to try my judgment out," Mark said. "I'll see you later."

She watched him, struggling to hold back tears, as he crossed the street to Daniel's house. Behind her, the screen door squeaked open.

Steve came out and slid his arms around her waist. "Is everything all right?"

She leaned back against him. "Yeah, I just think you might have been a little too hard on him."

He let her go and she turned around and saw the tension tightening through him. "Me, too hard? What did I do?"

"I think maybe you expect too much of him too soon. I think Annie's right. We need to cut him a little slack."

"I'm willing to cut him some slack. I just don't want him to make another mistake."

She slipped her fingers through his belt loops and drew him closer.

"Maybe we can't really keep him from doing that. I mean, as long as he doesn't go out there and ruin his life, maybe we need to let him make a little mistake or two."

"We're not talking about a little mistake or two," Steve said. "Dropping out of school could be a life-altering decision."

"Steve, a GED is not like dropping out. It's not that easy. He'll probably have to go to school and study for it. And he could still get into the community college here. Lots of colleges accept GEDs. If he does well in that, he could go on to a four-year college."

He picked up a weed eater leaned against the wall and hung it on its hook.

"I'm afraid he won't *want* to go to college. I have a bad feeling that if we let him drop out of school to get his GED, he's going to wind up getting a job and he's going to think he's making a fortune when he's only making a little above minimum wage." He set his hands on his hips. "And you know what worries me the most? I worry that he won't get a job at all, that he'll just want to hang around here all the time and do nothing."

"Well, what would be so wrong with that for a few weeks? He had a really bad year."

"But coddling him now is going to undo whatever jail did for him. I don't want to see you do that." He picked up Tracy's bike and took it to its assigned place on the other side of the garage.

"He's become a Christian, Steve. He's changed."

"But that doesn't mean he's all of a sudden going to have good judgment and wisdom coming out his ears."

She didn't know why he couldn't see things the way she did. Tears sprang to her eyes. "I know that. Don't you think I know that?"

"Well, you act like we need to do everything he wants."

She crossed her arms. "I'm just trying to show a little compassion. You remember that, don't you? Compassion?"

Her comment stung him, and she saw his face shut down. "That was low. Just because I'm the voice of reason, suddenly I'm devoid of compassion?"

"The voice of reason?" she asked. "Come on, Steve. What am I the voice of? Stupidity?"

"No. I'm just saying that you're thinking with your heart instead of your head."

"Which is exactly what *you* do when you're dealing with Tracy. It's a little different when it's *my* child involved."

Now he was insulted. "I don't do that with Tracy. I'm treating your kids exactly the way I treat mine."

She let out a sarcastic laugh. "Think again. I don't see that."

His face twisted with indignation. "What have I done? Give me an example."

"She threw a napkin and hit me in the face, and you didn't even bat an eye. If one of my kids had done that and hit you, you'd have been all over them."

He shook his head with disgust. "She was just playing. Give me a break, Cathy. What do you want me to do? Beat her?"

"I'm just saying that it's a double standard. You want to think that you're treating the kids the same, but you're not."

"Besides, Tracy wouldn't have done that if your kids hadn't started it. And while we're on the subject, it does concern me that she's picking up some of your kids' behavior. It's hard to punish her when she's seen your kids do so many of the same things."

"Oh, brother." She turned away. "This conversation isn't really going anywhere. I can see it going downhill from here."

He kicked a skateboard out of his way. "Not one of our better moments."

Cathy tried to keep her voice steady. "Maybe we'd better just cool down and talk later."

"Good idea."

Steve stormed into the house and slammed the door behind him. He headed for the bedroom.

"You do that again, I'm taking the door off the hinges!" Cathy yelled.

When he didn't respond, she burst through the screen door again and slammed it harder than he had.

But it didn't help her anger or her sense of injustice. And she wasn't sure if anything would.

CHAPTER *Eight*

Sylvia waited until nine o'clock to make sure that Harry was home from the clinic. León, Nicaragua, was on the same time zone as Breezewood, so she knew that he would be waiting for her call. He usually worked very late, treating all the poverty-stricken people who came to him for help. By now, he was probably unwinding, eating his dinner and reading his Bible, basking in the quiet. He also probably worried about her.

She dialed the number, listened for the ring, then heard Harry's voice. "Hello?"

"Hi, honey. How was your day?"

"Blessed," he said, as he always did. "Any better and I'd have to be twins. So tell me about your doctor's appointment. How did it go?"

"It was fine." She had practiced this phone call, and kept her voice level, just as she'd rehearsed. "Everyone at the hospital said to tell you hello."

Harry wasn't easily distracted. "What did he find, Sylvia?"

She drew in a deep breath. "Well, he found that I'm anemic. Said that was the reason for the fatigue."

"Anemia?" She could tell he wasn't satisfied with that. "I could have found that myself."

"Yeah, if you had a lab. And technicians to work in it."

"So that's all it was, huh?" He still didn't sound convinced.

Sylvia thought of saying yes, that was all it was, and switching the conversation from her defective body to the children she missed so much. But he had a right to know. "Harry, there was one other thing."

He got quiet, and she knew he braced himself. She wasn't sure if he needed to or not.

"When he was examining me, he found a lump in my breast."

Silence hung on the other end of the line. Sylvia hurried to fill it in. "He sent me for a mammogram. Jim Montgomery was the radiologist. He sends his regards. Says he's really missed you over at the golf course. His daughter's getting married next month."

Harry clearly wasn't interested in Jim's daughter's nuptials. "Sylvia, what did he say?"

"He showed me the lump, upper outer quadrant on the left breast."

"And?"

"And . . . I'm going for a biopsy tomorrow. No big deal. It's probably nothing."

Silence hovered over the line. "Honey, it's going to be all right. God's in control."

He cleared his throat. "I need to come home. I want to be there."

"That's ridiculous. Honey, I'll have the results in a day or two. It's probably nothing."

"Sylvia, I don't think I have to remind you that your mother died of breast cancer. You're at high risk. I should have seen it coming. I should have made you get mammograms while we were here. You could have gone to Managua to get one. It was important, but I just let it go."

"Harry, you are not responsible for my body. I'm a grown woman. I should have known to get mammograms, but we've been busy. The Lord understands that. I think I would know if my body was betraying me that way. I'd have some sense of it, you know? Some premonition or intuition that things weren't right."

"Sylvia, you know better than that. It's not like your body sends warning messages to your brain. Not in every case, at least. Not this way."

"I just don't think it's anything to worry about."

Harry's voice quivered slightly. "I would still like to be there. I could catch a plane tomorrow morning."

"Harry, I won't let you do that. I want you to stay right there and go on with your work, and in a few days I'll be there to join you."

Silence again. "You're not going to keep anything from me, are you? If I think that for a minute, I'll be on the phone calling every doctor who has anything to do with this."

Sylvia sighed. "You're going to do that anyway, Harry. You know that."

When he didn't deny that, she laughed softly. "I have a positive attitude, honey. Just like you've always told your patients to have. I'm not going to let this get me down. There's no reason for it. When we get the results, we'll find out it was no big deal. I don't intend to waste my time worrying. I'm having too much fun being back."

"I want to pray for you, Sylvia. Right now, before another minute passes."

"Okay, Harry."

She heard the silent prelude to the prayer, as Harry prepared his heart for speaking to the Lord. He always prayed the way the Israelites entered the tabernacle. He stopped at the bronze altar to deal with his sins, then washed in the cleansing water of the brass laver, then slowly approached the Holy Place . . .

"Lord, you know what's going on with my beloved bride . . ."

Sylvia swallowed the tears in her throat, glad he couldn't see her. She listened as her husband lifted her up to God's throne, laying her on the mercy seat.

When he said amen, she could hardly speak. With great effort, she forced her good-bye to sound upbeat and normal.

But when she got off the phone, she sat there a moment, staring down at it, wondering what would happen if indeed this lump in her breast proved to be malignant, as Jim suggested it could be. Would she be able to have quick surgery to remove it, then return to her work in León? Or would their ministry have to be shut down altogether? She couldn't fathom the idea that God might want them to come back home, not after it took so much for her to leave in the first place. Not after she'd given her life so totally to the work God had given her.

As she got ready for bed, she walked through her house, thankful that they hadn't sold it in all the months that they'd tried. It was a comfort to be here, back on Cedar Circle, sur-rounded by people who loved her. Cathy had called after their prayer meeting tonight and insisted on driving Sylvia for her biopsy. What a worrier. Yet she was glad for the offer. It would make things easier.

No, she wouldn't worry, she told herself as she climbed into bed. She was too tired to worry. She could do that tomorrow.

Exhausted, she fell off to sleep, but she dreamed of doctor's offices and hospital gowns . . .

At two A.M., she woke up and stared at the night. The clock ticked out its passing seconds, its red numbers glowing. She turned it around so she couldn't see.

Her mind wandered to the immediate future. Would she have to have surgery? She had planned on visiting her daughter and holding that grandbaby one more time before returning to Nicaragua. Would she have that chance now? She mentally tallied the commitments on her calendar. She had planned to meet with the realtor, to talk about lowering the price on the house, in hopes of making it sell. She wanted to be back in León by August fifteenth, when they planned the big work day to renovate the church that had been damaged in the hurricane. Until now, they hadn't had the supplies to do it, but recent donations had made it all possible. She'd planned to take some of the older children from the orphanage and let them help paint. They were all looking forward to it.

Maybe if she did have to have surgery, she could fly back to León for the work day, then come back and have the surgery done afterward.

But would it be wise to wait? If she did have cancer, was it growing with every passing moment? Should she get it ripped out of her before it spread?

She lay her hand on the offending breast, mashed it, and tried to feel the lump. Had her breast betrayed her? Was it her enemy now? Would she have to have it removed to keep it from killing her?

What would that kind of surgery mean? Pain ... difficulty lifting her arm ... emotional upheaval ... frustration at having to find a prosthesis to wear over a healing wound, so she wouldn't be lopsided and call attention to herself ... self-pity and anxiety about her husband's disappointment that one of his favorite parts of her body would be gone? And if the truth were known, it was probably one of *her* favorite parts, too.

Or would that be the least of it? Surgery on other organs? Chemotherapy?

Would the surgery be the beginning of her death, or the start of her cure? Would she go downhill from here, through a form of hell, before she came out on the other side?

She thought of getting up, turning on the light, and beginning her day, just to banish these thoughts from her mind. But she wanted ... needed ... to sleep, so that she could cope with the day ahead of her. She didn't want to be tired and emotional and fall apart when the doctor told her the results.

It looks like it's malignant.

She turned to her side, fluffed her pillow, and pulled the covers up to her chin. Would she handle his answer with dignity and faith, or would she fall apart and feel sorry for herself and whine to everyone who would listen? She'd always been fairly healthy. How would she behave as a sick person? Would she get angry and bitter, or would she accept this as one more of the human trials God warned us of, another offshoot of the Fall? Would the Lord allow her to get well so that she could continue to bear fruit, or did he intend to bear fruit through her death?

Finally, she did get up and went into the kitchen, flicking on lights as she went. She poured herself a glass of cold water, then sat at the kitchen table, staring down at it.

She recalled the Scripture about having not because you ask not, and asking with wrong motives. Did she have wrong motives? Would those hinder her prayers?

She started to examine them, desperate to find any unrighteous reason for her prayers not to be heard. Why did she ask God to take this from her? Was it because of the inconvenience and pain and illness it would bring to her life? Was it because she loved this world more than him? Was it because she tried to hold herself out of God's reach, refusing to trust him with her life, whatever happened?

Was it because she wanted to see her children grow into mature adults? Wanted to attend her grandchildren's school plays? Was it because she didn't want her children to suffer?

Or was it because of the children at the orphanage, who had so few people in the world who loved them? Was that a selfish motive?

Or was it because of Harry? Didn't she trust God with her children, her husband, her life?

She examined those motives, wearily trying to find some fault within them. They were human, normal motives, borne of uncertainty. Didn't God understand?

She asked the Lord to show her what lay in her heart. She asked him to forgive her for the selfish motives, the ones that were more for her than for God's kingdom and his plan. Then she asked him to let the tests come out negative for cancer.

"Let it be a wake-up call," she whispered. "I'll get my annual mammograms from now on, and exercise and eat better and give up Nutrasweet and sugar and flour and whatever else I have to."

But she still prayed without confidence, because she understood God's sovereignty, that his ways were not her ways.

"Not my will, but thine be done," she made herself say. Then she added quickly, "But please don't have it in your will to do this to me."

She went back to bed, curled up under the covers that gave her some comfort, and tried to put these things from her mind.

Be anxious for nothing . . . She knew better than to let herself wake up worrying in the wee hours of morning. But knowing better didn't always make it so. Sometimes fear came in before the morning. It was fear of the unknown, mostly. Fear of what lay beyond the certainty.

Finally, as daylight seeped in through the window blinds, she checked her alarm. One hour before it would go off. Slowly, she drifted back into sleep, before she had to get up and face what the day held.

CHAPTER *Nine*

I don't need the hand-holding, but I appreciate the company." Sylvia smiled at Cathy as she drove. "We can have lunch afterward."

"Sounds good to me. And I'm not coming to hold your hand. I want you to hold mine."

Sylvia laughed. "You're not worried about this, are you?"

Cathy shrugged. "A little. What did Harry say?"

"Oh, he wanted to drop everything and fly home. I told him not to, that there's no reason to panic until we get the results of the biopsy. Then I'll be flying to him."

Her bravado seemed to lighten Cathy's spirits, but when they reached the doctor's office, Sylvia's own spirits began to flag. She looked around at the others in the waiting room, wondering who there might have a tumor, who was having a biopsy, who had already gotten the results, whose life would be forever changed. Her hands felt ice cold again, so she slipped them under her thighs.

Cathy seemed to have thoughts of her own swirling through her mind, for she didn't bother to pick up a magazine or strike up a conversation.

This was craziness, her pretending not to worry, when she wasn't fooling anyone. She needed to come clean, she thought, and be honest with Cathy. "Have I ever told you that my mother died of breast cancer when she was about my age?" she said in a low voice.

The alarm in Cathy's eyes was unmistakable. "No, Sylvia, you've never told me that."

"She did. I don't bring that up because I think that it means I have it. I feel sure that my body would have told me if I had something terrible like that, but it does seem relevant, doesn't it?"

"You've told the doctor, haven't you?"

"Yes." She breathed in a deep breath, let it out hard. "The thing is, I've known I was at high risk for getting it myself. I don't know why I let it go for the past couple of years."

Cathy took her hand. "You're cold."

"Freezing."

"It's nerves, you know. You're not as tough as you act."

Sylvia started to laugh, and Cathy joined her.

Sylvia closed her other hand over Cathy's. "Let's talk about lunch. Something beyond this biopsy."

"Okay. Where do you want to go?"

Sylvia thought for a moment, trying to picture herself and Cathy relaxing over a chef salad. "Alexander's. I've been wanting to go there."

"Alexander's it is. And you'll have to have steak, you know."

"Why is that?"

"Well, we need to build your blood back up, get some iron pumping through your veins."

Sylvia nodded.

A nurse came to the door and Sylvia looked up. "Sylvia Bryan," the woman called. Sylvia didn't move. She looked at Cathy, and Cathy gave her a reassuring look and patted her knee. Finally, she leaned over and grabbed her purse.

"Guess I'll see you in a little bit."

"I'll be praying."

A little while later, Sylvia returned to the waiting room. "That was easy," she said.

Cathy looked up at her. "Any results?"

"No. They said tomorrow."

Cathy grabbed her purse. "Okay. How do you feel?"

"Fine right now. The local anesthetic hasn't worn off yet."

"And emotionally?"

Sylvia examined her own heart. "Well, I can't say I won't think about it again until the results come . . . but let's just have lunch and not talk about it."

"Okay," Cathy said. "Whatever you say."

At the restaurant, Cathy accommodated Sylvia's wish to avoid the subject of cancer, and told her instead of the fight she and Steve had had last night. "It's not like the marriage is going badly." She stirred more butter into her potato. "I'm really happy with Steve. I love him and I love Tracy, and I think things are going well . . . basically . . . but I can't help wishing that he'd go easier on Mark. He's trying to be Mark's father, but Mark doesn't appreciate it much. He's having trouble adjusting to coming home to a different family, and all of a sudden having to do what Steve says. I'm in the middle, you know, like I'm being torn in two."

"Nobody said it was going to be easy." Sylvia set her fork down. "Marriage never is. And a blended family is a lot harder than a normal marriage."

"Tell me about it." Cathy took a bite, shaking her head. "The thing is, Steve expects me to make my kids act just the way he wants them to, but then he overlooks the things that Tracy does. Don't get me wrong, she's not bad. But occasionally he needs to call her down, or punish her even. But he doesn't even notice it. It goes right past him. Yet he notices *everything* my kids do. He knows how Mark has changed and he knows what a struggle he's going through since he got out of jail. He knows that Mark is trying to decide exactly where he fits back into this world. It's not easy for him. But he just doesn't seem to understand that I need to give Mark a little more time. And he got his feelings hurt last night when I asked him to go a little easier. I don't know why it has to be so hard. Why can't we just love each other's kids the same?"

"Because you're not really Tracy's mother and he's not really your kids' father."

Cathy studied her potato. "I wish there was some magic key to having a happy second marriage, but if there is, I don't know what it is."

"Oh, there is one." Sylvia dug into her salad. "It's the same key to having a successful *first* marriage."

Cathy set her fork down and leaned back. "Okay, hit me with it."

Sylvia smiled. "It's easy. Die to yourself."

Cathy's eyes narrowed. "Die to myself?"

"That's right. Die to yourself. As soon as you and Steve each figure that out, your marriage will be a success."

"Well, what does that mean?" Cathy asked. "How do you die to yourself?"

"You decide that the other person's needs are more important than your own. If there's ever a question between your doing what you want and your doing what *he* wants, you do what *he* wants."

"Wait a minute. That doesn't sound like happiness. It just sounds like a lot of sacrifice."

"Well, sure, it's sacrifice. That's what marriage is about."

Cathy opened a pack of butter and dropped the square onto her plate.

"All right, sacrifice, maybe. But it's not supposed to be martyrdom. I mean, how far do you go in fulfilling his needs? Do you not eat or sleep or buy anything for yourself?"

Sylvia dabbed at her mouth with her napkin. "Cathy, you know better than that. I'm not talking about lying down like a doormat and inviting him to walk all over you. The fact is, you married a man who is not going to do that anyway. But he is the head of your household, biblically speaking, and when there's a question of your will against his will, you need to let him win."

"What if he's wrong?"

"Well, you pray for him every day," Sylvia said. "You pray that God will guide him, that he'll have a heart that's fertile and teachable, and that he'll listen to God's prompting."

Cathy crossed her arms and tipped her head. "That didn't answer my question. I asked you what if he's wrong? How do I submit to him ..." Her voice was rising, and she looked around, wondering if anyone had heard. Quickly, she lowered it. "How do I submit to him if he's flat wrong?"

"Easy." Sylvia took a drink of her iced tea and brought her eyes back to Cathy. "Watch Brenda. She's been submitting to David for years, and he's often wrong. Most of the time she lets him lead. But when it comes down to doing his will or God's will, she goes with God. It's really simple."

"But I can't say that Steve's going against God. He's just mistaken. Misguided. *Wrong*." She took a few more bites, as she thought through what Sylvia was telling her. "That dying to yourself stuff is hard, Sylvia. Who wants to die?"

"No one does," Sylvia said, "but I'm telling you, that's the key. You have to die to yourself if you want to be happy in a marriage. Period."

The advice only frustrated Cathy more. She tried to visualize what the advice meant, but it evaded her. She told herself it didn't matter.

The important thing was that she had gotten Sylvia's mind off of her biopsy, at least for a little while.

CHAPTER *Ten*

The night of the church program came with a flurry of activity at the Dodd house. Brenda lined Joseph, Leah, and Rachel up in her bathroom, and applied the heavy makeup that would make their fair skin look less pale under the harsh lights.

Joseph had a strange look on his face. "I'm nervous. I might throw up."

"You're not going to throw up." Brenda wiped her makeup sponge under his eyes. "You're going to do it just like you've done at rehearsal, and you'll be wonderful."

Leah stood in front of the mirror, spraying her spiked hair. "This is so embarrassing," she said.

David stood, grinning, in the doorway. "What is?"

"That Rachel and I have to be Spencer's entourage. Like we'd really follow around some eight-year-old kid like we were in love with him."

"He's dressing like Elvis," Brenda told David. "He's so cute. And Leah and Rachel have to follow him around like groupies."

"Okay, you've got to videotape this for me," David said.

Brenda shook her head and went for the blush. "David, I can't. I'm helping backstage."

"Then let Daniel do it."

"He's working the lights. I'm sorry, honey, but if you want to see it, you'll have to come." She brought the blush brush to Joseph's cheeks, but he jerked away.

"Huh-uh, Mama! You can't put that on me!"

"Why not? I'm just trying to give you a little color."

"I'll look like a girl!"

"Joseph, all actors wear makeup."

"Not me," he said. "This mud all over my face is bad enough, but I do not want all that pink stuff on my cheeks."

Rachel gave Joseph an assessing look. "Mama's right. You need contour, Joseph. Here, let me do it."

Joseph grabbed the brush out of his mother's hand so Rachel couldn't get it. "I'm finished, Mama. I have all the makeup I need. Please don't let her touch me."

Brenda laughed and took the brush back. "All right, Joseph. Go put on your suit, and be careful not to get the makeup on your white shirt."

She left the girls primping in the bathroom and grinned up at David. "This is going to be some kind of night."

"I can't believe there's no one who can tape this. What about Tory and Barry? If Spencer and Brittany are in it, surely they'll be videotaping."

"They might. But Tory's helping backstage, too. And I think Barry is helping with the props."

She stuck her head in Joseph's room and saw him carefully unbuttoning the white shirt on its hanger. He already had his pants and shoes on, and she saw the thick scars from his heart transplant on his chest. Stepping into the room, she helped him get the shirt on without getting makeup on his collar.

"I can't wait to get this stuff off my face."

"You can go right from your curtain call to the sink," Brenda said.

David grew quiet as the activity grew more frenzied, and by the time she had loaded everyone into the van, she could see the dejection creeping over him.

He'd made his choice not to come, she thought, and as she backed out of the driveway and left him standing alone on the porch, she tried to silence the yearning in her heart. He was missing some of the major moments in his children's lives. Their baptisms, their choir solos, their testimonies, their Bible drills, their plays . . . All because they happened within the walls of a church. In the interest of upholding his principle not to participate in church events at all, he had violated his principle to support his children in the most meaningful events of their lives.

But he didn't see it that way.

As she drove the chattering children to church, she prayed that the Lord would work in David's heart tonight, and help him to realize what he was missing.

David made himself a sandwich and tried to watch a ball game, but his mind kept drifting to his children.

The blueprint of the limousine lay on the coffee table, and he picked it up and wondered how it would work. Would it roll the way it was supposed to? Would it hold together? Would it add to the program, or detract from it?

He set the picture down and thought how excited the kids would be when they came home tonight. Daniel's pride at a job well done, Leah and Rachel's giggles at the way the congregation would probably respond to Spencer's Elvis impersonation, Joseph's funny stories about everything that went wrong on stage. They would remember this night for decades. When they came home years from now, with their spouses and children, they would sit around the table talking about tonight's event with fond memories.

One of those memories would be that their father hadn't been there.

He hated being a disappointment to them, and he hated even worse disappointing his wife. But he was an honest man, and he didn't believe in pretending to be something he was not. For him to walk through the doors of a church, when he'd vowed years ago never to do it again, would be like betraying himself.

He thought of how cruelly his own church had treated his mother and him, when his father, the pastor, had run off with the organist. Instead of loving them through it, helping them, and praying for them in their grief, the church had treated his mother like she had somehow caused her husband's infidelity. They had asked them to leave the parsonage to make room for a new pastor.

He and his mother had taken a garage apartment, and his mother had gone back to work. He'd spent many long, angry hours alone in a stuffy apartment, praying for his father to come back. But those prayers had never been answered.

When his mourning played out in anger and childish rage, the church had proclaimed him "possessed." They'd insisted on casting the demons out of him. That, too, had failed according to them.

He remembered those tragic, mixed feelings of fear that they were right, that hateful demons occupied his mind and heart, that God had turned away from him for some unknown reason, just as his father had abandoned him.

Those feelings fed him for the next couple of years, until he finally reached the point of not believing anymore. The God of his father, his mother, and his church did not exist, he had decided. And if he didn't believe in God, then he didn't have to believe in the demons, either. In some ways his atheism had set him free from the burden the church had placed upon him. But he'd never been able to fill the void left in his soul.

He'd vowed never to return to church—any church—and when Brenda became a Christian, he held to his vow. When she'd convinced him to let her raise their children in the church, he'd remained faithful to that vow.

Now he wondered if keeping that promise was such a noble thing after all.

He hated being left out. He wanted to see his son star as the Good Samaritan. He wanted to see Leah and Rachel following Elvis across the stage. He wanted to see Daniel doing magic with the lights.

He wanted to be a part of this memory.

He took his plate to the sink, set it down, then headed back to the bedroom. Quickly, he changed his clothes, then got his keys.

His hands trembled as he drove to the church. The parking lot was full, so he parked on a side street. The small sanctuary would be packed, he thought. Parents and grandparents had probably come to laugh and applaud at their own children's roles.

He hurried to the front door, hoping he hadn't missed too much. He opened the door, and heard the opening song that Joseph, Rachel, and Leah had sung for weeks around the house.

He stepped in and saw the colorful set and all the children in their various costumes. Leah and Rachel stood behind Spencer, who was hamming it up in a white sparkly Elvis jumpsuit, while Joseph stood on the other side of the stage, dressed like a businessman. He glanced up at the landing at the back of the room, where Daniel sat, flicking switches and moving spotlights.

He slipped into the back pew and grinned as the play began with a boy on a skateboard, gliding across the stage, and gangsters coming along to beat him up and leave him for dead. The story of the Good Samaritan began.

David was glad he had come.

Brenda watched the show from behind the curtains on the side of the makeshift stage. The children were in top form. The butterflies in Joseph's stomach seemed to have settled, and he was hamming it up.

When the opening scene ended, Joseph rushed toward her.

"Mama! Dad's here. He really came!"

Brenda was sure Joseph was mistaken. The lights made it difficult to see the audience clearly. "Are you sure, honey?"

"Yes! He's sitting at the back."

Brenda peeked around the curtain, but the church was too dark.

The audience laughed raucously as Spencer strutted across the stage, Leah and Rachel prancing behind him, at least two heads taller than the small Elvis.

When Leah and Rachel's scene ended and they came behind the curtain, they both began to jump up and down. "Mama! Dad's here."

It must be true, Brenda thought. *Please let it be true!*

Tory scurried backstage to congratulate her son. He high-fived her, then accepted her fussy hug.

"Don't mess me up, Mommy. I have to go out for the end."

Tory laughed and let her son go. "Brenda, you didn't tell me David was coming."

Brenda swallowed the emotion in her throat. "He didn't tell *me*."

"Well, he's out there laughing his head off."

As Tory hurried back to her seat, Brenda touched her chest and whispered a heartfelt prayer of thanks. God had managed to get David through that door.

Maybe it was just the beginning.

CHAPTER *Eleven*

Sylvia was up before dawn, three hours before the doctor's office would open. Even after that, it could be hours before they called.

She made her coffee and took it outside.

Sitting on her back porch, she watched as the sun came up over the mountains, first in a gray light that slowly gave way to a pale blue, then to a bright blue, then to a burst of orange as day exploded. A cool breeze blew through her brown hair. She had let it grow too long in León, and the frosted color she had left with had slowly evolved into the brown she'd had growing up. It was easier to color over her gray with a solid color than to highlight it every few weeks. Sarah, her daughter, had sent her the L'Oreal products from the States every month or so. Getting her hair cut was one of the items on her agenda before she went back.

She swept it behind her ear and pulled her thoughts back to God's art. Whatever man tried to do was a poor imitation.

Everyone needed to see at least one Smoky Mountain daybreak to appreciate true art.

She went back in and refilled her coffee, checked the time. Only seven o'clock. She had to stop this. She couldn't sit here and wait . . .

She went to the front window and looked out on the driveway. That phantom paperboy who only communicated through an envelope in the Sunday edition had already left today's paper. Though their subscription had been canceled long ago, he'd left her one since she'd been home, no doubt hoping she'd resubscribe.

She went outside, up the lonely driveway, and retrieved it. She heard a door close and looked around, waiting to see who might be coming out.

Annie strode out of her house in a baggy shirt and a pair of shorts. Barefoot, she headed up her own driveway and grabbed the paper.

"Up early, Annie?" Sylvia called across the yard.

Annie started. "You scared me. I didn't expect anybody to be out here."

Sylvia crossed the grass. Annie's long brown hair looked as if she'd just gotten out of bed, and her eyes were sleepy and unadorned. She had seen Annie that way every morning for the year they'd been together in León. Her heart burst with love for the girl.

"I've missed you." She reached out and hugged her.

"Me too," Annie said. "I got so used to getting up early down there that I can't sleep late to save my life. It's just not right, you know? People my age are supposed to sleep till noon."

Sylvia laughed. "Well, since you're up, you want to go for a walk with me? Or did you have your heart set on reading that paper?"

Annie glanced down at the paper and raked her hand through her tangled hair. "No, I can read it later. Just let me go get my shoes on."

"I'll be on my back porch."

Sylvia watched as the girl ran back into the house.

"Thank you, Lord," she whispered. Annie was just what she needed today.

Annie bounced around the house a few minutes later, her hair brushed back into a ponytail and her tennis shoes on.

Her face was brighter than it had been moments before. "I'm ready. Where do you want to go?"

"I thought we'd walk out to the barn. I haven't been back there since we sold the horses. Then we can walk through the woods, unless it starts getting too hot."

"Hot?" Annie laughed as Sylvia came down from the porch. "This is nothing compared to where we've been. I can't wait for winter. I missed snow. Imagine if we could gather up all our kids from León and bring them here for the winter. Wouldn't they get a kick out of the snow?"

"Oh, that would be so much fun. I'd love to watch little Juan build a snowman. I read him *Frosty the Snowman* once. He was captivated."

Annie reached the barn before Sylvia and opened the door. "I wonder what they're doing today. It's Thursday, so they have art."

"Yeah, and music. They're working on their program. It's just a few days away."

Annie shook her head. "Man, I hate missing that."

Sylvia stepped into the barn and looked around at the empty stalls. It still smelled of horses and hay, even though the place hadn't been occupied for almost four years.

She went to the stall where Sunshine, her favorite horse, used to be.

"Do you miss the horses?"

"Sometimes." She rested her arms on the stall door. "But we sold them for a good cause."

"For Joseph's transplant." Annie's voice was soft, nostalgic.

"We would have had to sell them eventually, anyway, when we left the country."

Annie got quiet, and Sylvia realized that melancholy was setting in again. "Let's go walk and see what's in bloom."

They followed the old path where Sylvia used to ride her horse. The sun had grown bright, and dusty rays cut through the tree branches and cast a golden light on the path ahead of them.

"Look at that," Sylvia said. "'A light unto my path ...'"

"'A lamp unto my feet,'" Annie finished. "Maybe it's a sign."

Sylvia glanced over at her. "A sign?"

"Yeah." Annie broke off a branch and began peeling off its leaves. "For today. You know. The phone call you're waiting for."

Sylvia stopped and faced the girl. "How did you know I'm waiting for a call?"

"Well, I knew you were getting the results today. *I'd* be waiting." She dropped the stick and dusted her hands on her shorts. "I just meant that maybe God lit up our path like that to tell you something."

Sylvia smiled. "What, Annie? What is he telling me?"

"That whatever happens, you won't go into it alone. You won't be groping through the darkness. He'll light your way."

Sylvia looked at the path again. "Thanks, Annie. I think that's just what he's saying."

"I mean, I'm not expecting the news to be bad or anything," Annie said. "Not at all. It's probably going to be good news. I've just been a little nervous because you've been feeling so bad lately ... Bad enough to come home."

"It's anemia, Annie. That's probably all."

"Yeah, I know." But Sylvia knew she didn't believe that for a moment. Annie turned away, scanning the trees. She knew the girl was hiding tears, and for the first time she wondered if her worry for Sylvia was what had gotten her up so early today.

"Whatever the news is, I'll be okay," Sylvia said. "You know that, don't you?"

Annie still didn't look at her. "I know." She wiped her eyes, then quickly looked back toward the house. "Shouldn't we go back? It's probably almost eight by now. They could call."

Sylvia looked at her watch. Annie was right. "I guess so. The sooner I get that call, the sooner we can all breathe a sigh of relief and I can get back to León."

Annie's smile was strained. "Wish I could go."

They started walking back, slower than they'd come. "Are you excited about school, Annie?"

"A little. I'm looking forward to it, but I feel like I've left so much undone back in León."

"I know the feeling."

"I want to go back again," Annie said. "I'm going to start saving now."

"We'd love for you to come back."

"I would have just stayed, you know, but I missed my family and my friends. And I figured I'd never meet a guy if I stayed there. I really want to marry an American, and I wasn't likely to meet one there, unless I happened on a tourist."

"No, Annie, you did the right thing. You have plenty of time for the mission field if the Lord calls you to it."

Annie's grin was back as they emerged out of the woods. "Since I've been back, though, I've realized that I don't really like any of the guys I used to date. They're not right for me. I wonder what I ever saw in them."

Annie was growing up, Sylvia thought. She had learned to see her life through more mature eyes.

"I want a godly man, like Dr. Harry," she said. "Like Steve. A man who answers to God. That way I'll know he'll never cheat on me."

Sylvia knew Annie had a hard time trusting men because of her father's infidelity. Her family had been torn apart because of that.

But Annie would be okay. She was too precious to fall through the cracks, and Sylvia would never stop praying for her.

They got back to Sylvia's porch, and Annie hung back. "Well, I'd better get home before my mother starts wondering where I am. If she notices I'm not there, she'll think I was abducted by aliens or something."

Sylvia smiled. "I enjoyed our walk. Thanks for coming with me."

"Anytime." Annie gave her a hug. "I'll be praying for you today."

"Thank you."

Sylvia watched as the girl tromped across the yard and headed home.

Somehow, she didn't feel the heaviness she had felt earlier that morning. She felt equipped now for the wait that lay before her, because she knew that one of God's favorite children was praying.

It was after lunch before the phone finally rang. Sylvia snatched it up. Her hand trembled as she tried to punch the "on" button. "Hello?"

"Mrs. Bryan, this is Dr. Phillips' office." The woman spoke in a flat monotone. "Dr. Phillips would like to speak to you. Could you hold a moment, please?"

"Of course." She held her breath as her doctor came to the phone.

"Sylvia, hi." His voice was low, serious.

She swallowed. "Hi, Al. Any news?"

He sighed. "I'm afraid the mass in your breast is malignant."

It was as if she sat in an echo chamber, and that word reverberated around her. *Malignant. Malignant. Malignant.*

She tried to center her thoughts back on his words. Something about getting her an appointment with the surgeon, about possible mastectomy, about radiation and chemotherapy, but none of it registered. The word still rolled around in her head trying to plant itself. *Malignant. Malignant. Malignant.*

"Sylvia, are you listening?"

She cleared her throat. "Yes. What's my next step?"

He seemed to understand that she hadn't heard a word he'd said. "I'm making you an appointment with Dr. Jefferson. You remember Sam, don't you?"

"Yes, I remember him."

"He specializes in breast cancer surgery, Sylvia. He's the best in town. I'm going to try to get you in for tomorrow. As soon as I tell them who you are, that you're Harry Bryan's wife, I'm sure they'll get you right in."

"Yes. Thank you."

"Sylvia, I recommend that you go to the bookstore and get some books on this, try to understand what your different options might be so that when Sam recommends them you'll understand. And remember that breast cancer is usually pretty slow-growing, so you have time. You don't have to make a decision in the next few hours. You have time to get Harry home and to talk things over with him and get some second and third opinions."

The thought of telling Harry snagged her mind. He would have questions. He'd want details. What would he want to know? "Al, can you tell how bad it is?"

"I can tell you that the tumor looks to be about three centimeters. That's larger than I would have liked. It has poorly defined margins, which is also not a very good sign. I'll know a lot more when we get a pathology report on the tumor itself after it's removed, and Sam will probably want to take some lymph nodes." He paused. "Sylvia, are you all right?"

She ran her fingers through her hair, trying again to focus. "Yes," she said, "I'm fine. Thank you for calling, Al."

"No problem. Sylvia, I'll call Harry if you want me to. I can explain things to him."

"No, that's all right. I'll do it. I just don't want him to rush home. His work there is so important."

"Sylvia, he needs to come home. How much surgery you have is up to you and the doctor, but I wouldn't go through this alone. Harry wouldn't want you to. Tell him everything, Sylvia. Don't hold it back."

Her eyes stung with tears by the time she got off the phone, and she sat there staring into the air. Moments ticked by, and she didn't move.

The phone rang again, startling her.

"Hello?" It didn't even sound like her voice.

"Sylvia, it's Al again. I just wanted to let you know that Dr. Jefferson's office had a cancellation this afternoon. You can go at three o'clock if you'd like."

She nodded, as though he could see. "Yes, I might as well get this over with."

"I'm sure you'll have a lot of questions," he said. "I'd recommend that you take a tape recorder with you so you can remember everything later. You might take a friend, too, just to be there with you."

Her hand trembled as she brought it to her forehead. "I'm not ready to tell anybody yet. I'm going alone."

"Whatever you think is best. And, Sylvia, call me if you have any questions. Harry, too."

"I will."

She hung up the phone and decided that she didn't have time to stare into space. Her problem was in her breast, not her brain. She had a tumor, and it could be removed. She might not even need a mastectomy. Lumpectomies were just as successful these days. Maybe they could quickly pull it out on an outpatient basis, and she wouldn't have to have radiation or chemo or anything. The sooner she took care of it, the sooner she could return to Nicaragua and pick up with her work as if nothing had ever happened.

But as she prepared for her appointment she realized that that probably wasn't the case. *Poorly defined margins.* She knew what that meant from dealing with her mother's cancer. It meant that the cancer wasn't contained in a bubblelike wall. It had seeped out, into the tissue. It wouldn't be as easy to remove as it would if the margins were well-defined.

The phone sat on the desk before her, like a live being challenging her. She needed to pick it up and call Harry, but she knew he would panic and drop everything to come home. No, she needed more information before she called him. She would wait until after the appointment with Sam Jefferson. She looked in the mirror, struggling with the surprising anger that her body had betrayed her in such a way. Her intuition had failed her.

Pulling herself together, she drove her rental car to Radio Shack and bought a little handheld recorder to take with her.

The doctor's office felt like Montreal in January. Though it was August, and the thermometer outside read eighty-five degrees, Sylvia wished she'd worn her coat.

Sam Jefferson seemed pleased to see her. "How have you and Harry been?" he asked as he ushered her into his office.

"We've been fine." She took a chair while he settled behind his desk. She tried to keep her voice level, polite. "Working hard, though."

"Yeah? Harry practicing cardiology down there, or has he branched out?"

"He's more of a general practitioner now. He has a medical clinic that takes care of everything from sore throats to gangrene. He puts in about twelve hours a day. We've really come to love the people."

The doctor smiled and looked down at her chart. "Well, you guys really have guts doing what you're doing. I've thought of doing a medical mission trip. It sounds really rewarding."

"I'm sure Harry would love to have you come to León for a couple of weeks if you ever want to."

She was stalling. She knew that, but she wasn't sure she was ready to jump into this discussion. What if she couldn't handle the truth?

But they couldn't go on making small talk forever.

Finally he got around to the subject at hand. "Sylvia, I've looked over your X rays and your biopsy report, and as I see it, we have several options."

She got out her recorder, switched it on, and set it on the chair next to her.

"With many of my patients I offer the option of a lumpectomy or a partial mastectomy to preserve as much as we can of the breast. That's certainly an option for you, but because of the irregularity of your tumor's margins and the type of cancer cell it is, I can't recommend that. I would recommend a mastectomy."

Her stomach sank like lead. "My mother had a mastectomy over thirty years ago," she said.

"Well, the good news is that it doesn't have to be as bad as hers was. Back then, we did radical mastectomies, where we took the breast, lymph nodes from the armpit, and the muscles in the chest. Today we can do a modified radical mastectomy, where we leave the muscles alone. That makes the surgery less disfiguring and easier to recover from." He handed her a couple of books and pamphlets about mastectomy surgery. "These will explain the procedure in more detail and answer your questions."

"If I have a mastectomy, will that take care of all of it, or will I have to have chemo?"

"I'd recommend that you follow up with chemotherapy, especially if it's spread to your lymph nodes."

She thought of her mother with her bald head and paper-thin skin, suffering through intense nausea and weakness.

"You said options. What are the others?"

"Another option I'd recommend you consider is a bilateral mastectomy."

"Both breasts?" Her ribs seemed too small for her lungs, and she tried to catch her breath. "Why?"

"The fact that your mother died of breast cancer causes me some worry," he said. "A bilateral mastectomy would virtually ensure that you don't get future tumors in the contralateral breast."

Tears sprang to her eyes, but she fought them back.

"It's not absolutely necessary," he said. "As I said, it's just an option. Some women choose to do that to be safe, to prevent recurrence, or to prevent a new cancer from growing. But it's your call."

"Do you think the cancer has spread?"

"The undefined margins mean that it's spread into the tissue around it, but it could be confined only to the breast. The lymph nodes will tell us a lot."

Sylvia cleared her throat. "If I have a lumpectomy, it might get it all. Right?"

"Possibly. But you're not a good candidate for that, Sylvia. You'd be taking a chance."

"But if we found out it didn't get it all, we could always go back and do a mastectomy, couldn't we?"

"That's possible. Again, I don't recommend it."

Sylvia felt herself shrinking back into her chair. She suddenly wished she had waited until Harry could be with her. She tried to prop herself back up and sat straighter.

The room seemed to be moving, and Sam's face blurred.

"I don't know what I want to do yet," she said. "I have to think."

"Of course you do," he said, "and you can take a week or two to decide."

Sylvia got up and walked to the window, looked out. In the hospital courtyard, she saw children playing while their mothers sat and smoked cigarettes, the smoke rising on the breeze and disappearing.

"This is not a decision you need to make quickly. It's your body and your life. But my main concern right now would be trying to get as much of the cancer out of your body as possible so that any additional adjuvant therapy is easier and most successful. You need to talk it over with Harry and decide what you want to do. And if you'd like to get a second and third opinion, my secretary will help set those up for you."

She glanced back at the doctor, trying to remember what it was she'd wanted to ask. The questions just whirled through her mind and she couldn't settle on one.

"If you choose the mastectomy, we need to decide whether you'd like to have reconstruction surgery at the time of the mastectomy. Or you may want to wait until later when you're finished with your treatment, and then go back and do the reconstruction. You may even decide you don't want the reconstruction at all. Some women prefer to have their battle scars to remind them how hard they fought and how much they've overcome."

Sylvia had once believed that if anything like this ever came up in her life she would know quickly what to do. But everything seemed muddy and unclear.

He leaned forward on his desk, crossed his hands in front of his face. "I have to tell you, Sylvia, that the biopsy report shows that these are aggressive cancer cells."

"Aggressive?" She turned back from the window. "Really?"

"Yes."

Her hand came up to her breast. "But you said I had time. Two weeks, you said."

"You do. But we shouldn't wait longer than that."

She rubbed her face. "Well, I'd like it out now. Right this minute. Can you do it now?"

He smiled. "Take a little time, Sylvia. Get Harry home."

She wondered how she would sleep that night knowing that this monster called cancer moved aggressively through her body, conquering new territory, staking its claim.

The doctor gave her some books on breast cancer and instructed her to read them thoroughly before she made up her mind. She walked in a haze back to the secretary, her arms overloaded with the books and her purse and the legal pad she hadn't used and the tape recorder clutched in her hand. The woman started talking about second and third opinions, plastic surgeons, possible operation dates.

But Sylvia couldn't make her mind focus. She wished she had followed Al's advice and brought a friend with her today. Someone who could think clearly while her thoughts roller-coasted out of control.

Failing to make any appointments at all, she left the building and went to her car.

CHAPTER
Twelve

Sylvia didn't go straight home to call Harry or share her news with her friends. She had errands to run. She had to go to the post office, the bank, the cleaners. She had to get things done.

The post office wasn't busy, so she went right up to the counter and bought her stamps. As she walked back to the car, she breathed in the sweet mountain air. The breeze felt like freedom on her face, but she was anything but free. She got into her car and drove to the cleaners. *Malignancy, mastectomy, aggressive cancer cells . . .*

She shoved those words out of her mind and told herself that she wouldn't fall apart until she got home. She would finish her errand list.

She went to the counter at the cleaners, and the college girl behind it asked, "Name, please?"

"Sylvia Bryan," she said.

The girl checked her slips for Sylvia's name one by one under the B's, then turned the spinning rack and checked some more.

"Bryan?" she asked. "B-r-y-a-n?"

"Yes," Sylvia said. "Sylvia Bryan."

"I'm sorry. I don't find a Sylvia Bryan."

"I brought them in Monday." *After I found out I might have cancer*, she wanted to add. "You told me they'd be ready today."

"Just a minute. Let me check." The girl went to the back, then reemerged and punched on the computer. "What's your phone number?"

Sylvia gave her the number and waited, tapping her fingernails on the Formica surface. The girl disappeared for five minutes while Sylvia waited. *Malignant . . . mastectomy . . . aggressive cancer . . .*

The girl finally came back. "I'm sorry, Mrs. Bryan, but we seem to have misplaced your clothes. Could you tell me what they were?"

"A green dress, a black skirt, a pair of white slacks." Her voice broke off and she desperately tried to remember what else she had brought, but she couldn't concentrate on her wardrobe. Her mind kept lunging back to reconstructive surgery, chemotherapy, death. Her mouth started to tremble and her eyes filled with tears.

Horrified, the girl caught her breath. "I'm so sorry, ma'am. I'll go look again."

But Sylvia couldn't wait. She turned and ran from the building, got out to her car, closed and locked the door, and humped over her steering wheel.

She screamed out her rage and fury, then wept loudly for several moments. Finally, she pulled herself together enough to start the car.

She couldn't stop railing as she drove. "Lord, what are you doing? This wasn't part of the plan. I didn't even *want* to go to the mission field but you changed my heart, you made me want to go, and now that I'm there, now that it's my life, why would you take it from me? Why would you stop us in our tracks and bring our work to an end like this? I don't understand."

She wept as she drove home, praying all the way, and when she pulled into the cul-de-sac, she prayed that none of her neighbors were waiting outside. But that prayer wasn't answered either.

Cathy stood in her driveway. Sylvia drove past her, gave her a quick wave, then pulled into her garage and closed the door behind her.

CHAPTER
Thirteen

Cathy knew something was wrong when she saw Sylvia close herself in the garage. She never did that. Whenever Sylvia saw that anyone was out, she would get out of her car and walk down the driveway and spend at least a few minutes talking.

Cathy's stomach plummeted. She was certain Sylvia had gotten bad news.

She ran back into the house and called upstairs. "Annie? Annie, come down. I need you."

Annie bounced down the stairs. "What is it, Mom?"

"I need for you to come with me and baby-sit Tory's kids. I need to gather her and Brenda up, so we can go see what's wrong with Sylvia."

Annie's face changed. "Did she get her results?"

"I think she must have. She looked upset."

"Oh, Mom, you don't think it's cancer! Tell me it's not cancer. It couldn't be cancer."

"I don't know, Annie, but I need to get over there."

Cathy bolted out the door, Annie close on her heels. "Mom, please let me come with you. I've been praying so hard for her."

Cathy crossed the street and ran up Brenda's porch steps to ring the bell. "Annie, please. Tory will need a sitter so she can come without Hannah. She trusts you."

The door came open, and Joseph took one look at Cathy's face and yelled out, "Mama!"

Annie hadn't given up. "Mom, if it is cancer, what will happen?"

Brenda dashed to the door. "Cathy, what is it?"

"Something's wrong with Sylvia," she said. "She drove right past me and closed her garage. I think she got the results."

"Oh, no."

"We need to get over there. Annie's going to baby-sit for Tory."

Brenda burst out of the house. "Let's hurry."

As they crossed the empty lot between the Dodds' and the Sullivans' houses, Cathy glanced back at Annie. Tears were rolling down her face. Cathy stopped. "Oh, honey."

Annie came into her arms. "Mom, I'm scared. Nothing can happen to her. She's too special."

Cathy held her and stroked her hair. "It's going to be all right. Look, if you really want to, you can come with us. Tory could just bring Hannah with her . . ."

Brenda touched Annie's shoulder. "I could get Leah and Rachel to sit for Spencer and Brittany."

Annie considered that, then stepped back and wiped her eyes. "No. I'll do it. She really needs the three of you. I'd probably turn into a basket case and get her even more upset." She dried her hands on her jeans.

"Thank you, sweetheart. I'll come tell you the minute I leave her."

They headed into Tory's garage and knocked on the kitchen door.

She answered quickly—Hannah on her hip—and stared at the looks on their faces. "What is it?"

"We have to go to Sylvia," Brenda said.

Tory brought her hand to her mouth. Annie took the baby, and the three of them hurried on their way.

CHAPTER *Fourteen*

Sylvia knew who it was the moment the doorbell rang, but she wasn't up to talking to anyone. She tried to ignore the bell, but her neighbors weren't going away.

Finally she grabbed a Kleenex, blew her nose, dabbed at her eyes, and decided that she might as well get it over with.

She opened the door, and Cathy, Brenda, and Tory stood there looking intently at her as if they already knew the verdict. Unable to utter a word, she reached out to hug all three of them. They came into her arms and clung.

For the moments that they embraced, Sylvia was sure that they were the only thing holding her up, keeping her from collapsing completely.

"Have you told Harry?" Cathy asked as they each let go and stepped back to look at their friend.

"Not yet. I wanted to tell him first but I dread it so much. I'm going to have to have surgery in the next week or two. I've got so many decisions to make. This ruins everything, you know."

"What does it ruin, honey?" Brenda asked.

Sylvia walked away from her and started flipping through the mail that sat on the counter.

"Our mission work. Harry's going to want to rush home, and what's going to happen to the people who need him? And the children are expecting me back. I don't understand this." She threw the mail down and flattened her palms on the counter. "What is God doing?"

Her voice broke off and she pulled a chair out from the kitchen table, lowered into it. Her friends sat down, Tory and Cathy across from her, Brenda next to her.

"Sylvia, what exactly did the doctor tell you?" Cathy's voice was soft, careful.

Sylvia propped her forehead in her hand. "Cancer in the breast," she said. "Poorly defined margins. Aggressive cells. I have to decide whether to have a lumpectomy or a mastectomy, and what *kind* of mastectomy, or even a bilateral mastectomy . . ." She hated that they'd come when she was so upset. She'd wanted to be stoic, philosophical, gracious. "I'm sorry, girls. I don't mean to get you all upset. I handled myself really well in the doctor's office. I really did. And then I went to the post office and the cleaners." She hadn't handled herself well at the cleaners, but she didn't tell them so.

"You know, this really makes me sick, the way I'm responding. It's not at all what I would have envisioned."

"What in the world did you envision?" Tory asked.

"I pictured myself being tough and godly, taking it all with some sense of divine power working in my life. I thought I was grounded enough in my faith that I could accept whatever God decided to throw my way, that I wouldn't fall apart."

Brenda hugged her. "Honey, you haven't fallen apart. You've just been given the worst news of your life. You're supposed to cry."

Cathy took her hand. "Sylvia, what would you say if it was me, if I had just come home with a cancer diagnosis and I was crying? Would you think I was weak?"

Sylvia lifted her chin and took in a deep breath. "Of course not. I'd probably cry with you, and say something totally inane. I'd probably give you some platitude like 'This, too, shall pass,' or quote you Philippians 4:13: 'I can do all things through him who strengthens me.' And I'd tell you that God will never leave or forsake you, that I wouldn't either." Tears assaulted her again and she wiped them away. "But, please, I'm begging you—don't say any of those things to me."

Tory smiled. "They're all true, you know."

"I know," Sylvia said. "I know they're true, and I'll hold on to them as this progresses, but right now I'm angry and confused, and I have too many options, and I don't know what to do."

"Well, let's break it down," Cathy said. "One thing at a time. First, you need to call Harry."

Sylvia nodded. "I know. But this is going to be the hardest thing I've ever done. How will I convince him to stay there?"

Brenda got up and looked down at her. "Stay there? Sylvia, you *can't* convince him to stay there. He needs to be here with you."

"But his work is more important," Sylvia said. "Don't you understand? Some of those people would have died without him. They can't do without him."

"Somehow they can," Tory said. "Sylvia, they can do without him because God put this in your path right now. He didn't do it so you could go through it alone while Harry works for the Lord. There are times when our work has to stop and we have to deal with things that come into our lives. This is one of those times."

"You know he's going to want to come." Brenda handed her a box of Kleenex. "Don't give him a hard time about it. Just let him do what he needs to do."

Sylvia knew they were right. She tore a tissue out of the box. "Oh, I hate breaking Harry's heart. And I hate not being there to comfort him when he hangs up the phone."

Sylvia blew her nose again and grabbed another one to wipe her eyes. "Who would have thought? When I came home feeling tired and weak, who would have thought I had cancer?"

"Maybe Harry did," Brenda said. "He sent you home for tests, didn't he?"

"Harry never suspected cancer," she said. "Not in a million years. And it turns out that the fatigue and the weakness are not even about the cancer. It's stupid anemia."

"Well, be thankful for it," Cathy said. "It was what got you back here so they could discover the breast cancer. God is working."

Sylvia got up, putting distance between them. "I know I should be thankful. It's just hard right now. I guess I've got to call him. I can't put it off any longer. I know he's waiting to hear."

"Honey, do you want us to stay or go?" Cathy asked.

Sylvia stared at them all for a moment. Part of her wanted to deal with this alone in a dark closet where she could curl up on the floor and scream out her anger and misery and confusion. But she knew it was better for her if they were here to walk her through this.

"Why don't you wait in here and let me go call him in the bedroom? I might need you when I come out."

The three women nodded and sat where they were as she headed into the bedroom.

Harry picked up on the first ring. "Hello?"

"Hi, honey." She forced her voice to sound upbeat, but feared that her stopped-up nose would give away her distress.

"Sylvia, what did you find out?"

She tried to draw in a breath and cleared her throat. "It's malignant, Harry."

Silence followed, and she pictured him covering his face, struggling with tears, trying to clear his own voice. "How big is the tumor?"

"Three centimeters," she said. "And the margins are poorly defined, and the cancer cells are aggressive." There. It was all out.

Harry didn't say a word. She knew he was letting it sink in, running it through his database, lining it up with all of his medical knowledge. She knew he was shaking, rubbing his face, frowning, and struggling with tears.

"Have you told the kids?"

"No, not yet. I don't want to, Harry. It'll scare them to death. I'd rather wait until some things are decided. Then I can give them more information, and maybe it'll soften the blow."

His sigh was shaky. "That's my Sylvia. Always thinking about others."

She could hear in his voice that he was taking it hard. "Harry, we have some decisions to make." Oh, she didn't want to cry right now, but her throat grew tight and she felt that emotion creeping up, waiting to ambush her. "It's so confusing. He recommended a modified radical mastectomy because of the size and nature of the tumor. But I'm thinking about maybe having a lumpectomy and radiation, and then if that doesn't get it all, I could go back and have a mastectomy later."

"Sylvia, that's not wise. You'd be giving this cancer the chance to metastasize."

She squeezed her eyes shut. "He also suggested that I could opt for a bilateral mastectomy just to keep from taking any chances with the other breast. Harry, I want to do the right thing, but this is all so unreal. I feel like I'm watching a Monday night movie."

"I don't," he said. "I feel like my bride is in serious jeopardy, and I want to get home to her as fast as I can."

She longed to tell him that he didn't need to come, but she knew it was all in vain. He was probably throwing things into his suitcase even as they spoke.

"Harry, what's going to happen to the mission work, to the clinic, and to the orphanage?"

"Sylvia, it was God's plan to send us here in the first place. Do you think he doesn't have a plan now that we're leaving?"

"But why would he get us there only to make us come home?"

"He knows what he's doing. And he's got replacements for us. We've got to trust him. But right now I've got to get home to you."

"Harry, my biggest wish is that you would stay there and keep doing the work and let me handle this. The girls will take care of me. I can handle it."

"Sylvia, I can't think of anything more torturous than to be here while my wife is suffering at home. God doesn't require that of me."

"I'm not suffering. I'm doing just fine. I don't have any pain."

"You will after the mastectomy. You're part of me, Sylvia, and when we suffer, we suffer together. That's all there is to it. I don't want to hear another word about it."

She closed her eyes. Tears streamed down her face. "When will you be here?"

"I'll get the first flight out of Managua tomorrow," he said.

"You don't have to rush. You can take a day or two."

When he spoke again his voice wobbled. "They said it was aggressive, Sylvia. I want it out of you as soon as possible. I'll see you tomorrow. Until then, honey, I want you to relax and not worry."

"How do I do that?"

"Call on the girls. Get them to come over and have popcorn and watch a funny movie."

She shook her head. "No. What I really need to do is read about breast cancer. I need information, Harry. I think I'll feel better if I know what I'm doing."

"All right, whatever you need to do. But I'm here, okay? If you need to talk tonight, just call me." His voice broke off and she knew he was crying. Anger surged through her again.

Lord, why would you break his heart like this?

"I love you," she whispered.

"I love you, too. I'll see you tomorrow, honey."

She hung up the phone and grabbed up his pillow, mashed it against her face, and wept into it, hoping her friends in the living room didn't hear. She sat there like that for a long time, spending her tears, venting her anguish. Finally she went into the bathroom and washed her face. Quickly, she reapplied her makeup. Then, taking a deep breath, she went back into the living room.

Cathy, Tory, and Brenda had been crying. Their eyes were red and puffy. They were all huddled together on the couch, and she sensed they had been praying.

She stood in the doorway, her hand on the casing. "Harry's coming home tomorrow."

"Good." Cathy's smile was overbright. "That will help a lot."

Sylvia nodded and averted her eyes.

"So what do you want to do to get your mind off of this?" Brenda asked.

"I don't want to get my mind off of it," Sylvia said. "I want to keep my mind on it. I want to read the stuff the doctor gave me, and go to the bookstore and get every book I can find on the subject. And I want to stay up late tonight reading until I feel like I have a better handle on this. I know that God is in control. There's no doubt about that. And I know that he's faithful. I'll hold onto that as I go. But I feel like a certain amount of this is under my control, and I need to know more to make the right decisions."

"Okay," Cathy said, "then let's go."

Sylvia looked around at them. "All four of us? What about the kids? What about Hannah?"

"Annie's got the kids," Tory said, "and she's great with Hannah."

"She'll be fine," Brenda added. "You trained her well in León."

So they headed off to the bookstore on a mission to find the information that could help save Sylvia's life.

CHAPTER *Fifteen*

Harry's hands trembled as he sat at his old desk at the back of his clinic and dialed the number for the airline. When they put him on hold, a screaming sense of injustice shivered up inside him. Jeb Anderson, one of the other missionaries who ran the orphanage, stepped into the doorway. Noting the sweat on Harry's brow and the expression on his face, he asked, "Harry, you talked to Sylvia, didn't you?"

Harry nodded quickly, as if he didn't have time to answer.

Jeb stepped closer. "Was it malignant?"

Harry raked his hand through his hair. "Yes, it was. I'm going home tomorrow, Jeb." He looked up at his friend and saw the dread on his face.

"Of course you are." Jeb crossed the room and looked into Harry's face. "Harry, don't worry about anything. I've been talking to Carlos Gonzales, and he thinks he can run things here while you're gone. He's been on the phone with some churches back in the States, and he's trying to get some doctors to come here on medical mission trips to fill in while you're gone."

Harry's eyes widened as he looked up at Jeb. "You were anticipating the worst."

"We know how bad Sylvia's been feeling."

"It's not supposed to have anything to do with the cancer. But if they're wrong and it does, then it's more advanced than we think."

The airline clerk finally answered the phone. *"Le puedo ayudar?"*

"Yes. Uh ... I need to get the first flight for the United States out of Managua tomorrow morning," he said in Spanish. He fumbled through his wallet for his credit card.

When the flight was finally booked, he hung up and leaned back.

"Harry, are you all right?" Jeb asked.

Harry evaded the question. "I've just got a lot to do tonight. I need to put things in the clinic in a little better order so that anybody who comes in here can take over. I need to check on Mrs. Hernandez and make sure she has enough antibiotics to get her through her infection. And I'd probably better go by and see baby Maria. She wasn't doing well and I was worried she wouldn't even make it through the week." His voice broke off and his shoulders began to shake.

"They'll be all right, Harry," Jeb said. "I'll go see her every day and make sure they're giving her the medicine."

"They sell it, you know." Tears began to stream down his face. "They sell it to buy food. And can you blame them? But they don't seem to understand that without it she could die."

"I'll make sure," he said. "In fact, if you want me to ration it out and take it daily one dose at a time, I will."

"Could you do that? That's what I've been doing. It was the only way."

"Of course. Harry, if you'll make a list of what needs to be done, I'll do everything that doesn't require a doctor. You need to be with Sylvia. You don't have to feel guilty about it." He came and sat down next to him, put his hand on Harry's back. "The Lord is still in control, you know."

"I know," Harry said. "I know he is. I would never want to suggest that he isn't. But my wife . . ."

He was going to lose it. He was going to break down right here in front of Jeb. He couldn't handle that, so he got up and headed for the door. "I've got a lot to do, Jeb. I have to get home and pack."

He took off without another word, walking as fast as he could to the old Fiat parked out beside the clinic. He realized that he had just contradicted himself. He'd said that he needed to organize supplies so that the medical missionaries could come in and take over, then he'd headed off to pack.

Jeb would understand.

He got to his house and went in, looked around at all the things that screamed Sylvia's name. The smell of her lingered on the air, and he suddenly felt a sense of deprivation, as if she'd already been snatched from him and he didn't know why. He went to the bedroom, pulled her pillow out of the bed, lay down and curled up with it . . . and began to weep. After a while, he got off the bed and knelt beside it to pray.

"Please," he begged his almighty God, "heal her. Please don't let this be the end. We've tried to be obedient, Lord. We've tried to do everything you've said. Father, please don't take her. I'm begging you. I've never asked you for a lot, not anything really big. This is the first time, Lord. Please save my wife."

He fell prostrate on the floor, pleading and crying for God's help and mercy.

CHAPTER *Sixteen*

It was eight-thirty the following night when darkness began to dominate the sky. Steve had finished mowing just before daylight gave up its ghost. Cathy took a glass of cold lemonade to him in the backyard. His sweaty T-shirt stuck to his chest and back. He grabbed the towel that hung over the lawn mower handle and wiped his face, then took a long swig of the drink.

"I like a wife that brings me lemonade."

She smiled. "I like a husband who mows the lawn. I haven't done it since you moved in."

"See? Marriage does have its perks."

"Lots of them." She lowered to the chaise lounge chair under the covered patio and looked up at him. Steve touched her neck. "You've been quiet today. Have you talked to Sylvia?"

"No, she made herself scarce, said she wanted to read and think about the decisions she had to make. And I think she's out picking Harry up at the airport now."

"You didn't sleep much last night."

"Hope I didn't keep you awake. So many things were going through my mind. Sylvia and Mark..."

He took another drink. "What about Mark?"

"Well, I've been thinking a lot about this GED thing. We're getting down to the wire. School registration is the end of the week, and I found out that a new GED class is starting up next week. He would have the choice of going nights or mornings."

"If he went nights, he could work during the day."

Cathy sighed. "Yeah, but I don't know if I want him doing that. Working all day and going to school at night? That's a lot of stress."

Steve nodded. "It is, but I thought it might be beneficial for him to work like a dog for a few months, and find out how valuable that college degree is."

"You have a point," she said. "Only you realize, don't you, that if he's doing a full-time job with other high school dropouts, he could be influenced by them? I mean, kids usually drop out because they hate the rules, want to party all night, take drugs and drink..."

"That's true," Steve said. "But haven't *all* those in the GED classes dropped out of school? Morning or night, it doesn't really matter."

"You're right." Cathy rubbed her forehead. "And I know there is something to having him work really hard. I do want him to realize how much he needs his education."

"Cathy, why not just make him finish school the traditional way?"

"Because I've been trying to put myself in his place. I understand why he doesn't want to go back to high school. That's where he met the kids he started doing drugs with in the first place. And I can understand why he doesn't want to study with Brenda anymore. I think he's insecure and feels stupid, because her kids are so advanced."

"But that would challenge him. And you know Brenda needs the money."

"She's done without it for a year. I'm not even sure she wants him back. We haven't really talked about it. And, Steve, he may be able to get his GED *now*, even without the class. I mean, he has gone to school straight through. Brenda put him a few steps ahead, and then he had school at River Ranch. He may very well know enough to pass it."

Steve finished his glass and set it down next to him. "I don't like it much, Cathy, but if you have peace about it, go ahead and let him. The goal is to get him to go to college, and the GED shouldn't hurt in that area, not if he plans to go to the community college first."

"All right," Cathy said, "I'll let him. Now all I have to decide is whether he should go to the morning or night class."

"And he has to start looking for a job."

"Right. A job." Cathy held his gaze for a moment. "Do you really think that making him take the class at night and work during the day is the right choice?"

"Depends on what you want to accomplish."

Cathy smiled. "I want him to hate the kind of work he can get and go to college."

"Then let him work his tail off for the next few months," Steve said. "Guaranteed, he'll be in college by the next semester."

CHAPTER
Seventeen

The moment Harry stepped off the plane Sylvia felt as if the parallel planes of her life had finally converged. She could get through this now.

He started to cry as he walked toward her, and she took him into her arms and held him as if he were the diseased and she were comforting him. They stood there like that for a long moment, him weeping into her hair, her weeping into his shirt, while the hustle and bustle of the airport life moved around them. Then she took him back to the house he hadn't seen since they'd left it to go to the mission field.

The "For Sale" sign still sat in the front yard. Harry got out of the car, and instead of going toward the door, he headed to the sign.

"Harry, what are you doing?"

"Taking the sign down." He moved it in the dirt, loosening it so he could pull it up.

"No, don't. We have to sell the house, Harry."

The sign came up. "Not until this is resolved. Honey, God is obviously working here. He didn't let us sell it because he knew we'd need it. We can put the sign back up when the time is right."

She watched as he laid it on a shelf in the garage—one more reminder that their plans and dreams had been derailed.

Harry went back to the car and got his suitcase. He carried it into the kitchen and looked around. "Home," he whispered. "I didn't even know how much I'd missed it. Isn't God good for not letting us sell?"

Sylvia put her arm through his and led him through the house. "The Gonzaleses did a great job of taking care of it. Since they left, Brenda and Tory have come over here every now and then to keep it dusted."

She led him into the bedroom, and he set the suitcase down and sat on the bed. "Are you tired, Harry? You could rest and we could talk tomorrow."

"No." He got up and fixed his eyes on her. "I want to see the pathology report and the X rays. You brought them home, didn't you?"

"Yes," she said. "They knew you'd want them."

"And I don't want to waste any time. We need to go for second and third opinions."

"I've already got the appointments booked," Sylvia said. "I called today and Dr. Jefferson's secretary set it all up. Monday we see Dr. Thibodeaux."

Harry nodded. "The oncologist?"

"That's right," she said. "And before that appointment I've got an appointment with Dr. Simon, the plastic surgeon. Then a second-opinion appointment with Dr. Hartford."

He stepped into the dining room and saw the breast cancer books spread out across the table. "You've been studying."

"Yeah, I've learned a lot," she said. "I at least have a little better understanding than I did yesterday."

He sat down and read the pathology report. His face betrayed his tension and strain as he flipped through the pages the doctor had sent home for him. Finally he looked up at her.

"Sylvia, I don't want any more talk about a lumpectomy. I want you to have a mastectomy. If it weren't such an aggressive cancer and if the margins of the tumor were more defined, I might not say that. But this report convinced me."

She closed her eyes. "They'd be cutting off a part of me, Harry. I don't know if I can deal with that."

"Don't think of it like that." He took her hand and made her sit down. "Think of it as them cutting out the enemy."

She met his eyes. "But my body will be different. That will change *us*."

He leaned forward and looked hard into her eyes. "It's not your breasts I'm in love with. It's you. It's going to be all right, Sylvia. Every time I look at that scar, I'll remember how close I came to losing you. If that scar is what saves your life, it will be beautiful to me."

"Let's just see what they say in the other opinions," she said. "I'm not ready to make up my mind just yet."

"Okay." He pulled her onto his lap and held her for a long moment. "We need to tell the kids, honey. Sarah and Jeff need to know."

"Not yet," she whispered. "Not until we've made some decisions. They'll take it so much better if they know what we're going to do about it. Please, Harry. Let's wait."

He nodded, his mouth straining to hold back his weary, raw emotions. "Whatever you think."

They went to bed soon after, Sylvia exhausted from the hours of study she'd put in that day, and Harry wiped out from a sleepless night and the trip home from Nicaragua. He reaffirmed her body and his love of it before falling off to sleep.

Sylvia lay next to him, watching his face in repose. She touched her breast, the offending one, and let her hand cup over the shape of it. In just a few days it would be gone. But if she could exchange it for the peace of mind she lost the day she found out she had cancer, she supposed it would be worth it.

Finally she drifted off into a sweet sleep, curled up warm next to her husband.

CHAPTER
Eighteen

Some of the heaviness lifted from Sylvia's heart as she sat in the plastic surgeon's office looking at the before and after pictures of breast reconstruction.

"We have several reconstruction methods," he was saying. "We can reconstruct using your own tissue from other parts of your body. With the TRAM flap we pull up fat, muscle, and tissue from your abs."

"Ouch." Sylvia turned a page in the photo album. "That sounds painful. Does it look real when it's finished?"

Dr. Simon took the album from her and flipped through its pictures. He found one and pointed to it. "You tell me."

She studied the picture. "So you get a tummy tuck as part of the package?"

"That's right. Or we can take the tissue from your gluts."

Harry wasn't impressed. "What are the risks?"

"Well, there are some. Sometimes the flap develops necrosis."

Sylvia looked up at him. "What is that?"

"The tissue dies," Harry said. "They'd have to remove the flap then, and that could cause you to be in worse shape than you were before the reconstruction."

"We could do a LAT flap, where we take muscle and tissue from the upper back and move it to the breast area."

"Still sounds painful. I'd have incisions in front *and* back." She looked at the picture the doctor offered her.

"We supplement this procedure with an implant."

Harry still wasn't satisfied. "What about not doing any of the flaps and just doing a synthetic implant?"

Dr. Simon nodded. "Yes, we can put an expander bag under her skin." He picked one up and showed it to them. "It has a valve at the bottom, and every week or two you come in and let me inject saline into it. Slowly, it will stretch your skin into the shape of your other breast. When the skin is properly stretched, say in six months or so, we can put in the permanent implant."

Sylvia liked the "after" pictures of that one. She showed them to Harry. "What do you think?"

He stiffened. "I think reconstruction isn't that necessary. That maybe we need to cross one hurdle before we move on to that one."

Sylvia shook her head. "But I'll have more hope if I think my breast is someday going to look normal again."

"It's just a lot of extra pain to go through, when you're already struggling."

"But, Harry, if I wait I may never do it. I'd rather get it all done at once."

Harry got quiet.

The doctor leaned forward on his desk. "When we get the permanent implant in, then we can do some skin grafts to finish the cosmetic appearance. It actually looks very good."

Sylvia looked at the "before" picture of the woman with an incision that cut from her sternum around to her back, leaving a flap. She swallowed the lump in her throat. Then she saw the "after" picture. The reconstructed look was more than she could have hoped for, but she knew better than to expect the best-case scenario.

She frowned. "I want to see a picture of one that didn't turn out like you hoped."

"I understand what you're saying." He flipped through the pictures, then brought out one that was a little less symmetrical. Even that looked better than she thought it would.

She glanced at Harry. "If this is the worst it will be, I think I can live with it. It's a lot better than not having anything at all."

Harry leaned forward. "Bob, I want you to tell us something honestly. Don't these surgeries and implants increase the risk of infection during the chemo?"

"That is a risk," the doctor said. "But it's minimal."

"What about recurrence? Would an implant keep us from being able to see new tumors?"

"Not at all."

Harry wasn't finished. "So you'd have to be there at the time of the mastectomy. Would this delay the surgery date at all? Coordinating your schedule with the other surgeon, I mean?"

"When are you planning to have it?"

"Early next week," Harry said.

Sylvia shot him a look. They hadn't talked about that. She hadn't even told the children yet. She hadn't prayed about it enough. She wasn't ready.

"Yes, I can work it into my schedule. If we choose an autologous tissue reconstruction, it'll take an additional five or six hours of surgery. The expander implant takes less time. But I'll need to know as soon as possible so we can schedule it."

Sylvia swallowed. "Can we schedule the surgery before I know for sure what I'm going to do?"

"Yes. We could hold the time for you. I'll check with Dr. Jefferson, and by the time we work out the time, maybe you'll know what you want."

As they drove away from the office, she recognized the tension on Harry's face. He was going to require some convincing, but she already had her mind made up. She reached across the seat and took his hand. "Honey, it's going to be all right."

He smiled. "I'm supposed to say that to you."

"But you're not sure it's true, are you?"

He focused on the car in front of him. "Of course I am."

"I'll probably have the mastectomy, but I want the reconstruction, Harry."

"I know you do. And it's your body."

She watched the way he worked his jaw, and knew that he still had serious reservations. "What's your main concern?" she asked.

"The unnecessary pain you'll be in, wherever they take the grafts, when you're already suffering from the mastectomy. Possible infection. Longer surgery. Harder recovery."

They were all valid concerns, she thought. She had always deferred to him in matters of medicine for their family. But there was something else here that she couldn't quite explain. She was losing a part of her body, and she needed to know she could get it back. Even if it was a poor facsimile of the real thing, just the shape and the contour would do so much for the way she felt about herself.

But she had to think of Harry's needs, too, and she didn't want to cause him unnecessary anxiety.

But that anxiety was impossible to hold at bay as they went for her appointment with her oncologist. He explained the process of chemotherapy to her, how necessary it would be to kill any cancer cells left in her body after the surgery. The strength of the chemo and the number of treatments would depend on how many lymph nodes were involved.

The only good news she could filter from his words were that she'd have a four-week period to recover from her surgery before starting the chemo treatments.

Their visit didn't make her decisions any simpler.

There was still so much to think about. It ought to be easy to decide these things. You had cancer, so you had it cut out. Took medicine to prevent recurrence. Took measures to cope with the side effects. But none of what she'd read or heard in the last couple of days made the choices easier.

She let her gaze drift out the window as they wound their way back up Bright Mountain. She didn't know why she was so adamant about reconstructing her breast, when there were so many more important things to think of. What if she didn't survive this? How would her children take it? They weren't ready to be motherless, even though they were both grown and out of the house. Even in Nicaragua she e-mailed them every day and spoke to them often. Sarah still called her for recipes and baby-raising tips. Jeff still wanted her advice on the women he dated.

And there was the grandbaby. She'd been so thrilled to have her, and now to know that she might not live to see her start school, star in her school play, accept Christ as her Lord.

There was no more frightening feeling than that of leaving her children behind. Death would be fine—absent with the body was to be present with the Lord, according to Paul. This was not her home. But she couldn't help the bonds that held her so tightly to her kids.

And her husband.

"You're awfully quiet." Harry's voice was raspy, hoarse.

"I was just thinking about the kids."

He nodded. "We have to tell them."

"Yes," she said. "I'll call them when we get home."

CHAPTER
Nineteen

Sylvia employed the three-way-calling feature she'd never used in her life, and got Sarah and Jeff on the phone together. When she told them the news, they both sat silent for a long moment.

Finally, Sarah spoke. "Mom, I'm coming home tomorrow."

"Me too." Jeff's voice was heavy, thick.

"No, you're not," she said. "Sarah, you've got the baby. And, Jeff, what about your job? I don't even know yet when the surgery will be scheduled. It's foolish to come here now. I'm going to be fine. I'm having surgery sometime next week, and then, according to the oncologist, I'll have four weeks before my chemotherapy starts."

"Chemotherapy?" Sarah sounded as if the breath had been knocked out of her. "Oh, Mom."

"Oh, Mom, what?" she asked her. "Honey, don't you realize that chemo is a blessing? What if they didn't have it? I know it's going to be hard, but I'm ready for it. I want to do everything possible to kill the cancer." She sighed. "Guys, it's going to be okay. Really."

"How's Dad?" Jeff asked.

"He's fine. Preoccupied, as you can imagine. We have a lot of decisions to make about the surgery. But we'll make them."

"But I want to do something!" Sarah cried.

"You *can* do something. You can pray."

"Mom, as soon as you know when the surgery is, let me know. I'll come so I can help Dad take care of you when you get home."

"How long before they'll know if it's spread?" Jeff's question rippled over the line.

"I won't know right away. Probably a couple of days."

"I want to be there when the results come back," he said.

She closed her eyes and tried to think of those results coming. If the cancer hadn't spread to the lymph nodes, they'd have a wonderful celebration. But if it had . . .

She didn't want her children there hurting that way. She didn't want to see the fear on their faces . . . the dread of her demise.

On the other hand, she didn't want them hearing about it on the phone.

"All right, you can come after the surgery," she said. "But only if you bring the baby, Sarah. And, Jeff, I don't want you missing more than a couple of days of work."

"Mom, are you sure you want me to bring her?" Sarah asked. "You won't be feeling well. Her crying and fussing might make you feel worse. I could leave her with Gary."

"Absolutely not," Sylvia said. "I have to have something to look forward to, don't I? If you bring her, I won't have time to feel sorry for myself. I'll have a little treasure to keep my mind off those results."

"All right," she said. "I'll bring her."

"And Jeff, no long-term absences from work, okay? I can't wait to see you, but your father and I didn't put all that money into your education to have you run off and leave your job."

"I hear you, Mom."

"So you'll call us when you schedule the surgery?" Sarah asked. "The very minute?"

"You know I will."

When she finally hung up the phone, she felt as if the last vestiges of her strength had drained right out of her. She got up and went into the living room and found Harry sitting in his favorite chair, staring out into the air.

"I told them," she said. "They insisted on coming after the surgery. Sarah's going to bring Breanna."

Harry only looked at her. "Something to look forward to," he whispered. "How did they take it?"

"Just like you'd expect."

He nodded and reached for her hand. She went to him, and he pulled her into his lap. There, she curled up in his arms, holding him and loving him, and praying silently that God wouldn't bring too much pain into the heart of this beloved man who had been such an obedient servant of God, and such a precious husband to her.

"There's something we have to do," he said, "before we go another day."

"What?"

"We have to call for the elders of the church and get them to pray over you, just like the Bible says."

Sylvia looked down at his serious face. "Are you sure? Do they still do that? I never hear of it." She got up and moved to the chair across from him.

"No, it isn't done that much in churches like ours, though if someone asks for it, they do comply." He got up and got his Bible, opened it to James 5, and read verses 14 and 15. "The Bible tells us that if anyone is sick he must call the elders and let them pray over him ... that they should anoint him with oil ... and that the prayer offered in faith will restore him. But there's a dispute as to whether the Greek word that's translated 'sick' really means 'sick.'"

"I don't understand. Isn't it clear?"

"Not really. The word translated 'sick' is *kamno*, which means 'to tire . . . faint, sicken, be wearied.' So it *can* be translated 'sick.' But it could also mean someone who is weak in conscience or weak in faith. And the problem is what we've seen. People who are prayed over by the elders don't always get well. Some of them still die, no matter how strong their faith is. This would imply that everyone who has strong faith and prays will have perfect health. But that's not so."

Sylvia was more confused than ever. "So why should we do it?"

Harry looked down at his Bible again, then brought his eyes up to her. "Because what if they're wrong? What if it really does mean 'sick'? What if God really does assign some extra power to prayers prayed by the elders? What if God wanted to heal you that way?"

Sylvia lifted her chin. She didn't need any more convincing than that. "Then we'll do it. But when? I've always wondered at what point it should be done. If you hurt your back, should you do it then? If you have the flu? If you break your leg? Or is it just for terminal illness? And even then, do you do it at the beginning of the illness, when there's a chance that modern medicine could cure you, or do you wait until there's no hope left?"

Harry shook his head. "I don't know the answer to any of those questions, honey. I really don't. All I know is that now is the time for us. And I'm going to call the elders tonight, and ask them to meet us tomorrow."

Sylvia took the Bible from him and read over those verses again. "It says that 'the prayer offered in faith will restore the one who is sick.' Does that mean that we trust in the healing and don't follow with the surgery or the treatments?"

"No, of course not. That would be like demanding that God heal you, not taking no for an answer. In that case, if he chose not to, it would shake our faith and make God the bad guy somehow. No, God doesn't want us testing him or demanding things of him. He simply wants us to pray. I have total faith in his ability to heal you this way if he chooses."

"Then how will we know if he healed me, or if the surgery or chemo did?"

"If you're healed, Sylvia, it will be God who did it, regardless of how he chooses to."

The hope in his eyes was intense, and she could see the pleas his mind and heart were already sending up on her behalf.

"After the surgery," Harry said, "if there's no cancer in the lymph nodes, I think we can assume that the elders praying over you really worked."

"And if it is in the lymph nodes?" she asked.

He cleared his throat and looked down at his hands. "If it is in the lymph nodes, then we assume that God heard the prayers of the elders, and has chosen to answer it according to his will. Whatever that will is."

Her eyes filled with tears again. He stood up and pulled her to her feet, framed her face with his hands, and gazed into her wet eyes. "Whatever happens, Sylvia, we know that God loves you more, even, than I do."

She nodded. "I know. And whatever he chooses, it's for some great purpose that we can't even imagine."

A tear rolled out of Harry's eye and ran down his cheek. "We'll pray that we can accept that, whatever it is."

"Yes," she whispered. "And that we'll be thankful, even if it means suffering."

It was more than she had the power to do . . . more even than Harry was capable of offering. But she was sure that they wouldn't have to rely on their own power to do that. God would give them what they needed, as they needed it. Comfort when it was needed, and healing if it was part of his plan.

CHAPTER
Twenty

After a couple of hours of having the elders pray over her, Sylvia told Harry that she felt the peace of mind to make the right decision. She had weighed every possible choice carefully, and she chose a modified radical mastectomy of only one breast, and reconstruction using the expander implant. Once the decision was made, Harry pulled every string he had and finally got a surgery date of the following Wednesday.

On the day of the surgery Brenda, Cathy, and Tory assembled in the waiting room at the hospital with Harry, and waited for word on how things had gone. They prayed and paced and worried until the surgeon finally came back out and took Harry aside.

Harry was silent as he followed his old friend into a consultation room. He sat down, studying the surgeon's face as he took the chair across from him. "Be straight with me, Sam."

Sam Jefferson met his eyes. "Harry, the surgery went well. You know I'd tell you if anything had gone wrong. They sent the tissue to the pathologist. We also took out ten lymph nodes and we should know if any of them are positive within the next seventy-two hours. But the surgery went very well. The incision looks good, and Bob did a fabulous job on the reconstruction."

"How did the tissue look?"

"Like cancer, just as we thought. But there's no way of telling whether it's spread until we get the results back."

Harry had never been particularly good at waiting. "When can I see her?"

"Probably in the next thirty minutes or so. We'll let you know."

Harry headed back to the waiting room. All three faces turned to him. "She's fine," he said. "Surgery is over. Everything went well."

"And the cancer?" Tory asked.

Harry shook his head. "We won't know anything for seventy-two hours or so."

Cathy got up. "Why so long?"

"It takes a while to get the pathology reports back," he said. "Meanwhile, we'll just help her recover from the surgery and not borrow any trouble until it comes."

"Harry, what's the best-case scenario?" Brenda asked. "Is it that they got all the cancer and it's not in the lymph nodes?"

"That would be good news to me. If it is in the lymph nodes we'll have more to worry about."

Cathy slapped her hands on her thighs. "Well, it won't be. I just know it."

But Brenda and Tory grew quiet as he gathered his things and headed to the recovery room to see his wife.

Sylvia slept peacefully on the bed in the recovery room, and Harry stepped up to her and kissed her forehead. She looked pale and lifeless, but the warmth of her skin reassured him.

He saw the bandage on the left side of her chest and under her arm, the flat place where her breast had been . . .

His heart sank at the grief he knew she would suffer.

Her eyes fluttered open, and he whispered, "Hello, sweetheart. How do you feel?"

"Fine. Is it over?"

"It's over. You came through it great."

Her voice was hoarse from the tube that had been in her throat. "Do they know anything yet?"

"Not yet, honey."

She brought those tired eyes up to his. "How do I look?"

He leaned over and kissed her dry lips. "You're still the most beautiful gal in the joint."

Sylvia didn't seem to buy that. She looked down at herself, saw the bandage over her incision.

"When did they say we'd know about the lymph nodes?"

"Seventy-two hours. It's going to be a long wait."

Sylvia swallowed and closed her eyes, then opened them again. "Then let's just pretend they got it all, Harry. Let's pretend that the worst is behind us."

"Okay, sweetheart," he whispered against her face. "That's what we'll pretend."

CHAPTER
Twenty-One

When Tory dropped Brenda off, she saw that Leah and Rachel sat on the front steps, playing jacks. The moment they saw her, they launched from the steps and ran toward her.

"Mama!"

Joseph came out the front door and waited on the porch, and Daniel came around from the backyard.

"How is Miss Sylvia?" Leah asked.

"She's okay. She came through the surgery fine."

Leah blocked her way up to the front, a dramatic look on her face. "Is she gonna die?"

Brenda sighed and put her arms around her twin girls. "Now why would you ask a thing like that? She had surgery so she wouldn't die."

Rachel laid her head against her mother's shoulder. "We studied about cancer, Mama. It kills people."

"But not all of them. We have lots of new drugs that can fight it. Lots of people survive the kind that Miss Sylvia has. So don't you worry."

She looked at Daniel, who stood near the driveway, and Joseph, who leaned against the post on the porch. Both boys had somber looks on their faces. "Come on into the house, kids," she said. "Let's talk."

David was in the kitchen when she came in, painting mustard on the corn dogs that had just come out of the oven. They sat around the table, and Brenda looked at each face, moved by how seriously they were taking Sylvia's illness.

"Miss Sylvia's going to be okay," she said, "at least for now. They took her breast off hoping to get all the cancer, and we won't know for a few days if they did or not."

"Why not?" Leah asked. "Couldn't they see it and make sure?"

"They can't always see it. Sometimes it gets into the bloodstream. We're waiting to see if it has, but we're hoping for the best."

Joseph blinked back the mist in his eyes. "We've been praying for her, Mama."

"I know, sweetheart." She touched Joseph's flaming red hair, tried to stroke it into place. "You keep praying. The same God who healed you is hearing these prayers, too."

Satisfied that Sylvia was not in immediate mortal danger, the children took their corn dogs outside to eat them at the picnic table.

Brenda and David were left in the kitchen alone.

He took her hand. "You sure you're okay?"

Renegade tears burst into her eyes. "No, I'm not okay. I hate it when someone I love is suffering."

"She's not suffering," David said. "She's going to be all right. It may be better than you think. There's no need to worry."

Brenda got up and put the pan that had held the corn dogs into the sink. "We're totally out of control, you know. I feel as helpless as I did when Joseph was sick. It's completely in God's hands." She wiped her tears and came back to the table, her wet eyes fixed on her husband.

"What can I do to help?"

She shook her head. "It would be so great if I could pray with you. Two or more gathered in prayer . . ."

"Brenda . . ." The word had that long-suffering sound, like an admonition, and it closed the discussion. He got up and grabbed some napkins and got his glass. "Let's go out with the kids."

"Okay," she said. "I'll be right there."

She watched him as he headed out, but she made no move to go. Instead, she cried into her hands for a few minutes, partly for Sylvia, and partly for David . . .

Then finally, she cleared the evidence from her face, and joined her family outside.

Three gathered that night in prayer—Tory and Brenda and Cathy—sitting on Brenda's porch where they'd prayed as a foursome so many other times in their lives. They all wept as they prayed, asking God to spare Sylvia's life.

As they brought the prayer to an end Brenda wiped her face, but the tears kept coming.

Cathy reached for her hand. "Honey, are you okay?"

Brenda shook her head. "Just . . . seeing Harry and Sylvia's approach to this disease has made me long for the day when David wakes up . . . and sees the truth about Jesus." She dabbed at her eyes. "I've prayed for him for years. It seems like it's never going to happen."

"You have to trust the Lord for it," Cathy said. "You just have to claim it."

Brenda rolled her eyes. "Oh, Cathy, trust the Lord for what? I trust him with everything, my life, David's salvation, *every-thing*. But he never *said* he was going to save David, so I don't know why people think all I have to do is expect it and it will happen. God's ways are not our ways. I don't believe in name-it-claim-it."

"Well, neither do I," Cathy said. "But I'm just saying that you need to believe God for it."

Brenda's face twisted in anger. "What does that mean, 'Believe God for it'?"

Tory looked uncomfortable at Brenda's response and reached out to touch her arm. "Brenda, she didn't mean anything."

"No, I'm serious," Brenda asked. "Cathy, I need to know what you mean by 'believe God for it.' That's like a demand of God, a presumption on him, that he has to keep some bargain he never made."

Confusion shone on Cathy's face. "You don't think God wants to see David saved?"

"Of course he wants to see David saved," Brenda said, "but he's not going to force him into it. He doesn't bang the door down. He just stands at it and knocks. There's nothing in the Bible that says that I can believe God for anything I want and it will come true."

"It does say ask and you will receive. That anything you ask in his name will be given."

"Yes, it does, but that's according to the will of God and his timing. I can't order God around with my prayers. I can't just believe he's going to do something because I asked him to, and think that it somehow obligates him to do it. Jesus asked God to take the cup of suffering and death from him, but he didn't. Paul asked him to remove the thorn from his flesh. He said no. They didn't just 'believe God for it' and expect it to come true."

Cathy leaned forward, her face soft as she looked at Brenda. "I guess you're right, Brenda. All I meant was that you have to have faith and keep praying."

Tory nodded. "Jesus said, 'You have not because you ask not, and when you ask you do it with wrong motives.' Brenda, the Lord knows your heart, that you're not asking with wrong motives. And we know that it's not his will that anyone should perish. So why wouldn't he eventually answer this prayer? You're praying right, according to his will, with pure motives. God will hear you and answer you, Brenda."

Brenda knew she'd never shown this side of herself to her friends before. Even when Joseph was sick, she'd had such strength and faith. But as serious and frightening as that was, she considered David's eternity to be at much greater risk.

"It's just that, after all these years of praying, it hasn't happened yet. And I want it to happen now." Her voice broke off. She rubbed her hands through her hair and sank back onto her chair. The cool wind from the Smokies blew up, ruffling it into her face.

"I'm sorry, Cathy. I'm sorry, Tory. I just want so much to have the kind of intimacy with David that Sylvia and Harry have. And you, Tory, and Barry. And Cathy and Steve. To be able to hold his hand and pray with him and know that we are agreeing in prayer and that God's hearing us."

"He hears you anyway," Cathy said. "He hears when you pray alone, and he hears when you pray with us."

"I know he does, but sometimes I just need that support, you know? I need a spiritual leader. Up until now it feels like it's been Sylvia. My mentor. My spiritual mother. But what if something happens to her?" Brenda wiped her face. "Oh, that's so selfish. I can't believe I'm saying these things. She's up in that hospital fighting for her life, and I'm sitting here worried about me."

"We're all worried about us." Tory put her arm around Brenda, leaned her head against hers. "We've all wondered what it would be like without Sylvia. Even when she was in Nicaragua, we still had her. We could e-mail her anytime, pick up the phone if we wanted to."

Brenda's face twisted. "But if anything happens to her ..."

"It can't," Cathy cut in. "Nothing is going to happen to her. God wouldn't do that. She's too important to his kingdom. Trust me. He's going to keep her alive."

Brenda turned her sad eyes to Cathy. "Honey, God takes people all the time. Death is a part of life. It's a part that is hard for us to accept, but it is. And sometimes he takes them when they're young, and sometimes he takes them with disease. And sometimes we don't know the reason."

Cathy's eyes flashed. "He's *not* going to take Sylvia, and that's all there is to it. You mark my word. He cherishes her."

"All the more reason to take her home," Brenda whispered.

CHAPTER
Twenty-Two

Harry, sit down," Sylvia said two days later as Harry ran around the room arranging the flowers that had been sent. "You haven't gotten a moment's rest since my surgery. Please sit down. You're wearing me out just watching you."

"Well, what else am I going to do?" Harry asked. "That's what I'm here for."

"You're not here to wait on me hand and foot. You're here to hold my hand. That's all I want from you, Harry."

He came to the bed and leaned over her, took her hand. "You look beautiful, you know."

Sylvia rolled her eyes. "You don't have to appease me with compliments, Harry. Nobody looks beautiful two days after surgery."

"I know. You're an enigma. I'm thinking about writing you up for a medical journal. It's probably a first or something."

A knock sounded on the door and they both turned to it. It cracked open and their daughter, Sarah, stepped inside. "Mom?"

"Sarah!" Sylvia sat up in bed. "Oh, honey." She reached her good arm out for her, and Sarah came to her and gave her a careful hug. "How are you, Mom?"

"I'm great, now that you're here. Where's that baby?"

"They wouldn't let her come up."

Sylvia gasped. "So you left her alone?"

Sarah laughed. "Right. She's fourteen months old, and I left her toddling around in the lobby. What kind of mother do you think I am?"

"Well, where is she then?"

"She's with her daddy, downstairs."

Another knock turned her attention to the door, and her son ducked in.

"Jeff! I didn't think you were coming until tomorrow! Come in! Oh, sweetheart, you didn't have to take off work on a Friday. You could have just come for the weekend."

"Like I'd just go on with things and forget that my mother is laid up in the hospital?" He leaned over and kissed her on the cheek. She recognized the way he avoided looking at her chest. "How you feeling, Mom?"

"Better than I expected." She reached up to hug him, and winced as the incision on her left side pulled.

They both went to their father and hugged him tight and hard. Neither of them had seen him in over a year, not since the baby had been born. Sylvia saw the emotion on his face.

"Okay, that's it. I'm going to get my grandchild," he said. "I need to see her, and your mother needs to see her."

"Oh, can you, Harry?"

"Of course I can. I know people. I can pull strings."

He rushed out, looking for his son-in-law and grandchild.

Sarah watched her father go, then turned her serious face back to her mother. "Are you sure you're all right, Mom? You look a little pale."

Sylvia tried to look shocked. "And your father told me I looked beautiful."

"Pale in a good way," Jeff said. "Like one of those porcelain-looking women in those antique paintings."

"Antique?" Sylvia swung at him. "Give me a break." Again, the incision pulled, but she wouldn't let herself wince.

"So have you heard anything yet?" Sarah asked.

"No, not yet." She took her daughter's hand. "We don't expect any news until tomorrow. But since tomorrow's Saturday, it might have to wait until Monday. Until then, we just assume that the cancer hasn't spread, that they got every bit of it in the surgery, and that I've already been through the worst part of this."

"Okay, Mom," Sarah said, but Sylvia didn't miss the look that passed between her children.

CHAPTER
Twenty-Three

Sylvia hated eating in front of an audience, but the next morning as she ate her breakfast, Harry, Sarah, and Jeff watched. Dr. Jefferson came in before she'd even finished her yogurt.

She set her spoon down and stared up at him. His face was somber, and she didn't like it. Harry introduced him to their children, then asked him point-blank, "You have the results?"

"That's right," he said. "Maybe we should talk alone . . ."

Jeff started to get up, but Sarah was more stubborn. She stood her ground, wanting to hear.

"That's okay." Sylvia held out a hand to stop Jeff from leaving. "I want them to stay. You can talk to me in front of them."

With all her heart, she hoped she was doing the right thing. They couldn't be sheltered from this. They were adults, after all. And they needed to know the truth. Keeping it from them would serve no purpose.

"Very well." He pulled up a chair and sat down next to the bed. Harry stood up, jingling the change in his pocket. He didn't even know he was doing it.

Sarah and Jeff didn't move a muscle. They didn't even seem to breathe.

Sylvia was glad she'd taken the time to put on makeup and fix her hair this morning. She didn't want to look sick when the verdict came down.

"Let's go ahead," she said. "Be blunt. I want the truth."

He shifted in his seat and opened her chart, as if seeing the results for the first time. Sylvia knew better. "It turns out that six of your lymph nodes are positive for tumor cells." He said it matter-of-factly, as if it held no particular significance. It was the way surgeons had of cushioning the blow.

She would have expected to start screaming out "no!" She would have pictured herself demanding that he run the tests again. Tears, at least.

Instead, she sat there numbly, staring at his face, wondering if that scar over his lip had happened in childhood, or if it had been recent. Had stitches been involved, or plastic surgery, or just a Band-aid?

Harry cleared his throat, shaking her out of her rambling thoughts. He was beside her now, taking her hand. It felt like ice, though she wasn't sure if it was his or hers that needed warmth.

"Six positive lymph nodes," she repeated. "What does that mean?"

"It just means that the cancer cells have spread. That we have to be a little more aggressive with treatment."

Sarah moaned and covered her face, and Jeff took her hand.

"Let me see the report," Harry said, and the doctor handed it to him.

"The cancer cells are also hormone receptor positive," the doctor went on.

Sylvia's mind groped awkwardly for the information she'd gathered. She had read about the hormone part of this, but for the life of her, she couldn't remember it now. "What does that mean?"

Harry rubbed his eyes and handed the report back to Sam. "They look for a particle of protein on the surface of the cancer cell to see if it's sensitive to estrogen," he said. "If it is, the cell is triggered into growing and dividing when it's stimulated by estrogen. Most women over fifty have that. Isn't that right, Sam?"

"That's right. That means that we'll have to treat it with hormones after the chemotherapy."

"For how long?" Sylvia asked.

"For at least five years, but possibly the rest of your life."

She swallowed, wondering how long that would be.

The doctor explained, "The hormone therapy will keep the hormones from triggering the cells into growing."

"What about the breast tissue?" Harry asked. "Can I see that report?"

The doctor flipped through the file and found the pathologist's report on that. "He determined that her breast tissue is poorly differentiated. No surprise there. The tumor is three centimeters, as we thought."

Harry took the report and studied it. His face was pale, and she felt his hand tightening over hers. He didn't realize how strong he was. Often, when they prayed together, he would hold her hand so tight that it would go numb. He did that now.

"As we told you going in, Sylvia, your cancer cells are very aggressive," Sam said. "That means that our chemo treatment is going to have to be aggressive, too. It's not going to be a picnic."

Sylvia thought of her hair falling out, her eyebrows bare . . .

Tears stung the backs of her eyes, but she told herself she would not cry in front of her children. She wasn't finished teaching them lessons, even in early adulthood. They were learning from watching her. Everything she did, every expression, every word, would be forever etched in their memory.

So she rose to the occasion. "I'm up for it, Sam. Bring it on."

He smiled weakly.

"What do we do next?" Harry asked. The paper in his hand trembled as he handed it back to Sam.

"I'm going to send Sylvia for scans of her head, chest, abdomen, and bones to determine if there's cancer anywhere else in her body. That should give us a good indication of what we're dealing with."

"More tests," Sylvia said. "How long does all this take?"

"We hope to get all the scans done today."

She nodded and looked at her children. Sarah had tears running down her face. Jeff's face was red and as serious as she'd ever seen it.

"When will I be able to start killing this cancer?"

"We can't start chemo until a month from now. We've got to give your body time to heal from the mastectomy."

She didn't like that answer much. "I know the oncologist warned me of that, but it seems like we need to do it sooner. Those cells are dividing and growing."

"It's okay," he said. "Even with aggressive cancer you have time to heal."

She looked at her children again, saw the terror on Sarah's face and the rock hardness on Jeff's.

"All right," she said, "I'm ready for those scans anytime you are."

"We'll schedule them for this afternoon." He closed her file and got up. "My secretary is making you an appointment about two weeks from now with your oncologist, so that you've had a little time to heal and we've gotten all the results back."

He patted Sylvia's hand. "Don't worry. We're going to be walking alongside you in this. We wouldn't mess up for anything, knowing Harry the way we do." He chuckled, and Harry forced a smile.

He started to leave, but Sarah came to her feet. She looked like a child lost at the mall. "Doctor?"

He turned at the door.

"Is my mother going to be all right?"

"We'll know more after the scans," he said. Without offering any more in the way of commitment, he headed down the hall.

CHAPTER
Twenty-Four

By the time Sylvia had finished all her scans, the kids had gone home to give the baby a nap. Sylvia tried to sleep, but the pain in her chest and under her arm was so great that she couldn't relax.

But it wasn't the pain keeping her awake. It was the fear. She'd already had bad news once today. If the scans showed tumors in other organs . . . Well, she couldn't even think past that.

Harry had gone to see the film and gather the reports. Once again, she thanked God that he had pull in this hospital, and that she didn't have to wait through another long night.

When he finally came back into her room, his eyes were bright and dancing.

She caught her breath. "Good news?"

"Yes," he said. "The cancer doesn't seem to have spread to any other organs."

"Oh, thank you, God." She brought her hand to her fore-head and gave in to the tears that had threatened her all day. "Thank you."

Harry's eyes were wet as he bent over her bed. "You're going to be fine, sweetheart," he said. "What the surgery didn't get, the chemo will."

She reached up and framed his face with her hands. "Oh, Harry. Are they sure?"

"They're sure and I'm sure."

She sat up, slid her feet off the bed. Wiping her eyes, she said, "Okay, then that means I can get on with this. I need to go home, Harry. I need to shop for a prosthesis to wear under my clothes. I need to look for a wig for when my hair falls out. I need to start physical therapy so I can move my arm again. I need to spend time with my grandbaby. I need to get on with things."

"I already talked to Sam about releasing you. He told me you can go home tomorrow."

She got up and pulled Harry into a one-armed hug, and melted against him. "You're going to be all right, sweetie," he whispered again. "You're going to be all right."

But the good news didn't outweigh the bad, and that night, as she tried to sleep one more night in the hospital room, with the bright night-light over her head and nurses coming in and out to take her blood pressure and temperature, she thought about those cancer cells that had already gotten past the filters of her lymph nodes. Where had they gone, and where were they headed? Would they take up residence somewhere in her body before the chemo could nuke them out?

Once again, she kicked herself for thinking this way. There was so much to be grateful for. How could she overlook the bless-ings of the normal scans and only concentrate on the negative?

But as hard as she tried to banish them, the thoughts wouldn't go away. She almost wished she hadn't insisted that Harry go home tonight. He was exhausted from sleeping on the sofa next to the window, and with Sarah's family and Jeff in the house, he needed to be home.

Besides, she was a big girl, and the uncertainty had passed. She knew where she stood now, what to expect, what would come next. It could be so much worse. People recovered from breast cancer all the time. It was treatable, and she had the best doctors anyone could want.

Yes, she told herself. She had much to be grateful for.

She reached for the Bible that Harry had left on her bed table, and turned to the Psalms. There would be comfort there, she knew. There always was.

She turned to Psalm 42 and began to read. When she reached verse five, she knew the Lord was speaking to her.

> *Why are you downcast, O my soul?*
>   *Why so disturbed within me?*
> *Put your hope in God,*
>   *for I will yet praise him,*
>   *my Savior and my God.*
> *My soul is downcast within me;*
>   *therefore I will remember you*
> *from the land of the Jordan,*
>   *the heights of Hermon—from Mount Mizar.*
> *Deep calls to deep*
>   *in the roar of your waterfalls;*
> *all your waves and your breakers*
>   *have swept over me.*
> *By day the LORD directs his love,*
>   *at night his song is with me—*
>   *a prayer to the God of my life.*

She hung on the last words of that passage ... His song would be with her tonight ...

Yes, she thought. She should sing that song. She should praise him, even from her despair.

Softly, tentatively, she began to sing about entering his courts with thanksgiving in her heart ...

She sang it slowly at first, haltingly, in a quiet voice that belied the words of the song. But then her heart lifted, and she sang in a faster rhythm . . . over and over . . . until joy did fill her heart like a prayer.

When she finished the song, she smiled and snuggled under her bedcovers. Yes, that was what she needed, she thought. The words of Psalm 104:33 whispered from her lips. "I will sing to the LORD all my life; I will sing praise to my God as long as I live."

Sweet sleep wrought from the Lord's presence fell over her, and in spite of the light and the cold and the pain and the intrusions, Sylvia slept better than she had in days.

CHAPTER
Twenty-Five

Sylvia was home two weeks when she decided to lead a Bible study of the book of James for the ladies of Cedar Circle. Tory couldn't have been happier. Since Hannah's birth, she'd spent so much time obsessing over the child that she hadn't taken enough time for Bible study.

The late August heat hung heavy over Breezewood, so they met in Sylvia's cool air-conditioned living room.

Tory sat at Sylvia's feet as her friend taught her about "considering it all joy" when you encounter trials. Sylvia was still weak from the surgery, and Tory could see the pain on her face when she moved a certain way. But she seemed to be doing well.

As she taught from James, Tory realized that the choice of books was as much for Sylvia as for them. They had all gone through trials of one kind or another, but Sylvia's was one of the worst of all. Tory couldn't imagine how she had the energy to concentrate when so much uncertainty hung over her.

But the study gave Tory comfort, and she could see that it was helpful to Cathy and Brenda, too. When they ended with prayer, Tory sighed. "You know, the more I learn about the Bible, the more I realize I don't know."

Brenda laughed. "Isn't that the truth? I feel the same way."

Cathy, curled up with her stocking feet beneath her on Sylvia's couch, waved them off. "You guys are way ahead of me. I came into this Christian thing too late."

"Don't be ridiculous," Sylvia said. "It's never too late."

"But I don't know *half* of this stuff."

"Well, you will. We're going to work through it together. It'll keep me going."

"Yeah," Cathy said. "Every time you get discouraged and don't want to teach us, you'll realize what heathens we are and decide that you've got to keep going."

Sylvia laughed. "That wasn't what I meant."

Cathy moaned and dropped her feet. "But it's true. I feel like a downright pagan when I start studying. All these things start coming up that I've never even heard."

Tory laughed. "And the worst part is that you're accountable for the things you know. So in a way, ignorance is bliss, right? If you don't know it, you're not accountable?"

"Hey, you're accountable, all right." Sylvia held her Bible up. "Everything you need to know is right here. You're accountable because all that information is available to you. There's no excuse for having it and not reading it."

"Ouch," Tory said. "You can be so brutal."

Sylvia's laughter lilted through Tory's heart. It was music.

Sylvia led them into her kitchen where she'd baked a cake earlier that day. They cut it and took their saucers to the table. "So, Tory, what have you decided about the job?"

Tory shrugged. "I haven't decided yet. But I do need to let Mary Ann know by the end of the week. She's got to hire someone else if I don't take it." Never one to eat much of anything with calories, Tory picked at her cake. "I just feel like I need to stay at home with Hannah. I don't like the idea of putting her in a nursery."

"But it's not just any nursery," Sylvia said. "It's a nursery that challenges her and helps her grow. She needs that, Tory. I wouldn't feel guilty about it at all."

Cathy dug into her cake with gusto. "And think of the benefits to you, getting to work with the older kids. You'll have so much hope about what Hannah is going to do eventually. I think Mary Ann sounds like a genius. You were the perfect choice for that."

Tory cut the icing off and took a small bite of cake. "The truth is, I'd really like to do it. And Barry wants me to."

"Then what are you waiting for?" Brenda's question sounded so reasonable. "I don't even know what's making you hesitate."

Tory smiled. "Do you really think I should?"

"Of course I do," Brenda said. "What's the downside?"

"Well, I wouldn't have as much time for Bible study with you guys. If I have Hannah in the nursery in the morning, I don't want to leave her again at night."

Sylvia wasn't satisfied. "You'll only be working Tuesdays and Thursdays. This is Monday. It's doable, Tory."

Tory considered the passion on Sylvia's face. She needed this study to get her mind focused for her upcoming chemo, and Tory needed it to have the strength to go on with her mothering of Hannah. "I'll probably take the job," she said. "And I'll try to keep up with the study. But the homework you're giving us is pretty substantial, and I'm not sure how much time I'll have to do it. There are some pretty complicated concepts in James."

"Well, you can't let the complicated concepts make you forget that the salvation message is very simple," Sylvia said. "'Believe in the Lord Jesus Christ and you will be saved.' That's all there is to it."

"But there's so much more," Tory said. "We know that works can't save you. Only faith can. But then James says that faith without works is dead. So there's more than just 'believe on the Lord.'"

"There's not more to salvation," Sylvia said. "Just to growth and sanctification."

"Holiness," Cathy said, pointing her fork at Tory. "Now that's the hard part."

"It is hard," Sylvia said, "but when we stay in the Word we can figure out how to be holy. And the great thing is that it's not our holiness that we need, but Christ working in us."

"Amen," Tory agreed.

That night, with her decision made and the Bible still fresh in her heart, Tory snuggled up to Barry.

"I think Sylvia's going to be all right," she said. "She's already back to herself. She's visiting the oncologist tomorrow but she doesn't even seem to dread it."

"I think she'll be all right, too," Barry said.

"And I'm looking forward to my job. I guess I'll start Tuesday."

He kissed her. "I'm excited for you. I think it will be good for you to think about someone other than Hannah for a change."

CHAPTER
Twenty-Six

Harry went with Sylvia to her first post-surgery visit with the oncologist the next day. They sat across his desk, a stack of books and articles on the table next to them.

"What's her chance of recurrence?" Harry asked.

Martin Thibodeaux, the oncologist, drew in a deep breath and thought for a moment. "I'd say fifty percent."

Sylvia gasped. "Fifty percent? I thought my chances were better than that!"

He shook his head. "We'll fight the recurrences if and when they come, Sylvia. But the number of lymph nodes involved raises the stakes."

She felt herself wilting in her chair. Harry's hand closed over hers.

"I'm recommending six months of chemo," the doctor said, "with treatments every three weeks."

"Which chemo?" Harry asked.

The doctor told him the name of the drugs they'd be using.

Sylvia saw by the look on Harry's face that the choice didn't please him. "What is it?" she asked.

"It's a really harsh chemo." The lines of his face deepened. He looked as if he'd aged ten years in the last few days, despite his attempt to keep her positive.

"We need to be harsh," the doctor told her. "Like you've already been told, it's a very aggressive cancer."

Sylvia closed her eyes. "I don't even feel sick. I feel like I've had surgery, but I don't feel like I have cancer. Not the kind that needs the big guns."

"Just keep in mind that we're only doing it for six months. And then because we had six positive lymph nodes, I recommend radiation to begin six weeks after the chemo has ended and the hormone therapy has begun."

Sylvia felt as if facts flew around her head like debris in a tornado, threatening to crash her skull if she didn't duck at the right time. "Harry, I'll never remember all this," she said. "I hope you're getting it."

"I am." She realized that Harry's knowledge of what she was about to embark on made it even more stressful for him than her. Maybe it was good that she didn't know all the horror stories that he knew.

"So when does she go for her first treatment, Martin?" he asked.

"Two weeks. I'm going to go ahead and set up her appointment. She should have healed well enough by then."

The doctor handed her one of the books off of his stack. "I want you to be sure and read this before you come. The first chemo treatment probably won't be quite as bad as you've read. But the effects will accumulate with each treatment. Your hair probably will fall out. And you probably will have a hard time tolerating the drugs. You'll probably have nausea. You might get sores in your mouth. You might get headaches. You'll probably feel pretty rough for a week after each treatment, then you'll have a couple of weeks to get your energy and your blood count back before we do it again."

Sylvia just stared at him and wondered if she was really ready for this. What if she just let it go? Took her chances? Left the chemo to those who could handle it?

"Honey, are you all right?" Harry was stroking her hand, watching her face.

"I just don't know . . . if I'm up to this . . ."

"You are." He put his arm around her shoulder and pulled her close. "Honey, you are. You're strong and brave, and you can do this."

Her mind reeled through pictures of herself pale and sick and bald, sitting on the bathroom floor waiting for the nausea to move her again. Funny how the very drugs that were supposed to make her live would make her sicker than she'd ever been in her life.

But it was the provision God had given her, and somehow, she had to search her soul and find gratitude for that.

CHAPTER
Twenty-Seven

When Tory, Cathy, and Brenda came over that night to hear what the oncologist had said, Sylvia tried to put on a happy face again.

"I was just thinking about my hair," she said. "Since it's going to fall out, I'm ready to shop for a wig."

The girls were silent, just watching her, and she knew they were on the brink of tears.

"I want you all to come with me Saturday," she said. "There's a wig store in Chattanooga that specializes in wigs for people with cancer. I want you guys to come with me and help me pick one out. I don't want to look like a hag while I'm retching my guts out."

No one laughed.

Brenda touched her arm. "Sylvia, are you sure you don't want to do this alone?"

"I'm absolutely sure," she said, "and Harry's no help. He'll just tell me everything looks great. I want some serious help on this. I know you three will tell me the truth. Besides, it'll be fun. We can go first thing in the morning, then stop for lunch on the way back. It'll be a girl trip. We've never had one of those."

Cathy smiled. "Count me in."

"Me, too," Brenda said.

Tory had to think a little longer. "If Barry can keep Hannah, I'll come," she said. "I would sure hate to miss a day with my three best friends."

"Come on," Sylvia said. "When's the last time you went hair shopping? It's the chance of a lifetime."

That Saturday, they all gathered for breakfast at Sylvia's, then took the short drive to Chattanooga, chattering all the way about anything but cancer. But as they went into the store with wigged Styrofoam busts on shelves around the walls, they all grew quiet.

Sylvia was first to break the silence. "It's a little creepy, isn't it?"

Cathy began to laugh. "It's just hair."

A plump woman popped out of the back, wearing a hot pink crepe dress and a black Cher wig. "Hi, girls! I'm Trendy. Are you looking for wigs?"

Sylvia tried to keep a straight face at the name. "Hi, Trendy. Actually, I am. I'm starting chemo in a couple of weeks, and I'd like to be ready."

"Of *course* you would." Trendy had a little-girl voice that lilted with enthusiasm. "And you'll be so glad that you took care of this before you started it. Trust me. After the hair falls out, most women get desperate and hit that wig store at the mall— you know, the one with all that synthetic hair? And they put it on their bald little heads and, besides having a perpetual bad hair day, they might as well have 'I have cancer' written across their foreheads, because it's obvious they're wearing a wig, because real hair doesn't really look like that. Our hair is one hundred percent real, and it *looks* real. You'll love it."

She led Sylvia to a dressing room with mirrors all around, and sat Sylvia down at the dressing table. She pulled chairs up close for Tory, Cathy, and Brenda.

"So, is your color out of a box, or are you one of those lucky gals who never grays?"

"Box." Sylvia glanced with amusement at her friends' reflections in the mirror. "Definitely a box."

"Great. Then we can use the same color to dye the wig you choose. That is, if we don't have the style you like in your color." She stood behind Sylvia, looking at her in the mirror. "Now do you want to keep this style, or do something different?"

Sylvia sighed. "Well . . . I'd kind of like to look like myself. But then again, it might be fun to have something different. Maybe one of those new styles that's bigger on the top and thin around the neck."

"Oh, honey, we have those. I'll bring a few of each."

"Or . . . maybe I could go longer. I've never been able to let my hair grow out. Maybe I could have a big head of hair. You know, the kind that hangs down around the elbow. Maybe like yours."

Trendy snatched her wig off of her head, revealing a short cropped pixie underneath. Cathy howled with laughter and fell against Tory. "Here, try this while I gather up several more choices."

Sylvia looked horrified. "I didn't mean to take the hair off your head!"

Trendy waved her off. "Oh, honey, I have plenty more. I was itching to pull a Nicole Kidman today, anyway."

Sylvia's eyebrows popped up. "Nicole Kidman? Red and curly? I might like to try that, too!"

Brenda's mouth fell open. "Sylvia, you really want to go red and curly?"

Sylvia thrust her chin out. "Maybe."

"Bring one of those," Cathy called. "And do you have a Meg Ryan like she was in *Sleepless in Seattle*?"

"Do I ever!" Trendy said.

Tory and Brenda leaned into each other, giggling. "Sylvia, you're crazy."

Sylvia winked at them in the mirror. "Hey, it doesn't hurt to try them."

Trendy spun around, her dress flowing behind her. "You girls come try some, too. You never know when you might need them. And it's the only surefire way not to have a bad hair day, ever. You may just want to take one home your own self."

The girls scooted their chairs closer to the table as they caught the dream. "I want to be a blonde," Tory said. "Marilyn Monroe."

Brenda ran her fingers through her hair. "I've always wondered how I'd look with short hair. One of those new styles, maybe, that flips up?"

"Got it," Trendy said. "And what about you?" She looked at Cathy.

Cathy thought for a moment. "Got any dreadlocks? I've always wondered how I'd look in dreadlocks."

Sylvia loved it. She laughed hard and loud, and the others joined in.

"I can't believe we're trying this stuff on," Tory said. "It's not like we'd buy it in a million years."

"Really?" Sylvia feigned disappointment. "Didn't you hear about the little boy who had chemotherapy and his hair fell out and everybody in his classroom shaved their heads so that he wouldn't feel bad about the way he looked?"

Cathy narrowed her eyes. "You're not expecting us to shave our heads, are you?"

"You mean you're not willing to? Not even for me?"

Tory couldn't hold her giggles back. "Sorry, Sylvia. I love you, but not that much."

Cathy cleared her throat. "See, I have to keep hair so the animals at my clinic won't get scared of me. Plus there's that pesky law that vets have to have hair."

"Oh, yeah," Sylvia said. "I've heard of that law." She looked at Brenda. "Et tu, Brenda?"

Brenda wiggled her shoulders. "I'll shave. But I don't want a wig. I just want a tattoo of a butterfly right on top."

The four of them screamed at the image.

"Oh, forget it," Sylvia said finally. "I can't have that much change in my life. Just try on the wigs, but keep your own hair."

Within moments the saleslady had come back with about twenty wigs on Styrofoam stands. The women set about putting them on their heads and making fun of each other in the mirror. Sylvia had brought a camera, just to help her remember what she'd bought if she couldn't bring it home today.

She got a shot of Tory in a blonde Marilyn Monroe, Cathy in her Jamaican dreadlocks, Brenda in a short cropped wig.

By the time they had gotten the silliness out of their system and chosen a serious wig for Sylvia, three hours had passed. She'd finally picked a style that was more modern than her own hairstyle. It was blonde now, but she would leave it for Trendy to dye to match her color. This wouldn't be so bad, she thought. She would look younger and perkier as she suffered through her chemo. Already she felt better about herself as she and her friends headed out to have lunch.

Chapter
Twenty-Eight

The morning Tory was to start her new job, she set her alarm for 6:00. Waking up wasn't a problem, since she hadn't really slept much at all. She had lain in bed listening to the rhythm of Barry's breathing and wondering if she was doing the right thing by taking Hannah to the nursery for several hours at a time. Of all the people in Breezewood, she trusted the lady who would be caring for Hannah. But she still worried.

She'd be right down the hall. If Hannah got upset or sick or hurt herself, Tory would be just feet away. It wasn't as if she was leaving her at all. And she needed this.

Despite her trepidation, she'd been a little excited about working with the older children who had the same affliction as Hannah. She wanted to hear how clearly they could speak. She wanted to see what concepts they could grasp, how much they could learn, whether they had skills of reason and logic.

"Why are you up so early?" Barry's sleepy voice sounded slightly irritated.

"I'm sorry," she whispered. "I didn't mean to wake you up. I just have to get ready for work."

"You don't have to be there till nine."

"Yeah, but I thought I'd run a couple of miles first, read my Bible, do a couple of loads of laundry, make the kids a good breakfast . . ."

"Tory, are you gonna do this every day?"

"Nope. Just the days I work. I refuse to neglect my family for an outside job."

Barry sat up and turned on the lamp. "You're not neglecting your family, honey. Brittany and Spencer will be at school. They'll never even know you're gone. And you can do the laundry on your off days."

She slipped on her shorts and sat down on the bed to pull on her running shoes. "I just want to start out right."

"You'll be exhausted by the time you get there."

"Don't worry about me." She came around the bed and kissed him, then turned the lamp back off. "Go back to sleep. Your alarm doesn't go off for another hour."

He pulled the covers up over him again and settled back on his pillow.

Tory scurried out of the room.

She went to the laundry room and started a load, then hit the floor and began her stretching.

When she was finally warmed up enough to run, she took off out the door. The dark morning air was full of dew, but summer still hung on, making it warm. She left the cul-de-sac and headed down the mountain road, easily making the distance she had marked off so long ago. She ran hard and fast, and when she reached the one-mile point, turned around and headed back uphill.

The run back was more punishing than the first half had been, but it was important to her to stay fit and slim. She couldn't stand the thought of getting plump and lumpy. It wasn't vanity. It really wasn't. She just expected more of herself, had a higher standard than most. She wanted to be her best.

By the time she got back home, it was 7:00, and she was soaked with perspiration. Barry had already gotten up and had put in a second load of laundry. Scrambled eggs and bacon fried on the stove.

"You're cooking," she said with a grin.

He nodded. "Not the kind of thing you eat, but the kids'll like it."

She kissed him. "I promise not to wake you so early every time I work."

"It's okay. You're nervous."

She got a towel out of the laundry room and wiped her face. "Am I? You think this is nerves?"

"I know it is."

She leaned against the doorway. "So why am I nervous?"

"Because you're not sure you're doing the right thing."

She smiled. He knew her too well. "Am I?"

"Yes." He grabbed the waistband of her shorts and pulled her close, until her nose touched his. "You're doing the right thing, Tory. I want you to say that fifty times while you're in the shower."

She grinned and brought her sweaty arms around his neck. "If you say so."

"I do. And you'll see."

She felt better as she got into the shower. Barry was on her side, Brittany and Spencer wouldn't know the difference, and Hannah . . .

She heard Hannah crying as she woke up, and Barry called out, "I've got her!"

As the warm shower rained down on her, soothing her jitters, she smiled. It was going to be okay.

༈

Class was already going full tilt when Tory finally left Hannah in the nursery and went to her classroom. The children, age six to nine, all with Down's Syndrome, sat at a table, already hard at work. Their teacher, a woman named Linda Shelton, sat with them as they shaped Play-Doh blobs into things only they could identify.

"Hi, Miss Tory," the teacher called out in a singsong voice as Tory came into the room. "Children, say hi to Miss Tory."

The children looked over at her while still molding their Play-Doh and muttered things that sounded a little like "good morning."

"Good morning, boys and girls." She wondered if Linda called them "boys and girls," or if they even knew that they were boys and girls.

Then she told herself to stop obsessing. These children were forgiving. If she made a teacher faux pas, they probably wouldn't notice.

She pulled a chair up to the table and sat down. Ten children sat around two tables. Two of them sat in wheelchairs, and three others had braces on their legs.

But the other five she had often seen running down the hallway on their way to lunch or recess.

"Thank goodness for your help," Linda said. "We'll get so much more done with you here. And frankly, I was thrilled when Mary Ann told me you're a Christian. It's not a requirement for working here, you know. But I love the fact that most of the teachers here are. And I like for the kids to have that kind of influence. Some of their parents aren't believers. But they really need Christ, I think. Don't you?"

"Of course," Tory said. "But I didn't think we could talk about Christ in the classroom."

"Sure we can," Linda said. "This is a private school. And even though it isn't a Christian school, the people who run it are believers, too. So they're just fine with our passing our faith on to our precious children."

Tory looked at the children working so hard on their blobs, and wondered if they even had the capacity for faith, but she didn't say so. It seemed to make Linda feel better to think she had an impact. And who was she to say Linda didn't?

The little boy next to her tore off a glob of Play-Doh and thrust it at her. "Thank you," she said. She looked at the teacher. "What's his name?"

"Ask him," Linda said. "He'll tell you."

She asked him his name, and the boy said, "My name Bo."

"What are you making, Bo?"

"Haws."

"A horse?" she asked, delighted that she'd understood.

"I make a ball," one of the other ones said, and she oohed and aahed over the ball. A couple of the others muttered things that she could not understand, but the teacher managed to translate as she helped them work on their Play-Doh creations.

Already, she tried to picture Hannah sitting at this very table in this very room hammering on a piece of Play-Doh and explaining what her vision for it was. Would she be one of those in the wheelchairs or have braces on her legs, or would she walk and talk like Bo? Tory didn't know, but just being here gave her peace that she hadn't had before. Sylvia and Barry had been right. She was glad she had taken the job.

CHAPTER
Twenty-Nine

Sylvia grew more serious as the day of her first chemotherapy treatment approached in the second week of September. She'd been warned that the treatment would be given intravenously and could take three hours.

When the day came she packed a couple of novels, her Bible, and some magazines, and Harry drove her to the Cancer Center.

The place looked different than she'd expected. Decorated in warm shades of green, with accent lighting in strategic places around the room, it looked more like someone's living room than a sterile hospital room. Recliner-like vinyl chairs were spaced about three feet apart in the large room, and soft classical music piped through the sound system.

Several other cancer patients occupied those chairs, their own medication dripping into their veins. A couple had on Walkmans, and leaned back with their faces pale and sunken eyes closed. Would she look like that a few months from now?

The nurse led her to a chair next to a woman who stared in front of her with dull, lifeless eyes. The woman's hair had already begun falling out, and thin, lifeless wisps hung into her face. She had a yellow cast to her skin, and dark circles hung under her eyes.

Sylvia tried to get comfortable as the nurse drew blood to check her count. When she disappeared to take it to the lab, Sylvia shivered, and wondered why they kept it so cold in here. She didn't know what it was about doctor's offices, but it seemed that the moment she stepped over the threshold, her circulation cut off, and her extremities flirted with frostbite.

The nurse returned with her IV pole. Sylvia trembled as they inserted the IV needle into her arm and began the drip of the poisonous fluid that would kill the cancerous cells in her body. She looked over at the woman next to her and saw that her eyes were closed. She wasn't asleep, though, for she had a frown on her face. Sylvia could see that she was already beginning to get sick. Sylvia reached over and took the woman's hand. Her eyes flew open.

"Are you okay?" Sylvia asked.

"No," the woman said. "I hate this. It's going to kill me."

Compassion welled up in Sylvia's heart. "No, it's not. It's going to save your life." She smiled. "My name's Sylvia."

The woman's frown melted. "I'm Priscilla."

"Hi, Priscilla. How many treatments have you had?"

"Three before this one." The woman glanced at her hair. "Is this your first?"

Sylvia nodded. "I'm very nervous."

The woman let go of Sylvia's hand and touched her balding head. "I would have worn my wig, but my skin feels so irritated during the treatments . . ."

Sylvia swallowed. Would she have three whole treatments before her hair started falling out? "It's cold in here," Sylvia said.

"They'll bring you a blanket if you need it. I don't. This stuff has brought on early menopause for me, and I seem to live in a perpetual hot flash."

Sylvia had been taking hormone replacement therapy since her own menopause, but the doctors had taken her off of it after they detected the breast cancer. She'd struggled with those symptoms herself, and Harry had warned her that they would likely get worse.

She looked at Priscilla. The woman was probably in her early forties. "What kind of cancer do you have?"

The woman sighed. "Breast, but it's metastasized to my lungs. You?"

"Breast, too."

Priscilla shook her head. "I have three kids. I have to beat this. But cancer can make you feel out of control. All my efforts still might not work."

"God's in control," Sylvia said.

Priscilla started to cry then, as if she wished that were true but didn't quite believe it.

Sylvia's head was starting to hurt, so she laid it back against the seat. Her stomach churned, and a nauseous feeling seeped through her. *Focus*, she told herself. *Think about something else.*

Slowly, she started to sing. "Jesus, Jesus, Jesus ... sweetest name I know ..."

Priscilla looked over at her.

"Do you know the song?" Sylvia asked.

"Yes."

"Sing with me," she said. "Come on. It'll get your mind off of it."

Sylvia started to sing again, and finally her new friend joined in with a weak, raspy voice. Sylvia watched the woman's countenance lift.

Priscilla's treatment ended an hour before Sylvia's. By the time her new friend was gone, Sylvia needed all her energy to get through her last hour.

When it ended, she found that she wasn't as ill as she'd expected. Headachy and queasy, she checked with the appointment nurse to see when the woman's next treatment was and scheduled hers at the same time. Maybe they could help each other again, she thought. Then she returned to Harry, who'd waited patiently in the waiting room.

He sprang up the moment he saw her. "How are you, honey?"

"Better than I expected," she said. "Just a little headachy, but that's all."

He took her shoulders and looked into her eyes. "Are you sure you're not feeling sick? You have this way of putting on a happy face for everybody, but I don't want you putting one on for me."

"You don't think I can hide it, do you? I mean if I start throwing up, I can't very well pretend that I didn't. And don't start wishing bad symptoms on me, Harry. When I say I'm okay, believe me."

As they drove home, she felt the fatigue seeping into her bones. She needed a nap, she thought, but that was all. She had much to be thankful for. But she didn't delude herself into thinking that it wasn't going to get worse. She knew that the next treatment might not be so mild.

CHAPTER *Thirty*

The second chemotherapy treatment seemed to have come too soon. Three weeks had passed way too quickly. Priscilla looked pleased to see her.

"My new friend," she exclaimed as Sylvia got comfortable in the seat next to her. "God is good for sending you to help me through this."

But it was Sylvia who needed help this time, and as her head began to ache and she began to feel that desperate, nauseous sense rising up into her throat, Priscilla started to sing. Sylvia joined in and tried to concentrate on the words and the concepts therein, praising the Lord and keeping her eyes on him as she grew sicker and fainter. By the time they got the needle out of her arm she was retching into the bowl they had brought her.

Harry had to walk her out to the car and into the house. She lay in bed curled up in a fetal position for the next few days, concentrating on feeling better.

The neighbors brought food that she couldn't eat. Friends brought books on alternative treatments, information they got from web sites, tapes on positive thinking, and diets that helped fight cancer.

Strangers she couldn't place for the life of her called her to see how she was doing. She didn't feel like talking to any of them, but on the rare occasion that she answered the phone, she felt as if they were only looking for gossip.

"That's not true," Harry said when she voiced that to him one day. "They just want to know how to pray for you and offer their support."

"Some of them, maybe," Sylvia said, "but people I've never talked to on the phone are calling, people who hardly even speak to me at church. People who didn't even realize we'd been gone to Nicaragua. It's like I'm a celebrity now, and people want to get to know me. Where were they when we were trying so desperately to raise money for our mission work?"

Harry didn't argue, but part of her knew that her attitude wasn't very charitable. People did, indeed, care. She just didn't have the energy to deal with them.

She began to feel better the next week and her sweeter nature crept back in . . . as her hair began to fall out. When she woke in the mornings, strands lay on her pillow. She found it sticking to her clothes, collecting on her furniture, gathering on her carpet.

"I feel like a dog that's shedding," she told Harry. "I think it's time to bite the bullet and shave my head."

Harry looked stricken. "You're not going to do that, are you? Not really!"

"Why not?" She ran her hand through her hair and pulled out a wad. "Look at this. By the end of the week it'll all be gone, anyway. If I shave I'll at least feel like I have some control. And I won't have to vacuum six times a day to get it all up. Then I can start wearing my wig and stop obsessing over my baldness."

She called Cathy as soon as she saw her car home from work. "I need you to come over with your grooming shears," she said.

Cathy laughed. "For what? You don't have a dog."

"I want you to shave my head."

There was silence for a moment. Then Cathy said, "Oh, Sylvia!"

"Don't sound so shocked. My hair's falling out so fast that one good tug would just about do the trick. I have to do something. I'd rather just get it all over with."

"Sylvia, I've never shaved a human head before."

"I promise to be a lot more compliant than your usual subjects. Oh, and call Brenda and Tory. We might as well make a party of it. And tell them to bring a camera. I'm making a survivor scrapbook, and I want a picture of this. Someday when I'm well I'll look back and remember how far I've come."

Cathy hesitated a moment. Then, in a voice packed with amusement, she asked, "This isn't a trick, is it? You're not going to shame us into shaving our heads, too, are you?"

Sylvia laughed hard. "That, my dear, is up to you. Just get over here, and let's get this show on the road."

∽∾

By general consensus, the three decided again not to shave their own heads for Sylvia.

"There are other ways to support you, Sylvia," Tory said as she bounced Hannah on her lap. "I'll walk ten miles in a walkathon to raise money for cancer research. I'll bring you food. I'll take you for your treatments. But I will not shave my head."

Sylvia gave her a look of mock disgust. "Some friend you are."

The shears over her head began to buzz. She swallowed hard and clutched the arms of her chair.

Brenda sat on the porch swing, her hand gripped around the chain from which it hung. "Sure you want to do this?"

"Absolutely." Sylvia looked back over her shoulder. Cathy stood there, holding the buzzing shears and staring down at her hair.

"Oh, Cathy. Don't look so nervous. You can't mess this up!"

Cathy tried to smile. "Okay. But you won't hate me for this, will you?"

"Of course not."

Sylvia turned back around. The buzz moved closer to her head. Cathy lifted the hair at her neck . . . and began to mow through.

Brenda covered her eyes. "I can't look."

"You have to," Sylvia said. "I want you to take pictures. Cathy, give me a mohawk before you shave it all off."

Tory screamed. "A mohawk? Sylvia!"

"Just for a minute," Sylvia said. "For one picture. I'll send it to my kids. Heaven knows they need a good laugh."

Sylvia held her breath as Cathy buzzed off one row after another. She watched as the breeze blew it off across the yard.

"The birds'll love it," she said. "It'll cozy up their nests."

A strand blew past Hannah, and the baby laughed. But Tory's face was red as she stared at Sylvia.

"Okay," Cathy said. "Just let me lengthen the clip so the mohawk will stand up." She buzzed again.

"Oh my gosh," Brenda shouted.

"It's you," Tory said. "Quick, take a picture!"

Sylvia struck a pose and Brenda snapped the picture. Cathy handed her the mirror.

A demented stranger stared back at her, and she howled out her laughter.

When the laughter had settled, she sat back down. "Okay. Finish it off."

Cathy cut off the last row of Sylvia's hair, then buzzed around her head trying to find places she had missed.

"There," she said in a quiet voice. "It's all done." Brenda and Tory's faces grew more serious as Cathy handed her the mirror.

Sylvia raised it and looked at her reflection. The sight startled her, jolting her heart. She looked . . . awful. Not stylish or trendy . . . not even particularly brave. Just sick and pale and bald.

She tried to think of something funny to say, but nothing came to mind. It didn't seem that funny anymore.

"So that's what my head looks like. I've always wondered what it was shaped like. You know all those times when you see *Star Trek* and see those bald-headed women with the perfectly shaped heads? I always had a feeling that mine was probably egg-shaped and lumpy."

"It's not." Tory's voice was weak.

Sylvia kept staring into the mirror. "No, it's not, is it? I should have done this years ago."

Brenda laughed again, but it was a forced, strained laugh, and it didn't fool Sylvia. She stared at the shape of her head and at the soft, smooth, peach-fuzzy feel of the buzz cut.

"Put the wig on," Brenda said softly. "You haven't tried it without a mane of hair underneath."

But Sylvia couldn't speak. She felt the tears rising up in her throat, her voice getting tight. "Why do I feel such shame?" she asked. "It doesn't even make sense."

"Shame?" Cathy asked, coming around to face her. "Honey, what are you ashamed of?"

"I don't know. I guess it's just that I *look* like I have cancer now. It announces it."

Tory got up. "Where's the wig, Sylvia?"

"On that Styrofoam head in my bedroom."

Tory headed in. "I'm going to get it."

She came back a few moments later sporting the wig they had spent so much time choosing. Still serving as the designated hairdresser, Cathy put it on Sylvia, straightened it, finger-combed her hair. Sylvia raised the mirror and examined herself.

"Not too bad, is it?" she asked.

"Sylvia, it looks beautiful," Brenda said. "When your hair grows back, I think you should style it like this."

Sylvia's tears backed out of her eyes, and her throat relaxed. "I do like it. It's just hard to get used to."

"Pretend you just had a makeover," Brenda said.

"And think of the bright side," Cathy added. "No more hair drying, no more rollers."

Tory shifted Hannah. "Like Trendy said, no more bad hair days."

"No more dandruff," Cathy added. "Or can you get dandruff when you're bald?"

"You wouldn't think so," Sylvia said, "since you can put lotion on your scalp. That's a good thing."

"Think how much less time it'll take you to get ready in the mornings," Brenda said.

Sylvia sighed. "Okay, Brenda. Take a picture of the alien Sylvia." She pulled off the wig.

Brenda held the camera up to her eye. Sylvia smiled, showing all her teeth, as Cathy snapped the picture.

"Now on with the wig." She pulled it back on, straightened it with her fingers, then posed up at Brenda. "Not bad for a sick woman, huh?"

"Not bad," Brenda said. "Sylvia, I think you look even better than before."

"See? Chemo becomes me."

The others laughed, but she knew that it was hard for them. Once again, tears threatened the backs of her eyes and hung in her throat. But the wig really did look good. Things could be so much worse.

She suspected they soon would be.

CHAPTER
Thirty-One

The image of Sylvia's shaven head, and the pale yellowish color of her skin, implanted itself in Brenda's mind. She remembered seeing Joseph looking that way, weak and shaky and not quite right. The knot that seemed to tighten in her chest every time she saw her dearest friend had grown bigger today.

Instead of going into her house, she went out to the swing David had hung on a tree on their back lawn, and looked out at the trees that lined their yard. She hadn't wanted to cry in front of Sylvia, not loud and hard like she'd needed to. Now she let the tears come.

She prayed for Sylvia, that the chemo was doing its job, that there wouldn't be any trace of cancer left in her body. She prayed that her friend wouldn't have to suffer or grow weaker before her eyes. She prayed that Sylvia would have the strength she needed to get through this.

"You all right?"

She looked over her shoulder and saw David. She wondered how long he had been watching her. "Yeah, I'm fine. Just a little down."

He grabbed a lawn chair and set it in front of her. Sitting down, he looked into her eyes. "Bad time with Sylvia?"

"No, actually, it was a good time. She made Cathy give her a mohawk. You should have seen it." She laughed, but more tears rolled down her face. Finally, she gave in to the tears and let them twist her face. "Oh, David."

He slid his arms around her and held her, and she wept against his shoulder. "You're really scared, aren't you?"

"Not scared, so much," she said. "Just upset that she has to suffer."

"Is she really suffering already?"

She thought about that, and realized that she wasn't. Not yet. "She just looks weak and pale. And her hair . . ."

"If she's okay about her hair, then you should be."

"That's just it," she said. "I don't think she is okay. She's just so . . . Sylvia. Putting on a happy face. Trying to make everybody think she's just having fun. But she shaved her head today, David, because the chemo was making it fall out. She shaved her head!"

She wilted against him again, and he held her quietly. She was thankful that he didn't accuse her of overreacting. She hadn't expected to feel like this. She wondered if Cathy and Tory were crying somewhere, too.

Finally, she got up, and David walked her into the house. He was gentle with her for the rest of the day, helping with the kids and the house and the laundry, as if she was the one with cancer, and not her friend.

But she couldn't get the sight of Sylvia's bald head out of her mind.

CHAPTER
Thirty-Two

Sylvia stood in front of the mirror Sunday morning a week and a half after her second treatment, trying to adjust the prosthesis so that she wouldn't look lopsided or call attention to what wasn't there. Her incision was still a little sore, but it was worth the discomfort to look normal.

When she was satisfied that it looked fine, she adjusted her wig. She had ventured out a few times since she'd started wearing it, and the few people who had seen her commented on her new haircut and how good it looked. She wasn't sure if they were being kind, or if they really meant it. She'd rather they didn't mention it at all.

"You sure you want to go to church?" Harry asked.

"I'm sure," she said. "I need to worship. I can't hide forever."

He came up behind her and slid his arms around her. "You've never needed to hide. You're still the best-looking dame in the joint."

Sylvia found herself sitting in the service next to a pleasant young man in his early twenties. He looked like a soap opera star, with dark hair and brown eyes behind a pair of intelligent wire-framed glasses. Just the kind of young man Annie would like. He greeted her politely during the greeting time, and she made note of his name, Josh Haverty, and learned that he was a medical student. With delight, she realized he was the son of a couple she'd known for years.

From time to time throughout the sermon, she glanced to her side. Josh kept his Bible open and took copious notes.

As they started out of the sanctuary, Sylvia nudged Harry. "That young man is perfect for Annie. He's George and Sally Haverty's son. I've got to come up with a scheme to get them together."

"Sylvia, no matchmaking," he said. "Come on. You've got better things to do. Besides, Annie probably already knows him from youth group."

"I doubt it. He told me he'd been away at Vanderbilt for the last four years. But he's going to medical school here. I love Annie, and I want to make sure she marries well. Introducing them is the least I can do for her."

"Let Cathy worry about marrying Annie off."

"Well, I'll sure let her in on it. But can't you just see the two of them together? I was thinking we could have a get-together, invite both of them, and see what happens."

Harry rolled his eyes. "Sylvia, you're not up for a get-together."

"Yes, I am," she said. "You just watch."

The weekend before her third chemo treatment Sylvia had a dinner party. She invited Annie, Cathy and Steve, Tory and Barry, Brenda and David, and Josh and his parents. The young man came into the house completely oblivious to the fact that the whole thing had been arranged for this meeting between him and Annie, but she noticed the amused, accusing look in Annie's eyes as the fact dawned on her.

"Miss Sylvia, tell me you didn't," she whispered in the kitchen.

"Didn't what? Honey, would you grab that tray of hors d'oeuvres?"

Annie grabbed the tray. "You had this party to set me up with that guy!"

"Who?" Sylvia asked. "Oh, Josh? He *is* close to your age, isn't he?"

Annie popped one of the hors d'oeuvres into her mouth. "You are incorrigible."

"But isn't he cute? He's a med student. And he's very polite, and he took notes like a madman during church last week."

Annie's mouth fell open. "That's why you picked him for me? Because he took notes in church?"

"No, because he seems like a godly young man. The kind you deserve. Just give him a chance, Annie."

Annie groaned, but Sylvia knew she wasn't mad. "What if *he* doesn't like *me*?"

Sylvia put on a shocked face. "Well, that's the silliest thing I've ever heard. Why on earth wouldn't he like you?"

Annie grabbed a napkin and dabbed at her mouth. "You're good for a person's ego, you know that? Do I still have lipstick on?"

"Yes, you look lovely. Now get out there and talk to him."

Sylvia watched Annie walk around with the tray, offering hors d'oeuvres to everyone in attendance. She saved the young man for last, then stood talking to him in the corner as the conversation went on around her.

Sylvia brought the tangy citrus drinks out and passed them around, and tried to listen in to Cathy's conversation.

"So we figure the first step is helping Mark learn to drive, so he can get his license," Cathy was saying. "But I have to tell you that I dread it with all my heart. Remember what happened when Brenda was teaching Daniel to drive?"

"Oh, yeah," David said. "He wrecked our van and my parked truck the first time he pulled into the driveway."

Brenda started to laugh. "Not one of our better moments. Cathy, you could hire one of those private teachers to come and teach him."

"We thought of that," Steve said, "but Mark balked. Said he didn't want to sit in the car with some stranger yelling at him."

"I'd rather be beaten than teach my strongest-willed child how to drive," Cathy said.

"Well, let me teach him," Harry said.

Everyone looked at Harry.

"Well, don't look so shocked," he said. "I taught Rick how to drive, didn't I?"

"Well, yes, but that was a while ago. Mark's got a little more edge."

"I can handle Mark," Harry said. "Can't I, Sylvia?"

Sylvia chuckled. "You'd better let him do it. He needs a project."

"Guaranteed, I'll even teach him to parallel park, and that's no picnic."

"They don't require that on the driver's exam anymore," Cathy said. "But I require it. I told him no license until he has enough skill to do that."

"Good call." Harry was getting excited. "Come on, let me do it. I would consider it an honor."

"Well, all right." Cathy looked at Steve. "You didn't have your heart set on it, did you?"

Steve laughed. "No, I didn't. Harry, you're a lifesaver."

Harry chuckled. "I've been called that before."

"Yeah, but in your medical hat. We're talking real life-saving here."

As the dinner party went on, Sylvia watched the two kids out of the corner of her eye. They seemed to be getting along well. Everyone there was having a good time. She only hoped that her efforts were not in vain.

CHAPTER
Thirty-Three

A week after Sylvia's third chemo treatment, when she felt human again and was able to ride in a car without getting sick, Harry decided to take her along on a driving lesson with Mark. He'd already taken Mark out numerous times, starting with country driving, then moving into city driving and even highway driving. Today was the day he'd teach Mark parallel parking. For fun, Daniel, Brenda's son, rode along next to Sylvia in the backseat.

Harry instructed Mark as he drove the streets of Breezewood, then braved the interstate. When he was satisfied that Mark knew what he was doing, it was time to teach him the art of parallel parking, to satisfy Cathy.

"All right," Harry said in a calm voice as Mark drove gently along the street heading to the coliseum's parking lot. "That's not bad. Now I want you to make a right turn up here. Put your blinker on. Easy. Easy. Slow down. All right, now turn. That's great, Mark. You're a natural."

Mark grinned and drove like he was the king of the road. They got to the parking lot of the coliseum, and Harry got out and set up an obstacle course of two-liter pop bottles he'd filled with sand. Mark wove through them as adeptly as if he'd been driving in the Daytona 500.

When he'd woven through them several times, Harry was satisfied. "I think you're doing fine, Mark. You'll get your license in no time. Now all we have to do is learn to parallel park."

He got out and set up another obstacle course with bottles a car's width apart, then he got back in. "Now, Mark, I want you to pull up to half a car's length in front of the spot you're trying to get. Half a car's length now. There you go."

"I can do this," Mark said. "Piece of cake."

"Now start backing up slowly. Now cut your wheel hard to the right. There you go. Now let your rear end go all the way in, then cut hard back to the left and straighten it out."

They heard a pop, and Mark slammed on his brakes. "What was that?"

Harry got out and looked. "You hit three of the bottles, Mark. If that had been a car . . ."

"I can do it," Mark said. "Let me try again."

He pulled out, straightened the car, and began backing up again.

"Cut hard now," Harry said. "Pull in . . ."

Another two pops, and Mark stopped again. "Man, those bottles are too close."

Sylvia started to laugh, and Daniel did, too.

Mark grinned. "Don't make me turn this car around."

Sylvia fell against Brenda's boy, raucous laughter coming from both of them.

"Hey, I can do better." Mark pulled the car back out and started over again. This time he didn't turn quite so sharply. He pulled into the parking space, then tried to slam on the brakes. His foot accidentally hit the accelerator and he mowed down the cones. Sylvia yelled.

"Hey," Mark said, "that was an accident, okay? I realize that if that had been a real car I would have totaled it. But it wasn't a real car, and now I'm sure of the difference between the accelerator and the brake. Man!"

Harry shot Sylvia an admonishing look. "If you can't stop laughing, we'll have to put you out of this car."

Sylvia dabbed at the tears in her eyes. "I'll be good. I won't laugh." She looked at Daniel, her lips closed tight. They both spat out their laughter.

By now, Mark was laughing too. "Is this hopeless?"

"No, it's not hopeless," Harry said. "It just takes practice. Nobody can do it on the first try." He got out of the car and righted the mangled plastic bottles. He got back and put his seat belt on. Bracing himself, he said, "Okay, Mark, try it again."

Slowly, Mark made it, this time slipping into the parking space without killing any hypothetical others.

"Now let's try it about twenty more times," Harry said, "and then maybe you can convince your mom to let you get your license."

CHAPTER
Thirty-Four

When Mark got back from practice driving, he got Annie to take him to the local grocery store. She waited in the car while he went in and found the manager.

As soon as the man came to the front, he rolled his eyes. "Mark, I told you I'm not going to hire you."

"I know." Mark held up both hands. "But I wanted to try again. October's almost over and I still haven't found a job. I thought I'd have one by now. I've applied just about everywhere."

"That happens when you've been to jail, Mark. It limits your choices."

"But I can bag groceries!" Mark said. "My brother worked here for years, and my best friend works here now. You know my mother. I made a few mistakes, but I've changed, and I really need a job."

The man shook his head. "I don't hire kids with records. I've kept that policy for years, and it's worked well for me. I have enough problems with the good kids."

Mark swallowed. "I'm a good kid. I know you wouldn't know it from my past. But if nobody ever gives me a chance, how can I prove it?"

"I'm sorry, Mark."

Giving up, Mark shuffled back out to Annie's car and slammed into it.

"No luck?" she asked.

"Nope."

"Bummer."

"Annie, don't be cute. This is my life, and it's not going very well."

"Mark, you'll get a job soon. It's no big deal."

"It is to Steve. Every single day he asks me where I looked and what my prospects are. I'm getting sick of telling him how many times I've been turned down. I'm starting to feel like a loser again."

"Well, you're not one, okay?" Annie pulled out of the parking lot. "Maybe God just wants you to concentrate on getting your GED."

"Yeah, well, that's another thing. I took the test as soon as my class started. I didn't tell Mom or Steve because I wasn't sure I'd pass. And I was right."

"You failed?"

"Yeah. So I'm stuck taking this class until I can try again. This isn't turning out like I hoped."

She shook her head. "You should have gone back to school, Mark."

"No, I shouldn't have. I still think this could work out, if I could just get a stinking job. Isn't there anybody out there with compassion? Somebody who messed up once himself, and understands that one stupid act shouldn't mean a life sentence?"

Annie pulled back onto Cedar Circle and whipped into their driveway. "There is somebody like that, Mark. Just keep looking. And pray. God'll work things out."

Mark was quiet as he went into the house and hurried up to his room to start studying before class.

CHAPTER
Thirty-Five

Though she wasn't feeling her best, Sylvia continued with the Bible study she'd started in her home. The effort of keeping it going had been good for her. It had forced her to stay in the Word when her instinct might have been to wallow in her own problems and forsake the very book that gave her strength.

It also gave her a reason to see her friends. It seemed that the only time they came around now was on Bible study night, and before they did, they always called to make sure she was up to having company.

Of course I'm up to it, she thought. Did they think that she enjoyed being a hermit? She thought back to the day when she'd shaved her head. It was the last time they'd really laughed and shared together. Since then, they seemed to walk on eggshells around her, like they feared they would say exactly the wrong thing to send her over the edge.

She leaned back on the couch, trying to get comfortable, and looked at Tory who sat next to her. "So tell me about your job," she said. "You haven't talked much about it."

"Well, it's great," Tory said. "The kids are sweet. They keep me busy, but I like it."

She looked at Cathy. "And what about your family? How's the whole stepfamily thing going?"

"Good," Cathy said. "Great."

Monosyllables, Sylvia thought. Why couldn't they answer her in paragraphs instead of sentence fragments?

"And Brenda? What's new at your house?"

"Just the same old thing," she said. "Nothing new, really."

She sighed and opened her Bible and flipped to the page they'd be studying tonight. For a moment she just stared down at the page, feeling the grief of lost friendships.

But that was crazy. She knew they were still her friends. They weren't sharing their lives with her for one simple reason. They didn't want to burden her. They felt that her problems were so huge that she couldn't handle the weight of theirs too.

She knew all that, but it didn't make it easier. So many things had changed. She hated the cancer that had altered her world so drastically. Oh, for the day things would be normal again!

She started reading the passage they were studying, and silently asked God to clear her mind and make her stop feeling so sorry for herself. And slowly, moment by moment, she got over the hurt of being shut out of her friends' lives, and concentrated on the Word of God.

CHAPTER
Thirty-Six

Days after her fourth treatment, Sylvia curled her body more tightly into the fetal position she'd been in for the last five days. She lay still, focusing on the backs of her eyelids, hoping that if she didn't move, the room wouldn't begin to sway and she wouldn't have to launch out of bed like a toilet-seeking missile.

Vaguely, she remembered the days in León when she'd worked from daylight until dark helping out in the orphanage, a surrogate mother to the broken and abandoned children. She'd hardly ever given a thought to her balance or her equilibrium, her energy or her metabolism. Health had been a given. She'd never even thought of it as a gift.

How she longed for that now! She would never again take it for granted.

Sores bubbled on her lips and in the soft tissue inside her mouth, making it hard to eat or swallow. Yet somehow she'd still managed to gain weight. How could that be? She could hardly stand anything in her mouth other than ice chips or water, and almost inevitably, whatever she did swallow came right back up. So how was it that she'd gained almost ten pounds since her treatments had begun?

Just another perk of cancer, she thought. She doubted the disease was going to kill her, but she felt certain the treatment would.

When the doorbell rang, she pulled herself tighter into a ball and tried to figure out what day it was. Monday, she thought, but she wasn't sure. Visitors didn't often come on Mondays.

She hoped Harry would send them away. She had no strength to be on display for anyone who'd come to get a first-hand glimpse of her suffering. The grapevine was going to have to be adequate for anyone looking for gossip.

You've grown bitter, Sylvia.

The self-admonishment was no more welcome than the ringing doorbell. She didn't care if she was bitter. She had every right to be.

But the moment that thought crossed her mind, she took it captive. How dare she be bitter? She had always claimed to trust in God, whatever he brought her way. Now he had brought her something difficult, something challenging. Was she going to spit in his face now?

She heard Mark's voice in the living room, laughing and talking as if he'd just won the lottery. He must have gotten a job, she thought. He must have passed his GED.

Then she heard "driver's license," and she carefully lifted her head to hear more.

"The guy testing me said I was the best he'd ever seen."

She heard Harry laughing. "You've got to be kidding me. Let me see that license." More laughter, and she realized Daniel was with Mark.

"I told him not to smile," Daniel said, "but he stretched up like that monkey on that commercial and showed all his teeth."

"Hey, I was proud."

Sylvia smiled.

"We wanted to tell Miss Sylvia. Does she feel like visitors?"

"Uh ..." His voice dropped. "Sylvia's not really feeling well right now, guys. Maybe you should come back later."

But she didn't want them to come back later. Mark was excited *now*. As sick as she felt, she didn't want to miss one of the boy's best moments.

She raised up on her bed and straightened the robe she'd been wearing. "Harry," she yelled out with as much strength as she could muster. Harry stepped into the doorway.

"I want to see them," she said. "Give me a few minutes, then let them come back."

She forced herself to get off the bed, grabbed her wig, and pulled it on. She straightened her robe, then sat down on the mattress. "Come in, guys," she called, "and let me see that license."

Mark looked around the doorway and stepped in tentatively, and Daniel followed. Mark brandished the license as if it was an FBI badge. "You believe this, Miss Sylvia? I'm a licensed driver."

"We've got some celebrating to do." Sylvia took the license in her shaking hands, and started to laugh. "Mark, the teeth—"

"I was just kidding," he said. "I didn't know they were about to snap the picture. But they're tricky. They make you think they're not ready yet, so you sit on that stool and look around, and then they tell you to look at the camera. They wait for, like, the stupidest expression you could make, and then they snap it. I was trying to get a laugh out of Daniel while they were setting up, but next thing I knew they were herding me off the stool."

Daniel joined in. "Mark begged and pleaded for them to give him another chance, but they felt they'd gotten the dumbest expression he had, so they kept it. I'd say they were right."

Sylvia hadn't felt like laughing in days, but now her shoulders began to shake with the joy of these kids.

"Yeah, Miss Sylvia. I'm like, 'Nobody's gonna recognize me in this picture.' I look like that chimpanzee in that pager commercial. It's cruel, I tell you. Cruel."

Sylvia handed the license back. "But the instructor said you were ... what was it you told Harry? That you were the best he'd seen?"

"Well, not the best, exactly," Mark said. "But really good."

Daniel shoved him. "What he really said was, 'Fine job, kid.'"

"Yeah, well, he doesn't say that to everybody, does he? He urged me not to stop with my private license. He said I was so good I should get my commercial license and drive for a living. He practically handed me a commercial license."

"Practically?" Sylvia asked.

"Well, almost."

Forgetting her nausea, Sylvia pulled her feet up on the bed and leaned back on her pillows. "This fish is getting bigger and bigger, Mark."

Mark threw his head back and laughed. "Okay, so he just said, 'Fine job, kid.' The important thing is that he passed me."

"That's right. What does your mother say?"

He shrugged. "She kind of turned white when I asked her if I could use the car tonight. I don't think she's real keen on me being out there on my own behind the wheel yet, but she'll get over it." He slid the license into his wallet. "Hey, Miss Sylvia, I really like your hair."

Sylvia grinned at him. She wasn't sure whether he was pulling her leg again. It was quite possible that Cathy hadn't told Mark about her shaved head. "Thank you, Mark," she said.

"No, really. It looks great. I thought you were supposed to, like, lose your hair or something when you had chemo."

Sylvia smiled, and Harry stepped into the room behind them, watching for her reaction. "Some do, some don't. Maybe I'm one of the lucky ones."

Mark seemed satisfied with that. "Well, we'd better go. We just wanted to show you."

"I'm glad you did, guys. I'm so proud of you. Even if the DMV man didn't say you were the best he'd ever seen, I'm sure he thought it."

When the boys were gone, Harry came back into the bedroom and sat on the bed next to her. "See? I told you no one knows it's a wig. It looks great."

She smiled. "Why is it that young people can lift my spirits so when no one else can?"

"You miss the kids in the orphanage, don't you?"

She nodded. "I wonder what they've been told about me."

"They've been told that you're sick and won't be able to come back until you're well. They're praying for you. I e-mailed Julie with the dates of your chemo, and they're praying hard on each of those days."

"I don't want them worrying about me," she said. "I think if I feel better tomorrow, I'll go buy them all something and send them a big box from Mama Sylvia. I was thinking about Beanie Babies."

"They'll love them."

"That way they'll know I'm still kicking." She sighed. "I wish I could go visit them between treatments."

"Sylvia, there's no way. Your immune system is too weak. And look at you. You haven't gotten out of bed for days."

"I know." She slipped back under the covers and curled up. "But it's terrible to be without them for so long."

"They're being well cared for. You're not the only one who loves them."

"Thank God for that." She laid her head back on the pillow.

"Do you think you might be able to eat now?"

She thought about it. "Maybe. I'm not making any promises."

"Okay. I'll bring you some soup."

"Not too hot," she said. "My mouth is so sore."

He started out of the room, and Sylvia closed her eyes and wished she had the energy to sit at the table with him. But the room was beginning to spin again.

Still, she was thankful for those two silly boys who had come by to lift her spirits. It was the first time in five days she'd seen hope that she'd emerge from under this pall of sickness. Maybe by tomorrow she could actually get out of bed.

Cathy was in the kitchen when Mark came in, closing the back door softly behind him.

"Mom, is Miss Sylvia going to die?"

Cathy turned around, startled to see tears in her son's eyes. "Why do you ask that?"

"Because I was over there," he said, "and she looks awful. Her face was so pale, and she's got these sores on her mouth, and her hands were shaking."

Cathy abandoned what she was doing and pulled a chair out from the table. Mark sat down across from her. "We just have to pray, Mark. We just have to hope that God will spare her."

"And why wouldn't he?" Mark asked. "I don't get it. I thought God blessed his children. Why would he let them suffer like that?"

Cathy sighed. Hadn't she asked the same question herself a million times? "God doesn't just take the lives of the ones he doesn't like. He takes those he loves, too. Sylvia is not immune to death by disease. None of us is. But I think she's going to live, Mark. I know five or six people who've survived breast cancer just fine. It's highly curable. The chemotherapy is the worst part, but she'll get through that."

Mark was quiet for a long moment. "Mom, I know you're uncomfortable with my driving by myself yet, but have you decided yet if I can borrow the car?"

Cathy stared at Mark, amazed at how fickle a teenager's mind could be. One moment they were talking about death, and the next he was thinking of going for a joyride. She sighed. "What for?"

"I want to buy a box of Popsicles before I go to class tonight," he said. "I was thinking that Popsicles might be something Miss Sylvia could eat. Those sores are bound to hurt."

So he wasn't thinking about joyriding, after all. He wanted to do something for their neighbor.

Tears misted her eyes as she leaned over and pressed a kiss on his forehead. "Yes, Mark. You can borrow the car. Go buy Miss Sylvia Popsicles."

CHAPTER Thirty-Seven

That evening when Steve came home from work Cathy hit him up with what had been on her mind for several days.

"Steve, I've decided I want to buy Mark a little car so he can get to his GED classes and to work as soon as he gets a job. That way we won't have to keep taking him everywhere he has to go."

Steve dropped his keys on the counter. "Cathy, that's not a good idea."

"Why not? He needs one, and I got one for Rick and for Annie when they started driving."

"I know, but I've always thought a kid should save up at least half the money before he gets a car."

"Do you know how long it would take Mark to save that kind of money? And it's an endless cycle. He can't get a job unless he has transportation, and he can't get transportation unless he has a job. I want to help him. He *needs* some help."

"Cathy, we can get him to class. But how are you going to teach him about the drudgery of minimum wage work if he's not having to pay any bills of his own?"

"He's sixteen, Steve. I don't want him to have bills! Besides, it's not fair for me to buy a car for Rick and for Annie, then when it's his turn tell him that I've changed the rules."

"What rules? You have a rule that you have to buy him a car?"

"You know what I'm saying. It's not fair if he doesn't get one, when they did. He shouldn't get passed over just because I remarried!"

Steve stared at her for a moment before his face shut down. He turned to the refrigerator, opened it, and scowled inside. "Fine then. You've got your mind made up. I don't even know why you asked me."

Cathy rolled her eyes. "Come on, Steve. I asked you because I care what you think."

He slammed the refrigerator door, knocking the bottles inside against each other. "Only if I think what you want me to. Go find him a car, Cathy. I won't say another word about it."

"Steve, you don't have to get mad. I wanted to talk about this. Am I not allowed to make my case?"

"Of course you're allowed. But you already have your mind made up, and you're not going to take no for an answer."

"Well, why would you *say* no? I can understand your position if we were starting when Mark was ten years old, and he knew ahead of time that he'd have to save for his own car. But you don't come up when he's sixteen and say, 'Oh, by the way, I may have gotten cars for your brother and sister, but you're going to have to save for yours.'"

"So even if what you're doing is wrong, you do it just to be fair?"

"Why is it wrong?"

"Because Mark needs to learn responsibility."

"He will. Rick and Annie have responsibility. They both work and make good grades. Mark will too."

Steve breathed a derisive laugh. "Are you kidding? I don't even think he's looking for a job. He's been home three months, and all he does is sleep till noon and watch television all afternoon. Then he pulls himself together and goes to class."

"He *has* been looking, Steve! You're not here all day. You don't know how he's spending his time."

"Where has he looked? Name one place."

"I don't know, but he has. He does want to work, Steve. But his record is getting in his way. He'll get a job soon."

"I'll believe it when I see it."

She tried to calm her voice before she set him off again. "Would you just come and look at this car I found? I'm not sure if it's reliable enough."

"So you didn't really need my opinion at all. You've not only made up your mind, but you've found the car."

"No, I haven't found the car. I found *a* car, and I wanted your input."

"Fine." He grabbed up his keys. "Let's go."

Cathy had hoped to change out of her jeans and tennis shoes and the baggy shirt she'd been wearing to pull weeds out of the backyard. But she knew better than to detour Steve now. She followed him out to the car and got in.

He brooded as they drove to the car lot. She didn't like him when he brooded. It reminded her too much of her ex-husband, when he would use his passive-aggressive silence to keep her in line.

Steve rarely did it, so when he did, it had a greater impact.

She brooded back, not willing to give him the satisfaction of melting into a rambling idiot trying to make up with him.

When they got to the car lot, she led him to the little Civic she had chosen. For Mark's sake, she broke the silence. "It seems to be in great condition. It's four years old. I thought he'd like it."

Steve was quiet as he looked under the hood, examined the belts, and checked the engine for leaks. He got under the car and checked its underside, as if he would look until he found something wrong.

Cathy bit her tongue and waited patiently for him. Finally, he stood up and brushed his hands off.

"It looks like a good enough car," he said. "How much is it?"

She told him and he rolled his eyes. "Cathy, don't you think that's a little expensive for a kid's first car?"

"It's not like it's a Cadillac. I just want him to have something reliable, okay? I don't want him breaking down somewhere."

"You could probably get an older model that might not be in perfect condition for a whole lot less money."

For a moment, Cathy wondered what this moment would be like if Steve were Mark's real father. Would he want the same thing she wanted for Mark? Would he be more interested in seeing the joy on their son's face than in grinding out some lesson on responsibility?

Or did original parents bicker over these things, too?

She supposed she would never know. "I want to get him this one," she said. "This is the one I like."

He breathed a frustrated laugh. "Then why did you bring me here? I thought you wanted my opinion."

"I did want your opinion," she said, "about whether it was reliable or not."

"Oh, I see. You wanted my opinion about its reliability but not about the wisdom of buying him the car."

"I thought we'd already been through this!"

"We have," Steve told her. "I'll be waiting in the car while you do your business. You let me know what you decide."

She stood there at the car, hands on her hips, as the salesman strode toward her.

"So, you want me to write it up for you, ma'am?"

She felt as if the wind had been knocked out of her, and crossing her arms, she shook her head. "No, I think I'm going to have to come back."

"He didn't like it?"

She shot a look at the car. Steve had a look of granite on his face as he stared out the side window. "No," she said, "he didn't."

"Well, what didn't he like about it? Maybe I could show you something else."

She shook her head. "No, he doesn't want to see anything else."

Without another word she headed for the car, got into it, and slammed the door. She snapped her seat belt into place and crossed her arms.

He looked at a spot on his windshield. "Are you going to buy it?"

"No, I'm not."

"Why not?"

"Because I don't want to have to deal with your attitude."

"My attitude?"

She ground her teeth. "Before I married you, Steve, I could buy anything I wanted for my children. I didn't have to ask anybody's permission."

"Well, you knew when you married me that we were pooling our finances *and* our children. That was the plan, anyway. I thought you valued my input." He started the car and pulled off of the gravel lot.

"I do value your input, Steve, except when you're wrong."

"Oh, that's just beautiful." He set his mouth, and she was glad she couldn't read his thoughts.

But she spoke hers out loud. "I don't know why you have it in for my children."

His eyes flashed as he turned to her. "I can't believe you would accuse me of that."

"I'm not accusing you. I'm just pointing out the truth."

"The truth is that I have it in for your children? Give me a break, Cathy. I've been nothing but good to your children. Even when Mark was in jail I was the one who was mentoring him. I thought you appreciated that."

"I do." She knew he was right. He had made such a difference in Mark's life. "I really do, Steve. But why can't I do things for my children? You do things for Tracy."

"I'm not going to buy her a car."

"Well, why not? When it's her turn I'll be just as generous with her as I am with my kids. I don't understand why I can't buy my son a car."

"Because it builds character to have them pay their own way."

"Well, that's fine," she said, "except for the last few years Mark hasn't been interested in paying his own way. And for the last year he's been in jail so he couldn't possibly have saved for his car. He got out with a new attitude, Steve, and he's trying to change his life. I want to help him. Is that so wrong?"

His face softened as he stared at the road in front of him. "No, it's not wrong, Cathy, and I do understand your intentions. And if you want to buy him a car, go ahead. I don't want to stand in your way. I just think that one is a little bit too expensive."

"I'll pay for it," she said. "Come on, Steve. I earn plenty of money, and you earn plenty of money. Together we don't have financial problems to speak of. Why can't I splurge a little bit with my son?"

"Okay, now we're down to it." Steve set his mouth again. "I should have known we weren't really pooling our resources. It comes down to yours and mine. The first time I balk at something you want to buy, you all of a sudden want to take your half back. Is that how it's going to be?"

She grabbed her ponytail and tugged on it. "No! I'm just saying that if I work hard and earn my share, why can't I spend it on my son? I don't know why everything has to be so hard."

"Everything is hard?" he asked. "I thought we'd done pretty well, Cathy. For the last six months we've done really, really well. Until Mark came home."

"Are you saying that Mark has caused all this trouble? Because he hasn't done anything. He's been a perfect angel."

"He's been a good kid," Steve conceded. "I'm not saying he hasn't. I just think that maybe we were sailing along too smoothly until we had more kids in the house, and now that we've got Annie back home and Rick dropping in and out at all hours . . ."

"And Tracy," Cathy added. "Don't forget that you have a child in the mix, too."

"I know that," he said. "It's just that we have different parenting styles and different philosophies on what a kid needs as they grow older."

"Well, we're going to have to find some common philosophies," she said. "We're going to have to agree on some things before Tracy gets any older. But right now I can't go back and undo everything I've done with my children."

He banged his hand on the steering wheel. "But you can change a few things now."

"What if I don't think things are wrong?" she threw back.

He got quiet then. "Look what we're doing to each other."

"What?" she snapped.

"We're turning on each other, all because of the children. All that premarital counseling, and we thought we could beat those blended family problems they warned us about. But we haven't. They're sucking us under, too."

"You're changing the subject." Cathy looked out the window. "I want to buy Mark the car."

He leaned his head back on the headrest. "Then go for it."

"I will."

They didn't say another word for the rest of the way home.

When he went into the house she got behind the wheel, backed out of the driveway, and headed back to the car lot to make a deal on the car.

CHAPTER
Thirty-Eight

Cathy surprised Mark with the car the next day before he went to GED class. Steve had made himself scarce since he'd come home from work, and now he busied himself washing his truck. He'd hardly said a word to her since the night before, and each of the children had noticed and mentioned it at least once. The house was tense, for all of the kids had noticed the strain between them.

When she blindfolded Mark and led him out to the driveway, Steve looked at her across the roof of his truck. His eyes accused, indicted, punished. But they did not convict her.

Mark's excitement shivered through him. "Can I open my eyes now?"

"Just a minute." She positioned him in front of the new car. Annie and Tracy came out behind him and gasped at the sight of the car in the driveway.

"Open your eyes," she ordered.

Mark's eyes opened, and for a moment he stared at the car as if he didn't quite understand.

"It's for you," Cathy said. "I bought it last night."

Mark gaped at her. "The car? The whole thing?"

"No, Bozo." Annie shoved him. "Just the steering wheel."

"I don't believe it. Mom, I love it!" He laughed and threw his arms around his mother, then danced to the car and opened the door. "It's beautiful. I never expected anything so nice. I figured you'd get me a clunker like you did Annie and Rick."

Annie turned on her. "Yeah, Mom. What's up with that?"

Steve shot her another look and went to turn off the hose.

"Well, I figured you deserved a nice car. I wanted you to have something reliable."

"Mom, it's fantastic." He got behind the wheel and cranked it up, listened to the engine. "Listen to it purr," he said. "It's beautiful. Look, and it's got a CD player. Oh, man."

"Way to go, Mom." Annie gave her a high five.

Tracy jumped up and down and ran around to get in the passenger's side. "Take me for a ride, Mark!"

Drying his hands off, Steve came around the truck. "Not yet, Tracy. Let's let Mark get a little more practice under his belt before he starts taking passengers."

"I'm a good driver," Mark said. "You should see me."

"I know, but I just prefer that Tracy didn't ride with you for a while."

"Well, he can take me, can't he?" Annie said. "I'm a licensed driver. I can correct him when he messes up."

"I'm not going to mess up," Mark said. "It's like I've been driving for years. I can parallel park and everything, can't I, Mom?"

Cathy smiled. "He did a knock-up job at the driver's test. The instructor was sure impressed."

Steve didn't say anything. He turned back to the truck and began drying it off.

When Mark drove off with Annie, and Tracy had gone back into the house, Cathy stood in the driveway and regarded her husband across the truck. He seemed to be intent on polishing it to perfection. The silence screamed at her, and she hated it. She'd hated it last night when he'd gone to bed without a word, and she'd stared at his back all night. Several times she had almost touched him and tried to make up. But to do that, she would have had to give in to him, and Mark wouldn't have gotten his car.

But now that the deed was done, she didn't feel as thrilled as she thought she would. If she could consider today a victory, it was a hollow one. Mark was happy, but she was left feeling alone and shut out.

She watched Steve drying his truck, and wondered if he hated the silence as much as she did.

"Can we be friends again?" she asked him.

He breathed a laugh. "We're friends, Cathy. We're husband and wife."

"But you're not real happy about it right now."

He just kept drying.

She went around the truck. He was bent down now, drying the lower part.

"Honey, I'm sorry for all this," she said to his back. "I still don't agree with you. I don't think I've done anything wrong, but I don't like us being mad at each other."

He straightened. "I don't like it either, Cathy, but your attitude the last couple of days has been really hurtful. You've accused me of being mean to your children, of not wanting them to have things, of standing in your way of parenting them. And you've tried to take back your part of our money, separating it out like I have nothing to do with it. That really hurt, Cathy, because when we got married I thought we were two becoming one. You said we were joined at the heart. But it doesn't feel like we're very joined at all right now, and I don't know what to think about that."

She took the wet towel out of his hands and slid her arms around him. "I love you, Steve. I didn't want to make you mad. I'm just a mother bear trying to protect her cubs."

"I'm not a threat to your cubs, Cathy."

"I know, but I want so much for Mark right now. I want to encourage him. I want to give him things to give him a head start. I don't want him suffering anymore. It's done now. Can we get past it?"

"Is that how it's always going to be? You're just going to do it and then I'm going to have to accept it?"

"No." She pulled back. "I'll try to be more sensitive to your feelings from now on. Please. I love you. I don't want us to be mad at each other. It's hard on the kids and it's especially hard on me."

He looked at her for a long moment. Finally, his expression softened. "I'll try to get over it, Cathy. I don't want to be mad, either, but it doesn't go away just like that. It's hard to shake off the things you said. Once they're out of your mouth, you can't really take them back."

"But can't I be forgiven?"

"Sure you can be forgiven," he said, "but I just don't think you're very sorry."

She backed away, crossing her arms. "What do you want me to do, Steve? Get down on my knees and beg?"

"No."

"Well, do you want me to snatch the car back out from under Mark and take it back to the dealership and tell him that I was wrong, that I don't want it?"

"Oh, that would really make me look like a hero," Steve said. "I've tried to be a good stepfather, and somehow I've wound up being the bad guy. It didn't start out that way."

He was right. Cathy dropped her arms and looked down at the water under the car. "No, it didn't," she said. "You don't deserve that."

"Well, thank you for that."

She looked up at him and saw the love in his weary eyes. He reached out for her. She went willingly into his arms and held him, thankful that his love was strong enough to survive these storms. But in her heart she knew that he wasn't completely over it.

That evening when they went to bed, she could tell that he was still tense, still upset about the things that had occurred between them, and she wasn't sure that she could make it right. She couldn't undo what had been done. Mark had the car now, and Steve didn't want to be the bad guy by making him give it up.

And after all was said and done, she still didn't feel she'd been wrong.

With that hovering in her consciousness, she fell into a deep sleep ... but the space between Steve and her on the king-size bed seemed wider than it ever had before.

CHAPTER Thirty-Nine

The drugstore was crowded, full of shoppers with coupons, and the line at the photo counter was almost as long as the line at the pharmacy. Brenda fidgeted as she waited to talk to the pharmacy's cashier. While she did, her mind clicked through calculations of her checking account balance, the checks about to clear, and the cost of Joseph's medication. Getting the medicine was critical. Transplant patients couldn't do without it. But how would she pay this time?

She went through this every month, when she came to get his drugs refilled. Sometimes David's work had netted enough to pay outright. Those were the good months. But other months she juggled between paying by credit card or adding to her store account. This month both were almost maxed out.

She got up to the cashier, said Joseph's name, and the woman scurried away and came back with a bag of medicine. She scanned each bag. "That'll be $553. Cash or credit card?"

Brenda's hands trembled as she fumbled with her check-book. "Uh, is there any possible way you could put this on my account? I know I already owe a lot, but . . ."

The woman punched her up on the computer, studied the account like a million-dollar banker disgusted with the riffraff. "Can you pay any of it at all?"

Brenda wondered why they kept it so hot in here. "I can pay $300 if you could put $200 on my account."

"Okay, we could do that," the woman said, "but you really need to make a payment pretty soon."

Brenda drew in a deep breath and started writing the check. "I know. I will. We don't have very good insurance because my husband is self-employed."

The woman wasn't interested. Brenda tore out the check and handed it to her. "Thank you so much."

"Uh-huh." The woman chomped her gum and typed into the computer. Then looking past Brenda to the next customer, she asked, "May I help you?"

Brenda went back to her car and sat behind the wheel, staring at the windshield and trying to decide what she needed to do. She couldn't go another month like this. At some point the drugstore would insist on being paid for the tab she had run up. She couldn't take the risk of having them cut off Joseph's supply of medication.

Once again, the idea of getting a job loomed in her heart. Not just any job, but a good one, one that had insurance bene-fits and paid well. Always before when she'd thought of getting a job she had looked for things that were small and insignifi-cant, part-time work that she could squeeze around her home schooling. The job she'd had as a telemarketer at night had been an ordeal and she didn't relish the idea of repeating it. When she had home schooled Mark, Cathy's payments had helped with the medication, but even that hadn't been quite enough.

Always before, she had found it critical to stay home with her children. But the fact was that Joseph, their youngest, was twelve now, and David was home working in his workshop all day long. It wasn't like the children would be unattended or unsupervised. She could get a normal job with normal work hours, and give them assignments to do during the day. Then she could home school them at night when she got home.

It wasn't ideal, but it was necessary. Sometimes sacrifices had to be made.

She had never stopped trusting God to provide for her, but she realized that sometimes God provided by leading you to work. Maybe it was time for her to do just that.

She started the car and pulled out of the parking lot. Her mind drifted to Sylvia's plight, and she wondered what Sylvia and Harry would have done without adequate insurance. Thankfully, their denomination had offered that when they'd gone to the mission field. What if cancer struck the Dodd family? How would they ever pay? In a family of six, someone would get sick, someone would need surgery. There would be tonsillectomies and appendectomies. She and David could be struck with disease, or there could be an accident. They had to be ready.

But David would never go for it.

How would she convince him of the wisdom in her going to work?

And if she did convince him, would he urge her to put the children back into the school system? They would balk at that for sure. Besides, they'd be bored to death because her schooling had gotten them way ahead in their studies. Rachel and Leah were probably already two years ahead of their counterparts in school, and Daniel probably could have graduated by now and headed off to college. Joseph had almost caught up with Leah and Rachel.

No, they needed to stay home and keep studying in the way that worked for them. It would just be more challenging now, but they could do it.

She drove home, holding back the tears in her eyes, trying to psyche herself up for her talk with David. If he saw any trepidation or dread in her face, he would put his foot down and kill himself trying to work even longer hours than he already did. He'd start talking again about going to work for someone else, where there were benefits and a steady income.

But David loved what he did, and she liked having him home. No, it made more sense for her to work. Somehow she would convince him.

She got home and took the medicine inside, then stepped out the back and found David in his workshop. She went inside.

David didn't hear her. His power saw buzzed through a flat piece of lumber, and Brenda waited until it came to a stop.

"Hey there," she said.

He pulled his safety glasses up to his forehead. "Hey. I thought you were at the drugstore."

"I'm back." She picked up one of the pieces he'd just cut, and blew off the sawdust. "Listen, I need to talk to you."

"Shoot." He pulled the safety glasses completely off. "What is it?"

"David, I had an epiphany."

"Uh-oh."

She smiled. "I want to get a job. But not a part-time job like I've tried before. Not a night job. I want to work full-time at a place that has benefits."

She saw the distress darkening his pale features. "Brenda, we've talked about this."

She tipped her head to the side and softened her voice. "No, we haven't. Not really. We've never considered a serious job. David, I haven't had any income since I quit teaching Mark fifteen months ago. There's no reason I can't work."

"There are *four* reasons," he said. "Daniel, Leah, Rachel, and Joseph." He crossed his arms and sat down on one of his sawhorses. "Brenda, is this about Joseph's drugs?"

There was no use denying it. "David, it's getting harder to pay for them. Even the most affluent family would have a hard time paying a monthly drug bill like ours with no drug coverage."

"We could get another credit card," he said. "Or change drugstores and open a new account somewhere else."

"David, we don't *have* to go deeper into debt. I could help. I've figured it all out. I could give the kids assignments in the mornings, and you could look in on them all during the day. When I get home, I could do the one-on-one teaching. It could work."

"The kids would be unsupervised most of the day, Brenda. I'd rather put them back into school than do that."

She crossed the room and stood in front of him. "David, they're good kids. If I gave them enough to keep them busy ..."

"Brenda." He said it in that tone that brought a halt to the conversation. "I don't like the idea. It won't work."

She felt tears pushing to her eyes, tightening her throat. Staring down at the floor, she said, "David, I want to do this for Joseph, and for the rest of the family. I *need* to do this. It can work if we make it work. When have we ever backed down from anything just because it's hard?"

He stared at the jigsaw hanging on the wall, his teeth set. "I'll figure something out, Brenda."

She had heard that before, but there wasn't anything to figure out. The answer was obvious. "Honey, I know that you have a hard time with this. But it's not your fault. You've been working out here fourteen hours a day. You're a wonderful provider. But who could have expected us to have a child who needs hundreds of dollars' worth of medication to stay alive? You're not the only one who has to make sacrifices, David. I need to make some of them, too."

David set both palms on his worktable and let his head slump down. "You're great at what you do, Brenda." His voice was barely audible. "Ours are the luckiest kids in the world. I want you to keep doing what you do best."

That did it. The tears rushed her eyes, stung her lids, trembled in her throat. She crossed the room and slid her arms around him.

"That's so sweet," she said. "But they're older now."

"They're not grown. They still need you."

"And I'll still be here at night and on weekends. And you'll be here too. We could try it, David. Just to see. If it doesn't work out, we could find a Plan B."

"That is Plan B."

"Okay, then, Plan C or D . . . on down the alphabet. We Dodds can handle a challenge. All of us."

David held her, and after a moment, he kissed her hair. "All right, honey. Go ahead and look for a job. It doesn't hurt to look. We'll see what comes up."

She rose up and kissed him. "Thank you, David." She touched his face. "It'll be okay. You'll see."

He nodded silently, then put his safety glasses back on. The saw buzzed behind her as she stepped out of the workshop.

CHAPTER *Forty*

Friday afternoon, Cathy was in the middle of administering heartworm medication to one of her regular patients, a German shepherd she'd treated since he was a pup, when her secretary came around the door.

"You have a phone call from a Harry Bryan."

Cathy finished with the dog, then hurried to the phone.

"Harry?" she asked when she picked it up.

"Hi, Cathy. I hope I haven't bothered you."

She closed her office door with her foot and sat down. "Is everything all right?"

He didn't answer. "I wanted to talk to you about Sylvia."

"Sure." She leaned forward on her desk. "How's she feeling?"

"Pretty bad," he said. "That last chemo treatment really did her in. She's getting her energy back now, but she's been depressed. And she told me yesterday that she feels left out of your lives because nobody's talking about themselves. You come over and you're totally focused on her. I wanted to ask you if you would gather up Brenda and Tory and come over and visit her after work today. She needs some company."

"Well, of course." Cathy swept a strand of hair behind her ear. "We've been trying to stay away because she's been so sick. We thought it took too much energy for her to have us over."

"She needs a reason to get out of bed," he said. "So come over and tell her all your problems, tell her what's going on with Mark and with Rick and Annie, tell her how the marriage is going. Get Brenda to tell her what's going on with the family, and let Tory update her on Hannah. In fact, tell her to bring Hannah with her."

"Harry, we really don't want to burden her."

"You're not burdening her," he said. "You'd be helping her."

She sighed and pulled on her ponytail. How many times over the last few days had she wished she could run to Sylvia for advice? "Well, I can sure give her an earful tonight."

"Good," he said. "Just come whenever you're ready."

"How about seven?"

"All right. I'll tell her so she'll be ready."

Sylvia sat in the living room when the trio came in. Cathy hesitated at the door as a rush of emotion tightened her throat. She looked worse than Cathy had ever seen her. Her skin had a yellow cast to it, and her eyes seemed sunken in. But the moment she saw Hannah on Tory's hip, she reached for her.

"Give me that baby."

Tory set her in Sylvia's lap. Sylvia laughed as Hannah smiled up at her. "Oh, you sweet thing."

"How do you feel, Sylvia?" Tory asked.

"Better than I look. Aren't you glad?"

"You look great." Brenda's weak statement didn't ring true.

Sylvia waved her off. "I feel like I've aged twenty years in the last two weeks."

Cathy sat down next to her. "Is it the chemo?"

"Yes. The cancer and I were getting along fine until they started shooting that stuff into my veins. But I don't want to talk about that." She sat back and put her feet on the ottoman. Hannah settled her head comfortably against Sylvia's chest. "So what's going on with you girls? Cathy, how's Mark settling in?"

"Oh, all right."

Sylvia gave her a knowing look. "That doesn't sound good. He's not getting into trouble, is he?"

"No," Cathy said. "It's just that Steve and I don't exactly agree on everything about Mark. In fact, we've been at each other's throats."

Sylvia's eyes speared her. "Tell me everything, Cathy. What's going on?"

Cathy looked from Brenda to Tory, and realized that they were watching her with great interest.

"Well, let's hear it," Tory said. "I thought you two were the happiest couple in the cul-de-sac. What gives?"

She sighed. "Steve's really mad at me."

"About what?" Sylvia asked.

"I bought a car for Mark," she said, "and Steve didn't think I should. He thought I should make him save up for half of it. But the thing is, he can't get to work if he doesn't have a car."

"Where's he working?" Brenda asked.

"Well . . . nowhere yet. That's another sore point between Steve and me. But he will have a job soon."

"So you bought him the car," Sylvia said, "against Steve's will?"

"Not really. I mean, he says he's not upset that I bought the car, but that I bought the one I did. He thought it was too expensive."

"Was it?"

"No," she said. "I earn good money, Sylvia. I work hard. I should be able to buy my son something if I want to. Mark's been through a rough year. I wanted to do this. I don't know why he wanted to stop me."

"It doesn't sound like Steve to sulk over something like that."

Cathy took off her shoes and pulled her feet beneath her. "He says he's mad because of the way I did it, because I told him that he was interfering with my parenting of my children. And then when I started talking about how I earned enough money to be able to do things for my children, he felt like I was splitting our finances down the middle and taking my half back."

"Sounds like it to me too." Sylvia's calm declaration shot through Cathy.

"That's not true. Sylvia, I know all about submission and everything, but Steve was off base."

"It's like I told you before, sometimes he will be. But the Bible didn't say submit to your husband when you're sure he's doing the right thing. I doubt if Steve would have pressed the issue if he knew how you really felt. He probably would have gone out and bought Mark a car himself, if I know him."

"Well, it didn't seem like he was heading in that direction, Sylvia. Trust me."

"I'm just saying that maybe you jumped the gun. Maybe there would have been a meeting of the minds if you'd just waited a little while."

"But I wanted to buy him the car now."

"I know you did," Sylvia said. "And look where it got your marriage. Honey, when are you going to learn that you've got to die to yourself to have a happy marriage?"

The baby started to squirm, and Tory took her back. "She's right, Cathy."

Cathy turned on Tory. "How can you say that after what you went through with Barry during your pregnancy? When he wanted you to abort Hannah? You didn't submit to him then."

"That was different," Tory said. "I wasn't willing to sin against God to make my husband happy. But you're talking about a car, Cathy. Not a life."

Cathy turned to Brenda. Surely she was an ally. "What do you think?"

Brenda smiled. "I can understand how you feel, Cathy. But I think Sylvia's right, too."

Cathy got up and set her hands on her hips. "I have a problem with dying to myself when it comes to my children. I'm not doing this for me, Sylvia. I'm doing it for Mark. Don't you agree that he deserves a car, that he needs something to help him get a head start so that he can get a good job and get his GED and get on with his life?"

Sylvia shook her head. "That's not the point, Cathy. It's like I told you. Steve probably would have come around and it wouldn't have been a bad thing then. But now you've got a strain between you. That's not going to help Mark in any way."

Cathy just stared at Sylvia, then Tory, then Brenda. "All right. When I get home I'll die to myself so hard that you'll have to plan my funeral."

Sylvia laughed. "That's my girl."

Cathy plopped back down and propped her feet on the coffee table.

"So, Tory, how's your job?"

"I love it," Tory said. "It's the greatest decision I've ever made. You should see the kids. They're so precious. They celebrate every victory, from washing their hands in the sink to scribbling on paper."

"I'm so glad you like it," Sylvia said. "Has it changed your perspective about Hannah's future?"

"Some. But mostly it's changed my perspective about me. They have no self-consciousness at all. They don't have the same critical tapes playing in their heads that I have. Nothing inside them is censoring them or scolding them. They just go for it. If they can't do it, fine, but if they can, you should see the joy on their faces."

"We could all learn from that," Brenda said.

"Really." Tory got on the floor and set Hannah down. "There's this little guy named Bo who loves to learn. And he loves for me to teach him. He always wants to sit by me. When we go outside he wants to hold my hand. He has the sweetest heart."

Sylvia's eyes glistened at Tory's enthusiasm. "Do you think they might let me come when I'm feeling better, and read to them or something?"

Tory looked up at her. "Well, sure. We always need help."

Brenda set her elbow on her knee and propped her chin. "Are they hiring, by any chance?"

Tory glanced up at her. "Maybe. They have all the teachers they need, but they might need some part-timers."

"Too bad." Brenda straightened. "I need full-time."

"You?" Cathy's question was too blunt. She'd known that Brenda and David were on a tight budget, but she didn't know Brenda was looking for full-time work.

"Yes, I'm looking for a real job with benefits."

Sylvia leaned forward and got a pretzel out of the bowl Harry had put out. "Brenda, are you sure you want to do that?"

"Yes, I am." Brenda got a pretzel of her own and seemed to examine it. "I've got to find a way to pay for Joseph's drugs. Most part-time jobs don't have benefits, so I'm going full-time."

Cathy couldn't picture David going along with that. "How does David feel?"

"Well, he wasn't thrilled about it at first. But he knows it's necessary. I'll be giving the kids assignments to do while I'm gone, then I'll home school at night."

Sylvia shook her head. "Honey, you'll wear yourself out."

"I'll be fine."

Tory slid Hannah back onto her lap. "Have you found anything yet?"

Brenda ate her pretzel. "No, not really. I've put in applications at about a dozen places. Since I've been at home for the last sixteen years, they act like I have no skills."

"No skills?" Sylvia laughed. "Brenda, that's ridiculous. You have more skills than someone who's been in the workforce for twenty years."

"That's right," Cathy said. "You have medical experience, lots of it."

"True," Brenda said.

"And you're a teacher," Tory added.

"Yeah, but not a licensed one. Home schooling momhood doesn't count."

"You can type," Sylvia said.

Brenda nodded. "Yes, I'm a really fast typist."

"You could be an office manager," Tory said. "You've organized your family for years."

"Or a bookkeeper," Cathy said. "Aren't you the one who handles the finances?"

"Some of them."

Sylvia took another pretzel. Cathy watched her, wondering if she'd been able to keep much down for the last few days.

"Looks to me like you're a candidate for just about anything out there," Sylvia said. "I just hate to see you doing it. Maybe you could find something you could do from your home."

"I'd love that," Brenda said, "but it wouldn't pay benefits. That's the main incentive. I have to have insurance."

Sylvia stared into the air for a moment as if she was thinking, then ate another pretzel. "We need to pray about this," she said finally. "God has something just right for you."

"I'd appreciate those prayers," Brenda said.

Cathy saw through Brenda's smile and knew it was a facade. Her friend didn't have much peace about this, but she was doing what she had to do. Cathy wished she could help her, but she had offered her money before, and Brenda had been insulted. She wished Mark were still home schooling with her so she'd at least have that income.

But it still wouldn't solve the problem of the insurance.

"I'll put some feelers out," Cathy said. "Maybe I'll hear of something."

"Me too," Sylvia said.

Tory nodded. "I'll check at the school."

"Don't worry," Cathy said. "You'll be gainfully employed before you know it."

"Maybe," Brenda said. "But I don't think it's the best time to look for a job, right before Thanksgiving and Christmas."

"In God's timing," Sylvia said. "By the way, what are you all doing for Thanksgiving?"

Tory pulled some plastic keys out of her diaper bag and handed them to Hannah. "We're going to have dinner with Barry's mom and brother."

Cathy shrugged. "I think we're going to stay home. It's getting kind of complicated. Mark can't decide whether to have it with us or with his dad, though Rick and Annie both want to stay home. And Steve's parents want us to come see them, but my kids don't really want to do that . . ."

"Nothing's easy with you guys, is it?" Tory asked.

"Nope. Never is."

Cathy looked at Brenda. "What about you, Brenda?"

Brenda smiled. "We're having our traditional pilgrim dinner. The girls dress like pilgrims, and the boys are Indians, like the first Thanksgiving."

Sylvia laughed. "You never stop teaching, do you, Brenda?"

"Oh, it's fun. Sylvia, why don't you and Harry join us?"

Sylvia shook her head. "Can't."

"Why not? Are you going to Sarah's or Jeff's?"

Sylvia's smile was weak. "They're coming here, just for the day."

Cathy's heart swelled, and she took Sylvia's frail hand. "If you need help with the meal, let us know," she whispered.

"It's all under control," Sylvia said. "It's going to be a good day."

CHAPTER
Forty-One

As Cathy walked home from Sylvia's, she thought about what her friends had said about dying to herself and submitting to her husband. She was tired of the tension between Steve and her. Someone was going to have to break it, and she knew it had to be her.

When she got inside, Steve sat in the living room watching a ball game on television while he folded a load of towels. Steve rarely just sat back and relaxed. If he allowed himself the time to watch television, he always tried to accomplish something else while he did. Cathy was thankful for the help he gave her in running the household.

Tracy sat at the kitchen table behind him, trying to polish her nails. So far, she'd gotten more polish on her cuticles and fingers than she had on the nails themselves. Cathy touched Tracy's hair. "How's it going there?"

"Not too good," Tracy said. "I think I'll have to take it all off and start over."

"Why don't you let me do it for you?"

"Would you?" Tracy looked up hopefully at her.

Before Cathy pulled out the chair to sit down, she looked at her husband. They had talked some since their fight about the car, but she could still see the tension in his back and neck as he kept his eyes on the game.

She went over to him and pressed a kiss on the back of his neck. He glanced back at her and forced a smile. "Sylvia okay?"

"Yeah, all things considered."

"Good." He folded another towel, set it on the stack.

Cathy sat down and helped Tracy take the polish off, then slowly, painstakingly, began her manicure.

"You do a good job," Tracy said quietly as she watched each stroke down her nail. "I don't know why I can't do it."

"It's hard to do it to yourself," Cathy said. "Sometimes a girl just needs someone to help her."

"But my friends all do it themselves, and they don't look like freaks when they're finished."

"Just takes a little practice."

They both got quiet as Cathy finished up, blowing on them to dry them. "Now," she said, "how's that?"

Tracy looked proudly at her nails. "Much better."

Cathy propped her chin on her hand. "Time to get ready for bed."

Tracy moaned. "But can't I watch TV awhile? I'm not tired."

"Tracy, it's late."

"But I'm twelve. I should be able to stay up."

Cathy sighed. She needed to talk to Steve and couldn't do it with Tracy sitting here.

"Besides," Tracy added, "it's Friday. I don't have school tomorrow."

"But you said you were coming to work with me in the morning. You need to earn some money, remember? I don't want to have to scrape you off of the bed. So go on, kiddo. Hit the sack."

"Okay. In a minute." Tracy went around the couch and plopped down.

Cathy looked at Steve. He still watched the game and folded the towels, as if he hadn't heard the exchange at all. If he had, he certainly wasn't going to rebuke his daughter.

So she tried a different tact. "Steve, can I talk to you alone?"

"Sure." He finished the towel he was working on, and handed Tracy the remote control. Taking the stack of towels, he headed for the bedroom. Cathy followed him.

"What is it?" He put the towels away, then sat down on the bed and started to take his shoes off.

Cathy stood, watching him. He didn't meet her eyes—she tried to remember if he had even once since their fight. "Steve, I was talking to Sylvia and the girls tonight about the car and everything . . . and I just realized that I've made a lot of marital mistakes lately. I should have waited and given you time about the car. I should have tried to compromise and maybe come to some kind of agreement with you. And I shouldn't have expected you to get over it with my belated apology."

He put his shoes in the closet, then leaned against the door. "I accept your apology. Again."

Could it be that easy, she wondered, or were his words only one of those lip-service things that wouldn't pan out in his behavior?

But then he crossed the room and pulled her into a hug. "I miss you when I'm mad at you," he said.

All her tension and anger melted away. She laid her head against his chest. "I miss you, too. That bed is so big when we're mad. You're a good-feeling husband."

He smiled. "You're a good-feeling wife." He kissed her, then looked into her eyes. Really looked. That distant gaze was gone. "I hope you know I wasn't trying to make Mark's life hard for him."

The truth was, she didn't know that. She released him and stepped back. "I think sometimes you do want things to be hard for him so he'll be tougher or have more character. I'm just not sure you're right."

It was the wrong thing to say, and suddenly, Steve's soft look hardened. "Wait a minute. I thought you just apologized. What was it exactly that you were apologizing for?"

"For overriding you. For doing it when you didn't agree that I should."

He nodded, like he just now understood. "Okay. So you're sorry you did that, but you still stand behind your reasons for doing it."

"Not exactly."

He breathed a laugh and shook his head. "Well, excuse me for being dense. It's just that an apology doesn't sound very heartfelt when it's followed with more argument."

"I'm not arguing, Steve. I'm just asking if it could even be possible that I'm right for once?"

He narrowed his eyes and stared at her. "Did you think you were going to apologize, and that would lead me into saying, 'No, no, *I'm* the one who's sorry. I should have jumped on board with the car, because you were absolutely right'? Is that what prompted the apology?"

"No. Of course I didn't expect that. And the apology was prompted because I don't want you mad at me."

He sat back down on the bed and stared at his knees. "Good, because that's not going to happen. I still think that *you* were wrong. You think you have to make it up to Mark for the year he was in jail. But you're wrong when you start trying to spoil him and make things easy for him. He still needs structure and firmness. He needs to have to strive for things and know the satisfaction of achieving them. It's not good for him to just lie around the house when we've told him he needs to get a job."

"He's looking, Steve. You know that. And he's studying."

Cathy heard Nickelodeon blaring from the living room, and she stepped to the door and peered out into the living room. Tracy still hadn't turned off the television. Instead, she sat on the floor in front of it.

"Tracy, I told you to turn off the television and go to bed," she called out, then turned around to Steve. "Why are you so tough on Mark but you let Tracy get away with murder?"

"Get away with murder?" he asked. "What are you talking about?"

"She's disobeying this very moment, and you haven't said a word about it."

Steve sprang off of the bed and headed to the doorway. "Tracy, turn off the television now and get to your bed!" he yelled.

Cathy hadn't expected that. She watched Tracy turn around with startled eyes. "What did I do, Daddy?"

"You didn't mind Cathy. Now do what I said."

She turned off the television and headed quickly up the hall.

When he turned around, he looked like the wind had been knocked out of him. "Are you happy?"

Cathy grunted. "See how it is? You hate disciplining her, but you don't mind being hard-nosed with my kids. I understand your points about Mark, but Tracy's disobedience goes right over your head. You treat my kids differently than yours."

He started to protest, then caught himself and sank down on the bed. "It shouldn't be different," he said. "I don't mean for it to be."

"Well, it is, and it's normal. I do it, too. I'm soft with my kids, but less tolerant with Tracy. There's grace involved when you're parenting your own child. But there's more law between the stepparent and the child. God is a lot like our parent, and the law is like our stepparent. When we have the Holy Spirit it's pure grace, but when we're under the law, it's hard-nosed and objective . . . but without grace."

He got quiet and tried to process that. "Grace versus law. That's an interesting perspective."

Relieved, Cathy wondered where her words had come from. She'd never thought of the situation exactly in those terms before, and yet the words had spilled out of her mouth. But there was wisdom there, she thought. And it might be the key to learning how to make their stepfamily work.

"Think of it," she said. "Think of it from Tracy's perspective. I told her to go to bed, and she didn't. You didn't see any reason why she couldn't stay up. So I get mad at you for not taking action . . ."

"I just didn't see any harm in letting her watch TV when it's Friday night."

"And I didn't see the harm in buying Mark a nice car. It's grace, Steve. You give grace to Tracy, and I give grace to Mark. I'm not suggesting that you get tougher on Tracy. I'm just saying that if we could treat each other's kids with more grace and less law, we'd have a happier family."

He looked down at his sock feet. "You may have a point."

"I'm trying to learn, Steve." Tears shone in her eyes, and she went to sit next to him. She slid her arm across his shoulder. "I'm really trying to understand about dying to myself and submitting to you. It just doesn't come easy, not for a woman who's been going it alone for so long."

He reached for her hand at his shoulder, and laced his fingers through it. "It's okay. We're both still adjusting. We're going to make it. We've just got a few glitches to work out."

"Do you think so?" she asked. "Are you sure we aren't going to be mad at each other for the rest of our lives?"

He smiled and looked at her. "I couldn't be if I tried. You're just too irresistible."

Grace instead of law. It was the nature of their marriage, too.

CHAPTER
Forty-Two

Sylvia woke soaking wet. The hot flashes had been almost debilitating for the past few weeks, even when she was having her good days after the treatments.

She got out of bed, careful not to wake Harry, and went into the bathroom. Her clothes needed changing again. Exhausted from her constantly interrupted sleep, she turned on the shower, shed her clothes, and got into it.

The cold water ran over her body, washing away the perspiration and cooling her off. Despair rolled over her too, threatening to pull her under. She leaned against the shower's wall, letting the water spray into her face.

And softly, she began to sing. "A mighty fortress is our God . . ."

It wasn't a magic formula that made her symptoms stop, cured her cancer, or solved her problems. It just made her feel better to adore her God and remember that he was her defender and her refuge against the enemies assaulting her. It got her mind off of herself and onto him.

It didn't happen right away, and as the depression hung on, she told herself that she didn't feel like singing. But she sang anyway.

Finally, by the third verse, she felt the depression dripping away like the sweat that had awakened her. Her spirits lifted, and hope seeped back into her bones.

She got out and dried off and tried to focus ahead. She would probably feel all right by Thanksgiving, just six days away. The kids were all flying home just for the day, because Jeff and Gary, Sarah's husband, had to work the Friday after. Harry had insisted on letting a local restaurant cook the dinner, so they'd just have to warm it up before the meal. She hoped she'd have more energy to put into Christmas. Her sixth treatment date fell just three days before Christmas, but her doctor had agreed to postpone it until the following week, so that she would feel good. She was thankful for that.

Breanna would be eighteen months by Christmas, and Sylvia couldn't wait to see her toddling around their house, fascinated by their tree, tearing into the presents.

It was dreadfully important to have the best Christmas she'd ever had this year. But to do it, she would have to start now.

With thoughts of decorations and food and family coming to visit, she went back into the bedroom.

Harry had the lamp on and was changing the sheets.

"Harry, I didn't mean to wake you."

"It's okay, honey. I wanted to change the sheets for you."

"They were soaking wet," she said. "Another hot flash."

He smoothed the fresh sheet out. "All dry now."

She sighed. "Until the next one."

"We have more sheets," he said. "Plenty of them."

She crawled back into bed and curled up next to her husband. Gratitude filled her heart again for the man who had chosen to be her life partner and had never faltered in fulfilling that promise.

She had much to be thankful for.

As hard as Sylvia tried to put on her best face for Thanksgiving Day, she realized that her children saw her as a sick, possibly dying woman. The look on Sarah's face when Harry brought her in from the airport spoke volumes.

"Oh, Mom ..." She burst into tears and threw her arms around Sylvia. Sylvia held her, rocking back and forth. Sarah just cried.

And then Jeff came in, and she saw the startled look on his face. He quickly rallied. "Hey, Mom. You look great."

She hugged him. "Don't give me that. I must look awful, judging by the looks on your faces. Come on, I spent all morning fixing up for you. Now where are Gary and Breanna?"

Sarah wiped her eyes. "Gary's getting her out of the car seat." She touched Sylvia's face. "Mom, are you sure you're all right?"

"Yes!" she said. "Chemo is no picnic, but I'm doing fine. It's not the cancer you see, honey, but the side effects of the medicine. I've gained a little weight, so I might look a little puffy. And my skin color would make Elizabeth Arden cringe. But it's temporary, guys. It's going to be okay."

Harry burst through the door, carrying the baby in his arms, and Gary came in behind him with the suitcases. Sylvia gasped and reached out for the child, and as she got to know her grandchild, the seriousness faded, and the joy of Thanksgiving filled the house.

When they sat down for the meal, Harry asked them each to tell what they were most thankful for in the past year. Sarah muttered something about her child and marriage, Jeff said he was thankful that they could all be together today, Gary said he was thankful for Sarah and Breanna, and Harry said he was thankful for all the opportunities the Lord had given them to serve him.

When it was Sylvia's turn, she hesitated a moment and looked from her daughter to her son. They watched her, waiting to see if she could truly be thankful for anything in this state. So she surprised them.

"I'm thankful for my cancer."

Sarah's face twisted. "Mom, how can you say that?"

"It's easy," Sylvia said. "God gave it to me as an opportunity . . . a gift. I can use it. I'm not sure how yet . . . he hasn't revealed all that to me. It might be to support other cancer patients when I've gotten through this. Or it might be just to prove his faithfulness. But whatever the case, he's going to use it to bear fruit through me. I know he is. And that's what I'm here for, isn't it? To bear fruit. If I can do that better because of my cancer, then why shouldn't I be thankful for it?"

Her words didn't bring a smile to either of their faces. Gary reached over and took Sarah's hand, a silent gesture of support as she struggled to hold back her tears. Harry patted Jeff's shoulder, as her son stared at the turkey at the end of the table.

Breanna began to bang on her tray, demanding attention and food. It broke the ice and made them all laugh, and she became thankful for that, too.

As they dug into the meal, she silently asked the Lord to make her even more thankful. The cancer *was* a gift, she knew. She just needed the courage and strength to use it fully.

Thanksgiving came and went, and Sylvia felt good about the facade she'd shown the kids. They had put them back on their planes that night with smiles on their faces, and promises to see them next month for Christmas.

But her fifth treatment knocked her out again.

Still, as soon as she was able, Sylvia forced herself out of bed. She had too much to do to get ready for Christmas, and she wasn't going to let her cancer ruin it.

She made her way through the woods at the back of her property, a garbage bag in one hand and a pair of pruning shears in the other. Now and then she would spot a tree that was perfect for trimming branches that could be made into garland, or the wreath that she had made every Christmas for years.

Harry trudged through the woods behind her with his own garbage bag and shears, but she knew he wasn't interested in the live wreath that she planned to create. He had come just to make sure she didn't fall in the woods.

"Honey, you know this isn't necessary," he said. "We could go to one of those craft stores and buy a bunch of fake garland this year. Everybody else in the world does it. Some of it is really beautiful."

Sylvia shot him a disgusted look. "I do real garland, and I've been known to make the most beautiful wreaths in Tennessee. I'm not going to stop now."

"But I'm not sure you're up to this. I don't even know how you've made it this far out here."

"I'm fine." The truth was, she wasn't fine. She had spent the night throwing up, and she hadn't been able to eat a thing this morning. Her legs shook with each step, but she was determined. "I want the house to look just like it always looks at Christmas. The kids are scared enough. I want normalcy, joy, excitement this Christmas."

"They would understand this time. In fact, they'd probably love to help decorate."

"By the time they come for Christmas, it's going to be done. We have a grandbaby this year. I want her to walk in and see the wonders of Christmas."

Harry didn't argue anymore. She found a stump and sat down, tried to catch her breath. A feeling of nausea rose up over her, but she fought it until it was gone. The brisk air against her face made this a little easier.

When she had gotten all she needed, she went back to the house for a nap. She would rest for a while, then get up and wire the garland together and make her famous wreath. In fact, she might just make one for each of her neighbors.

She heard Harry in the garage, pulling out boxes of lights. She knew he did it just to please her. Usually, she had to beg and plead with him to get it done by the second week in December. December was still two days away, but Harry was getting it done.

In bed, she prayed that the Lord would give her uncanny strength to make this a wonderful Christmas for her children and her grandchild, because she knew he had given her no guarantees that there would be another one for her.

CHAPTER
Forty-Three

What're you doing, Dr. Harry?"

Harry turned from the lights he was hanging on the bushes in front of their house and saw Joseph standing with his hands in his pockets.

"Hanging lights. Wanna help?"

"Sure." Joseph unwound the spool on which Harry had wrapped them the last time he'd taken them down, and fed it to Harry. "It's early for Christmas lights, isn't it?"

"Sylvia has her heart set on getting it done early. I think she's worried she won't have that many good days, so she's giving herself plenty of time."

"I know what her problem is."

Harry turned back to the boy. "You do?"

"Yes. She's not having any fun. She needs to have fun. When I was sick, my mom tried to make me have fun, and it helped. It gets your mind off of your problems."

Harry finished the bush and plugged it in to test it. The lights came on. Satisfied, he unplugged them again. "So what do you suggest, Joseph?"

"Well, what's the most fun she's ever had?"

"She likes playing with our granddaughter. And all the kids back at the orphanage in León."

"But they're not here." Joseph kept unwinding the lights. "Miss Sylvia used to have a lot of fun when she rode your horses."

Harry smiled and took the strand of lights from him. "Yes, she did. But that was quite a few years ago."

"She'd still like it, I bet." He got to the end of the strand and handed it to Harry. "I wish you hadn't had to sell them for me."

Harry turned back to the child. "Joseph, everyone in town was trying to help out with your transplant expenses. It was the least we could do, especially when we were about to go to the mission field."

"Yeah, I know. And I appreciate it. I really do. But maybe you could get another horse for Miss Sylvia, just until she's better."

Harry wrapped the lights, letting that idea filter through his mind. "I don't know, Joseph. She might be too weak to ride."

"But it would get her out into the fresh air, because she'd want to talk to it and pet it and feed it and stuff. And I could help, you know. When you two didn't feel like feeding it or cleaning the stables, I could do it. I remember how."

Harry crossed his arms and looked down at Joseph. Brenda had always said that Joseph had an uncanny wisdom that few children his age had. Now Harry believed it. "You know, you could be right, Joseph. Maybe it would be good for her. Give her something else to love. Something to take care of."

Joseph nodded, his round face very serious. "Because she had to give up so much, leaving Nicaragua and all. She's probably mourning for all those kids and stuff. And if you got her a really good horse, she'd fall right in love with it."

"But what about when she's well and we go back to Nicaragua?"

"You could sell it," Joseph said. "Maybe I could buy it. I could start saving now . . ."

Harry grinned. "What about riding it? Do you think you could ride it for us if Sylvia didn't feel like it? Just to give him exercise?"

"Sure." Joseph's whole face grinned. "I'd love to do that."

Harry had caught the vision. He pictured Sylvia sitting out on the back porch, instructing Joseph in brushing the horse, cooling it down, putting on the saddle and taking it off. It would go so far in getting her mind off of her illness. She might even bounce back faster from her chemo if she got the fresh air and exercise she needed.

"Joseph! Supper!" Brenda's voice cut across the yard.

"I gotta go," Joseph said. "Sorry I couldn't help more, but I can come back after supper."

"No, I'm almost done," Harry said. "Besides, you did help a lot. I'm going to think about what you said."

They slapped hands, then Joseph took off running across the yards. Harry watched, moved, at the exuberance and health in the boy, when he'd come so close to death not so long ago.

Maybe he did, indeed, know what Sylvia needed. But if he got her a horse, would she be strong enough to ride? Maybe if he found a gentle mare, she'd be able to do it. It would certainly give her something else to think about.

Boxing up the leftover decorations, Harry went into the house to search the classifieds for a horse.

CHAPTER
Forty-Four

Full-time job openings were sparse this time of year, and Brenda wondered if she'd have to wait until January to find work. That would make Christmas awfully tight, and she dreaded that next trip to get Joseph's refills. She sat poring over the want ads at the kitchen table, when Daniel came in.

"Mama, I've got a plan," he said. "I want to see what you think."

David, coming in from his workshop, went to the sink to wash his hands.

"Dad, you need to be here, too. I was telling Mama about my plan."

David gave Daniel a look over his shoulder. "Shoot," he said. "We're listening."

"Okay, here's the thing."

Whenever Daniel started anything with "here's the thing" they knew that it was going to be good. Brenda closed the paper and put her pen down.

Daniel's eyes danced with excitement. "You know how Mark is taking the GED course? He'll be literally out of high school soon, and then he can go to college or get a job or do whatever he wants to, right?"

Brenda looked at David. "Well, something like that."

"Well, I was thinking that since Mama plans to go back to work, and she doesn't have so much time for home schooling, that I could take the GED test, too. Then I'd be finished."

"Why do you want to do that?" Brenda asked. "Why don't you just want to finish school and get your diploma?"

"Well, what difference does it make? I'm home schooled. It's not like I'm going to put on a cap and gown and walk through the high school."

"We do have a home schooling graduation, Daniel. You know that."

"Yeah, but that would be another whole year and a half, and I don't want to do it. I could be finished now."

David chuckled. "Daniel, is this about Mark getting out of school before you? Are you jealous or something?"

"No, I'm not jealous." Daniel's ears pinkened. "But it's not fair. I'm a better student than he is. It's like he's getting rewarded and I'm not."

"You'll be rewarded when you finish school the way you're supposed to," Brenda said. "Lots of people get GEDs and it works out fine, but you don't have to do that. You're too close to graduating."

Daniel turned his pleading eyes to his father.

"No," David said. "I agree a hundred percent with your mother. You are not going to finish early."

"Great." Daniel threw himself back into his chair. "It's like I'm being punished because I never went to jail."

"What?" Brenda's mouth fell open. "How can you say such a thing?"

"Well, look what's going on with him. I mean, he spends a year in jail. He gets out and they throw this great big party for him. You've never thrown a party for me. And then he doesn't have to go back to school. He gets his GED. And they hand him a car on a silver platter when I have to work like a dog to pay for mine."

David bristled. "Son, I paid for part of yours."

"I know, and I'm glad, Dad, but sometimes it just seems like he's getting a better deal."

"You think it was a good deal when he had to spend a year locked up?" Brenda asked. "Come on, Daniel. You're not thinking clearly."

He drew in a deep breath and let out a sigh. "It's not fair, that's all. He gets out of school before I do, and he didn't even apply himself. He didn't even try."

"He's trying now," Brenda said.

"Not very hard," Daniel threw back. "And if he'd come back to home schooling with us, we'd have more money and you wouldn't have to go to work."

Brenda met her husband's eyes. "That's not true. I'm going to work for the insurance benefits." David's expression was somber, and she knew his pride ached that his wife was joining the work world.

"We need more money than I could have made with Mark, anyway, Daniel. Don't you understand that?"

He propped his chin on his hand, sulking. "Yeah, I guess. Joseph has all that expensive medicine to take."

"Well, that's right," she said, "and it's a small price to pay to keep him alive. I'm willing to go to work to do that."

"Well, I'm just saying if I got a GED then I could go to work and get some insurance and I could pay for it."

"It doesn't work that way, Daniel. They don't let you put your brother on your insurance. Or your parents. It's a sweet thought, but we'd rather have you at home studying so you can get scholarships to college."

David patted his shoulder. "You're going to be fine, Daniel. You'll go at the normal pace, and you'll be in good shape for college entrance exams. You'll probably qualify for all sorts of scholarships. College is going to be a breeze for you."

"Well, maybe I don't want to go to college," Daniel said.

Brenda gasped, and David sprang up from his chair. "Young man, I don't want to hear that again. You *are* going to college."

"But you didn't, Dad."

David gritted his teeth. "Son, that's the worst mistake I ever made."

"But you've made a good living as a carpenter."

"I love being a carpenter, and I probably would have been had I gotten a degree or not, but I don't have the options that I would have had if I had gone to college. And I want you to have better."

"But Mark isn't going to get better."

"That's up to Mark," Brenda said. "We have a different plan for you."

"Well, what if it's not the plan I have for myself?" Daniel asked.

Brenda could tell he'd been talking this over with Mark. She rubbed her temples. "Daniel, quitting school and skipping college is not a plan."

David shook his head. "Daniel, when you become an adult you can make up your own mind about what you're going to do, but for right now we're going with our plan. You will finish school. Do you understand?"

Daniel scraped his chair back and got up. "Yes, sir."

"And you will go to college. Is that clear?"

He hesitated, then muttered, "Yes, sir."

"Fine. I'm going back to work." David headed out of the room, ending the conversation.

Daniel turned his eyes to Brenda. She took his hand. "Your father is right, Daniel. Do you understand why?"

"No, ma'am, but I'll do it."

"Good," she said. "You're a very wise boy."

CHAPTER
Forty-Five

The snow that covered the ground infused Sylvia with a burst of energy the week of Christmas. The kids would be home Thursday, the day before Christmas Eve, and she needed to get ready for them. Harry had gone to run some errands. Left to her own resources, she went up into the attic and found Jeff and Sarah's old crib. Knowing she couldn't get it down herself, and unwilling to wait until Harry got home, she called Cathy's house.

"Hello?" Mark's voice was soft across the line.

"Mark, this is Sylvia. How are you?"

"Hey, Miss Sylvia. I guess I'm okay. How are you?"

"I'm great. Nothing like the last time you saw me. By the way, thanks for the Popsicles."

"Sure. Did they help?"

"They sure did. In my book, you're a downright hero."

"Cool," he said. "Too bad I can't put that in my resumé."

"Still no job, huh?"

"Not yet. Man, you'd think I was a convicted killer or something. I'm never gonna get away from my record."

"Yes, you will, Mark. You'll see. As a matter of fact, that's why I'm calling. I want to hire you myself, just for the afternoon. I need someone to come get some things out of the attic for me."

"Sure, I can do that," Mark said. "Only, I can't take money for it."

"Then I'll have to find someone else. Maybe Daniel's available."

"No, I can do it." Mark laughed. "Man, you drive a hard bargain."

"Is Annie there?" Sylvia asked. "I could use her help, too."

"Yes, ma'am. She just got home from school. Do you need us now?"

"As soon as you can get here."

"Okay," he said. "We'll be right over."

In moments, Mark and Annie stood at her door. She welcomed them in with hugs. "Mark, I think you've grown a few inches since you've been home."

He stood straighter. "I think I have, too. I'm five-eight now."

"You are not," Annie quipped. "I'm five-five, and you're not that much taller than me."

Sylvia turned to the girl who was so special to her. "Annie, you just grow more beautiful every day. Look at you." She took her face in her hands and kissed her cheek. "So tell me about that boy Josh. Has he called you?"

Annie cocked her head and crossed her arms. "Miss Sylvia, you *were* trying to fix me up with him, weren't you?"

"Of course I was," Sylvia said. She led them through the house, to the attic stairs. "Why wouldn't I? When I meet a wonderful boy, wouldn't I want him to meet the most precious girl I know?"

Annie grinned and shot a look at Mark. "I told you."

"You should listen to her," Mark said. "I'm getting to know Josh at church. He helps out with the youth group. He's pretty cool."

Sylvia started up the ladder. "So has he called you or not?"

"Not." Annie followed her up. "Big bummer. I thought we hit it off, too."

Sylvia waited until Mark was up, then led them to the crib. "Well, maybe I need to get creative. Have another party or something."

Annie laughed. "No, Miss Sylvia. It's okay. If he doesn't like me, he doesn't like me. I'm okay with it. There are other fish in the sea."

"Sharks, you mean." Mark snickered. "The guys you pick are more like great whites."

"I'm only nineteen," Annie said, ignoring him. "I'm in my first year of college. I'm not looking for a husband, okay?"

"Okay," Sylvia said. "But you should know that I met Harry in my first year of college. We didn't get married until four years later, but I knew."

"I like Josh, but not that much, Miss Sylvia. I didn't go out shopping for a wedding dress the day after we met."

Sylvia shook her head and grinned at Mark. "They're not cooperating with me, Mark. What's a woman to do?"

"I don't know," he said. "But if you see any cute girls and want to fix me up, I promise to cooperate."

When they had gotten the crib down, she had them bring down the boxes of baby things that she had put up so many years ago. When it was all down, she paid Mark and sent him back home. Annie stayed behind to help her decorate one of the bedrooms for the baby.

As they sat on the floor digging out motherhood memorabilia, Sylvia got misty-eyed. She pulled out a threadbare homemade doll and gazed down at it. Sarah had carried it around until it had fallen apart. Sylvia had completely reconstructed it three times.

She reached into the box and pulled out a tiny baseball cap. Jeff had never wanted to take it off. Most nights, he'd fallen asleep in it, and they'd slipped it off without waking him. It seemed like so long ago.

"Don't rush your life, Annie," she whispered. "It goes by so fast. You just have to hang on to every single moment."

Annie smirked. "Hey, you're the one trying to marry me off. I'm not in any hurry."

She set the doll down and pulled out a worn-out blanket that had covered both her babies. "When your kids are young, you're tired and busy, and you just think they'll be that way forever. And then one day, you find yourself sitting on the floor looking through all the stuff that had so little meaning before ..."

She looked up at Annie and saw the tears in her eyes. "Miss Sylvia, are you sure you want to do this?"

She tried to rally. "Yes, I'm sure. I want to fix this room up for little Bree. Last time she was here, she had to sleep in a playpen. This time I want her to have the crib. They're coming for Christmas, you know."

Annie looked around at the decorations she'd already arranged. Small Christmas trees in every room, real garland strung all over the house ...

"Miss Sylvia, how did you get the energy to do all this? It would make Martha Stewart proud."

Sylvia knew she was right. She had done a good job this year. "My kids are really worried about me," she said. "I don't want them coming home to a sick house. I want them to be excited here, happy, like they were so many other Christmases. I want them to forget about my cancer."

Annie's soft eyes fell on her. "How long are they staying?"

"Until the day before my next treatment on the 27th. I'm so blessed that the doctor let me postpone my next treatment until after Christmas. I'm at my best this week. Isn't God good?"

Annie's face sobered. She pulled some blocks out of the box, stacked them up on the floor. "Yes, he's good." But her face belied the statement.

Sylvia pulled the crib bumper pads out of the box. They were wrapped in a garbage bag, carefully preserved so they wouldn't yellow and collect dirt. "Look at these. They look as fresh as they did the day I packed them up."

Annie wasn't listening. She hugged her knees. "Miss Sylvia, do you ever just get mad at God and ask him why?"

Sylvia set the pads down and looked fully at her young friend. "Why would I be mad?"

"The cancer." Tears filled the girl's eyes. "Because sometimes I do. It just seems like you're supposed to be blessed when you're serving God. Not cursed."

"So you think my cancer is a curse?"

"Don't you?"

She smiled and recalled her declaration to her children on Thanksgiving. She had meant it then . . . and she meant it even more now. "No, I don't think it's a curse, Annie," she said. "I think my cancer is a gift."

"A gift?" Annie wiped a tear as it rolled down her cheek. "How?"

"It's a gift that gives me new opportunities. Think about it. If I'm healed, then I'll have a testimony about how God brought me through a fatal disease. I'll be able to help others with terminal illness. I'll know how to relate to them, in a way that others can't possibly know."

"And if you're not healed?"

The question was blunt, but Sylvia knew that Annie didn't mean it maliciously. She had grown so close to her over the year she'd spent with her on the mission field. And Annie wasn't one to hold much in.

"If I'm not healed, if this disease takes me, then I can guarantee you one thing. I'm not going to go without taking a lot of people with me."

Annie frowned. "What do you mean?"

"I mean that if I'm going to leave people behind, I'm going to make sure they'll be coming to join me someday. I'll make up my mind to win every single soul I can to Christ before the Lord takes me home. A woman who's ill is taken a little more seriously when she talks about matters of the soul, don't you think?"

Annie nodded. "So you really think it's a gift?"

"Yes, Annie, I do. It is a gift. And I need to be thankful for it."

Later, when the crib was up and the baby's room was decorated, and Annie had gone home, Sylvia sat out on the swing on her back porch, watching the sun set over the Smokies. Yes, she thought. Her afternoon with Annie had given her clarity. While she planned to fight her cancer with everything she had in her, she also planned to use it. She had always said that the Lord doesn't give gifts that he doesn't equip one to use.

That meant that the Lord would turn her cancer into a tool. A tool for winning souls.

She heard Harry's car pulling into the garage and suddenly realized how very tired she was. But it was a good kind of tired. She had accomplished much today. And there was much more to do.

CHAPTER
Forty-Six

Sylvia managed to pull off the Christmas she'd planned for her family. Within a couple of days of being home, both Sarah and Jeff seemed to forget their mother was ill. They stopped walking around with somber faces, trying to keep the baby quiet, and watching every word they said to her.

By Christmas Day, the family had relaxed completely, and it felt like old times. Sarah helped her in the kitchen while Harry played with Breanna, and Jeff and Gary watched a ball game in the den.

By the time the dinner was served and eaten, chemo exhaustion was pulling at her. Harry insisted on cleaning the dishes so that Sylvia could lie down for a nap, while the kids went to visit high school friends from town.

That night, as her children continued to visit with friends, Sylvia joined the neighbors at Tory's house for her annual Christmas night celebration. The Christmas paper had all been thrown away and the presents were no longer new. It was the perfect time to gather and relax from the harried pace of the season.

They sipped eggnog and munched on Chex mix and watched Tory's Christmas morning video of Spencer and Brittany and baby Hannah tearing into their presents. Harry read the Christmas story from the Bible, while David sat quietly, tolerant of the observation. Sylvia sat with baby Hannah on her lap, and Joseph leaned next to her on the couch, patting her arm in a quiet affirmation that he knew what she was going through.

All seemed right with the world. Her abundant blessings were too many to count.

That night as Brenda and David and the kids headed back to their house, David put his arm around Brenda and kissed her on the cheek. "I love you," he whispered.

Brenda smiled up at him. "I love you, too."

"Watching Harry and Sylvia made me think," he said. "You can just see how much they love each other. He's worried about her."

"He is going through a rough time."

"Yeah, but I'm just amazed at her attitude." David stopped in the yard between the two houses, and grabbed the chain to the big porch swing he'd built to hang beneath the arbor. As he always did when he passed it, he tested it to see if it was safe. Joseph, Leah, and Rachel horsed around just ahead of them, their cheeks and noses red in the cold night air.

"Joseph seems so drawn to Sylvia," David said.

Brenda sat down on the swing. "He's never forgotten how close he came to death. But Sylvia does have a good attitude. She has her down moments, but mostly she just has a lot of hope."

David sat down next to her. "What if she dies?"

Brenda tried to picture Sylvia facing death head on. "I'm sure she's hoping for a cure, David. But if it turns out the other way, if she's going to die from this cancer, I think she'll be ready for that, too. She has a lot of faith."

"Faith in what?" he asked. "I mean, if she's going to die anyway, wouldn't that faith be misplaced?"

Brenda looked at her husband, and felt his breath warming her face.

"This life is temporary, David. I wish you understood that. There's a lot more on the other side."

"Let's see if you feel that way if Sylvia dies."

She knew he didn't mean to be cruel. In a way, she suspected his words were a kind of plea. Whether he admitted it or not, she was pretty sure he relied on the stability of her faith.

"You've seen me suffer over impending death before," she said. "I got to the point where I thought we were going to lose Joseph, and so did you. Did I ever despair?"

Tears misted his eyes and he shook his head. "No, you didn't."

"I won't this time either, but I'm still hoping that Sylvia is almost out of the woods."

David looked down at his feet. "Yeah, me too. I'm really hoping that."

He took her cold hand, pulled her to her feet, and snuggled her against him as they went into their house to get warm.

CHAPTER
Forty-Seven

That night after the party, Steve and Cathy felt the warm sense of contentment that Christmas night brings, when all the work and celebrating are done. Annie and Tracy had gone home from the party with Sylvia to help her make a pot of soup for her family. Both Rick and Mark had signed up with their church to work at the local soup kitchen tonight, cooking for and serving those who didn't have Christmas dinner.

While Steve started a fire in the hearth, Cathy curled up with a cup of hot apple cider. When the fire was going strong, Steve joined Cathy on the couch.

Propping his feet on the coffee table, he said, "Ah, this is one of the nicest parts of Christmas."

"Yeah," she said. "No deadlines, no food to prepare, no gifts to wrap. When it gets quiet and slow."

Steve pulled her close. "You sure you're not upset that the kids aren't here tonight?"

She smiled. "They were here all last night and most of today. It's nice to have quiet, especially when I know they're doing something good. Can you believe Rick signed up to work at the soup kitchen?"

"Sure I can," Steve said. "He's got a good heart. The miracle is that Mark is doing it. A year ago, would you have ever imagined it?"

"No," Cathy said. "God has done amazing things."

She heard a car door slam, then another.

Cathy got up and looked out the screen door, and saw Mark coming toward the door. Someone else walked behind him, but he was taller than Rick.

"Looks like we're about to have company," she told Steve.

Mark opened the door into the kitchen, and as his companion stepped in behind him, Cathy recognized Josh, the young man Sylvia had pegged for Annie.

"Josh, hi," she said. "It's good to see you."

"Good to see you, too, Mrs. Bennet."

"Josh gave me a ride home from the Stewpot." Mark winked.

Cathy only looked at him, wondering what the wink meant. Was Mark telling her that he had set this up for Annie's sake?

"Where's Rick?" she asked.

"He wanted to stay and help clean up," Mark said. "Josh was leaving, so he offered to bring me home."

Cathy grinned, wishing Annie would hurry home. "Did you have a nice Christmas, Josh?"

"Yes, ma'am. Did you?"

"Wonderful," she said.

Steve came and shook his hand. "So how was the Stewpot?"

"Great," he said. "My parents and I have been there all afternoon. We served five hundred people today. Mom and Dad are still there, closing the place down."

Mark brandished the Blockbuster movie he held. "I invited Josh to come in and watch a movie. I figured Annie and Rick and Tracy might want to hang out."

Cathy doubted that the twenty-two-year-old had accepted the invitation to spend time with sixteen-year-old Mark. She hoped that meant he wanted to see Annie.

"Annie and Tracy are next door. They should be home any minute."

Mark shot her a look that spoke volumes. *Call her and get her home, Mom. I didn't do this for my health.*

She slipped into the bedroom, and Steve followed. "I'm calling Annie," she said.

"I was just going to suggest that." Steve grinned. "Do you believe Mark did that?"

"Guess it's just a little belated gift for his sister." She punched out Sylvia's number.

"Hello?"

"Sylvia, it's Cathy." She kept her voice low. "Would you tell Annie that Josh is here?"

Sylvia gasped. "Really?"

"Yes. He brought Mark home from the Stewpot. He's in the living room watching a movie."

"She'll be home in two minutes," Sylvia said. "I'm throwing her out right now."

Cathy laughed as she hung up the phone.

Annie hurried Tracy out the door and across the yard. Back home, Tracy ran straight for the new computer the family had gotten that morning, but Annie gravitated to the living room. "Hey, guys," she said. "What you watching?"

Josh came to his feet. "Hi, Annie," he said. "Remember me?"

She grabbed a handful of the popcorn the guys had between them, popped it into her mouth. "Sure I remember. From Miss Sylvia's dinner party."

"That's right."

"We're watching *Monty Python and the Holy Grail*," Mark said. "And don't hog our popcorn, okay?"

Annie ignored him. "I love this movie." She came around the couch, picked up the popcorn, and plopped down between them on the couch. "Oh, good. I didn't miss the part about the rabbit."

Josh threw his head back and laughed. "I love the killer rabbit."

They started trading off lines they'd memorized from the movie, and before long they were laughing and chattering, and rewinding bits of it so that they could act it out again.

As the movie came to an end, Annie realized she owed her brother big.

She and Josh had a lot in common, and she enjoyed being around him. Maybe once again, Miss Sylvia had been right.

It was almost midnight when Josh got up to leave, so she walked him to the door.

"Thanks for the ride home, man," Mark said from the couch.

"Sure," Josh said. "Thanks for the movie."

"Bye, Josh," Annie said as nonchalantly as possible.

"See ya," he said. "Uh, could I get your phone number, by any chance?"

Annie grinned, but Mark spoke up. "Mine?"

Josh chuckled. "Either of yours."

"Same number," Annie said. "And either of us would be glad if you called."

She wrote it down for him, hoping she'd hear from him soon.

When Josh was gone, Annie turned back to her brother. Grinning, he lifted his hand, and she slapped it.

"Merry Christmas, sis," he said.

Annie leaned over the couch and kissed him.

CHAPTER
Forty-Eight

The week after Christmas Mark learned that he'd flunked his second GED test. His instructor had warned him that he still wasn't ready to take it, but he had insisted. Now he saw that he was going to have to finish his entire class in order to get it.

Trying to revive his sagging ego, he set his mind to applying for jobs. A guy in his class had told him that the building contractor he worked for was hiring, so he called ahead and made an appointment, then got dressed up and drove to the site.

"I'm looking for advancement," he told the builder. "I'd like something I could grow into, maybe work my way up."

The contractor rubbed his mouth. "You're how old?"

"Sixteen, but I'm mature for my age."

"Well, Mark, I'm not really hiring for any executive positions today. I'm looking for people willing to work hard for minimum wage."

Mark sat straighter. "Well, you have to start somewhere. But it's pretty cold out. What do you do when it rains?"

The man leaned back in his chair and propped his feet on his desk. "We don't work. And I don't pay you when you don't work."

Mark thought that stank, but he didn't say so. "How would you be able to pay your rent if it rained a lot that month?"

"That's your problem," the boss said. "Besides, you live at home, don't you?"

"Yeah, but I don't want to forever. But it's okay. I think I'd like construction work."

The man dropped his feet and looked back down at Mark's application. "Tell me about this year of incarceration."

Mark cleared his throat. "I sold some marijuana to an under-cover officer. It was stupid to smoke the stuff, much less sell it to somebody else. I served a year, but it changed me. It really did. I'm a different person now."

"Yeah, I've heard that before." The man closed his file and got to his feet. "Well, thanks for coming by, Mark. I'll let you know."

Mark left the office discouraged and headed for the mall. He went around and put applications in at several different stores. He had made up his mind not to lie about his conviction, but now he wondered if that had been a mistake.

He felt whipped by the time he got back home. Steve was home early and sat at the kitchen table reading the paper. He looked up when Mark came in. "What's up, Mark?"

Mark shook his head. "Not much. No jobs, that's for sure."

Steve put down the paper and looked fully at him. "You've been looking?"

"Yeah, but no luck."

"Where have you been applying?"

"You name it. I've been there." He poured a glass of milk and sat down across from Steve. "I was honest on all my appli-cations. Told them about my year at River Ranch. But maybe that was stupid. Maybe it wouldn't have hurt anything to keep that to myself."

"Honesty never hurts, Mark. I'm proud of you for telling the truth about it."

Mark took a drink, set the glass down hard. "Even if one of them does hire me, it'll be for a minimum wage grunt job. But I'm looking for something a little more permanent."

"Why? What's wrong with getting something temporary for now, even part-time?"

"Because you can't make a living doing that," he said. "And I don't want to go to college. I'd like to get a job I could grow into."

"Well, the problem is that unless you do go to college, you're not going to have as many choices."

"I know, but I want to do something a little more substantial than working an hourly job for minimum wage. I can do it. I'm a hard worker. I worked hard at River Ranch. I'm not afraid to get my hands dirty. But nobody will give me a chance."

Steve picked up the newspaper and flipped to the employment section. "Let's see. Maybe between the two of us we can come up with some ideas."

When Cathy got home from working at the clinic, she stepped into the kitchen and saw Steve and Mark huddled over the paper.

Her mama bear instincts kicked in, and she imagined that Steve had been lecturing the boy about pounding the pavement for work. "What are you guys doing?"

"Hi, honey." Steve rose up and gave her a kiss.

"Hi, Mom." Mark's voice was flat, and she could see that something was wrong.

"We were just talking about Mark getting a job," Steve said. "Trying to figure out places he could apply."

"Oh." Just as she'd thought. Mark had probably walked innocently in, and Steve had hit him with the classifieds.

She took off her coat and hung it up. "Steve, could I speak to you alone for a minute?"

He looked up at her, puzzled. "Sure."

Mark took the list they had been working on and began to study it as they headed for the bedroom. When they were alone, she turned on Steve.

"Why are you riding him about getting a job? He's been looking. I happen to know that for sure. He's applied at dozens of places."

Steve gave her a stunned look. "Why do you assume I'm riding him?"

"Because I can see what's going on. You're sitting there lecturing him and he looks like he's been hog-tied."

"Well, that would be your impression. And it's just possible it could be wrong."

"I don't think I'm wrong."

Steve's lips thinned, and he sat down on the bed. "Cathy, for your information, Mark came home after applying to about twelve places today and getting rejected at every one, and he was upset. He sat down with me and I started trying to offer him some suggestions. He's listening. It's not a pleasant experience for him because he hasn't had good luck so far. But he's not in a bad mood because of me."

She stood there a moment, letting the information sink in. "Oh. Guess I was wrong."

"Yeah, guess you were wrong." He got up and grabbed his keys off of the dresser.

"Where are you going?"

"Out," he said. "I think I need to put a little distance between you and me for a few minutes while I cool off."

"Cool off?" she asked. "I didn't mean to make you mad."

He swung around. "I know you didn't mean to, Cathy. It just comes naturally these days. I don't like being accused of riding your son. It makes me angry."

"I'm sorry."

"You *should* be sorry. This isn't the first time, and I know it won't be the last time. But I am not Public Enemy Number One to your son." With that, he strode through the living room and kitchen, and headed out to his car.

"Hey, where'd he go?" Mark asked. "We were in the middle of something."

Cathy stared at the door. "He had to run to the bank before it closes."

Mark got his list and took his glass to the sink. "I guess I have enough leads to keep me busy tomorrow," he said. "Man, I've *got* to get a job."

He headed up the stairs, and Cathy stood in the kitchen, realizing she'd made a terrible mistake. Once again, she had failed to give Steve the benefit of the doubt. She had shot first and asked questions later.

She didn't blame him for being so angry.

When Steve hadn't come back after twenty minutes, Cathy started getting angry again. They needed to talk this out, but if he didn't come home, how could they?

She didn't know why things had been so hard for them lately. When they were dating, it seemed that they had worked all of these things out. But now, only months into their marriage, it was as if the seams were coming unstitched.

She needed to talk to Sylvia.

Crossing the yard, she knocked on Sylvia's door. When no one answered, she checked the garage. The car was there, so they must be home. She knocked again.

Finally, Harry answered the door. "Oh, Cathy." His hair was tousled and his face looked tired and aged.

"Harry, what's wrong?"

"It's Sylvia. She's really sick. She had her treatment today."

"Oh, I forgot."

"Come in." He left her at the door and ran back into the house. She stood just inside the foyer for a moment, not certain whether to stay or go.

Finally, she stepped back toward the bedroom and saw Sylvia on the bathroom floor, retching into the toilet bowl. Harry bent over her, wiping her face and neck with a cold, wet rag.

He looked to see if she was there and called out, "Cathy, get me a couple more wet washcloths. They're in the linen closet."

She got them and held them under the faucet, squeezed them out, and brought them back to him. He set them on Sylvia's neck and forehead.

"If you wouldn't mind, go get her a Popsicle. She's got terrible sores. Maybe it would help."

Cathy grabbed a Popsicle and stuck it into a cup, then got some crushed ice out of the little dispenser at the front of the freezer.

Sylvia was retching again when she came back. When she stopped, she lay on the floor, her bare cheek against the cold tiles.

"Here, honey," he said. "Some ice chips. Just suck on these." Harry put them into Sylvia's mouth.

She lay there curled up on the floor, unable to move. He lifted her head gently and put it onto his lap.

Cathy stood speechless just outside the door, tears stinging her eyes. For the first time, she sensed the pall of death that seemed to hang over Sylvia. Rage rose in her chest. How dare death stalk her this way? How dare it torment her?

Harry seemed to have forgotten she was there. She watched as tears rolled down his face and plopped onto Sylvia's cheek.

Cathy started to cry and decided to let herself out. As she pulled the front door shut behind her and launched out across the yard, she saw that Steve's car was back in the driveway. Weeping harder, she realized that this petty argument she had come to tell Sylvia about was worthless. It was hardly a blip on the screen of a lifelong marriage that she hoped she would have with Steve. But here she was being petty, accusing him of things that he hadn't done, looking for the worst in him when she had married him because he was a precious, wonderful man just like Harry—a man who would sit on the floor next to her in her darkest hour and hold her head while she vomited.

Why had she attacked him in the way she had?

Die to yourself. Sylvia's words reeled through her brain. She *hadn't* died to herself. Instead, she still clung mercilessly to herself, feeding her own feelings of paranoia and suspicion and anger . . . but Steve didn't deserve any of it.

She went through the garage to the door into the house. She stumbled into the kitchen and saw that Mark was back at the table, studying his job prospect list and scoping them out on a map.

"Where's Steve?" she asked.

Mark looked up at her. "You okay, Mom?"

She sucked in a sob. "Yes . . . just . . . where's Steve?"

"In the bedroom, I guess."

She headed back to the bedroom and found Steve sitting on the bed staring into space.

"Oh, Steve!" She stood at the door, her face twisted and red.

He saw her grief and got up instantly, reached for her. She fell against him, clinging with all her might. "I'm so sorry, Steve," she wept. "I'm so sorry."

"It's okay, baby," he said. "It wasn't that bad. Why are you so upset?"

"Because I'm so stupid," she said, "and so catty. And Harry and Sylvia are over there struggling for her life. Harry's so afraid he's going to lose her, and here I am, picking at you. Just picking, picking, picking."

He touched the back of her head and pressed her closer to him. "It's okay, honey. It's okay."

"I promise I'm not going to accuse you anymore. You're the best thing that's ever happened to me or my children."

Steve held her and let her cry until her tears subsided. Then together they sat on the bed and prayed for Sylvia.

CHAPTER
Forty-Nine

A week after her sixth treatment, Sylvia lay curled up on the bed, wondering when she would ever get her energy back. Each chemo treatment seemed worse than the one before it, and took longer to recover from. And what if it was futile? What if she was putting herself through these grueling treatments, and the cancer grew in spite of it?

Harry came and sat on the edge of the bed. "You want to go for a walk?"

"No, I'm too tired."

"But you love the snow. And your favorite place in the world is the woods behind our house. Maybe it would be good for you to get some exercise, breathe some fresh air, get your mind off of how bad you feel."

"I can't, Harry. Not today."

But Harry didn't give up. "Sylvia, I've got a surprise out there I want to show you. A late Christmas present."

She rubbed her eyes. "I don't want any surprises. I don't have the energy for them."

"Come on. You'll love this one." He pulled her up, helped her to her feet.

She didn't want to go. Within a few days, she knew she would be back to herself, except for the debilitating fatigue. But right now . . .

He pulled her up, got her coat, pulled it around her shoulders. She didn't have the energy to fight him as he took her by the hand and led her out into the backyard.

Harry couldn't wait to show her his surprise. Ever since Joseph came up with the idea, he'd been looking for a gentle, older horse that would be right for Sylvia. If she had something to take care of, something that needed her, he knew she would feel better sooner after each treatment. He'd found the horse through a friend of a friend. Its owner had died, and the family needed to sell it.

Before he made an offer, he'd consulted with her oncologist. He'd told him it was okay for her to ride as long as she didn't overdo it.

He took her hand and walked patiently beside her, one step at a time. When he put his arm around her, he could feel her body trembling with weakness. He hoped he was doing the right thing.

"I've missed having the horses," he said as they headed slowly for the barn. "Haven't you?"

"Yeah, I really do."

He grinned. "Wouldn't it be nice to have one again?"

"Sure it would," she said. "But if we got one, we'd just have to sell it again when we went back to León."

That positive proclamation did him good. For the last few weeks, he'd worried that she was giving up.

"Well, I was thinking that this time if we got a horse, when we left we could just donate it to somebody."

She looked at him with dull, distant eyes. "Somebody like who?"

"Somebody like Joseph."

Sylvia stopped and looked up at him.

"Wouldn't that be like coming full circle?" Harry asked. "We sold the first horses to raise money for his transplant, and this one we'd give to him because he's so healthy he can ride."

"But Brenda and David could never afford to keep a horse for Joseph."

Harry shrugged. "We could work something out."

Sylvia smiled. "I like that idea."

He laughed and pulled her into the stable, and she heard something over in the corner where Sunshine, her favorite horse, used to live.

She frowned. "What's that? I heard—"

His grin was giving him away. "You'll see." He led her to the stall, where a tall, beautiful mare looked over the door.

She caught her breath. "Oh, Harry, what have you done?"

He laughed. "I bought you a new horse," he said. "Isn't she beautiful? Look at her." He opened the door and grabbed the horse's bridle, which he had put on a little while earlier. He pulled her out of the stall so that Sylvia could have a good look.

She started to cry and stroked the horse's chocolate coat. "Oh, Harry. I love her."

"I've been looking all over for just the right horse. I thought it would be good therapy for you to ride again. It's your favorite thing to do in the whole world, and you haven't done it in years."

The horse nuzzled her neck and she rubbed her face against it. "What a sweetie," she said. "Oh, Harry. Are you sure we can afford it? We don't have that much left in savings."

Their finances had been drained by their mission work. They'd funneled all of their savings and much of their retirement into medical supplies and food for the people of León.

"Sure we can," he said. "I've decided to go back to work at the hospital part-time. Joe Simmons wants me to join him in his practice, and I told him that I might be able to do it on non-chemo weeks."

Sylvia turned away from the horse and regarded him. "Does he understand that you're only going to be there a few months?"

"He understands," he said. "I'm not planning to take any long-term patients."

She hugged the horse as if he were a long-lost member of her family. "Can I ride her?"

"Of course you can." He grabbed down the saddle that had hung there for over two years, dressed the horse as Sylvia watched. Already he could see the energy seeping back into her, and her countenance had changed completely.

"Take it easy now the first time," he said. "I don't want you breaking any bones."

With his help, she got on the horse, sat for a moment. He saw the perfect peace passing over her face, as if she was finally home.

Her laughter was like a symphony. "Oh, Harry, you're a genius," she said. "I'm already feeling better."

"Now take it real, real easy," he said again as the horse walked out of the barn and into the fresh air. Big snowflakes floated down around them. "Don't underestimate your weakness."

"I won't," she said. "We're just going to get to know each other. What's her name?"

"Midnight," he said.

She patted the horse's neck. "Let's go, Midnight."

Then she walked the horse off to her favorite path.

Harry stood watching, and said a silent prayer that she would not hurt herself. But the surprise had accomplished his goal to get her out of bed and her mind off of her problems. She only had two more treatments. They were sure to get worse and more draining. Then, as she built her strength back, she would have Midnight to nurture and pamper.

It was the perfect plan. Harry just hoped God would go along with it.

CHAPTER *Fifty*

A week into the new year, Mark got up early to beat the bushes for a job. He went to each business on the list that he and Steve had forged. Some of the managers were not in, and he was only able to fill out applications. When he finally found one that would see him, he felt as if he had hit pay dirt.

It was a roofing company and paid a little bit more than minimum wage. It sounded like a good job, at least according to Steve, and Steve knew the guy who ran the company.

The interview was going well until Mark told him what he had done with the last year of his life. The open look on his face closed, and he leaned back in his chair. "You should have told me that up front, Mark."

Mark shifted in his seat. "Why? You wouldn't have even seen me if I had told you that."

"Well, I needed to know. It's kind of pertinent."

Mark felt his cheeks burning. "It's really not. I did a stupid thing a year and a half ago and I paid for it. But I'm different now. I don't do drugs anymore."

"Still, I don't hire ex-cons." The man got up and stuck the file back into the file cabinet behind him.

Mark knew he was being dismissed. He got up, slid his hands into his pockets. "It was River Ranch juvenile delinquent center." He kept his voice low, steady. "It's not like I was serving time in the federal penitentiary. Besides, I'm a Christian now. And if the almighty God of the universe can forgive me, then I don't see why somebody like you can't."

He turned and started back to the door.

"Wait a minute," the man said.

Mark stopped and turned around.

"Come back in here and sit down."

Mark slid his hands into his pockets again and came back.

The man sat back down and leaned his elbows on his desk. "I'll tell you what. I can see that you're a passionate young man, and that maybe you really do have it in you to change. And since you're Steve's stepson, I guess I can help out with that a little."

Mark started to tell him not to do him any favors, but thought better of it.

"If you're here tomorrow morning at seven o'clock, you can start working. Just report here and fill out all the paperwork, and then Myra, my secretary, will tell you where our work site is for the day. You can come over and we'll put you to work."

Mark slowly unfolded from his slump, and a grin crept across his face. Had he heard right? Had the man hired him? The man got up and held out a hand to shake. Mark got to his feet and shook. "Thank you, sir. You won't regret it."

"Let's hope not."

CHAPTER *Fifty-One*

Cathy hadn't seen Sylvia since her treatment just after Christmas, but one day in early January she spotted her sitting out on her horse, staring out at the hills behind her property. Something was wrong. Sylvia didn't move, and the horse beneath her stood motionless. Cathy hurried across the yard to see if she needed help.

As she grew closer, she saw that the color of Sylvia's skin was a grayish-yellow. She looked sick now, not just weak or frail. The systemic effects of the chemo were taking a terrible toll on her.

Sylvia didn't seem to hear as she approached. "Sylvia, are you feeling all right?"

Sylvia turned slowly and looked down at her. "Hey, Cathy. I was just going to ride, but I think my legs are too weak. Can you help me off?"

Cathy gave her a hand, and felt Sylvia's body trembling as she stepped to the ground. "How did you saddle the horse?"

"Joseph did it, then I sent him back home to study. I didn't realize I was still so weak."

Cathy let her lean on her and led the horse back to the stall. "This last treatment must be hanging on, huh?"

"Yes, but there are only two more."

Cathy wondered if those last two would completely do Sylvia in. It seemed cruel, injecting such a harsh drug into a cancer patient's veins, when there were no guarantees that it would even work.

But she supposed the alternative was even more deadly.

Sylvia took measured steps. The horse walked slowly beside them as if it understood that she was ill and could not hurry. Cathy took the horse into the stall and pulled the saddle off.

"Poor Midnight," Sylvia said. "She was all dressed up and ready to go."

"Well, you'll have plenty of time to ride when you're stronger. Won't you be glad to get these treatments behind you?"

"I guess."

Cathy set the saddle down and gaped at her. "You guess? What does that mean?"

Sylvia leaned her face against the horse's neck. "It's hard to explain, but I kind of feel like I'm doing something as long as I'm taking the chemo. When it's over, I won't be doing any-thing. What if the cancer's not gone?"

"It will be," Cathy said. "You know it will be. I mean, they probably got it all in the mastectomy. The chemo was just because of the lymph nodes, right? It hadn't metastasized anywhere."

"No."

Cathy took off Midnight's blanket and hung it over a rail. "Sylvia, I just know you're never going to have to deal with this again. When you finish, you'll be home free."

Sylvia sat down on a tack box and watched as Cathy started to brush the horse.

"Oh, I've got some good news for you," Cathy said. "Josh called Annie, and they went out on a date. They really seemed to hit it off."

Sylvia's countenance lifted. "We've got to help it along. Maybe I could have another dinner party, invite them both over."

"Sylvia, I don't think you can get away with that. Come on. It was weird enough for you to invite them both the first time. I think we should just let God do the rest. I'm not so sure I want Annie in a relationship right now, anyway."

"Well, I can understand that," Sylvia said, "but you know Annie. She's going to wind up in one before long. I just want to make sure it's with the right person."

"No arguments from me," Cathy said.

CHAPTER
Fifty-Two

January went by in a blur as Sylvia struggled through her seventh chemo treatment. Sarah came with Breanna to visit, and Jeff was able to come for a long weekend. Though she still had a few good days the week before her treatment, she was too exhausted to ride. Most days, Joseph rode Midnight for her as she sat out on her porch and watched. She carefully taught him how to groom and care for the horse and hired him to clean the stables.

The child gave her comfort when he was around, and since Brenda was spending so much time in a hunt for a job, she didn't feel she was taking him away from his schoolwork.

On the days after her treatment, when she could hardly crawl out of bed, Joseph cared for Midnight without her help. They'd given him permission to ride anytime he wanted without asking, and he kept the horse in shape.

At last in early February the day of her final treatment arrived. Sylvia was quiet as Harry drove her to the Cancer Center.

"Eight times," she whispered. "I can't believe I did this eight times."

"Six months," he said.

"I wouldn't wish it on anyone. I just hope it helped."

"It did," Harry said. "It had to." He took her hand, squeezed it as he drove. "Are you excited?"

She hesitated and looked out the window. "I'm a little scared."

"Scared? Why?"

"Because after this treatment, I go for all the scans. That's when we'll know for sure if it worked. And they said there was a fifty percent recurrence rate. I hate the chemo, but I hate the cancer worse. And without the chemo, the cancer could take a foothold."

"It won't though. You're going to be fine. After this treatment, you'll feel bad for a couple of weeks, but then you'll start feeling better, your strength will come back, your hair will grow back, the color will return to your face . . ." He pulled into the parking lot of the Cancer Center. "And the radiation and hormone therapy will still be battling the cancer."

Harry walked her in, and she took her place and waited as they put the needle into her vein.

An hour into her treatment, her head began to ache, and she dipped some ice chips out of the bowl on her lap and put them in her mouth to keep the sores from forming. Vertigo taunted her, and she felt slightly nauseous.

She closed her eyes and, quietly, started to sing. "Amazing grace, how sweet the sound . . ."

A woman's voice beside her joined in, and she opened her eyes and saw Priscilla, the woman she'd sung with during her first couple of treatments. Priscilla had been finished with her chemo for some time now, and her hair had begun to grow back in. She stood over Sylvia with a smile on her face and a vase of roses. "Hi there," she said softly.

Sylvia smiled, though dizziness wobbled over her again. "Priscilla."

"I knew this was your last treatment day," she said. "I wanted to bring you flowers to celebrate." She put the vase on a tray.

Sylvia touched her hand. "You're so sweet. How are you?"

Priscilla pulled up the rolling stool that the nurses used, and sat down facing Sylvia.

"I'm great. I seem to be in remission. We're very optimistic."

"You look great. Your hair is wonderful. You should keep it that short."

She ran her hand over the inch-long strands. "I'm tempted."

A wave of dizziness seemed to turn Sylvia's stomach, so she closed her eyes again.

"Sing with me," Priscilla whispered. "Come on, honey, sing. Just like you made me do those times. Amazing grace ..."

Sylvia sang along, trying to get her mind focused on the amazing grace of a God who sent a compassionate friend who'd suffered through the same thing, on the day that she needed her the most.

Priscilla stayed through the whole treatment, then helped her back out to Harry, and hugged her good-bye.

"We both made it through," Priscilla said. "We survived. The worst is behind us now."

Sylvia started to cry. She hadn't expected it, and didn't really have the energy to do it. Yet the tears came—deep, soulful, blubbering tears. "It's over," she whispered to Harry. "It's over."

Harry and Priscilla cried with her, as the joy of her release from the bondage of chemotherapy finally began to dawn on her.

CHAPTER
Fifty-Three

Several days after Sylvia's final chemo treatment—when she was finally able to get out of bed—she went to the hospital for CT scans of her head, chest, abdomen, and bones.

She prayed while she waited for the scanners to move over her body, searching for any more signs of cancer that had spread to other organs or bones. At the end of the day, she went for her blood test and prayed as they drew the blood that the tumor markers would not be elevated.

The results wouldn't be in until the next day.

Still tired and weak, Sylvia went home and tried to get her mind off of the tests. Cathy, Brenda, and Tory came over that night, and they watched *Harvey* on video and munched on popcorn and jelly beans.

But as Harry slept next to her later that night, Sylvia lay awake, praying for remission. She didn't know what she'd do if the test results showed that cancer had taken up residence somewhere else in her body.

So this is what Gethsemane felt like, she thought. Stark fear, heartbreaking dread. She'd heard her pastor say that Gethsemane was the word for "olive press," where they crushed olives to get the oil. In the garden of the olive press, Jesus had been crushed.

Tonight she felt as though she was being crushed, too.

As morning dawned and she gave up trying to sleep, Sylvia came to the place where Jesus had ended up that night.

Not my will, but thine.

She only wished she had more peace about it.

Harry took her back to the oncologist's office for the results. They waited, jittery, in the waiting room until he could see them in his office.

"Good news," Dr. Thibodeaux said as he hustled into the room. "Everything looks normal."

Sylvia gasped so hard it made her choke. "No. You're kidding."

"Not kidding," he said. "It looks like the chemo was successful."

Harry started to laugh, and she saw the tears glistening in his eyes as he hugged her. She threw her head back and laughed like a hysterical woman.

"You're not out of the woods yet, though," Dr. Thibodeaux said. "You still have to go through radiation and hormone therapy. But the chemo was the worst of it, and for right now the results look as good as they could possibly be."

Sylvia felt as if the olive press had been lifted off her back. "Thank you. Oh, thank you, Lord!" She almost danced. "Doctor, isn't there some way that I can have the radiation in Nicaragua so we can get back to our work?"

Harry shook his head. "Honey, that's not a good idea."

The doctor frowned. "Harry, I agree. I don't recommend that at all. I'd prefer she waited here until she was finished. There's a lot of danger of infection in the hospitals there, and the equipment is not up to par. León, Nicaragua, is not an environment that will help this process at all."

Harry gave her an apologetic look. "Sylvia, we can't go back to the field just yet."

She wasn't going to let that news get her down. "It's okay. Only a few more months."

As they walked out of the office with Dr. Thibodeaux, Harry stopped him. "Could I get a copy of her records to take to the plastic surgeon? It's time for her to have her expandable implant replaced with a permanent one, and he'll want to see where we are in the process."

Dr. Thibodeaux nodded. "Sure. I can give you all the records of the test results, but my dictation won't be back for a month or so, so you won't have my notes. It takes that long to get it transcribed."

Harry laughed. "The test results will be fine. You should try doing your notes the old-fashioned way like I do. Write them yourself."

"I see too many patients," he said. "It slows me down to handwrite them, and I tend to abbreviate my comments. I can be more thorough if I dictate. It just takes so long to get them typed. Our transcription service handles most of the doctors' offices in town, so there's a terrible turnaround time on them."

The germ of an idea planted itself in Sylvia's mind. "Have you ever thought of hiring your own typist for the office? That way you could have a one-day turnaround."

The doctor shrugged. "We haven't really given that any thought. We just do it the way we always have."

"You should think about it," Sylvia said. "If you made someone a full-time employee with benefits and everything, you could hire someone of quality. They could even work from home. Show up once a day to return the notes they've typed and pick up what you dictated that day . . ."

Dr. Thibodeaux gave Sylvia a knowing look. "Sylvia, you're not looking for a job, are you?"

Sylvia laughed. "Me? Heavens, no. I'm no typist. But I have a dear friend who would be perfect for a job like that. All you'd have to do is create it, and I bet I could convince her to take it."

His smile faded, and he stared at her for a moment as the wheels seemed to turn in his mind. "Tell you what. This might be an excellent idea. Let me talk to my partners, and then I'll give you a call. Maybe we could set up an interview with your friend."

"You'd better hurry before someone else snaps her up," Sylvia said.

She laughed as they walked out to the car, and all the way home she chattered and planned the party she was going to have for the neighbors that night to celebrate her good news. As she made her plans she felt as if the worst of her disease was behind her. What lay ahead was going to be easy in comparison. Soon cancer would be a distant memory in her life, and she would be able to get on with her work.

She decided to hit the ground running to prove to everyone that the old Sylvia was back.

CHAPTER
Fifty-Four

Since the weather was unusually warm, the neighbors had a picnic in the open lot between Tory's and Brenda's houses that night to celebrate the good news. The Dodd kids decorated the trees with toilet paper and balloons, and Cathy brought her karaoke machine.

Spencer tried to monopolize it, doing the Elvis impersonation he had become known for, but Leah and Rachel managed to get the microphone away from him to do a few numbers of their own. Brenda didn't remember when she had ever laughed more.

As darkness fell and the early March evening grew cool, they grabbed sweaters and turned up the grill and kept celebrating long into the night.

When Brenda got home that night, her excitement over Sylvia's remission left her floating on a wave of energy. As soon as the children were in bed, she hurried to her computer. David sat at the desk in the small room, working on the checkbook.

He looked up at her as she began to type. "What are you doing?"

"I decided to write a proposal to give to Dr. Thibodeaux at the Cancer Center."

He stopped working and turned his chair to her. "What kind of proposal?"

"A proposal of what I could do as the office transcriber. Sylvia said this would be a new job that they create. I don't want to rely on Dr. Thibodeaux's memory or imagination for this. I want to paint them a picture of what they could have if they hired me. Something Dr. Thibodeaux can take to his partners, so they can all catch the vision."

David smiled. "Good thinking. You're a genius."

"No, Sylvia is. It was all her idea. Can you imagine? She'd just gotten news that her body was clear of cancer, and what does she do? She starts campaigning for a job for me. And not just any job, but a job that doesn't even exist, a job that would be perfect for me and allow me to work from home and still have full-time pay and benefits . . ."

Her voice broke off as tears filled her eyes, and she brought her hand to her mouth. "Oh, David . . . do you realize what a blessing this could be?"

He leaned forward, putting his face inches from hers. "It will be, honey, but I hate for you to get your hopes up. What if it doesn't pan out?"

Brenda blinked back her tears and slapped her hands onto her knees. "I've thought of that. If they decide not to take advantage of my offer, then I'll submit the same proposal to every doctor's office in town. And in the proposal, I'm going to offer to do two days' worth of transcribing for free, just so they'll see that I can do it. And hopefully, they'll love the speed and the way it works, and hire me."

He grinned. "It could work."

"It will work, David. It has to."

CHAPTER
Fifty-Five

The final step in Sylvia's breast reconstruction was a minor surgical procedure that needed to be done before her radiation, since the X rays were known to inhibit healing and rob the skin of its elasticity.

She scheduled it for a couple of weeks before her first radiation treatment, then checked into the hospital, anxious to get her body back to as close to normal as possible.

Sylvia stood in front of the hospital mirror, assessing herself with a critical eye. Her hair had begun to grow in and it felt like peach fuzz on her head, much like her grandbaby's hair. Though it was gray, it was new, soft and fine, and it looked like it might have a slight curl as it grew. She hadn't had a curl before.

The breast implant had already been expanded to the size of her other breast—through her monthly saline injections—and under her T-shirt it looked as if she'd never had a mastectomy. Today they would remove the expandable implant and replace it with a permanent one, then make a few cosmetic adjustments to make it look more real.

But she couldn't help the delight surging through her at the idea that she was cancer-free and rebuilding her body. It made her feel that she was on her way to full and complete recovery. She would have the chance to watch her grandchild grow, see Jeff get married someday, and rock all the other grandchildren born into their family . . . and the ones she'd left in León.

A knock sounded on the door. "Come in."

Harry stepped into the bathroom. "They're ready to prep you for surgery," he said.

She nodded. "I'll bet I'm readier than they are."

He gave her a hug and kissed her on the lips, then sent her on her way.

The phone call Brenda had prayed for came Wednesday, the same day as Sylvia's outpatient surgery, less than a week after she'd sent the proposal to the Cancer Center. She'd been dissecting a video on calculus, in an attempt to help Daniel with his lesson, when the phone rang. She dove for it.

"Hello?"

"Mrs. Dodd?" It was a woman's voice.

"Yes."

"This is Sheila Morris, office manager at the Cancer Center."

Her heart jolted. This was it. This was the call.

"Dr. Thibodeaux asked me to set up an appointment for you. He said to tell you that he and the other doctors in the clinic had reviewed your proposal and were very interested in talking to you."

Brenda groped for a nearby chair and made herself sit down. It was happening. It was really happening. "Yes, of course. When would he like for me to come?"

"He was wondering if you could come in at 5:30 this afternoon, after the clinic is closed. The doctors have a meeting scheduled for that time anyway, and they thought it would be a good time to talk with you."

"Yes," Brenda said. "That sounds perfect."

When she got off the phone, she let out a whoop, then ran into the room where the children were working, and began laughing and dancing around. "I have an interview! It's really happening!"

Joseph got up and began to dance with her. "Mama, what kind of job is it?"

"It's the one I wanted, where I can work at home."

Leah and Rachel caught the excitement then, and they sprang up and began to jump up and down. Daniel just sat at his desk and grinned.

She heard the back door open, and David came in. "Hey, what's all the commotion?"

"Mom's got an interview!"

Brenda abandoned the children and threw her arms around David. "The Cancer Center, David! They called! They liked my proposal and want to talk to me today!"

David threw his head back and laughed then, and picked her up and twirled her around.

Brenda had calmed down by that afternoon, and with the assurance from Cathy and Tory that they would be praying for her, she dressed in a skirt and blazer and went for the interview.

It went better than she could have imagined, and within half an hour of arriving, she headed back to her car with a medical dictionary and each doctor's tapes for that day's transcription. If she delivered as she'd assured them she could, she could come in Monday morning to fill out all the paperwork, making her a full-time employee.

There was no doubt in her mind she could pull it off.

She sang praise songs as she drove home, filled with joy that the Lord had answered her prayers even better than she'd hoped or imagined.

She immediately set to work transcribing the tapes, and had them all finished by noon the next day. At the end of the day, she returned them to the clinic, and picked up another day's work. When she returned them at 5:30 on Friday, the office manager shook her hand. "Congratulations. Dr. Thibodeaux told me you're hired. You can come in Monday morning to do all the paperwork to get you on the payroll."

Brenda didn't need gas to get home that day. She could have made it on pure joy.

CHAPTER
Fifty-Six

Within a week of the reconstruction surgery Sylvia felt ready to resume her life. The children came home for a visit, and when they were gone she and Harry decided to start a class at their church, a Bible study for those who wanted deeper discipleship. Sylvia decided that they should do a study of Jesus in the Old Testament, so she and Harry had set about to design a curriculum.

They showed up at the church the night of their first meeting, hoping and praying that someone would attend. By fifteen till seven, the room was already full. Some of the men went out and began bringing in extra chairs.

Sylvia's heart soared as she saw Annie come in with Cathy and take one of the back row seats. A little while later, just after seven, Josh slipped in and took a seat across the room.

Harry started teaching, and Sylvia threw things in whenever something occurred to her worth adding. Together they managed to hold the class's rapt attention.

"That went well," Harry said as they drove home that night. "Who would have thought we'd have that big a group? Almost made me feel like we were doing as much good as we did in León."

"Me too," Sylvia said. "I've felt so unproductive for the last few months. This revived my need to be used. I want to do more than a once-a-week Bible study."

Harry grinned as if that didn't surprise him at all. "What do you have in mind?"

"I've been thinking about what I could do during the day," she said. "I was thinking that maybe I could volunteer at the Breezewood Development Center, where Tory works. I could teach the wordless book to the children with Down's Syndrome."

Harry studied the road. "Are you sure, honey? The radiation might take a lot out of you. You don't really want to commit to anything until you know how it's going to be."

"Well, it can't be as bad as the chemo," Sylvia said. "Besides, if I'm a volunteer I can not show up once in a while and it won't hurt anyone. But while I'm able, I want to bear as much fruit as I can."

"Do you think Down's Syndrome children that age would be able to understand the wordless book?"

"Sure they could," she said.

He stopped at a red light and leaned over to kiss her cheek. "I'm proud of you," he said. "Most people in your shoes would be finding ways to indulge themselves to make up for the last few months, but here you are, trying to think of ways to fulfill the Great Commission."

"That's what I'm here for. I'm going to go ask Tory as soon as we get home. She's probably got her children in bed by now."

Tory's garage was still open, so Sylvia knew it wasn't too late to knock on the door. They usually closed the garage as their last task before going to bed at night. She knocked on the door, waited, and after a moment Barry opened it.

"Hey, Sylvia. How's it going?"

"Couldn't be better," she said, stepping inside.

"How was your Bible study?"

"Just fabulous," she said. "You should have been there."

"Well, we were going to, but you know how hard it is for Tory to leave the kids with a sitter. So we've decided that maybe we'll take turns going starting next week. I'll baby-sit and let her go, and then the next week she'll baby-sit and let me go. Maybe we can keep up in the meantime."

"Sure," Sylvia said. "I was thinking about taping it anyway. Whoever doesn't come could hear the tape."

"That's a great idea," he said. "Come on in and I'll get Tory."

Sylvia walked into the spotless living room and sat down on the couch. Tory was a perfectionist and never left anything out of place. But tonight she saw that a few toys lay out in the living room. Tory was loosening up a little, and Sylvia was sure that benefited the whole family.

Tory came out of the back of the house. "Hey, Sylvia. How did the class go?"

"It was fun, and it just thrilled me to be able to do something again. And it sort of started me thinking."

Tory plopped down on a chair near the couch. "Thinking about what?"

"About what you're doing at the school, the children you work with. I'd love to meet little Bo."

"Well, come on up there," she said. "That'll be fine. We invite visitors."

"Well, what about volunteers?" Sylvia asked. "I was thinking about coming up there and reading to the children."

"Well, sure, we'd love to have you. And I know we're always looking for help. The only problem is they have very short attention spans and they're not very good listeners."

"Well, I had another idea," she said. "I have some special books that I used to use for the Nicaraguan kids, and I was thinking maybe it would be a good tool to use with your kids. Since it's a private school, they won't mind if I teach them about Jesus, will they?"

"No, they'll love it. The director's a Christian, and so are most of the teachers. Let me just clear it with the administration tomorrow and I'll get back to you. But I know it won't be a problem. If somebody volunteers to do something they don't have to pay for, they're going to be thrilled. They're constantly having budget problems. I was shocked that they offered to pay me."

"Well, I was just thinking I could come every morning at the same time and work with the children. And on my bad days I could skip and no one would be any worse off for it."

"I think it's wonderful," Tory said. "But, Sylvia, are you sure you want to do that? I mean, if I were you, I'd probably be focusing all my energy on getting well."

"I am getting well," Sylvia said. "It's all in God's hands. Besides, we're supposed to bear fruit in every season of our life. I don't plan to take this season off."

Tory looked down at her hands. "Sometimes I wonder if I bear any fruit at all."

"Of course you do," Sylvia said. "How can you think such a thing? Look at all the work you do with your children. That's bearing fruit. Some day they'll grow up and bear fruit of their own. You're doing your life's work right now. This is what you're called to."

Tory got up and started picking up the toys on the floor. "Remember when I wanted to be a writer?"

"You're still a writer," Sylvia said. "You write better than anyone I know. And those days are not over. But right now you're called to take care of Hannah and Spencer and Brittany, and the children at the school. If that isn't bearing fruit, I don't know what is."

Tory dropped the toys into a basket beside the couch, then hugged Sylvia. "When I grow up, Sylvia, I want to be just like you."

CHAPTER
Fifty-Seven

Sylvia got permission to read to the children at the Breezewood Development Center, so she ordered the wordless books she would need, and took them to the school the Monday after they came in.

Tory and Linda, the teacher, spent the valuable time planning their activities for the rest of the day, while Sylvia sat in a circle with the children. She started off trying to teach them "Jesus Loves Me." A few of them picked it up, but most of them only hummed and muttered words that sounded nothing like the words in the song.

Then she gave them each a wordless book, and began teaching them what each page meant.

"Red is for Jesus' blood," Sylvia would say, and the children would stare blankly at her. "And black is for the bad things we do, all the sin in our hearts. And white is for how clean we are when Jesus washes us."

On their way home, Tory voiced her skepticism that Sylvia's work would do any good. "It's hard for them to grasp concepts like Jesus' blood washing away their sins," she said. "I'm not even sure they understand sin at all."

"Oh, they'll get it before you know it," Sylvia said. "Within a few months I'll bet we have every one of them asking Jesus into their hearts."

Tory turned into Cedar Circle. "I don't know, Sylvia. That might be a little optimistic."

"Optimistic? Why?"

"I just sometimes feel that salvation isn't even a message that *needs* to be brought to these children. They're never going to reach the age of accountability, because they're mentally handicapped. They're already God's children. Their minds never really grow into mature adulthood. Don't you think that they're already saved by virtue of being perpetual children?"

Sylvia regarded her for a moment. "I'm sure that's true. But it never hurts to teach them the truth. And the best truth in the world that we can teach them is about Jesus' love for them and what he did to prove it."

Tory pulled into her driveway and let the car idle for a moment. Hannah slept in the back, so there was no hurry to get out. "I just think the concept of salvation is very complicated. They can barely even learn 'Jesus Loves Me.' Can they ever really grasp that Jesus died on a cross, and was raised from the dead?"

"Don't you want Hannah to?"

"Well, yes, of course. But I don't have much hope that she will. I think God will make a special provision for her."

"Of course he will. But I think you need to raise your expectations. Jesus said to come to him just like those little children. He wouldn't have said that if he meant it to be complicated. It's the adults who make it complicated."

Tory frowned. "You really think so?"

"Of course I think so. We teach them that we did bad things and God decided to send his Son to take our punishment, that when he died on the cross he bought our way into heaven. That's simple, Tory."

Tory looked back at Hannah, sleeping soundly in her car seat. "I know. But there's so much more, even beyond that. All the things I'm learning in the Bible about sanctification and obedience and bearing fruit."

"Those children can understand it on their own level. God isn't some phantom that hides from the innocent. He'll reveal himself to them. And it's good for us to share him with them. It grows *us* when we bear fruit."

As Tory took Hannah into the house, those two words rolled over and over in her mind. *Bear fruit. Bear fruit.* It was the main focus of Sylvia's life. Yet Tory wasn't sure it was a focus at all for her.

Hannah woke up as she started to put her down, so Tory got the wordless book Sylvia had given her. She had never tried reading to her before, never even thought it would have any effect, but maybe Sylvia was right. Maybe she could teach little Hannah about the love of Jesus. The result was completely up to God.

CHAPTER
Fifty-Eight

Mark slammed into the house in late March, sweating from head to toe, an angry scowl on his face. He looked as if he'd been dipped in tar. "This is absolutely the worst day I've ever had in my entire life!"

Cathy flipped the hamburgers she was frying and glanced at Steve, who leaned against the counter. "What is it, Mark?"

"It's a crummy job, that's what. I almost fell off the roof today, and it got so hot out there I thought I was going to die. Eighty degrees in *March?* It's some kind of record or something. And I couldn't take my shirt off because yesterday I took it off and I got so sunburned that I'm blistered. They work us daylight till dark and the money's crummy."

Steve winked at Cathy. "You'll get used to it. People always do. There are people who have been in that business for most of their lives."

"Yeah, but they don't do what I'm doing all those years. They advance to management, and the management guys don't even get up on the roof. They just go from site to site overseeing."

"Well, maybe you can work your way up to that."

Mark dropped his keys on the counter. "I don't even want to *be* in this business."

Steve cleared his throat. "Well, you know, it takes a lot of brains to do construction work, Mark. Reading and interpreting blueprints, making everything come out all right. And roofing is not a small thing. The roof protects the whole house . . ."

"Maybe so, but all I'm doing is hammering and getting tar under my fingernails." He stretched. "Every muscle in my body hurts."

"You'll build your muscles up," Cathy threw in. "After a while, you won't notice it anymore."

"There are better ways, Mom."

She turned from the stove. "Well, Mark, what would you like to do? It was your idea not to go back to school."

"I know. I'm just thinking maybe I need to look for a different job. The problem is, I don't have time because I'm so busy working at this one. By the time I get off I'm filthy and exhausted. I don't have time to go do anything else. Besides, nobody wants to hire a guy with my record. Even when I get my GED, it'll be practically worthless when it's balanced against the conviction."

Annie came into the room, munching on a celery stick. "Told you you should go to college. It's a breeze, Mark. Practically like a day at the beach compared to what you're doing."

Cathy shot Annie a look. "Annie, stop snacking. We're about to eat."

"Seriously, Mark. You'll have your GED in the next month or so. You should sign up for the summer term at the college. You'll have fun, especially after all this."

"I don't want to go to school," Mark said. "I just want a decent job, where they don't treat me like some kid."

"Well, you are a kid," Annie threw back. "Mark, you're only sixteen. Give me a break. What do you think they're going to do, let you become a stockbroker?"

Cathy grinned. "She's got a point, Mark." She got out the buns and put one on each plate. "The fact is, you're trying to grow up too soon. You need to slow down and take your time, do the things that a sixteen-year-old is supposed to do, like go to school and work for the grocery store bagging groceries. Take your time planning what you want to do for the rest of your life. You can do that, Mark."

Mark went to the sink and washed the filth off of his hands. "But I don't even know where to start. What if I can't even get into the community college?"

"I think you can, Mark. And if you make good grades, I'm sure you could get into a better college when the time came."

Steve handed Mark a towel to wipe his hands on. "Mark, I know you think your sentence will always hang over your head, but the truth is, if you have four good years of college with good grades and good behavior and no more trouble, people will forget that when you were in high school you made a few mistakes."

Mark slumped over the counter. "You think so? Because right now that's all they care about, like I'm some kind of drug dealer who's wanting to get on their payroll."

"People will forget," he said. "It's a lot easier to overlook a year at River Ranch when you've got four good years of college and good behavior."

"I'd definitely have good behavior," Mark said. "I'm not so sure about the good grades part. I've never been a very good student."

"But you're more mature now, Mark," Steve said. "You can do it. You've got it in you now. Look how much you've learned about the Bible on your own in just a few months."

"Well, that's true," Mark said. "I guess when I'm interested in something I can apply myself."

"Well, maybe you could make yourself be more interested in English and history and science when you realize that it's your alternative to getting up on a roof every day in the hot sun and hammering shingles."

Mark thought that over for a moment. "I don't know," he said. "I'll have to think about it."

"Why don't you run up and take a shower?" Cathy said. "We'll hold supper until you're finished."

"Good," he said. "The sooner I can get this filth off of me, the better."

They watched as Mark trudged up the stairs.

Cathy turned around, grinning, and Steve raised his hand for a high five. "It's working," he whispered.

Annie's mouth fell open. "You two planned this."

Cathy swung around. "What? Us?"

"Yes," she said. "You knew all along he'd hang himself with his own rope."

Cathy laughed. "Harsh image, Annie. We just hoped it would work out this way."

"Boy, you guys are slick."

Cathy almost danced as she set the table.

It started to rain about lunchtime the next day, and Mark was sent home from work. The house was empty when he got there, so he took a shower, cleaned up, and then decided to go to the local community college. Something had to give, he thought, and this hard manual labor was for the birds. It wasn't that he was too good for it. He wasn't. The other guys on the crew were hardworking men who did what they had to do to make a living. And there was something satisfying about working with his hands and coming home exhausted at the end of the day.

But he wanted more. His mind needed stimulation. He wanted to stretch it somehow, the way he'd done when he'd home schooled with Brenda. His GED test was this coming Saturday, and he felt confident that he'd pass it this time. Then he'd be ready to move on.

He drove over to the community college, found the administration building, and went in and got a catalog. Then he sat out in his car and flipped through it, wondering if he did go to college, what in the world he would study. He liked computers, he thought, and he liked to draw. Years ago before he'd gotten too cool to do it, he'd even been pretty good at it. He'd once considered being a graphic artist. His father had suggested architecture, but that seemed like a lofty goal, too far out of his reach.

He flipped through the catalog and looked up graphic art, then architecture, and saw that some of the basic courses were the same. Maybe he could have a broad target and start with both of those, then narrow it as his focus cleared.

Whatever he did, he felt an urgency to sign up for the summer term.

Man, he hated it when his parents were right.

CHAPTER
Fifty-Nine

Sylvia floated along for the months of March, April, and May, taking her radiation treatments and her Tamoxifen, volunteering at the school, teaching the Bible study with Harry at her church, and writing letters to the children in the orphanage in León. In the afternoons, she rode her horse, visited her neighbors, and prayed for those around her.

When her lower back began to ache, she told herself that she had pulled a muscle, and went on with her life.

She threw a neighborhood party for Mark when he got his GED, then celebrated again when he got into college for the summer term.

Though she was tired from the radiation and still had frequent hot flashes from the hormone pills, she felt as if the cancer was just a part of her past. She began counting the days until the radiation would end and she could return to her work in León.

But then the oncologist ordered blood tests at her three-month checkup. Her tumor markers were elevated, so he sent her for more scans.

And a sense of dread began to fall over her again.

The doctor's face was grim as he came into the office to deliver the results. "We've got some bad news, I'm afraid. The scans showed that the cancer has metastasized to your lower spine."

Sylvia sat frozen, not certain she had heard right. The cancer that had been cut out of her breast, blasted with chemo, burned with radiation, had now conquered her bones? She turned her stricken eyes to Harry.

She heard the groan that seeped out of him as he pulled her into his arms. "Honey . . ."

"Please don't panic," the doctor went on in a calm voice. "The skeleton is not a vital organ. This is still treatable."

Sylvia gaped at him. Was he crazy? Not a vital organ? Did he equate her bones to tonsils or appendixes? "Not a vital organ? We're talking about my skeleton. How can you say it's not a vital organ? I can hardly live without it."

"He's right." Harry's voice trembled. "The truth is, the prognosis can still be pretty good with this kind of cancer. If it were in your liver or your brain or your lungs, we'd have a bigger challenge."

So she should be grateful that it had only attacked her bones? All that time that she'd thought she was out of the woods, had it been laying ambush to her spine? Would it begin to attack her joints, her skull, her limbs? She didn't want to think about what was to come. She'd felt so good knowing the cancer had disappeared, that she had fought it back valiantly, and that it had fled. But now it was back, hunkering down in her body, waiting to attack other cells and organs. "What does this mean?" she managed to ask.

"Well, for right now I think the best approach is to change your hormone therapy," the doctor said. "We'll see how the cancer responds to that. Meanwhile, we'll just continue with the radiation and pray."

Sylvia was quiet all the way home, and so was Harry. She'd believed she was out of the woods, but now she felt so deep in them that she couldn't see her way out. The cancer could still kill her, despite her efforts to fight it.

She thought of her grandbaby, little Breanna. Would she watch her grow up after all? Would she be around when Jeff found the right girl and married? Would she hold any more of Sarah's babies?

And would she ever be able to return to her work, and hold little Juan and the Nicaraguan children who were so much like her own? Was all that behind her forever?

When they got home, Harry sat down. "Honey, talk to me."

She paced across the room, her arms crossed. "I can't," she said.

"Yes, you can."

"No. I just want to read. I want to get all the books I have about cancer and dig into your medical journals, and try to find out what my chances are."

"They're good, Sylvia. Very good. You can't give up yet."

Tears glistened in her eyes. "But I thought I was cured. I know they tell you not to think that until you've been cancer-free for five years, but I still thought it. I'm not prepared to fight metastatic disease. I'm afraid of this cancer, Harry! It's so aggressive, nothing can kill it."

"It can be stopped," Harry said. "Honey, you just have to have faith."

Sylvia finally sat down beside him. "I've presumed on God," she whispered. "All this time I've been sure that he would send us back to the mission field, let us resume our work, allow us to bear more fruit. But he's got other plans, hasn't he?"

Harry's mouth quivered at the corners, and she saw him struggling with the tears in his eyes. "Maybe for now."

"His ways are not our ways." She breathed a humorless laugh. "That makes me so mad. What is he doing?"

"I don't know." He pulled her forehead against his, and started to cry.

She touched the tears on his face, and pulled back to look into the agony in his eyes. "Oh, Harry." She hated seeing him so sad, and she knew that her own pain provoked that sadness. She had to pull herself together. If not for herself, then for him.

They wept together for a few moments, then finally, she dried her tears. "I'm gonna be okay," she said, drying his face with her fingertips. "I am, Harry. I'm going to fight and do everything that the doctors tell me to do, and I'm going to trust the Lord, whatever he chooses to do."

Harry swallowed and nodded. "That's my girl."

"We can't live in fear," she told him. "That's no way to live. We'll have to figure out a way to live life without constantly thinking about it."

He made a valiant effort to wipe the emotion from his face.

"Remember when I said that cancer was a gift God had given me?" she asked.

"Yes."

"I said that, believing it would go away. But it's still probably true. If God gave it to me, then it's a gift. An opportunity. I have to find a way to think of it as that again. Would you pray that for me, Harry?"

He didn't wait until he was alone. Instead he just held her, and began to pray.

CHAPTER *Sixty*

That night when she had her bearings, she called her children and each of her neighbors individually and told them the news. They were each crushed and quiet, and had little to say in the way of comfort. But Sylvia hadn't expected otherwise. They were as shocked as she, and it would take a few days to sort out all these emotions and figure out what to think.

That night as she and Harry lay in bed next to each other, neither tried to fool the other into thinking they were sleeping.

"The thing I hate most about all this," Sylvia whispered, "is that I've always hoped that if I ever came to a place like this where I had a terminal disease and was going to die . . ."

Harry cut in immediately. "You are not going to die."

"But you know what I mean, Harry," she said. "I hoped that if I ever had a terminal illness, I would handle it as a godly woman with a positive attitude and a cheerful heart. I hoped I would focus more on the people around me than on myself, that I'd worry more about whether their spiritual needs were being met than I would about my own physical needs. But that's not how I am."

He touched her face. "How can you say that? You're the most godly woman I know. Anyone would agree."

"But *anyone* doesn't know what's going on inside of me," she said. "I feel so angry and so out of control. I want to scream and holler at God and ask him what in the world he thinks he's doing. I want to yell at everybody who's healthy, that they'd better enjoy it while they can because it could be snatched out from under them at any moment. And I want to scream at all those complacent Christians sitting in the pews on Sunday mornings and doing nothing with their lives, wasting their talents and gifts God has given them when they could be out sharing the love of Christ."

"I feel the same way. Honey, it's not ungodly to feel all those things."

"But that's not what I want to feel," she said. "I want to be someone that God would be proud of. If I'm going to die, I want to go out with a bang, you know? And don't say I'm not going to die again because we're all going to die someday. Whenever it is, I want to do it right."

He wiped the tears off of his face with the top of the sheet. "Honey, God's going to give you whatever you need to get through this. You can believe that. The one thing we've learned over all these years is that God is faithful. Haven't we learned that?"

"Yes, we have." Sylvia let the tears run down her temples and through her hair onto her pillow. "I wonder if I'll live to see my hair grow all the way back in."

"Of course you will," he said. "It's long enough now that you could go without your wig."

She was quiet for a moment, trying to picture herself as she'd been before the surgery, with her body whole and her hair just the way she'd chosen to wear it.

"It's strange, going from thinking of myself as being healthy and healed, to realizing that my fight is not over."

"No, it's not over," he said, "but you don't have to worry, Sylvia, because you're not fighting it alone." He slipped his arms around her and pulled her close, and they wept together long into the night.

Instead of slowing Sylvia down, the news of her recurrence spurred her onward, faster, with more fierce urgency to do the things that she felt God had called her to do. Since the Breezewood Development Center didn't close for the summer, Sylvia spent more hours than ever at the school, working with the children. Little Bo began to meet her at the door each morning. "Miva," he would call her, in his own special combination of "Miss" and "Sylvia."

As if the Lord wanted to show her that her work did please him, the children had all managed to learn their own version of "Jesus Loves Me." The tunes varied, but the sounds of their awkward words hit close to the real words. Even their attention spans seemed to have broadened. Sylvia had a calming influence on them, and they loved to hear her read. She had advanced from the wordless book to reading actual stories. Still, each day she went over the wordless book again, until each child considered it his favorite book, the only one that some of them could "read."

Sylvia didn't stop with the children. In the afternoons, she spent time teaching Bible to Brenda's kids, while Brenda did her typing.

On Wednesday nights, she and Harry kept teaching the Bible study at church. And on Thursday nights she and her neighbors gathered to pray.

In between all her work, she wrote the children in the orphanage in León individual letters letting them know she loved them and missed them.

There was little time for self-pity, even though her back had begun to ache constantly as the cancer sank its teeth deeper into her bones. There was no kidding herself that the new drug was working.

She knew from deep within that the cancer was growing, occupying more territory, overthrowing her body.

But there was little that she could do, except press on, and trust that God had things under control.

CHAPTER
Sixty-One

The meteor shower that only occurred every thirty-five years or so was scheduled to happen at the end of May. Brenda suspended school that day and let the kids sleep late, so they could stay up late enough to see the heavenly display. At ten o'clock they took blankets outside and went up to Lookout Point at the peak of Bright Mountain.

Stars shot across the sky, delighting the children as they lay on their backs, clapping and cheering for each burst of light.

Brenda lay next to David, praying that the beauty and majesty of the shower would cause him to acknowledge his Creator. But he had made his salvation so complicated that the doorway was not only narrow, as Jesus had warned, but it seemed locked and bolted shut.

Still, she prayed and hoped. With every star that flew across the sky, she asked the Lord to let this miracle be the one that opened David's eyes.

"Isn't God cool?" Joseph asked, his head pillowed on David's chest.

Brenda laughed. "Very cool."

David's silence became his answer, but Joseph didn't let it lie.

"Dad, how could you not believe in God after you've seen this? It's just so obvious. All this stuff didn't happen by accident."

David expelled a long sigh. "I'm just not the kind of person who can have faith in what I don't see, Joseph."

Joseph sat up. "But you did just see it. It would take more faith *not* to believe than it does to believe."

David didn't answer.

"Wish we could have videotaped this," Daniel said from his place on the ground. "This is the most awesome thing I've ever seen."

David nodded. "It is amazing."

They lay quietly for a moment, listening to the music of the wind as it scored the spectacular showing in the sky. After a moment, Leah sat up and looked at her mother.

"Mom, is Miss Sylvia going to die?"

Brenda shivered. Forgetting the display overhead, she got up and went to snuggle between her twin daughters. "I don't think so, sweetie, but we're not sure yet."

"Do you think she's scared?" Rachel asked.

"Nope," Joseph said. "Not Miss Sylvia. She's not scared."

"How do you know?" Daniel asked. "Did she tell you that?"

"She didn't have to," Joseph said. "I just know, 'cause I was there once. How can you be scared when you know you're going to be with Jesus?"

Brenda met David's eyes, but he looked away. He slid his arm around his youngest son's shoulders and pulled him close. Once again she said a prayer for her husband to believe.

CHAPTER
Sixty-Two

When Annie called Sylvia to ask if she and Josh could come over to ride the horse, Sylvia welcomed the opportunity to spend time with the two kids she had chosen for each other. The horse needed riding, but her back ached too badly to ride today.

She met them out at the barn that afternoon and helped them saddle her and get her ready to ride. Josh had ridden for most of his life, so it all came easily to him.

They rode double on the horse, and headed off to the pasture beyond the trees. Sylvia sat on her swing and watched, smiling at how well things were working with them. She thought of herself and Harry, when they had first fallen in love. Every touch, every look, every smile had carried special significance. In so many ways, that hadn't changed today.

She thought of the way Harry had stood beside her during this illness, even though his own dreams had been interrupted.

But she knew he would have it no other way. How blessed she was to have him.

Lord, whether it's Josh or someone else, bring Annie a soul mate like that. Someone to stand by her for her whole life. Someone like Harry.

She heard footsteps and turned to see Cathy coming toward her. "Hi," Cathy said.

"Hi yourself."

She sat down next to Sylvia, making the chains creak. "How you feeling?"

"Not bad."

Cathy got quiet. Sylvia knew she was keeping a respectful distance from the subject of Sylvia's cancer. It was clear that she tried hard to let Sylvia set the parameters of their conversations.

"Looks like Josh and Annie are getting along really well," Sylvia said.

Cathy nodded. "Yeah. They don't need much help from us."

"I just think they'd be a wonderful couple."

"Well, don't rush them. You know Annie's still young."

"I know," Sylvia said, "but she's a precious young woman and she deserves the best."

She looked at Cathy and saw tears misting her eyes. "You know, there was a time when I didn't hold out much hope for Annie being a spiritual person."

"I know that. But God surprised you, didn't he?"

"Yes, he did."

"That's the thing with God. He always has surprises for us. He has so many plans and so many layers, and they're so rich in our lives ... if we just had enough faith to trust in them." She'd said too much, she thought, and now they were back on the subject of her cancer. She wished she'd kept that thought to herself.

"You have enough faith, Sylvia."

Sylvia frowned into the wind. "I don't know if I do or not. People tell me I'm brave, that they admire me for such a valiant effort, but the fact is, I don't have any choice. What do they think I'm going to do, just roll over and die?"

The wind was the only answer. It whispered through their hair and hung between them. Cathy looked down at her knees. "You're going to beat this, Sylvia. I know you are. So many people are praying for you."

"I know they're praying, but I'm not sure if they should be praying for healing."

"Why not?" Cathy asked. "Why would we pray for anything else?"

"Because it may not be God's will. He may have a whole different plan. And, you know, just because he takes one life and leaves another doesn't mean that one person is blessed over another, or that one person's prayers are more important to God. He's just got these ways that are so mysterious. Who can understand them?"

Her voice broke off and she looked up at the leaves over her head, focused on them as if she might find some answer there. "I just want to be faithful," she went on. "When I get to heaven, whenever that day may be, I want to hear those words."

Cathy smiled. She knew what those words were. "'Well done, my good and faithful servant.' You'll hear them, Sylvia. I know you will."

"The thing is, it's easy to stop running the race. Sometimes I feel like just resting on the fact that I worked in Nicaragua, that I helped a lot of people there. I feel like if I just curl up in a closet somewhere, never to be heard from again, it won't really matter. But that's not what the Bible teaches, is it?"

Cathy just looked at her.

"The Bible teaches that we should run the race until the end. And I'm not at the end yet."

Tears stung Cathy's eyes. She laid her head on Sylvia's shoulder. "Sylvia, how could you ever doubt that God is pleased with you?"

"Because I have all these conflicting emotions raging through my heart, and I don't feel very holy sometimes. I'm not the way I thought I would be if I ever faced a crisis like this."

"God asks us to be holy," Cathy said. "He doesn't ask us to be superhuman. Within your humanity, I think you're as holy as you can be. Don't forget that even Jesus prayed that the cup would be taken from him."

Sylvia sat there for a moment, taking that in. "He did, didn't he?"

"Of course he did. He wept and he railed and he sweat great drops of blood."

"I understand that," Sylvia said. "I've been there myself."

"If you're supposed to take this with all the stoicism of a statue, then why would God let us see the Gethsemane Jesus?"

Sylvia nodded as that truth became clear to her. "I guess he did it for me. Seems like I've been going through my Gethsemane for an awfully long time. Maybe I'll eventually come out on the other side and be able to do whatever it is God has for me to do."

Even if it's to die.

CHAPTER
Sixty-Three

Sylvia's Gethsemane didn't end for several weeks. During her times of serving others she managed to smile and laugh and get out of herself and forget those anguished pleas she sent up to heaven at night when she faced her illness head-on. But the pain intensifying in her back and hip told her the hormones weren't working. And when she started feeling pain where she knew her liver to be, fear overtook her again.

For several days she failed to tell anyone about it because she didn't want to be an alarmist. She had learned that when dealing with cancer, every pain had significance. If she got a headache, she assumed that the cancer had spread to her brain. If her wrist ached, she was certain it had gotten into that part of her bone. If her blood sugar was off, she was sure that it had advanced to her pancreas.

But finally when the pain grew more intense, she decided it was best to tell Harry. Harry didn't even respond. He went straight to the telephone and started to dial.

"Who are you calling?" she asked.

"I'm calling Dr. Thibodeaux."

"It's night," she said. "He's not at his office."

"I'm calling him at home."

"But, Harry, do you think it's anything?"

"It's probably not," he said, "but there's no use taking any chances. I wish you'd told me the minute you started feeling it."

She sat listening as he told the doctor what she felt, and the oncologist told them to be at his office first thing the next morning.

She went through another round of CT scans and blood tests, then endured another season of waiting. Her Gethsemane continued.

They returned to the doctor's office the next day to get the results. Sick of the place, she wished she could change the curtains and reorganize the furniture. Better yet, she wished the doctor would meet her and Harry in a restaurant that was crowded and bustling with activity and life, instead of in these offices full of other cancer patients waiting for bad news.

Dr. Thibodeaux had that look on his face again, the one that made her want to put her hands over her ears. "It's spread to your liver," he said.

Sylvia had expected crushing despair, but instead she just felt numb. The pain in her back had already convinced her that the treatment strategy was failing. The doctor was only confirming it.

He looked up at her, his eyes tired. She wondered if he'd been at the hospital late last night or early today. Oncologists carried such burdens. For the first time, she felt sorry for him.

"I'm so sorry, Sylvia," he said, "but this means that we have to change our approach. We have to get more aggressive."

Sylvia swallowed. "That would be because the liver *is* a vital organ as opposed to the skeleton. Am I right?"

"That's right."

She looked at Harry. The blood seemed to have drained from his face.

She forced herself to speak. "But what does more aggressive therapy mean? Chemo again?"

The truth was, more chemo was one of her greatest fears. Her dark night of suffering had finally come to an end. The thought of reentering it was more than she could bear.

"Yes." His voice was low, steady. She wondered how often each day he had to deliver this kind of news. "We'll have to put you on a more aggressive chemo this time," he said, "and you'll have to have tests after every three cycles. If it's not working, then we'll change the drug."

There it was, the crushing despair . . . the feeling that she had been kicked in the kidney.

"How long will you do this?" Harry asked.

The doctor cleared his throat, shifted in his chair. He met Harry's eyes across the table. "This time the treatment has to last until the cancer is gone."

She stared at him for a moment, dissecting his words. "You mean I could be on chemotherapy for another six months or a year . . . or two years?"

"We'll fight it as long as we have to."

She looked at Harry. His head was slumped down, and he stared at his feet. "You mean I could be on it until the day I die?"

"I'm not going to lie to you," the doctor said. "Liver cancer can be fatal. When the disease has metastasized this much, we're dealing with a lot bigger challenge than we've had before."

Harry took her hand. His was as cold as hers. Her breath was shallow, inadequate. *Breathe*, she told herself. *Just breathe.*

"Okay," she said. "Given this new development, what are my chances?"

He shook his head. "You know I don't do percentages, Sylvia. There's no point in that."

Her voice got louder. "But how many people die when they have what I have?"

"Some of them," he said. "But some of them live. And you believe in miracles, don't you?"

"Are you telling me it's going to take a *miracle* to pull me through this?"

His eyes looked almost as forlorn as Harry's. "A miracle would help," he said. "I'm telling you that we have good drugs and they work. It's going to be a struggle, but you're strong enough to take it. I know you are."

It sounded hopeful, even gentle, but Sylvia knew he'd just given her a death sentence.

Harry reached for her, but she sat stiff, unable to respond. "Harry, I don't know if I can go through with this."

"You can. Honey, you can. I'll help you."

She started to cry, and turned back to the doctor. "Will my hair fall out again?"

The doctor turned his compassionate eyes to her. "Probably. The side effects might be worse than they were before, but it's the best treatment we have. And, Sylvia, it often does work."

She wiped her nose and got up, looking helplessly for a Kleenex. Why didn't he have a Kleenex? "How long?" Sylvia asked. "How long do I have? I want to know."

He shook his head again. "I don't do that, Sylvia. I'm not going to tell you you have six months or a year."

"Six months or a year?" she asked. "Is that what I have?"

"I don't *know* what you have. You might have twenty years."

"Worst-case scenario?" she said. "If the chemo doesn't stop this cancer and it keeps spreading at the rate it has been, how long do I have to live?" She leaned over his desk, her hands balled into fists. "I need to know!"

He didn't answer, so finally, she turned and headed for the door.

"Sylvia, we still need to talk."

Sylvia turned back to the doctor. "Set everything up with Harry. I have to get out of here."

Then she ran up the hall, past the bookkeeper, out into the waiting room. She hurried out to the car and got in, and screamed out her rage, grief, and anguish. She could have torn the steering wheel off and slammed it through the windshield, broken glass all the way around, started the car and rammed it into a wall.

But she sat in the passenger seat, doubled over with her hands over her face ...

My children, she thought. *How will I tell my children?*

It would shake their faith. It would shake everyone's faith. So many were praying for her. They all believed she would be healed. Why would God let them all down?

She had said it was a gift—this cancer, this archenemy that occupied her body. She had even believed it, when chemo was a temporary torture and the cancer hadn't found another home in her body.

But now ...

The peace and joy she had once known had been banished, and stark fear took its place.

Where are you, God? Where's the victory in this?

She heard Harry at the car door and sat up, wiped her face. The sobs kept hiccuping from her throat, but she tried to get control.

He got in with several papers and the appointment for her first chemo treatment, twisted, and set them on the backseat. He looked at her, assessing her condition. She patted his hand, reassuring him that she had not completely fallen apart. But Harry looked old, frail ...

They were quiet as they rode home, and when they were back in their driveway, Sylvia got out of the car. "I have to go ride."

She started around the house and headed for the barn. Harry followed her. "Sylvia."

"You don't have to come with me," she called. "I can do this by myself. I need to be alone."

"But I don't!" Harry cried. "I don't want to be alone. I want to be with you!"

He followed her into the dark stable, and she opened her horse's stall. Going in, she slid down the wall onto the hay and covered her face with both hands. The horse dipped his head and nudged her.

"I won't survive the treatments, Harry," she cried. "They'll kill me faster than the cancer. If I'm going to die, I want to do it with dignity, not with nausea and fatigue and sores and a bald head and yellow skin and all my joints aching like I'm a ninety-year-old woman."

Harry sat down next to her in the hay. "Honey, I know it's a lot to ask. I know you don't want to go through this again, and right now you probably don't even feel that bad, just a little pain in your side and back. But, honey, that pain is your enemy, and it's *my* enemy, and I want you to live. I want you to do the chemo because there's a chance that you'll beat it. I don't think God's finished with you yet. There's still hope. I haven't ever asked you for much, have I?"

She shook her head. "No, not much. The last time you asked for something really important, you wanted me to leave all my memories behind and traipse off to Nicaragua to save the world."

"And you did, valiantly. You gave it all up, and the next thing I knew you were more passionate about doing our work there than I was. And there's so much more for us to do yet. I want us to go back to León together. I want us to see the children again. I want to take care of those people who depend on me," he said, "but I can't do it without you. I need for you to fight. I need for you to go through this chemo. I need for you to suffer a little longer just for hope of the good outcome. Please, Sylvia. Don't reject the chemo. I'm begging you."

Her face softened as she looked at her husband and realized this was the most important request he had ever made of her, even more important than forsaking everything and heading off to the mission field. This was life or death. Her life. Her death. And she owed it to Harry to fight.

She reached for him and pulled him against her, stroked the back of his head and breathed in the scent of him. She loved him so dearly. She would do anything for him. Even this.

Finally she pulled back and looked into his face. "All right," she said. "I'll give it the fight of my life. For you. And for whatever fruit is left in me to bear."

That night she fell exhausted into bed and drifted into a shallow sleep. Harry lay next to her for a long time, but sleep didn't come for him. Finally, he slipped out of bed, quietly got on his clothes, and headed out to the barn. Once there, he got down on his knees, face to the ground.

"Please don't take her," he cried to God. "I've never asked you that much before. I've been very accepting of the things you've wanted for us. I've given you our lives and I've been obedient, and so has she. I'm begging you now, Lord, please don't take her. She's my helpmeet, my soul mate. You chose her for me. I'm begging you, Lord. I know that death has to come at some point in our lives, but not now. Please not now. Please, God, answer this prayer. Give us a miracle. Save her life."

He wept until the wee hours of morning and prayed and wrestled with God. Finally, around three A.M. he felt a peace fall over him. It wasn't a peace that he would have the answer he sought. God wasn't making that promise. It was only a peace that God would walk with them through this shadow of death, and that they should fear no evil. It was a tall order, Harry knew, and he wasn't sure if either one of them was strong enough to follow it. But he had committed to trying, just as she had.

CHAPTER
Sixty-Four

The next morning Harry and Sylvia were quiet as they started their day over breakfast with tired eyes and long faces. "We have to tell the children," Harry said.

"I know, but not yet."

"When?" he asked.

"I think I need to spend some time in God's Word," she said. "I need to soak up all the strength I can. I need to find verses about why God lets us suffer, about death and dying, about what the future holds and whatever else God decides to show me. I need to be ready for their questions."

Harry rubbed his eyes. "That's a good idea, Sylvia. I'll do it, too."

"I was thinking that, once I feel I have enough strength, I want to call the neighbors over and have a dinner party, and try to be upbeat and positive as I tell them. And I want to call the children and tell them the same way. I don't want them to see us like we were last night, or even like we are right now. I want them to see a godly woman continuing to serve God even in the dying season of her life."

"It's not your dying season," Harry said. "It's just a dark season . . . but there's going to be light again."

"There's going to be light again whether it's my dying season or not," she whispered. But she couldn't be happy about that just yet.

"I wish I didn't have appointments today," he said. "I don't want to see patients."

"I want you to go." Sylvia took her plate to the sink. "I'm just going to stay in today and study the Bible. By the time you come home I'm hoping I'll feel better."

She spent the day weeding through the Bible, searching for passages that would give her comfort, passages she could pass on to others to give them comfort, too. By that night she still wasn't ready to tell her children or the neighbors, so she and Harry spent the time in prayer.

Harry took the following day off, and he spent the day with her poring through the Word. Finally by early afternoon Sylvia thought she could manage the announcement.

One by one she called Cathy and Steve, Tory and Barry, and David and Brenda, and invited them over for a dinner party that night. Nothing in her voice warned them what was coming. She didn't want it to be some horrible surprise. She just wanted them to see a smile on her face, a positive attitude, hope shining in her eyes, when she told them the bad news.

She set about to cook for them. While the lasagna baked in the oven, she called her children.

Heartbroken, they both said they would drop everything and come to be at her side, but she told them it wasn't necessary. She would let them know if things got bad, but until then she would just be pressing on with the things she had to do. All she needed from them now was their prayers.

Then she and Harry set about preparing for the dinner party. They hummed praise songs as they worked, decorating the house with fresh flowers, putting out hors d'oeuvres, arranging the tables, buttering the garlic bread.

By the time the doorbell rang, she was quite sure that she was ready.

Tory and Barry were the first to come over. Barry and Harry sat in the living room watching a baseball game that was almost over, while Tory helped Sylvia in the kitchen. Then Brenda and David showed up and David joined the guys in the living room, rooting for the Atlanta Braves as the last inning of the game wound down. Brenda came in and picked up a celery stick to crunch on.

"So how's the job going?" Sylvia asked her.

"I love it. Since it's summer and we're not doing school, I'm getting the work done earlier every day. It's working out great. I owe it all to you."

Sylvia waved her off. "I didn't do anything."

"Yes, you did."

The doorbell rang and they knew it was Cathy and Steve. They waited a moment until Cathy buzzed into the kitchen with hugs for everybody.

"Cathy, Brenda was just telling us how great her job is working out."

Cathy slid up onto the counter and looked at Brenda. "Isn't Sylvia a genius for giving the doctor the idea?"

Sylvia laughed. "Common sense, my dear. Those doctors have their minds so busy with people's diseases that they can't focus on little things."

"How does David feel about it?" Cathy asked.

"Fine now." Brenda glanced out the door to the men congregated around the television.

Cathy pulled open the oven and peeked in at the contents. "Mmm, Sylvia. You outdid yourself. The bread is almost ready."

Sylvia pulled it out and set it on the stove.

They chitchatted until the game was over, and when they heard the guys cheering in the living room at the victory of the Braves, Sylvia decided it was time to take the food to the table.

"All right, guys. Everybody come eat."

They headed in and took their places around the table, and Harry led them in a prayer. His voice broke as he spoke to God. He asked God to bless the meal and the conversation, and to give them all the strength they needed to get through the coming week.

Finally, they sat down and began chattering all at once as they filled their plates and passed the bread and salad. When they'd finished with their desserts and were ready to leave the table, she asked them all to assemble in the living room. She had some news for them, she said.

Harry helped her clear the table as the others quietly assembled in the living room, whispering. Harry took her into the kitchen, pulled her into his arms, and held her tight. She told herself she couldn't cry. She had to put a smile on her face and say this with bright eyes so that they would not feel dismal about what she faced.

Harry held her hand as he led her back into the quiet living room. They sat together on the love seat, as all six of their guests stared at them.

"What do you have to tell us?" Tory asked her.

"I bet I know," Brenda said. "Sarah's pregnant again. Right?"

Sylvia shook her head. "No, not yet." She looked down at her hands and realized they were trembling. "It's medical news." Her smile faded and she knew that her face was giving her away.

"Medical news?" Cathy stood up. "Oh, my gosh, Sylvia. What is it?"

She brought her face up. "Well, we found out that the cancer has spread to my liver."

Dead silence.

She looked around from one pair of shocked eyes to another. Brenda's eyes were already filling with tears, and David's face was turning red as he gaped at her. Tory looked angry and shook her head as if this couldn't be true, and Barry put his arm around her as if to support her. Steve got to his feet and slid his hands into his pockets, and she could see his jaw popping under the pressure.

Cathy's mouth hung open. "Sylvia, what does this mean?"

"Well, it's all right really. It's not as bad as it sounds." She knew they weren't buying any of it. She tapped Harry's leg, passing the baton to him.

"She's about to start chemo again," he said. "It'll be a lot more aggressive and it will continue until the cancer is gone."

"Oh, no," Brenda whispered.

"Is it still in the bones, too?" Tory asked on a wavering voice.

"Yes, it is, and it just keeps spreading."

She knew they all wanted to ask her what the prognosis was, what her chances were, how long she had to live, so finally she decided to address those points one by one.

"The prognosis is very iffy, guys," Sylvia said, "and the doctor wouldn't give me odds. Some survive this and some don't. And as far as how long I might have to live, it could be anywhere from twenty days to twenty years."

Tory collapsed against Barry and buried her face in his chest. He held her tight and she could see the tears taking hold in his own eyes. Cathy backed against Steve, and he slid his arms around her. Brenda seemed frozen with a look of horror on her face. David looked down at his knees.

"I wanted to tell you like this, because I wanted you to see that I'm okay and that I'm willing to do what I have to do to live. But if I don't live, God is still in control, and whether he plans to pull me out of this or take me home, I trust him absolutely."

David looked up at her and she met his eyes. She could see the questions reeling through his mind. *How can you trust?*

She uttered a silent prayer for David. *Lord, help me to have enough trust to make a difference in his life before I go.*

She cleared her throat and went on. "Now I know how things are going to be after this," Sylvia said. "You're all going to be upset, grieving my loss before I'm even gone, praying for me constantly, bringing me food and books and articles on alternative medicines. And that's all fine. But what I really need from you, and what I'm asking from you now, is that you don't cut me out of your lives just because you think I'm too ill to hear the daily activities. I want you to come visit me even when I'm sick. I want you to tell me what's going on in your lives. I want to know about every one of your children and what they're doing and what they're thinking and how they're acting. Those things keep me going, guys. I love hearing them and I don't want to be left out. And I don't want to always be talking about cancer. In fact, if I never hear the word again, it will be fine with me."

She saw the pain on their faces. They grieved already. They would go home tonight and cry and lie awake and wrestle with God.

She had never felt more loved. Her heart broke for them.

"It's going to be okay," she said. "All my life, I've told others about the principles of God. That he is faithful. That he supplies all our needs. Now's the time for me to test those principles, and prove whether I truly believe them to be true. We talk big, until our own rough spots come. But I intend to be a testimony of those principles, whether God chooses to heal me or not. God will not fail me now."

Her eyes met David's, and she saw the questions, the amazement.

Cathy got up and came over, sat down, and hugged her so tightly that she thought she would break. Then Brenda came, then Tory.

She wished she could spare them the pain.

When the couples had finally gone home, Sylvia felt a surge of relief as she turned back to Harry. "There. It's done."

"You did well."

She shook her head. "Maybe I should have told each of them privately."

"No, I think you did it exactly the right way. They saw you smiling. They saw your hope, your strength. They saw what you're made of."

That night they fell exhausted into bed. There were no more words to exchange. Harry just held her as she fell asleep in his arms.

CHAPTER Sixty-Five

Annie didn't take the news well. Cathy had taken her into her and Steve's bedroom when she got home, and told her what they'd learned.

Annie grabbed a pillow from the bed and hugged it against her. "No, Mom, it can't be. Tell me it isn't."

It was as if Cathy had just told her that she, herself, had been diagnosed with terminal cancer. "Honey, it's true."

"Mom, she's just got too many things to do. How could this be?"

Cathy pulled her into her arms and wept with her. "Honey, I know how much Sylvia came to mean to you when you were in Nicaragua, but she wants us to know that God is faithful and he's still in control."

"But I can't stand to see her suffer. I thought it was over. Oh, Mom . . ."

Cathy pulled back and looked into Annie's face. She hated seeing her daughter crushed like this. Her own grief was multifaceted. It wasn't just for Sylvia, but for herself and for the neighbors . . . for all those children who loved her from Nicaragua . . . for Annie.

"We're not going to give up hoping. We're going to keep praying for her and know that pretty soon this will all be behind us. This different chemotherapy she's going to try might really do the trick. We'll just have to have faith."

Annie grabbed a towel out of the laundry basket and wept into it, then flung it down. "This is worse than when Joseph was sick."

Cathy shook her head. "I don't think so, honey. I think it was horrible both times."

"But Joseph came out of it. God healed him."

"He sure did."

"Don't you think he'll heal her, Mom? Don't you think if we have enough faith that God will honor that?"

"God always honors faith, honey," she said, "but his ways are not our ways. And death is something that comes to all of us."

"But Sylvia's too young. She's just got too much to do. I don't think God would really want this." Annie plopped down onto Cathy's bed, grabbed a Kleenex out of the tissue box. "Mom, do you think this is something from Satan, that he's afflicted her, cast this disease on her somehow, just a form of spiritual warfare to keep her from doing the work she's supposed to do?"

Cathy thought that over for a moment. "I don't know, honey. I'm not smart enough to answer that question."

"I mean, God doesn't give people cancer, does he?"

Cathy looked up and saw Steve standing in the doorway. She hoped he could see how ill-equipped she was to answer questions like this. "Steve, come in. Annie has questions. We all have questions."

He nodded. "I have them, too."

"But you're the one who knows so much," she said. "You know the Bible way better than I do."

He got onto the king-size bed with them, leaned back against the headboard.

"I know what you're gonna say," Annie muttered. "You're going to say that cancer happens because of the Fall. But that doesn't explain anything to me. Why do people always say that?" She wiped her eyes roughly.

"I don't know if that's exactly what I was going to say, but that is part of it. The sin in the Garden of Eden did bring an awful lot of problems into the world."

Annie punched the pillow she held. "But it wasn't Sylvia's fault that Eve ate the apple. Why does *she* have to pay?"

Steve's face was compassionate as he looked at the forlorn girl. "We all have to pay."

"But I don't understand why that has anything to do with her getting cancer!"

"It's why cancer is even in the world," Steve said. "Before the Fall the world was a perfect place. No disease. No shame. No sin. And then when sin came into the world, all of a sudden we have death and decay. We have a world that gets worse instead of better. Things break down, *bodies* break down, people get sick and they die."

Annie slid off of the bed and slammed the pillow down. "Then it's better never to have been born at all."

Cathy got up and pulled her daughter into her arms. She felt Annie's sobs as she held her.

"Some people might think that," Steve said quietly, "but we're here for a reason, Annie. Sylvia has done a lot of good while she's here. You wouldn't suggest that the world would have been better off if she'd never been born."

Annie looked up. Her face was wet and raging red. "No, of course I wouldn't suggest that. But maybe to *her* she would have been better off."

"I don't think even she would suggest that," Cathy said.

Steve propped his arms on his bent knees. "The fact is, this world is not our home, and these bodies are not our home. Maybe God makes us real uncomfortable in them before he brings us home so that our new glorified bodies will be all the more exciting."

Annie still wasn't buying. "But what about us? The ones they leave?" She turned back to Cathy. "Oh, Mom, what are we gonna do without Miss Sylvia?"

Cathy didn't know.

"What am I saying?" Annie asked. "It's like I've given up on her. Like I've already buried her. I'm not giving up. I'm going to keep praying for healing."

Cathy nodded. "You do that, honey. I'll do it too."

They hugged again, and Cathy heard the bed creak as Steve got off of it and stepped across the room. He put his arms around both of them, and the three of them cried together.

CHAPTER
Sixty-Six

Sylvia's chemo treatment on the first day of August—almost a full year after her diagnosis—left her bed-ridden for three days. When she finally felt like emerging back into the world, Harry urged her to go to a cancer support group someone had started in their church. She had avoided it before, thinking it was a self-indulgent pity party.

But her first meeting surprised her. It wasn't a pity party or a place of sadness or despair. Instead, she met survivors of cancer, those in the throes of it like herself, family members and loved ones of those who had died.

They smiled and laughed and shared Scripture. And they shared strategies for coping with the various treatments and the fears plaguing them. By the end of the night, she had a little more energy to her step as she headed back home.

At the end of the week, Sylvia sat on the floor in the classroom as ten little Down's Syndrome children sat around her, two of them in wheelchairs, two propped in chairs, and the rest sitting on the floor with their legs crossed. They seemed glad to see her after she had missed several days.

They each brought their wordless book to the group, anticipating having her lead them through it again. Her hands trembled, and she felt so weak that the walk down the hall had forced her to stop and rest, but she was glad to be here. She picked up the wordless book and opened to the first page.

"What color is this, boys and girls?"

"Yewwo," Bo cried out.

Tory laughed and patted his head. "Very good, Bo."

"And can anybody tell me what the yellow stands for?"

"Heben," one of the children in the wheelchair muttered.

"That's right," Sylvia said. "You're so smart. It's heaven, because in heaven there are streets of gold. And the best part about heaven is that somebody we know and love very much lives there. Does anybody know who?"

"Dod," one of the children cried out.

"God. That's right," she said, "and the Bible tells us that God so loved the world that he gave his only begotten Son, that whoever believes in him should not perish but have everlasting life. Raise your hand if you believe in him."

Every one of them lifted their hands, and Sylvia laughed.

"Now tell me about Jesus. Who is he preparing a place for in heaven?"

"Me," one of the children cried out.

Sylvia clapped her hands with delight, and winked at Tory. The teacher who sat across the room working on the next project for the day laughed as well.

"But God is holy and perfect," Sylvia said. "And he can't allow anything into heaven that isn't perfect. So there's one thing that can never be in heaven. Can any of you think what that thing might be?"

The children got quiet. No one seemed to know the answer until she turned the next page. "What color is this?"

"Bwak," Bo cried out.

"Very good," she said. "And what does black represent?"

Bo raised his hand again, not wanting to be overlooked. "Bo, tell me what the black represents."

"My hawt," he said.

Tory turned her stricken eyes to the boy, then met Sylvia's eyes. It was working, she seemed to say. He was really getting it.

"That's right, Bo. Our hearts. They all have sin, right? We all do bad things sometimes. Everybody. Big or little, young or old. No matter where you live or who you are, you've done something bad at some point in your life. And we know that God punishes sin, doesn't he? He punishes all the bad things we do. But we don't have to be punished, do we?"

"No!" One of the children bound to a wheelchair spoke out, and Sylvia caught her breath. He rarely spoke at all, but lately she had watched him following along in his book. She turned the page.

"What color is this page?"

"Wed," someone cried out.

"That's right. And what does the red remind us of?"

"Deezus," Bo said.

"Yes, Jesus!" The energy was returning to Sylvia's limbs, lifting her spirits, reviving her body. "Because God sent Jesus to be born as a little baby and to live a perfect life. He never did anything bad, did he? But he took our punishment, so we wouldn't have to." She held up the cross they had made last week out of Popsicle sticks. "What is this?"

"Cwoss!" someone yelled out.

"Yes. Jesus died on a cross, to take our punishment. Isn't that right?" The children all nodded.

"And so now the heart that's in us that's black and bad can be replaced, can't it? We can have a new heart." She turned the page to the white page.

"The white reminds us of a clean heart, doesn't it? And how can you have a clean heart? You can ask God to take your black, dirty heart away, and give you a new heart."

The children hung onto every word, nodding their heads and looking down at the white page in their own books. She turned the page.

"And what color is this, Bo?"

"Gween," he said, proud of himself and grinning at all the kids around him.

"That's right," she said. "And green stands for things that grow, and when you have Jesus in your heart, you want to become more like him. Isn't that right?"

Bo nodded his head like he'd written the book himself.

"And so we pray, and we talk to God, and we read the Bible, and we tell others about Jesus, and we get our mommies and daddies to take us to church. Right? And whenever we do something bad, we can tell God we're sorry."

The children clapped their hands in pure delight, and for a moment, Sylvia forgot her cancer and the pain in her side and back, and her thinning hair, and the next treatment that would send her to bed. She forgot about her fears and her questions and her death. Because here, in this room, there was so much more.

Tory gestured excitedly as she drove Sylvia home. "I never dreamed these kids could learn colors this young," she said. "But you've not only taught them the colors, you've taught them the whole gospel message ... and they understand it. That's just a miracle."

"Well, God's in the business of miracles," Sylvia said.

Tory looked at Sylvia, her eyes bright with unshed tears. "I hope I can be like you, Sylvia. That I'll never underestimate the fruit I can bear in any situation."

"You will bear fruit, Tory. You will."

Exhausted, Sylvia lay her head back on the seat and closed her eyes, certain she would sleep all the way home.

CHAPTER
Sixty-Seven

Two days after Sylvia's next chemo treatment, Tory took Hannah over, hoping the baby would cheer Sylvia up and get her mind off of her illness. Harry greeted her at the door and led her down the hall.

Tory stepped into Sylvia's room. The lamp was on, but darkness still hung on. Sylvia lay in bed, a skinny heap of bones. Her skin was a pallid color, somewhere between death and life, and the hair that had begun to grow back had fallen out again.

"Sylvia," Tory said softly, "do you feel like visiting with Hannah and me?"

Sylvia opened her eyes and squinted up. Tory could see by the look on her face that she nursed a headache, among other things. She thought of leaving, but Sylvia rose up.

"Give me that baby."

Hannah smiled and kicked her feet as Tory laid her next to Sylvia on the bed.

But the child didn't want to lie still. Instead, she rolled over and raised up on her hands and knees.

Sylvia gasped. "Is she crawling?"

Tory smiled. "Just about. That's what I wanted you to see."

"Put her on the floor," Sylvia said. "Let me see what she can do."

Tory set her on the floor and coaxed her to crawl. Hannah laughed and rocked back and forth on her hands and knees. "While she's been in the nursery without me, she's developed this awareness of the kids around her. And she's started trying to do what they do."

Sylvia forced herself to sit up, but Tory wondered if that was wise. She looked as if she might collapse if the air conditioner blew too hard.

"Crawl for Miss Sylvia." Sylvia clapped her hands. "Come on, sweetie. Let's see you do it."

Instead of crawling, Hannah grabbed the bedspread, and started to pull up.

Sylvia reached for her, and the child stretched up. "Tory!" she said. "She's going to stand up."

"No way," Tory said. "She can't stand."

"Watch." Sylvia took the child's little fists, and pulled her up carefully, until her dimpled little legs locked beneath her.

Tory squealed and began to clap, and Hannah looked over at her, surprised. Sylvia picked her up like an Olympic star, cheering and clapping.

Tory started to cry. "Sylvia, she stood up. She stood up!"

"She sure did," Sylvia said. "Who would have thought this little thing could make me feel better?" She set Hannah on her lap, and made the baby clap her own hands.

"Do you know what this means, Sylvia? She'll walk someday. She'll walk on her own two feet, and her legs will hold her up, probably without a brace. Don't you think so? Don't you think she'll walk?"

"I know she will." She set her back down, hoping she would do it again. Tory helped the child pull back up as Sylvia lay back and watched.

When the child did it one more time, they both cheered, and Hannah laughed and brought her own fat little hands together.

Tory knew better than to stay much longer. Sylvia was waning.

"Well, I'd better get her home before she forgets how to do it," Tory said.

Sylvia smiled. "Thank you for bringing her over, Tory. What a gift."

"And who knew she was going to give it to you? Now if she'll only do it for Daddy. When I tell Spencer and Brittany, they probably won't leave her alone for the rest of the night. They'll insist on having her walking by morning."

"Don't ever underestimate her." Sylvia reached out for a hug, and Tory bent down.

"I love you," Tory said. "You get better, okay? Call if you need me."

"I'll be as good as new in a couple of days."

"Good," she said. "Because our class is having their school program, and I don't want you to miss it."

Sylvia's face brightened. "I'll be there," she said. "Nothing could stop me."

CHAPTER
Sixty-Eight

The package from León came on a day when Sylvia desperately needed it. A week after her chemo, she hadn't bounced back, and the pain in her liver had grown more intense. Her back had begun to hurt so badly that she could hardly stand up straight, and she'd started having headaches that wouldn't let go.

The package made her get out of bed, and when Harry pulled the video out, she actually managed to get dressed and put on her wig.

"Call Annie," she said. "I want her to come watch it with us."

Annie dropped everything and hurried over. She sat on the love seat next to Sylvia, watching the children they had ministered to so diligently for the last year of her life.

Each child had a message for Mama Sylvia. Juan, her favorite who rarely left her side when she was there, smiled into the camera. In Spanish, he blurted, "Mama Sylvia, one of the new doctor men gave us Reeses. I saved half of mine for you."

He held up the half-eaten peanut butter cup. "Please hurry back. It smells very good."

For the first time in days, Sylvia laughed out loud.

"I have to go back there," she said. "I can't even fathom the thought that I'm never going to see them again."

"Me, too," Annie whispered. "As a matter of fact . . ."

Sylvia looked up at her. "As a matter of fact, what?"

Annie sprang to her feet. "As a matter of fact . . . I've told Josh so much about León and the children and the clinic. And he's studying to be a doctor, you know. And then we found out that some of the doctors at our church were getting up a medical missions trip to work at Dr. Harry's clinic, and he decided he wanted to go with them."

Sylvia brought her hands to her face. "Are you serious?"

"Yes. And I'm going, too." She struck a pose, then screamed. "Can you believe it? I'm going back! We're going during Christmas break this year!"

Sylvia got up slowly, her face glowing with delight. "Oh, Annie. That's wonderful. You can help so much, since you know where everything is. You can take presents to the children from me, and bring back news."

"Oh, yeah. I'm going for the kids. I mean, it'll be fun going with Josh and everything, but he'll be busy at the clinic. I just want to spend the whole time at the orphanage, and hug those precious children, and get to know the new ones."

"New ones," Sylvia said. "I guess there are new ones. A whole bunch of them who don't know anything about me."

Annie's smile faded, and her eyes rounded. "I'll tell them about you. And that you'll be coming back soon."

Sylvia hugged her. "Now don't you two fall head over heels in love and go off and get married in Nicaragua. Your mother would never forgive me."

Annie laughed. "Yeah, that'll be the day. Talk about giving my mom a heart attack. I'd never do that to her."

"Don't do it to me either," Sylvia said. "I want to be at your wedding."

"Whenever it is, and whoever it's with, you'll be there, Miss Sylvia. I wouldn't have it without you."

But that night, as she lay in bed, trying hard to sleep through her pain, Sylvia had the shivering, dreadful feeling that she wouldn't make it to Annie's wedding day.

She might not even make it to Christmas.

CHAPTER Sixty-Nine

When Miva come back?" Bo's question came as he sat in the circle in their classroom, each of the children clutching the wordless book they kept in their cubbies. Tory looked around, wondering how much to tell them about Sylvia's decline. With each passing day, Sylvia grew more ill, but Tory could hardly speak of it without her throat tightening.

"Miss Sylvia's not feeling well. We've got to keep praying for her. And she would like it if we kept reading the book she gave us."

Carefully, Tory went through the wordless book, letting the students call out what each page meant, just as Sylvia had taught them. When she'd finished, she sent the children back to their desks. But Bo hung back, looking at her through the thick lenses in his glasses. She hoped he wasn't going to ask her about Sylvia again.

"What is it, Bo?"

"I wanna new hawt."

Tory's eyes rounded, and she bent toward him. "What did you say?"

"I want Deezus give me new hawt." He turned to the white page and pointed to it.

Tory got down on her knees in front of the child, and looked him in the eye. "You want a new heart? Why, Bo?"

He shoved his glasses up on his nose. "My hawt ditty."

Tears filled her eyes, and she touched his shoulder. "You're heart's dirty?"

He nodded. "Deezus give me *new* hawt."

Tory looked up and her eyes met Linda's. She saw the teacher grab the camcorder, cut it on. *Yes*, she thought. *This is one of those moments we'll want to remember.* She cleared her throat. "You can have a new heart, Bo. All you have to do is ask Jesus. Tell him to take your dirty heart out and give you a clean, new heart. And he will."

Bo grinned, and his eyes grew wider. "And he wive in me?" He tapped his heart. "In here?"

"That's right. He'll live with you in there. Right inside of you. Every day of your life."

"Den I go heben," he said.

"That's right. And then you'll go to heaven."

Tory struggled to keep herself from crumbling right in front of the child. What would Sylvia do now? she wondered. She would pray. Yes, she would pray with little Bo.

Her voice came out on a whisper. "Let's pray right now, Bo, and we'll ask Jesus to take out your dirty heart and give you a clean one."

The little boy knelt in front of her just as she had done, and folded his hands.

"Deezus," he whispered, and he began to pray his own Down's Syndrome version of the sinner's prayer.

When they came out of the prayer, Tory's face was wet, and she desperately needed a Kleenex. Bo went to tell his friends about his new heart, and Tory got to her feet. She looked at

Linda again. Still holding the camcorder, the teacher hugged Tory. "Do you realize what you just did?"

Tory laughed through her tears. "Do you realize what *Bo* just did? And all this time I thought these children weren't capable of making a decision for Christ."

"In Bo's case, you were wrong," Linda said. "I made this video so we could show it to his parents. I thought it would mean the world to them."

"Can we make a copy?" she asked. "I'd really like to show it to Sylvia. It's only right that she should see the fruit of her labors."

"You bet," Linda said. "I'll have you a copy made by the time you leave the school this morning."

CHAPTER *Seventy*

That night, Cathy, Tory, and Brenda got together to visit Sylvia. Pain twisted Sylvia's face, but she made a valiant effort to smile around it. When they showed her the video of Bo praying, she started to weep.

The other three passed a box of tissue around.

"You know something, Sylvia?" Tory got the video out of the VCR. "Other than Spencer and Brittany, Bo's the first person I've ever led to Christ, and you did most of the work."

Sylvia waved a hand, as if that was ridiculous. "Oh, I didn't. All I did was read him a book. God did all the work."

"But isn't it amazing," Tory said, "to think that a little boy like that with such a simple mind could grasp something so profound?"

Sylvia smiled. "God showed you this, Tory, so that you'd know that he'll be able to do the same thing with Hannah when she's older. This was God's way of telling you to instruct

Hannah in the ways of salvation, even though she'll always be so childlike. Let's watch it again."

Tory put the video back in and rewound it. While they waited, Cathy took Sylvia's cold hand. "Sylvia, you're my hero."

Sylvia frowned at her. "Why on earth?"

"Because even when you've been fighting the hardest battle of your life, you were out there teaching children about Christ."

Brenda concurred. "You were, Sylvia. Most of us would have been licking our wounds, but your mind has always been on everyone else."

Sylvia smiled. "If you only knew. I've thought about myself. Trust me."

They watched the video again, sniffling and wiping their eyes. Finally, when it was over, Sylvia said, "Let's pray. Come here, all of you. Let's get in a circle and pray like we used to on Brenda's front porch." The women came around her and held her hands.

"God showed Tory a miracle today," she whispered. "But I'm asking for one more." She knew they all expected her to ask for healing, but she had something else on her mind. "There's one more person that I want to see saved before I die."

"Who's that?" Cathy asked.

Sylvia looked at Brenda. "I want to see David come to know the Lord."

CHAPTER
Seventy-One

The cough that Sylvia developed in September was another clue that the chemotherapy wasn't working to stop the cancer. When the time came for her next round of scans, her fears were confirmed. The cancer had spread to her lungs.

The doctor changed the chemo once again.

Sylvia hardly noticed when Harry quit his job at the hospital. Suddenly he was with her every moment of every day, by her side when she retched into the toilet, helping her walk through the house when she was too weak to do so on her own. Every ounce of Sylvia's energy went into her survival. There was none left for conversation or thoughts of despair or worry of any kind. She just concentrated on getting through one moment at a time.

Soon her breathing got shallow and raspy, her fever spiked, and she lay for hours without the energy to open her eyes. She had a vague awareness of Harry bustling around her, putting cold compresses on her head and neck and arms and chest . . .

Harry's frantic voice into the phone . . . neighbors touching her and talking to her . . .

Limp as the doll that Sarah used to carry around as a child, she felt groping hands, stethoscopes, an IV going into her arm.

Then they rolled her into an ambulance. Harry held her hand and prayed over her for the long, jostling ride.

Sometime later, Harry sat helplessly in her hospital room, listening to her breathe beneath the oxygen mask. Urgently, he searched his Bible for some word from God, some sign that he was going to pull her out of this and heal her. It was God's way, he told himself frantically. Didn't he like making things look grim, so that it was clear a miracle had been done? Wasn't that what he'd done when Jonathan and his armor bearer had overtaken the Philistine army? God had thrust confusion into the Philistines' hearts, and they had killed each other. And when God was raising an army with Gideon as the leader, hadn't he sent everyone but three hundred men home, just to show the world that they hadn't done the work, but God had?

If cancer was their enemy—and it most definitely was—then maybe God was letting it look as grim as it could, so that he could do his miracle.

So Harry searched the Psalms for some word from God that he would deliver her, some sign that he would not make her suffer any longer, some indication that she would be restored.

But he found none.

When the doctor came by the room, Harry jumped to his feet and confronted him. "She's dying, isn't she?"

The expression in Dr. Thibodeaux's eyes gave him no hope. "She's very sick."

Harry wanted to put his fist through the man's face, grab him by the collar and tell him to get out of here and find a cure. He tried to keep his voice steady. "You've got to do everything you can to keep her alive. If you've heard of any kind of treatment that might work, any kind of clinical trials, I want to know about them. Alternative treatments. Experimental drugs. Anything."

"I've been looking, Harry, just as you have. But she's very, very ill, and this is an aggressive cancer that we haven't been able to stop. It's growing and spreading too fast."

Harry's lips compressed tightly across his teeth. "She can't die. Do you understand me? My wife cannot die. Not yet." But even as he said the words, he knew that the matter was out of the doctor's control. He might as well be waving his fist at God.

"We'll do everything we can for her, Harry. You have my word."

There was nothing more that Harry could demand of him. It was too late for medicine and science to work in Sylvia's body. It was going to take a true miracle. Only God could heal her now.

But for the first time, Harry had to face the fact that God might choose not to.

CHAPTER
Seventy-Two

From the depths of fevered unconsciousness, Sylvia felt as if she floated at the bottom of a warm ocean. There was no pain there, no drugs, no time ticking away . . .

A bright light shone through the opaque depths, and she swam toward it, but as hard as she swam, she got no closer to the light. It wasn't time.

Still, that light shone like an escape hatch through which she would soon pass . . .

And for the first time, there was no dread. Beyond that light her Father watched and waited . . .

Home beckoned . . .

She was not forsaken, but anticipated.

She was not abandoned, but summoned.

Soon, a voice seemed to say from that light, *but not yet. There's more for you to do.*

So she stopped swimming and floated there, limp and docile, as she began to rise to the top.

When they got the fever down and gave Sylvia a transfusion to get her blood count back up, she began to return to full consciousness. "How in the world did I wind up here?" she asked Harry.

Harry got onto her hospital bed and lay beside her, stroking her face. He'd spent the last two nights sleeping on the couch in her room, and fatigue had crept over him like a life-eating fungus. "An ambulance brought you." His eyes misted over. "I thought I'd lost you."

"That bad, huh?"

"Yeah, that bad."

She stared at him for a long moment. "Harry, I'm going to die."

The statement surprised him, and he closed his eyes and shook his head. "Don't say that," he whispered. "Please don't say that."

She touched his face, stroked her fingers across the stubble. "I have to, Harry. You know it's true."

He squeezed his eyes shut and pressed his lips together.

"Honey, it's okay," she whispered. "Don't cry."

This was all wrong, he told himself. He was supposed to be telling *her* not to cry. She was the one who hurt . . .

He steeled himself and forced his eyes open. "I'm supposed to be telling you that."

"But why? You're the one who'll be left when I go. The greater pain in this is yours. I'll just be going home." A tear rolled across her nose, and he wiped it away.

"Remember the night after we met with the surgeon, and we talked about the elders laying hands on me? Remember how we said that whatever happened, we would know that God had heard our prayers, and had chosen to answer according to his will?"

Had he really said that? Had he meant it? Had he even known what he was talking about? It had been easy then, at the beginning of this, when she wasn't so ill and there was so much hope. But now ... "Why is this his will?" he whispered. "It seems so hard."

She kissed his wet cheek. "It's not hard, Harry. Remember how you told me that, whatever happens, we know that God loves me even more than you do?"

He nodded.

"He does, you know. He's there making a place for me ... waiting for me ... He loves me, and he loves you. And I'll bet he's weeping with us. Hating that our hearts are broken. Hating that we can't see the big picture that he can see. But he loves us, Harry, and we can't doubt that."

"So what do we do?" His voice was rising in pitch ... he wasn't going to be able to hold strong for her. He felt like a brokenhearted child who'd just learned the meaning of death. "How do we handle this?"

"Medically, we keep fighting. Spiritually, we start accepting."

Harry let out a shaky breath. "I thought I could do that. But now I wonder how that's even possible."

Sylvia's eyes twinkled as her dry lips stretched into a smile. "When I take the chemo, I sing praises. It gets me through the fear and the sick feelings and the dread. It keeps me focused. So that's what I think we should do, Harry. I think we should sing."

No, not that. He didn't have a song in his heart. It was too heavy to work up a tune ... "I can't, Sylvia. I can't sing right now."

"Yes, you can," she whispered. "Come on ... sing with me."

He sighed. "I'm tired, Sylvia."

She stroked his thinning gray hair. "I know you are. You can rest in a minute. After you've sung one chorus with me."

He knew she wouldn't relent, so reluctantly he said, "All right. Pick a song."

He had hoped she'd, at least, pick a slow one ... one that reflected the sorrow in his heart. But she didn't. Instead, she chose the upbeat "Shout to the Lord," and started to sing softly, coughing intermittently as they went. He joined in weakly, trying to mean it, trying to make his mind focus on the Creator of the universe who could have healed Sylvia but hadn't.

By the end of the song, her eyes smiled with a serenity that he wished he had. But he feared he'd never know the feeling of peace again.

⚬⚭⚬

David and Brenda came to the hospital as soon as they heard that Sylvia had emerged from the fog of fever.

Brenda held David's hand as they made their way down the hall to her room. She glanced at his face, and saw in his misty eyes that he, too, was struck with the memory of their child lying so close to death in this very building.

They reached Sylvia's door. "Let me peek in and see if it's a good time," she whispered, and David stood back, waiting. "I don't want to disturb her if she's sleeping."

She cracked the door open and saw that the drapes were open. Sunshine streamed into the room, and she saw Harry sitting on the couch and looking toward the bed.

Instead of the sick silence of machines, she heard a song. Sylvia sang quietly . . . in her thin, raspy, breathless voice. "When Christ's sweet face I see . . . the suffering shall flee . . ."

Brenda caught her breath and stepped back. She put her hand over her heart and turned back to David. "She's singing!" she whispered.

David took a step toward the door, and listened.

"My trials will be worthwhile . . . when His face I see."

Brenda stepped inside, and Sylvia began to laugh at the sight of her.

David stood outside the door, unable to follow just yet. He stepped to the side and leaned against the wall, trying to contain himself.

How could Sylvia sing?

Joseph had been like that, too. As he'd grown closer to death, he'd grown closer to his God, and what seemed like passing into the end had only been a beginning to him. It was that way for Sylvia, too. He couldn't fathom how she could sing about cancer in her breast and bones and liver and lungs being worth it all . . . It was something he couldn't get planted in his mind.

But the truth of it was growing clearer every day. If there was ever a time in life when spiritual things were clear and the mind and heart were at their peak, he supposed it was when a person was about to die. He wondered how he would face it. He knew there wouldn't be a song in his heart. There would probably be anger and bitterness, helplessness and despair.

Unfamiliar tears trailed down his face, and he looked from side to side, then quickly wiped them away before anyone could see.

Then drawing in a deep breath, he made himself go into the room.

Brenda stood beside the bed, speaking to Sylvia in a soft voice. "Harry was your knight in shining armor," she said. "When you were so sick, you should have seen him spring into action. We were all there, trying to help him . . ."

Sylvia saw David entering the room. "Oh, David," she whispered, and reached out for his hand. "What a joy to see you!"

Again he found that it was too hard for him to speak, so he only held her hand with both of his and tried to smile.

She looked tiny in the hospital bed, with an oxygen mask that should have been over her mouth but now hung under her chin, an IV running out of her arm, and wires and monitors running from her body to machines around her bed.

He couldn't escape the certainty that Sylvia was dying, and there was nothing that medicine or technology could do about it.

For the second time in his life he wished he believed in prayer.

CHAPTER
Seventy-Three

The decision to stop the chemotherapy and put Sylvia into hospice care was the hardest one of Harry's life, but her body was too weak to accept the ravages of any further chemo, and her pain was too great. After many meetings with the doctors, he agreed to shift their focus from healing to comforting her and keeping her free from pain.

They set her up in a hospital bed in their bedroom, and a hospice nurse came to set up the equipment they would need to keep Sylvia as comfortable as possible.

Sarah and Jeff dropped everything and came to be with her. To Sylvia's chagrin, Sarah left the baby with Gary and showed up alone, looking like a porcelain doll with a dozen cracks just beneath the surface, waiting to shatter if it was jarred.

When Sylvia fell asleep, Harry took the kids into the kitchen and sat across from them. Jeff looked like a lost little boy, struggling to hold back his tears, and Sarah couldn't look at him.

"Sit down, sweetie," he told her as she gazed out the window toward the barn.

"I'm okay standing," she said.

He sighed. "I need to talk to you, honey. I need for you to look at me."

Slowly, she turned back around. Her face twisted with pain, and she covered her mouth. "Oh, Daddy, don't say it."

He forced himself to go on. "I have to. Your mother is going to die."

Sarah shook her head. "No, Dad! You're giving up! There are still things you can do! You can't just give in to this and let it have her!"

"I'm not giving up," Harry said softly. "I've just had to come to terms with it. She's going to die. She's suffering, and it's hard to keep her free from pain. It won't do me any good to lie to you and give you false hope. We need to prepare ourselves."

Jeff got up now, his hands hanging in fists at his sides. "How could he do this to her?" he asked. "How could God refuse to heal her after all she's done for him?"

Harry closed his eyes and swallowed back the tightness in his throat. "He will heal her, son." The words came hard, but he managed to get them out. "He's going to heal her in his way. Maybe even the best way. When she dies, she'll be with him and she'll be healthy and sound again."

"That's not healing!" Sarah said. "That's not what we prayed for. God knows what we're asking. He promised that if we delighted ourselves in him that he would give us the desires of our heart. Well, my desire is for her to live!"

Jeff turned his sister around and pulled her against him, and they held each other as they wept. Harry stepped around the table and put his arms around both of them. "She will live," he whispered. "Just not here, with us."

He knew it wasn't enough for them, not yet. They wept harder than he'd ever seen them weep before, and he wept with them, holding them and hugging them and reassuring them as the reality of their mother's life and death seeped into their spirits.

When Harry returned to her bed, he saw how still and life-less she lay. The morphine had knocked out her pain, but in her drug-induced state, he wondered if she would be able to sit up and have a conversation. Would she be able to pray? Would she sing again?

The morphine didn't last long, and each time it wore off, he heard the groaning in her throat and saw the pain on her face. He squeezed her pump, issuing more drugs into her blood-stream, knocking her out again until the medicine wore off and she gritted her teeth in pain . . .

That night, as he lay in the bed he used to sleep in with her, he watched the sporadic, labored pattern of her breathing in the hospital bed, and wondered if she'd make it through the night.

He lay there, exhausted from the struggle to keep her drugged before the pain took hold, and realized that he'd come to the absolute end of his hope. It was time to start praying according to God's will, and according to Sylvia's needs.

"I can't stand her suffering, Lord," he whispered into the darkness. "Go on and take her. It's okay with me. Just don't let this suffering go on."

Sleep didn't come for him that night. He just lay there near her, listening for every breath, every groan, every beep of every monitor, while the children slept in their childhood rooms.

He had never felt more alone.

Chapter Seventy-Four

For the sake of the children, Harry convinced the doctor to pull back on Sylvia's morphine, just long enough to get her coherent to give closure to the children. She would want it that way, he was sure. He could just hear her spirit sitting up in bed and shaking her finger at him. *Harry, don't you keep me so drugged that I can't say good-bye.*

The pain soaked her in sweat and made her body tremble, but she tried to smile as Sarah and Jeff came to her bedside.

They sat on either side of her, each holding one of her hands. Sarah leaned in, and pressed her forehead against Sylvia's face. "Mama, don't go," she whispered. "Please don't go. I need you. I don't know how to be a mother without you."

Sylvia let go of Jeff's hand and stroked Sarah's hair. "Yes, you do, sweetheart. You're doing a great job."

"But that's because I can pick up the phone and call you. You can walk me through it."

"But you have everything you need," Sylvia whispered. She swallowed with great effort. Even her throat had begun to feel cancer ravaged. "I've taught you everything I know. And you'll still have your dad. And Gary is so precious. I have perfect peace about leaving you with him. He'll take care of you. He'll help you through this." She turned Sarah's face up to hers, and made her look into it. She remembered when Sarah had wept inconsolably over a boyfriend who had broken her heart. She must have been sixteen then, Sylvia thought. Her face had looked like this, and Sylvia had wanted so much to be able to dry her tears and say the words that could heal her heart. But there hadn't been words then, and there weren't any now.

"Sweetheart, you're going to raise a houseful of godly children who serve the Lord and bear bushels and barrels of fruit. And when they ask about their grandmother, you're going to show them pictures of me and tell them that I'm in heaven, waiting for all of you to come and join me. Home, where we all belong."

Sarah's weeping broke her heart, but Sylvia didn't have the energy to cry her own tears. She looked at her son. His face was red and wet. She hadn't seen him cry since he was ten years old. She wished he had a wife now, one who could help him through this time, comfort him and cry with him. But he looked so alone.

She touched his face with her cold, trembling hand. "Jeff... my sweet Jeff... you'll be okay, too."

He could hardly speak. "I know, Mama."

"I've prayed so hard for you. God's going to send you a wonderful, godly woman someday, and you'll be a precious husband to her. You'll be just like your father. And when you have children, they'll be the most blessed children in the world. There will be generations of blessings for your family. I know that without a doubt, because I've prayed it since you were born."

A pain shot through her side, and she sucked in a breath, then started to cough. Sarah got up and tried to help her, but she turned on her side and kept trying to clear her lungs.

Jeff put the oxygen mask back on her face, and she was able to get some air into her lungs. She lay on her back, her eyes squeezed shut, as the nerves in her back seemed to break into attack mode, shooting bullets of pain through her body.

One of the children went to get Harry, and he came into the room. She saw him grabbing the morphine pump, squeezing it. She would slip into oblivion soon, she thought on a wave of panic. She hadn't finished saying good-bye.

When he leaned over her to kiss her, she grabbed his shirt. "Harry," she whispered. "I want you to get me the tape recorder."

"Why?" he asked. "What do you want to tape?"

She didn't have the energy to explain it to him. "Please. I'll rest for a minute, but don't pump the morphine again. Let it wear off so I can talk. Then bring me the tape player. I have some things to say to the people I love."

Harry straightened, and she saw the pain pulling at his face. As painful as her decline had been, she knew that he suffered even more.

"I want it to be played at my funeral," she whispered.

He looked so helpless. "Sylvia, I don't want you expending energy on that."

The morphine was taking hold, pulling her under, dulling the pain, but also dulling her senses. "Honey . . ." She knew her speech was slurred. "I have no intention of letting my death be the end of my fruit-bearing. The Lord has been too good to me not to do this last thing for him. I want to minister in my death, just as I've ministered in my life. I want my death to glorify Jesus. And I want to say good-bye."

She touched his face, felt the tired stubble. "Please, Harry. I have to do this."

He sighed, the heaviest, saddest sigh she'd ever heard in all her life. "I'll get the tape player."

When the morphine wore off, and the pain sank its teeth into her again, Harry sat her up, tried to make her comfortable, and pinned the microphone onto her gown. Then he turned the tape recorder on and left her alone to say her final good-bye to the people she was leaving behind.

CHAPTER
Seventy-Five

With each day that passed Sylvia declined further, until finally those who loved her began to pray her home. No matter how much morphine they gave her, it wasn't enough. She flailed and jerked and trembled in bed. Days had passed since she'd been able to speak or look anyone in the eye.

In many ways, she was already gone.

Harry didn't want her to linger in this place between life and death for his sake . . . or the sake of the children. Instead, he wanted her to go where she could shed the pain like an old garment she wouldn't need anymore.

He prayed for the Lord to take her, night after night after night . . .

But when the time finally came that the doctor warned him she wouldn't make it through the night, he found that he wasn't ready. It was a funny thing. Sarah and Jeff had suddenly developed the strength they needed to make it through their mother's death . . . but he . . .

He didn't know if he could really let her go. The thought of her still being here in some form was preferable to having her disappear from the earth, no longer a part of his world.

He didn't dare pray for God to give her more time. That would be selfish. Instead he prayed for strength. He would need God's arms around him, propping him up, moving his feet as he walked through these final hours. He could not do it on his own strength.

He knew that the neighbors needed to see Sylvia one last time, and in some way, he felt that she would know they were there. Sarah called, and found them at Brenda's house, praying on the front porch. David called them in to the kitchen and they sat around the telephone listening to her stopped-up voice.

"They don't expect Mama to make it through the night," she said. "My dad said that it would be all right if you'd like to come over."

"We'll be right there," Brenda whispered.

They were at the door in moments, and Harry could see that they'd shed as many tears tonight as he and the kids had done. They came silently into the house, hugged everyone quietly, then followed Harry into the bedroom.

As they went in, Sylvia opened her eyes. Harry rushed to her bed. "Honey?"

Her eyes looked glazed, distant, but then she focused on him.

"Honey, the girls are here. Brenda, Tory, and Cathy came to say hello."

❧

Sylvia felt as if she swam through Jell-O, fighting her way to the top where she could get air. She heard Harry's voice ... sniffing ... the whisk of tissues pulled from their box ...

" ... girls are here ... came to say ..."

She had to talk to them, she thought. She had to see them one last time. *Please, Lord, pull me up ... one last time ...*

And there they were, standing around her bed, Cathy on one side next to Harry, Brenda and Tory on the other. Sarah and Jeff stood at the foot of her bed. They looked like they hadn't slept in days.

She locked into Cathy's eyes, then turned to Brenda and Tory. "Best times," she whispered on a thin breath. "Tell me . . . best times . . ."

They had always done it. It was their ritual after an ordeal. When Joseph survived his heart transplant, when Tory had given birth to her Down's Syndrome baby, when Cathy got Mark safely home from jail. They had always run down the list of the very best moments . . .

There were so many.

In stark silence, the three women made herculean efforts to control their tears. She felt sorry for them, and wished she could touch them and impart some kind of peace.

Finally, Cathy spoke up in a raspy voice. "Watching when you came home with my Annie," she whispered, "and I saw how changed she was. That was a best moment."

Sylvia smiled. "Good one," she managed to say.

Brenda patted her hand and tried to put on that cheerful face that came so naturally to her. But it didn't look natural when her face was covered with tears. "When we went trying on wigs," she said.

Sylvia breathed a laugh. "So silly."

"Yeah, we were silly," Brenda said. "But it was definitely a best moment."

Tory squeezed her hand. "When little Bo accepted Christ."

She squeezed back. "Priceless."

"Yeah," Cathy agreed. "The look on your face as you watched the video of him giving his life to Christ."

Sylvia closed her eyes and remembered.

"The best moments weren't just in the last year," Cathy said. "They go back for several years. Remember when you realized you were supposed to go to the mission field, and surrendered to Harry's call?"

Sylvia opened her eyes, laughing weakly.

"And the moment I met Steve," Cathy said.

That was a good one, Sylvia thought.

"Barry," she whispered.

Tory nodded. "I was just thinking of that. When Barry came back home after we'd been separated. That was one of the best moments."

"And Joseph's heart." Sylvia almost couldn't get the words out. She hoped they heard.

"Yes." Brenda's voice wobbled. "When he woke up from surgery with all that color in his cheeks."

"Good moments ...," Sylvia whispered. "Best moments."

She started to cough, and they all gathered closer, as if their closeness could somehow help her clear her lungs. But it was no use. Harry put the mask back over her face, and she sank back into her pillow as the pain tightened its vice around her body.

She sensed the grief overtaking them all, and she wished she was a better actor, that she could pretend to be relaxed, serene, and pain-free. She tried to lie still, tried not to jerk or moan, tried not to wince with the shooting pain.

Then she felt the drugs sweeping over her, dulling the pain, relaxing her body, taking her out ...

But she wasn't ready ... not yet ... she had to pray for them ... they weren't ready. ...

Lord, please ... just another minute ...

Cathy thought she would collapse in grief, but somehow she managed to leave Sylvia's bedside. Sarah was there to hug her, and she felt the young woman's racking sobs as she held her. Brenda hugged Jeff, and Tory clung to Harry.

"Don't go."

Cathy turned and saw that Sylvia was awake again, reaching for them. Sarah and Jeff rushed for her, taking her hands, and Harry grabbed that pump again.

"Want to pray for you," she said on a shallow whisper. "Come ..."

One by one, they took each other's hands, until they stood in a circle around Sylvia's bed, tears flowing and noses running and hearts moaning ...

And then she spoke as clearly as if she'd never been sick. "Lord," she said, "help them to see the joy in this ..."

Her words trailed off, and her eyes closed. Her raspy breathing settled and stilled ...

... and all grew quiet.

The monitor beeped out a warning, and Harry fell over her, shaking her and touching her face, trying to make her open her eyes.

But she was gone.

Sylvia had gone home to be with Jesus, with a prayer for her loved ones still on her lips.

CHAPTER
Seventy-Six

Silence hung over the Dodd house as they got dressed the morning of the funeral. Brenda moved by rote, ironing shirts and preparing breakfast. But her mind remained in that bedroom at the Bryans' house, all of them crowded around Sylvia's bed, receiving a prayer of blessing before she passed into eternity.

Sylvia had prayed that they would see the joy in this, but so far, Brenda only saw the tragedy of losing her mentor and closest friend.

What would she do without Sylvia? Who would teach her? Whose wisdom would she call on?

She took the boys' shirts to their room. Daniel stood in front of the mirror, combing his hair. He'd been crying, she could tell. His eyes were red and slightly swollen, but he would have denied it if she'd acknowledged it.

He took the shirt, stared down at it.

She stood in the doorway, and remembered when Joseph hung between life and death, how Sylvia had come to stay with Daniel and the girls. She'd told Brenda how Daniel had done the only thing he'd known to do. He'd come down in the middle of the night to wash his own sneakers, so he could take them to Joseph the next day. The child's feet had been too swollen for his own shoes, and Daniel imagined that his feet were cold.

She knew that he had bonded with Sylvia that night, and was running those moments through his mind. What had once been a sweet memory now burned with the bitterness of death.

She took the other shirt and headed to Joseph's room. Leah and Rachel were coming out of theirs, their eyes swollen and pink.

"Mama, tell Rachel she's supposed to wear black. It's rude to wear color to a funeral."

Brenda looked at Rachel's choice of the yellow dress she'd worn on Easter. "Mama, do I have to?"

Brenda forced a smile. "I think it's fine for you to wear yellow, honey. Miss Sylvia wanted us to see the joy in this. Yellow is a joyful color, don't you think?"

Leah crossed her arms. "Well, should I change into a color?"

"You look beautiful." She kissed Leah's forehead, then Rachel's. "Both of you do. I wouldn't change a thing."

She took the shirt into Joseph's room, and saw him sitting cross-legged on his bed in his T-shirt and pants, the Bible open on his lap.

He looked up when she came in. "Mama, look. The gates of heaven are made of one gigantic pearl on each gate. And there's a sea of glass, and there's no need for light, because God is so bright."

She put her fingertips over her mouth, and nodded.

"And the disciples are there, and the apostle Paul, and Moses and Abraham ... Do you think Sylvia's had the chance to ask them questions yet?"

Brenda forced her voice to remain steady. "What questions?"

"Like what Paul's thorn in the flesh was, and what Jesus wrote in the sand, and what was going through Abraham's mind when he went to sacrifice Isaac."

Brenda pictured Sylvia at the feet of the fathers of their faith, getting the story behind the story. The thought made her smile. "I think she probably has."

Joseph nodded. "Because it says that right now we see through a mirror darkly, but someday we'll see face-to-face. Seems like everything should be clear to her by now, huh?"

Brenda wished her youngest son could have been the one to preach Sylvia's funeral. He seemed to have the most perfect perspective of all of them.

She gave him his shirt, then went to finish getting ready.

David was putting on his tie. His hands trembled as he did, and she caught his reflection in the mirror. The lines around his eyes were deep. He hadn't slept much the last two nights. Last night she'd heard him get up in the wee hours of morning, and he had never come back to bed.

He was taking Sylvia's death harder than she'd expected. She thought of that prayer that Sylvia had prayed some time ago, for David's salvation.

It had not been answered, and the pain of that rose up high in Brenda's chest, twisting her grief and bringing her close to despair.

But she had no choice but to trust that God had heard that prayer, and had every intention of answering it . . . someday.

She wondered if Sylvia still prayed from heaven.

She went into the bathroom and sprayed her hair, put on earrings and her watch. Then she checked the time, and saw that they needed to go.

It was time to lay Sylvia's body to rest.

CHAPTER
Seventy-Seven

Next door, Tory tried valiantly to get her family ready. She had taken Hannah in to the school this morning, to be cared for while she attended the funeral. The faces of all the teachers had been grim, but the children, who had been told yesterday, played as though nothing had happened. They didn't understand, she thought. How could they?

When she spoke to Bo, he looked up at her with a smile. "Miva in heben," he told her matter-of-factly.

"Yes, she is," Tory said. "She's in heaven, all right."

"Bo see her dere."

"That's right. Someday you'll see her there."

There was no grief on his face, no crushing sense of loss. Only joy, pure and undefiled, as he imagined Sylvia's new situation. Time had little meaning to him. As far as he knew, he'd see Sylvia tomorrow, when Jesus returned for him.

As she left the school and headed back home, she realized that Bo had it right. There was no need for grief. Sylvia wasn't suffering. She probably had great hair in heaven, and a twenty-five-year-old body, and a brain sharper than it had ever been.

Still, the grief pulled at Tory like quicksand.

As she got Spencer and Brittany ready for the service, she struggled to keep from letting that grief suck her under.

"I'm choking," Spencer said as she knotted his tie. "I can't stand this."

"Spencer, you need to wear it. Now don't give me a hard time."

Barry stepped into the room and touched her shoulder. "Here, let me."

She stepped back, and watched her husband sit on the bed in front of the boy. "We want you to wear a tie today, Spence, because it's an important time, and we want you to look like the little man that you are."

Spencer seemed to stand taller. "And because Miss Sylvia might be able to see me?"

Barry met Tory's eyes. "I don't know," he said. "I don't really think so. The Bible says there are no tears in heaven. If she could see how sad Dr. Harry is, she might cry. So I doubt that she can watch."

"Yeah." Spencer stuck his chin out as his father straightened his tie. "She probably has too much to do, anyway. Checking out her new mansion, and talking to Jesus, and all that stuff."

Tory stood back at the door, listening to the quiet conversation. God was using the mouths of babes today, to show her the joy in Sylvia's passing.

Just as she'd prayed before her spirit left her body.

Come to me as little children, the Lord seemed to remind her. *See what they see. Understand as they do.*

She went to Brittany's room and saw her eleven-year-old, already fully dressed, struggling with her hair in front of the mirror. She'd grown so beautiful in the last year ... still a child, but almost a woman.

Tory came to her rescue. "Let me help."

She pulled her hair up out of her face.

"What's gonna happen, Mom?" she asked. "Will we see Miss Sylvia?"

Tory shook her head. "No, honey. She asked Dr. Harry to have a closed casket. She wanted us to remember her as she used to be."

"She was *always* beautiful on the inside," Brittany said. "I think we can remember her all the ways that she was, even when she was sick."

Tory turned her daughter around and hugged her. "I'm glad you understand that, sweetie. Sylvia was never more beautiful than she was at the very end. Skinny and sick and bald . . . she was the most beautiful woman I knew."

"She's even more beautiful now," Brittany whispered.

Again, from the mouths of babes . . .

Barry stuck his head in the room. "We should go. It's getting late."

Tory nodded, but wasn't able to speak as she got her purse and headed out to the car.

CHAPTER
Seventy-Eight

At the Bennett house, Cathy tried to console her daughter.

Annie was already dressed, but her eyes were so swollen and wet that Cathy had brought her ice packs in hopes of making her look more normal at the funeral. But the girl couldn't stop crying.

"Mom, why did they ask me to speak, of all people? There's no way I can do it. Look at me. I'll fall apart."

Cathy shook her head. "Annie, you spent a year with Sylvia, doing what she loved most in the world. Who better to tell about her?"

"But I just don't get it." Annie held the pack against one eye, but her tears countered the work it did. "Why did she have to die? Aren't we all here to bear fruit? Why would God take somebody who bore more than anybody else I know?"

Cathy drew in a deep breath. "Last night I was reading my Bible and trying to find peace . . . and I read something that

Jesus said. He said, 'Unless a seed falls in the ground and dies, it cannot bear fruit.' I don't think he meant that you can't bear fruit when you're alive, obviously, but I do think he was saying that sometimes death brings even more fruit."

"How?"

Cathy stroked Annie's hair. "Honey, there will be a lot of people at that funeral today. Harry's even having it videotaped for the memorial service they're having for her in León. Think of all the unbelievers who will hear the testimony of Sylvia's life, and embrace Jesus for the first time. Then they'll tell people, and they'll tell people ... her fruit could keep reproducing for years."

Annie nodded and brought the ice pack down. "Generations even."

"That's right."

Her face twisted again. "But what if I let Dr. Harry down? What if I mess this up and make him more upset than he already is?"

"You won't, honey. Just read what you've prepared. If you cry, that's all right. We'll all be crying with you."

She left Annie alone to get her bearings, then checked on Rick. He had come home for the funeral, and stood in his room now, staring out the window at Sylvia's house next door. She stepped into his room. "You almost ready, honey?"

He turned around. "Yeah, Mom. How are you?"

The sweet question brought tears to her eyes, and she nodded. "I'm okay."

"Good."

"You okay with being a pallbearer?"

He nodded. "I think so. I'm a little nervous. This isn't the kind of thing they teach in college."

"You'll do fine." She walked into the room and reached up to kiss him on the cheek. "I'm proud of you. Dr. Harry chose his pallbearers well."

Rick shrugged. "I can see him picking David and Barry and Steve. But me and Mark and Daniel?"

"You're the men of Cedar Circle," she said. "Why not you?"

When she'd left him alone, she went to Mark's room and saw that he was already dressed. His cheeks were mottled pink, as they always were when he was nervous or upset.

"You ready, Mark?"

"Yeah." He looked up at her. "Mom?"

"Uh-huh?"

"I know the Bible says that we're not supposed to grieve as those who have no hope. But do you think it's a bad witness if we cry at the funeral?"

Cathy breathed a sad laugh. "Of course not, sweetheart. Jesus wept at Lazarus's funeral, even though he knew that he was going to raise him from the dead."

"Yeah," Mark said. "I've wondered about that. Why do you think he cried if he knew it was going to have a happy ending?"

"Because his heart broke for Mary and Martha . . . just like it's probably breaking for us." Her voice broke off, and her own tears rushed to her eyes. She tried to hold them back.

Mark hugged her, and she clung to him, so proud that he had become a young man who cared about God's Word.

"Mom, I know this is gonna be hard for you," he said as he held her. "Miss Sylvia meant so much to you."

She swallowed. "I owe her a lot." She pulled back and wiped her tears. She had to get herself together. With Annie as upset as she was, one of them was going to have to be strong.

"I'm worried about your sister. She's so upset."

"I could go in there and torture her a little bit. Make her forget her troubles."

"Generous offer." Cathy laughed softly. "But I don't think so."

He looked at his watch. "We'd better get going."

Cathy drew in a deep breath. "Yeah. Let's go."

She went down the stairs, and found Tracy in the kitchen, loading the last of the breakfast dishes into the dishwasher.

"Tracy, look what you've done. Thank you, sweetie."

Tracy got a sponge and began wiping the counter. "I got ready early. It was something I could do."

Cathy kissed her cheek. "That was very thoughtful."

The girl turned her face up to Cathy, and gazed at her with big, round eyes. "I'm sorry you're sad, Cathy. I wish I could make it better."

"You just did," she said.

She found Steve in their bedroom, sitting in the rocker with his elbows on his knees, his head bowed, his eyes closed.

She knew he was praying, so she stood quietly in the room, watching him, so thankful that she had married a godly man who knew where to turn when he hurt.

After a moment, he looked up at her. "You ready?"

She nodded, but those tears rushed her again. He stood and took her into his arms, held her for a long moment.

"I miss her," she whispered. "I miss her so much."

"Me too." She felt his tears on her neck, and clung tighter to him.

A knock sounded on the door, and Annie stepped into the doorway. "I'm ready, Mom," she said.

Cathy wiped her face. "All right then. Let's do this."

And quietly the family piled into the car.

CHAPTER
Seventy-Nine

The casket at the front of the church was closed, and on top of it sat a lovely picture of Sylvia, before she'd gotten sick. Her eyes laughed in the framed photograph, and her smile spoke of love and joy. A bright spray of autumn flowers lay across the casket, proclaiming life rather than death. It was just as Harry had ordered it.

The neighbors of Cedar Circle gathered with the family in a back room as the church filled with mourners. Harry led them in prayer, and asked that this funeral minister in her death just as Sylvia had ministered in her life.

"Lord," he prayed, "let this funeral not be a time of glorifying Sylvia. She wouldn't have wanted that. Let it glorify you, from its beginning until its end."

His voice broke off, and for a moment he struggled to get the knot out of his throat and finish the prayer.

"Lord, we have so much to be thankful for. Thank you for healing Sylvia in the most complete way possible. Thank you for all the years we had with her. Thank you for what she taught us, how she loved us, the way she modeled you. Thank you for letting her touch our lives. And thank you for assuring us that we will see her again, when we see you in all your glory, and we're all finally home."

Harry waited as the family and neighbors filed into the first few rows of the church. All three of Sylvia's closest friends huddled close together, holding hands. Their husbands and sons who would serve as pallbearers sat in the front row, their faces grim.

As Harry walked in, he met David's eyes. He was the only one among the pallbearers who didn't believe. How sad, how crushing that grief must be, Harry thought. And as he took his seat, he prayed the prayer that Sylvia had prayed until her dying day.

Lord, save him.

CHAPTER Eighty

As the funeral began, and the full choir of the church sang "Because He Lives," anger swirled up in David's heart. The funeral was supposed to be about Sylvia, a woman so many in this room mourned. He couldn't fathom why they would put so much emphasis on Jesus. The fact that Harry had prayed for that very thing baffled him.

When Annie got up to speak, his anger faded. He knew that she would talk about Sylvia rather than the God she believed in.

She looked as if she'd been crying for days, but as she got behind the podium, she stood like a portrait of poise and maturity.

"I spent a year with Miss Sylvia and Dr. Harry in Nicaragua," Annie began, her voice wobbling. "And as I was trying to decide which things to tell you about her, and which to leave out, I realized that there was too much for me to choose. We'd be here all day. So instead I e-mailed León, and asked that the children of the Missionary Children's Home, the orphanage where she worked, e-mail me back with the things they wanted you to know about the woman they called Mama Sylvia. Here's what they said."

She began to read the heartfelt notes—translated into English—from children of all ages, telling how Mama Sylvia had taken them in when they were alone and frightened, how she'd loved them when they grieved over parents killed in the hurricane, how she'd taught them and nurtured them. Every single note spoke of how she had led them to Jesus, and how they knew they would see her again. The final note, dictated by a six-year-old boy named Juan, came like a blow to David's heart.

"All I can say now is, 'Please, Jesus. Hurry up and come. Take me there, too, so I can see Mama Sylvia's smile again. And you, because you're the reason for her smile.'"

Tears stung David's eyes, and he looked back at his wife. Brenda sat between Tory and Cathy, holding their hands and weeping. Her heart was broken, but the tears weren't angry or bitter. She grieved without despair, just as Harry did.

When Harry got up and went to the podium, David sat straighter, watching, listening.

"My wife . . ." Harry stopped and cleared his throat. Finally, he went on. "My wife planned her funeral. She told me who she wanted to preach it, who she wanted to speak, who she wanted to sing. She had very specific instructions."

He stopped and brought a handkerchief to his nose. "A few days before her death, she asked me to bring the tape recorder to her room. She had some things she wanted to say to all of you. So here . . . in her own voice, and her own words, is my wife's message."

He went back to his seat and wiped his eyes, stuffed the handkerchief back into his pocket.

David glanced at Brenda again. Her face looked stricken as she waited for the tape to begin.

Then David heard the hiss of the tape. He stared down at his hands, listening.

"Hello, friends."

It was as if she stood in the room with them, standing at the microphone, her smile lighting up the place.

"When you hear the rumors of my death, don't you believe them."

He looked up, frowning, and locked eyes with the picture of her on her casket.

"By the time you hear this, I will be in the presence of Jesus. I'll be free of this sick, earthly body, and I'll be laughing with more joy than I've ever known on earth. And I've had lots of joy. John 16:22 says, 'Now is your time of grief, but I will see you again and you will rejoice, and no one will take away your joy.'

"So don't cry for me. Remember the happy times, the times when God worked in our lives, when he taught us precious lessons, when he used us together. Remember the best moments."

David met Brenda's eyes, and wished he could be beside her.

"And think ahead to that day, not so far from now, when I'll be there to greet you, as you come home, too.

"Harry, I can't express how much I've loved you. God chose you for me when we were very young, and you have been a model to me of how much Christ loves me. My love for you has not died. It remains and lives on.

"Sarah, what a beautiful daughter you've been, and what a precious mother. You're my treasure, and my hope. Everything I had I put into you. I can't wait to see all your crowns when you get here. Gary, take good care of her and little Breanna, and all those other children that you and Sarah will have.

"Breanna, know that your grandma loves you. You won't have memories of me, so let me tell you what's important to know, and what I want you to tell all the other grandchildren yet to come. Tell them that my life was worth it. Everything, all of it, was worth it, because of the unsurpassed joy that Christ has on the other side.

"Jeff, my son, my precious boy . . . You're a man after God's own heart, and I'm so proud of you. Someday you'll marry and have children, too, and though I won't be there to see them, I'll be ready to make up for lost time when they get here.

"To my dear neighbors, and my very closest friends in the world, I've loved you so much."

David felt tears ambushing him, catching in his throat, pulling at his face. He closed his eyes.

"Cathy and Steve, God has brought the two of you together, and joined your two families. You've been joined for a purpose, all of you. I pray that you'll learn the art of dying to yourself, living for each other, and bearing much fruit for the Lord who gives you everything you need.

"Annie, you were right all those months ago. When God lit up our path that day, he was telling me that he would light my way. I know you're thinking that my prediction didn't come true, that I'll never dance at your wedding. But when Christ comes to get his Bride, I'll be with him. I'll see you in that white gown, after all."

Annie covered her face and pressed a wad of tissue to her eyes.

"Mark and Rick, you're turning into such godly young men. You'll be wonderful fathers and husbands some day. I'm so proud of both of you. And Tracy, what a precious child. I know you'll grow into a godly woman.

"Tory and Barry . . ."

Next to David, Barry leaned his elbows on his knees and dropped his face into his hands.

"Your faith has grown so much in the last few years. The Lord has done mighty things in your lives. I know he'll continue those mighty works. I know that your children will grow to become people of God—Brittany and Spencer, and even little Hannah, who will one day invite Jesus into her heart. There's no doubt in my mind. Always remember to have the simple faith of that little child, and you can't go wrong.

"And Brenda and David . . ."

David looked up, staring through his tears at that picture again. It was as if Sylvia's eyes were fixed on him.

"What a dear family you have, and God has done amazing works in your lives. I expect multitudes to know Jesus, because of Joseph's sweet, priceless heart, and Daniel, Leah, and Rachel's abiding faith. Brenda, you've done a wonderful job with them. Never let the worries of the world interfere with your life's work.

"Joseph, I want you to have Midnight. Dr. Harry and I have arranged for you to keep her at a stable nearby. Her rent and food are paid for for the next five years. I think God meant her for you all along ..."

David smiled and looked at his son, saw that Joseph smiled through his tears.

"And David ..."

He snapped his gaze back to the picture.

"David, I want you to know that God does exist, and he loves you. I want to see you in heaven, David. I want to see the joy in your eyes as you walk down the streets of gold and behold the light of the Lord's glory. All of your family will be there. David, don't be left behind."

It was as though a stake had been driven through his heart, killing something inside him, crushing the core of who he believed himself to be. From Sylvia's perspective, he was an incomplete man, a man who hid from obvious truth, a man with a void the shape of hope in his heart.

He couldn't stop himself as grief—for Sylvia, but even more for himself—conquered him completely. He set his elbows on his knees and dropped his face. Barry straightened beside him and touched his shoulder. Daniel patted his knee.

The rest of the service went by in a blur, as the preacher gave a message that once again pointed to Christ rather than Sylvia.

Someone sang, someone read a poem ...

But none of it registered in his mind. All he could hear was Sylvia's voice ringing in his ears. *David, don't be left behind.*

He pictured that day, when his family went to heaven and greeted Sylvia again. Joseph, running and jumping in some divine meadow, Leah and Rachel glowing like angels, Daniel rejoicing, Brenda laughing and laughing and laughing ...

But he was not in that picture. Like the night they had all headed off for the program at church, the program that he'd almost missed, he would be left out.

David, don't be left behind.

The pallbearers stood, and shaking himself out of his reverie, he stood with them. Leaving the casket where it was for now, they filed out of the room. Harry and the family, and Brenda, Tory, Cathy, and the kids all lined up behind them and left the room.

He couldn't talk to anyone, couldn't look in their eyes, couldn't make small talk about what a wonderful service it had been. Instead he went into the rest room, bent over the sink, and splashed water on his face. Slowly, he dried it off, and looked at his reflection in the mirror.

David, don't be left behind.

He left the bathroom, and went back into the sanctuary. It was empty now, except for the casket. Sylvia's picture had been taken down, but the autumn flowers still draped across its lid.

Tears that seemed to come from some aged place in the deepest part of his soul rushed up to drown him, and he twisted his face and let it go.

Slowly, he fell to his knees at the altar behind the casket.

"David?" It was Harry's voice behind him, and he looked up at the man who should have been the one doubled over in grief.

He started to rise up. "Harry, I'm so sorry . . ."

"It's okay." Harry knelt beside him. "Talk to me, David."

David tried to stop the slide of his anguish. "What she said on that tape . . ."

Harry smiled. "Tough stuff, huh? It was very serious business to her. Your salvation has been on her heart for a very long time. Just as it's been on Brenda's."

David didn't know how so many tears could be pouring from his eyes, while his throat seemed so dry. "Harry, I saw a picture of heaven in my mind during the funeral. And I wasn't there." He sucked in a sob and wiped the tears from his face.

Finally, he looked Harry in the eye. "Harry, I don't want to be left behind."

Out in the church foyer, Brenda searched the faces of the departing mourners for David. Soon they would be loading the casket into the hearse, and the cars would line up for their procession to the grave site.

She knew he was upset. She'd watched his profile as Sylvia spoke directly to him, and she'd seen the pain on his face. As much as she wanted Sylvia's words to penetrate his heart, she hated the thought that he was hurting or embarrassed, somewhere alone.

She found Daniel standing with the other pallbearers. "Honey, where's your dad?"

"I don't know," he said. "Somebody said they saw him go back into the sanctuary, but I don't know why he'd do that."

Frowning, Brenda hurried down the hall. As she neared the sanctuary, she saw the funeral director standing just outside the door.

"Is anyone in there?" she asked him.

"Yes," he said. "I was going to roll the casket out, but Dr. Bryan and another man are having a private conversation."

Another man. She knew it was David. She bolted through the doors and into the large room. She saw her husband kneeling at the altar, with Harry beside him.

She stood silently as he prayed. She couldn't hear the words, but her heart soared with hope. *Lord, are you answering my prayer?*

After a moment, the prayer came to an end, and David looked up. Harry hugged him tightly, and both men came to their feet.

As David turned to her, she saw the tears on his face. "Brenda," he whispered.

She ran into his arms, and clung to him with all her strength.

"I'm so sorry, Brenda."

"So sorry? For what?" she asked. "What have you done?"

"I've failed you all these years," he said, "by not believing the truth that was so obvious. The truth about Jesus Christ. He's real. I've seen it so many times, but I chose to reject it. All the things you've stood for all these years are right, and I don't know why I've been so blind."

He broke down, and Brenda kept holding him. "It's okay, honey. It's okay."

Harry put his hand on both of their backs. "Tell her what you did, David."

He pulled back and looked down at her. "I asked Christ to forgive me and change me," he said. "I want to live for him from now on, like Sylvia did . . . like you do. When I die, I want to leave good things behind. And I want to be a spiritual leader in our family, because you deserve that. I want to be a new person."

Brenda suddenly knew the joy that Sylvia had prayed for. There *was* joy in her death. Fruit had come from it. David was a believer!

As she wept and pulled Harry into their circle, she saw that Harry had that joy, too. All of Sylvia's prayers had now been answered.

CHAPTER
Eighty-One

The Lord seemed to have adorned the world for Sylvia's burial. The autumn trees wore an explosion of colors, from yellow to bright red, and the early November breeze whispered gently across the hills.

The neighbors of Cedar Circle stood hand in hand at the burial, their husbands behind them. Next to Cathy stood Annie, Rick, and Mark, each struggling with their own open grief. Brenda and David stood on the end with Joseph, Leah, Rachel, and Daniel beside them, and Tory and Barry had Brittany and Spencer standing quietly in front of them.

When the burial service was finished, all of the funeral attendees went back to their cars. Harry and the kids stood near the cars, talking softly to the mourners.

"It was a beautiful day," Brenda whispered. "Sylvia would have liked it."

"Yeah," Cathy said. "She would have been clipping leaves to use as Thanksgiving centerpieces."

"Riding Midnight," Tory added.

A gentle wind whipped up, blowing their hair and drying their tears. But more came.

"I can't do this," Tory whispered. "I can't say good-bye."

"Yes, you can." Brenda squeezed her hand. "We said it when she went to León. We knew we'd see her again. It's no different now."

"It feels different," Tory said.

Harry came back and gave them each a flower from the top of the casket. One by one, he kissed their cheeks. "We'll go on," he told them. "It seems impossible now, but we will. There's work to do."

Cathy took his hand. "You're going back to León, aren't you?"

"Yes," he said. "I want to be back for their memorial service next week. The kids are joining me there for Christmas. I think it'll be good for them to see the results of their mother's work."

"We'll miss you," Brenda said.

He couldn't answer. His eyes strayed to the casket, still sitting beside the grave it would be lowered into after they were gone.

"She would tell us to sing," he whispered. "Don't you think she would?"

There was a long silence . . .

Then Brenda began to sing. "It will be worth it all, when we see Jesus . . ."

Cathy joined in . . . then Tory picked up . . . and Harry followed.

The song lifted on the breeze, carried across the grave sites, rose up the hills on the other side . . .

From the depths of their grief came a fragile joy . . . and from the hollow of their good-bye . . .

. . . A distant hello.

For their story would not end, until they met again.

Share Your Thoughts

With the Author: Your comments will be forwarded to the author when you send them to *zauthor@zondervan.com*.

With Zondervan: Submit your review of this book by writing to *zreview@zondervan.com*.

Free Online Resources at
www.zondervan.com

Zondervan AuthorTracker: Be notified whenever your favorite authors publish new books, go on tour, or post an update about what's happening in their lives at www.zondervan.com/authortracker.

Daily Bible Verses and Devotions: Enrich your life with daily Bible verses or devotions that help you start every morning focused on God. Visit www.zondervan.com/newsletters.

Free Email Publications: Sign up for newsletters on Christian living, academic resources, church ministry, fiction, children's resources, and more. Visit www.zondervan.com/newsletters.

Zondervan Bible Search: Find and compare Bible passages in a variety of translations at www.zondervanbiblesearch.com.

Other Benefits: Register yourself to receive online benefits like coupons and special offers, or to participate in research.

ZONDERVAN®

ZONDERVAN.com/
AUTHORTRACKER
follow your favorite authors